Not by Bread Alone

By the same author:

Mercy on Trial

Wendell B. Will

Not by Bread Alone

International Institute of Trading Mastery, Inc.
Publishing Division
Raleigh, North Carolina

Published by
International Institute of Trading Mastery, Inc.
Publishing Division
8308 Belgium Street
Raleigh, NC 27606
919-362-5591 (voice)
919-362-6020 (fax)
http://www.iitm.com (internet)

Library of Congress Catalog Card No.: 97-70381

ISBN 0-935-219-080

Design and typesetting: Craig A. Conley

It is written that man shall not live
by bread alone.
—*Luke 4:4*

I do not believe that the Creator
meant for us to have perfect
happiness.
—*Thomas Jefferson*

What do you do after you have it all?
—*Lady Mavis Ashley*

A starving man does not worry
about the meaning of life.
—*Michael Hollingsworth*

For everything its season, and for
every activity under heaven, its time.
A time to seek...
A time to love...
—*Ecclesiastes 3*

I have observed that people are
about as happy as they make up
their minds to be.
—*Abraham Lincoln*

Contents

PART ONE   1

PART TWO   47

PART THREE   137

PART FOUR   213

PART FIVE   299

PART SIX   387

PART SEVEN   513

Preface

It is customary to assert that characters and events are purely fictional and that any resemblance to actual persons or events is purely coincidental.

While Mark Stevens and the other characters who people *Not By Bread Alone* were created wholly out of my imagination, they are very real. They live in my mind, my emotions and my creativity.

Mark and the women so important to him, Priscilla, Christina and Mavis, traveled with me on countless airplane journeys, attended the theater with me, read books with me, exchanged ideas with me, indeed veritably lived with me. We experienced life together. While they are fictional they are real. They are as real as the people I see everyday. The fact is, I know them better than anyone I have ever known.

While I do not like Jonah, Derek and Henry, I understand them and what makes them the way they are. Such people exist and we must deal with them.

I prefer, as friends, people like Rolf and Rodney. As with old friends, Mark, Rodney and Rolf have been through the wars together.

I like men of noble spirit such as Mark's teachers, John Hall and Richard Dawbarn.

I need to add that while the characters in my book are real, they and their events are fictional. They are not copied from, nor based upon, flesh and blood people. With the exception of the historical events and public figures, any similarity is purely coincidental. After all, people are similar the world over.

When you have finished *Not By Bread Alone*, I expect that the characters will linger on, continuing to live in you as they have lived in me.

Acknowledgments

I express my appreciation to the many people who have graciously assisted my work, including:

Rachel Ballon, Los Angeles
Philip Berry, Clerk of the Schools, Oxford University, Oxford
Margaret Collins, London
Dr. Leo J. Fishbeck, San Diego
John J. Harris, Examiner of Questioned Documents, Los Angeles
David Joergensen, Washington
Dr. John A. Letiche, Professor Emeritus School of Economics University of California, Berkeley
Anne Loudon, Chelsea, London
Clarence F. Lyons, Jr., National Archives, Nixon Presidential Materials, Alexandria
Paul McCracken, Chairman President Nixon's Council of Economic Advisors, Ann Arbor
Alan Loy McGinnis, Author and Psychologist, Glendale, California
Allan Newman, Barrister, London
Marjorie Aaron Quittner, Hypnotherapist, Los Angeles
Rolls-Royce Motors, Crewe and London
William Safire, Presidential Speech Writer
Sara Seacome, Solicitor, London
Richard Smethurst, Provost of Worcester College, Oxford University, Oxford
Sebastiano Sterpa, Glendale, California, formerly of Rome
A nameless street corner preacher on Rodeo Drive, Beverly Hills

Wendell B. Will

Historical Notes

In October of 1963 the ocean liner, *Ile de France*, transported all twenty-eight American Rhodes Scholars to England, where they commenced their two-year course of study.

On January 30, 1965 a special rail car bore Sir Winston Churchill's remains on a portion of his journey from London to his final resting place near Oxford. That rail car is now permanently located in the city of Industry, California.

In August of 1971 the world faced a financial crisis of epidemic proportions. Heavy demands were being placed upon the gold reserves of the United States. If something was not done soon, the U.S. would run out of gold, threatening to throw the world's financial system into ruin. On the weekend of August 13-15, 1971 an emergency secret meeting was called for Camp David to address the crisis. The President invited his leading advisors and experts in the global financial system. As a result the President in a televised address told the nation that he was adopting radical measures creating a new system and averting the crisis.

On Friday, November 21, 1980 a catastrophic fire occurred within the MGM Grand Hotel in Las Vegas, Nevada. The fire and smoke killed 84 human beings. (Note: Subsequently the hotel was retrofitted with modern fire prevention and detection equipment. Thereafter the hotel was sold and its name changed. Sometime later a new and completely different MGM Grand Hotel was built and operates today.)

On December 8, 1980 John Lennon was assassinated outside his residence on New York's upper west side. The next night and early the following morning a huge crowd gathered in adjacent Central Park. The mourners sadly sang songs all night long.

Part One

-1-

"Race you to the barn!" shouted Christina Movelli. Her horse, Madera, instantly responded to the digging of her spurs and sped toward the barn.

"You're on!" cried Mark Stevens, but Christina was already 40 yards ahead. Mark had heard she was a calculating woman, who never would have challenged him without having the advantage. But even though her husband was the owner of Movelli Winery and Vineyards, where Mark's father was the foreman, he was determined to win the race.

Mark knew his horse could not catch Madera, but he had trained Whisk to run cross-country. He pulled the reins toward the fence. "Jump, Whisk. Jump," he shouted.

"Where are you going?" Christina shouted back in her Italian accent. Seeing Mark's horse leap the fence, she quickened Madera's gallop down the dusty road, determined to win despite his unexpected maneuver. In a few hundred yards she would make a sharp turn onto the straightaway to the horse barn. Long blond hair flying, Christina and her horse were a breath-taking sight, as she put to use every bit of her expertise.

Excited by the challenge, Mark rode Whisk like a steeplechase champion, jumping irrigation ditches and dodging the rows of vines. The black horse leaped the fence into the orchard where it raced onward.

Christina did not know that Mark had run this course many times since her husband had given him the colt for high school graduation nearly four years ago. Mark knew every row of vines and every tree in the orchard. She was dead wrong if she thought he would back away simply because she was mistress of the Movelli Compound.

Hooves flying, Whisk made his last leap over the white-slatted fence onto the straightaway, just as Christina came abreast. They raced nose-to-nose, charging the barn door at full gallop. The door was too narrow for two horses, but neither would give way.

Galloping side by side, they were but 100 feet from the door. A collision was inevitable.

"Whoa, Whisk! Whoa! Now!" commanded Mark, as he yanked the reins.

Dust flying, Whisk reared on his hind legs, just short of the door. Christina ducked her head and hugged Madera's back as they plunged through the door, miraculously avoiding slipping on the concrete floor. She jumped from the horse, threw the reins around a post and stood defiantly, hands on her hips, as Mark led Whisk into the barn.

Mark stood to his full six feet and bowed to Christina. "Ladies first, Mrs. Movelli," he laughed, deliberately implying he had let her win.

"I don't believe that for a minute," she said with her Italian accent. "I had you beaten. You're the one who lost his nerve." Saying not another word, her long blond hair bouncing on her shoulders, Christina strode from the barn toward her husband's mansion.

What they say is true, thought Mark. That woman is absolutely crazy. She was willing to destroy the horses and injure us both. What on earth is she up to?

Christina Movelli slipped into her tub of hot water, sensuously reveling in the feel of the scented bubbles on her skin. She was 26 years old last December and had been married to Antonio for three years now. She had promised him she would accompany him on his annual trip to Italy, but two days ago had begged off.

"Surely you can live without me for two weeks. You know how I hate airplanes. Besides, think of how much you'll want me when you come home," she had cajoled, running her fingers though the wiry white hair on Antonio's chest as they lay in bed. She was bored sick with his endless reminiscing with his cronies in his home town of Pinerolo, in one of northern Italy's wine growing regions.

"But I want you with me. I'm proud of you," the 58-year-old Antonio had protested. But indulgences were the nexus of his marriage to Christina and he had given in. This morning she had driven him to the San Francisco airport in her new red 1963 Thunderbird, where she had dutifully kissed him good-bye.

Christina got out of the tub and looked in the mirror, as she dried herself with one of the huge orchid-colored bath towels she had bought on Union Square. Her body was slim and beautiful. The truth was, she was bored with her life here. She had to admit that Antonio had filled his end of their bargain, but she was restless. Life was passing her by.

Mark was grooming the sweat-soaked horses in the barn. His radio was playing a single of a new English group called the Beatles. The song was "Please, Please Me." England seemed very far off. Mark thought again about the Rhodes Scholarship he had applied for at Professor Hall's urging. He was uncertain whether he would accept the prestigious honor, even if it were offered. He was anxious to go to New York and get on with his career.

The wind was whipping up the hill from below the barn, as the sun sank low in the sky. Mark hurried with the horses, because he had heard on the radio a thunderstorm was expected in the Sonoma Valley at any time. He was eager to return to his parents' house in the Movelli Compound before the storm broke.

As long as Mark could remember, he had loved the smell of clean fresh straw. The warmth of the horses gave him a feeling of commonality with the animals as he touched them. It was the same as when he was small and would get in bed with his parents. He sank his face into Whisk's side and stroked the horse's black coat with his hands. Animals gave him such a sense of peace, a respite. Animals were freed from the intense ambition that had been such a part of him since he was a teenager.

Mark had always loved the simplicity of the Sonoma Valley, the Valley of the Half Moon, as it was called. It was home to him, but he was anxious to get back to Berkeley, where he would graduate in June. Even though it was Easter vacation, he had been reading an economics book by Milton Friedman. As far back as Sonoma High School, he had read everything he could find about finance and economics.

He could not afford to go to Palm Springs with his college friends. His vacation was being spent helping his father's crew with the winery equipment. Jonah, his father, had treated him even worse than last summer, when they had constantly quarreled. Jonah's words rang in Mark's ears. "I want you out of the house the minute you graduate." The feeling was mutual. Even if Mark postponed New York and went on to graduate school at Cal next fall, he would have to stay at the fraternity for the summer, because he could not stand living in the same house as his father.

"Please, please me," sang the Beatles' recording. Mark liked the new music. It had an exciting feeling to it. That was what he wanted to do with his life. Something exciting. Something far beyond what his parents were. Even far beyond Antonio Movelli.

Suddenly, he sensed someone was present. He looked up and was startled to see Christina standing at the open barn door. The glare of the sun was at her back, creating a corona-like light through the edges of her blond hair. Against the sun, he could clearly see her legs through her long pale lavender cotton skirt. Her darker lavender loose top exposed her tanned midriff. Mark swallowed hard. He was stunned at Christina's sensuous beauty.

Previously her afternoon rides had been alone, but today, for reasons that puzzled him, she had insisted that he ride with her. Then there was the race to the barn and now this. Christina had a reputation for being a wild, unconventional woman, but that she might want to seduce him had not entered his mind. She was the lady of the manor, the aloof wife of Antonio Movelli, his mentor and employer of his family. Yearnings for the wife of such a man were unthinkable.

"Mark, I'm glad you're still here. I need your help with something." Her request sounded innocent enough.

"Sure, Mrs. Movelli. I was just finishing up here." Mark could not bring himself to call her Christina to her face. Even after three years, his mother and father still called her Mrs. Movelli.

"I want to rearrange Madera's trophy shelf. I need you to hold the stool for me." The trophy shelf, which was covered with dust, was across the aisle from Madera's stall. "Would you see if you can find it, please." Her delicate perfume was different from that of any woman he had dated at Berkeley. He stood in awe of Christina and yet he was delighted that this marvelously feminine woman had returned to the barn.

She climbed the three steps of the stool and busied herself with the feather duster. "Please hold the stool steady. I wouldn't want to fall." Her Italian-accented tone was subtly flirtatious.

Looking up as she worked, Mark saw that under her loose blouse she was wearing no bra. My God, he thought, her breasts are bare. Totally bare.

He was startled and confused. Did she realize she was exposed? Good Lord, this was Antonio's wife. What if she caught him looking? Quickly, he looked down at the floor.

"I'm through. Here, take this duster, while I get down." She handed him the feather duster.

Suddenly, Mark sneezed, causing the stool to wobble. Christina grabbed his shoulder to steady herself. "Oh, I made you sneeze," she laughed and scampered down the steps.

If it had been any woman other than Christina Movelli, Mark would have assumed that her overtures were not innocent, but his thoughts raced in opposite directions. Christina was the most sensuous woman he had ever seen. But she was married to Antonio, the man who had paid for his college education. He could not imagine her being unfaithful to Antonio, least of all with him.

Christina took him by the arm. "You are not the same young man as when I first came here. You know that, don't you?"

"Well, I . . ." He still was uncertain about what was on her mind. After all, she knew of his long relationship with Antonio. When he was home from college, she often watched as Antonio and he continued their tradition of playing chess. Surely Christina was only showing her wild, fun-loving side. No doubt that was all there was to it.

She turned to him. "I have an idea. Since you haven't eaten yet, why don't you join me for dinner? I had Mona leave some of her pasta for me. It's her day off."

"Well, I was expected at home." He knew that Mona, the Movelli cook and housekeeper, made excellent pasta.

"Oh, come on. I get lonely with Antonio away."

In all these years neither Mark nor his mother or father had ever dined at the Movelli mansion. Antonio and his first wife, Anna, had been childless and had extended special treatment to Mark, but they drew a clear social line. Even when they played chess, it was always after dinner while Antonio smoked his Italian cigarettes and they listened to opera.

Christina placed Mark at the head of the large dining room table. Surely this is Antonio's chair, he thought. He felt out of place in his dirty work jeans and shirt, especially with Christina so clean and beautifully dressed.

When the meal was on the table, she lit the candles and handed him a wine bottle. "Please open the wine for us tonight. It's a Barbera 1945—very special." The wine bore the Movelli label.

Mark expertly opened the bottle and filled their antique wine glasses. "Here's to the Movelli Vineyards and Winery," he said, raising his glass.

"No, no. Here is to your *graduation*. The University of California class of 1963. Tonight my thoughts are far from the Movelli name." They drank from their glasses. It was a very tasty Barbera. "What are you going to do after June?"

"I have two or three options," he said. "I could go to New York right away. That's where most of the investment bankers are. Or I could stay on and get my master's at Cal. That's assuming Antonio would keep helping me financially."

"He's very proud of you."

"Then there's Oxford. My professor at Cal got me to apply for a Rhodes Scholarship, but that's a long shot."

"I'm impressed. Oxford would be wonderful. I've never known anyone who's been to Oxford."

.   .   .

With the free mention of Antonio's name, Mark felt less ill at ease. Surely Christina would not so readily talk about her husband, if she had some surreptitious plan. He had been off base to imagine anything else.

The meal was delightful. They laughed and joked and talked for a long time. She had insisted that he stop calling her Mrs. Movelli and use Christina. "At least when others are not around." She told Mark that like Antonio she had been born in Pinerolo, although of course years later. She had been working in Rome, but was visiting her mother in Pinerolo, when Antonio had met her on his first visit after Anna had died. "And what about you, Mark? Tell me about your dreams for the future."

"The truth is, I want to be like Antonio someday."

"Like Antonio?"

The wine made Mark speak more frankly than he would have. "I'd like to be respected like Antonio. Live in a mansion like this. Maybe have a wife like you. Everyone in Sonoma respects Antonio Movelli. It shocked people when he married you, but he got by with it because they respected him."

"Do they respect him because of his money?"

"I suppose the answer to that is yes. When it comes right down to it, it is money. After all Antonio would be no one, if it were the 'Stevens Vineyards and Winery' and Antonio were the foreman."

"But surely there's more to it than money," she said.

"That's true. You know my father. He hasn't a friend in the world except his buddies at the bar. If he owned the winery, he wouldn't have the same respect as Antonio. Even so, if it weren't for the Movelli Vineyards and Winery, Antonio, would be just some kindly old man. No, I think when it comes right down to it, it's money that tells the tale."

"And exactly what do you plan to do to get so rich?"

"As I say, it's investment banking. And that means New York . . . eventually."

"I don't know what an investment banker does."

"I don't know that much about it myself, but Dr. Hall says the best chance for economists is in investment banking. They float stock issues. Futures trading. Things like that."

"Why New York? Why not San Francisco?"

"New York's where the money is. San Francisco is tough. The business is all sewed up. The real opportunity is New York. Besides, I'd get away from my father that way."

"Everybody knows you don't get along, but I always rather liked Jonah."

"Oh, sure, women love him. He's a handsome bastard. He's always nice to women."

"Amanda says you're at the top of your class at the university."

"Did she tell you that? Well, yes, I guess I am. Professor Hall says I have a good chance at the Rhodes Scholarship."

"What do you think of the idea of going to England?"

"I don't know. I'm anxious to get started in business. I've been a student all my life. Oxford would take two more years."

They had each had more wine as they talked. This was the first time Mark had ever really talked to Christina since she came to Sonoma three years ago. Mark had been at Cal when Antonio had brought the stunningly beautiful Christina back from Italy and announced their intended marriage. At the wedding reception Mark's friends from his high school days had gossiped about Antonio's taking the young bride. She was only slightly older than Mark, while the bridegroom was more than twice her age. Mark had indignantly refused to participate in the gossip and jokes, finding it offensive. Secretly though, he had not known whether to admire Antonio or feel that he had made a fool of himself. The truth was, even though Christina publicly showed affection for Antonio, Mark could not imagine them in bed together.

"Mona made some zabaglione for dessert. Shall we have some?"

"I never turn down Mona's zabaglione." When baking for the Movellis, Mona often supplied the Stevens family with her freshly baked special desserts and pastries. Mark could not remember a time when Mona did not work for the Movellis.

Any ambiguity in Christina's intentions toward Mark that evening was dispelled after dinner. When they finished the dessert, she got up from the table.

"You must feel uncomfortable in those clothes. Would you like me to draw you a bath? You'd feel so much better. I'll find a robe for you."

Mark felt as if his mouth had dropped open. Even a fool would understand that this was more than an invitation to bathe. As he searched for an answer to her suggestion, conflicting thoughts again invaded his psyche. He was a normal male college senior, who would leap at the thought of sex with such a woman. He wanted to grab her. To hell with a bath, where is the bed? But what about Antonio? He would not even permit a joke about Antonio and Christina, and now was he going to jump into bed with her?

"Are you sure all the servants are gone?" he answered, trying not to disclose his inner conflict.

"Yes, they're gone. Come with me." She took his hand and led him up the mahogany paneled staircase.

"I've never been upstairs in the mansion before," he said.

Mark's conflict persisted as Christina led him into the bathroom and turned the hot water tap of the marble tub.

"Christina. I . . . Are you sure Mona won't come home?"

"Shush. Now you be quiet. Mona's not coming home. Here, let me help you with your clothes." She helped him remove his shirt and then his work jeans. He took off his undershorts himself, as she sprinkled scented bath salts into the swirling, rising water. She saw that he had no erection, as she glanced at his tall naked body.

"My, you are a handsome man," she smiled. "When the water is right, you can get in. I'll be right back." Her voice contained a promise of something to happen.

As the tub filled, Mark stirred the foaming water with his hand. He felt embarrassed about being naked like this in Antonio's bathroom. On the other hand Christina was not concerned about Antonio. Perhaps he should not be either.

When the water reached the right level, Mark lowered himself into the tub. He liked the warmth of the water and the slippery feeling of the bubbles. He took in the odor of lilacs. For him a bath was masculine, to wash away the residue of work, but this bath was feminine, enticing him into Christina's world. He reveled in the experience, as he lay soaking, waiting expectantly for her return. He looked at the bright colors of the floor and walls of the bathroom, which were in the style of the '30s, when the Movelli Compound had been built. Someday he would have a house like this. The curtains, the rug, the towels were all in Christina's lavender. The shelves were loaded with figures of carved soap and with colored jars filled with soaps and bath crystals.

"You don't look at all relaxed." Christina had returned and stood next to the tub in a lavender-colored floor length peignoir. She had taken down her hair, so that it nearly touched the shoulders of the sheer garment. My God, she was enticing. How could any man resist such a woman? He could understand why Antonio had risked the jokes and gossip to make her his wife.

"I guess I am a little tense."

"Why don't I join you? Perhaps that will relax you."

She slipped the peignoir to the floor and entered the tub. He hardly had a chance to absorb her naked body before she too was under the water. They were at opposite ends, their legs entangled under the bubbles.

Playfully, she poked his chest with her foot. "You look so grim. You should be happy."

"I'm sorry. I keep thinking about Antonio."

"Please don't talk about Antonio tonight. You know nothing about the way we are. Nothing about . . ." She did not continue. "I know what you must be thinking, but we must forget about Antonio, at least for tonight."

"All right," Mark said, but he could only pretend.

They lay silently in the water for a minute, as if waiting for their minds to catch up. She slid her fingers up his leg to his crotch.

"You are still so small," she laughed. "Don't you like Christina?"

"No, I like you. It's just that I . . . I didn't expect all this. I'm sorry."

"Don't be sorry." Abruptly she sat up, the soapy bubbles slipping from her body and showing her well-shaped breasts. "I know what to do."

She turned the handle, allowing the water to begin to drain. Sitting on her haunches, she watched him as the water continued to drain, until it only half covered his body. Mark's heart beat strongly with anticipation, as he looked at her. Her darker but still blond pubic hair was so thin that he wondered if she trimmed it.

She turned the handle stopping the flow of water. "I want you to spread your legs for me, so that I can get close to you." Mark did as she wanted and she lowered her head toward him.

She began with her tongue and, as he began to become erect, she took him into her mouth. He slid his finger up her slippery thigh, while she brought him to a full erection. Fleetingly, he wondered how many times she had done this to Antonio, done this to other men, but then in a few moments he did not care if she had done it to the whole Italian army.

"You certainly are ready for me now. Just look at you," she laughed.

Any feelings of guilt about Antonio were forgotten as his lust for her took complete control. He pulled her slippery body on top of him. "I want you Christina. I want you now."

"No, no. The tub is too small. Come with me. Let's go to the bedroom."

Giggling at his impetuousness, she reached for a towel, vainly trying to dry herself as they hurried toward the bed.

Mark had never made love with a woman older than himself. At first it seemed that she was in charge. Christina knew what she wanted and freely told him. "Wait for me," she said. And then later, "Hold still."

Once, her desire to be in control and her sharp commands caused him to lose his erection. "Roll over on your back," she ordered and quickly brought him erect again with her mouth.

Moments later Mark had entered her again. "*Più su Marco, ancora più su*, she shouted.

Soon it was over for them both.

Mark lay on his back, catching his breath. For the first time he noticed the silkiness of her lavender sheets on his skin. "Here," said Christina, a new gentleness in her voice. "Let me put this pillow under your head."

Until now he had been oblivious to the storm that had struck outside. Through the open windows, he heard the sound of the hard rain splattering on the trees and ground. Distant lightning flickered in the wall mirror.

"Listen to that rain," Christina marveled. She got out of bed and closed the windows, muffling the sounds of the storm. Still desirous of her, he admiringly watched the feminine movements of her naked body. Lying on his back, he stroked the skin on her arm after she returned to the canopied bed. For the three years she had lived in Sonoma she had been forbidden to him. He had watched her from afar, never expecting that one day he would be touching her naked skin.

Christina spread her hand on his belly. "In Italian we call a tummy *la panza*." She was light-hearted. "Your *panza* is so young and flat." Mark knew she was comparing him to Antonio, who had developed a paunch. For the first time he was aware of a competitive voice inside him that was reveling in the fact that he had screwed Antonio's wife. Not only had he had screwed her in Antonio's own bed, but she had found him more desirable. Still guilty, he shoved the ugly thought out of his mind, or he thought he had.

"This will be my last week at the compound," Mark told her.

"I was afraid of that," she said. "It's your father, isn't it?"

"You've heard us arguing, then."

"Maybe we can find a way to be together at Berkeley."

Mark was surprised at her suggestion. He had assumed this would be a one-night affair.

"Why does Jonah hate you so?"

"I don't know . . . Ever since the accident."

"I never knew about an accident. Tell me about it."

"I was 11. He was driving the tractor. You know where the pasture road turns off the main road?"

"Yes."

"I was riding on the hitch."

"What happened?"

"His temper. He got mad. A wagon ahead was going too slow for him."

"Yes?"

"It isn't easy to talk about."

"I'm interested. Go ahead."

"There was a car coming. He had to go into the ditch. I was thrown off. My leg was hurt . . . It was very bad."

"Is that where you got your limp?"

"He wouldn't take me to the hospital. My mother wanted to, but he wouldn't let her."

"So what happened?"

"Finally, she defied him—took me to the doctor, but it was too late. I'll always have this limp."

"You hardly notice it."

"Well, I know it's there. It's a living reminder."

She ran her hand down his left leg. "It's this one, isn't it?"

"Yes. It's a bit shorter. That's where the limp comes from."

"It gives you . . . what do you say? . . . an air of mystery."

"The son of a bitch didn't even say he was sorry."

"Some men can't say they're sorry."

"He acted like it was my fault. He actually ridiculed me because I couldn't play football in high school after that."

"Reminds me of my first husband."

"Your first husband?"

"I was only 18. We never lived together. Someday I may tell you about it."

When they made love a second time, she was less demanding, less intense. Mark was more sure of himself, less troubled by guilt and fear. When they were finished, Christina pulled the lavender sheet over them and they fell asleep.

It was long after midnight when she was awakened by the wave of rain and thunder. "Mark. Mark, dear, wake up."

Startled, Mark sat up. "What is it? What's wrong?"

"You'd better go home. They'll wonder where you are."

Mark quickly dressed in the bathroom. His clothes were stiff and uncomfortable. He was glad that she had awakened him. His father would be as mad as hell. He would have to make an excuse for not coming home for dinner. My God, if Jonah ever found out, there would be no telling what might happen.

.   .   .

When he returned to the bedroom, Christina had put on her peignoir. "I would like you to be here again. Can you be here tomorrow morning at eleven?" She was whispering.

His mind raced ahead. Tomorrow he was supposed to be working with his father and the crew, cleaning the winery vats. He never knew he could feel so strongly toward a woman. He knew the affair was pure danger and that it must stop immediately, but he also knew he would figure out a way to be back at eleven.

"Yes. I'll be here."

-2-

Mark was jolted awake by the noise of the alarm clock. It was seven o'clock. His first thoughts were of Christina and yesterday. He realized how naive he had been not to recognize her intentions from the very beginning. He remembered how they had talked in the dining room and then made love in Antonio's bed. He had felt so complete as they had exchanged confidences afterward. Aroused by the thought of seeing her again at eleven, he began to have an erection.

Suddenly, there was loud knocking on his door. "Get your ass out of bed. There's work to be done." Christ, he thought, it was his father.

Without further warning, Jonah Stevens burst into his son's bedroom. "I'll bet your fucking professor don't teach you how to clean wine vats."

"Take it easy. I'm getting up." Instantly his erection disappeared. He could hardly wait until the end of the week to get out of this place.

"We're starting half an hour early," said Jonah in his blustery manner. "If you'd come home like your mother was expecting, I'd a told you last night"

"You could have left a note, you know." As Mark had gotten older, he had stood up more to Jonah.

"Where the hell were you anyway? I'll bet you aren't too good to go fucking the town girls."

"Okay, okay. I'm up." Mark gave up trying to talk to his father. Naked, he got out of bed.

"Hurry it up. Your mother's making breakfast. I don't want you keeping her waiting." Jonah glanced at his son and shut the door.

Silently Mark shook his fist at the closed door. "Since when do you worry about my mother?" he wanted to shout at him.

He turned on the shower. That son of a bitch, he thought. If he did not need the money, he would desert the compound right now, work or no work. As he hurriedly showered, his mind returned to his eleven o'clock rendezvous with Christina. The thought of her eager naked body stirred him. He would find a way to be with her, no matter what the risk.

"Mark, I'm putting your waffles on," Amanda shouted upstairs when she heard the shower water stop. "Better hurry."

If it were not for his mother, he would have stopped returning home for vacations a long time ago. Despite her miserable life with Jonah, Amanda made things bearable. He wondered what would happen to her after his graduation.

His parents had already started breakfast at the familiar oil cloth-covered kitchen table when Mark came hurrying down the stairway. They had eaten there together since he could remember.

"Antonio's coming home in two weeks. We'd damn well better have the winery looking good when he gets back." Jonah's black tee shirt showed the ace-of-spades tattoo on his arm that he had had done in a carnival when he was a teenager in Vallejo. Jonah was proud of his muscular arms and body. He was disappointed that his son was slim and unathletic. Jonah took a drink of his black coffee and returned to his breakfast steak. At 48, Jonah did not have a trace of gray in his black hair, unlike Mark, who already was graying slightly at his temple. At five feet ten, Jonah was shorter than his son, but he knew damn well that if it came down to it, he could give the younger man a good licking. Jonah was a ruggedly good-looking man who had always attracted women.

"The men and me, we've got to work 12 hours a day if we're going to get the job done. I've decided we're going to work half a day Sunday . . ."

"But Sunday's Easter," Amanda interrupted.

"I don't give a damn if it's Christmas. We're going to get this place back in shape." Jonah turned to Mark: "And I want you working Sunday too . . . though I'm not too damn sure you're going to make one hell of a lot of difference. Staying out all night and . . ."

"Jonah, dear," Amanda said. "You're too hard on Mark." Stuck in a marriage that had gone bad years ago, Amanda had made Mark the light of her life. When she was 20 she had fallen head over heels in love with Jonah Stevens, who was a strong, good-looking shipyard worker. Amanda had always been a churchgoer, but had given in to Jonah's sexual demands because she was afraid she would lose him. She was pregnant with Mark when they had married. Soon after, Jonah had taken a job with Antonio Movelli and they had moved from Vallejo. Amanda was still a slim, attractive woman, who wore her dark hair in a bun as did her mother before her.

"Yeah, well, you're too easy on him," Jonah said.

"I'm sorry, Dad. I must have forgotten to tell you. I'm supposed to meet Rolf in town at ten-thirty." Rolf Williams was Mark's high school friend, who was also graduating from Cal this June, where they were fraternity brothers. "His Dad needs help unloading some stuff at the store."

"Yeah, well, let Rolf's old man get somebody else. I need you here."

"I can be back by twelve, twelve-thirty."

"Please, Mark, help your father. He's worked hard supporting us all these years. You men get along with each other now. For once stop being at each other's throats every minute."

Mark was angry. He was trapped. His lie about helping Rolf Williams' father was not going to work.

"Come on," Jonah demanded, "the men will be waiting."

"But he hasn't finished yet," Amanda pleaded.

"There's always another breakfast. The work won't wait."

Mark was angry, but left his half-finished breakfast and, not saying a word, followed his father to the winery. He would have to figure out some other way to meet Christina.

The winery, as all buildings in the Movelli compound, was made of white stucco with a red-tiled roof. The half dozen waiting men were smoking, and joking in Spanish when Jonah and Mark arrived. Their faces and hands mapped a lifetime of hard manual labor. They lived in the small dormitory-like buildings at the edge of the compound. Some had their families with them, while the others had left them in Mexico.

"All right, men," Jonah began. "My college kid here has decided he'll help us. You've all got to speak English, or he'll report you to immigration." The men laughed at Jonah's joke.

"All right, you sons of bitches. Enough talk. We've got work to do."

"Yes, boss," said one of the men. They showed no resentment at Jonah's disrespect. He was their boss and they did what he said. They knew there was worse in Mexico. Besides, they knew that was Jonah's way. He was tough, but he was not afraid to get his hands dirty himself.

It took them three hours to clean the first vat. The men were covered with grime and smelled of wine residue. Jonah worked shoulder to shoulder with them, barking orders. He was in his element. "Come on, Jose, give it some elbow grease." He loved to prove that when it came to hard work, he was second to no one.

He took particular pleasure in working faster than Mark. "What's the matter, college boy, have you forgotten what hard work's like?" Mark had learned long ago to stay out of competition with his father. Even when Mark was better, such as when horseback riding, or the time they put new tile on the roof of the mansion, it only meant more bullshit from Jonah.

Mark was seething at his plight. Christina was expecting him in a few minutes and here he was stuck, cleaning a goddamn vat. He had to find some way to get out of this stupid situation.

"All right, everybody. Time for a break before we get our asses over to Vat Four. Go ahead with your cigarettes." In his element like this, Jonah was a commanding figure.

The men stepped outside and began smoking and talking. Since he had been a teenager, Mark had worked with laborers such as these. While he respected them, their plight seemed hopeless. Each was condemned to ill-paying manual labor until the day he died. They served as an inspiration to him. He wanted no part of a life like theirs, or for that matter a life like his father's.

Mark had begun walking toward the horse barn. He could pretend he was looking in on Whisk and sneak up the back way to the mansion.

"Not you," Jonah shouted. "You and I get no break. We're way behind. I want to get started on Vat Four right now."

Mark snapped. Jonah was thwarting his every plan to meet with Christina. "Why, you son of a bitch," he shouted at Jonah. "They have to take your shit, but I don't. I'm getting the hell out of here right now." While he was truly angry, at the same time he had found his excuse to get away.

"You do and you'll never set foot around here again."

"Fuck it," Mark mumbled.

"What was that?"

"I said fuck it," Mark shouted. Mark had never talked to his father this way. "I'm going to Sonoma to help Rolf, whether you like it or not. I promised."

The men stared in disbelief as Mark disappeared around the corner. "You can go fuck yourself," Jonah shouted. "You be back here in 10 minutes or you can get the hell out."

Mark heard his father raving as he got into his battered old Ford. A plan had popped into his head. He would pretend he was driving into Sonoma and circle back to the compound. He hid the car behind one of the outbuildings and slipped through the servants' entrance of the mansion.

He had hoped that Mona had not yet returned, but she was working at the center table in the huge old-fashioned kitchen. As

usual Mona was mumbling to herself and had not heard Mark
come in.

"Hi, Mona." Before she could turn around, he put his arms
around the large gray-haired woman and gave her a hug. "I'm
going to miss you. When I get rich, I'm going to live on Nob Hill
and you can come be my cook."

"What a start you gave me," she smiled. Mark was her favorite. "I thought you'd be working this morning."

"Dad and I had an argument."

"I can't remember when you two didn't have an argument."

"This time it was serious." Mark took a freshly baked cookie
from the tin, as he had so many times over the years.

"I've heard you say that before." Mona did not look up from
her work. She had often overheard Jonah and Mark argue. It was
strange, she thought, how Jonah would brag to her about Mark's
brilliance, yet to his face he was always so critical.

Mark sat down in the cane chair that was always in the kitchen.
He wondered if there were a way he could get upstairs without
Mona's knowing. "Some of our greatest times were on Friday nights,
when you'd serve your zabaglione."

"I still miss Mrs. Anna. She was so happy when you finally
beat Mr. Movelli at chess that first time."

"I miss her too." Mark knew Mona had never accepted Christina as the new Mrs. Movelli.

"I still think he should have waited at least a year." Mona had
once confided that she thought Antonio had married too quickly
after Anna's death. Mona opened the oven door to remove her
next tin of cookies. "Mrs. Anna always thought of you as a son.
She was the one who got him to promise to send you to college,
you know." Mona had told him this many times.

"Mrs. Movelli around?" Mark made his inquiry sound casual.
He wished Mona were still away. He did not like feeling guilty.

"I took her breakfast about nine, why?"

"Nothing. Just wondering."

"She should have gone to Italy. A wife should be with her
husband."

He kissed Mona on the cheek. I'm going to help Rolf and his
father. Want anything from Sonoma?"

Mark walked up the slope in back of the mansion, where Mona
could not see him from the kitchen. Christina stood at her open
bedroom window. He could see her silently mouthing something,
but could not understand what she was telling him. He was nervous that someone would see him, but he desperately wanted to

be with her. Christina leaned out of the window and silently pointed toward the iron fire escape ladder on the back of the house.

Mark hurriedly began climbing the ladder. His heart was pounding. He was a fool, he thought. If Mona came outside, she surely would see him. For all he knew, his father was angrily searching the compound for him right now. He knew he was asking for disaster, climbing the ladder like this, but he had no choice; he wanted her. Christina opened the hallway window and he managed to get inside.

His fears of discovery were forgotten when he saw her. She was dressed in a white negligee. She pressed her body against him as they embraced. This time he had no trouble getting an erection.

"Where have you been? Your clothes are filthy." She spoke in a whisper, until she closed the bedroom door.

"It doesn't matter. I'll have them off in a minute."

"I've got the bathtub all filled. The way you like it."

"To hell with a bath." He began removing his clothes. "It's you I want, not a bath. Besides, we don't have much time."

"Not much time? Why?"

"Jesus, Christina. Mona's downstairs. Who knows who may be looking for me!"

Their love-making was different this morning. Christina was more passive. She issued no commands, but followed his lead. Not once did Antonio even cross his mind, until it was over and they lay together. He was amazed at himself. Last night he was so troubled and guilty, but today all he worried about was getting caught.

When they had finished he caressed her skin. "I envy Antonio. He can have you whenever he wants."

"No. It's not that way any more. Antonio has been having trouble. It's been over a year since we have made love."

"I'm surprised."

"I think it's in his head, but he won't see a doctor."

They were silent. She spread her hand across his stomach, as she had last night.

"I remember when you first came to the valley," he said.

"And what did you think of me?"

"I thought you were the most beautiful woman in the world. I couldn't imagine you being in bed with Antonio."

"And now here you are here in bed with me. Is that it?" She ran her fingers softly over the gray streak of the hair on his head.

"I remember one time, just after you came here. Rolf and I were having a hamburger at Sally's in Sonoma. This guy we knew from high school started mouthing off."

"What did he say?"

"I don't remember exactly. Something about Antonio not keeping up with you."

She was lying on her side stroking his body. She leaned over and kissed his stomach.

"The guy must have thought I was crazy, the way I acted. Of course he was just trying to get my goat."

"What did you do?"

"I was mad as hell," Mark laughed. "I told him to shut up or I'd take him outside and knock his block off."

"Knock his block off?"

"Yes. His head. It's an expression."

"What happened?"

Mark was chuckling. "He could see I wasn't kidding. I don't know if I could've beaten him, but he backed off. He left Sally's."

Christina slid her hand lower, until Mark was aroused again.

"You are a crazy woman, you know." He slid on top of her.

"If you say so, I must be."

But they were interrupted by loud voices coming from downstairs.

"You can't go up there." It was Mona's voice.

"You get out of my way. I'll go up if I damn well please."

"My God, it's Jonah," Christina shouted.

"Jonah, you can't go up there," Mona argued. "It's only Mrs. Movelli up there."

Mark sat up, reaching for something to put on.

"Don't give me that shit," Jonah shouted. "My man saw Mark. He's up there all right."

"But that's not possible."

"You'd better get out of my way." Jonah's voice came nearer.

Christina was out of bed, struggling to put on her robe.

"Come back down here," shouted Mona. "You know you're not allowed up there."

Jonah burst through the bedroom door. "So you had to go to Sonoma, eh, college boy. What's the matter? Too good for the town girls?"

"What are you doing here? Get out of my house," Christina shouted.

Livid with rage, Jonah ranted on. "You got to fuck the boss's wife. Is that it, Mister Big Brain? Is that right, Mister Big Cock?"

"I'm sorry, Mrs. Movelli." Mona, puffing for breath, had caught up and stood behind Jonah. Embarrassed when she saw that

Mark was naked, she put her head down and backed out of the door.

Mark was bewildered and trembling with rage. He fumbled with the sheet, trying to cover himself. "You'd better get out of here," he shouted. "What I do or don't do is none of your business."

"We'll see about that!" Jonah slammed the door and stalked down the stairs.

Christina and Mark were stunned. She leaned her back against the door, as if to prevent a raging Jonah from returning. Dazed, Mark sat on the bed, the sheet partially covering him.

"We've got to keep him from telling Antonio." Christina nearly shouted with panic.

"Christina," he pleaded. "You saw what he was like. What the hell could I possibly do to stop him?"

"I don't know, but we've got to stop him. Antonio would divorce me."

"But you don't want to stay with him now, do you?"

"I don't know . . . I can't let him find out. I wouldn't know what to do, if he made me go away." Nervously, she took off her robe and began to get dressed. Mark stared at her absently as she put on a western shirt, without putting on a bra. Not bothering with her panties, she pulled on her riding jeans over her pubic hair and tucked in her shirt. Even in this terrible situation Christina was desirable. As she pulled on her boots, Mark began putting on his work clothes. He had to decide what he would do next.

"What about Mona?" Christina asked. "I'm sure she'll tell. She's never liked me. It'll be all over Sonoma by the time Antonio gets back."

"Mona won't tell. She would know Antonio wouldn't give me any more money for school. I'll explain to her."

Christina finished dressing. "I'm going riding. I want to think."

Head high and blond hair flying, she walked to the door. She looked defiant, the same as yesterday when she had won the race to the barn. Without saying another word, she left and closed the door behind her.

Mark sat on the bed, putting on his shoes. He was trying to think, trying to decide what he should do next. His father and he had had so many arguments in the past, yet he had never left home.

Christina suddenly reopened the door. She pointed her riding whip at Mark. "You tell Jonah if he doesn't keep his mouth shut, I'll tell Antonio something that will cost him his job . . . his house, his pension, everything." Before Mark could respond, she turned and closed the door as abruptly as she had opened it. Then she spoke loudly through the door: "You tell that to that sweaty farm worker! You tell him that for me!"

Mark went after her, but by the time he had opened the door all he could see was Christina's bouncing hair and her whip disappearing down the stairs.

He was puzzled by what Christina had said. He had learned as a teenager that his father had ways of skimming money from Antonio, and forcing kickbacks from the men to keep their miserable jobs. One time he had overheard Jonah on the telephone, demanding a kickback from a grape buyer. Although he did not know how Christina could have found out, perhaps it was that that she was using as a threat, or perhaps it was only her anger wildly exploding at Jonah.

Head down, Mark walked the pathway from the mansion to the foreman's house. He dreaded confronting his father, but he knew he had to return to the cottage for his things, and to try to explain himself to his mother. He knew Jonah would be waiting to unleash a lifetime of anger against him. In times past, when his father yelled at him, Mark had felt a subtle safety in knowing he was being unjustifiably treated, but this time his father was completely justified. Jonah would not be holding back.

"Dinner will be on the table in a few minutes," said Amanda. As was her custom on work days, she had prepared a large noon meal for the two hungry men so central to her life.

"Did he say anything to you?" Mark asked his mother.

"No. What? He's acting so strange. Did you two have another fight?"

"Yes, a bad one."

"You get your ass in here," Jonah shouted from the living room. "I'm surprised you had the guts to show up." He stood belligerently, like a prize fighter.

"Dad, I don't want to talk about it. I just came back to talk to Mom."

"It's not that easy, smart boy." Threateningly, he stood close to Mark. Mark knew Jonah delighted in his ability to turn his anger off and on as if flicking a switch. Jonah enjoyed the power being angry gave him.

"Jonah, what's the matter?" asked Amanda, wiping her hands on her apron as she entered the living room.

"The problem is your son, that's what the goddamned problem is." Jonah was like a prosecutor who knew he had an open and shut case.

"Dad, please don't. Let me . . ."

"Your son's been screwing Mrs. Movelli. Your Mister Pure son has been fucking the boss's wife. That's what the problem is."

Amanda's eyes grew wide at the accusation. She was too stunned to respond.

"Listen, Dad. I don't want to argue."

"Is this true? Is your father telling the truth about you and Mrs. Movelli?" Amanda sat down, nervously wrapping her hands in her apron.

"I'm sorry, Mom, it is true. She was . . . I'm sorry, I've got no excuses."

"Mark, how could you? After all Mr. Movelli has done for you."

Mark said nothing. There was no satisfactory answer to her question.

Arms folded defiantly, Jonah stood with a look of self-satisfaction.

"Why did you? When did it start?"

"What difference does it make, Mom? I can't undo what we did."

Bewildered at the awful news, Amanda put her hands to the sides of her head.

"We're having this thing out," Jonah interrupted. "This could cost me my job."

"It won't, if you keep quiet about it."

"It would be worth it just to see Antonio kick your ass out of college. Always sucking up to him, as if you was more his son than mine. Those fucking chess games."

"He was more my father than you ever were." They were shouting at each other.

"No kid of mine is going to keep his nose in a book when there's work to be done. You remember that, goddammit. You're my kid, not his." His fist raised in anger, Jonah was screaming.

"Some father you are. At least Antonio helped me with college. You never gave me a dime." Mark refused to back off the way he usually did. He stood with hands on his hips, matching Jonah word for word.

"I could've been twice as rich as Movelli, if your mother hadn't gotten herself knocked up. I had plans . . . big plans."

"Jonah," wailed Amanda. "You promised you'd never tell."

"It's all right, I figured it out years ago," Mark said. "Don't worry about it."

"You and me's going to have this out. You've never done a man's work around here. Let's see if you can fight like a man." Mark had never seen Jonah so enraged. He swung his fist, striking Mark on the side of the face as he turned away, trying to avoid the blow.

Even with the years of abuse and this unexpected provocation, Mark could not bring himself to strike his father. Hands at his side, he stepped away.

Like an animal, Jonah grabbed Mark's shoulder and jerked him around, so they faced one another. He tightened his fist, as if to strike Mark again. In a burst of rage, Mark shoved off the blow with his left hand, then with his right he struck his father hard on the jaw.

Hardly noticing the blow, Jonah became even more enraged that Mark would dare strike him. He yanked open the glass door of his rifle case and took out his well-used Winchester. "All right, you Christina-fucker. Get out of my house right now before I shoot you in the nuts."

"What about you? Everybody in town knows you screw a different whore every Friday night."

His face red with rage, Jonah pointed the rifle at Mark.

"Jonah," screamed Amanda. "You put that gun down." Amanda was trembling with fright as she confronted Jonah. "You put it down this instant, or I'll call the sheriff."

With such words from the normally passive Amanda, Jonah took his eye off his son.

Mark grabbed the gun and twisted it from Jonah's struggling grasp. He made no effort to point it at his father, but went to the door and flung the weapon as far as he could. It clattered on the asphalt driveway.

"You get out of my house right this minute and I mean forever. Do you hear me? Forever!" shouted Jonah. "And as for you," he turned to Amanda, "I forbid you to ever see him again. Do you understand me?"

Defying her husband, Amanda rushed out of the house after Mark. She caught up with him at his car.

"I'm sorry about everything. Sorry about Christina."

"It can't be helped now," Amanda sobbed.

"I shouldn't have said that about him seeing whores. I don't think he really does."

"I don't care what he does any more." She was still crying.

"I'm sorry. I'm going back to Berkeley. I never should have come." He kissed her and put his arms around her.

"When will you call me?" Amanda was trying to regain her composure.

"As soon as I can."

"Study hard."

"Okay."

"I'll come to your graduation, no matter what your father says."

"I want that too."

"Remember, I love you."

"I love you too, Mom."

Mark got into the Ford and spoke to his mother through the rolled-down window.

Just remember, one day I'll buy you a house twice the size of the mansion." He pointed at Antonio's house.

Amanda smiled. "I don't want a big house. I just want my son happy."

Tears streamed down Mark's face as he drove down the road. "I'll never go back," he said aloud. "I'll never go back there again."

-3-

Head down, Mark walked to Wheeler Hall, the main classroom building for Cal's School of Economics. Over a month had passed since the fight with Jonah. He had one more week of classes, followed by final exams and graduation.

Mark had been very depressed since the events of Easter vacation. It was impossible to concentrate on his studies. The morning haze had not yet cleared as he entered the campus from fraternity row. Head down, he was wearing his jeans and battered "California Bears" sweat shirt. He was hurrying for his eleven o'clock class in international economics that was taught by Dr. John A. Hall. The course, 180 B, International Economic Policies, had 15 students. In the past month Christina had been constantly on his mind. He found himself writing her name on the margins of his textbooks. He had telephoned her twice from the fraternity house, but each time Mona had answered. The first time he had hung up, but last week he had asked Mona to tell Christina he had called. "I'll tell her, but you know it's wrong," Mona had scolded. Mark knew he should not try to see her, but his days were so empty without her.

Mark had taken several courses from Dr. Hall in the past four years. This year Hall, a tall, thin, gray-haired man, had given him a job grading freshman quizzes. It paid little, but provided considerable prestige. Once when Hall was called to Washington, Mark had given Hall's lecture in a first-year course. It was Professor Hall who had urged Mark to apply for the Rhodes scholarship to Oxford, even though Mark planned to continue on to U.C.'s Graduate School in economics, unless he went to New York. Hall took a great deal of interest in his senior students, frequently advising them on career decisions.

Mark took his seat in the familiar classroom, Wheeler Room 200. He opened his notebook and sat back to listen. His concentration had been poor since Easter. He knew he had to shape up, if he were to do well on finals. This last month he had been drift-ing—doing just the bare minimum.

This morning Hall's subject was international monetary ex-change. He was continuing yesterday's discussion of the Bretton Woods System for setting the rates by which the currency of one country, say Britain's pound, was valued against the currency of another, such as the United States' dollar.

This was Mark's favorite subject. Hall always encouraged in-dependent thinking in his students, and Mark had frequently chal-lenged some of the traditional views about the exchange system. But today his mind was not on the lecture. He was barely listen-ing to Hall as he again found himself printing Christina's name in his notebook.

"Mr. Stevens," repeated Dr. Hall. At first Mark did not know that Hall was calling on him, but suddenly he realized he had drifted off.

"Yes, sir. I'm sorry, sir."

"Are you with us, Mr. Stevens?"

"I'm sorry sir. I seem to have . . ."

The other students turned and looked at Mark. They were not used to this from him.

Hall turned to another student. "Miss Altmann, I'll ask you the question, if I may. Assuming a floating exchange rate system, what factor would be the most important in determining the value of a given currency?"

Mark was embarrassed by his lapse. He took pride in his reputation as Hall's brightest student. The question snapped him back into reality.

"You mean if Bretton Woods were abandoned?" Miss Altmann asked. She, too, was a very bright student.

"Yes, and no gold standard."

"To some degree it would depend on the new system, but if I had to select one factor, I suppose it would be interest rates."

"What about the cost of living in a given country? How many goods could be bought for a dollar or a pound?"

"Of course that would have an effect, but I think in the last analysis we'd find that money would tend to move to the country that paid the highest interest rate."

"And why would that affect exchange rates?"

"Well, for example, if higher interest rates were available in the U.S., investors would be buying dollars. That would drive the dollar upward." Mark was annoyed with himself. He knew that he, too, could have answered the question.

Soon the class was over. Mark intended to have lunch at the fraternity and then study all afternoon.

"Mark," Dr. Hall said, seeking his attention. "Could I have a word with you?" Hall had put his notes in his brief case. They walked down the stairs together as they talked. "Are you all right? You don't seem to be yourself these past few weeks."

"Well, I . . ." Mark didn't know what to say. He did not want to tell him about Christina. "I guess I do have a few personal problems. I didn't realize it was that obvious."

"Your work, your class participation, has not been what it should."

"I'm sorry."

They neared the Faculty Club, an older, shingle-sided building where many of the faculty lunched. "It's nothing to be sorry for. I inquired because I thought I might be able to help." They paused because they were at the walk that Hall intended to take to the club.

"That's thoughtful of you, but I don't know what you could do."

"Maybe nothing, but I think we should give it a try. What do you say?"

Mark nodded tentatively. "Couldn't hurt, I guess."

"I'll spring for lunch. How about one o'clock tomorrow, right here?"

"All right." Mark looked depressed. "Tomorrow."

As Hall neared the entrance, he turned. "Have you heard from Oxford?"

"No, not yet."

"Any day now, I suppose. See you tomorrow."

Mark turned onto Piedmont Street, Berkeley's fraternity row. He remained depressed. Not only had he not contacted Christina, but he was cut off from his family. He had called his mother twice, trying to time the calls when Jonah would not be around, but their conversations had been brief and furtive. Then too, his monthly check from Antonio was two weeks late. He worried that Antonio had found out about Christina and had cut off his money. He was late in paying his room and board bill to Alpha Zeta.

The day's mail was lying on the entry table at the Alpha Zeta house when Mark arrived. Mark's high school friend, Rolf Williams, was looking through the mail.

"Sorry, buddy, nothing for you from Oxford," Rolf said. Rolf had been accepted at Boalt Hall, Cal's law school, and planned to stay on at the Alpha Zeta house for the next three years. Rolf was the only person in Berkeley Mark had told about Christina.

Mark looked through the mail himself to see if Antonio's check had come, but it was not there.

"Mark," Rolf said, looking around to be sure they would not be overheard. "You haven't acted like yourself lately."

"I'm okay." But Mark's depressed expression belied what he said.

"You aren't still involved with Mrs. Movelli, are you?"

"No, but the truth is I can't get her out of my mind." Best friends since Sonoma High, Mark and Rolf often shared confidences.

They were interrupted by another fraternity brother who had just come in the door. "Mark, there's a lady parked outside. She wants to see you. What a beauty!"

Mark looked out the window. It was Christina's new red Thunderbird. The white convertible top was up, so he could not see for sure that it was Christina, but it had to be her.

He rushed outside and bent down to look into the car. "Christina, is something the matter?"

"I'm afraid so," she said nervously. "We've got to talk. Can you get in the car?"

With Mark in the passenger seat, Christina began aimlessly driving.

"Tell me, what is it?" he asked.

"Is there someplace we can have coffee?"

"The Durant Hotel is right around this corner. They have a coffee shop."

Mark asked the waitress for a table in the far room of the hotel restaurant. His pleasure at seeing Christina was overshadowed by the ominous news she was carrying. They took a table in the distant far corner, where they would be reasonably alone.

Even though she was distraught, Christina looked beautiful. She was dressed in a purple silk top and close-fitting black slacks with black high heels. Her blond hair was tied back with a scarf that matched her blouse. She was stunning. It was no wonder that he had not been able to think of anything else for the past month.

"What is it?" Mark asked again.

"The menus are already on the table," the waitress interrupted. "I'll be back in a few minutes."

Christina waited until the waitress was gone and burst forth, "Antonio knows about us." Nervously, she removed a cigarette from a nearly fresh pack. Mark had never seen her smoke before.

"I was afraid of that." Mark felt as if he had been punched in the solar plexus. It took him a moment to go on. "How did he find out?"

"He wouldn't tell me, but I'm sure Jonah told him."

"Jesus Christ."

"We had an awful scene."

"How long has he known?"

"Two weeks."

"So he didn't find out right away?"

"No."

"Did you sleep together?"

"Yes, of course. He would have been suspicious." She looked away, avoiding Mark.

"Then you had sex with him."

"He's my husband, you know."

"I thought you said he couldn't."

"He'd been away a long time."

Mark had no answer. He could not stand the thought of Antonio's making love to her.

"He wants a divorce."

"A divorce? Jesus, he wants to divorce you?"

"It's all been arranged."

"How could you do everything in two weeks?"

The waitress returned. "Are you ready to order?"

"I don't want anything, Mark. I'm not hungry."

"How about some coffee?"

"Okay."

"Make that two coffees, please," Mark told the waitress. "Maybe we'll order later."

When the waitress left, Christina went on. "It was easy to arrange. You see, we never were married, legally."

"What do you mean? I was there myself. I saw you get married."

Christina took a deep breath, as if gathering her courage. "I was never legally divorced from my first husband, in Italy."

"My God, Christina!"

"Antonio and I have never been legally married. We both knew I didn't have an Italian divorce."

"But why not?"

"It was only recently they even allowed divorces in Italy. You have to be separated for five years. It hadn't been that long."

"Jesus!"

"I told Antonio, but he wanted to get married right away."

"But where does that leave you?"

"We're not married. I guess it's as simple as that."

Mark sighed and leaned back in his chair. "What are you going to do?"

"Antonio made me a generous offer. I've just come from his lawyer's office in San Francisco." She pointed to her purse. "I've got my copy of the paper right here."

"Paper?"

"He pays me $2,000 a month for three years. I can live in Italy very well on $2,000 a month."

"In Italy? What are you talking about?"

"Antonio put two conditions in the agreement."

They were interrupted by the waitress with their coffee, and waited until she left.

"The first condition is that I must move to Italy. He says he could never stand it if I stayed in California."

Mark sighed. He could not believe what she was telling him. "And you've agreed to all this crap?"

"The second condition is I never see you again."

Mark nearly spilled his coffee. "That vindictive old bastard!"

"Vindictive? I don't know that word."

"Vindictive. Wanting to get even. It doesn't matter."

"Antonio's very upset with you. Even more upset with you than with me."

"What a mess!"

"If I had been with someone else, he might have been able to forgive me, but not when it was with you."

"I can't believe my father would tell him."

"Who else would it be?"

"I don't know."

"I suppose he thought he was getting even."

"He's brought the roof down on everybody," Mark mused.

"There's something else."

"Even more?"

"Antonio never wants to see you again. He's cutting off your money."

"I was afraid he had done that." Nervously, Mark ran this fingers through his hair.

"What are you going to do?"

"I don't know."

"Can you get a scholarship or a loan?"

"I don't know. I have to think." Mark was stunned.

Christina reached across the table and took his hand. "I wish there were something I could do."

"You've got enough problems of your own."

"I'll be all right," she said.

"Maybe the Rhodes Scholarship will come through," Mark mused.

"You haven't heard yet?"

"Not yet. I'm seeing Dr. Hall tomorrow. He'll know about student loans."

He drank some of his coffee.

"There has to be some way out of this," he went on. "Maybe Antonio would change his mind about the divorce if I talked to him."

"Nobody can get him to change his mind, least of all you. He actually threatened to get his gun and kill you."

"God, Christina! It all started with going for a horseback ride."

"No, it started long before that. It started when I married him."

"What do you mean?"

"I shouldn't have married him if I couldn't be faithful to him."

"But you're so young. You can't be expected to give up your life for him."

"And why not? That was what I promised I would do."

They sat silently for a long time. It did not seem as if there were anything else to say. Finally Christina excused herself to use the ladies' room.

Mark watched admiringly as she left the dining room. She certainly was an attractive woman. He realized he had fallen in love with her. He leaned back in his chair, fondling the pack of cigarettes she had left.

The recent series of events was incredible to him. A few weeks ago his future was well planned and assured. He would graduate in the top of his class, go on to graduate school at Cal, get a good job in New York and be well on his way to earning the million dollar fortune he had always dreamed of. It seemed impossible to believe that in one short month his plans, his whole world, had collapsed around him. He had no idea what he would do or how he would go about doing it. Nothing had ever diverted him from his goals before, but this month had set a world record for disaster. Idly, he glanced out the window. There, parked on Durant Street, was Christina's red Thunderbird. Christina belonged in a car like that. Maybe one day he could buy her a red Ferrari. She would look even better in a Ferrari. There was an old gray convertible with its top down parked behind the Thunderbird. A man, he looked like a student, opened the door for his girl friend. She was a pretty redhead. She looked like a student too. The man got in on the driver's side and, after jockeying a few times, the couple drove off. They looked happy, Mark thought. Maybe they would graduate next month too. Maybe even get married and start a family. He wondered if the man could possibly enjoy screwing the redhead the way he did Christina. Perhaps he should find a girl like that. He was stupid to have allowed himself to be thrown off the track like this because of Christina. There were plenty of pretty women. Plenty who were not married. Especially not married to Antonio Movelli.

But then Christina moved back into view. His heart leaped at the sight of her. He knew he would never be satisfied with some pretty redhead as long as Christina inhabited the earth.

He rose while she took her chair. She had combed her hair and freshened her lipstick. She looked better now. Less apprehensive.

"You looked very beautiful coming in just now."

"Thank you, Mark. I haven't felt very beautiful these past weeks."

"Christina, listen to me." He took her hand. "I want to be with you. I want to rent a room here at the hotel so we can be together."

Their love-making was very different this time. This time Mark was the initiator. This time he had new emotion for her. Adding to the sexual excitement was his feeling of being in love with her. He would never get enough of her. Despite the bad news that had brought her to Berkeley, he marveled at his good fortune at making love with her. After they finished he held her longingly, wanting to be as close as possible. There had to be some way to reverse this foredoomed course of being apart. Within 15 minutes he was making love to her again. It was as if when he possessed her sexually she belonged to him and would never leave. When they finished, Christina pulled the sheet over them.

"Mark, you didn't ask me when I was leaving for Italy."

"You're going to tell me it's soon. Aren't you?"

"Yes, my dear, I'm afraid it is soon."

"When?"

"Tomorrow morning. My flight is at eleven. The car is packed. Mona will be shipping the rest of my things."

Mark grimaced. "At least we have until then."

"I have a reservation at a hotel at the airport tonight. Antonio thinks I took today's flight, but I wanted to see you."

"Cancel the hotel. I want you to stay here with me tonight."

Mark was starving when he woke up. Naked, he went to the window. Their room was on the sixth floor of the Durant, so he could see across the campus to the clock on the Campanile, Cal's landmark tower. It was nearly six o'clock. With no lunch, it was no wonder he was so hungry. He looked at the sleeping Christina. What a risk she had run to be with him. If Antonio found out, he would stop her $2,000 a month.

When Christina awoke they decided to have dinner in the room. "Order some wine. Barbera like we had our first night," she cheerily called out while Mark was speaking to room service. He would have barely enough money for the hotel bill and would not have enough to last the semester, but this would be the last time he would be with Christina.

Both were sexually spent from the afternoon, so after dinner they talked. They carefully avoided discussing the ominous fact that tomorrow morning they would be saying good-bye.

In his jeans and Cal sweat shirt, Mark sat in the chair, putting his bare feet on the coffee table. Christina lay on the bed, wearing her white robe, with her head propped against the pillows. She fondled her package of cigarettes, occasionally removing one, but she had not actually lit a cigarette since supper. She began telling Mark about her first marriage.

"I was only 18. He was 19. I wouldn't let him have sex with me until we were married."

Mark listened intently. He hadn't asked about her first marriage, but she seemed to want him to know.

"In Italy it is very important that a girl be a virgin. But I wasn't, and I knew if I told him—his name was Alfonzo—he wouldn't marry me."

"What a primitive custom."

"Maybe so, but that's the way it is, especially in small towns like Pinerolo. I thought I could fool Alfonzo. On our wedding night I told him I had hurt myself as a child, climbing a fence, but he wouldn't believe me. Looking back on it, I can see that it was a stupid story."

"What happened?"

"He left me in the hotel room and ran back to the wedding party. They were all drunk. He told everybody. He said he would get an annulment, but he couldn't get one."

"What did you do?"

"I went to Rome. I had studied some French, so I got a job at the French Embassy there in Rome."

"How did you meet Antonio?"

"When I got promoted at the embassy, I went back to Pinerolo to visit my mother. To celebrate. Antonio was there. He had known my father."

"After Anna died everybody thought Antonio had gone back to Italy to marry his old sweetheart."

"Then you had heard that story?" she asked.

"People were suspicious there was another woman. He kept going back to Pinerolo and Anna wouldn't go with him."

"That's pretty close to the truth. My mother said the reason he left for America in the first place was because he had gotten this girl pregnant."

"Oh, so that was it."

"She had a little boy," said Christina. "Antonio always sent money. The boy was killed in the war. Libya, I think."

"My God, it's hard to believe. Antonio had a son. Do you know his name?"

"It was Antonio, too. They called him Tony."

"Did he know who his father was?" Mark asked.

"That I don't know. You would think so. Everybody else knew."

"Maybe it was because of his son's being killed that Antonio took such a liking to me."

"That could be, I suppose."

"So it was little Tony's mother that Antonio went back to see every year," Mark observed.

"Everybody in Pinerolo knew about it. Anna must have too."

"I'll be damned! And here they had no kids of their own."

"So when I was visiting my mother in Pinerolo that weekend Antonio was seeing his old sweetheart now, that Anna was dead. Everybody assumed he would take her back to America."

For Mark the story was like a curtain opening and letting in the sun. "That's amazing. Absolutely amazing."

"But then Antonio took a liking to me and . . . well, you know the rest."

Once near sunrise Mark woke up. There was enough light so that he could make out Christina's form sleeping next to him. This past month seemed like a dream. He was so fortunate to have her there with him. He reached over and took a lock of her hair in his hand. Softly, so as not to awaken her, he slid the sheet down from her shoulder. She was so beautiful. What turmoil she must have been going through. He moved the sheet so he could see her breast in the dim light. It would be worth any sacrifice to be with a woman like this. She stirred and rolled over. He got up from the bed and looked out. Christina's Thunderbird was still parked on the street. He wondered if the man with the red-headed girl friend was sleeping peacefully.

When they made love later that morning, it was with a strange lack of enthusiasm. All Mark could think of was that this was the last time for them. He wondered if she was thinking the same. As he watched her dressing afterward, his mind wandered to Antonio's cutting off his money, and to his meeting this afternoon with Dr.

Hall. Perhaps, too, Christina was thinking about her new life in Italy.

They decided to have breakfast in the coffee shop before leaving for the San Francisco Airport. Their conversation was strangely stilted and lifeless.

"Where does your plane stop?"

"In New York."

"When do you get to Rome?"

"You know, I didn't even look at my ticket."

"Is anyone picking you up?"

"No."

"Are you going to stay in Rome, or going to your mother's?"

"I'll go to Pinerolo for a while. I've been thinking of trying to work for the French Embassy again."

Mark handed her a piece of paper. "You'd better give me your mother's address."

It was as if they had withdrawn from each other in order to save themselves the pain of parting.

Mark headed for the hotel desk to pay their bill.

"Mark, you don't have much money. Here take this." Christina tried to hand him some folded money, but he refused.

"No, I want to pay. I don't want you to pay for our last time."

Their conversation remained forced and empty as they crossed the Bay Bridge and took the Bayshore Freeway toward the airport.

"So you're seeing Professor Hall for lunch."

"Yeah. One o'clock."

"I hope he can help."

"I do too."

At the airport Mark let her out at the curb with her luggage. He planned to park and meet her inside. As he watched her walk into the terminal, a flood of emotions struck him. He was a fool to let her go like this. A man could go an entire lifetime and never feel this way for a woman. No goal, no ambition, was worthy of losing her.

Hastily he parked the car and ran into the terminal looking for her. Frantically, he looked up and down, fearing that she might have already boarded. Then he spotted her sitting on a bench waiting for him and ran to her.

"Christina, I've been a fool. I don't want you to go."

"I know how you must feel, but we're doing what we have to do."

"But I love you, Christina."

She smiled. "I love you too."

"Then we have to find a way to be together. I'll come to Rome. I'll do anything. Christina, I'll never find another woman like you."

"Don't you see, my love? It cannot be. We have separate paths we must take."

"But you said you loved me."

"I do love you, Mark. But loving you doesn't mean that fate will let me be with you. The human heart is capable of many loves. This is not our time."

"It's money, isn't it? It would be different if I were rich like Antonio."

"Money is a very important part of the world. If we tried to be together you would soon hate me. You must go on with your career. Find a way to go on with your studies. Go to New York and fulfill your dreams. Someday I want to see you on a magazine cover. Can't you see we both want the same for you?"

"Promise me something."

"What?"

"You'll keep watching the newsstands in Rome."

"Okay."

"You'll see. One day I'll be on the cover of *Time*."

Mark sat at the bar watching Christina's plane, still at the gate. He could not afford it, but he ordered a Rob Roy. He wished he knew which was her window on the plane. Finally the 707 was pulled away. It was when he started to pay for his drink that he discovered the money Christina had slipped into his pocket.

Her plane came into view again just as it lifted from the ground. He watched as it headed east over the Bay. He hated what she had said about each of them finding their own separate paths, but he knew she was right.

"*Arrivederci*, Christina," he whispered. "*Arrivederci*." Fifteen minutes had passed when he finished his drink. By then the tears on his face had dried.

-4-

The drive from the airport to have lunch with Dr. Hall was melancholy. Mark knew that he had to be practical. Christina was right in returning to Italy and he must find a way to go on with his education. Despite this his mind continually tried to find ways he could be with her. Perhaps she could find a job in California. But secretaries made only $500 a month and Antonio would be paying her $2,000. Maybe she could stay in Berkeley without Antonio's discovering her and still get the $2,000 a month, but that would not work for long. He realized too, it would be impossible for him to live in Italy. But most disconcerting was the recurring suspicion that Christina really wanted to return to Italy, to make a new life without him. Why would a woman like Christina ever want him, a penniless student, when she could have her choice of men? He remembered her words: "A woman can love many men." Perhaps their affair was nothing more than a fling. Nothing to her but a temporary escape.

Dr. Hall and Mark were dining at a table on the porch of the University of California Faculty Club. It was very pleasant sitting outside near the huge trees that bordered the club. Most of the faculty were eating inside, but Hall had suggested the privacy of the porch. As the students walked by, Mark felt sentimental about Cal. These had been wonderful years. He only wished he knew where he would be next fall.

"I thought I should talk to you," Dr. Hall began. "Something must be bothering you."

"Why do you say that?"

"Your mind seems to be someplace else lately. I even had some first-year students complain about the way you corrected their papers."

"I'll be better. It's going to be different, I can assure you."

Momentarily a feeling that he might burst into tears moved through him. A flood of tension inside waited to burst forth.

"Don't you think it would be best if you told me about the problem?" Hall asked.

The invitation was all that Mark needed. He spilled out the story of his brief affair with Christina and how Antonio had canceled his financial support.

"I don't know what I'm going to do," he faltered, barely getting out the words. "I know what I did was wrong, but I had no idea that my whole life would go down the drain this way."

"It happens. I remember a colleague of mine, years ago, getting involved with a student. It nearly ruined his life. His wife couldn't handle it. She got a divorce so fast it would make your head swim."

"Well, it's over now. I just took her to the airport. She's gone back to Italy."

"Permanently?"

"Oh, yes, permanently. That was clear."

"And what about you? Financially, I mean."

"I can't even pay my room and board for the rest of the semester."

"I wouldn't worry about it. The university has emergency student loans."

"Really?"

"I'll look into it tomorrow."

Mark had hoped Dr. Hall could help. "Would you? It would be a big load off my mind."

"I'll find out whom you should see." Hall leaned back in his chair. "Do you remember when I first met you?"

"Sure. It was Econ 201."

"Was it then?" Hall asked.

"I'll never forget your explanation of 'future time preference.'" Mark was relaxing a bit.

Hall laughed. "Really? It's funny what will stick in your mind."

"I remember the tables were arranged like a 'U.'"

"Oh yes, I remember."

"You sat inside the 'U.' I remember thinking 'What kind of a crazy man is this?' You kept turning around in a swivel chair as you lectured. You were explaining the difference between people with high future time preference and those with low future time preference."

"I hope I was good at it."

"You were." Mark laughed at the recollection. "I remember you called on me. You asked me which I would rather have, a dollar now, or five dollars a year from now."

"And you took the five dollars?"

"Of course. You said that meant I had high future time preference. But then you asked me what I would do if I hadn't eaten for
a week and I needed the dollar for a meal."

"Knowing you, you would have starved yourself to get the five
dollars."

"Of course. Once a high future time preference man, always a
high future time preference man."

While they laughed, the waiter came by and filled their coffee
cups. Mark felt better. It seemed a year since he had laughed.

"Have you decided what you're going to do about next year?"
Hall asked.

"What would you say to my skipping graduate school and going to New York right away? Where the big money is."

"Stick with your education. An advanced degree will mean a
lot to you." Hall took a sip of his coffee. "Still no word about the
Rhodes Scholarship?"

"No."

"That's surprising. You should have heard by now."

"What do you think about a student loan if I stay at Cal next
fall?"

"I think it would be a real possibility. You're going to live in
Berkeley this summer?"

"I certainly can't stay home. Unless I decide to go to New York,
I'll live at the fraternity for the summer and get a student job
someplace."

"Oxford is by far your best bet. Two years' full scholarship.
The most prestigious university in the world. Oxford is very tough
academically, but you'd get an excellent education. Have you written them asking why you haven't heard?"

"No. I've been looking for a letter."

"Something's wrong, but I wouldn't take that as bad news.
They would have written, even if they had rejected you."

"If I stayed at Cal next fall it would be only for one more year,
not the two it would be at Oxford. I could get started in New York
sooner."

"Yes, but Mark, Oxford would open doors to you that Cal
couldn't hope to do. We gave you a wonderful education here, but
to be a Rhodes Scholar! Believe me, I'd give up a lot to be a Rhodes
Scholar."

"Do you think I have what it takes to succeed there? England
is a long way away. I wouldn't know a soul."

"What a perfect time for you. Your family, this man Antonio,
they've all cut you off. Even your lady friend. You have nobody,
no ties. What a time to start all over again. I envy you, young
man."

"I don't mind telling you the whole idea frightens me."

"Of course it does. It would frighten anybody. But you can't back away just because it frightens you."

"I suppose not."

"Remember, the mark of a good man is how he reacts to trouble. Don't go find a cave and lick your wounds. This is the time to stake out your claim to the future you want. My advice is go for it."

"I guess I'll write to England."

"Would a letter have been sent to your home?"

"I suppose it's possible. I might have given them my home address. But Mother would have called me."

"I see."

"Oh, my God!" Mark shouted, attracting the attention of others on the porch. "My father."

"What about your father?"

"Don't you see? If they sent the letter home, my father might have gotten it first."

"But surely, he would have told you about it."

"Not if it came after Easter vacation." Mark stood from the table. "Excuse me, Dr. Hall, but I have to leave."

Mark rushed to the fraternity house. Frantically he telephoned home. No one answered. Without knowing what he would do when he got there, he jumped into his old Ford and headed toward Sonoma. The fastest he had ever made the trip was 55 minutes, and that was late at night when there was no traffic. It seemed as if every red traffic light took forever to change. Impatient, he simply ran the red light near the freeway entrance. He continually changed lanes on the freeway, going as fast as he dared. He had no idea what he would do when he got home. If that son of a bitch had intercepted the letter from Oxford, he would kill him. He knew his mother would have telephoned if she had seen the letter. In his anger no other explanation for not having heard from Oxford was possible. His father must have seen the letter. He exited from the freeway and made his way around the north end of the Bay, toward Sonoma. The fact that no one had answered the phone meant that his mother was in Sonoma. They never took the car together, so Jonah must be around the property someplace. Finally he was through Sonoma and nearing the Movelli Vineyard and Winery. He would rip the place to shreds, if he had to, to find the letter. He looked at his watch. He had made the trip in 54 minutes.

The family car was not in its usual place—confirming that his mother was in Sonoma. Mark raced into the foreman's house.

Desperately he ran from room to room. The house was empty. He was right, his father was working outside someplace. He had no idea what he would do. The fact that if Jonah had intercepted the letter, he might have destroyed it, did not occur to him. The fact there might have been no letter from Oxford did not occur to him. To his angry mind the letter must be in the house someplace.

Mark ran into his parents' bedroom. Ever since he could remember he had been forbidden to open his father's chest of drawers. He yanked out the two top small drawers and hurriedly dumped their contents on the bed. There was no letter. He knew his father might return at any minute, but he did not care. Frantically, he searched the other drawers, spewing their contents helter-skelter over the floor. Again there was no letter.

He knew his father kept one of those cheap metal document boxes, but he did not know where it was hidden. Maybe Jonah had put the letter in the box. He started for his mother's chest of drawers. Maybe Jonah had hidden the letter there. The top drawer held his mother's inexpensive costume jewelry. He was overcome with the feeling of invading Amanda's privacy and stopped. Besides, if Jonah had hidden the letter there, surely Amanda would have found it. He looked around the rest of the house for hiding places, searching, looking, but to no avail.

Then he remembered a secret drawer in the bottom of his father's rifle case. Maybe that was where the metal box was kept. He took out two of Jonah's rifles to get at the drawer and hurriedly slid it open. There inside the drawer was the old green metal box.

He tried to open the box, but it was locked. He put it on the floor and grabbed his father's rifle. He smashed down on it with the rifle butt. He smashed it again, as hard as he could. With the blow the box and the rifle butt both broke apart. He bent over and picked up the smashed box.

"What are you looking for, college boy?" It was Jonah leaning against the door casing, a smirk on his face. Mark jumped with shock.

"My God! Dad!"

"I thought I told you to never set foot in this house again."

"I'm looking for something that belongs to me."

"It wouldn't be a letter from England, would it, college boy?"

Mark was still holding the rifle by the barrel. "So, you did see the letter."

"It wasn't addressed to anyone who lived here. So I send it back. 'Not known at this address.' or maybe it was 'Moved left no forwarding address.' Who gives a shit?"

"That was my letter. You had no right." Mark picked the rifle up over his head, as if he was about to swing it at his father.

"Go ahead. You wouldn't dare hit me."

Mark lowered the rifle at least for the moment. "What did the letter say?"

"How the fuck should I know? I told you, I sent it back."

"When did it come?"

"A month ago. Right after I caught you fucking Christina Movelli. Who the hell knows? Who the hell cares?"

Dropping the rifle, Mark scooped up the metal box and hurried to the kitchen. He wanted to telephone Dr. Hall. He would know how to find out about the scholarship.

"You can't use that phone," shouted Jonah. "Get the fuck out of here."

Mark started to leave, to go to the mansion and use Mona's phone, but Jonah stood in his way.

"You give me that box. You have no right," Jonah shouted. He yanked at the box, dislodging it from Mark's grasp. The box dropped to the floor, spilling its contents. From the way Jonah scrambled after the spilled papers and envelopes, Mark realized there was something there Jonah did not want him to see.

"You get away from there," Jonah cried, trying to block Mark with his body while picking up the papers.

But Mark was quicker. He snatched the papers from his father and, turning his back, quickly rifled through them. There it was. There was the letter with "Rhodes House" printed on the return address. He dropped the rest of the papers and fled from the house.

"You come back here with that," Jonah cried.

"It's mine, you son of a bitch," he shouted and ran for his Ford.

Mark waited until he was a mile down the road before he pulled over and tore open the letter.

> *We are pleased to announce that you have been awarded a scholarship. You should present yourself at Worcester College, Oxford on 5 October 1963 where you will be assigned your rooms. Transportation will be provided on the* Ile de France *departing New York 31 September at noon. The enclosed packet will supply you with complete details.*

"My God!" Mark shouted. As he drove back through Sonoma, his spirits were elated. It was over 10 minutes before his hands stopped shaking and his pulse calmed down. He knew this would be the shortest summer of his life.

Part Two

-5-

Mark stood on the deck of the *Ile de France*, excitedly taking his first look at England. The mood of the passengers was festive as the great ship docked at Southampton. It was cold and foggy and he was happy for the heavy gray sweater his mother had given him for graduation last June. All of the 29 Rhodes Scholars aboard stood together, fascinated at the activity on the dock below. They had rooms on the same deck and had dined together on the Atlantic crossing. By now all were well acquainted. One of them spotted the bus that Rhodes House had arranged to transport them to Oxford.

Mark was the only Rhodes Scholar from Cal and would be the only one attending Worcester College, one of over 30 separate colleges in the University of Oxford. Mark had enjoyed the fellowship on the voyage, but was uneasy. Most of the men had scholastic records every bit as good as his and were from prestigious universities, such as Harvard and Yale. Many were from wealthy families with connections assuring future positions. Inwardly he felt they were from a class above him, with their better clothes and affluent life styles. A common topic at bull sessions aboard ship had been how difficult Oxford would be. At Cal Mark had never doubted his success, but as he prepared to disembark from the *Ile de France* he knew the competition would be stiff. He was not at all sure how he would measure up.

The Rhodes Scholars worked their way through the crowd toward the bus. A small crowd surrounded fellow passenger Peter Sellers, seeking his autograph. One of the Rhodes Scholars was saying good-bye to his shipboard romance, a petite member of a traveling dancing troupe which had an engagement in London. The scholars had attracted the attention of the ship's other passengers and many were wishing them well as they departed.

Mark had always wanted to see London, but the bus driver told him their route was not near the capital city. London would have to wait until another day. The young men looked out the windows as the vehicle made its way toward Oxford. The representative from Rhodes House, called the Warden, worked his way up the aisle explaining procedures and answering questions. Mark was fascinated by the countryside, so green compared to the dry hills of California. He was both excited and apprehensive about the adventure ahead of him.

The bus worked its way through Oxford's heavy traffic. Charles Billings from Princeton, who had bunked above him on the ship, was dropped off at Christ Church College. The others in turn gathered their luggage and were wished well as the bus stopped at their colleges. Being at the edge of town, Worcester College was the last stop.

"Here you are, Mr. Stevens, Worcester College," said the Warden. It was the first time Mark had heard an Englishman say the word "Worcester." He seemed to be pronouncing it "Wuster." "The entrance is right across the street there." He pointed at the very old stone building. "Good luck to you, my good man."

"Thank you, sir," Mark responded, as he helped the driver unload his luggage.

"If you have any questions be sure and ring me at Rhodes House."

"I will. Thank you again."

Mark stood on the sidewalk watching as the bus pulled into the busy traffic. It took him two trips to get his luggage across the street. He found it very confusing with the traffic being on the opposite side of the street from that in America. He found himself looking in the wrong direction for oncoming cars. Finally with his suitcases at his feet, he stood looking up at the gray three-story building that was the main building of Worcester College. He felt a thrill go through his body. What all summer had been only a featureless, faraway place had now taken reality. He liked Worcester already. The events that had so disrupted his life were in the past now. He was excited and looking forward to the new challenge.

Mark entered the old front door to the college. Inside was a small glass-windowed room, sort of a guard's post where the student mail was collected.

"I'm Mark Stevens, a new student," Mark told the man who was in charge.

"Yes, Mr. Stevens, I'm James, the porter here at Worcester College. We've been expecting you. Did you have a good journey?" Mark was impressed that the man knew him without checking any paper work. "Your rooms are in the Terrace. Staircase Four, Room Eight. It's on the third floor of that large newer building to your right from the cloisters."

Mark took the keys and started through the building with one of his suitcases, intending to return for the others. "Oh, Mr. Stevens," the Porter called after him. "You have a letter."

Eagerly Mark looked at the letter. Seeing his mother's hand-writing drove home how far away from home and familiar sur-roundings he was. He put the letter in his pocket to read when he got to his room. Struggling with his luggage, he walked through the building that opened up onto a large grassy quad, surrounded by old buildings and a high brick wall. It was peaceful inside the quad. The noise of the city traffic was shut off by the buildings. The only sound was the English-accented chatting of the students returning for the new term.

Mark struggled with his luggage up the narrow wooden stairs of Staircase Four. He was confused. There was no Room Eight, yet he could swear he was on the third floor as the porter had told him. As he pondered his plight, he heard the sound of someone coming up the stairs.

"Are you having some difficulty, old chap?" It was a large young man about his own age.

"I can't figure out where my room is. It's supposed to be here on the third floor, but I can't find Room Eight."

The man laughed heartily. "I'm in Room Nine—across the hall from you. It's one more flight up."

"But that would be the fourth floor," Mark protested.

The man again laughed good-naturedly. "That would be true if you were in America, but we English never do anything like other people. You see over here the first floor is one above the ground floor. The second floor is two above the ground floor, and so on. I must say, I think your system has it right."

Mark laughed too. "No, I wouldn't say that. Your system has its point."

"Allow me to introduce myself. I'm Rodney Ashley. You must be our Rhodes Scholar. I suspect we'll get to know one another before this year is over."

"Yes. I'm Mark Stevens. I'm from California."

"Here, let me help you with those cases." Rodney picked up two of the suitcases and started up the stairs. He looked to be about five feet ten and must have weighed nearly 250 pounds. With Mark following, the Englishman was puffing by the time he reached the top of the stairs.

"Here you are. I trust you will enjoy your stay here at Oxford."

"Thank you. I'm sure I shall."

"I'll tell you what. Why don't you come by after you've got yourself settled. We'll have a beer at the buttery before dinner."

"The buttery?"

"Yes. It's our name for the beer hall."

"The college has its own beer hall?"

"It wouldn't be Worcester without the buttery. Come by my room when you're ready."

The "third" floor was the top floor in the Terrace. Mark looked out his gabled window down onto the grassy quad. In the distance he could see the fortress-like towers of buildings of other colleges. The porter had referred to the Terrace as a newer building. It had to be 150 years old, but he could see that the building across the quad was much older than that. He looked around his room. It was depressingly tattered and bare. Each student in the Terrace had two private rooms. The larger was his study or living room, which was furnished with a writing desk under the window, an old sofa and two upholstered chairs. He tinkered with the fireplace, which looked as if it had not worked in a century. He looked at his tiny bedroom. It was furnished with an old, free-standing wardrobe and a single bed. For shaving and washing up, it had hot and cold running water over a porcelain basin. It too was dreary. There was not a single picture or other decoration in either room.

He plopped down in the old sofa and opened his mother's letter. As they had agreed at graduation, Amanda had obtained a post office box in Sonoma. They wanted to keep their letter writing secret from Jonah, who persisted in his edict that she have no contact with her son. Amanda wrote of her church work, the weather, the grape harvest and that neither Jonah nor Antonio ever spoke of him. She had little news, but clearly she missed him. As he finished the letter he realized that perhaps with the exception of Rolf Williams, his mother was the only person alive who cared what happened to him.

Mark read the letter once again and began to unpack his things. Perhaps the rooms would look better with his belongings in them, he thought. He needed some posters like those he had had at the Alpha Zeta house. As he unpacked he remembered landing at New York's Idlewild Airport and taking the bus across Manhattan to the waiting *Ile de France*. From the bus, New York was very busy and exciting. One day, when he was finished at Oxford, he would have a large office with a prestigious investment banking firm. To be a partner in such a firm was worth any sacrifice, including living in these depressing rooms for two years and standing up to the rigorous competition he knew he faced here at Oxford. Ruefully, he wondered again about Christina. Where would he be today if he had never gone on that horseback ride with her? All summer, while he had worked at the Berkeley restaurant, he had not been able to keep his thoughts from her. Despite his better judgment, he had finally written to her in Rome the news of his Rhodes Scholarship and given his Oxford address. Even though Oxford was thousands of miles closer to Rome, he felt much farther away from her. He knew he should stop thinking about her. He wished he could.

When Mark finished his unpacking he decided to take up Rodney Ashley on his offer for a beer. He changed his shirt and put on his sweater. There were only three rooms on Mark's floor. Rodney's room was directly across the hall. The room had two doors: an outer door, which was open, and an inner door, which was partially open. As Mark reached to knock he was struck by self-doubt. He would be living across the hall from Rodney for two years and he wanted to get started on the right foot. Yet he had the impression that the English were very proper and a little stuffy. He was not sure how to act with Rodney. Taking a deep breath, he knocked. There was no answer. He cocked his head and looked through the partially opened door. He could see Rodney sitting in his chair. Rodney had seemed sincere when he invited him over. He knocked again.

"It's me, Mark Stevens." He paused. "From across the hall."

Mark could see that Rodney was reading a newspaper, but he still did not answer. For a moment he thought he might have misunderstood the invitation, and considered returning to his room.

"Come in. Come in. By all means come in," bellowed Rodney.

Mark pushed the door completely open. Rodney was seated in a tattered easy chair, his feet on a footstool and with a newspaper in his hand. He lowered the newspaper and peered at Mark.

Mark saw that Rodney was wearing only a pair of shorts—red shorts. He had a bath towel over his shoulders. Mark stared at Rodney's protruding belly. His head was massive and striking, with black hair, still wet and uncombed. Rodney reminded Mark of a young Santa Claus. He had lived with 40 other men at the Alpha Zeta house, but had never seen anyone like this before.

"I came by for that beer," said Mark.

"Damned *Times*! I don't know why I read it. All it does is make me angry." Rodney continued reading. "Look at this! Just where in blazes do they think the government is going to get all the money for those blasted programs? It's all rubbish." Mark hesitated to go into the room without an invitation.

Rodney tossed his newspaper on the floor. "Please come in and sit down, old man. Sorry, I got so involved with that bloody newspaper. If they had their way this country would never recover. Spend, spend, spend! He vigorously pointed at the newspaper on the floor, as if he had killed a snake.

"I see you're not dressed. Would you like me to come by later?"

"What? Oh. Don't mind me. When my outer door is open, it means I'm at home for visitors."

"Oh, I see."

"I just had my bath and got involved with this bedamnable paper," Rodney said, laughing. "I'd love to have a pint with my friend from the New World. Spare me a moment while I put on some clothes."

Mark stared at Rodney's massive form he as walked into his bedroom. Rodney's rooms were exactly like Mark's, except that Rodney's were nicely furnished with pictures on the walls, new lamps and a new rug.

"I see you're wearing a woolly. Did anyone tell you we all wear jackets and ties to dinner?"

"No. No one told me anything about that. They never wore suit jackets at Cal." All Mark had was his gray sports coat that he had worn every night on the *Ile de France*.

"Why don't you sit down until I get dressed for dinner? We can have a sherry while you change, if you like. We have plenty of time."

Mark was annoyed. If it had not been for Rodney, he would not have known about coats and ties and would have been improperly dressed for dinner. He certainly did not want to wear the same sports coat every night for two years. He would have to squeeze his budget and buy an extra one or two.

Rodney reentered the sitting room. He looked thinner in his rumpled plaid sports coat that concealed his belly. Actually, he was rather good-looking with his straight black hair combed back smoothly, off-setting his striking head and face. He was holding three or four ties in his hand.

"Here, tell me which tie looks best with this jacket."

"The plain blue one. You really should wear a plain tie with plaid."

"Bloody hell, Mark, all my jackets are plaid or some sort of pattern. I'd never wear some of my ties, if that were the case," said Rodney, laughing heartily. Mark noticed the way he pronounced "pattern," like "patt'n."

Looking in the mirror above the fireplace, Rodney knotted and adjusted the plain tie. He pulled a bottle of sherry from a cabinet and poured two glasses. Mark did not like sherry, but certainly was not going to tell his host.

"Here's to hands across the sea and all that," said Rodney, smiling and handing Mark a glass, at the same time raising his own in a toast.

"Yes, here's to hands across the sea," answered Mark, touching glasses.

As they walked across to his rooms, Mark felt that he had made a new friend.

"The man who had this room last year failed his prelims," said Rodney.

"Prelims?"

"Yes, preliminaries. First-year men take prelims to see if they are getting on all right. They're tests—as you call them. He failed them, poor chap, but I suppose it's better to fail early, rather than later."

"But since Rhodes scholars start out in second year, I would be exempt from prelims wouldn't I?" asked Mark.

"That's right. Prelims are only given in the first year."

"What's this I've read about Oxford not giving exams each term? That seems strange to me."

"Our only really important exams are given at the very end of the third year, just before graduation."

"That's a little frightening. Not having any idea whether I'm going to pass or fail, until two years from now."

Rodney laughed. "Well, they do have what we call collections. They're not examinations, but you'll be warned at collections if you are doing badly. Oxford figures if you're good enough to make it to your second year, you're going to get your degree all right."

"I suppose that's comfort of sorts."

"Don't worry. As long as you're not lazy or stupid, you'll do all right on the examinations. How well you do determines what sort of degree you get—first class, second class or third class. I'll probably get a third, perhaps a second."

"Doesn't that put a lot of pressure on those final exams?"

"Only if you're not satisfied getting a third."

Mark sipped his sherry. He was trying to imagine the pressure there would have been at Cal, if all his grades had depended on one set of final exams at the end of four years. What was more, he knew he would never be contented with a third class degree. He wondered if Rodney had family money or connections, so that he did not need to be concerned as long as he graduated. Mark took his sherry into his bedroom and changed his clothes.

"How do I look?" he asked when he came back into his sitting room wearing his gray sports coat and dark trousers.

"Super. But what about your gown?"

"My gown? What are you talking about? My gown?"

"Your academic gown. You know cap and gown and all that."

"You're joking!"

"We wear our gowns every night at dinner over our jackets," said Rodney.

"Come on over to my rooms and I'll put on mine." Rodney's black gown was different from the one Mark had worn at the Cal graduation exercises. Rodney's was not as long and did not completely cover his suit coat.

"I'm sorry, but I don't have any gown."

"You are certainly in a fine pickle my friend," laughed Rodney.

"Surely they'll let me eat dinner without a gown."

"Wait. I have it. I have an extra gown. I kept my old one in case I needed to clean my good one." He returned to his bedroom. "Yes, by Jove! Here it is."

Mark laughed to himself. He thought Englishmen said "by Jove" only in movies—Dr. Watson and people like that. Mark put on Rodney's gown. It hung like a tent over him. At six feet, Mark was only two inches taller, but Rodney weighed at least 60 or 70 pounds more.

"Thank God, I didn't have to borrow your sports coat," laughed Mark.

"I have a picture of that," said Rodney.

They both looked at each other and laughed heartily.

"Come on. Let's go downstairs and have those pints," said Rodney.

"Who lives in Room Seven?" asked Mark, as they clattered down the stairs. He was referring to the third room on their floor that, being in the back of the building, faced the other direction.

"Derek. Derek Harden. He's reading for P. P. and E. Went to Eton with me. I knew him well there."

"What's P. P. and E.?"

"Philosophy, Politics and Economics."

Mark was studying Philosophy, Politics and Economics too, but he had not heard the abbreviation.

"I suggest you be careful of Derek," Rodney added mysteriously.

"What do you mean, be careful of Derek?"

It was beginning to rain, so they walked under the protection of the cloisters. "Perhaps I've said too much. You should judge for yourself, but I've found him to be very difficult. A quarrelsome fellow."

They scurried down the ancient outdoor granite steps just as the students who had been sitting there were driven into the buttery by the increasing rain. The buttery was packed with students and a couple of faculty members.

Cigarette smoke filled the air. The room was small, perhaps 20 feet by 20 feet. The walls were richly paneled with dark wood and covered with trophy shelves, plaques and old photographs of athletic teams. The two took their glasses of beer from the bartender. The room was very crowded with students talking, smoking and drinking. As there were no chairs or benches, everyone was standing. All wore coats, ties and academic gowns.

"Here's to happiness in paradise *and all of that*," said Rodney exaggerating his last words and holding up his glass.

"Yes, cheers and *all of that*," retorted Mark, chuckling.

Mark was grateful for his new friend, but he realized that he still felt the outsider with the other students, as he had on the *Ile de France*.

Rodney introduced Mark to another student, John, who joined them. They talked of America and Cal. "Tomorrow is my first tutorial," John said.

"I'm supposed to see my tutor at ten o'clock," said Mark. "I know Oxford doesn't use the classroom lecture system we use in America, but I have only a vague idea what a tutorial is."

"A tutorial is simply a meeting with your tutor," said Rodney.

"My tutor is my professor then?" asked Mark.

"Right. Whom do you have to see tomorrow?" asked John.

"I don't know," said Mark. "The paper was just signed with his initials. R.A.D."

"That's Richard Dawbarn," said Rodney. "He's the best we have at Worcester."

"I wonder who your tutorial partner will be?" John inquired, sipping his beer.

"What's a tutorial partner?" asked Mark.

"Simply the student who attends your tutorials with you," said John. "You share the same tutor."

"Dawbarn assigns your tutorial partner," said Rodney.

"It's important that you get the right sort of chap," said John. "Last year one of my tutorial partners was very unpleasant. In actual fact it was quite a miserable experience."

"I guess I'll find out more tomorrow," said Mark. Today had been a day of learning English customs: driving on the left side of the road, the floor-numbering system, the coat and tie and now this tutorial partner business. He would have to take these things in his stride.

The number of students in the buttery was thinning out as the dinner hour neared.

"We'd better go up to the dining hall now," said Rodney.

The buttery was below ground level in a very old building near the dining hall. The three left together and climbed the outside

stairs to the cloisters, near the entrance to the dining hall. The
rain had stopped and some students were finishing their beer in
the small courtyard outside the buttery. Others were still talking
while standing on the stairs. The three joined the short line of
students filing into the large high-ceilinged dining room.

Once they were inside the dining hall, the din was very loud.
The conversations of a couple of hundred chatting students echoed throughout the room. The young men were seated at four
long tables, which stretched out the length of the room toward the
head table. Mark was thankful for the borrowed gown. As in the
buttery, all of the students wore gowns over their coats and ties.
Chandeliers added to the light from the sky, that came through
the large windows. The noise made it very difficult to hear someone who was not sitting very near.

Suddenly a procession of faculty and dignitaries shuffled up
the aisle. The students stood at their places as the procession
circled the head table, which was on a raised platform. Then
absolute silence came over the hall.

"*Nos miser homines et egeni, pro cibis quos nobis ad corporis
subsidium benigne es largitus,*" prayed a strong male voice, a student at the second table over.

Mark felt a rush of emotion that tingled along the back of his
neck. So this was Oxford! As he stood with his fellow students,
he felt a part of centuries-old tradition. His high school Latin was
not good enough to understand more than a few words of the
prayer, but in this academic setting he felt a deep connection between generations of persons who held dear the finest in culture
and civilization. He knew he was privileged to be here at Oxford,
furthering his quest to become an educated man.

The benches scraped loudly on the floor as everyone sat down.
Then the din of low-pitched male voices resumed. The waitresses
and waiters in their black uniforms included skinny women, fat
women and little old men, who began serving large dishes of food
for the students to pass to one another along the long tables. Tonight the fare included rather overcooked slices of hot beef along
with beets, turnips and boiled potatoes.

"Pass the biscuits, please," Mark asked.

"We don't call them biscuits, my friend. Biscuits are what you
call cookies," smiled Rodney. "We call these rolls."

Something else for Mark to get used to. At the end of the meal
a dessert was served and dinner was over. Many students lingered to talk, but others left the dining hall as soon as they finished eating.

"Must go," said the young man across the table. "I'm off to the Duke of Cambridge for a pint with my Somerville College bird. Haven't seen her all summer."

"Are there many women's colleges at Oxford?" asked Mark.

"A few, but I'm afraid not enough. Many of us don't have women friends at Oxford, just at home," said Rodney.

Some of the students were going to the movies, others to pubs, some to the television room and still others remained to chat.

"Care to join my bunch at the cinema?" asked Rodney.

"I'd better not," said Mark. "I got a letter this summer. I was supposed to 'take a look at' a list of books during the summer. I gathered that 'take a look at' means 'damned well better read.'"

"All those reading for P. P. E. got that," said one of the students. "No one takes it very seriously."

"Thanks, but I've only got about 40 pages to go in the last book," said Mark as the group began to leave. "I'd better finish it before tomorrow."

As he walked up the stairway toward his room, he wished he had accepted the invitation to go to the movies. Unlocking his outer door, he thought of changing his mind. At that moment the door to Room Seven opened and there stood a man his own age, nattily dressed in a sports jacket and tie.

"You must be Derek Harden. I'm Mark Stevens from America. I'm in Room Eight here. I guess we share the bath and loo." Mark walked down the few steps to the landing that separated them and extended his hand.

"Yes. Well, I can tell you're an American from your accent, can't I?" Derek only perfunctorily grasped Mark's outstretched hand, as if he would rather not.

"Yes, I suppose you can," laughed Mark, nervously withdrawing his hand, uncertain whether Derek meant to slight him.

Derek stood by his door, head held high, and holding a small thin cigar. He was a good-looking man with very curly blond hair. He was shorter than Mark and more athletically built. Making no attempt at conversation, Derek took a puff from his cigar and acted as if he wanted Mark to get out of his way so that he could leave.

"Well, I'm turning in for the night. I have a book to read," said Mark, backing away so that Derek could get by.

"As you can see, I'm going out." Derek turned his body to get past Mark and started down the stairs.

"Good night," managed Mark.

"Good night," mumbled Derek. Mark disliked the cocky swagger in the man as he disappeared down the stairs.

As the sound of Harden's steps faded, Mark shook his head and walked into his room. He wondered what it was that made

Derek so obnoxious. He resolved that the thing to do was stay out of Derek's way.

He fumbled for the switch on his desk lamp and looked out his window. The rain had completely cleared. He could see a few students still chatting on the steps near the cloisters. Across the quad, lights were on in some of the rooms in the Cottages building. There was still some late sunlight on the distant spires of Oxford. He stood watching for several minutes. Despite his experience with Derek, he liked Oxford. He was fortunate to be in such a beautiful place. He opened his book, *The European Economy Since the War*, and began reading.

-6-

Mark was shaving in the lavatory in the corner of his tiny bedroom. He had finished his book last night and was eager for his tutorial this morning at ten o'clock. The radio was playing the recent Beatles single, "She Loves You." As he looked at himself in the mirror, he remembered he had dreamed about Christina. All he could remember of the dream was that he had been in the Durant Hotel, desperately trying to tell Christina something, but not able to get out the words. From the dream he knew Christina was still not out of his system.

As he went down the staircase for breakfast, he noticed that Derek's outer door was closed. He was glad there had been no contact with him this morning. Sometime he would have to ask Rodney more about Derek.

The line of students that waited for breakfast under the cloisters outside the dining hall was very short. At breakfast the students came and went at any time after eight. Coats and ties were not required. Mark took some juice and cold cereal and looked for a place to sit. He saw John, one of the students from the buttery yesterday.

"Hi, John, how's it going this morning?"

"Sit down, Mark, won't you?" John invited. "Let me move over a bit."

John and he chatted pleasantly. John's first tutorial of the Michaelmas term was this morning at nine. He was in his third and final year. Mark had noticed last night that John had an accent different from Rodney's.

Mark took the plate of two poached eggs on toast, offered by the elderly waitress. The water from the bland eggs had soaked into the toast. Although the plate was garnished with a boiled tomato, it looked rather unappetizing.

"Try some of the bacon with your eggs," John suggested.

"Thanks. I believe I will." Mark took two slices of the rough, thickly sliced bacon. "Smells good."

"I must apologize. We English aren't very imaginative when it comes to food," he said.

Mark laughed. "Listen, after the food at Cal, I can eat anything." The truth was the food at the Alpha Zeta house was much better.

"I can only say you haven't eaten a real breakfast until you've had a full English breakfast on a Yorkshire farm," said John. "You see I was brought up in Yorkshire. My parents are farmers. Perhaps you'd stay with us some time and try my mother's cooking."

So it was a Yorkshire accent that John had. Mark liked John. He seemed like an ordinary sort of fellow and apparently his background was similar to Mark's.

"Do you know Rodney well?" Mark asked.

"I know him here at Worcester, but otherwise not too well. You do know about Rodney's family, don't you?"

"His family? No. He didn't say anything about his family."

"Rodney wouldn't. His father is a Lord. His mother is also from a very prominent family. Very wealthy."

"I didn't know that." A picture of Rodney reading the newspaper in his red shorts passed through Mark's mind.

"Rodney is an exceptional person. He accepts everyone for what he is."

"I gather he doesn't think much of Derek though."

"No. No one thinks much of Derek, except his little clique of friends."

"What's Derek's problem anyway?"

"I doubt that anyone knows. Rumor has it his mother and father had a very messy divorce years back. I hear his father has made millions, import-export, something like that. It's made Derek too big for his trousers."

"He was certainly rude to me last night."

"That sounds like Derek Harden all right."

The best part of the breakfast was lingering and talking over coffee, with toast and marmalade. Mark poured himself another cup of the thick coffee and diluted it with plenty of milk.

"No more black coffee for me. You English make it too strong for my taste," Mark laughed.

"I don't blame you. No Englishman in his right mind would go without milk in his coffee."

"I'm surprised to hear what you said about Rodney. So his father is a Lord."

"Don't let on I told you. It would embarrass him."

They chatted for some time. Mark was surprised at John's knowledge of America and his intense desire to travel there. "I'm hoping that when I finish Oxford, I can get the money together to visit America. It seems to be a place where you can get ahead, no matter what your background."

"When you do go to the United States, you must visit me," said Mark. "I expect to be living in New York. Let's keep in touch after we leave Oxford."

After several minutes John pushed his bench back. "I must leave now for my tutorial. It's nearly nine," he said. "I want to wish you the best of luck. It would be a pity if you didn't get a decent tutorial partner."

"Where can I buy a newspaper?" asked Mark, as the two rose to leave the hall.

"At any news agent. There's one down Walton Street." John pointed out the direction. "But they've got the morning papers in the Junior Common Room." He smiled quizzically as he headed for his tutorial. "If you go there be careful of the ghost of Amy Robstart. She haunts the place." Mark started to ask John what he meant, but he was already gone.

The Junior Common Room was on the first floor of the Cottages, the old building across the quad from Mark's room. Mark climbed the rickety stairs that led to the JCR, as it was called. A handful of students sprawled on some of the couches and chairs that filled the spacious old room. Ancient paintings contributed to the comfortable but dreary air. Mark took one of the newspapers from the long wooden table at the edge of the room and sat in a large chair that faced the empty fireplace. He smiled at the thought of the ghost of Amy Robstart. This was a perfect room for an English ghost.

Mark was eager to find out about the World Series. There had been no news on the *Ile de France*. He smiled. The paper he had selected from the table was *The Times*. He was curious to see what it was about the Times that had upset Rodney. He searched for the sports section, but there was nothing in it about American sports. There was coverage of soccer, cricket and plenty of horse race results, but nothing about the World Series.

He turned to the front page and worked through the paper. The paper was flat and unappealing. There were no columnists as in the *San Francisco Chronicle* that he usually read at the fraternity. He noticed the crime stories. They were about crimes in unknown sections of London and cities in the rest of England. He never thought he would miss reading about some murder in the Bay area, but he did. He read one of the editorials, but could not see what had upset Rodney so much.

Mark took another paper from the table. It too was flat and dull, with little news from America. It was going to be a long two years without knowing something about what was happening at home.

He remembered a student on the *Ile de France* mentioning a newspaper published in Europe for Americans. He walked the five minutes to the news agent and found the paper. It was the *Herald Tribune*. He eagerly began reading as he walked back on the sidewalk. Los Angeles had won the World Series from New York four games to none. President Kennedy was asking for a large appropriation for the space program. Perhaps we would reach the moon one day. To have some news from home made him feel less alienated. He read until it was time for his tutorial.

He wanted to be early for his tutorial. The sheet said he should report to the room of his tutor, Richard Dawbarn, in the Nuffield Building at ten o'clock, but he had no idea how to find Nuffield. He walked completely around the quad, but there was no building called Nuffield. He looked around the old building that housed the buttery, but still no Nuffield. He had used up the extra time he had allowed and was getting nervous about being late. Finally, he stopped a student, who directed him to a low tunnel under the Cottages. The narrow tunnel was barely large enough for his head to clear and he had to be careful not to bump the students coming the other way.

He was amazed when he emerged into the daylight at the other end of the passageway. There was much more to Worcester than he had realized. The tunnel went under the Cottages and then opened onto a beautiful field with extremely green grass and huge trees. There were several more buildings that he had had no idea existed. Hurrying, he found Nuffield, which was a three-story building on the left, facing the field. He looked at his watch. He would barely avoid being late. He found the building directory and rushed up the stairs to Dawbarn's rooms.

Mark was perspiring as he knocked on Dawbarn's door. A student opened the door. "We're nearly finished," the student said. "I see your tutorial partner isn't here yet. He should be along in a minute." Relieved that he wasn't late, Mark sat down to read the *Herald Tribune* in the dim light of the hallway.

As he read, he heard footsteps on the wooden stairs. He assumed they belonged to his tutorial partner. He shifted his eyes from the newspaper to the blond curly-haired young man who stood before him. He was shocked. It was Derek Harden. Of all people at Oxford, Derek Harden was his tutorial partner!

"It's you. That American from next door," said Derek, glaring at Mark. "What bloody bad luck!"

Flustered, Mark was searching for words, when the two students from the previous tutorial exited the room, talking to Dawbarn as they left.

"Come in. Come in," said Dawbarn heartily. "Sit down. How was your summer, Harden?" Not waiting for an answer he turned to Mark. "I'm Dawbarn. Richard Dawbarn. I'll be your Economics tutor."

Dawbarn was a short, vigorous man in his early 50s. John had explained that Dawbarn was a widower until recently, when he had married a younger woman, who retained her government post in London. His hair was already totally white, as was his mustache. Mark wondered if his own white streak would spread so that his hair too would be totally white. Dawbarn wore a rumpled suit with vest, and a plain brown tie. The sporty look of his patterned cream-colored shirt did not go with his suit.

"Thank you, sir. Thank you very much," said Mark.

Finally Derek answered Dawbarn's question about his summer. "In actual fact I had a very delightful summer. I traveled with my parents. My father had business in New York. It was my first trip to America since I was a child. I used to live there with my mother."

"If I recall, your father is in import-export. What sort exactly?" asked Dawbarn.

"Father was looking into importing whiskey from America. Bourbon actually. It's made in a place called Tennessee. I can't abide the stuff. The American taste is abominable."

"Mark here is from America. A Rhodes Scholar from the University of California. Tell me, Mark, do you drink bourbon?" asked Dawbarn.

"Bourbon, especially sour mash bourbon, is very good, but I'm more of a wine drinker. I was brought up on a vineyard in California," said Mark.

"I never drink California wine. French is the only proper wine," said Derek haughtily. "Did your father export the wine from his winery?"

"My father doesn't own the vineyard, Derek. He only works there. My father is the foreman."

"Oh, I see. We have the American success story here. Workman's son to Oxford. Well, you Americans certainly are busy taking over the world." Mark took a deep breath, containing his anger at Derek's sarcasm.

Dawbarn ignored Derek's remarks. "Tell me, Mark, do you know what we do in a tutorial?"

"Apparently Derek and I are tutorial partners. That's about all I know, Mr. Dawbarn."

"Toward the end of the hour I'll give you both a reading list. Next week you are each to submit an essay. I'll assign the subject this morning. We won't have time for each of you to read your essays, so you'll alternate from week to week."

"What are you looking for in the essays?" asked Mark.

"I'm glad that you asked that. Many Americans have difficulty getting accustomed to our way of writing. We want it short. We want it pithy."

"I see."

"We aren't particularly looking for original ideas in essays. I don't expect some new theory from you." He made a face as he finished his cup of tea. "This bloody tea is cold." He put down his cup. "I will assume that you've read the subject, so I don't want you merely to tell me what you've read. Be succinct. As I say, be pithy. Then tell me what you think of what you've read. Draw conclusions. Have your own opinion. Tell me what you think the situation is."

"All right."

"I'm interested in your truly comprehending what you've read. Perhaps Derek, here, will help you from time to time."

Mark looked at Derek, who looked into the fireplace and said nothing.

"I hope it won't be needed, sir," said Mark, looking again at Dawbarn. The last thing he wanted was help from Derek.

"I'll make us more tea before we begin," suggested Dawbarn.

Dawbarn walked to the adjacent room to fill the kettle with water. Mark looked around the study, avoiding looking at Derek. The walls were covered with bookcases packed to overflowing. The wooden floor was partially covered with a large beige rug. Uncomfortable being alone with Derek, Mark looked out the window at the park-like area, which was bordered by Worcester buildings. Beyond in the distance he could see water.

The two said nothing to each other as Dawbarn returned and plugged in the full tea kettle. Mark looked at the photographs standing on the mantel. The attractive dark-haired woman must be Dawbarn's new wife. The room, the books and the photographs gave him a feeling of knowing Dawbarn. He already liked this man who would be so important to him for the next two years. The trouble was, he could not say the same about Derek.

"There, that will take just a minute," said Dawbarn of the kettle.

With a large cloth he began to erase the chalkboard that covered most of the wall opposite the windows. Mark recognized the economic terms scrawled on the board which Dawbarn was erasing. Comparative advantage. Terms of trade. Ricardian model.

Many were circled and some had arrows vigorously pointing to other words.

"Today I want us to talk about comparative advantage. Mark, I assume that you have previously studied something about comparative advantage."

Indeed, the subject had been included in his third-year international economics course with Professor Hall. "Yes. We studied it some." Mark was reassured. International economics had been his favorite subject at Cal. Although he was on the other side of the Atlantic, he knew he would feel at home discussing the subject.

The kettle loudly clicked off and belched forth its steamy whistle. "What kind of tea, gentlemen?"

"Darjeeling," said Harden.

"The same," said Mark, not knowing one tea from another.

"There, that will make this exercise in learning a little more palatable," said Dawbarn, sipping his tea.

He then launched into a discussion of comparative advantage before his attentive audience of two. "Every country has certain products that it can make better or more cheaply than another country. That country is said to have a comparative advantage over other countries. It might be due to the easy accessibility of cheap raw materials, or perhaps cheap labor, or even very highly skilled or specialized labor, such as used in English china or French wine.

"Let's say Ruratania makes ties more cheaply or better than the United Kingdom." Dawbarn pulled his necktie from under his vest. "If that is so, why should the U.K. make its own ties? Why shouldn't the U.K. import all its ties from Ruratania?"

Dawbarn feverishly scrawled a caricature of a necktie and circled the words "Ruratania" and "U.K.," drawing arrows back and forth between the two countries.

"All right then, Mark, what does the Association of English Tie Manufacturers demand of Parliament?"

"They demand a tariff on foreign ties, so that Ruratanian neckties can't compete with U.K. ties," said Mark. He was having fun getting in the spirit of Dawbarn's Ruratanian example.

"And Derek, what does the Tie Workers Association argue to support the new tariff?"

"They want Parliament to protect the jobs of the tie workers," answered Derek. "Tariffs protect employment." Mark knew Derek had given a good answer.

"Remember, the M.P.'s in tie-making districts are much more vocal than the vast number of unorganized tie buyers, who won't protest too much about paying a pound more under the tariff," said Dawbarn, getting up from his chair and drawing a stick man representing a Member of Parliament waving his arms.

"Well, someone had better protect the consumer, or we won't have any trade at all," said Mark.

"Correct. And that someone is you," said Dawbarn, plopping down in his chair and tucking his tie inside his chalk-marked vest. "This morning, Mark, you are Reginald Maudling, the Chancellor of the Exchequer. Your task in Parliament is to justify the government's new lower tie tariffs." Mark was puzzled as to what was expected of him, but Dawbarn continued. "First to speak will be Derek Harden, Member of Parliament from Tieshire, who will now question the Government."

Derek stood, confidently facing the other two with his back to the chalkboard. He was now an M.P., addressing the House of Commons. He cleared his throat and began.

"Unemployment in Britain is already dangerously high and now Mr. Maudling wants to throw the tie makers of my district out of work—good, solid people who have been tie makers for generations. Where will they go? What will they do?" Derek pointed his finger at Mark. "Mr. Maudling is unfeeling and uncaring towards my constituents." Derek was taking the matter seriously.

"Perhaps ties are a little more expensive, but after all they are made in Britain," Derek continued. "We must protect our own. Surely these good people should be making ties and paying taxes, rather than collecting redundancy benefits. All this just to save a pound on a tie? Mr. Maudling forgets that we aren't in America. In this country we care more about people than money." Derek sat down.

Dawbarn loudly clapped. "Very good Derek, very good indeed. Now it's the turn of the government. Mr. Maudling, the government's position, if you please."

Mark took his turn standing by the chalkboard. He wasn't nervous. He knew what he wanted to say and he was glad for the chance to show he knew economics. "The Right Honorable Harden is quite right supporting the small necktie makers and the workers of his district." He wasn't sure about the "Right Honorable." "But I have a larger duty. My duty is to all of the people of the United Kingdom. It is true that if there were no tariffs on ties, some workers would be displaced, but I am here representing two constituencies. My first is the millions who must pay more than necessary for their neckties to support Mr. Harden's inefficient workers. The government has programs to teach them more competitive jobs."

"And your other constituency, Mr. Maudling?" asked Dawbarn.

"My other constituents are the British workers who make products that are exported to foreign nations. After all, if we keep out Ruratanian ties, you can't expect Ruratania to allow our dairy products into their country. If they did, it would mean the end of a vast number of Ruratanian farmers' jobs," Mark finished.

Derek jumped to his feet. "In other words, let my tie makers starve to death. Is that right Mr. Maudling?"

Mark, still standing, spoke. "We must foster free trade or we can't have a growing economy. If every country had high tariffs, Britain would never be able to sell its products overseas." Mark felt as if he were on a roll. "With high tariffs we couldn't concentrate on what we're good at. We must be able to sell in other countries. Britain is in enough trouble as it is."

As Mark spoke, Dawbarn had finished his tea and had taken a cigarette from a black package. He clapped loudly. "Perhaps not put as politically appealingly as it might, but very good nonetheless. Now, Mr. Harden, do you wish to say more?"

"I certainly do." Derek took his turn, again standing. "Let them starve. That's what Maudling would do. Warning to workers: 'If the government finds you inefficient, out you go—fend for yourselves.'"

Mark answered eagerly: "I do care. The lower tariff will be phased in. There will be retraining programs, so that workers can get better jobs." He was very much involved in the debate.

"That's rubbish and he knows it. He'd make the tie workers leave their homes and move to London, where it's already overcrowded," said Derek.

"It's that kind of talk that keeps the British economy in the doldrums. Protectionism may be politically appealing, but it's bad economic policy."

The two had been heatedly wrapped up in the debate.

"Gentlemen, you have done a good show of some of the issues involved in trade legislation, but it's five minutes to eleven," Dawbarn interrupted. "Now for your essay next week. I want you to refine the arguments for and against high tariffs. Discuss tariffs to protect infant industries. Be certain to include the problems of tariffs on major industries, such as automobiles and farm products." He listed several other points he wanted covered. "Here's the reading list."

The tutorial had ended. Derek and Mark walked down the staircase together into the bright sunlight. "So long, Derek. Maybe I'll see you in the dining hall," said Mark, hoping he might somehow engineer a rapprochement with Derek.

"You listen to me, Stevens, I'll not have you showing me up the way you did in that stupid debate." Derek pointed his finger at Mark's chest as they stood in front of Nuffield.

"I didn't show you up, Derek. I thought you did a good job."

"You know very well Dawbarn deliberately gave me the tougher end of the debate. He's always deferring to you Americans. As for the dining hall, I suggest you not come near me."

"I don't know what your problem is, Derek, but I'm telling you you're way off base." Mark was angry as he watched Derek storm along the walk toward the Terrace. He could see now there would be no getting along with him. The man was crazy—out of his mind. The only thing to do now was to live with the situation for eight weeks, until the term ended and Derek was someone else's problem.

Mark decided to take a look at the lake he had seen from Dawbarn's window. He wanted his anger to settle down. He walked the several hundred feet through the park-like grass to the water's edge. The tiny lake divided the college proper from the cricket and football fields. A small bevy of ducks caused ripples in the serene water. He sat alone on one of the benches at the water's edge for several minutes. He knew he had done well in today's tutorial, but was already thinking about his essay for next week. He looked at the suggested reading list that Dawbarn had given and decided that he had better get started with it right now.

He walked through the narrow passageway under the Cottages and past the students who were chatting on the cloister steps. He would like to join them, but was determined to get started on his reading. He climbed the spiral staircase, which would take him to the library above the dining hall. He wanted to write the best essay on tariffs Dawbarn had ever heard.

Mark smiled grimly. So Derek Harden thought he had deliberately showed him up, did he? Well, he could hardly wait to see Derek's expression next week, after he had heard Mark's essay.

-7-

It was a Friday late in November. Mark walked with his shoulders hunched against the damp, chilling wind that swept the quadrangles of Oxford. He wore his new leather jacket over the sweater his mother had given him and, even then, he shivered. Never in his whole life had he experienced such raw weather. During the past six weeks Derek had continually tried to provoke Mark with his scornful remarks, but Mark was determined to hold his tongue until the term was over.

Tuesday had been Derek's turn to read in Economics and yesterday Mark had read in Philosophy where, thank God, he had a pleasant tutorial partner. In two weeks the Michaelmas term would end and he would be rid of Derek Harden.

Mark walked the half-dozen blocks to the Bodleian Library. When it was cold like this, his old leg injury ached and he was glad to be inside the huge stone library building nicknamed the "Bod."

He sat in a small quiet room reading a biography of John Maynard Keynes, Britain's chief delegate to the 1944 Bretton Woods Conference in Vermont. Dawbarn had assigned Bretton Woods for next week's essay and Mark wanted to learn about the powerful personalities who had devised a new system of international monetary exchange. It intrigued Mark that world leaders deferred such great power to economists like Keynes because international economics was such an unfathomable mystery to them. As he read, he admired Keynes' impact on British economic policy and eventually on Roosevelt's New Deal. One day he would like to make his own mark on history as Keynes had done.

The author of the Keynes biography was Roy Harrod, who had also attended the Bretton Woods Conference in '44. Harrod was now on the faculty of Christ Church, Oxford's largest college, and was famous in his own right. Mark decided that he would see if he could study with Harrod, perhaps next year, when he could take a special elective course. He was fascinated with Bretton Woods and the men who had created the new world economic order.

When he finished reading, it was past one o'clock and he had missed lunch. He plunged his hands into his jacket pockets and walked along Broad Street toward Worcester. He stopped at Blackwell's for a moment to look in the window. The inviting old book store tempted him. He decided to browse in the economics section. Blackwell's was such a wonderful place. Mark had been there many times. Often, he had leafed through a book and found himself sitting on the floor reading for 15 minutes or more. He had never yet been disturbed by a sales clerk. After browsing and reading, he left Blackwell's with a book on economics and another on traveling in Britain.

Mark decided to have lunch and a pint of beer at the Eagle and Child, a pub which students nicknamed the "Bird and Baby." The pub was crowded with students. He found a table in the back room and returned to the counter for his food. The sight of the fire in the fireplace warmed him. If it were this cold in autumn, he wondered what winter would be like.

As he ate his hot lunch, he looked at the pictures in his new travel book. One section was about Yorkshire, where his friend, John, lived. The scenes were silky green and beautiful. He recalled John's invitation to visit his parents' farm. Perhaps he would visit there this summer and have that Yorkshire breakfast John had offered.

Mark was distracted from his book by an attractive woman at the next table. She was a good-looking blonde, old enough to be a graduate student. Her male companion was younger, more Mark's age. She listened intently to what her friend was saying. Like a shot, Mark felt an immediate connection to her. It was the same feeling that he had with Christina.

Christina had been less and less on his mind as the term had progressed. Engrossed in his studies, he had shifted to another mentality, a frame of mind that excluded women and sexuality. However the sight of the blond woman suddenly rekindled the emotions in him that had been dormant since Christina had left.

Except for the color of her hair, the woman did not look at all like Christina. Perhaps the connection was because the blonde was older than her male friend, the same as Christina and he. As she animatedly talked, she twisted and turned her body, causing her miniskirt to show her thighs. His heart quickened. She radiated the same female sensuality as Christina.

The couple gathered their belongings and left the pub, each with an arm around the other. Mark hastily put on his jacket and followed them. He was embarrassed by what he was doing. What if they realized he was following them? What did he hope to accomplish? He lingered for a moment so that they would not see him. God, she was sexy as she walked along St. Giles in her short skirt—it must have been five or six inches above her knees. As he followed the couple, cutting through the walk by the St. Giles churchyard, he noticed the sign announcing that Sunday's sermon would be "Lust After Life." Indeed at this moment, it was lust that he was feeling for the blond woman.

The couple turned and walked up the Banbury Road. Mark crossed the busy road so they would not think he was following them. They hesitated in front of the quaint hotel and went inside. Despite the cold, Mark stood thinking and watching the hotel. He envied the young man. The woman was so much like Christina. He wondered where Christina was now. Was she still in Rome? Was she with someone new? He thought of the hotel in Berkeley and wished he were there with her again.

He stood waiting in the cold for five more minutes. It was just as well they didn't come out. He should not be following them anyway.

He walked back through the churchyard and continued to Worcester. He had to forget the feelings the blond woman had aroused in him. Christina was gone from his life. He knew it was for the best. He should not let himself be diverted from his studies.

He entered the front door at Worcester, where he had struggled with his luggage that first day in October. He walked under the cloisters and up Staircase Four to his room. It was good to get in from the cold.

Mark sat at his desk writing his Bretton Woods essay. He wanted next week's tutorial to be a good one, but as he worked he was distracted by thoughts of the blond woman. He found himself wondering how he could meet her. Finally he gave up trying to write. He put on his Beatles record and idly looked across the quad at the Cottages. Next Thursday would be Thanksgiving at home, but it would be just another Thursday in England. He would miss being with his mother and, oddly, even miss his father. He remembered when his grandmother and grandfather used to drive to the compound from Vallejo for Thanksgiving. Sonoma seemed so very far away from Oxford. Maybe he would get together with some of the other Rhodes Scholars from the *Ile de France* on Thanksgiving. They had been gathering occasionally at the Nag's Head pub not far from Worcester. The students found that the meetings alleviated their homesickness.

When the Beatles record was finished, Mark decided that a visit with Rodney might chase away his lonely mood. The two had developed a deepening friendship these past weeks. Nearly always they went to the dining hall together and frequently chatted in their rooms.

"Sorry, old man. I was taking a snooze." Rodney's abundant body was covered by a robe that came to his knees.

"Are you okay? You look a little sleepy," Mark asked.

"I'm all right. Come on in and I'll put on some tea." Rodney clicked on the kettle.

"I just can't seem to concentrate on my essay," said Mark. "My mind wanders."

"You sound to me like you're ready for a holiday. Only two weeks to go. Tell me, what are your plans? Vacation lasts six weeks, you know."

"I don't have any special plans. One of the Victoria League ladies told me that each Rhodes Scholar gets invited to stay with a family. I suppose I ought to get busy and call her," said Mark.

"It sounds perfectly dreadful."

"I would like to see something of London, if I can."

"I've got it," said Rodney. "Why don't you stay with us for a few days before Christmas? We always spend Christmas in the country, but we won't be going there for a week or two. You could stay with us in Chelsea."

"Where's Chelsea?"

Rodney smiled and poured Mark a cup of tea. "Chelsea, my friend, is a part of London. We have a house there. You'd like it, I'm sure. We're only a block from the mod crowd action."

"I suppose I ought to do some of my reading for next term . . . but it sounds wonderful. What would your parents say?"

"Oh, it'll be all right with them. I've brought home plenty of friends over the years."

"You're on. I've always wanted to see London."

"Fine. It's settled then. I'll call Mother. We'll go by train."

"I can do my reading after I visit you. You're sure it will be all right with your parents?"

"Let me tell you, Mark, most anything I do is all right with my parents *as long as*." He smiled.

"What do you mean *as long as*?"

Rodney laughed. Let me give you a short list. First *as long as* I finish Oxford even with at least third class honors, then anything I do is all right with them."

Mark laughed as Rodney continued.

"Then *as long as* I go into some respectable business, I can do anything."

"Are there more?" Mark asked.

"Of course. *As long as* I marry the right girl." Rodney stopped and held up his hand. "Wait. There's more."

"More?"

"Yes, more. There's *as long as* my private life stays out of the newspapers, I can do anything I want. There are plenty of others, but that will do for now."

"You've never talked much about your parents. I gather you've got to behave yourself."

"Oh, I'm not complaining. They're quite fair with me. They'd not even protest if I came home drunk, or if I smashed the family car." He laughed. "'Smashed the car *again*,' I should say. I already smashed it once this year."

Mark laughed along with his friend.

"In actual fact, Mother and Father are very liberal with me. They simply don't want me to break with family tradition. When Father came to Worcester instead of Madgalen College as Grandfather and Great-grandfather had done, it was shocking. It would have been unthinkable if he'd gone outside Oxford, let alone if he hadn't gone to University at all. They want me to be like them."

"Sometimes I wonder if that's not what's behind my father's being so angry with me," said Mark.

"What do you mean?"

"He knows I'm never going to be like him . . . a laborer . . . no education . . . never much money. I'll never forget his calling me a smart-alec college kid."

"What's your father like?"

"His name is Jonah. The truth is, I really don't like him very well. Can you imagine not liking your own father?"

"It would be very difficult—at least for me."

"Dad's a strong, good-looking guy, all right. Lots of muscles. A lot of women really like him. But he's always screaming at people, especially me. I think he's afraid of getting old. He drinks way too much. He's always whoring around. He even gave my mother V.D. once, if you can believe that."

"And he wants you to be like him?"

"I don't know if that's what's bothering him. It's just that every time I try to get ahead, he cuts me down."

"My parents just want me not to disgrace them. To be sure, it would be fine if I became the P.M. or the Foreign Minister, something like that. But they don't expect me to make money. Certainly not to be like Derek or his father . . . you know they wouldn't want me to go into some sort of commercial enterprise."

"Seems strange to me—not to want to be better than your parents. Since I was a teenager I've wanted to live better, to be better than my father. But then, if my father were like yours . . ."

"I've never thought of being anything different from my father. We've always had more material things than we ever needed. Mother and Father never spoiled us though. We never got just anything we wanted. In actual fact though, we knew that one day we could have anything we wanted. I guess money simply isn't an issue with me, Mark. Here do you want some more tea?"

Mark held out his cup as Rodney poured. "That's easy when you're well off, but I'm on the outside looking in."

"Maybe I'd feel that way too, if I were on the outside looking in, as you put it."

"I'm here to tell you that you would." Mark helped himself to the milk and sugar. "The only successful man I ever knew was Antonio. Except for him, I didn't even know anyone who was well off."

"Antonio?"

"Antonio Movelli. He's the man who owns the vineyard and winery where we live—kind of a second father to me. We always lived in the foreman's cottage on Antonio's compound. He has the biggest house in the Sonoma Valley. A huge two-story Spanish place." Mark gestured.

"Maybe half as long as the Terrace here. Until last year, my goal had always been to be like Antonio."

"What happened last year?"

Mark was hesitant to tell Rodney about Christina. While he enjoyed the openness that had developed between them, he was not yet ready to tell him about the affair.

"Let's just say that Antonio got angry with me. As angry as a man can be. The problem is I deserved it. All the good times went down the drain. I remember Antonio's library, where we played chess on Friday nights. I can still feel the touch of those leather books—hundreds of them. He never read them, but how that man prized his books. He wouldn't let anybody but me touch them. I'd take a book home nearly every week. *David Copperfield, Jane Eyre, Tom Sawyer.*"

"It sounds as if Antonio was an important influence on you."

"I wanted so much to be like him instead of like my father, but I always knew Antonio's money was what made him an important man. Everyone on the compound respected him because he owned the place. Even though he was old, he could have almost any woman he wanted because he was rich."

"He must be a powerful chap," said Rodney.

"He is. He once told me he was leaving the whole Movelli compound to me in his will," Mark sighed, "but I'm sure that's all changed now."

Rodney got up and went to his cabinet. "What do you say to a glass of sherry?"

"Thanks. Sherry sounds great." The chat had changed his lonely feeling. He sipped the sherry and continued, "All this is why I'm here at Oxford. Someday I'm going back to the compound. First I'm going to look my father square in the eye. Then I'm going to tell him, 'Look at me you son of a bitch, I've got it made. I'm better off than you could ever be.' Then I'm going up to Antonio's mansion. 'Look at me,' I'm going to tell him. 'See, I made it without you. I can buy a dozen of your mansions.'"

"I can tell how strongly you feel."

"I know of only one way to get what I want and that's to get the best education I can. I'll work 20 hours a day for 20 years if I have to, but I'm going to get there."

"I believe you will too. I've seen how hard you work."

They sat for a few minutes drinking their sherries, only occasionally speaking. Mark drew a deep breath. "Let's go down to the buttery."

"I could do with a pint myself," agreed Rodney.

Soon they were climbing down the staircase to join the others in the buttery. Mark wore the academic gown he had recently purchased on High Street. He had become much more comfortable with Oxford life and was included in group treks to pubs and movies. Tomorrow night he would attend the new production at the Oxford Playhouse, provided he got in a good bit of studying tonight. Over beer in the buttery, they were joined by John and two others. After dinner the din of the male conversations quieted, and Mark and several students lingered to talk.

"Come on, Mark. We're going to the cinema. Tonight it's Van Heflin in *Cry of Battle*. You must join us," said John.

"No, I goofed off all afternoon. It's the library for me tonight. I'm finishing my Bretton Woods essay."

Mark said good night to the others and climbed the circular staircase to the library.

He had been reading only a few minutes when he looked at the library clock. It was just past seven o'clock. He planned to go through various books, then go to his room and write the rest of his first draft.

"Mark! Mark!"

He turned around. The urgent voice was much too loud for the quiet library. It was Charles Billings, the Princeton Rhodes Scholar from the *Ile de France.*

"Shush, not so loud! What's the trouble?"

"Have you heard?" Charles asked.

"Heard? Heard what?"

"It's the President! President Kennedy! He's been shot!"

Mark and Charles walked quickly together through the night to the Nag's Head, where they thought other Americans might be gathering.

"I can't believe it, Charles."

"Neither can I."

"How did it happen?"

"All I know is that he was in Texas. He was in a motor-cade . . ."

Mark and Charles sat down in the pub with several subdued Americans, who were already there. Soon more Americans joined them, some arriving singly, others in groups of two and three.

A radio was tuned to the BBC. Mark helped push the tables together so that they could feel they were together as they listened. Each new arrival was brought up-to-date on the tragic events.

The President was shot as his motorcade went through Dallas, reported the radio.

"Quiet!" said a student. "Let's listen to the radio."

Stunned, the students looked at one another with blank expressions.

Mrs. Kennedy was with him in the limousine at the time of the shooting, and accompanied the President to Parkland Hospital.

The wait for news of the President's fate seemed interminable, although Mark could not see how Kennedy could survive.

Governor Connally of Texas, who was in the Presidential party, was wounded. His condition is not known.

"Doesn't look good," said one of the students.

Vice-President Johnson was not in the car with President Kennedy and apparently has not been shot.

"Oh, my God!" said a student. "Do you suppose it's a conspiracy to get them all?"

We have a report that the Secret Service is protecting Vice-President Johnson.

"None of this seems possible," Mark said.

"Remember how President Wilson lived so long after his stroke?" asked a student.

Finally, the news that they had dreaded came.

President Kennedy died at 1:00 p.m., Dallas time. He was shot at 12:25.

Everyone was quiet. Then followed gentle murmuring and occasional conversation.

"How can it be?" one asked.

"Who could have shot him?"

"What will happen now?"

"He was so alive and now he's going back to Washington in a goddamned box," said Mark.

We have a report of a policeman having been shot . . .

Vice-President Johnson has been sworn in as the new President . . .

Air Force One will soon take off with President Kennedy's body and the new President on board . . .

"I wish I could get to Washington somehow," said a student with tears in his eyes.

Another was softly crying. "I want to be home with my family."

The British were having their own reactions to the radio announcements. They sat in small groups at the various tables, listening carefully and sharing feelings. Several approached the Americans to offer consolation and express their sorrow.

"How perfectly awful!" said one.

"He was such a vital young man," said another.

"Ghastly!"

"What will the free world do without him?"

Suddenly Mark heard a loud dissonant voice. "Drivel. Absolute drivel!"

Surprised, Mark looked up. It was Derek Harden striding toward the Americans.

"Who the hell is he?" asked Charles.

"Derek Harden. He's my tutorial partner. A real pain in the ass!"

Derek stopped a few feet from Mark. He was well dressed as usual.

"Look, Stevens, no man can be glad about this sort of thing, but I must say I can't join in all of these phony banalities!" It was obvious that Derek had been drinking.

"Derek, for Christ's sake! Our President has been killed! For once keep your goddamned prejudice against Americans to yourself!" Outraged, Mark stood facing Derek. He felt like hitting him.

"Hold on, Mark. Don't let him get to you," said Charles, who jumped to his feet and grabbed Mark by the shoulder.

"This is my country and I'll say what I bloody well please," said Derek loudly.

"Listen, Harden. He was our President and I'll not take any of your crap," said Mark. His anger was at the snapping point.

"Kennedy's no martyr. If I hear the word 'martyr' again, it will make me ill. He was on a blasted political trip to Texas, not being a martyr. You Americans have no right to lead the free world. You're nothing but a bunch of bloody cowboys, killing whomever you want."

Mark was beyond restraint. He yanked himself free from the grasp of his friend, and hit Derek as hard as he could.

Derek staggered and fell to the floor, holding his jaw. He looked up at Mark in surprise. A beer had spilled over his clothes. Everyone was looking at him. "Why, you're a bloody cowboy yourself, you fool."

"Get up, you bastard," Mark shouted. "I'll hit you again."

Charles and another American restrained Mark.

"Cool down, Mark."

"Take it easy."

"You mark my words, Stevens; you'll never finish Oxford. I'll see to that." Derek's female companion helped him get up from the floor and wiped the blood from his face. "The provost will hear about this in the morning," Derek shouted, as the two left the room.

Several Englishmen stepped forward to Mark.

"Sorry," said one.

"He doesn't speak for us."

"The bugger deserved it. I was about to hit him myself."

Before Mark could absorb what had happened, the evening was over and everyone was leaving the Nag's Head. Several were shaking Mark's hand.

Charles and Mark left the pub and walked back through the chill air together.

"I'm glad you hit him. The bastard deserved it."

Mark wondered what the provost might do. Could he possibly be disciplined for striking Derek? He thought about the weeks of insults and the venom Derek had spewed out toward Kennedy. Derek acted the way his father would.

"I'm glad I hit him too," Mark said. "Damned glad!"

-8-

Mark was exhilarated as he walked from his last tutorial of the term. It was a cool, bright, December morning. He felt like a colt kicking up his heels. No longer would he have to deal with Derek. For six whole weeks he would be free of tutorials and studying. He was excited about going to London.

The days since the Kennedy assassination had been filled with intense studying until two and three o'clock in the morning. Mark was bone weary from the regimen, but today he was charged with new energy. Light-heartedly, he walked across the grassy area to the lake and sat on his favorite bench, watching the ducks paddle busily about. "Hey, ducks", he said out loud, oblivious to whether others were overhearing. "Listen to me. Do you know I go to London this afternoon? *Quack, quack, quack.*"

Mark had been concerned that Derek might make good on his threat to make trouble with the provost, but he had heard nothing from the provost.

He was proud of his recent essays in both Philosophy and Economics. In last week's Econ essay, he had postulated an idea about reforming the Bretton Woods system of monetary exchange. He doubted that his ideas were anything new to Dawbarn, but he had been pleased when the tutor had complimented him, especially since Derek was present. His early fear of failing at Oxford had been replaced by confidence in his work. He had gotten the hang of doing well at Oxford and had even been thinking about the possibility of graduating with first class honors.

The ducks were swimming to the other side of the pond by the cricket field. Ducks never worried about the Dereks of the world or first class honors. He felt good inside today. He got up from the bench and stretched. "Good-bye, ducks. I'm going to pack my suitcases for London now. See you in a few weeks. *Quack, quack, quack.*"

.   .   .

It was two-thirty as Mark and Rodney watched the powerful diesel train for London pull to a stop at Oxford station. Mark handed the luggage piece by piece to Rodney, who had jumped on board first and was lifting their suitcases onto the luggage shelves of the coach.

"I didn't think I had to bring everything," Mark complained. "I thought I could leave some of my stuff in my room."

"No, we have to clear out our rooms every December for potential students. Poor devils converge on Oxford from all over Britain to take their entrance exams. I did it myself. For a good many, this is as close to Oxford as they'll ever get."

The two talked animatedly as the train passed through the countryside out of Oxford. "I telephoned Mother last night. They've been in Nice for two weeks and only just returned. They're going out tonight, but you'll get to meet them before they leave."

"I feel I know them already. You talk about them so much."

"I know you'll like them, especially Mother. She's the thin one. You'll see for yourself. I look more like my father."

They walked forward to the next coach to buy coffee.

"Tonight is when we see the Beatles," said Rodney.

"Can we see Big Ben and Buckingham Palace tomorrow?" As they made their way back to their seats on the lurching train, they tried not to spill their scalding hot coffee.

"We'll see them Monday, when we go to the House of Lords."

"The House of Lords? You hadn't told me we could see the House of Lords."

"Father is a member of course. He'll leave us passes for the Members' Gallery. We're lucky. The House of Lords normally wouldn't be in session, but there's some sort of special ceremony going on."

Mark was impressed. A few months ago he had been cleaning wine vats in Sonoma and now he was going to be the guest of Lord Ashley, a member of the House of Lords.

They talked until the 60-minute journey ended with the train's pulling to a stop at Paddington Station.

Mark unloaded the luggage and stood on the long platform, waiting for Rodney to find a porter. The vast station appeared to be over 100 years old. He looked up at the cavernous roof supported by a lattice work of iron girders. Everything in England was so old! When Paddington was built, San Francisco barely existed.

"Here we are." Rodney had found a porter who was pushing a cart.

They followed the porter through the crowd toward the taxis. Mark dodged the hurried but polite crowd, which was scurrying for the pedestrian tunnels leading to different Underground trains.

They passed various British Rail advertising posters. Paris, Rome, Munich, Amsterdam. To be so close to all these places made them very real. Maybe he could see them this summer. Mark was surprised that the line of a dozen or more black Austin taxicabs was actually inside Paddington Station. The porter filled the luggage area next to the cab driver and still needed more room.

"Here, put the rest in back," directed Rodney. "We don't want to take separate taxis. Driver, take us to Chelsea Square."

Mark climbed into the crowded cab, but there was not enough room for the corpulent Rodney. Laughing at their plight, they took the baggage out of the taxi and rearranged it. This time they both made it inside the cab with their legs stretched over the luggage, which was jammed on the floor, and with a large suitcase stashed on the seat between them. Laughing, they were thrown back against their seats as the taxi pulled forward out of Paddington.

Meanwhile, back in Oxford, Derek Harden was meeting with the Provost of Worcester College, where he was lodging a complaint against Mark.

"Let me understand this, Derek," said the Provost, a pleasant man in his 50s who was the head of the college. "Mark Stevens and you had a quarrel the night of the Kennedy assassination, and he struck you. Is that correct?"

"Yes, sir. Totally without provocation."

"I find that hard to believe, Derek. Surely you said something to him."

"Nothing to justify his striking me."

"What was it you said?"

"I merely pointed out that Americans were a violent lot, as they had shown in Dallas."

"And you expect me to do something about this altercation?"

"Well, sir, I would hope you might call him in and . . ."

"Derek, you've been at Worcester over a year now. You know very well that such matters are not the business of the college."

"But this was very serious. He actually knocked me down."

"If you have a complaint, I suggest you make it to the landlord of the Nag's Head, not to me."

"But sir."

"I would suggest you forget this whole matter. These things happen, you know."

Derek was very angry as he walked back to his room. I have no intention of forgetting the whole matter, he thought. I'm going to make Mark Stevens a sorry man if it's the last thing I do.

"I've got it," said Rodney as the taxi entered traffic. "Let's show you Buckingham Palace on the way home."

"To the palace it is," joked Mark, his spirit of adventure riding high.

"Driver, take us by way of Buckingham Palace."

Mark stared out of the taxi window at the sights of the busy city. Traffic was very heavy, interspersed with many red double-decked buses, carrying signs indicating their destinations.

"What odd names," commented Mark. "Eastcheap. Elephant and Castle."

"Odd? I never thought of those names as odd. Now here comes what I call odd. That's Speakers' Corner. It's those fellows over there that are odd. They stand there endlessly spouting out their paranoid theories. I think maybe the people who listen are a bit daft too."

A traffic light changed, but a young woman in an extremely short skirt ran in front of the traffic to catch her bus. "Look at the legs on that one, will you?" cried Mark.

"I'm busy looking at a bird here on my side." Rodney was delighted with their banter.

The cab turned right onto a faster moving street. "Down that street over there, a couple of blocks, is the American Embassy." Rodney pointed. "That's Hyde Park on your side."

Mark was overjoyed with London. He liked Oxford well enough, but London had a big-city excitement. "I can't believe this city. I've never seen anything like it."

"Then let me show you Piccadilly. Wait, driver, turn down Piccadilly."

Rodney's impulse was a mistake. The traffic ahead was hopeless and the car stopped.

"I've heard of Piccadilly, but I don't think I know what it is."

"Piccadilly is the name of the street. It runs to Piccadilly Circus."

"I still can't believe I'm here." There was an aura about London that excited Mark. He was in a whole different world. Hundreds of taxis, cars and red double-decked buses crowded Piccadilly. Yet the people were not frenetic. No horns blew. Pedestrians waited for the signals, instead of surging against the light. For all the excitement, there was a gentility, a civility.

The taxi, with its passengers comically stretched across their luggage, made very slow progress down Piccadilly which, typical of London, was lined with four- and five-story buildings.

"God, it feels great to be out of Oxford! At least for a while," said Mark. "I didn't realize how much I needed a vacation."

A light changed ahead and their taxi made some progress. "The church here on the right. It's St. James's Piccadilly Church. Mother goes there. It's a metaphysical church."

"I have only a vague idea what metaphysical means."

"Ask Mother sometime. But be careful. She'll talk about it forever if you give her a chance."

"It's certainly an attractive old church."

With a light change, the taxi was able to move. "This is Piccadilly Circus," said Rodney. "Most people would say this is the center of London. Here and Trafalgar Square are where the crowds celebrate—as when the war ended."

"Like Times Square on New Year's Eve."

Piccadilly Circus was filled with people crossing streets or going downstairs to the Underground. A few young people stood listening to a group of musicians. "Everything is so different from anything I've ever seen."

The taxi turned onto another street.

"All right, driver, let's go to Buckingham Palace."

"Yes, sir." The taxi turned and picked up speed. In a few minutes they arrived at Buckingham Palace."

"It looks almost like an office building. No turrets and moats as I had imagined."

Rodney smiled at Mark's naivete. "We have our share of that sort of thing, but this is a palace, not a castle."

"Can we see the changing of the guard?"

"Certainly we can, but not today. That's at eleven o'clock every morning. We'll see it when we visit Parliament."

They stood outside the huge wrought-iron gates, looking at the palace and its famous guards. Mark was moved by the tradition, the power and the wealth he was witnessing. "Can you imagine people living in a place like that?" he asked.

"Of course, the real power is over at number 10 Downing Street, but there is something about the majesty of the monarchy, isn't there?"

It was getting dark now, but Mark lingered by the big gates, reluctant to leave. "We'd better go," said Rodney. "You'll see it again Monday." They crawled over the crammed luggage into the taxi. They drove past the palace and began to gather speed, when suddenly a guard walked into the street, halting traffic and bringing their taxi to an abrupt stop.

"What is it, driver?" asked Rodney.

"It's the Royal Mews, sir. A car must be coming out."

Several more guards stopped traffic in both directions. A large black limousine slowly pulled out from the palace.

"It's a Rolls-Royce. I think it's the Queen," Rodney said, matter-of-factly.

Mark leaned forward in anticipation.

"Yes. It is the Queen—and Prince Philip," said Rodney.

"You're right! It is!" said Mark excitedly. "I recognize them!"

"There must be an official engagement somewhere. They never use the Rolls unless it's an official engagement."

The car came within a few feet of their taxi, its famous occupants in full view.

"I never thought I'd see the Queen of England," said Mark, turning and watching through the rear window as the car disappeared. "Their Rolls doesn't even have a license plate."

As fast as it had happened, it was over, and their taxi headed for Chelsea.

"You didn't seem very excited. Have you met the Queen before?" Mark asked.

"Not actually met her, but Mother and Father have, several times. I have seen her a few times from a distance."

"I've never seen a car so long."

"Rolls-Royce makes it especially for the Queen."

"I wonder if anybody could buy one. If he had the money I mean."

"I suppose so. Probably not one just like the Queen's, but one just as lovely, I'm sure."

"Can you see the look on my father's face if I drove up in one of those with a chauffeur and the whole bit?" asked Mark.

"Knowing you, you'll have a car like that someday, if you set your mind to it."

Mark settled back in the taxi. "When I was in high school I had a little mite of a teacher. Miss Zackem was her name. Miss Zackem was the only person I ever knew who had visited England. She described everything so vividly. I remember her telling us about the Tower of London and all the kings and queens getting their heads chopped off. She had me listening to every word, and now I'm actually here."

"I had a teacher like that once, at Eton."

"It was because of her that I took English History at Cal. I've been here less than an hour and everything she told me about is so real. It's as if I've lived in London before."

"My mother would say you were a Londoner in a prior life."

"Does your mother believe in reincarnation?"

"She says she does. I don't know how serious she is about it. Here's Chelsea Square now. You'll meet her in a bit." Rodney spoke to the driver. "Number 101, please."

The dwellings on Chelsea Square were not pretentious. Most were town houses, built close to the street. Mark had expected something larger, but he realized that homes with large grounds must be few in London, as in San Francisco.

"Here on the left," Rodney said to the driver.

The three stories of the large house rose up beyond the high red brick wall bordering the street. Rodney pushed the buzzer by the gate. It was answered by a middle-aged servant. "Robert, this is my friend from Oxford, Mr. Stevens. He'll be staying with us. Please attend to the luggage."

"Lady Ashley told me to expect Mr. Stevens, sir. The guest room is ready."

The gate opened onto a three-car garage at the side of the big house. Although it was dark now, Mark could see a beautiful dark green sports car through the open garage door.

"That's Mother's Aston Martin. She must have just got home." Robert took their luggage in the servant's door and Rodney led Mark around to the front of the house. The red brick house was considerably larger than it appeared from the street. Shuttered windows and a slanted roof gave it the appearance of being two stories, instead of three. The front entrance was approached from a courtyard, also made of red brick in a herringbone pattern. A large wooden gate gave the courtyard privacy from the street. Mark could see through the ground-floor windows into what he took to be the living room.

Mark was apprehensive about meeting Rodney's mother and father. He was not in the same class as people who lived in such a magnificent house. He feared that Lord and Lady Ashley would look at him as if he were a stray brought home by their overly friendly son.

The young men entered the large, marble-floored entry. Two large paintings on opposite walls dominated the hall.

"I'll see if I can find Mother and Father. Have a look about. That's Mother," he said, pointing to one of the paintings. "The other is her family's country home." Rodney disappeared up the carpeted stairs, while Mark turned to the paintings. Unzipping his jacket, he looked intently at Lady Ashley's portrait.

The large painting was of museum quality. Lady Ashley, in her early 30s, was seated, wearing a black dress with a low cut bodice and a single string of pearls around her neck. Standing beside her was a small boy, who was probably Rodney. They were in front of a large fireplace with a grand piano to one side. Mark backed up beyond the center of the hall to get a better perspective. Lady Ashley was certainly a striking woman. She reminded him of Gene Tierney. The high cheek bones of her face and her closely sweptback black hair accentuated her dark eyes. The artist had caught a certain restrained sensuousness in his subject, but the overall impression was one of elegance. Mark swallowed hard at the breath-taking impact of the painting on him. She was an extremely attractive woman indeed. He could not imagine Rodney, or anyone else, having a mother like that. The small metal tag on the frame said "Lady Mavis Ashley-1946." She would be 17 years older now, he calculated. No doubt she would be less attractive now, more what one would expect the mother of a person his own age to be.

His attention turned to the other painting. The subject was a huge mansion, very much larger than Antonio's. The feeling was of grandeur, yet of peaceful ease. The edge of a small lake was in the foreground. A tree-lined road curved around the lake toward the front of the home. A car from the 20s was moving toward the mansion. So this was Lady Ashley's family home. The very size of the house astonished Mark. It made Antonio's mansion look like a foreman's cottage. The metal tag said simply "Castle Enfield."

Mark heard voices on the stairway as Rodney and his father descended.

"Father, I'd like you to meet my friend from the New World, Mark Stevens."

Lord Ashley looked to be 65 years old, perhaps older. He was a large man, but not fat like his son. Like Rodney, he had a large, magnificent head. Lord Ashley completely fit Mark's notion of an English Lord. He was about five feet ten inches tall and wore a tuxedo. He walked with a limp and carried a carved walking stick. Mark wondered how he had been injured. Lord Ashley's full head of hair was white, as were his sideburns. His step was vigorous as he advanced to shake hands. His blue, penetrating eyes looked directly into Mark's as he spoke.

"Rodney has told me much about you. I'm very pleased that you have become such great friends. Welcome to London. It's jolly good to have you visit us."

"How do you do, sir? I've been looking forward to meeting you," said Mark.

"Shall we go into the drawing room?" Lord Ashley asked, gesturing towards the room Mark had seen from outside. Ashley was a striking, dynamic man. Mark could imagine him being a prime minister in the last century. The room was very large and had a beautiful formal fireplace with a black marble surround. Its comfortable furniture was arranged in several conversation areas. The walls were hung with paintings of traditional landscapes and still lifes. Mark accepted Lord Ashley's gestured invitation to sit on the large sofa facing the unlit fireplace. Father and son each sat on single chairs on either side of Mark.

"I'm sorry we aren't going to be home tonight. We're going to a blasted banquet. Lady Ashley will be downstairs soon."

"That's all right, Father. We're going to a concert tonight in Wimbledon."

"A concert?"

"Yes. A new singing group called the Beatles."

"Never heard of them. Well, I'm sure you'll have a splendid time. Would you care for tea, or perhaps a sherry?"

As they talked Mark soon saw the warmth and friendliness of Lord Ashley's personality, despite the formidable appearance and manner that he presented.

"Rodney tells me you live near San Francisco. My brother-in-law lives in San Francisco too. Pacific Heights, I believe it is."

"I'm from Sonoma, about 60 miles north. Actually, I don't know San Francisco as well as I should."

"Ah, Sonoma! The wine country, isn't it? We visited the wine country when we visited Henry. Lovely place."

"I told Mark he must meet Uncle Henry if he's to be an investment banker," said Rodney. "What is the name of Uncle Henry's firm, Father, do you recall?"

"Enfield and Company, or something like that. Your mother would know. What on earth is keeping her? Rodney, would you ask your mother if she will join us for sherry. Mind you, don't tell her that I'm being impatient again."

"I'll take her glass of sherry up while you and Mark have a chat." Rodney went upstairs, carefully carrying the two glasses of sherry.

"Rodney and I have had many a long talk in the Terrace," said Mark.

"Ah, the Terrace! I lived at the Terrace for my first year at Worcester. That's why Rodney chose it. Some happy memories there. Rodney's a decent lad. He tries very hard."

They sipped their sherries.

"Are you active in any sports at Oxford?"

"No. I did get in some golf at Cal, but I've been pretty busy so far at Oxford. Maybe this summer I'll learn cricket. Everyone seems to enjoy it."

"Rodney tells me you are a brilliant student, that possibly you'll get a first."

"That's very kind of him, sir. I don't know that I'll get a first. It's only the end of my first term, but I'm working as hard as I can."

"And so you should, so you should. Let me tell you, young man, don't wait until you're an old man like I am to enjoy life. My father always said a man should enjoy himself on the road to success."

"I'll remember that, sir." Mark knew Lord Ashley meant well, but with his money, a beautiful wife and two huge homes, it was easy to give advice. He knew that as far as he was concerned he would have to wait to enjoy life until he had achieved the success he wanted so badly.

"Mother will be downstairs shortly," said Rodney reentering the room. "Where is your banquet tonight?"

"The Royal Garden Hotel. A bore really. But your mother wants me to go." Ashley struggled a bit to get up. Blasted leg! Injured it in the Great War," he told Mark. "That's why I don't sit on those bloody low chairs. Too difficult to get up."

Lady Ashley entered the room from the staircase. "Hello, hello", she said, and strode purposefully across the room toward Mark. "I'm Mavis Ashley. I welcome you to London. Tell me, what do you think of our city?"

Her bearing was of confidence and ease. She wore a floor-length black evening dress. Glimpses of her plain black suede high-heeled shoes could be seen as she walked. Her shoulders and back were bare except for two slim straps. Her unblemished English skin, so very white, was beautiful. She wore a diamond necklace. Her black hair was arranged as in her portrait. Mark could see the same quality of latent sexuality that the artist had captured. She seemed innocent of her mien. Although older, she was every bit as attractive as in the painting.

"Actually, Lady Ashley, today is my first day in London—and to answer your question, I love your city."

"I think Mark has fallen in love with London," Rodney laughed.

"Really now, that is a compliment. I'm afraid those of us who live here take London for granted." Lady Ashley laughed along with her son. A delightful, hearty, not unfeminine laugh. "There's nothing wrong with falling in love with a city. Nothing wrong at all."

"Mark is from the California wine country," said her husband.

"No doubt Rodney told you my brother lives in San Francisco. His partners asked him to go to America before the war to start another office."

"I'm from the Sonoma Valley, just north of there."

"We were in California in 1958 for my sister-in-law's funeral. I remember dining at a golf club near Napa. Isn't it Napa? A beautiful, white, southern mansion building. And the little villages to the north were so delightful."

"Yes. Sonoma is the next valley over. It's called the Valley of the Moon."

"Oh, I recall very well. Do you, Stanley? Henry drove us through one valley and we returned to San Francisco through the other. What a wonderful city, San Francisco. 'Baghdad by the Bay,' isn't it called?"

"Yes, that's right. You must have driven right through Sonoma that day. My parents and I lived on a vineyard near there. 'Fifty-eight you say? That was when I was in Sonoma High School. You probably drove right past it."

He was captivated by Mavis Ashley. She was stunning. He knew that she moved in entirely different circles than he, yet she made him feel very much at ease. Her politeness was not superficial. There was no pretense about her.

"Rodney, I do hope you and Mark will stay in for dinner tonight. I happen to know Margaret has roast beef in the oven for Robert and herself. I told her I would try and persuade you to dine here." She spoke and moved with such elegance and grace.

"I'm sorry, but we're going to a Beatles concert. Perhaps Margaret could serve dinner early. I certainly miss her cooking."

"The Beatles. Isn't that the new group from Liverpool? Weren't they on the telly?

"Yes. They're all the rage. I was lucky to get tickets," said Rodney.

"Well, you young men have a good time," said Mavis.

"What banquet are you and father attending tonight?" asked Rodney.

"The Merit Book Awards in Kensington. We honor the best British book of fiction for the year. The best political book. That sort of thing."

"That's the group your mother helped found when you were small. We expect Sir Winston to be at our table tonight. He's to get a special award, if he's feeling well enough to come, that is."

Sir Winston? Sir Winston Churchill? Mark was amazed. It was a big deal the time the mayor of Antonio's home town in Italy came to visit, and here the Ashleys were, eating with Winston Churchill and only casually mentioning it.

In five minutes the Ashleys finished their sherries and were leaving for the banquet.

"I look forward to more conversation this weekend. Pity we're going to the country Monday, but Rodney will show you a bit of London, I'm sure," said Mavis Ashley.

Robert had brought a sedan to the front door and Rodney and Mark walked with the Ashleys to the car.

"The house is yours. Remember what I said about enjoying yourself on the way," said Lord Ashley.

Rodney smiled. "Father has told me that since I was a boy."

Lord Ashley got behind the wheel, with his wife next to him. Robert opened the gate, and the car drove away.

The two friends ate Margaret's meal in the dining room, hurrying so as to be on time for the concert. "My parents like you. Mother especially."

"They were very pleasant to me."

"They're pleasant to everyone. But they liked you. Take my word for it, my friend."

The Wimbledon Palais dance hall was jammed with 3,000 Beatles fans. The noise of the screaming teenagers was incredible. It was as if a football stadium full of cheering fans had been crammed into the room. When the Beatles finally came out onto the stage the noise was so loud that Mark and Rodney covered their ears and looked at each other in amazement. Mark enjoyed the Beatles, but these fans had taken leave of their senses. They seemed absolutely crazy. They pressed against one another, trying to get closer to the Beatles. Some danced to the music, either by themselves or with whomever was near. A few fainted. The females all wore miniskirts and the males bell-bottom trousers and other mod clothing.

John Lennon and Paul McCartney sang "I Want To Hold Your Hand." The screaming crowd rushed toward the specially built cage separating them from the four young performers. This morning's newspaper quoted John Lennon as saying that last night's crowd at Southampton was among the wildest yet of their autumn tour. For security reasons the management of the Palais had decided to encase the Beatles in the large wooden and mesh cage they had constructed around the stage just for tonight's performance. There would be no repeat of the Birmingham fiasco, where the Beatles escaped only by disguising themselves as policemen.

Paul McCartney sang "Long Tall Sally" and then Lennon did "Twist and Shout." Since the Beatles' appearance on television in October, students had been kicked out of school for letting their hair grow long, Beatles-style. The huge speakers on the platform emitted the sounds of the electric guitars and the songs that were sweeping England.

Mark had read a *Telegraph* editorial accusing the Beatles of "filling the empty heads of their fans the way Hitler had done, and causing mass hysteria." A lord had demanded that police protection be denied the Beatles. Tonight Mark was witnessing the mass hysteria he had read about. He was enthusiastic about the performance, but the crowd reaction was the show. Rodney and he had early on given up talking to one another and were using hand signals. England amazed Mark. Here, a few miles from the quiet dignity and luxury of the Ashley home, he was in the middle of some sort of revolution. He preferred the world of Oxford and Chelsea, but he was fascinated by what he was seeing.

Finally, the Beatles closed with "Please, Please Me" and the performance ended.

"Ladies and gentlemen, the Wimbledon Palais is pleased to announce that the Beatles will be happy to greet each and every one of you." The crowd went crazy with shrieks of glee. "Ladies and gentlemen . . . Ladies and gentlemen . . ." The fans would simply not let him speak. "Sorry . . . but if you want to greet the Beatles, you will have to listen to me." The man had come outside the cage, holding his microphone. Finally the crowd quieted. "If you will form a queue, please, and then pass by the bar, the Beatles will stay on until you've each had your chance."

"Do you want to stay?" asked Rodney. It was the first time they had been able to hear one another since the concert had started.

"I wouldn't miss it for the world."

It took them over an hour before they finally neared the four entertainers, who stood behind the bar so as to separate themselves from their frenetic fans.

"These guys are going to be absolute millionaires and they're only our age," said Mark.

"They have something new that everyone wants," responded Rodney.

Suddenly, they were in front of the four newly famous performers. The last was John Lennon. Mark reached across the bar and shook Lennon's hand. "I'm from California. When are you going to America?"

"We signed with Capitol Records only yesterday. Thanks a lot."

And with that the reception line had ended and with hundreds of others they were making the long walk to the tube station. "It's amazing," said Mark. "If Lennon can make it big at his age, why can't I?"

"I have no doubt that you will," Rodney responded. "No doubt at all."

It was after midnight when Mark and Rodney stepped off the escalator at the Sloane Square Underground Station, on their way back to Chelsea.

"I think we're better off walking than waiting for a bus," said Rodney.

"I'm game for a walk. How far is it?"

"A mile or so—down Kings Road over there." He pointed to one of the several streets that came together onto Sloane Square.

A number of young people had gotten off the Underground and, although the businesses on Sloane Square were closed, there was plenty of pedestrian and motor traffic. It was not as cold as it might be for a December night, but people wore winter clothing and walked briskly.

Mark was surprised at the late night activity on Kings Road. The two-lane road was still filled with slowly moving cars.

"Kings Road is where young London shows off its cars," said Rodney.

One shop after the other catered to the fanciers of mod clothing. Even at this hour, miniskirted customers were still inspecting clothing in some of the shops. The window displays showed miniskirted mannequins, wearing boots and leather hats. Others wore flared trousers, cut low below the waist, and other extreme styles that Mark had not seen at Oxford.

"This and Carnaby Street are the main shopping areas for the new clothes—for young people, I mean. My mother's friends would not be seen in these shops."

Several of the shops were for men's clothing and others sold shoes for both sexes. After they walked six or eight blocks they began coming across groups of people their own age spilling out of the restaurants and hangouts, smoking cigarettes and chatting. Mark was certain he recognized the aroma of marijuana, which just had begun to make its appearance in Berkeley.

There was no letup of the stylish cars crowding Kings Road. They passed several more groups of young people filling the sidewalks. "What do you think?" Rodney asked.

"Everything in London is so old and conservative. I would never have expected something like this."

"It's a completely different Britain all right. No one could ever call this conservative."

"Where is all this happiness coming from? Everyone seems so free. They're not worried about studying or money." They passed another group standing on the sidewalk, laughing at a remark one of them had made. They turned a corner off Kings Road onto the side street leading to Rodney's house. "Interesting people," Mark continued. "I've never seen anything so wild and crazy. I wonder where they get the money to live on. In some ways I envy them."

"Envy them? You?"

"Yes. They don't have a care in the world."

"Don't kid yourself. You could never be happy living the way they do. Those blokes have ordinary jobs or maybe no jobs at all. You'll never be happy until you're the head of some giant organization or have millions of your own."

"I suppose you're right. But when I saw Kings Road tonight I wondered a bit . . . They're so happy already. Without doing anything . . ."

"They don't need the success and all the millions, but you do."

"Maybe you're right."

Mark lay awake, recounting his exciting day. He would give anything to have a family like the Ashleys. They had teased him about falling in love with London, and he had, but he had also fallen in love with the Ashley family. Perhaps one day, he would have a wife like Mavis Ashley and a house like this. Rodney was right about the people on Kings Road. He could not be contented for long to be like them. He wanted more. 'He wanted to be successful like Lord Ashley. He did not want to be known as the son of Jonah Stevens. He wanted to be invited to banquets with people like Winston Churchill. He wanted a big house and an Aston Martin, maybe a Rolls-Royce. Maybe he would go to conferences like Bretton Woods. He wanted people to say, "There goes Mark Stevens. I wish I were like him."

-9-

An entire year had passed since Mark's first visit to London. In a few months he would graduate from Oxford. In the past year he had been a guest at the Ashleys' Chelsea home on several more occasions. By now Rodney had shown him most of the sights of London.

Last summer the two friends had toured much of the continent, staying at student hostels and with Rodney's relatives in Brussels. Included had been a three-day stay in Rome. There Mark had confided to Rodney about his affair with Christina. They rang the bell at the address she had given Mark, but she had moved without leaving a new address. In a way he was relieved. Since she had never written him, he half-expected she had forgotten him.

Throughout the past year he had sublimated his feelings for Christina into studying all the harder. But just when he thought he had her out of his system, he had seen the blond Oxford woman again.

This time the blonde was not with her boyfriend. Mark was hurrying to Christ Church to Sir Roy Harrod's lecture when he realized that it was she up ahead, looking at a shop window. He pretended to look in the same window, then followed her at a safe distance. His heart thumped as she turned onto the walkway that would take her across Christ Church Meadow. With his forefinger he felt the perspiration on his forehead. The blonde was very desirable in her miniskirt, with her hair flowing down her back. She aroused him. Quickly, he looked at his watch. The lecture would start in five minutes. He wanted to follow her, to run after her and to catch her. He wanted to ask her name and to see if she would have tea with him. Maybe, if things went well, she would even one day go to the hotel with him. He followed her for only a few yards, but stopped. He knew he had to go to the lecture. He knew if he were to succeed at Oxford, he could not get involved with her. Wistfully, he watched as she walked across the meadow. When she was gone from sight he turned and went back to the lecture.

On his most recent trip to Chelsea, Mark and Mavis Ashley had talked for over two hours on Sunday afternoon. She had returned from her church on Piccadilly, looking elegant in a simple dark dress and bright hat. She unpinned her hat and joined him at the table. Mavis was a vital and interesting woman. She kept Mark absorbed in metaphysics their entire time together. Before Rodney and he left for Oxford, Mavis invited him to join the family for Christmas at their country home in the Cotswolds, not too far from Oxford. Mavis made Mark feel a part of the Ashley family and he was looking forward to Christmas.

Mark was relieved that during the past year he had rarely seen Derek Harden. Derek was no longer living in the Terrace and apparently that unpleasant part of Mark's Oxford experience had ended, although he remembered Rodney's warning that Derek was the sort of person to get even when he could. While at Eton Rodney had learned that when Derek's parents had divorced, his mother had surreptitiously taken Derek to live in America with her new American husband. Ever since, according to the rumor, Derek had hated Americans and everything American. Eventually his father, who had become wealthy, had gained custody of Derek from his mother and put him in Eton.

Mark's studies had been going very well. He often dropped by Richard Dawbarn's rooms in Nuffield for unscheduled chats. Dawbarn had become Mark's mentor the way Dr. Hall had been at Cal. They often talked about issues of the day and points that had come up in Mark's economics studies. Mark was writing an essay about various ideas for reforming the Bretton Woods System of foreign exchange. It was an Oxford credo that the test of an idea was to put it to paper. Writing caused good ideas to crystallize and flaws to be seen in bad ideas.

Tonight in the Bodleian Library, Mark had read several articles by economists discussing foreign exchange problems, and was returning to Worcester. While he was very tired, he planned to begin rewriting the draft of his essay so he could submit the final version to Dawbarn on Monday.

As he entered Worcester, he checked for his mail. He had not heard from his mother for a while. He wished there were a way he could see her at Christmas, but knew that a telephone call would have to suffice.

There was a letter for him, but it was not his mother's handwriting. His heart leaped as he recognized the large loops in

Christina's writing. The postmark was blurred, but when he made out the words, *ROMA FERRAVIA*, he knew the letter was from Christina.

He was eager to open the letter, but was strangely calm as he climbed the stairs to his rooms. He recalled how unrealistically calm he had always been when his grades had arrived in the mail in Berkeley. He would take them upstairs to his desk and, in his own good time, slowly open the envelope. He recalled too that after the tractor accident he had been oddly calm while waiting for the doctors to tell him whether his limp would be permanent. For a moment he stared at the letter. Irrationally, he feared its contents. Then, hand trembling, and mouth dry, he opened the envelope.

> *My Dearest Mark,*
>
> *I am writing you from the small apartment I share with another woman here in Rome.*
>
> *I have waited over a year now to be rid of my memory of you. To be rid of my memory of our first night of love and of our time together at the Durant Hotel. I try to forget the morning that your father burst in on us. Such a crude and awful man.*
>
> *I have not been able to forget these things. I am frightened in writing you, because you may have forgotten me. I am sorry I did not answer your letter, but I was trying to forget you.*
>
> *You must be very busy with your studies at Oxford and probably are in love with some beautiful English girl by now. I know if I truly loved you, I would hope you are happy with another, but the truth is I want you to remember me.*
>
> *Today, I'm taking the train to visit my mother in Pinerolo and will mail this letter from the railway station. I have been working at the French Embassy. They are sending me to Paris for several days to take a seminar. Mark, could you possibly get away from your studies and join me in Paris for the weekend? Forgive me, but I am unable to forget you. I will be at the Hotel Montmartre, 44 Rue Caulaincourt, starting Friday 24 November. I know there is not time for you to write, so I will just pray that you want to see me one more time. Please accept the enclosed fifty pound note. I know that you are a student and will need the money for train fare.*
> *Love,*
> *Cristina.*

.   .   .

Mark stared out his window. In his heart he knew that there was no question he would go to Paris, but he needed to think. Following his heart had nearly ruined his life once before. That was why he had resisted the blond woman. He wanted to finish his essay this weekend and he had other studying to do. He could not afford the time, but he knew that, despite this, he was going to see her. He needed to be near her, to touch her, to make love to her. He held her letter tightly in his hand. No matter what the consequences, he was going to Paris on Friday.

The train clacked across the tracks leading to Dover and the channel crossing. Wearing his leather jacket, Mark was slumped with one foot on the opposite seat, in the half-empty third class section. His overnight bag jostled on the rack above him. As he watched the cows grazing in the hilly pastures, his eyelids began to droop. He had worked until four this morning, finishing his essay, "The Future of Bretton Woods." He felt great pride as he placed the 30 handwritten pages of yellow paper in his desk drawer. The document was easily his best work at Oxford. He had made an analysis of the strengths and weaknesses of the present monetary system and had set forth his own and others' ideas for a new system. As the rules required, Mark had taken great pains to give credit to other authors in instances where he had used their writing. At Oxford it was considered highly unethical to make use of another's writing without proper acknowledgment.

Mark's train was an express, passing through many country village rail stations without stopping. He watched as they passed villagers waiting for the local train. It was cloudy and looked as if it might rain today. Mark wondered if it might rain in Paris. The train slowed as it approached the blue water of the English Channel. He watched with interest as it worked its way slowly to a stop, not far from the waiting ferry. On the walk from the train he turned and looked back. So these were the famous white cliffs of Dover.

In Oxford the figure of a young man walked up the Terrace steps to Mark's rooms. Because lunch was being served in the dining hall, there was no one about except for the mysterious figure. He pulled a long pointed tool from his small black leather bag and inserted it into the lock in Mark's outer door. Quickly, he also picked the lock to the inner door and was inside without being detected.

Mark sat near the front of the ferry so that he could watch as France came into sight. When he finished being processed by the French authorities, he paused for several moments before boarding the waiting train. That he would see Christina soon was now real to him. He knew he had made the correct decision in coming to Paris.

The figure searched each of the drawers in Mark's desk. He came across the neat stack of 30 sheets entitled "The Future of Bretton Woods." He placed the essay into his black bag, taking care not to fold the yellow sheets. Carefully, he locked the doors as he left, silently descended the staircase and left the Worcester grounds.

Mark had read that England and France were once joined together, before prehistoric glaciers had gouged the English Channel. Perhaps that explained why the lay of the land he was seeing from the train was not much different from England's. However, from the buildings he was seeing, there was no mistaking he was in France. The train passed through fields of farm land divided by hedgerows and through many villages, whose buildings with their bright colors and distinctive architecture looked characteristic of French paintings.

Mark was startled by the sound of rushing air as a vendor opened the door and came into the coach. The lady across the aisle bought ice cream sticks for herself and her child. He was getting hungry, so he bought an ice cream stick for himself. Despite being so tired, he was too excited to sleep. His excitement grew as the train pulled into the Gare Du Nord railroad station in Paris.

The Gare Du Nord was a madhouse, with passengers dashing for trains in all directions. The feeling was entirely different from that of Paddington. The strange surroundings and the French language made him feel very much alone. He followed the picture-signs indicating the taxis, and made his way through the scurrying crowd. He was dismayed to see that there were 40 or 50 people in line for taxis. He stood in the slowly moving line for 10 minutes, but decided to try the Metro. Taking the escalator to the depths of the Metro station, he studied the wall map of the system. From what he could tell, the exit he should take to the hotel was Lamarc Caulaincourt. Much later, having twice gotten off at the wrong transfer station, Mark climbed the long flight of steps from the Metro to Rue Caulaincourt.

He had emerged into a different world. The pace of the street was much slower than at the Gare Du Nord. Pedestrians paused in the small food shops along the street, picking out fruits and vegetables. Restaurants and shops lined Rue Caulaincourt. The buildings along the heavily traveled street were all about five stories high. It was a neighborhood quite unlike a downtown area. He looked at the address on a nearby building—number 57. Christina's hotel, number 44, would not be far down the street.

"Madame Movelli is expecting you," said the Montmartre Hotel desk clerk in English. She is out right now, but she said that I should leave you her key if you arrived. It's Room 203. Up the stairs to the right, if you don't want to wait for our old-fashioned elevator."

Mark took the key and climbed the stairs. She had not given him the knowing look that he half-expected from a hotel clerk. He wondered what she would think if she knew the story behind his being here. She had probably heard every love story there was to tell.

The small room was almost totally filled by the double bed. Light from the windows facing Rue Caulaincourt cheered the otherwise gloomy room. Mark saw that a note written on the hotel stationery lay in the middle of the flowered bed spread.

> *My Darling Mark,*
> *I wasn't certain that you would come to Paris, but I have left a key for you. I would have waited if I had known for sure you would come. I will return no later than twenty past five.*
> *I love you,*
> *Cristina*

He put the letter to his mouth and gently kissed it. It would be so wonderful to be with her. He looked around the room. Christina's clothing was hanging in the small clothes closet. He fingered her lavender robe and took it out of the closet, holding it up by its hanger. It looked like the very same lavender robe she had worn in California. He wished she were with him right now. In the bathroom he took the cap from her toilet water and smelled the familiar scent. He sighed. He was tired, so very tired. In a few moments he was lying on the bed, fast asleep.

Mark was awakened by Christina's kissing his cheek. Before he knew what was happening she was kissing him on his lips. Eagerly, she rolled onto his drowsy body.

"Darling, you're here," she murmured. "You got my letter. You came to Paris." Excitedly, she rolled back and forth on his body, putting her fingers in his hair, kissing him again and again.

Awake, he held her close. He remembered the pleasure of stroking her long blond hair that cascaded delightfully across his face as she lay on him. He could detect a trace of her toilet water. It had been so very, very long since he had held her this way.

Since he had opened her letter in Oxford, he had imagined what he would say to her. He would ask her what she had been doing. Had she been seeing other men? Had she changed her mind about living with him, even marrying him? But now that he was holding her, he asked none of those questions. He had imagined that they would have sex almost immediately, but that was not what happened either. Instead, they simply lay on the bed facing each other and holding one another. He continued stroking her hair. She kissed him on his eyelids and frequently kissed him long and hard on his lips, excitedly framing his face with her delicate hands.

"The white streak in your hair is getting larger. Soon you will look as old as I am," she teased, kissing him again.

"I missed you so much—the pleasure of looking into your eyes. I never feel closer to you than when I look into your eyes."

"Why have we been so stupid as to be apart?" she asked.

"Everything I do, everything I want to be, is so that I can be with you someday." He wanted these feelings to last forever.

He began to undress her slowly, kissing her and running his hands over her body. He reveled in the sight of her soft, feminine flesh. It was difficult to realize that he was actually with her.

Mark was more in charge of their love-making than their first time in California, when she had been the initiator. This time he had no difficulty with an erection. In fact, he came almost immediately.

"I'm sorry," he whispered. "I couldn't wait for you."

"That's all right, darling."

In a few minutes, however, they were making love again. This time each wanted it to last forever.

"Life just isn't the same when I don't have you," Mark said, holding her face in his hands and looking deep into her eyes.

"I missed you very much," she responded.

When they finished, both were satisfied.

They lay side by side under the sheet on the old double bed. Their bodies rolled together into the sag of the mattress.

Mark laughed, "With this stupid mattress, we're going to be closer than we want this weekend."

Christina laughed with him. "We can never be close enough, as far as I'm concerned."

She lit a cigarette, but put it out after only one puff. "You're different. You seem so much older."

"I've been working very hard."

"You're more confident now. That's what it is. I like you this way." She rolled over on her stomach and played with the hair on his chest. "Tell me all about Oxford."

He told her about Worcester and Oxford. He spoke of his friendship with Rodney and the trips to London.

"Lady Ashley sounds delightful," she said. "I'm afraid she'll steal you away from me."

"You don't understand. We were just friends that weekend. She's my best friend's mother." He could feel his face flush at her suggestion.

Christina playfully shook her finger at him. "Don't forget, you were Antonio's godson too, but I still wanted you. I know all about these older women." He thought she was kidding, but was not sure.

"Come on, Christina. Not everybody is as crazy as you."

He told her the whole story about Derek, and how he had knocked him down the night of the assassination. Christina became very angry with Derek. "*Quel bastardo!*" she shouted. "You did the right thing. I would have torn out his eyes."

He told her about how important his Bretton Woods essay was to him. "This could be the first step toward making a name for myself. One day I'm going to be rich. Then I can have you and tell my father to go to hell."

"One day you'll be richer than Antonio. I know it."

"I'd buy the Movelli Vineyard. I'd fire my father and buy my mother a house in Sonoma. We could move into the mansion."

"You don't need to dream." Naked, she stood up and extended her arms upward. "Look at me. See you have me already. Right here in Paris." She knelt on the bed and put her arms around him. "When we made love, I wanted you in every part of my body. I wanted you everywhere at once inside me, in my mouth, even in my ears."

Christina's words aroused him. Mark had never before made love to a woman with his tongue, but he had never felt the way he did tonight. With his tongue inside her, it was as if her femininity had become his own. Christina reacted to him as never before. Her soft sounds of sexual pleasure gave way to near shouts of intense gratification. Any remaining reserve was completely abandoned by both of them. At this moment he felt his sole purpose for being alive was to give his lover pleasure and that her sole purpose was to receive it. When she climaxed he watched the involuntary spasms of her abdominal muscles. Not wanting his exquisite sense of oneness to end, he continued despite her or-gasm. Finally, after another climax, and still a third, she said, "Please darling. You must stop. I'm exhausted."

He lay with his head on her abdomen and slid his arms under her back, holding her soft shoulders. For the moment he felt at peace with his inner discontent.

"I love you, Christina. I want to be with you forever."

Quietly, they held each other, until she said, "Now let me make love to you."

He knew what she meant and rolled over on his back. She perched herself between his legs and took him with her mouth. He held her breasts in his hands, until with intense pleasure, he closed his eyes and dropped his arms. "I'll never let you out of my sight again, never."

"Promise me that. Promise me you will never let me go, no matter what I tell you I must do."

He knew she was referring to leaving him in California and going to Rome. "I'll never let you go away again."

They held each other until they fell asleep.

Mark awakened several hours later and looked at Christina's naked body in the light from the hotel sign. He had never experi-enced such joy. The long absence had created new feelings for her. In the morning he would make her see that she should move to Oxford with him. They could manage somehow. Perhaps he could take her to the Ashley country house. He would be so proud to introduce Christina to Rodney and to Mavis Ashley. After he fin-ished Oxford she would inspire him to success no matter where in the world they chose to live.

He lay there watching her. She had turned so that her bare breasts were visible. He knew if he could not persuade her to go to Oxford, he would go with her wherever she wanted. He knew if he had to he would give up Oxford, even his career, for the woman next to him. To do without her would be to go on without a part of himself, a part that was more important than anything in the world.

He put his arm around her and went to sleep again.

-10-

When Christina awoke, she saw by the light of the hotel sign that Mark was asleep. The clock on the nightstand indicated 3:00 a.m., and she knew she was not going to get back to sleep. She wished now that she had not written Mark. It had been a mistake to ask him to Paris. She had never intended to hurt him, but now that was inevitable. She had only wanted to see him one last time. Until last night she had not realized the depth of Mark's love for her, nor the full extent of her own for him. There was nothing to do now but wait until he awakened.

It was daylight when Mark stirred. He lay there for a few moments before he realized he was in Paris and Christina was next to him. They were both naked under the bed covers as he drew himself to her back, gently taking her breast in his hand.

But she pulled away, sitting up in bed, covering herself with the blanket. Looking away, she spoke hesitantly, "I have to tell you something. I've been awake for hours. It's very difficult for me."

"What's the matter, sweetheart? We don't have to make love right away. Is that it?" He was puzzled by her expression. She looked frightened.

"I must tell you something. Something that is going to make you very angry."

"What is it Christina? I don't understand."

"God, this is so hard to say. I've just got to say it and be done with it." She paused. "*Mark, I'm going to get married.*"

Her words struck him like a thunderbolt. "What did you say?"

"I'm sorry, Mark. Very sorry."

"Jesus! When? What are you talking about?" He could not believe what she had told him.

"Please don't be upset. It's next Thursday—in Rome." Her voice was shaking with fear. Head down she avoided looking at him.

"Why didn't you tell me last night? Was last night all a lie?" His dismay turned to anger.

"No, it was not a lie," she said defensively. "I wanted to tell you, but I was afraid."

"But why are you getting married? My God Christina, why? How could you marry anyone but me?" He could see her bare shoulders shaking, but felt no compassion for her—only anger. "Don't you love me?"

"Yes, I do love you. That's what makes it so terribly difficult to marry someone else." In the face of his anger, she had squelched her tears.

"That's crazy! I suppose that's why you wanted me to come to Paris. You love this guy, so you want to see me. I don't understand you, Christina." He was nearly shouting. "You don't make sense, lady! No sense at all! You can't love both of us." The words frantically tumbled out.

"When I asked you to come to Paris I wanted to be with you once more—one more time before I got married," she pleaded defensively. "Don't you remember? I told you in Berkeley that even though I loved you I wouldn't marry you."

"Who is this guy, anyway? Why in the hell would you ever marry him?"

"Please, Mark, calm down." She got up from the bed and looked out the window to avoid his flashing anger. Still trembling, she wrapped herself with the blanket. "You frighten me so when you get angry."

"What kind of crap is that? First you tell me you're going to get married, and then you tell me to calm down. Don't pull that shit on me, Christina!" He paused. "How old is this guy anyway?"

She turned from the window and looked at him. "His name is Otello Bagliani. He's from a powerful newspaper family in Rome. I feel safe when I'm with him."

"You're afraid to tell me how old he is, aren't you?"

"I am not afraid," she said hesitantly.

Mark shook his finger at her across the room. "The hell you aren't! All your men have to be rich, don't they? Well there's one thing he can't give you. He'll never give you what we have together." Mark took a step toward her. He felt like hitting her. "Goddammit, you're selling yourself Christina. You don't love him. You love me." His voice was bitter.

"How *dare* you say I'm selling myself?" she screamed. "You know what it's like to be without money. I married the first time for what you call love. Well, I was a fool. He treated me like a whore." She gestured wildly, still managing to keep the blanket around herself. "I'm not the first woman to marry a rich man. Don't you *ever* accuse me of selling myself." She lost her hold on the blanket and it slipped to the carpet. Her body visibly shook as she turned her back to him, retrieving the blanket. For an instant he wanted to hold her in his arms to stop her trembling, but he was still far too angry.

"How can you do it? I know I can't give you things, but Jesus Christ! How can you possibly marry someone you don't love just because of his money?" He shouted out the words. In despair he plopped down on the bed, as if to give up on her. He looked up at her, his eyes flashing his anger. He still could not comprehend that all this was happening.

"Poor Mark! You still have the same young man's idea of love you had before." Her voice was calmer now. "You didn't think I loved Antonio, but I did. Don't you see I can love Otello the same way?"

"Yeah, you loved Antonio all right." His anger had turned to sarcasm. "The minute he went to Italy you wanted me in his bed. Well, I'm not going to hang around waiting, until this new guy lets you out of his sight."

"That was a filthy thing to say, Mark Stevens," she screamed. "I would have been faithful even after Antonio couldn't make love any more if he had shown me some kindness. But, no! He got nasty, as if it were my fault."

Mark said nothing in response.

"I had been thinking about you for months before we went on that horseback ride. I would never have come back to the barn that afternoon if Antonio had been halfway decent to me." When she finished, her shaking had nearly stopped. She was twisting a Kleenex in her hands.

"You never intended to leave Antonio. I was just somebody who happened to be there. You would have stayed with him if we hadn't been caught."

"You don't understand. I *needed* you. I needed you in my very soul!" She spoke with her head down, avoiding his eyes. "I needed you so much it destroyed my marriage, but that's not going to happen with Otello. I'm not a whore." Her voice rose. "Do you hear me? I am *not a whore!*"

"I suppose you're not being a whore when you fuck me and know you're going to marry him."

"Otello knows I'm here," she shouted. "He knows all about you. I told him I had to see you once more, or I wouldn't marry him."

Her revelation shocked Mark.

"I can't believe what I'm hearing. You tell him you're coming to Paris to fuck the kid. Only there's one problem," Mark screamed. "You don't tell the kid."

They did not speak to one another for a long time. He was so angry he was nearly exploding.

Finally, she broke the silence. "I'm sorry, Mark. It would've been best if I hadn't told you."

"No, it would've been best if you had never sent that goddamned letter to Oxford. Better if I had just heard that you were married, when I got back to California next year."

"I want to explain things to you. I don't want you to think I don't love you."

"Christina, I don't want to hear any more. Do you understand me? I don't want to hear any more."

"Listen to me! I tossed and turned all night. I feel miserable." Still wrapped in the blanket, Christina sat down in the only chair in the small room, and finally brought herself to look directly at him. But angrily, he broke away from her gaze.

"You've got to understand why I'm marrying him."

"That's pretty obvious, isn't it Christina?" He said disgustedly.

"Surely, you can understand how badly I want to be something besides what I am. That is what you want to do too, isn't it?" Depleted, she leaned back in the chair.

"Maybe, but I'm not going to get it by letting some rich old fart own my body."

"That's not the way it's going to be. He loves me. He knows I don't love him. All he wants is that I be faithful to him after we get married. And I will be faithful, so help me God!"

"Yeah, and he gets out of the deal the youngest, best-looking wife of any of his rich friends. Doesn't it bother you to make such an unholy bargain?"

"It's not a bargain. Don't you see? It's the only way I have to escape. You've got your brain. You don't need anybody else the way I do."

"Yeah. What you need to do is struggle like the rest of us poor bastards."

"You're wrong. You think everybody ought to be smart like you. Well, I'm not. The only thing I've got is that I'm pretty. I can speak French and that gets me 75,000 lira a week. That's not even $100. I can't live on that. I have to share rooms with another woman who works at the embassy. My divorce money is going to run out before I know it. Mark, I'm trapped. Otello is my only way out."

"Why can't you wait for me? I'll have money someday. You know I will."

"I can't wait that long. It would take you 20 years. I'd have to wait all that time. You would forget me. I'd be almost 50 years old by then. No, I've got to do it while I'm young."

"I'll have money before 20 years. You just wait and see." But he knew it was futile to argue. She had made up her mind.

She looked determined. Neither would give ground as they stood face to face, he naked, and she wrapped in the blanket. She had finally stopped quivering. "No, Mark, my decision is final. I'm sorry. You were right. I shouldn't have written you. I'm going to shut out my feelings for you. It's a price I'll have to pay."

"But Christina . . ."

"It's no use. Thursday I'm marrying Otello."

The finality of her decision stunned him. "Last night I was ready to give up everything for you." He struggled to express himself. "You were me. I was you. We weren't separate people any more. Don't you see? I had a little bit of peace for the first time since I was a kid. Now you're taking all that away." He felt like crying, but he would be damned if he would.

She put her hands to her face. "Mark, I wish to God I could give up everything for you. I really wish I could. You must believe me when I tell you I understand the way you feel. But, my darling, your emotions will go away. I know what I'm saying. First they will lessen a bit, then finally they will disappear altogether. They might even be gone before the next sunrise."

"Well, I'll never know, will I? You're taking everything away from me without even asking."

She moved toward him as if she wanted to put her hands on him, but his anger made her think better of it. "It would be no good for us to be together when you have so much ahead of you. It wouldn't take long before your ambition would make you restless again." She was attempting to convince herself as well as Mark.

Mark despised his feeling of helplessness over his future. He could see that Christina had made her decision to marry even before she wrote him. He never had stood the slightest chance with her. He had been a fool to think he might leave Oxford for her.

"Damn it, Christina, you were playing with me last night. Well, no more. Two can play this game." He vowed he would never get in this position again, as long as he lived. Never again would he rely on someone else for his happiness.

"No, Mark, it wasn't that way at all. I just wanted to see you one more time."

"Goddammit, woman! It hurts too much to love you. From now on it's going to be different. From now on I'm going to be Mark, the stud, and you'll be Christina, the . . . I don't know what. That's all you want, isn't it? Mark, the stud?" As angry as he was, he inexplicably felt a strong desire to hold her close. "You can't have it both ways."

"I don't want us to end this way." She put one hand on his shoulder, holding the blanket around her with the other. "Let's go out for breakfast. You'll feel differently."

"For God's sake, Christina! Do you really think having breakfast is going to change anything?" Still angry, he grabbed the blanket from her and threw it to the carpet. Roughly, he pulled her to him, pressing their bodies together, and then kissed her, hard. She put one arm around his neck and tumbled backward onto the bed with him, reaching out so that they would not fall.

They made love wildly, as if they had not seen each other in a year, as if sex were the only way they knew to say what they had to say.   Shortly they finished and silently lay side by side, covered with perspiration.

Finally Mark broke the silence: "All right, Christina, I'll have breakfast with you. But I want you to understand, I'm still mad as hell at you."

In Oxford the mysterious man waited in the queue to use the library's copy machine. When it came his turn he looked about to be certain that no one could see what he was copying. When he was finished he carefully placed the original and the copy of Mark's Bretton Woods essay into his black bag, and left the library.

"Clinette, We're going up to the Montmartre. Please have my room made up."

"Yes, Ma'am," said the desk clerk as they walked into the morning Paris air. Saying very little, they walked along busy Rue Caulaincourt and climbed the stairs up the mountain to the steep narrow streets and the Place du Tertre.

"The Place Du Tertre is really a tourist trap, but it's fun seeing the artists hawking their paintings. I think maybe they are all painted by the same Frenchman in some little village in the Pyrenees." Christina was nervously chatting, attempting to put their quarrel behind them. She took Mark's arm as they entered the square from a narrow side street. Having sex had not diminished his anger in the slightest. She wore a short black skirt, with high heels, and her lavender blouse. He decided he would treat her as if she were some pretty woman he had met at a party last night. A woman who would disappear from his life when the weekend was over.

"Let's have breakfast at that restaurant with the outside tables." He pointed across the square.

The artists were pitching their cheap paintings to the few tourists in the square this morning. The waiter did not speak English, and so Mark knew Christina would have to do the ordering.

"I don't want much. Just coffee," he said. His anger had not abated. That old Italian son of a bitch could have Christina; he didn't give a damn. She was not going to get him down. He was crazy last night to think he loved her. He knew exactly what he would do next. As soon as they got back he would screw her again. Screw her until her eyes popped out! Then he would be through with her forever. He hoped that rich, old fool really knew his wife fucked someone else right up until they got married.

When the waiter brought the bill, she slipped Mark a 20 franc note. "Come, I want to show you the Sacre Coeur. It's one of the most beautiful churches in Paris." She was hoping that Mark's angry mood would change with more time.

Mark was aroused at the idea of having still more sex with Christina, knowing that next week she would be marrying someone else. The thought of it piqued his erotic instincts. Hell, he did not want to see any church! What he wanted was to get her in the hotel room again. But if she wanted to see it, he had better go along.

"If that's what you want, we can see the church," he agreed. To hell with her and her calculating ways. So she had only wanted him for one last fling, had she? Well, that was fine with him. One last fling was exactly what he wanted.

Christina was fetching as she struggled with her high heeled shoes on the cobblestone street leading to the Sacre Coeur. He looked down from the heights of the Montmartre at the magnificent view of Paris.

"Let's stand here and look at the funicular," she said. "See there, those little cars taking people up and down the mountain." The tracks dropped steeply down the mountain, beyond the protective railing at the edge of the cliff.

"Is that the Seine?" he asked pointing toward the distant river, not really caring, but managing a pleasant tone.

It was a clear day. They stood for several minutes, leaning against the railing and talking about the sights of Paris. Christina pointed out the spires of Notre Dame. She was talking as if they had never argued, as if nothing had been said about marrying Otello. Mark wondered if the conversation was as much pretense for her as it was for him. He put his arm around her waist and slid his hand over the side of her hip.

"You look very sexy."

"Aren't you ever satisfied?"

"Only for a while."

"Are you over being angry with me?"

"Yes, I guess I am. I know you were right. I should never have thought of leaving Oxford." Christina was indeed a very desirable woman, he thought. If she could make her bargain with this Otello, he would make a bargain to conceal his anger.

They climbed the steps to the huge Sacre Coeur and sat in a back pew until their eyes became accustomed to the dim light inside. They walked down the long center aisle and sat in a pew not far from the front.

The all male choir, dressed in clerical robes, was chanting with its blending of masculine voices. They had listened for several minutes when Mark put his hand on Christina's knee. "Let's go back to the hotel. I want you again."

"My, my, you are anxious. Let's wait until this song is finished." She put her hand on his. "I like you better when you're not so angry."

He ran his fingers along the inside of her leg and whispered. "I want you, Christina. Let's do it right here in front of the choir."

"Please, Mark. They'll see you." She took his hand from under her skirt. "I'll make it up to you. Let's go."

A taxi was waiting near the church. "Taxi! Taxi!" he shouted.

"But it's only a few blocks," she said.

"I don't care. I'm in a hurry," he said.

"Okay. Okay, Mark."

The taxi driver braked sharply to a stop as they pulled up to the hotel, showing his displeasure at the short trip.

"To hell with it. I'll give him a big tip. That will make him happy."

The maid passed them as they went up the stairs. She said something in French.

"*Merci*," said Christina to the maid. "She's finished with the room now," Christina told Mark.

They went into their room, and Mark sat on the edge of the bed holding both her hands.

"I want to watch you while you take off your clothes. One thing at a time."

"Anything to make you happy, my darling." She started to remove her shoes.

"No, not your shoes. Your high heels excite me."

She unbuttoned the back of her blouse and slipped it off. She was wearing no bra.

"Do you like me with no bra? I only wear one when I'm at the office." She smiled provocatively.

"You knew I wouldn't be able to take my eyes off you. You knew no matter how much we argued, I'd still want you." He was appealing to the tigress within her that had wildly ridden her horse that late afternoon in Sonoma.

He turned her around and kissed her bare back. "I thought you wanted me to take off my own clothes," she said impishly.

He turned her again, kissed her nipples one at a time, then kissed between her breasts. "You're right, I do." He sat in the chair and watched her as she stepped out of her skirt and put it on the bed. She had worn no panties.

"Leave your shoes on when we make love." He began to remove his own clothing.

Christina was entirely different in their love-making. She was only aggressive in her desire to please Mark. Perhaps she wanted to make up for the wound she had inflicted upon him. "I'm sorry I hurt you," she said, when once they stopped for a few moments.

Today he had little interest in giving Christina pleasure. Still indignant, he wanted everything possible from this woman who had so callously spurned him. There was something about this Otello that aroused his vengeance. Yesterday Christina had said that she had wanted him in every orifice of her body. Today that was what he wanted. When he was through with her Otello could have her.

"I want you to turn over," he said.

"What do you want?"

"I want to put it in your ass, that's what I want."

"Yes, yes," she whispered. "I want that too."

He was aroused as he had never been before. He had never had sex this way and never had he felt so erotic. He had warned her that he would be Mark, the stud, and not Mark, the lover. That was exactly what he was doing.

After they caught their breath, she broke the silence, "I've never let a man do that before. Did I please you?"

"Yes, you did. It was what I needed."

"I know. I wanted you to be happy."

"That's one thing I give you, Christina. You know how to please your man."

He got up from the bed and began to dress.

"What's the matter?" she asked, panic in her voice.

"This is good-bye, Christina. I'm going now."

Shocked, she reached for her robe. "But you don't have to leave until tomorrow."

"Christina, we've done all there is to do. We've fucked every way there is to fuck, and now there isn't anything else to do."

"But we could see Paris. We could make love as much as you'd like. Please stay with me. I'm sorry for what I've done."

"What's the point in my staying? Everything's settled. Next week you'll have what you want. There isn't anything more to do or say."

"But it's too late to leave for England."

"I may have to sleep in a train or on a boat, but I've got to go right now."

"Please don't, I beg you! You know it's you that I really love. Don't leave me this way." She wrestled Mark's half-packed bag from him, spilling its contents on the bed.

"Christina, don't," he demanded. "I want to remember you the way we were at the airport in San Francisco."

Apologetically, she tried to help him repack his bag. "I'm sorry, Mark. Don't go." She was nervously crying and clutching her robe as he finished packing.

"Good-bye, Christina."

"Promise me that someday we'll see each other. Please promise me," she pleaded.

"No, Christina. I'm never going to let you hurt me again."

"At least kiss me then," she said, raising her lips to him.

Mark did kiss her. He did his best to be responsive, but he was drained of any passion for her.

"Good-bye, Christina."

"Good-bye, Mark."

He closed the hotel room door and walked down the stairway.

"Are you leaving us so soon, sir?"

"Yes, Clinette. Thank you for everything."

As he hailed a taxi on Rue Caulaincourt, he looked back at the second floor window. Christina was watching him from behind the curtain.

As he had done yesterday, the figure waited to enter Mark's rooms until the students were in the dining hall. He took the original of the Bretton Woods essay from his black bag and carefully replaced it in the same desk drawer. In a few moments he was down the stairs, and quickly walked under the cloisters to exit from

*the grounds. One student, however, was late for dinner, and passed
the figure at the front door.*

"Hello, Derek. Haven't seen you in a while," said the student.

"Yes. Quite. Good to see you, John."

*I wonder what the bloody hell Derek Harden is doing here at
this hour, thought John, but then dismissed the incident from his
mind.*

It was very late as Mark's train from Dover approached London's
Victoria Station. The return trip from Paris and the channel crossing had been uneventful. He was glad that he had left Paris early.
Christina was behind him forever. Never again would he think of
her in the middle of his studies. No longer would he wonder if
there might be a letter from her in his postal slot. As far as he was
concerned Christina Movelli existed no longer.

But at Victoria he thought he saw Christina ahead on the
Underground escalator. "Christina," he started to shout. But he
knew it could not be her. When the woman on the escalator turned
her face, he saw that she looked nothing at all like Christina. Like
the woman in Oxford, the only thing she had in common was her
blond hair.

At Paddington he caught the last Oxford train with a few minutes to spare, and sat silently in the empty coach thinking about
the aborted weekend. The lonely train jarred into movement. Only
yesterday he thought he was in love with Christina, and now it
was obvious he was better off without her.

At Didcot he waited on the dreary platform until the connecting train arrived. It was nearly 1:00 a.m. as he looked out the
window into the night. He could see tears in his reflection next to
the "3" for third class. His hair had more gray than the last time
he had looked. He could not understand why he was crying. After
all, he wanted to be rid of her. But no matter how much he ratio-
nalized, he could not rid himself of the powerful yearning inside
him. If only somehow a smiling Christina would be waiting to
greet him as he walked out of the pedestrian tunnel at Oxford
Station.

-11-

"Mark. Mark. Are you there?" Rodney pounded on Mark's door.

"Just a minute," Mark groggily shouted from his bedroom.

Not quite yet awake, Mark opened the door.

"What time is it?" asked Mark. Too exhausted, he had slept in the clothes he had worn on the train from Paris. He had not even shut his drapes, and was so tired that the morning sunlight had not awakened him.

"It's past eleven. How was Paris?" asked Rodney.

"A disaster. Christina's going to marry someone else. All she wanted was one last fling. Can you believe that? He's some old guy from Rome."

"I'm sorry to hear that, but maybe you're better off without her."

"She really gave me the business."

"I'm afraid something else very unpleasant occurred this weekend," said Rodney, looking grim.

"What's happened?"

"You got a telephone call from America." Rodney spoke hesitantly, as if he were reluctant to tell Mark more.

"What do you mean, 'a telephone call'? Was it something about my mother?"

"No, nothing about her. It was your mother who rang."

"Am I supposed to call her back?"

"Yes, she wanted you to call as soon as you returned."

"I'd better call right away. She'd never spend the money unless something important had happened."

"I'm afraid she rang with some dreadful news."

"What do you mean, 'dreadful news'? How do you know?"

"When you weren't here, she asked for me."

"It was about my father, wasn't it?"

"Yes, Mark, I'm afraid it was." It was very difficult for Rodney to tell Mark what he had to say.

"What did he do now? He didn't hit her, did he?" Mark suddenly was angry. "He's been on one of his binges, hasn't he?"

"No, it's not that, Mark." Rodney was somber. "I have some very bad news. Your father is dead."

"*Dead?* You say he's dead? I can't believe it!" Mark was stunned. He sat down, nervously running his hand along the white streak in his hair. "Are you sure he's dead? I can't believe it!"

"They think it was a heart attack."

"My mother. Is my mother okay?" He was dumbfounded by the news.

"She seemed all right, but you'd better call her right away."

Mark looked at his watch. "Let's see, it's three in the morning there. I'd better wait." He paused, taking a breath. "My God, I just can't believe it! Where was he when it happened? Did she say? "

"In Sonoma? Could that be what she said? Mark, I'm very sorry I had to tell you this."

"Yes, that's where he goes all the time. Especially on weekends. He was probably there, all right. I still can't believe it."

"Will you go home for the funeral?"

"Jesus! I hadn't thought of that." He was only beginning to realize his father was really dead. He hated the thought of the long plane ride and going to the funeral.

"I sure don't want to," he mumbled. Mark had always dreaded the thought of one day looking at his parents in their coffins. He had assumed that the morbid day would be very far off, but now he was going to have to do it. He continued to run his hand across his hair.

"I suppose mother will need me," he continued. He paused for a moment, thinking. "How did she sound? Did she sound all right?" He was overwhelmed at the thought of the funeral.

"She seemed very alone to me. Maybe you'd feel better if you called right now, even if you do wake her up," Rodney advised.

"I'd better wait."

"I'll make some tea. You look as if you could do with a good chat."

"I guess I'd better be with my mother."

"Come on over to my room. We'll have that tea."

"At least I have my essay finished." Mark went to the drawer and took out the yellow sheets. "I suppose I could hand it to Dawbarn tomorrow. After all, this is the last week of the term. I can go home if I have to."

"Come on now, Mark, you get dressed and I'll see you in a minute."

"Damn it, Rodney! The last thing in the world I want is to go to that man's funeral. All he ever did was cause me trouble—nothing but grief my whole life." Mark's hands trembled as he gestured, still holding his essay.

When he spoke again it was without feeling, "Funny, I know I should feel like crying, but to be honest with you, I don't think I'll ever cry for him."

Amanda was waiting as Mark emerged from the ramp at San Francisco International Airport. It had been a tedious flight, including a long wait in New York. Mother and son embraced and they made their way to Jonah's car after gathering Mark's single piece of luggage. He drove the car up the Bayshore freeway toward San Francisco as they talked.

"I'm so happy that you came home, son. Mr. Movelli has been very kind, making the arrangements and all, but I never could have managed if you hadn't come."

"It's okay, Mom. I didn't want you to be alone."

"What about your school work?"

"I had already finished my last essay and my tutor said it would be all right."

Downtown San Francisco came into view as they drove around a bend in the freeway. The late afternoon sun made the tall buildings and the famous hills sparkle. Mark was not yet ready to talk about his father's death. "I remember the first time Dad and you took me to San Francisco. We took someone to the airport."

"I remember that time."

They exited the freeway and picked their way through the traffic to the Golden Gate Bridge and home. San Francisco gave him a different feeling from London. San Francisco was exciting too. It was every bit as urbane as London without the same heavy crowds and traffic. Perhaps he should give some thought to working here. After all, his mother would need him now.

Finally, when they were nearing Sonoma Mark decided he could no longer avoid talking about Jonah.

"How did he die, Mom?"

"It was definitely a heart attack. There was an autopsy."

Mark pictured Jonah's body on a slab, being cut up by a coroner wearing blood-smeared surgical garments. "Where was he?"

"Oh, Mark, you don't really want to know."

"Yes, I do. When Rodney told me it was in Sonoma, I figured it was in a bar or something."

"Yes, I'm sure he had been in a bar."

"Is that where he died? In a bar?"

"I wish that were so."

"Where did it happen then?"

"You want the truth don't you?"

"Sure, the truth."

"He was with a prostitute. He's been seeing her for years."

"I didn't know you knew."

"I'm sorry if that hurts you."

"Mom, it's not me that it hurts, it's you. I knew about her. I just didn't know that you knew."

"I've known too, but what was I supposed to do?"

"I don't know, Mom. I really don't know." He wanted to ask her why she had not left him long ago, why she ever stayed with such a man, but he did not. There was no point.

They each remained silent for long periods of time as they neared Sonoma, each keeping their own thoughts. His father never even had the decency to keep his hooker secret from his mother. He thought of the tractor accident and Jonah's refusal to take him to the hospital. "Hell, the boy's not hurt. He'll get over it soon." He could still hear his father's know-it-all, belligerent voice.

He thought about Jonah's body lying in the funeral home that he would have to visit. He was extremely tired when they reached the Movelli compound.

"You look like you've lost weight."

"Maybe a few pounds. I've been working very hard."

"Remember, success won't do you any good if you don't live to enjoy it."

She made him sit down, while she unpacked his suitcase. Even though he protested that he had eaten on the plane, she insisted he eat the dinner she had started preparing for him that morning.

Without eating, she sat opposite her son at the old kitchen table, as she had done for so many years. "I want you to tell me all about Oxford."

He told her about Rodney and his trips to London. He told her about Lord Ashley and Mavis.

"Oh, my goodness, a real lord and lady!"

"My friend Rodney, at Oxford, has an uncle who lives in San Francisco. I'm supposed to phone him before I go back. He has an investment banking firm in the Financial District."

"Is that the kind of company you'd go to work for?"

"Yes, but most of the big companies are in New York."

"My goodness, I hope you don't go to New York."

"I hope so too, Mom." He was reluctant to tell her that he might have to choose New York if he were to get the sort of job he wanted.

She patiently listened as he enthusiastically told her about his essay on the future of Bretton Woods. To Amanda Stevens, economics was making her allowance last until next payday. But she was proud, and hung on his every word about Dawbarn and Harrod, and about his hopes for a first class degree.

When Mark went to bed that night, his boyhood home seemed strange and empty without his father's dominating presence.

As they drove to the funeral home the next day, Mark's extreme dread of seeing his father's body intensified. The idea terrified him. The palms of his hands perspired as he entered the room where his father lay. Reluctantly, he approached Jonah's bier alone. Amanda was talking to the few friends, who were seated near the entrance.

His fear eased as he stared at his father's remains. He felt superior to the long-feared form that lay there so still. He was alive and Jonah was helpless in the satin-lined box. No longer could his father bark obscenities at him. No longer could he throw him off a tractor and shout at him for not jumping off in time to save himself. Never again could Jonah crudely burst into his bedroom. Mark did not feel even a slight possibility that he would cry for his father.

As he looked at Jonah he could not remember when he had last seen his father in his only suit. If Jonah had come to his high school graduation, he would have worn the same dark well-tailored garment, but he had not. "Too busy in the winery," he had said. God, how he had wanted his father to come to that graduation.

Jonah was a good-looking bastard. He had to give him that. There was not a hint of gray in his black hair. Even in death one could see he had been muscular and strong. Ready to skin a rabbit in a minute, or to shoot a pheasant with an unerring shot. If he could Jonah would sit up in his coffin, show you his tattoos, and tell of his exploits with women. He was a man who would be self-righteously angry if his son was not the same kind of man as he. Well, the feeling was mutual, Mark thought. The last person in the world he wanted to be like was Jonah Stevens.

The next day the black Oldsmobile sedan followed the hearse from the funeral home through the gate to historic Mountain Cemetery, not far from the center of Sonoma. Mark had been there last for the funeral of Anna Movelli. It must have been seven years ago, because he had been a junior at Sonoma High School. That gloomy winter day it had been raining. Antonio had invited Mark to walk beside him as they had followed the pall bearers, who were carrying Anna's coffin up the hill to the grave site. Today Antonio's car was one of the handful making up the small proces-

sion.   Antonio, who had sat in the last row of the funeral home
chapel, seemed so much older. Amanda had asked him to be one
of the pall bearers. When the casket was laid over the fresh grave,
Antonio stood well back from Mark and his mother.

As the minister said his hypocritical words about Jonah, Mark
looked at Antonio out of the corner of his eye. Antonio, far more
than Jonah, had been a father to him when he had most needed
guidance and encouragement. He remembered the time Antonio
had asked him to stand by Anna's bedside when she was so ill.
"Anna and I have decided we want you to go to college. We want to
pay your way. We want you to learn to make your way in the
world with your mind, not with your hands, as we did."

He wished that the minister would stop his phony praise for
Jonah. He wanted to speak to Antonio, Antonio you were the only
father I really had. The only one who loved me. I know I don't
deserve to have you even speak to me, but I need you. I wish we
could play chess in your study again. I wish that Anna were not
buried on that slope. I wish she could bring me cookies, and
watch us play chess. I wish you would reach for your Italian
cigarettes once more, while we listen to the opera.

When the minister finally finished his lies about the man who
had never set foot in his church, Antonio was the first to offer his
condolences to Amanda.

"Mr. Movelli, I appreciate your coming," she said. Hesitantly,
Mark stood back from them as Antonio comforted the black-garbed
Amanda, all the time ignoring Mark.

"Jonah was a loyal foreman," Antonio told her. "Without him
the vineyard won't be the same. I had thought that Jonah and
you would take care of me now that I'm old, but now . . . I'll see to
it that you're taken care of. Don't you worry. You'll have a job
with me as long as you want," he assured her.

Antonio began making his way to his car as Amanda turned to
talk with her church friends. Mark mustered his courage and
quickly caught up with him. "Antonio, I would like to talk to you
for a minute."

"Listen to me, young man. I'm here out of respect for your
mother and father. I'm warning you, do not try to take advantage
of this situation." Antonio may have grown feeble, but his resolve
was strong.

"But, Antonio, I never intended to hurt you. If only you could
forgive me."

"Forgive you? How could I ever forgive you?"

"You always meant so much to me. I'm sorry I hurt you. Can't
we go back to the way we were?" Mark pleaded.

"You should have thought of that before you got into bed with my wife. How can I possibly forget what you did to me?" His voice showed its old power. "I loved you like a son and you betrayed me. You put out the light in my life." His voice broke with emotion. "You took away the one thing that was important to me. I have nothing left." He turned and hurried down the hill to his car.

Mark walked up the cemetery road to be away from the others. He cried his first tears of the week, as the hate-filled old man started his car and accelerated out of the cemetery, tires spinning on the gravel. If only Antonio could know what Mark knew about Christina. He would know they were both better off without her. But it was too late. He had lost two fathers. One he had loved and one he had hated.

-12-

Jonah had been buried for three days when Mark telephoned Henry Enfield. Enfield asked that Mark come to his office in San Francisco.

As Mark approached from the north, he exited the freeway at the vista point, so as to look at the spectacular view of the city across the Golden Gate and the Bay. It was from here that he had first seen San Francisco when he was a boy. He had never imagined that one day he might be inside one of those tall buildings. It was windy as he stood by the rail looking at Angel Island and Alcatraz. The sailboats were making their eccentric patterns on the foamy bay. He recognized Coit tower and the hotels and apartments on Nob Hill. He wondered what it would be like to live on Nob Hill.

"Enfield & Co." was emblazoned in gold lettering on the impressive, double wooden doors to the full floor suite. It was an ornate, older building on Montgomery Street in the Financial District. Henry Enfield's personal assistant ushered Mark directly into his private office.

"My sympathies to you on your father's death," Enfield offered.

"Thank you, sir."

"My sister, Mavis, is very impressed with you, young man. She called me from London when she heard you would be here for the funeral. She tells me you are thinking of being an investment banker yourself."

Henry Enfield was 15 to 20 years older than Mavis. Mark wondered if she had been born of a second marriage. Enfield reminded him of pictures of Edward V, England's pleasure-seeking king of the early 1900s. He was smiling and gregarious, with bushy red hair, gray at the edges. Mark imagined him turning out for a wedding, in morning clothes, and even wearing a diplomat's wide, red ribbon across his chest.

"I was sent here by my London firm before the war. It turned out I loved San Francisco and, as you can see, I stayed."

He took Mark on a tour of the suite, introducing him to various men dressed in conservative suits. The more senior men had offices with windows, while the younger ones were in the center, with their work areas separated only by half-partitions made of wood and glass.

"My company frequently participates in underwriting stocks and bonds."

"I have only a general idea about what underwriting means, Mr. Enfield."

"That's quite understandable for a student. Quite understandable. We come into the picture when a large corporation wants to sell new stock to raise capital."

"Surely, you don't buy their stock yourself, do you? That would take a tremendous amount of capital."

"That's exactly what we do Mark," Enfield chuckled. "We and a group of other investment bankers commit ourselves to buying the stock. Naturally, we expect to sell it immediately to our investor customers. For a profit, I might add."

"That sounds awfully risky. What if you can't sell the stock except at a loss?" asked Mark.

"You're right about that. It is risky," laughed Enfield, putting his large hand on Mark's shoulder, and guiding him back toward his office. "But we do our best to protect ourselves."

"How do you accomplish that?"

"We have all sorts of clauses in our contracts with the corporation that's issuing the stock. Clauses that let us out of our commitment if the market drops. There is always an element of risk though."

"I suppose reward follows risk."

"As little risk and as much reward as possible," laughed Enfield. "But enough of me. What are your interests Mark?"

"I hope to specialize in monetary exchange. I've just finished an essay on the problems of the Bretton Woods System. My Cal professor always said to find some narrow area you like and specialize in it."

"I must say Bretton Woods is one subject I don't understand at all."

Enfield sat behind his large wooden desk in his huge corner office. They talked at length about London, Oxford and San Francisco. Enfield had attended Magdalen College in Oxford, as he jokingly put it, "sometime before the American Revolution." He was obviously very prosperous. Mark wondered whether the Enfield family money he, no doubt, had shared with Mavis had paved his way to success.

"Look out this window," invited Enfield. "There's Berkeley over there." Across the Bay the light from the winter sun reflected off some of the windows on the hills near the University. "It's a very long way from university learning to the practical world of business. Get all the education you can, but remember, young man, it's in offices like these where the important decisions are made."

What Mark would not give to have an office like this, to be a partner in a firm such as Enfield & Co. They were in the business of using money to make more money. He had never really known much about investment banking. It had just been one of the things you could do for a living if you had an economics degree. But meeting Enfield made the profession come alive, something he could see. As they talked he pictured himself in one of those small offices, striving to become a partner. Something like that would be his opportunity to get rich.

"I would like you to join us for dinner. I'd be delighted to have your company. My sister was so enthusiastic about you."

Mark was bowled over by the invitation. "I don't think I can. I really shouldn't impose. My mother is expecting me home."

"Fiddlesticks! I told cook to expect you. There's only my daughter, Priscilla. She's home for the holidays. I've been a widower for five years now, and we don't often have dinner guests."

Mark hesitated, but decided he should accept. He knew this was no invitation to turn down.

Henry Enfield's limousine pulled up to entrance of the Enfield mansion. In San Francisco style, the grand marble-facaded house was built close to the street. As with many of the other houses, the mansion was decorated with Christmas lights. The two got out of the car under the magnificent two-story porte-cochere. Mark stared at the bronze statuary that lined the marble railing at the edge of the slate driveway. A huge, hanging ornate lamp illuminated the entry. He was astonished at the great wealth that Enfield must have in order to live this way. They entered the mansion into a large ornate living room, with windows on both the street side and the back of the house.

"Come, look at our view," said Henry Enfield.

Mark stood agape at the view of the Golden Gate Bridge with its striking orange iron work. Ahead and to the right was San Francisco Bay. Traces of fog were coming in from the ocean.

"This is magnificent, Mr. Enfield. Your home reminds me of an old Cary Grant movie I once saw on television."

Enfield chuckled. "My wife and I lived here for so many wonderful years that I'm afraid I took the house for granted, until she died. Now I appreciate every moment here, especially when my daughter is home."

As they spoke Priscilla Enfield came down the marble staircase to the living room. She was red-haired like her father, although her hair was darker, more auburn. Mark thought she was very pretty in a conservative way. She wore a sweater with a skirt longer than he was accustomed to seeing and low-heeled shoes.

"Priscilla, dear, I would like to introduce you to Mark Stevens. Mark is cousin Rodney's Oxford friend I mentioned. Mark, this is my daughter, Priscilla." Henry smiled broadly, obviously proud of her.

"How do you do, Mark? Father tells me Aunt Mavis thinks the world of you."

Mark felt both pleased and embarrassed by Mavis's praise. "That's very kind of her. Rodney and I have become great friends."

"And how do you like Oxford?"

"It's been a wonderful experience."

"Mavis says you are an excellent student," said Enfield.

"I'm afraid the Ashley family is too generous with their praise."

"They are a wonderful family, indeed," said Enfield. "We spend Christmas with them. Unfortunately, this year there is such a flurry of new business I'm afraid we're postponing our trip until summer."

"Are you in college, Priscilla?" Mark asked.

"Yes. I'm a freshman at Wellesley. I'm home with Father for the holidays."

Mark thought that Priscilla looked as if she belonged at Wellesley or Stanford. She certainly would never fit in at Berkeley.

"Dinner is served, Mr. Enfield," said the cook. As far as Mark could tell, the only servants were the chauffeur and the cook. It must be lonely for Enfield with Priscilla away at college.

The dining room was as magnificent as the living room. It had a large marble fireplace with a painting of what Mark presumed to be an ancestor, dressed in the garb of two centuries ago. Twelve luxuriously upholstered high-back chairs surrounded the massive wooden table on which there were two ornate candelabra. Enfield sat at the end of the table near the fireplace, and Priscilla and Mark sat opposite one another next to him. She was an excellent conversationalist for so young a person.

.   .   .

"Priscilla, dear, please show Mark around the place. I'll wait for you in the study," Enfield said affectionately when they had finished dinner.

The upstairs library, with its magnificent light wood paneling and view, and the master bedroom, with its huge canopied bed and ornately painted ceiling, were striking rooms. Although as large as this, Antonio's house was very plain compared to Enfield's spectacular residence.

"When do you finish at Oxford?" Priscilla asked.

"Next summer."

"Will you be coming home?"

"I'm not really certain. I like San Francisco well enough, but New York is where the action is."

"I hope you stay here. I can tell Father likes you. If you lived in San Francisco, perhaps you'd visit us."

"I'd like that."

"This old place is so big and lonely. Many of Father's friends are moving to condominiums on Nob Hill. He'd be right across the street from his club, but Father is so set in his ways. I doubt if he'll ever sell."

What a contrast between Christina and Priscilla, Mark thought. Priscilla seemed so safe and proper compared to Christina. She did not have Christina's sex appeal, but perhaps she was the type of woman he should begin thinking about. "What do they call you besides Priscilla? What's your nickname?"

"I wish I had a nickname, but no one has ever given me one."

"Well, I'll fix that. I'll think of one for you," he laughed.

"When will you tell me what it is?" she responded happily.

"The next time we have dinner together," he laughed.

"Well, if you ever want to have dinner alone with me, you'd better not tell Father."

"Oh, really, why is that?"

"Father can be overbearing at times. He's very possessive of me. The only man good enough for Henry Enfield's daughter is the Prince of Wales." They both laughed. "And the Prince of Wales isn't likely to call." They laughed again.

When they returned to the living room Henry was having a cigar as he looked over the darkened bay.

"Priscilla, dear. Would you play something for our guest?" he asked.

"Certainly, Father."

Priscilla sat at the large concert grand piano and played while they listened. She played a lengthy concerto and concluded with a popular number. She laughed gaily when she finished, and the two men applauded.

"That was wonderful, my dear. I think of your mother whenever you play. You must do it more often." Henry approached her as if to kiss her on the cheek, but she deftly pulled away from him.

"Please, Father, you know I can't stand cigars."

"Oh, yes, of course. I'm sorry." Henry turned to Mark, smiling to cover the hint of hurt that crossed his face. "Let's all go into the study now."

The three sat down comfortably in the book-lined study, which also overlooked the bay. Enfield offered Mark a cigar. Though Mark did not like cigars, he took one to be sociable. Without inhaling, Priscilla smoked a cigarette as Mark and her father talked.

Mark was surprised at Enfield's grasp of the academic side of economics, even though he had professed ignorance of Bretton Woods. He understood full well the economic principles Mark had been studying. "As I said in my office, you need to understand that what you learn at university may not mean a bloody thing in real life business."

After a time Mark realized that Enfield was deftly probing him about his knowledge of economics. Was this only casual conversation, Mark wondered, or was Enfield looking at him as a possible associate in his firm?

"I agree with your professor. You should pick some area of expertise. But I must say that I'm not so sure that foreign exchange is the right choice. May not be too practical in the investment banking world. But as he says, pick something and learn as much as you can about it."

"Well, sir, first I'd like to see what my tutor thinks of my Bretton Woods essay."

In the next few months Mark would many times think of Enfield's next remark. "Get a first class degree, if you possibly can. Many people will tell you that a first is not important. Well, it bloody well is. No matter what, people will always know you have a first from Oxford. Having a first is a small club. You'll never be sorry you're in it."

As the evening neared its end, Enfield said, "If you see my sister, tell her I'm sorry about not being there for Christmas."

"Actually, I'm going to Castle Enfield for New Year's. I'll see her then. I was invited for Christmas, but because of my father's death I'll be with my mother.

"Jolly good. You give them all my best. I want you to keep in touch with me, young man. Ring me up next summer, and I do hope you get your first."

"Good-bye, Mark. It was such a pleasure to meet you," said Priscilla, allowing Mark to grasp her hand.

"Thank you both for a lovely evening."

Alone in the back seat of Enfield's limousine, taking him downtown to his car, Mark reflected on the evening. He thought about Priscilla. She was so different from Christina. Attractive, but in a different way. He thought about Enfield's advice about first class honors. Was it his imagination or was Enfield thinking about offering him a position? If he got a first it would make seeing Enfield next summer much more interesting. Next summer also he might just call Priscilla about that secret dinner they had kidded about. It would be interesting to get to know the daughter of a man like Henry Enfield.

Meanwhile, at the Bodleian Library in Oxford, Derek Harden checked out an unpublished doctoral thesis from the clerk and took it to a table. As part of his plan to discredit Mark, Derek had spent several days searching for the right thesis covering the Bretton Woods conference. It was strictly against library rules to remove doctoral theses from the Bodleian.

Derek sat at the table, carefully examining the bound volume, as he had done last week when he had first discovered this thesis. Yes, there was no doubt that this was the thesis best for his purposes. He surreptitiously removed from his bag a counterfeit volume. Its cover would fool the clerk into thinking that the original was being routinely returned to him. With any luck at all, the counterfeit would remain undetected on its remote shelf, until vacation was over and Derek was ready to return the original to the unsuspecting clerk. That bloody Mark Stevens would be forever sorry he had humiliated Derek Harden. He walked from the Bodleian with the stolen thesis in his bag.

-13-

The day after tomorrow Mark would return to England. Amanda was rapidly adjusting to her new life as a widow. Antonio had asked her to remain in the foreman's cottage to be in charge of the mansion. She was happier than Mark had seen her in years. Mark was restless and was anxiously looking forward to New Year's at the Ashley country home and to the new term in Oxford.

Since the funeral he had been disconcerted. He could not shake the troubling feeling that Jonah was with him. Sometimes Jonah seemed distant, as when Mark was in Berkeley. Other times it was as if his father were with his every move and thought. It was as if Jonah were trying to speak to him from his grave. For several nights now he had been awaked by the sense that his father was with him in his bedroom. As he lay awake he was frightened. It was different from a dream. There was no explanation for the dreadful feelings plaguing him. Each night after an hour or so sleep had returned, but in the mornings he was still uneasy.

Once when Antonio was away for the day Mark rode Whisk on one of the back trails. He had an inescapable feeling that his father was riding beside him. Of course he knew Jonah could not possibly be present, but it was so real he stopped Whisk and looked around. The unworldly experience troubled him. He was all the more anxious to return to England, where he hoped this unwelcome feeling would stop.

While Amanda was preparing breakfast, Mark told her what had been happening.

"I'm worried about you. You've been studying too hard," she said. "I know how you felt about your father, but it's not good for you to keep hating him."

"I can't pretend what I don't feel."

"Reverend Mitchell says we need to forgive. Forgiveness isn't for the sake of the other person. It's for our own sake."

"I'll bet that Reverend Mitchell didn't have a father like mine," Mark retorted bitterly.

"Mark, you can't spend the rest of your life hating your father. You'll make yourself sick. He's dead now. Let him rest in peace." She broke the eggs into the frying pan. "The dead deserve to rest in peace."

Neither pressed the matter further. Knowing from long experience when they had reached areas too sensitive to discuss, they made small talk until breakfast was over. Mark rose from the table and took the car keys from the kitchen drawer.

"I'm going into Sonoma for a while, Mom."

"You think about what I said."

"I will, Mom. Be back soon." He kissed his mother and walked to the car.

When Mark arrived at the cemetery, there was a funeral in progress near the parking lot. He drove the car up the steep narrow drive in the unique cemetery, until he was very close to Jonah's grave. The fresh, gravelly dirt was partially covered with wilted flowers. Mark stood, reflecting on the site. He did not want to be here, but he had to try to rid himself of this sense that his father was always with him. He looked around to be certain no one could overhear him.

"Mother says I should forgive you, but I can't," he said aloud. "She says my anger against you is tearing me apart." He felt strange. It was as if he were actually talking to his father. "But, don't you see, I can never forget the way you treated me. I can never forget the way you treated Mother. If Antonio won't forgive me, why in hell's name should I forgive you?"

Upset at himself for what he was doing, Mark turned away from the grave and looked down the hill at the graveside service in progress near the parking lot. He took a breath and turned back, staring at Jonah's grave and its dead flowers. Without warning, the feeling of his father's presence came over him again. It was as if Jonah's voice were inside of him, actually speaking to him.

But you don't understand me. I know I shouldn't have done those things, but if you could only understand why I did them, the pleading voice within Mark said.

As he had the other night, Mark knew it was not his father actually speaking inside him. Of course it could not be. It must be a long-buried part of himself, wanting to understand his father.

"Shut up!" he said out loud. "I don't want to hear your excuses. What about that time you took me to that whorehouse over in Napa. Christ, I was only 14 years old! You made me go with her. I didn't want to. I had to learn to be a man, you said. Well, you son of a bitch, I went to the room with her all right, but I was so scared I couldn't even get it up. You didn't know that did you?" Mark suddenly realized he had been nearly shouting. He quickly looked around, checking to be sure no one was near.

Then Jonah's voice within him spoke again. It was so real, as if he were actually defending himself.

You were so smart in school. I thought you were going to be a doctor or a lawyer or, hell, maybe even President of the United States. Do you know how that made me feel? Like shit, that's what! Jonah's voice continued, *A man isn't a damn thing, when his son isn't like he is.*

Mark was shocked as he stood there. For the first time he saw some sort of an explanation for the way his father had been.

Do you realize what it's like to have your wife love your son and not love you any more? the Jonah voice continued. *When that happens you're mad as hell at everything, especially your son.*

Mark nearly shouted his answer. "Every time I tried to be like you, every time I tried to love you, you put me down. You always got mad at me for nothing. I tried to do my chores as well as you, but I never could. You yelled at me about everything," Mark continued, sobbing as he spoke. "The only goddamned thing I was any good at was school. Even then I wasn't good enough for you."

Mark sat on his father's grave, slowly picking the petals from the flowers, one at a time. He did not care if anyone had heard him shouting down his father's defense. He supposed no one deliberately decided one day to be mean to his son for the rest of his life. No one, unless he were totally crazy. But it didn't matter what made his father act that way—he was a horrible man. Maybe Reverend Mitchell had been right. There was probably something in the Bible about not carrying a grudge, but whoever wrote the Bible had not grown up with Jonah Stevens as a father.

Mark sat on Jonah's grave for over an hour. He did not pretend to understand what had just happened. He had no explanation for Jonah's voice within his head, but maybe now these feelings of Jonah's presence would finally stop. He had had enough of them to last a lifetime.

Amanda and Mark were driving around the Bay from Sonoma toward San Francisco and the airport. Today he was returning to England.

"It won't be long, Mom. I'll be home in seven months."

He had been thinking a lot about the possibility of a job with Enfield & Co., or at least getting an introduction from Henry Enfield to help find a job with some other San Francisco investment banking firm. New York remained a serious possibility, but he had been impressed by Henry Enfield's office and his Pacific Heights mansion. Now that Jonah was dead, he did not feel as strongly about living away from the Bay area.

"Do you know whatever happened to Christina Movelli?" Amanda asked.

"I don't know, Mom," he lied. "Rodney and I tried to look her up in Rome last summer, but she had moved." He had wondered when she was going to bring up Christina.

"It's for the best, believe me."

"You're right. I was just curious, that's all."

"She's an evil woman, that Christina Movelli is."

"Come on now, Mom. She's not an evil woman. I was just as much at fault as she was." Even now Mark did not like his mother's criticizing Christina.

"I'm telling you, she's an evil woman." It was not like Amanda to be so fervent.

"Don't worry about it." He was glad he had not told her about Paris, or she really would have something to talk about.

"I'm warning you, Mark, don't ever let that woman tempt you again." She hesitated, as if undecided whether to say more. "I know what she did to me."

"What, Mom? Come on now. What did Christina ever do to you?"

"She slept with your father! That's what she did!" Amanda's long-kept secret was out.

"What are you talking about?"

"They didn't think I'd find out, but I did." Amanda was gesturing vigorously, and shaking her forefinger as she spoke.

"I don't understand what you're talking about," said Mark, still not comprehending his mother.

"It was that last summer you were home."

"What do you mean, she slept with Dad?"

"I mean just that. They were having an affair. Big as life, they were having an affair."

"An affair? With Dad? What do you mean? When?"

"Just as I said, that last summer."

"My God, you mean the same summer we had the affair?"

"That's exactly what I mean. They were together all that same summer your father caught you in bed with her."

Mark pulled the car off the highway. It was the two lane road, before they reached city traffic. His hands were trembling on the steering wheel.

"I . . . I . . . Let me understand."

"She's a bad, bad woman, Mark. She was carrying on with your father all that same summer. I caught them in the horse barn."

"My God!" Mark cried out. What his mother was telling him finally had begun to penetrate his brain.

"They'd ride their horses up near Jack London Park. She'd be with him everywhere. They didn't even stop after I caught them. It was all so terrible."

"Oh, my God! How awful!" Mark was incredulous, still not believing.

"Jonah knew I couldn't tell Mr. Movelli. He knew I was afraid we'd be fired. Your father taunted me, Mark. He actually taunted me with his dirty affair." She began sobbing.

They had gotten out of the car and were standing in the weeds at the edge of the road.

"How terrible!" he said, holding his mother as she cried.

"Then she got tired of him. She got rid of him. She got rid of him for *you*, Mark." She trembled as she looked at her son.

"My God, it can't be true!" Mark was stricken. "First she had Dad and then me?"

"I'm afraid it's all true. They were even together in Mr. Movelli's bedroom in the big house. It was after he went to Italy. They were there all night together once."

Mark put his hands to his head. "I can't believe it of her. The same room as where she was with me later." It was incredible. The full impact was beginning to dawn on him.

"They had a quarrel. He came home in the middle of the night. I could tell they had been fighting. He was very angry. When I asked what was the matter, he shoved me. He said it was none of my business."

Still standing by the car, they stopped talking briefly while Amanda composed herself. "He went to the mansion the next morning, but Christina wouldn't see him. It was that very night that you worked late in the barn and didn't come home. I just knew she had gotten you to stay with her."

"And I fell for it. God what a fool I was!" Mark was stunned at Christina's cunning.

"It was all right. You're a young man. I can understand how it can happen," she said. "Your father paced up and down all that night. Then he wanted sex with me. I never refused your father before, but that night I wouldn't. Then he hit me, Mark. He hit me on the face." She pointed to the side of her face. They stood together, crying and trying to comfort one another, as the traffic went by.

"Then the next morning, when you were supposed to be cleaning the vats, your father came to the house looking for you. When you weren't there, he stormed up to the mansion. That's when he broke in on Christina and you. It was all so terrible."

Mark turned away from Amanda. Suddenly the full impact of the horrible revelations hit him. He felt violently sick to his stomach. It just could not possibly all be true, he thought. How could Christina do such a thing?

Suddenly and without warning he fell to his knees, vomiting.

If his father had not been already dead he would have killed him with his bare hands. He wanted to race back to the cemetery and finish his retching on Jonah's grave, to tear up the ground and get at him. If only he could find Christina, he would choke her, choke every breath from her.

"My God, I hurt!" he cried aloud. "I hurt so goddamned much!"

He stayed on his knees in the tall weeds, sobbing with anger and distress. Amanda stood with her shoulders rounded, stroking the white in her son's hair, until he finally finished crying.

As his airplane waited to take off for England, Mark looked out the window, reflecting on these last tumultuous days. His mother may have followed Reverend Mitchell's advice and forgiven Jonah, but even if he could, he would not. He only wished that somewhere there were a wise man, a man the complete opposite of Revered Mitchell, who could tell him how to get even with the dead.

Part Three

-14-

Mark's 707 flight sped toward London. It was midnight, San Francisco time, and he was trying to sleep. He removed the arm rest between two seats and the stewardess gave him a blanket, but he could not fall asleep. He was tormented by thoughts of Christina and Jonah together. That Christina and his father had shared the same bed the night before she had made love with him, revolted him. He felt tricked and used. It was even worse than in Paris when she knew she was going to marry the Italian newspaper man.

Mark adjusted his position in the airplane seat. What mystified him was that he knew in his heart she had genuinely loved him. He never would understand Christina. He felt naive and stupid for falling in love with her. He must stop thinking about her. He must get her out of his system. At least he had learned a lesson. If he ever fell in love again, it would not be with a woman like her. It was only when dawn's light filtered around the plane's closed window shades, that he finally fell asleep.

At Heathrow dozens of people were greeting passengers. Some held signs bearing the names of their parties. Others were tour directors, behaving like hens gathering their chicks about them. Still others were eagerly inspecting the arriving passengers, hoping to spot friends or relatives. Mark looked for Rodney, who had agreed to meet him and drive to the Ashley country home.

"Mark! Mark! Over here," shouted Rodney.

It was good to see his friend's overweight shape. "I didn't think I'd ever live to see the day when I would be glad to see an Englishman," joked Mark.

"Now, be quiet there—let me have your case," Rodney rejoined.

They chatted as Rodney carried Mark's suitcase through the maze of ramps and corridors. He was driving his mother's Aston Martin that he had parked in the far corner of the top deck to be away from other cars. Although it was chilly the sun shone brightly, and there were only a few billowy clouds in the sky. A huge jet noisily took off as Rodney expertly steered the luxurious sports car through the Heathrow traffic. Mark slid down on the seat, relaxing in the sumptuous leather of the interior. Until now he had not realized the terrific pressure he had been under these last weeks.

"What a beautiful day for December. It's great to be back in England."

"It's been very cold until today."

"I met with your Uncle Henry in San Francisco."

"And how is my dear old Uncle Henry?"

"A very interesting man. I think he was hinting he'd like to interview me for a job after graduation."

"Really? He has a very important firm. Famous for new stock issues, you know."

"He was taken with the fact that I'm reading economics at Oxford."

"Ah, yes, he would be. Uncle Henry has always been a good one for maintaining old ties and that sort of thing."

"He was sorry that Priscilla and he wouldn't make it to England for this weekend."

Rodney accelerated the Aston Martin, as they pulled onto the A419 toward the Cotswolds. It seemed odd to be driving on the left side of the road again.

"Pity. As long as I can remember, even before Aunt Margaret died, he's come to England for the holidays. It's been a family tradition."

The conversation shifted to Jonah's death. "Mark, I'm very sorry about your father's death. Was the funeral as unpleasant as you expected?"

"I'll put it this way: I made it through. His death had a strange effect on me."

"How do you mean?"

"It's hard to explain. I guess it brought up a lot psychological stuff."

"Oh?"

"Yes. Not getting along with him, that type of thing." Mark wanted to tell Rodney about Jonah's presence following him, and about his father's affair with Christina. He wanted to tell him, but he simply could not.

As they left the A419 onto a country road near Castle Enfield, their conversation shifted to the events of the coming weekend.

"I'm sure you'll want to sleep off your jet lag today. You'll need to be fit for the dance tomorrow night," said Rodney.

"Will I know anyone there?"

"No, but there might be an interesting bird or two. Which gives me a chance to tell you my big news."

"I'm sorry. Here, I've been telling you all about my trip and haven't asked about you. What's your news?"

"Rebecca and I are going to announce our engagement New Year's Eve."

"That's wonderful, Rodney. Congratulations." Mark had not met Rebecca, but Rodney had spoken of her many times.

"Rebecca is a marvelous girl. I'll be fortunate to have her as my wife."

"She's the fortunate one. When do you plan on getting married?"

"We haven't decided. Perhaps as early as this summer."

"Well, I'll be damned! I can picture it now—Rodney the old married man. There will be no more midnight bull sessions for you, my friend."

Rodney laughed. "I'm anxious for you to meet her. She's coming up from London with her parents tomorrow. They're staying over the weekend."

"This is a surprise to me, although a pleasant one. I didn't realize you were that serious about Rebecca.

"She's prettier than I deserve. My mother and father approve and that's very important to me."

"She sounds like the sort I should find for myself. All the Christinas of the world do is break your heart."

"Maybe so, but I envy you having the affair you had. The closest I ever had to anything like that was a girl I knew in Oxford two years ago." Rodney took his eyes from the road to glance at Mark. "The truth is, if it weren't for Madeline, I'd still be a virgin. I really was in love with her for a time, but it was no good. She wasn't the right sort for Mother and Father . . . and I guess for me."

"You never told me about her."

"It was my first year at Worcester. Madeline was a waitress at a little restaurant over on High Street. I used to go there all the time. She was a plucky little thing. Trying to survive on her own. She was the first girl I ever met who really cared about me."

"And your mother and father didn't approve?"

Rodney smiled. "They never knew about Madeline. I knew they would think she wasn't the right sort—not from the right family and all."

"So, getting serious with Madeline was out of the question?"

"Yes. At least it seemed so at the time. If I had to do it over again, perhaps I'd do things differently," said Rodney sadly. "But, no matter. I've got Rebecca now." Rodney paused thoughtfully. "You know, I really do love Rebecca, Mark. It's true I don't have the same passion for her I had for Madeline . . . and indeed I suspect the same is true of her, but she is from the right family."

"What does being from the right family mean? Having money?"

"It might look that way," answered Rodney, looking down with embarrassment. "But it's more than that. As long as I can remember, Mother and Father have made it clear to me that I should be careful to marry the right sort. Always very subtle of course, but the message was there. The bedamnable truth of it all is that they're quite right. I knew they were right when I fell in love. I loved Madeline, but I could never marry her."

"Well, my congratulations to you both." Mark admired Rodney for being so open. He wished he could be the same way.

Rodney had been driving very fast along the country road. "Anyway, I want to ask you a very important question."

"Shoot," said Mark. "Anything you want."

"I want you to be my best man when I get married. I don't have a better friend than you."

Mark was taken back by Rodney's expression of friendship, and hesitated, searching for words.

"I know you don't have much money, so I would be pleased to pay for your way here from California for the wedding," continued Rodney.

"My friend, if we were both beggars, I would find a way to return to England to be your best man. It's as simple as that."

"Thank you for saying 'yes'. I appreciate it more than I can say."

"There was never any doubt."

They drove on in silence, each keeping his thoughts to himself. Rodney turned the Aston Martin sharply onto a narrow road that was nearly hidden by giant trees. They crossed over a picturesque one lane stone bridge, and Castle Enfield came into view across the small lake. It looked as it did in the painting in Chelsea, except that it was much larger in life. Mark was astounded by the size of the house. It was a veritable hotel. He had never imagined anyone could have enough money to live in a place such as this.

"Lady Ashley is in the garden, sir," said the servant to Rodney. "She asked that you and Mr. Stevens join her."

Mavis Ashley saw the two young men as they emerged from the rear of the house.

"Rodney! Mark!" she shouted across the garden. "I'm here."

She was even more attractive than Mark had remembered. From a distance she indeed could be mistaken for Gene Tierney.

She had the jet black hair and the beauty of the actress. She looked very stylish in a tight-fitting heavy black sweater over her bright yellow slacks. Mark was truly happy to see her again.

"I found him all right at Heathrow," Rodney called to her.

The view from the back of the house was breathtaking. Beyond the terrace, which was to one side of the vast U-shaped building, was a tennis court, and then a small stream, which was crossed by another picturesque stone bridge. Beyond were beautiful gardens stretching to the creek and beyond, perhaps a quarter of a mile to the bare trees of the woods.

"It's good to see you Mark. It's such a beautiful December day I thought I'd walk in the garden a bit."

"Thank you for having me here this weekend. It's wonderful to be back in England. I'm looking forward to some relaxation."

"Let's join the others inside. It's a bit more chilly than I had expected."

Mavis led them through a door directly into a large paneled and book-lined room. At one end was a fireplace and, nearby, four people at a card table.

"Would you care for a drink or perhaps some tea? Lunch will be in about half an hour. You must be tired and hungry after your flight," she said.

"We had breakfast on the plane, but I could do with a beer, at least if Rodney will join me."

"No need to ask me twice," said Rodney.

"Good for you. I do believe I'll have a tonic and join you," Mavis said.

A servant, who had been hovering near Mavis, went for the refreshments.

"Charles, perhaps you should bring some chips for these young men," she called after the servant.

"Yes, madam," Charles answered.

"I was so sorry to learn of your father's death. How perfectly awful for you to have to leave university on a moment's notice to attend the funeral."

"It was my mother I was concerned about. As I've told you, my father and I didn't get along very well." A few months ago, when Mark had discussed with Mavis his plans for the future, he had been frank with her about his relationship with Jonah.

"I suppose the truth is many of us have old scores with our parents. All we can hope for is that we'll have them settled, before they die."

"Well, Mother, I don't know that I have any old scores to settle with you," said Rodney lightly.

"I don't believe a word you say," she said, laughing merrily.

Mavis introduced Mark to the card players. The couples were in their 40s. The men wore sports jackets and ties, and the women were dressed in tweedy-looking outfits.

"Rodney tells me that you're a Rhodes Scholar. How perfectly lovely," said one of the women holding her cards down."

"How do you like England?" inquired the man next to her.

"England's wonderful. I'm actually beginning to learn the language," responded Mark. They all laughed politely.

Much of the conversation centered on Mark. "I'm from the California wine country north of San Francisco," Mark said in response to a question.

"And what are you reading at Oxford?" asked the other man.

"Economics. I intend to be an investment banker, perhaps in San Francisco, or maybe New York."

"The others will be gathering in the French Dining Room. Let's join them," said Mavis.

They walked into a very large living room with a blazing fireplace at one end. "We've seen you so often, I quite forget that you've never been to Castle Enfield. Perhaps Rodney will show you around after lunch."

The living room was in the style of an elegant hunting lodge, with large beams rising to the peak of the ceiling. There were several groupings of furniture. Paintings of Mavis and Lord Ashley hung on either side of the main window, which looked out the front of the house onto the motor court. Along one side of the room, toward the paneled entry, was a group of four suits of armor, helmets and all, lined up as if to defend Castle Enfield from marauders. Mark was impressed. He could not get used to the idea that he knew people who actually lived like this. The living room was filled with guests, chatting, reading newspapers, and the like. As if on cue, they began moving toward the dining room when they saw Mavis.

The French Dining Room was at one end of the house, overlooking the lake and the formal gardens that led down to the woods. The room was incongruous with the rest of the house. The high ceiling was very ornamental as were the table and plush chairs with their carved legs. A large, fancy mirror hung on the main wall. The exquisite chandelier and long table dominated the room. One expected Louis XIV to step to the head of the table.

As the meal progressed they talked of the various parties they all had been attending during the Christmas season, as well as tomorrow night's dance and Saturday's fox hunt here at Castle Enfield. The group was extremely polite and even cordial to Mark, but he could not escape feeling he was not from their class. They all came from wealth and privilege. They took for granted playing tennis or riding horses on their friends' palatial estates. They, no doubt, had large country houses of their own. Even as a brilliant Oxford student, he was a guest, not one of them.

What was more, he felt he could never be one of them. Even if he became the richest man on earth and had a dozen estates like this scattered across the world, he would never be admitted to their society, because their relationships were based far more on class than money.

The meal was barely finished when Mark stood and sought out Mavis at the end of the table. "Lady Ashley I'm afraid I must excuse myself. I simply cannot hold up my head for another minute. By my body clock time it's something like seven in the morning."

"Of course, Mark. Rodney, you must show Mark to his room. I expect that you'll sleep through dinner, but if you awaken in the night just ring and the servants will fetch you something to eat."

"Good-bye, everyone. I'm afraid jet lag has got me."

Mark was too tired to notice very much of the huge house as a servant, carrying his luggage, led the way up a large stairway and down a hallway lined with rooms. He looked out the window at the vast grounds of Castle Enfield before pulling the drapes and collapsing into bed.

Mark awakened from a frightening dream. His body was covered with perspiration. He had been standing on Christina's grave. While dreaming, it seemed it was his father's grave and not Christina's, yet he knew, in the dream, it was she who was buried there.

Crying uncontrollably in the dream, he had wildly stamped on the fresh flowers. A shadowy figure of a woman had come toward him. At first, he had thought it was his mother, but then he could see that it was Mavis Ashley. Mavis had put her arms around him and comforted him.

As he reflected, he recalled that Mavis had been wearing a provocative nightgown and that he had been very much sexually attracted to her.

When he woke again hours later, he was still troubled by the dream. He was left with a feeling of grieving for Christina, as if he had been to her funeral. Then there was the part about Mavis. First she had been comforting him the way a mother would do, yet he knew they would have become lovers if he had not awakened.

He turned on his light and saw that it was time to get up. The others would be having breakfast. Maybe the dream was telling him, now that 1964 was at an end, he should put Christina and his father in his past.

.   .   .

Yesterday Derek had laboriously typed two key pages of Mark's Bretton Woods essay onto paper that was exactly the same as used in the doctoral thesis he had pilfered from the Bodleian Library. He even bought a used Olivetti typewriter that was the same model as used in the original thesis. Today the London bookbinder he had hired inserted the two pages into the bound volume.

In his room at Oxford Derek smiled as he admired the bound volume. He had very carefully determined where the pages from Mark's essay could be inserted to fit the context of the thesis. Now for all intents and purposes, when one read the thesis it would appear that key parts of it were word-for-word exactly the same as Mark's essay.

All that remained was to return the book to its shelf in the Bodleian. As far as anyone could tell, Mark Stevens had copied an essential part of his essay directly from the doctoral thesis. No one would ever guess what Derek had done.

He leaned back and closed the leather-bound volume. The next step would be to report anonymously to the provost that Stevens had plagiarized the key part of his essay, then let events take their course.

The New Year's Eve dance had started at nine o'clock. Mark danced with a dozen women in the ornate ballroom that had been added to the mansion by Mavis Ashley's grandfather in the last century. The women ranged from Rodney's 15 year old cousin to a portly neighbor, who had insisted on dancing "with Rodney's brilliant American friend." He was having a good time. The orchestra played a number of waltzes, which made him glad for the eighth grade dancing class he had taken. It was great fun whirling around the dance floor to the waltzes and to the Glenn Miller music. The men were dressed in tails, the ladies in long dresses. Rodney's father had loaned Mark an old set of tails that did not fit too badly. It came as a surprise to him when the older-looking musicians played several rock and roll numbers. In fact once he danced to a Beatles number with the portly neighbor.

It was now one minute before midnight. "Ladies and gentlemen," announced Rodney, standing with Rebecca and gesturing to the orchestra leader to stop the music. "Tonight is a very special night for me." Rebecca's mother and father stood on one side of him and Lord and Lady Ashley on the other. They all smiled broadly at the some 200 guests who filled the room, guessing at the purpose of the announcement. "It gives me great pleasure to announce that Sir Andrew Wilson and Lady Wilson have given me the hand of their beautiful daughter, Rebecca, in marriage."

"But only with my consent. I had something to say about it, you know," joked Rebecca to the assemblage. They all laughed at her pretended protestations.

"I'm sorry, my dear, if I didn't make that clear. You see I've never been engaged before," laughed Rodney. He turned to the group. "We haven't set the date yet, but it will be sometime in 1965, we assure you." Rodney looked at Mark in the crowd. "I'm happy to tell you that my friend, Mark Stevens, has agreed to be my best man."

Everyone applauded and made their way to congratulate the couple.

"We wish you all a happy 1965. May it be as happy as ours," Rodney shouted over the buzzing of the crowd. The orchestra played "Auld Lang Syne" and a few of the couples kissed, amid horns tooting.

Mark had met Rebecca and her parents at tea that afternoon and liked her. He took her by the hand. "Now that you are engaged, are you permitted to dance with single men?"

"These are the '60s Mark," Rebecca laughed. "Even married ladies can dance with single men."

To the music, they moved out onto the crowded dance floor.

"I can't tell you how happy I am for Rodney. He's a fortunate man," said Mark.

It was a rock and roll dance and they had only periodic moments when they were close enough to have fleeting bits of conversation.

"I'm the one who is fortunate."

As they danced, Mark thought of the first time he had seen Rodney in his red shorts in his favorite chair. They had become such good friends in the months since then. He wondered if Rebecca had been attracted by the same qualities he liked in Rodney. His loyalty, his genuineness, his sense of humor. When Rodney liked you, you knew it, and you never doubted his sincerity.

"I think it's wonderful you are going to be Rodney's best man," said Rebecca as they danced, but the music was so loud he could not make her hear his response.

The music stopped and they joined in the applause for the orchestra. They found Rodney, who was getting another drink at the bar. "You must consider our home to be your home, whenever you visit London. You do plan to return to England often, don't you?" Rebecca asked.

"Are you joking?" Rodney chimed in. "The way Mark loves London, he'll be here every chance he gets."

"You're right about that," Mark laughed.

"Well, you'll always have a home with us when you visit London," said Rodney before Rebecca and he moved onto the dance floor for the last dance of the evening.

Mark thought that Rebecca was quite pretty as he watched them dance. The tight bodice of her long dress showed her attractive figure. He mused over Rodney's Oxford waitress. Perhaps that was the way it should be, he thought. Marry the right woman and let the love come later.

There were 30 or 40 guests who stayed over for the long weekend. The next day was a Friday and the big house was quiet until late afternoon, when conversation and drinking began. The guests were content to spend the day lazily loafing about, recovering from yesterday's festivities—knowing that Saturday was to be the fox hunt.

Mark had never had the intention of being in on the kill, but he enjoyed the chase of the fox hunt. As with the formal clothes, Lord Ashley had supplied Mark with his extra red-coated hunting garb. There was something exciting about a bunch of rich Englishmen riding off though the woods together. It hardly mattered if there were a fox. The scene could have been in a two or three hundred year old painting hanging on a museum wall, or in the long gallery of Castle Enfield that he had seen yesterday.

Although his horse was in the very middle of the group of riders, Mark felt more like an observer of the scene than a participant. The most fun of the day was caused by a persistent group of trespassing protesters, shouting and waving their "SPARE THE FOX" signs. All the protesters did was frighten the fox that darted off in the opposite direction, followed by hounds and red-coated riders.

At the feast that evening the plight of the protesters was the subject of much laughing and joking. "Did you see that woman from the village waving her sign?"

"If she had stayed home, the fox might have gotten away."

Nearly all the guests were gone by late Sunday afternoon. Mark and Rodney were alone in the library.

"Mark I must see Rebecca back to London," said Rodney. "Would you mind awfully if I left you here for a day or two?"

"Why, no, I really ought to leave for Oxford myself." Mark felt he was imposing, although he had been invited for the whole week.

"Nonsense. You know perfectly well you can't stay at Worcester this early. I'm the one who should be embarrassed leaving you this way, but I didn't think you'd mind."

"I don't mind at all. I just don't want to overstay my welcome."

"I've already spoken to Mother. She's delighted to have you stay. Father has already gone up to London. Some sort of business. You two seem to get on so well, I thought you wouldn't mind."

"Why, no, not at all." In truth Mark felt ill at ease about being alone with Mavis.

"Mother said she wanted to get to know you better. I'm warning you . . ." Just then Mavis walked into the room and Rodney laughed, " . . . watch out for Mother's lectures on God and metaphysics. She'll talk forever if you let her."

Mark and Mavis walked to the auto court to wave goodbye to the engaged couple as they left in the Aston Martin.

"Don't worry, Mark. My metaphysics lecture isn't all that long."

-15-

Before dinner Mark joined Mavis, in the ground floor study, for sherry. She looked very attractive in her silk blouse, conservative black skirt and stylish low-heeled shoes. Mark wore the new sports jacket his mother had bought for him at Christmas. Mavis asked him polite questions about his boyhood and his years at Cal, but they discussed nothing of substance. Mark felt awkward being alone with her and was glad when the sherry was served.

A servant announced dinner and they moved to the dining room. "This reminds me of your brother's dining room in San Francisco." Like Henry Enfield's dining room, it had a beautiful marble and carved-wood fireplace. Portraits hung on the walls.

"That's not surprising. Henry loved Castle Enfield. I think what he missed most about moving to America was this house. He spent most of his time here as a boy. By the time I came along Henry was married and on his own. Perhaps you didn't know, in actual fact he's my half brother. You see Henry's mother died when he was a teenager."

They talked more about Mark's recent visit with Henry and Priscilla. "I was very impressed with his investment banking firm. My ambition is to be a partner in a firm like that one day," he told her.

"Henry is always complaining that most of the really promising young men want to work in New York. They think that's where the opportunities are. Perhaps you should ask him for an interview."

"To tell you the truth, I thought he was already sizing me up for a job."

As the meal progressed, their conversation remained largely predictable; they discussed such subjects as Mark's reaction to life at Oxford and whether New York dominated America as London did Great Britain. By the time the servants cleared the table for dessert, Mavis and Mark had consumed most of the bottle of red wine. Both were more relaxed and their conversation more convivial.

"Mark, I want to ask you a favor. Would you please call me Mavis? I've had quite enough of Lady Ashley for the evening," she laughed.

"But the servants . . ."

"I don't care about the servants. You're my friend, and my friends call me Mavis."

"All right, Mavis."

"Tell me how you first met Rodney," she asked.

Mark told of their first chat that day in Rodney's room. As the servant brought them a fresh bottle of wine, Mark told about Rodney's wearing nothing but his red shorts. "I can still see him sitting in his big chair, cursing the *Times*," he chuckled.

Mavis laughed without restraint. "What did you think?"

"I was hoping most Englishmen wore clothes." Mark laughed along with her.

Mavis chatted about her memories of Rodney as a boy. "I think Rebecca is a wonderful young lady, but I've been worried about his choosing a wife, when he has so little experience with women," she continued. "As far as I know Rodney never even had a date with a girl until he began seeing Rebecca. She's such a proper girl. I just wish he had more experience with the opposite sex." Obviously Mavis had not heard about Madeline, Rodney's waitress friend.

"Oh, I wouldn't worry about Rodney's being experienced."

"Indeed! You think I shouldn't worry," she raised her eyebrows in surprise. "Are you quite sure?"

"I'm very sure, Mavis—very sure."

"Why, that young devil," she laughed. "Here I've been worrying for no good reason. I'm very relieved. It would be dreadful for a man to marry the first woman who came his way."

Perhaps it was the wine that accounted for their increasing candor as dessert and coffee were served. The conversation led to Mark's problems with Derek Harden. He spoke of Derek's insolence and the fight on the night of the Kennedy assassination. "Looking back on it, I was very naive. I guess I assumed all Englishmen were gentlemen."

Mavis laughed at his confession. "Don't forget history. England has always had more than its share of knaves, especially in its kings."

"Well, Derek is one knave who lost a fight. I never heard from him again."

.   .   .

But Mark was seriously mistaken. At that very moment in London Derek was completing his plan by typing an undated anonymous letter to the Worcester College Provost.

"Sir: This is to advise you that I have regretfully learned that Mark Stevens has copied much of his essay, "The Future of Bretton Woods," from the doctoral thesis entitled "Questions About Bretton Woods" that bears Bodleian number 45 RST 3502E. I understand that this copying was done without proper attribution to the author of the thesis. I feel it my duty to make my inadvertent discovery known to you."

Derek decided that the best time to mail the letter would be after examinations in June. The timing would be perfect. Just as Mark would be expecting to graduate, this bombshell would strike.

The topic of conversation changed to Mark's interest in the Beatles.

"I have a surprise for you," said Mavis. "Since Rodney and you attended that Beatles concert, I've been collecting their records. Let's go up to the music room. I'll show you."

Mark had not expected that a person of Mavis's age would be interested in the Beatles. She drew the new single release, "She's a Woman," from her collection and placed it on the turntable. She was very knowledgeable about the Beatles. She knew of their beginnings in Liverpool and, later, in Germany, and even about their introduction to America on the Ed Sullivan show. When "She's a Woman" came to an end, Mavis got up and looked through the remaining records on the shelf.

"How about 'I Want To Hold Your Hand'?" she asked. As the album played, they sat side by side on the couch between the stereo speakers. When the record was finished, she played it a second time. Animatedly they sang, snapping their fingers to the music. When it was finished they laughed, realizing they had the lyrics completely memorized. Their carefree fun had melted away their age difference. When the record was over she filled their brandy glasses and they laughed and talked about the Beatles.

"Let's listen to some of my longhair music," she said looking through the record albums on a different shelf. "How about some Puccini?"

"Okay by me," said Mark. He remembered Puccini from the days he played chess with Antonio.

When the record was finished she put a Bach album on the player. After listening for a minute, she got up and lifted the phonograph arm. "Bach just doesn't fit our mood tonight. How about some violin? Did Rodney ever tell you I play the violin?"

"The violin? No, he didn't."

"Every proper English girl must do something musical and I wasn't very good at drums," she joked. "I haven't played for months, but I'd love to try, if I wouldn't bore you to tears." Self-assuredly, she took her violin from the case on top of the piano. After tuning the instrument and warming up, she began playing.

From attending string performances at Worcester, Mark realized that Mavis was very skillful. When she finished he applauded and cried "More! More!"

She leafed through her sheet music and selected another number that she played beautifully.

"That's quite enough for one night. I'm afraid I got carried away and was a bore."

"I'm very impressed. To tell the truth, I wasn't expecting you to be so good."

"When I was a girl I practiced constantly. I even gave a recital at Albert Hall, along with some other students. In actual fact I once had serious aspirations for the violin."

"Really? You should have gone on. What happened? Why did you stop?"

"As with so many things of that time, it was the war. I got engaged to an R.A.F. fighter pilot. When he was fighting in the blitz, we got married on very short notice. I became a full-time volunteer. Mostly helping in the blitz in London."

"Was that Lord Ashley or was that before you met him?"

"No, Stanley was in the first war. He's my second husband. My first husband was Jimmy. It was Jimmy who was the fighter pilot. He was shot down in the blitz. Killed." Mavis filled their brandy glasses and sat on the couch, rejoining Mark.

"I'm sorry. It was none of my business."

"It's all right. I was so shaken I didn't think I'd ever get over Jimmy's death. That's when I first became interested in metaphysics. It saved my life really. That and meeting Stanley Ashley."

"You met him during the war?"

"No, I had known him years before. He and his first wife were family friends. She died in '39 just months before the war. After Jimmy was killed, dear, sweet Stanley was there for me."

"I never would have guessed you were married before."

"And why is that?"

"I don't know. The portrait. You were so young. I would have thought you always loved the same man."

"I certainly do love Stanley . . . but Jimmy was once in a life-time. Never to be repeated."

Mark was surprised that she would disclose such an intimacy. With such a mother, he understood how Rodney had come to be so straightforward. "Yes, I think I understand."

"My mother and father were not too keen on my marrying Jimmy, but it was very romantic. The war and all. He could be killed any day. We were together every chance we got, but it was never enough."

"Couldn't you have felt that way again? For someone else?"

"I don't know. I don't think so. Stanley was there when I needed him. I thought I'd never be able to feel again, so it was the most natural thing in the world to marry him when he asked."

"I see."

"He's been a wonderful husband, and then of course we have Rodney."

Mark was moved by her openness and apparent trust in him. "You seem to have a very successful marriage."

"Have you ever been in love, Mark?"

The confidences she had shared prompted him to begin relating the painful story of Christina.

"Yes, I have been in love. Her name was Christina."

"Christina. What a very beautiful name. Was she an American?"

"No, she was from Italy. The most beautiful woman I have ever seen."

"If you want to tell me about Christina, I would like to listen." She spoke with soft understanding.

"I would." Mark swallowed with emotion. "I never thought I'd be able to tell anyone."

"Perhaps it would take away some of the pain if you did."

Mark started at the beginning, telling her about Antonio and Anna. About the nights of chess and Italian opera. How Anna had died, and Antonio had returned from Italy with the beautiful Christina.

"I was a senior in high school. There wasn't a man in the valley who wouldn't have followed Christina to the end of the world. It never entered my mind she would ever be interested in me."

"It must have been wonderful to have your fantasy come true."

"Wonderful? It all happened so fast I didn't have time to think of it as wonderful. No sooner had we made love than the trouble started."

"But wasn't it worth it? Think about the joy she brought into your life."

"No, it wasn't that way at all. The first thing I knew my father was kicking me out of our house."

"Why would he do that? Your own father!"

"Because he was *screwing* her, that's why. Can you imagine that? My father had actually been screwing Christina." He faltered momentarily. "Mavis I didn't even know about it until after his funeral."

"Poor Mark," she said, touching his hand.

"It was my own fault. After all she was Antonio's wife."

"And you have never forgiven yourself."

"Well, I know Antonio sure as hell won't forgive me. He made that clear at the funeral."

"Mark, please listen to me. It's you that needs to do the forgiving. If you can forgive yourself, it won't matter what Antonio does."

"Well, I paid the price for betraying him," he said, not comprehending what she meant. "Even after Antonio threw her out, she didn't want to stay with me. I was only a toy to her."

"What happened?"

"I didn't hear from her for over a year. Then a couple of weeks ago she asked me to come to Paris. I had thought of her every minute that whole year. I can't tell you how much I loved that woman. I would've done anything for her. Quit Oxford—anything! But she wanted to marry someone else, some rich bastard." Mark spoke coldly, attempting to keep his boiling anger under control.

But Mavis could see the angry pain in his eyes. "Remember, you had something important with her. Something many people never know."

"Believe me, I can do without it. She led me down a dead end road I'll never go down again. I'll never marry anyone like Christina."

"But, Mark, every woman isn't like Christina."

"I was watching the women my age at your dance the other night. They seemed like nice young women who wouldn't jump into the next man's bed every time they got the chance. I'd rather have one of them than Christina."

"Yes, but you'd have to love one before you'd marry her, wouldn't you?"

"Listen, I've been taught by the master. Christina told me once loud and clear. I can still hear her words, 'There are many people you can love. Just because you love someone doesn't mean you marry them.' Christina taught me you can marry for good sound, practical reasons."

"A very cynical woman, your Christina."

"Maybe, but I think she was right. I've been looking at your guests here this weekend. I'll bet there wasn't one couple that were married because they couldn't keep their hands off one another. From what I could see they were all married for the 'right' reasons. Social. Class. Money. Position. If I ever get married, it will be to a woman who'll fit in with the type of life I'm going to lead."

"Aren't you overreacting because of Christina?"

"I don't mean to be impolite, Mavis, but look at you."

"What do you mean?"

"I know it's none of my business, but Lord Ashley must be 25 years your senior. Wasn't that a case of overreacting?

"That's how I know what I'm talking about. I gave up love for security. You should only marry for love, Mark. Believe me, once you have known what love is like, it's hell to spend the rest of your life without it."

Mark nodded, indicating that he was listening and that he wanted her to continue.

"Do you have any idea what it's like to be married to a perfectly wonderful and respected man—a member of the House of Lords, for God's sake—and to have the urges I have? I used to lie awake, crying, after Stanley would go back to his bedroom. I simply couldn't respond to him the way I wanted. I couldn't cope with the enormity of my plight."

Mark felt helpless. There was nothing he could say that would help. He wished there were some wisdom that he could offer, but there was not. He reached out and took her hand. With the other hand Mavis took a tissue, dabbing at her tears. "I ached to feel the touch of a man like Jimmy. To have him make love to me. To respond to him. My God to *feel* again! To *feel* the passion in my body that I hadn't felt for so long."

Mark had conflicting emotions. He was aroused by her confession, but, at the same time, he felt compassion for her plight. Who would have thought Lady Mavis Ashley harbored such unhappiness?

"Isn't there anything you can do? Is divorce totally out of the question? At least you could have had an affair or something."

"I would never divorce Stanley." She hesitated, as if gathering nerve to go on. "The truth is I have often wondered what it would be like if Stanley died. God forgive me, but once I even imagined him dead. Imagined his funeral, with me in black." More composed, she put the tissue aside. "Yes, I've even thought about an affair once or twice. I doubt if I could, though. The fear of discovery, the guilt would be too much. I would *never* take the chance of hurting Stanley or my family." She returned her hand to his arm.

"But he leaves you alone all the time. You could have an affair if you wanted. Look at us now. We're absolutely alone and it's the middle of the night."

"There was one time I might have been interested, but the man seemed intimated by Stanley and the Ashley name. Or maybe he wasn't interested in me. I don't know for sure. When you're in my position, it's not as easy as you might think." She took her hand from his and sat back looking at him. "For example, as you say, here we are absolutely alone and yet you would never dare ask me to make love, would you?"

His heart raced at her remark. He doubted she was intending to proposition him. More likely she was merely pointing out the futility of her plight.

"You make a good point, Mavis. I would be afraid to ask you."

They talked endlessly on other subjects. He told her more about Jonah and his mother. She talked of her spiritual beliefs. The sharing of an intimacy by one led the other to share something more, until finally she asked, "Do you know it's after three o'clock in the morning?"

"There's something about talking to you—I can't get enough of it."

"I've never been this way with anyone either," she said. "I feel safe telling you things. I'm sorry the evening is over."

They stood and gently held one another close, carefully, only barely touching their bodies. Mavis gently patted him on his back.

"Good night, Mark. I'll see you tomorrow. Maybe we can have a walk before the others return. We could talk some more."

"I'd like that," he said.

Mark could not get to sleep. Endlessly, he recounted the events of the evening. It was hard to believe that they had spent over seven hours together. My God, he thought, the subjects they had discussed. He never would have dreamed he would have told anyone what he had told Mavis. She had met it all with such understanding, never once judging him.

He thought about her as he snapped on the light and looked for something to read. He could have talked until the sun came up. It had been as if nothing stood between them, none of the customary walls that separate people.

He tossed aside the old issue of *Country Life* magazine. The antique clock on the fireplace mantle showed four o'clock. He had expected to have a predictable time this weekend, and then to get ready for the start of the Hilary Term at Worcester; he certainly had not expected this.

Sometimes at Oxford when his mind was whirring this way, he would go for a long walk. After trying again to get to sleep, he decided he would try a walk outside.

He quietly walked down the stairway from his third floor bedroom and along the wide portrait-lined hallway to the top of the grand staircase. His heart quickened when he saw a light under the door of the room at the other end of the hallway. It had to be Mavis's bedroom. She had headed in that direction when she had said good night. She must not have been able to sleep either, he thought. Perhaps the evening had affected her the same way it had him. Did he dare knock? His heart pounded as he stopped outside her door. He wondered if he should turn around and go for his walk or if he should knock. Perhaps she would want to see him too. Perhaps she would join him on his walk.

He was shaking as he softly knocked on the door. There was no response. He knocked louder. "Mavis. It's me. Mark."

"Just a minute," she said through the door. Several moments passed before she opened it. She was dressed in a white silk robe, contrasting with her long, black, freshly combed hair. She looked beautiful.

"I shouldn't be here, I know, but I couldn't sleep. I was going for a walk around the grounds when I saw your light. I wanted to see you again tonight."

"I never dared hope that you would come," she whispered. "Come in, Mark. I couldn't sleep either." A lighted cigarette curled smoke from an ash tray. An open book lay on the chaise longue.

"I didn't know you smoked," said Mark.

"I try not to, but I'm so nervous tonight." She motioned for him to sit on one of the chairs.

"Nervous? Why are you nervous?"

"The whole evening. Our conversation. It made me realize . . ." She stopped.

"Made you realize what?"

"I've been deceiving myself." Her fingers shook as she crushed out her cigarette. She sat on the edge of the chaise longue, facing the fireplace. Mark sat on the chair next to her.

"About what, Mavis?"

"About what I'm really like inside." Her voice cracked with emotion. "Excuse me," she said, suddenly crying and rushing from the bedroom.

Mark started to go after her, but he was too late. She had closed her bathroom door. He lit the firewood in the fireplace while he waited for her to return. He did not understand what was upsetting her. Perhaps he had made a mistake in knocking on her door. He stared at the fire as he waited.

"Sorry," she said, when she reentered the room. "For a moment there I really understood what I've given up for this good, safe, practical life of mine." She stood next to him by the fire. He saw that she had dried her eyes and freshened herself.

"What is it you gave up, Mavis?"

"I gave up *me*. Don't you see? It was *me* I gave up." She lit another cigarette. "Oh, it was my fault all right. Poor Stanley was just an innocent participant." Mark took the cushions from the chairs and arranged them on the floor, back from the fire that had begun to crackle. They sat looking at the burning logs.

"But you have a wonderful, successful husband, a marvelous son. You have all the status and money anyone would ever want. On top of that you're a beautiful woman. What more do you want? What was it you gave up?"

"My *lust*. Don't you see? It was my *lust* that I gave up!"

Now Mark understood why she had cried. "It is as if I lived never having known Christina—isn't that what you're saying?"

"Oh, no. It's much worse than that. Ever so much worse than never having known."

"Worse?"

"Don't you see? I *did* know Jimmy. It is so much more diffi-cult to give up something once you've known it. With Jimmy I knew the *lust* in me. I reveled in it. My God, Mark, once we made love under the Christmas tree in this very house. Once in May, the year he was killed, we were driving in the north of England. He had a few days leave. I had him stop the car. I grabbed a blanket and we went behind a stone wall beside the road and fucked, yes I said 'fucked'. Does that shock you? We fucked our bloody heads off."

She had stood up gesturing while she talked. "Don't you see?" she plunged on. "I knew what lust was. I bloody well knew what it was. I had explored my own lust in ways I think most women never know. *And then I gave it all up.* Don't you see? *I gave it all up. I sold part of Mavis Enfield as surely as if I were a slave trader.*" As her emotions spilled out Mark expected her to cry, but she remained in control.

She sat on a pillow and they silently looked into the fire. "Do you realize what it's like to wake up one morning as I did? I had been married six years. I knew that my husband loved me and he was beyond reproach. I was on top of the world, but it was not enough. As I lay there in bed I thought of Jimmy and the way we were by that stone wall, and I cried inside. I knew I could never betray my husband, but I knew I was dissatisfied down to my soul."

Mark turned from the fire and looked into her eyes. "Mavis, I want to say something serious to you."

"Serious? What is it, Mark?"

"I know I shouldn't say this. Maybe it's the booze talking. Mavis, I'm very attracted to you."

"Oh, Mark, you flatter me. You would never be interested in someone so much older than you."

"I have been from the very beginning. I would have chased you around your Chelsea house as soon as we were alone if it hadn't been for that sign on your chest."

"Sign on my chest," she smiled putting her hand on her chest, "What sign?"

"There was a great big sign on you. Right across the front of your dress. Maybe I put it there, I don't know. But I saw it there all right."

"And what did this sign of yours say?" she asked quizzically.

"'Hands off.' That's what it said, in large letters. Then under that, in smaller letters, it said: 'You may think I'm vivacious and desirable, but I'm also Rodney's mother.' And then under that there were even smaller letters: 'I'm also Lord Ashley's faithful wife, rich, prominent and absolutely unapproachable.' The wording on the sign was so clear, I knew I had to stay away from you for the rest of my life."

"Then the next day, there was a different sign," he continued. "It said. 'But it's okay to talk, as long as it's strictly intellectual talk.'"

"Have there been any other signs?" she asked flirtatiously.

"Yes, two more. That first day in the garden, here at Castle Enfield, there was a new sign."

"And what did the new sign say?" she asked.

"The 'hands off' part was still there, but the small lettering had changed. It said, 'It's okay to be friendly with me.' Then tonight in the music room you had another new sign on."

"Still another? And what did it say?" she asked, amused.

"Well the 'hands off' was a lot smaller and the rest of the sign said, 'I'm a human being, even a very special friend.'"

"Do you ever wear a sign?" she asked softly.

"Yes, in fact I have one on right now. Do you see it?"

"Yes, but I can't quite make it out," she pretended to peer at the sign. "The lettering isn't too good. What does it say?"

"It says, I'd like very much to kiss you." He was talking with total disregard of the risks.

"Don't you see that I have a new sign on tonight?" Her voice was barely audible, as the fire crackled.

"Oh, yes. Now I see." He pretended to hold a sign that hung from around her neck. He squinted his eyes at the sign, as if he could not read it, and held it to the light. "Why it says, 'I want you to kiss me too.'"

They kissed passionately, holding tightly onto one another. Long kisses followed by short kisses, then more kisses. For him they were more delicious than he had known even with Christina, and for her more sensuous than any she remembered.

"I can't pretend I don't want to go to bed with you. The truth is I wanted to when we were in the music room," she said.

"But we shouldn't." He kissed her again, as the fire rapidly consumed the logs in the fireplace. "I want to have you as a friend for the rest of my life. If we made love, we'd lose that."

"It wouldn't have to be that way," she said. "We could just have this once together."

"Someday I want to sit around a fire like this one with you and Rodney and Rebecca, and talk philosophy. I'd listen to you play your violin for your grandchildren while I hold them on my lap." But even as he spoke, he knew very well he desperately wanted to make love with her.

"I want that too. We could have both."

"But we couldn't. I would always want to be with you, yet we'd never be able to make love again. How could we possibly do that?

"We'd have to. There would be no other way."

By the time they had made love the first time, the logs in the fireplace had turned to embers. They lay on the thick bedroom carpet, near the hearth. With her fingers Mavis gently smoothed over the beads of perspiration that had formed on his body.

"I wish our lives were somehow different. I wish we could suspend time and be together whenever we wanted, without hurting anyone else," she said, kissing the dampness on his skin.

He kissed her breasts. He wanted to remember what her naked body looked like, so when he saw her at Rodney's wedding and at dinner parties, he could picture her under her dress.

With the embers dying, they moved across the room to her bed. They wanted as much of each other as their single night together would allow. Their early intensity diminished and their pace slowed, as they reveled in each other. Mark freely used all he had learned with Christina. He wanted to please Mavis and to fulfill her long denied yearnings, for tonight he loved her.

Finally their time was ending. Each knew they would have to return to their own rooms to avoid discovery by the servants. Mavis broke the long silence by laughing.

"What are you laughing about?"

"You know, you did things Jimmy didn't even know about."

"His bad luck was never knowing Christina."

He dressed to leave. They talked near her door, like a young couple not wanting to leave one another.

"Thank you for this night. I'll always remember it. And you don't need to worry. I'll live up to my promise and not pester you," she teased.

"You mean tomorrow it's back to talking metaphysics?"

"Yes, and someday I'll play my violin for you, while you hold my grandchildren on your lap."

"Do you mind if I think of you absolutely stark naked, while you stand there with your fiddle?" he asked.

"I wouldn't have it any other way."

-16-

It was January 30, 1965, the day of Winston Churchill's funeral. Mark was in his in his Worcester College rooms, reading for his Philosophy tutorial. He turned on the BBC radio:

We shall go on to the end, we shall fight in France, we shall fight on the seas and the oceans, we shall fight with growing confidence and growing strength in the air, we shall defend our island, whatever the cost may be, we shall fight on the beaches, we shall fight on the landing grounds, we shall fight in the fields and in the streets, we shall fight in the hills; we shall never surrender . . .

It was the recorded voice of Britain's wartime prime minister, giving his famous speech after the defeat at Dunkirk. Prior to the funeral in London, BBC was broadcasting some of Churchill's speeches, and tributes from commentators and statesmen from around the world.

The Hilary term had barely begun. Mark was scheduled to meet with his tutor, Richard Dawbarn, this afternoon. Oxford, like all of England, was deeply affected by Churchill's death. Some shops had removed their window displays and exhibited Churchill's portrait. One on Cornmarket displayed a dozen roses that were painted black and lay under a photograph of the great man. In front of the Randolph Hotel, Churchill's beloved union jack was at half mast. Although expected, Churchill's death had deeply affected England. Political differences were forgotten as Englishmen shared personal memories of the man who had led them through the blitz and to victory. Throughout the U.K., speeches were being given, eulogizing the beloved symbol of Britain's triumph after its dark hours. Last night in the buttery Mark listened as the students, too young to remember the war, talked with admiration for the crusty old man who had won their respect.

It had been a month since the weekend at Castle Enfield. Mavis had not contacted him, and he had made no attempt to reach her. He realized full well that she had been serious in her resolve that they make love just that once. He had no intention of invading that resolve, nor did he have any expectation that she would contact him. To be sure, the next time they met their relationship would be at a new and deeper level. They could never erase the openness they had shared, let alone the fact that they had experienced sex together. He looked forward to seeing her and having long talks with her again. Probably he would be invited to Chelsea or Castle Enfield sometime during spring vacation. Perhaps some day, before too many years had passed, he would listen to her play the violin for her grandchildren.

Mark climbed the staircase to Dawbarn's rooms. As he knocked on the door he remembered his dismay when he had discovered that Derek was his tutorial partner. He rarely saw Derek, even at a distance, and then they managed to avoid one another.

"Mark, I want to talk to you about your Bretton Woods essay," said Dawbarn, plugging in his teakettle. Mark had come to have a great deal of affection for this comfortable man, with his white hair and white mustache. Mark had figured out that Dawbarn had two suits and two sports jackets. Today he was wearing suit number two, which was brown with a vest and had the usual Dawbarn rumpled look. He would miss him after graduation. "It's a marvelous essay; a brilliant piece of work."

"Thank you, Dick. Thank you very much." The time Dawbarn had invited all the P. P. and E. students for a dinner party at his home, he had asked Mark to call him by his first name.

"You're certainly not the first student to suggest that we should dispense with the Bretton Woods System, but I want to congratulate you on your analysis."

"Some of those ideas have been kicking around in my head since I first studied international economics in Berkeley."

Dawbarn poured the tea for each of them, and eased into his chair near the window. "I should make it clear that I don't much agree with your conclusions, but you marshaled every argument in your favor that's ever been discussed, to my knowledge, and added a few new ones. Arguments I have to admit I'd never thought of."

Mark's spirits soared. While a fair man, Dawbarn was not one to be liberal with his praise. He assumed that Oxford students were the best and didn't need their egos stroked. To have Dawbarn tell him this made him feel like dancing down the hallway.

"I thought 30 odd pages was way too long, but then who am I to question genius?" Dawbarn laughed heartily.

"I was trying to do something special."

"And you did—you did, indeed. It was very original. I'm certain you realized it was much more innovative than we customarily look for at Oxford."

"Professor Hall at Berkeley told me a long time ago that I should specialize—pick some field and become as good as I possibly can."

"That's perfectly good advice." Dawbarn was looking out the window at the trees and lake in the distance.

Mark got up from his chair and looked out the other window, taking in the familiar scene. "I've decided to specialize in foreign exchange. I want to learn everything I can about it. That's why I wrote the essay. That's how I want to make my mark in the world."

"Well, then, I have an idea for you."

"An idea?"

"That's why I made this appointment, but we need more time to talk. How about driving with me to meet Churchill's funeral train. I didn't want to fight the bloody crowds at the procession in London."

"I didn't know about the funeral train."

"Yes, Churchill is to be buried at his little church over at Bladon. The newspaper says the burial is only for the family, but I've decided at least to meet the train that brings the casket from London. If you'd care to come along, we can talk about my idea for your essay, and you can see a little of English history in the making."

"I'd be honored to go." Mark was thrilled to see part of the historic event and was flattered that Dawbarn had asked him.

Together they drove in Dawbarn's car to the nearby village of Handborough.

"Churchill was born at Blenheim Palace, not far from Oxford. That's why he's being buried so nearby," said Dawbarn.

"My friend took me to Blenheim. Huge place," said Mark.

"The Oxford newspaper said that they have maintained the old rail line all these years, just for the funeral train. It hasn't been used for years. Quite remarkable!"

"Just for his final trip. What a tribute!"

As they waited in Handborough with the small crowd for the train to arrive from London's Waterloo Station, they talked about Mark's thesis.

"I think you should submit your essay for a university prize."

Mark had only a general awareness that there were various prizes that were awarded at Oxford. "Do you really think that I might have a chance at a prize?"

"Yes, I do. You've created a very original piece of work. You might want to make a few changes here and there, but I'd give it a go."

"I'm flattered you feel that way."

"I've been thinking about it. I suggest you try for the Linde-Ewell Prize. It's not a very large monetary sum—about 100 pounds—but it's a very prestigious award. I see no reason why you shouldn't enter. All the entries are done anonymously."

"What are the criteria for that prize? You say the Linde-Ewell Prize?"

"Yes, that's it. The winner is supposed to have written something original. Created some unique ideas, as you have in your essay."

"Is the prize awarded every year?"

"It hasn't been. The judges are very particular."

"Who would be the judges?"

"The Bulldog Professor and another member of the Oxford faculty. In actual fact I suspect in some years there may not be many serious entries." They heard the whistle of the arriving Churchill train in the distance.

"I'd submit my essay anonymously?"

"Yes. You'd give your essay a secret name. Rather like a race horse is named. It may be, oh, let's say, 'Dancing Lady' or something like that."

"So the judges would simply choose 'Dancing Lady' as the winner and then someone else tells them who 'Dancing Lady' is?"

"Right. The prize has proven to be very prestigious, both to the winner and to his college."

"I think I'll do it. I think I'll give it a try."

"Good for you."

"You've given me an idea for a name to use."

"Yes, go on."

"I'll use the name 'The Violin Lady.' It has sentimental meaning for me."

"Ah, a lady?"

"Yes, a lady."

Mark and Dawbarn watched as the old yellow and black train slowly pulled to a stop. After several minutes Lady Churchill and their son, Randolph, emerged from one of the cars.

"They named the locomotive the 'Winston Churchill'," commented Dawbarn.

"Can you imagine having your country keep a special old railway car for years, just to take you home to be buried?" remarked Mark.

"Yes, and keeping up an obsolete railroad track for you."

They were silent as the bearer guards slowly carried the coffin from the train, placing it on the caisson for the short trip to the burial ceremony, which was to be in the yard of the old church at Bladon.

"I was in Whitehall during the war. I saw him once, walking around after the all-clear had sounded." Dawbarn was watching the proceedings with great reverence.

"I've seen photos of him in the blitz, with a cigar and holding up his fingers in the Vee sign," said Mark.

"That's the way he was the day I saw him. I'll never forget it. As long as I live, I'll never forget it." Dawbarn took a handkerchief from his jacket pocket and unashamedly brushed tears from his eyes.

In the car back to Oxford Dawbarn continued to reflect. "He always took full advantage of his gifts, even when he was out of power—painting—writing. I think that's the mark of greatness. Never let circumstances hold you back."

Mark had not seen the sensitive aspect of Dawbarn that was evident today. It gave him a deeper respect for his tutor.

"He bided his time, waiting for his turn." Then, as if he felt he had dwelled enough on Churchill, Dawbarn changed the subject. "I think you should give some thought to being a teacher. You have the very valuable gift of explaining complex subjects in simple terms. Of course, it's obvious from your essay that you are capable of original thinking."

"I don't know about teaching, Dick."

"If you got a first, you might even have a chance to teach at Oxford. Remember only about five percent get a first. If you decide to teach I would recommend you do some post-graduate work."

"I've always been in a hurry. I'm afraid I'm too anxious to get into business."

"Teaching has it compensations, you know. There's a great deal of satisfaction. If it's prestige you're after, you might well be asked to give advice to government." Dawbarn edged his small car into the traffic circle.

Mark had not known that Dawbarn thought he had the potential to teach at Oxford. "I'm very flattered by what you say. I'll admit that I've always wanted to be in a position of a man like Sir Roy Harrod, advising say, your Trade Minister or our Secretary of Treasury."

"You really ought to give it some thought."

Mark paused before responding. "I suppose I should. I'm reluctant to tell you, but I've always wanted to be a player in big business. To live in one of those big houses I've only been able to visit. I've some goals that are important to me. I'm afraid being a teacher wouldn't do that for me."

"Don't be in such a hurry. You don't want to end up having the big house and nothing else."

"I appreciate your advice. I will think about it." He glanced out the car window. "It sure would require a complete about-face for me."

"I know Mark. That's exactly why I thought I should mention it. Look what Churchill accomplished. I hardly think he had making a lot of money on his mind. Give it some more thought, will you?"

"I will, sir. I promise you, I will." But the truth was Mark knew what he wanted and teaching would not provide it. Churchill was different. His family had all the money he ever wanted.

Outside Oxford they stopped at a pub for beer as the short winter day ended. They talked for hours and ultimately had dinner there. Although Dawbarn's world did not offer what he wanted, he respected his teacher. He hoped that they would keep in touch. It was a good idea to keep the door to the academic life open. Who knows, perhaps one day when he had done what he had to do, he would return to Oxford.

That evening in his room Mark idly wrote on his yellow pad. "Mark Stevens, Linde-Ewell Prize Winner." Not bad. Not bad at all.

-17-

Three months had passed since Mark had submitted his Bretton Woods essay for the Linde-Ewell Prize. At Oxford the last term of a student's final year is devoted to review for the all-important examinations. Mark had been working day and night, reviewing all two years of his Oxford work. While most students would be satisfied with second class honors, Mark was putting all his effort toward obtaining the coveted first. He would be writing exams this week and then finishing up next week.

This morning was his first examination. He entered the imposing Examination Schools on High Street, where the university gave exams to students from all the Oxford colleges. The grand interior of the building was filled with scurrying students, all wearing their required caps and gowns. Mark climbed the stairs to where 250 nervous young men were busy finding their alphabetically labeled desks in the large hall. He was tense as he read the first question.

Second Public Examination
Honour School of Philosophy, Politics, and Economics
Trinity Term 1965
ECONOMIC ORGANIZATION
Thursday, 3 June   9:30 a.m. - 12: 30 pm

ANSWER FOUR QUESTIONS

1. Discuss the reasons for the greater fluctuations in company profits than in total factor incomes in the United Kingdom in recent years.
    . . .

As Mark read the 14 questions from which he would choose 4 to answer, he gained confidence and his anxiety waned. He felt a burst of confidence and began writing. The questions required a great deal of judgment and sophistication. Frequently there were no right or wrong answers. He loved the competition and the feeling that he was covering points that other students were missing. He enjoyed analyzing the questions and applying the knowledge his studying had given him.

The large "L" shaped hall presented a dramatic sight, with the formally gowned students watching the strategically placed clocks as they wrote. Grim faced men, called Invigitators, slowly paced the aisles to remove any temptation to cheat.

When Mark finished and walked onto the street he let out a sigh, and with it some of the tension that had built up for this fateful week. This evening he planned to study for tomorrow's Politics exam.

He walked toward Worcester on the familiar streets that he had grown to love. He would miss Oxford. Despite himself, Christina often came to his thoughts. He assumed she had gone ahead with her marriage to the Italian. While his anger had cooled and he could see that he had been foolish to think about giving up Oxford to be with her, he could not shake the memories of her.

Wearing his academic gown, Mark stood, head bowed, in the Worcester dining hall as the Latin prayer was said. He joined Rodney and John for dinner at the table.

"How did you fellows do on the exams?" he asked.

"Not very bloody well," answered Rodney. "At first I wasn't sure I was in the right examination room."

"Dawbarn was looking for you," said John. "He's at High Table. He wanted to see you right away."

"Why does he want to see me?" asked Mark. " Do you think I should go right up to High Table?"

"I wouldn't. You'd better wait until dinner is finished," answered Rodney.

"Something must be wrong. Why else would Dawbarn want to see me so urgently?"

"Here's your answer now," said John. "Here's a note for you." A folded paper bearing Mark's name had been handed down from the High Table.

Mark hurriedly unfolded the note.

> *"Mark:*
>
> *Congratulations. Violin Lady has been awarded the Linde-Ewell Prize. Worcester College is proud of you. Dawbarn."*

"Violin Lady" was his code name. He had won. "Yippee!" he shouted at the top of his voice."

Nearly everyone in the room stopped talking, wondering what could account for his unusual behavior. Taking advantage of the silence, Dawbarn rose to his feet, tapping a glass with his spoon for attention.

"Gentlemen, I see that you are wondering what has come over Mr. Stevens. I'm here to tell you that there is indeed a justifiable reason for his behavior." Dawbarn was smiling broadly as he spoke. "It gives me a great deal of pleasure to announce that Mark Stevens has been awarded the Linde-Ewell Prize for his original essay 'The Future of Bretton Woods.' Mark, you have brought great honor to Worcester College. We thank you and extend our heartiest congratulations."

Pandemonium broke loose. Students and High Table occupants alike stood, cheering and clapping for Mark. Smiling, he stood, accepting their adulation. Soon a line of students extended more congratulations with handshaking and backslapping. When the noise died down, the sound of silverware clanging on glass could again be heard. This time it was the provost who commanded their attention.

"Gentlemen, we are all proud of Mr. Stevens for the honor he has brought both to himself and to Worcester College." The provost was interrupted by more applause and shouts of "Hear, hear." "In honor of this occasion I have asked that The Blue Peter be passed around."

Mark had never heard of the Blue Peter that was carried forward to the provost at High Table. The Blue Peter was a large Georgian silver loving cup filled with beer. The group cheered loudly as the provost took a drink of beer from the cup and passed it to Dawbarn, who stood next to him. The cup was passed around the High Table, until each had taken a drink. From the High Table the cup was passed to Mark. The cheering reverberated in the hall while Mark took his turn and passed The Blue Peter to Rodney for its trip around the room.

Standing to one side, not participating in the cheering, was Derek Harden. Now was the time to send his anonymous letter, he decided. If there ever was an opportune time to spring his trap for Mark, this was it.

When exams were over Mark stayed with Rodney at the Ashley house in Chelsea. Both were on pins and needles during the long weeks they were forced to wait for the exam results to arrive in the mail. At Oxford if the three examiners of their papers could not agree on the class of honors to be awarded, students face the further challenge of comprehensive oral questioning, called *viva voce* exams, nicknamed "vivas."

Mavis and Lord Ashley were staying in the relative cool of the country for the summer, but tonight Lord Ashley was in Chelsea on business. When Mark had visited Castle Enfield during the spring vacation, Mavis and he had not spoken of their night together, but tonight as he chatted with Lord Ashley and Rodney he felt ill at ease.

"Rodney tells me you were awarded a prize at university. My heartiest congratulations."

"Thank you sir. I'm to get it just before I go home."

"I think he's odds on for a first too, father," said Rodney proudly.

"It's a remarkable achievement. Lady Ashley and I were discussing it only this weekend."

"Thank you, sir. I'm very flattered," said Mark, still feeling party to a deception on Lord Ashley.

"She made a suggestion which I thought was jolly good."

"What did she say?" inquired Rodney.

"She thought I might invite Mark to make a few remarks at the Blue Sheep club next week. Is that agreeable to you, Mark? I'll invite some of my friends from the financial community here in London. They could use a few new ideas."

"I've never spoken before a group before. I'm not sure . . . "

"Nonsense! I'm sure anyone who has won such a prestigious prize will do a capital job."

Mark had agreed, and had been preparing all week for the speech tomorrow night. He was nervous, but if he were going to get into the big time he had to do things like this.

"Mark, it's Richard Dawbarn on the telephone. He would like to talk with you," Rodney called upstairs. Mark was shaving in the bathroom that had become his when he stayed at the Chelsea house.

He took the call on the extension. "Mark, something very serious has come up about the Linde-Ewell Prize. I'm afraid I must ask you to come up to Oxford as soon as possible," said Dawbarn.

"You sound ominous. Can't you tell me what it is?"

"I hate to say anything at all without seeing you. I don't want to upset you unnecessarily."

"But you can't just leave me dangling."

"I'm certain you have a proper explanation for the problem."

"The problem? Proper explanation for what problem?"

"I had wanted to wait until you got here. I'm sorry, but you've been accused of cheating."

"Cheating? What do you mean cheating?"

"Mark, I'm sorry. Please. Not over the telephone. Can you come right away?"

"I don't understand what you're telling me."

"I'm certain you have an explanation. Please just get here as soon as you can."

"It's eight now." Mark gave up on getting more out of Dawbarn. "I can be at Paddington by nine."

"Good. Come to my rooms the minute you get here."

Mark practically ran the mile from the Oxford railroad station. It was raining lightly, but he had not brought his umbrella. He was breathing hard as he raced up the Nuffield stairs. Contrary to his usual practice Dawbarn, did not click on his teakettle, but abruptly motioned to Mark to take his usual chair. He commenced immediately.

"I don't know what to say, or even how to go about saying it." Dawbarn was obviously distressed.

"I don't understand. How am I supposed to have cheated? Does somebody think I cheated some way on my essay?"

"Somebody wrote this anonymous letter to the provost. He gave it to me yesterday morning." Dawbarn held the letter in his hand.

"How could it say anything? I haven't done anything wrong." Whatever the letter said, Mark knew there had to be some simple explanation. He could clear this up in a few minutes.

"This letter says you copied part of your essay out of an unpublished doctoral thesis."

"An unpublished . . . What are you talking about?"

"I didn't believe the letter myself. I've known you two years now. You would never cheat."

"I didn't copy anything from any doctoral thesis. What is this?"

"I told the provost there had to be some explanation. At first I was going to dismiss the whole stupid charge out of hand. After all, an anonymous letter. A bunch of rubbish."

"What does it say? Let me see that letter," Mark demanded.

"*I have regretfully learned that Mark Stevens has copied much of his last essay of the Michaelmas term from the doctoral thesis entitled 'The Future of Bretton Woods . . . '*"

"What the hell is this?" Mark's hand was shaking as he read the letter.

*"I understand that this copying was done without proper attri-
bution to the author of the thesis . . . "*

"You've got to believe me! I wouldn't copy anything."

"It wouldn't be so serious if it were just an essay, but the Linde-
Ewell Prize!"

"But I didn't copy anything! You sound as if you think I did!"

"You did tell me it was your own thinking. It was on that basis
that I suggested that you try for the prize."

"See, you *are* beginning to assume I copied it."

"I'm not assuming anything. That's why I asked you to come
here." Agitated, Dawbarn got up and looked out his window, as
was his habit. "Mark, do you know the penalty for lying about
original research?"

"But I didn't copy anything."

"I'm sorry, I've no alternative but to tell the judges. If these
charges are true, I'm certain the prize will be removed. There will
be an announcement in the *Gazette*. You and the College will be
disgraced. The college may even send you down."

"Expel me?"

"I fear it might be."

"What the hell am I supposed to do? Just sit here and take it?
You can't go by some stupid anonymous letter." Mark was frightened and angry.

"I want you to look at what I found at the Bodleian. I got
special permission to remove it from the library." Dawbarn handed
Mark a bound volume. He saw the title "Bretton Woods Today."

"Open it to page 79. Start with the first full paragraph."

Mark found the place and started to read. The language on
page 79 was identical to his essay! He quickly finished reading
the page. Shocked, he looked up at Dawbarn. "It's the same."

"The same is true of the next page. It wouldn't be surprising to
find essentially the same ideas as yours in some other book or
thesis—no one has a monopoly on ideas—but the prize was
awarded because of your originality. What do you expect the judges
to believe when the whole page—nearly two pages—was copied
word for word?"

"I can't explain it. I need time to figure it out. You've got to
believe me, I've never seen this thesis before in my life."

"Mark, I need to give you some very difficult advice. I can
understand it if you copied. If you were trying to impress me, you
succeeded. But for God's sake, don't make matters worse by de-
nying it. Let them take back their prize. If you admit you made a
terrible mistake, I may be able to keep you from being sent down
by the college."

Mark felt like an innocent person facing the hangman. If he were Dawbarn, he would probably have drawn the same conclusions. He was stunned. What could he possibly do? "I don't know how I can convince you, but the truth is I've never seen this volume in my life. I can't admit to something I didn't do."

"I've got to show you these." Dawbarn reached in his desk drawer and handed Mark two sheets of photocopy paper. His expression was sad as he looked at Mark.

Mark took the sheet from Dawbarn's outstretched hand. "What is this supposed to be?"

"Check-out sheets from the Bodleian. Doctoral theses aren't allowed out of the library, but you can look at them in a room there at the Bod."

Mark slowly studied the papers. He was stunned. "They surely look like my signatures."

"These check-out sheets have to be signed whenever a thesis is taken from the shelves."

"But I didn't look at any doctoral thesis."

"Those aren't your signatures?"

"They can't be. Something's wrong someplace. Someone's made a terrible mistake."

On the train back to London, he stared blankly out the window at the countryside. If he could just think! He had to take time and think. He felt as he did when his father had burst in on Christina and him, only this time he had done nothing wrong. He felt panic. The evidence was overwhelming, but he knew he was innocent.

It was raining as he changed trains in Didcot. He stood in the rain on the platform with his umbrella unopened. He needed time to think, to apply his analytical mind. There had to be some rational explanation, but what it was he had no idea. He had to talk with someone. Then as the connecting train to London pulled into the station, he knew he should telephone Mavis. No matter what the appearances, Mavis would support him.

He raced for the telephone, not caring if he missed the train. He heard the "ring-ring, ring-ring" of the phone at Castle Enfield.

"Lady Ashley, please. Tell her it's Mark Stevens calling—tell her it's urgent."

"Lady Ashley went to Chelsea this morning, sir."

Without a word Mark hung up and dialed the Chelsea number.

.   .   .

"Mark, don't take the time to tell me any more on the tele-phone. I'll meet you someplace. There must be a solution to this," said Mavis.

"I've never been so upset about anything. It looks bad." Mark's voice shook.

"There's an Italian restaurant I know in Soho. It's called 'Quo Vadis.' Take a taxi from Paddington. The driver will find it. It's on Dean Street."

"Dean Street. 'Quo Vadis.' I'm writing it down now."

He paid the taxi driver and rushed into the restaurant. Mavis was having a glass of wine in the reception room of the Quo Vadis. "Thank God. you're here," he said, handing the head waiter his umbrella. "If ever I needed a friend it's right now." He sat oppo-site her at the small table.

"You'd better order a drink, and tell me the whole story from the beginning."

"Scotch whiskey." Mark said to the waiter. "With ice, please, and a little water. Better make it a double." He felt better being with Mavis.

She gently squeezed his hand momentarily under the table. It was early for dinner and there were no other patrons in the recep-tion room. "Is it the same essay that won the prize? The one for your speech at the Blue Sheep Club tomorrow night?"

"Mavis, I didn't cheat. I didn't copy the damn thing. I wish I'd never heard of the Linde-Ewell Prize!"

"You don't have to convince me of anything. Don't you under-stand? I really don't care if you did something wrong. If you say you did, then you did. If you say you didn't, then you didn't. It simply doesn't matter to me."

Her *carte blanche* support took him by surprise. He returned her squeeze. He wished Dawbarn had said something like that. "You don't know how important it is to me to have you say that." He swallowed, barely getting out the words.

"What makes them think you copied something?"

"Nearly two pages of my essay are identical, word for word, with a thesis in the Bodleian. I don't understand how it could be, but there it is. And they've got check-out slips too, with my signa-ture. Slips I never even saw before." He was distressed as he gulped a swallow of his drink.

"How perfectly awful! Something is terribly wrong someplace, isn't it?"

"Excuse me," the waiter interrupted. "Would you like to order now?"

"I don't know if I can eat."

"You'll feel better after a while. You'd better order something."

He agreed and they each ordered from the menu. "I want another Scotch whiskey," Mark told the waiter.

"What could happen to you?" Mavis asked sympathetically.

"They'd revoke the prize for starters."

"I'm sure that would be humiliating to you, but it's really very unimportant. Let them take back the silly prize." She patted his hand.

"I suppose so, but Dawbarn thinks they might even kick me out of Worcester. I guess I've disgraced the college."

"But they can't do that—after all your work! Who do they think they are?"

When their meals were ready the head waiter ushered them into the main dining room. They asked for a table in the corner.

"And tomorrow I'm supposed to give my talk to the Blue Sheep Club."

"Yes, I know," she sighed. "I wish you didn't have to."

"I feel like a hypocrite, telling them about my ideas on Bretton Woods, when they're claiming I plagiarized my essay."

"I'm afraid I'm the one who suggested the Blue Sheep Club to Stanley in the first place."

"Yes, I knew."

"What's more, I did worse than that. I invited Henry."

"Your brother, Henry? He's going to be there?"

"He was coming to England in a fortnight anyway, so I suggested he come early to hear your talk."

"All the way from California?"

"You told me he might want to hire you, so I told him about your talk."

"My God, what if he finds out?"

"There's nothing to find out, except that you're a very fine speaker."

"Let's walk for a bit," she said as they left the restaurant. The streets were wet, but it had stopped raining. They walked silently down Shaftesbury Avenue, through the early crowds of the theater district. After several blocks, she pointed out a taxi. "Please, can you get that taxi?"

Mark hailed the cab. "Where are we going?" he asked her.

"Do you mind awfully if we go to my church for a few minutes? I'd like to sit there with you for a time."

"It's all right with me."

"Driver, St. James's Church, Piccadilly, please. The Jermyn Street side."

.   .   .

There were a few people browsing at the book stall in the entry to the old Christopher Wren-designed church.   A hand-lettered sign indicated a class was being conducted in the bell tower. Mavis and Mark sat on one of the benches in the empty sanctuary, candles providing the only light.

"I come here often. It's my refuge. This is where I renew my strength," she said.

"Do you ask God for help, as my mother does?"

"In a way, but I don't like to use the word 'God.' It means so many things to so many people. I do believe there is a power that can help us with your problem at Oxford."

"So you want to pray, is that it? You want me to pray with you?"

"No, not pray. That sounds too much like beseeching some almighty being to give you something. I don't do that."

"What do you want to do then?"

"I want us to sit here.   Just sit here for a few moments to gather ourselves. I'm certain that there's an answer to this trouble."

They sat silently for several minutes.

"You see, Mark, we humans think that our intellects are all we have to solve our problems." She placed her hand on top of his.

"It's my intellect that works for me. That much I know," Mark responded.

"But the truth is there are times when our intellects are useless, absolutely useless."

Mark tentatively nodded, but he did not really understand.

"We think that because we can't see the answer, there isn't one. But I've come to believe that there are always solutions to everything, only we can't see them. Most of what I have thought were problems, didn't turn out to be problems at all when I saw them from a different perspective."

"But what god do you believe in?"

"I call it a force for good. It's not a person in the sky someplace. It's a power. When I trust it, it works." Mark was listening intently.   He respected Mavis too much to discard out-of-hand what she was saying. "It's a principle—like electricity. It's there for me to use. There's an answer to these plagiarism accusations. I don't know what it is, but I know there is one."

"But what should I do?"

"What you need to do, what we need to do, is release the whole business to that power. Not try to solve it with our intellects."

Mark had never heard anyone talk about their religion this way. Amanda had gone to church every Sunday that he could remember. Her religion had to do with being good, praying, and going to church. Mark had not seen church do much to help his mother, and when he was old enough he had stopped attending. He did not understand Mavis's religion, but he knew it was an important part of her life. As for him, religion would have to wait. He had other things to do.

After several minutes Mavis was finished meditating. "Thank you for indulging me," she said. "I appreciate your willingness to be here with me."

They waited for a taxi outside the church. The night air had been cooled by the rain. "Women aren't allowed at the Blue Sheep Club, but I want a full report on your speech tomorrow night."

Mark had no idea what he was going to do about the plagiarism charges. Perhaps Mavis's god would find a way out. He hoped so, because he had used up about all the faith he had in himself."

-18-

Mark was very nervous about his speech tonight. He had practiced three times in front of the mirror in his bedroom in the Chelsea house. The specter of the plagiarism charges was bad enough, but many Blue Sheep Club members had invited their bankers and investment advisors. He found it difficult to conceive of himself holding the attention of such an august group. On top of that he wanted to impress Henry Enfield.

The plagiarism charges were constantly on his mind. It looked as if the burden was on him to establish his innocence, yet he did not know where to start. He knew that someone must be guilty of foul play, but he had not been able to come up with an explanation for what had happened.

The Blue Sheep Club met in the St. James's section of London, only a few blocks from Mavis's church. The chauffeur dropped off Henry Enfield, Lord Ashley, Rodney and Mark in front of the small building, which reeked of tradition and old wealth. They joined the 40-odd members and guests drinking and chatting in the high-ceilinged reception room. The walls were covered with leather-bound books that had not been looked at in years. Mark sipped a whiskey, as Lord Ashley proudly introduced him. Ashley knew the name of every member and most of their guests. As Henry Enfield spoke convivially with many of those present, Mark overheard him mention that he too had once been a member.

"Gentlemen, dinner is served in the upper dining room," announced the butler. So much of English life reminded him of the way it had been in movies he had seen as a boy. The whole club scene looked as if it were from one of those movies. The butler looked like Arthur Treacher, an actor who always played the butler. He was tall, as Treacher was, and was dressed in tails, as were the members and guests. As on New Year's Eve, Mark had borrowed Lord Ashley's extra set of tails.

Just as Mark was about to climb the stairs with the others, he was interrupted by the head waiter. "Mr. Stevens, you have a telephone call."

"Who could that be?" he asked as the head waiter ushered him to the phone.

"Mark, this is Mavis. I'm sorry to interrupt you, but I have important news."

"What is it?" He half-expected more bad news.

"I went to see my solicitor this afternoon. I thought we needed professional advice."

"You mean about the plagiarism business?"

"Yes. Exactly. He's sure there is foul play of some sort."

"I'm sure too, but I . . . "

"He thinks we should see a handwriting expert."

"But those signatures—they look exactly like mine."

"That's precisely why we need help. I've made an appointment for tomorrow. A man he recommended on Charing Cross."

"Do you think there's some hope he can help?"

"I'm sure of it. And Mark . . . "

"Yes?".

"I know you'll do well with your speech."

The members and guests completely filled the several small tables in the dining room. The walls were covered with portraits, and at either end of the room were single statues portraying politicians making speeches. Mark sat at a table with Rodney and Lord Ashley. "God, I'm nervous! My mouth is so dry," Mark confided to Rodney when Lord Ashley was chatting with the man at the next table.

"Don't worry. Most of them come here to drink a little too much and be in their club. They haven't heard a good speech in years. You'll be smashing."

Mark picked at his food, sorry that he had agreed to give the talk. When the meal was finished and brandy was being served, Lord Ashley rose to his feet. "Gentlemen, in these times it gives us all pause to realize that there is a younger generation ready to take command of the reins of commerce and investment. Soon it will be time for us all to surrender those reins to the likes of my son, Rodney, here." He looked down at his son. "And to the likes of his friend from America, who has kindly consented to share his expertise with us this evening." Ashley paused to sip his brandy. "Some would say that it is a sad day for England when it is the Americans who come to our shores for the best that British education has to offer, and then are the ones who educate us, as will happen tonight."

"Hear! hear!" the group murmured.   From the lilt in Lord Ashley's voice and the slight smiles from the audience, Mark knew they were jesting.

"However, I am used to being educated by Americans. You see I lost my brother-in-law to America many years ago. However, I am here tonight to tell you that we English can survive the American onslaught." Lord Ashley gave no indication that he was not serious, yet everyone in the room knew he was joking.

"Hear! Hear!" Several raised their brandy glasses.

"Now for the business at hand. It is my pleasure to introduce Mr. Mark Stevens of the United States of America, the announced winner of the Linde-Ewell Prize, who will speak to us on his original work, "The Future of Bretton Woods.""

With the words "original work" still in his ears, Mark's knees wobbled as he stood to polite applause.

"Thank you, Lord Ashley. I thank you for the invitation to speak to your friends and colleagues." He was still very nervous. What would they think of him if the prize were revoked? He groped for the words he had practiced in front of the mirror.

"No matter where the future may take me," he began. "I shall always remember these two wonderful years in England. My friend Rodney Ashley will tell you that I was with him the first time I saw London. It was love at first sight. As a matter of fact if I had my way the engineers would build a London Bridge from here to California."

The group interrupted Mark with applause, making his nervousness disappear. He spoke for 30 minutes on economic problems on the international scene, keeping his subject as simple as possible. As he went on, he gained confidence in himself. His enthusiasm for what to most was a dry subject became evident. Although a few of the older men could barely stay awake, most listened with complete attention.

"And so I can foresee the day when America, because of the Eurodollar system, will be forced to abandon its long time commitment to the price of gold. But the solution is not to be found in shackling the Euro-currency markets, nor in legislating substitutes for gold, as some have argued. No, as I have explained, we need to move to floating exchange rates. I know for many of you that thought brings alarming memories of the 1930s. But the system I am advocating can be ameliorated by international cooperation, and by the development of foreign exchange markets.

"As I near the end of my stay in your country, let me repeat my gratitude to you all for having me here tonight and to Sir Cecil Rhodes for making it possible for me to take some of England back to America. It gives me great pleasure to tell you I shall be back in London soon. You see my friend Rodney Ashley has done me the honor of asking me to be the best man at his wedding."

The audience rose as one man to applaud him. Mark stood at the head table, smiling and acknowledging them. Lord Ashley shook his head and raised his hand, indicating a request for silence. "Let me express the thanks of the Blue Sheep Club for your remarks. Gentlemen, would you agree with me that with the likes of Mark Stevens the world economy is in good hands?"

"Hear! hear!" shouted several as the audience applauded.

"Gentlemen," cried Lord Ashley gaining their attention. "I suggest we adjourn to the downstairs, where I shall be only too happy to buy a round of drinks for you all." Several lingered to shake hands with Mark and chat while the others made their way downstairs, all the while talking and lighting their cigars and cigarettes.

Mark's spirits soared. The tension that had plagued him all day was gone. He had never imagined feeling this way. His speech had succeeded beyond any expectations.

When the others had finished congratulating him, Henry Enfield approached him. "Mark, may I have a word with you before we join the others?"

"Of course, Mr. Enfield."

"Mark, I think you know I was very impressed by you when you were in San Francisco. I had intended to ask you to interview the firm this summer, but after hearing you tonight, I don't want to wait."

"Yes, sir. You mean you want to interview me right now?"

"No, I'm not offering you an interview. I don't need an interview. I'm offering you a job with Enfield & Co. right now."

"I don't know what to say! You've caught me off guard. I'm very flattered . . . "

"I don't intend to lose you to one of those large New York firms. I need someone like you. You've won this prize. That's very important. Rodney says you may get a first, and I've never heard a better speech. I know my man when I see him and I want you."

Mark was elated, but he thought of the plagiarism charges and didn't speak for a moment.

"We can talk about the financial details in San Francisco," Henry continued. "But I don't want you even thinking New York. You, my good man, belong in my firm."

"Mr. Enfield, you're never going to regret tonight. I don't need to wait for my decision. I'd be proud to join your firm."

It took Mark a long while to fall asleep that night. He knew very well it would not take Henry Enfield long to withdraw his offer if the plagiarism charges stuck. If that happened, it would not be likely he could get a job with any of the top investment banking firms.

The next morning Rodney and Mark were at the breakfast table when Robert brought them the mail.

"There's a letter for me from Oxford," said Rodney excitedly.

"Nothing for me?" asked Mark.

"No, nothing." Rodney tore open his letter. "You are dispensed from attendance at *viva voce* examinations," Rodney read from the letter.

"What does that mean?"

"It means all three examiners agreed on what my grade should be. Probably a third class."

"Don't be so pessimistic, Rodney. It might be a second." Mark read Rodney's letter for himself. "So does this mean I'm to be vivaed?"

"Unless there's a delay in the post, which isn't very likely."

As they both knew, Rodney's class of honors, whether a second or a third, had been agreed upon; but there had been disagreement among Mark's examiners, which would be settled by the *viva voce* exams. Mark was quite certain that the issue was whether he would win first or second class honors.

At the viva voces in July, he would be examined orally on up to three questions, for 20 minutes each, and there was no way to predict which questions would be chosen. As with last month's written exams, he would have to study for all possibilities.

"My God, Mark, the pressure on you is more than I could take," commiserated Rodney. "The week after the vivas you have to see the Proctors about that bloody plagiarism business."

"All I can do is tell the truth. I guess if I were them, I wouldn't believe me."

"You should tell them to keep their wretched prize."

"The big question though is what Oxford would do? Dawbarn says the College might expel me."

"What are you going to do?"

"I was thinking about what Dawbarn said about Churchill . . ."

"What?"

"It sounds corny, but he never gave up. He kept trying no matter how it looked."

"And that's what you're going to do—keep trying?"

"What else is there?"

Mavis and Mark found the address of the handwriting expert, 45 Charing Cross Road. It was an old, well maintained office building, four floors high, in London's book store section.

"J. J. Harrelson, Examiner of Questioned Documents," stated the plain black lettering on the glass door.

"My solicitor told me Harrelson is the best there is. He says barristers all over the country call on him whenever they have a case involving questioned documents."

"Mr. Harrelson will see you in a few minutes. He's in his photographic lab right now," the receptionist said, gesturing in the direction of a door off the reception room. "I've strict orders not to disturb him. Won't you please be seated?" The short woman was 5 or 10 years beyond retirement age. She turned to her ancient typewriter as Mark and Mavis sat on the two hard wooden chairs in the small room. As the typewriter clacked away, Mark hoped it did not take modern equipment for Harrelson to practice his mysterious profession.

In a few minutes Harrelson burst through the lab door, carrying a handful of photographic documents. "Ah, you're here. Sorry to keep you waiting. Come into my office."

Mark and Mavis followed Harrelson into his small, cluttered office, taking chairs across the desk from the old man.

"Look at this will," he said, holding up a photographic blow-up of a document. "A clear forgery. I'm constantly amazed at what people will do for money." Harrelson looked to be 80 years old, but moved with the vigor of a much younger man. He was tall, with thinning white hair and white bushy eyebrows that rapidly went up and down as he talked. "Well, never mind this. You didn't come here to listen to me talk about someone else's will." Harrelson took a well-used pipe from the rack on his desk and began filling it with tobacco. "Tell me, what brings you to see me?"

Mark told the story of his essay and winning the Linde-Ewell Prize, while Harrelson listened. "I won it because my essay was original. At least I thought it was."

"Exactly what is it they say you copied?"

"Almost two complete pages from an unpublished doctoral thesis that's kept in the Bodleian Library. It was written two or three years ago. I didn't even know there were such things."

"Why do they think you copied from it?"

"Because over a page and a half of my essay is word-for-word what is in the thesis. A very important part right in the middle."

"And it couldn't be a coincidence?"

"Two pages? No. If the thesis weren't written before mine, I'd swear he copied from me. But obviously he couldn't have."

"What other evidence do they have? I want to see what we're up against."

"They've got my signature on two check-out slips, making it look as if I checked out the thesis. They're in my handwriting, but I never signed them." Mark was agitated.

"Mr. Harrelson, I know that Mark did not copy that thesis," said Mavis.

"And what is your interest in this matter, Lady Ashley?" Harrelson asked.

"Mark is my son's friend. It's very important to Lord Ashley and me that he be found not guilty. My brother has offered him a position with his firm in America."

Harrelson held a match to the bowl of his pipe and sucked his breath in. Finally he succeeded in getting the old pipe lit, and leaned back in his chair, sucking in the smoke.

"Mr. Harrelson, you've got to believe me, when I tell you that essay is my original."

"Mr. Stevens, I learned a very long time ago that what I personally believe is quite irrelevant. I've learned to trust the scientific evidence. In the last analysis, the only thing that counts is the evidence."

"What do we do next?" asked Mavis.

"I'll need some exemplars, examples of Mark's signatures. I want you to sign your name four times." Harrelson pushed a pad of paper toward Mark. "Sign naturally, and stop for a minute between each one. Typically, we don't sign our names the same each time." Mark began signing his name as they talked. "I'm going to call the Bodleian as soon as you leave. I think the man I used to know is still there. I want to have a look at this doctoral thesis; I'll need other samples of signatures you've written in the past."

"What sort of samples?"

"Your name on your identification papers, your library card, that sort of thing."

"Do you think there is a chance?" asked Mavis.

"Certainly there's a chance. If Mr. Stevens is innocent, then there's a decent chance I can find evidence to prove it."

"I hope you can, sir," said Mark. "I am innocent."

"I want you to think about one other point."

"Yes?"

"Is there someone who might want you to get sent down from Oxford?"

"I've been thinking about that the past few days."

"Have you come up with a name?"

"Yes, I have."

"Who could it be?" Mavis asked.

"The only one it could be is Derek. Derek Harden."

-19-

Mark fully realized that the mystery was little mystery at all. He did not know how Derek had managed it, but there was no doubt that he was behind it all. Derek must have forged Mark's name to the library slips. How nearly two pages from Mark's essay had found its way into a doctoral thesis written three years earlier was not easy to explain, but someone had been diabolically trying to frame him. That could only be Derek.

The meeting with J. J. Harrelson had given him hope. The crusty handwriting expert had promised Mark that he would complete his investigation in time for Monday's plagiarism hearing. If there were any proof at all absolving Mark, Harrelson would be the one to find it.

Doing his best to ignore the impending hearing, Mark had been busy studying for the *viva voce* exams. This morning he reported to the Examination Schools at nine to be assigned a specific time later in the day. Wearing their caps and gowns, the students from all of the colleges who were to be vivaed today trooped in to see the examiners, who would control their fate. The examiners could question any student on as many as three papers.

When Mark was assigned ten-thirty and the student following him was asked to return at eleven, Mark guessed he would be questioned on only one paper. One paper, a mere half an hour, would determine whether he would get his coveted first class honors.

There was nothing to do but endure the hour and a half of tension until ten-thirty. He decided to go for a walk. Soon he passed the shop where he had seen the blonde window shopping that day. He wondered what had ever happened to her. Had she left her young boy friend and, like Christina, married some older and richer man? He walked past Christ Church and down the walk where he had started to follow the blond woman. He supposed Christina was living in some big house in Rome by now.

The impending plagiarism hearing had overshadowed the seriousness of the vivas, but as Mark entered the small, ground floor examination room, he was nervous and tense. He had been studying for every possible question these past days, and had been getting only a few hours sleep each night. At least in a few more minutes it would finally be over.

"Mr. Stevens," said the chairman of the 12 examiners, "many students are unnecessarily nervous about vivas. In actual fact each of us would be most pleased to award you the higher grade. We are looking for ways for you to succeed here today. Please be at ease."

"Thank you, sir," said Mark. "I appreciate your consideration."

"The question we would like to discuss with you is number nine in the Philosophy paper before us," said the chairman. "What is the relationship between Spinoza's theory of knowledge and his theory of mortality?"

Mark knew, of course, that whether he received a first would depend a great deal on how well he knew Spinoza. Fortunately, Spinoza was Mark's favorite philosopher. The 17th century Dutchman had defied the beliefs of his time and had spent his life ostracized from society.

Still nervous, Mark began. "Sir, I believe that the truth of the matter is that there is no relationship at all between the two theories, except of course that both came from the same philosopher and from God, as Spinoza thought of God." Mark's nervousness abated as he got into his answer. "One can argue, I suppose that his theory of knowledge could be used to prove or disprove mortality." He had seen this sort of question before. It took confidence to challenge the premise that was assumed in the question. Other students might evade directly answering the question and instead use it as a springboard to tell all they knew about Spinoza, but Mark doubted that was what the examiners wanted in a student trying for a first. There were several follow-up questions—all on Philosophy papers. Soon the half-hour had ended and the vivas were over. None of the examiners had given a hint as to whether they were pleased with his performance.

As he walked from the ornate Examination Schools, the realization hit him that he was through with Oxford. Through with exams. Through with studying weekly essays. He had had enough of formal education to last him a lifetime. He felt like tossing his mortarboard into the air.

He stood in line at the red telephone booth near the post office. He wanted to call Harrelson to see if there was any news.

"Mr. Harrelson, I just finished my vivas. Have you found anything?"

"I can't say. I've just come from the Old Bailey on a bank fraud case. I've been exploring every possibility, but I don't want to be premature. I'll be in court again Monday morning for an hour or so and then I'll leave for Oxford. I'll be there, but you'll have to start without me."

"I'll do my best, but I don't have much to go on."

"Do whatever you can. It may be all you'll have."

Mark had not expected Harrelson to be so discouraging. If Harrelson could not help he was in deep trouble. There was not much of anything he could do except deny he had cheated. He would do his best to raise enough doubt so that the college would not send him down, but that was not a very realistic chance. Like it or not, his hopes were all on Harrelson.

The hearing Monday morning was in the Clarendon Building, a distinctive structure on Broad Street near the Bodleian Library. On his way there Mark tried to call J. J. Harrelson for a last minute update, but his secretary explained that he was in court and that she expected him to leave for Oxford immediately thereafter. While Oxford's disciplinary proceedings were reputed to be fair, they also were feared by the students. The proctors were steadfast and swift in enforcing the rules. Mark was shaking inside as he entered the old building. All weekend he had tried without success to devise a convincing strategy, but he felt that his cause was hopeless. He had reached the point where he would be happy just to have the day over with, no matter the outcome.

Mark waited in a stark anteroom, just off the hearing room. The formality of the proceedings was in itself threatening. As required by the rules, he held his mortarboard under his arm and wore a white bow tie with his academic gown. He was solemnly ushered into the main room by two serious looking men, members of the University police colloquially called "bull dogs," who wore dark suits topped off by bowler hats.

The two proctors who were to judge him sat at a table. They too wore full academic dress. Their ties were also white, but with long tabs hanging down from either side. Mark could see several wooden staffs arranged in a fan shape on the wall. His knees felt as if they would buckle. To him the grim proctors looked like veritable hangmen. Perhaps they intended to be fair, but he could tell by their looks that he was in deep trouble.

"Mr. Stevens, I'm George Denning," said the tall, thin and serious-looking older man. "I am the Senior Proctor. This is Mr.

Michael Power, the Junior Proctor. Mr. Power, would you please read the charges."

With considerable flourish, the Junior Proctor stood and read from a document. "Mr. Mark Stevens of Worcester College is charged as follows . . . " The charges were very specific setting, forth the exact title of the doctoral thesis and his Linde-Ewell essay, and accusing him of plagiarism. Power read the charges as if he believed every word of the indictment.

When he finished, Denning, the Senior Proctor, spoke, "Do you have any defense?"

"Yes, sir. I am completely innocent."

"Will you be presenting any witnesses?"

"Besides myself, I expect one other. He's coming from London and may not be here until after lunch. I also have a request."

"Yes, what is it?"

"I would like to ask permission for three of my friends to be in the room while you proceed."

"Who are these friends?"

"Lady Mavis Ashley, and my friends, Rodney Ashley and John Hartley, both undergraduates."

"Very well. They may be present."

The bull dogs brought the three into the room. They smiled their acknowledgments to Mark, and took chairs.

"Thank you, sir."

"Very well. We shall begin now. The first witness will be Richard Dawbarn."

The bull dogs left the room and escorted Dawbarn to the plain wooden chair near the Proctor's table, that evidently was to be used as the witness chair. Mark could not believe they were actually calling Dawbarn as a witness against him. Dawbarn had become his friend and mentor. This was incredible!

Power began the questioning, "Mr. Dawbarn, we appreciate your being here in what must be a very painful duty for you."

"Very painful, indeed. I've been Mr. Stevens's tutor at Worcester College for two years." Dawbarn looked very uncomfortable, as if he would rather be somewhere else. He avoided looking at Mark. "But it is my duty to tell you the facts as I know them."

"I certainly understand. Did you talk to Mr. Stevens about entering his essay in the Linde-Ewell competition?"

"Yes, I did. Mark . . . Mr. Stevens, had submitted a remarkable essay for the eighth week of the Michaelmas term this year. Actually, we were together to see Sir Winston Churchill's coffin arrive at the Handborough station, when I suggested it."

"Then you had been friendly with Mr. Stevens?"

"Very friendly. I'm friendly with most of my students. I have them to my home for dinner, that sort of thing. But Mr. Stevens was special, at times brilliant. I expected great things from him."

"And you discussed Mr. Steven's essay while you were at Handborough?" Power asked.

"Yes. His essay was about Bretton Woods. He had criticized the system. He predicted that circumstances would arise wherein America would be forced to withdraw its commitment to sell gold at $35 per ounce."

"Did Mr. Stevens's essay seem original?"

"Yes. That's the point, you see. His ideas were very original. I'm not sure that I agreed with him at all, but he had a new perspective on the problems inherent in any monetary exchange system. For an undergraduate it was remarkable, quite remarkable, if I do say so."

"And so you suggested that he submit his essay in the competition?"

"Yes, I did. The Linde-Ewell Prize. I congratulated him on his thinking. I told him the essence of the prize was originality. I urged him to submit his essay. He even told me what code name he would choose." Dawbarn still avoided looking at Mark.

"And what code name did he choose?"

"The Violin Lady, I believe. The Violin Lady had special meaning to him."

"Did you ask what it was? What the Violin Lady meant to him?"

"No, I did not."

Mark turned and looked at Mavis who hinted at a smile.

"Then Mr. Stevens knew full well that it was vital to the competition that his ideas be original to him?" Denning asked.

"Yes, he understood that."

"Do you have any explanation for the copying in this case?" Power had resumed the questioning.

"No, I'm afraid not." Dawbarn's voice dropped.

"Mr. Stevens, do you have any questions of Mr. Dawbarn?" asked Power.

"No, I guess not," said Mark, downcast. He did not know what he could possibly ask. "Wait. Yes, I do have a few questions." He had to try something, even if it did not work. "Mr. Dawbarn, have you found me to be a good student?" He felt himself trembling as he began.

"Yes, in fact one of the best."

"And have I always been truthful with you?"

"Indeed, you have." Dawbarn seemed relieved to show Mark his positive feelings.

"Have you seen any signs of plagiarism in my essays? Any signs at all?"

"Whenever you used other's materials, you always indicated as much. I have found you to be a very original thinker. Not always accurate, but very original." Dawbarn laughed at his last remark. Mark laughed too, as did the others in the room. Even the proctors smiled slightly.

"Did you suggest to me once that I consider teaching as a career? That I was able to express complex ideas in an understandable manner?"

"Yes, I certainly did. And when this whole terrible affair is cleared up, I hope that you still consider it."

"Even perhaps teach at Oxford?"

"Yes, even that."

"But this affair, as you put it, these charges, might prevent such a career?"

"Yes. I'm afraid they might."

"Might hound me wherever I may go?" Mark felt he was on to something.

"Yes, I fear so. It would be very humiliating."

"Mr. Dawbarn, tell me, do you think I copied my essay?"

"Mr. Stevens, I don't know. How can I possibly know the definitive answer to that? I would never have thought you would copy anything, but I can't explain this physical evidence. It's very damaging."

"Do you think I should be stripped of the Linde-Ewell Prize? Humiliated, as you put it?"

Dawbarn hesitated, obviously torn. "Well, I . . . "

"Perhaps sent down from the college?"

"No, I don't think that at all."

Power, the Junior Proctor interrupted, "Mr. Dawbarn you needn't concern yourself with that. The matter of punishment is our prerogative, not yours. Mr. Stevens, do you have any more questions of Mr. Dawbarn?"

"Yes, sir, I do. Mr. Dawbarn, do you know of anyone who would deliberately forge documents to make it look as if I cheated? Anyone who might want to get me kicked out of the college?"

"Why, no. I don't think so."

"Do you know of someone who became very angry with me because I lost my temper and struck him when he insulted President Kennedy, the night he was shot?"

"Yes, I do. As a matter of fact I had forgotten."

"Do you remember that person was my tutorial partner in your economics tutorial my first term in Oxford?"

"Yes. That is correct."

"What was his attitude toward me?"

"He seemed to hate you. I could never understand why, but I believe he despised you."

"What was the name of this person who hated me and tried to get the provost to kick me out of Worcester?"

"Harden—Derek Harden was his name."

Mark did not know whether he had proved a single thing, but he knew he had to keep on fighting, hoping that things would take a turn his way.

The next witness, a mousy man in his 60s, was ushered in by the bull dogs. "My name is James Mander. I work at the Bodleian Library."

Mander was pale, thin, and apparently very nervous.

"What are your duties there?" Power was conducting the questioning.

"Well, sir, I have several duties at the Bodleian."

"Confine your answer to the safekeeping of unpublished doctoral theses, if you would."

"Well sir, you see sir, doctoral theses are in separate, bound volumes. They are not to be taken from the library under any circumstances."

"Any circumstances?"

"Until this case that is."

"What do you mean?"

"I was told to deliver the thesis on Bretton Woods to Mr. Dawbarn." Mander sat with his hands nervously folded.

"I mean normally, except for the time to Mr. Dawbarn, would anyone be allowed to take the volume from the Bodleian?"

"Oh, no, sir. Only to the reading room sir. Except that last week my superior took it to his office."

"Your superior? Did he explain why?"

"He said someone else was to examine it in connection with this matter. A Mr. Harrelson, I believe."

"How would one obtain the volume to read in the reading room? Normally, I mean."

"He would sign one of those check-out slips, sir. One like those in front of you."

"What would he write on the check-out slips?" He handed the slips to the clerk.

"Just like here, sir. He would write the date, the name and number of the volume, his name and, finally, the desk number, where he would be reading it."

"And what is written on those three slips in your hand?"

"They're each for the Bretton Woods thesis. Three different dates, and all signed by Mark Stevens, sir. He checked it out all right, sir."

"Mr. Stevens, do you have any questions of Mr. Mander?" Power concluded.

"Yes, I do," Mark answered impulsively. "Mr. Mander, do you recognize me?"

"No, sir. I see a great number of students. I'm not very good at faces."

"Could anyone have taken out the Bretton Woods volume without giving you a check-out slip?"

"No, sir, absolutely not."

"Do the students sign the check-out slips in your presence?"

"Yes, sir. I keep a blank pad of slips right on my desk. I'm very meticulous about my work."

"I'm sure you are, Mr. Mander. What I'd like to ask is: did you actually see me sign these slips?"

"I must have, but I don't specifically remember."

"How do you know it's my signature — my writing?"

"Well, I don't know it for a fact, I suppose."

"Mr. Stevens," asked Denning. "You certainly aren't saying these are not your signatures, are you?"

"We have other copies of your signatures from various university records, and they are identical to those on the check-out slips," added Power.

"I admit they look like mine," said Mark, "but I didn't sign them. They have to be forged. You see I was out of the country on the dates in question."

"You what?" exclaimed Power.

"I was in Paris." Perhaps this was the chance Mark had been hoping for.

"In Paris? You certainly don't expect us to believe that, do you?" exclaimed Power.

"Mr. Stevens, do you have any proof of this claim? Any proof you were in Paris?" asked Denning"

Mark could feel his new hope slip through his grasp. He knew he had no proof. Christina had paid for everything, even to the cash she had sent him. He had thrown away his train ticket stub. He had kept nothing. How could he expect them to take his word that he had spent the weekend in Paris with a woman?

"I have no written proof, but Mr. Ashley here can vouch for the fact that I was in Paris."

"And how can he vouch for that?" asked Power. "Did he go with you?"

"No, sir. I told him that's where I had been."

"You told him that's where you had been. So, in effect, you are asking us to take your word for it?"

Mark stammered. "Well, sir, I have no other proof. Nothing that you would accept."

"Mr. Stevens," said Denning, "I don't see how you can expect us to accept such an uncorroborated claim. The evidence clearly shows that you must have copied from the thesis. After all, even you have to admit that the language is identical. How can we conclude anything else except that you checked out the thesis?"

This was the first time the proctors had said what Mark knew very well they must be thinking.

"Gentlemen, at this point I don't have any proof to offer you, except the simple truth." Mark had risen to his feet. "May I take the witness chair?"

"Certainly you may," said Denning, who turned to Power. "Do we have anything further?"

"No, let him testify."

Mark sat in the witness chair. He had to do something.

"Gentlemen, I did *not* copy a single word of my essay. I'm telling you the absolute truth. I did *not* know about the doctoral thesis. I cannot explain the check-out slips, except to say with every ounce of vigor and truth at my command that I was in Paris and could not have signed them. Maybe at some other time someone put them in front of me to sign, when I didn't realize what they were. I don't know. I do know that Derek Harden hated me enough to have set up all of this. I also know that I created my essay from my own mind. I repeat. I did *not* copy it. I wrote it at the end of the Michaelmas term in my own rooms in the Terrace at Worcester College."

Powers interrupted him. "Mr. Stevens, is the only evidence that you have your own denial?"

"I believe I'll have another witness. The one I told you about. He's Mr. J. J. Harrelson, but I'm not sure whether he'll be here before lunch."

"You go ahead with your statement, Mr. Stevens," said Denning. "I see it's eleven-thirty now. If he's not here, we'll break early."

"Thank you, sir." It was clear to Mark that without Harrelson, he was going to lose. "I'd like to convince you to consider this whole matter from my viewpoint. I did not set out to win the Linde-Ewell Prize. I just wanted to write the best essay on Bretton Woods I could. It was Mr. Dawbarn who suggested I enter the competition. If I had not won the prize, I would not have given it another thought. Of course, I was very happy with the honor, but why would I cheat for such a prize? To be very frank the prize is quite insignificant. It is the possibility of being stripped of the prize and publicly humiliated that is so significant. Why would I risk so much for so little?"

"But you can't very well expect us to ignore the evidence," said Power.

Mark was angry at his predicament. "That's another point. It is not fair that *I* be the one to have to disprove these charges. As far as I'm concerned, it is *you* who have barged into my life, asking me to explain these circumstances." Mark's face was flushed with his anger. "I apologize for being angry. I hope you will understand that my reputation is at stake." His voice calmed down. "I'm asking you to resolve your doubts in my favor in the name of this great university."

"Thank you, Mr. Stevens. I'm sure we'll give what you say every consideration," said Denning. No matter what Denning said, Mark knew the proctors were going to rule against him. Discouraged, he left the witness chair and resumed his place.

At that moment the hallway door opened and in walked J. J. Harrelson. Everyone turned to look. Harrelson's rapid gait belied his years. As he took a seat behind Mark, there was no indication whether he had found anything favorable.

"Mr. Stevens, it's not yet noon." said Denning. "So if the gentleman who has just arrived is your witness, perhaps we could proceed at once rather than wait."

Mark bent over and whispered to Harrelson. "What should I do?"

"Tell them I'll be ready in a few minutes. I'll need some help getting my equipment from the car."

"I couldn't help but overhear," said Denning. "We'll take a few minutes. We'll start again at 12:15."

Mark, Rodney and John went with Harrelson to his car, which he had illegally parked in front of the building.

"Have you found anything that will help?" asked Mark.

"A few things. Here, boys, take this equipment inside, will you?"

The young men carried Harrelson's overhead projector and other equipment down the corridor.

"Here, will you park my car?" Harrelson asked John, handing him the keys.

"You must have discovered something," said Mark.

"You may just be right, my young friend," said Harrelson with a lilt in his voice. "But I would recommend a little patience."

.   .   .

"Gentlemen, I would like to introduce to you Mr. J. J. Harrelson. Mr. Harrelson is an Examiner of Questioned Documents, who is very well known in the Inns of Court. He has agreed to look into my case. I ask your permission for Mr. Harrelson to sit in the witness chair."

"An examiner of Questioned Documents?" asked Power.

"Yes, sir. I'm sometimes called a handwriting expert. My job is to find out if documents are forged or have been fiddled."

"I've heard of such people, all right. Don't they usually testify against criminals?" asked Denning.

"I worked for Scotland Yard for over 20 years. Testified many a time in Old Bailey. I've been in private practice for many years now. Mostly civil cases. Even some abroad."

"Abroad?"

"Yes, I've testified in Canada, Hong Kong, even Australia. I just returned from Dallas, Texas."

"Texas? What were you doing there?"

"The Dallas police wanted me to take a look at some Lee Harvey Oswald letters."

"We are very appreciative of your being here, Mr. Harrelson," said Denning. "We don't have any formal procedure such as you are used to in court. We have been having the witnesses sit in this chair, if that is all right."

"Mr. Harrelson," said Power. "It seems obvious to a rank amateur such as myself that part of Mr. Stevens's essay was copied word for word from the doctoral thesis here." Power held up the bound volume.

"That's just it. It may be clear to the rankest of amateurs, as you put it, but it is perfectly clear from even a cursory examination by a professional that *such is not the case.*"

"What? Such is not the case?" Power was surprised.

"I don't understand. Isn't it perfectly clear that there has been copying?" asked Denning.

"You are absolutely correct. It is perfectly clear that two pages have been copied. But what is perfectly clear to me, and will be to you before I finish today, is that the doctoral thesis you hold in your hand was copied *from Mr. Stevens's* essay and *not the other way around, as you have presumed.*"

"What? What are you talking about?" exclaimed Power.

"Yes, would you please explain?" demanded Denning. "The thesis was done three years ago. Before Stevens was even in Oxford. How could it have been copied from Mr. Stevens's essay?"

"The thesis was prepared three years ago, all right, *all but the two pages in question,*" said Harrelson.

"Two pages of the thesis were written at a different time from the rest? That seems impossible," said Power.

"Not impossible at all. Pages 79 and 80 were typewritten by someone other than the original writer at a different time from the rest of the thesis—probably shortly after Mr. Stevens finished his essay."

"I don't understand," said Denning. "Would you explain?"

"Part of page 79 and onto page 80 contains material essentially the same as Mr. Stevens's essay. Is that correct?" asked Harrelson.

Power picked up the volume and looked at the page. "Correct," he answered. "It's the same, except for the beginning and the end."

"Yes and the beginning of page 79 and the end of page 80 were reworked by the forger to blend in contextually with the rest of the thesis. The forger removed pages 79 and 80 and changed just enough of the wording to cleverly fit in Mr. Stevens wording."

"How do you know that?" asked Denning, looking astonished.

"If I may have a few moments, I want to set up my side light, which I want to shine on the paper."

"Your side light?" asked Denning.

"Yes. The one I have here. It will show the watermarks on the paper in the bound volume."

"There's a socket here on the wall," said Denning, pointing.

Harrelson held the high intensity light to the side of a page in the book, so that the proctors could see. "The paper used in the thesis is of a high quality. It has watermarks. "There, you see? There's the 'Ashcroft' mark."

First Denning and then Power left their chairs to peer at the lighted sheet.

"All of the pages in the original thesis are Ashcroft," the old man continued, while the two proctors stood near the equipment.

"And the two pages aren't?" asked Denning.

"No, they're Ashcroft all right. The forger knew something about watermarks, and was very careful to use Ashcroft on the two pages."

"Well, then, how does that prove anything?"

"He slipped up."

"How is that?"

"If you note carefully, there is a little mark, a little lateral mark under the c in Ashcroft. Here, see?" Harrelson pointed with his pen. "They call it a bar."

"Yes," said Denning. "I see."

"Well now, let's look at the 'Ashcroft' on page 79." Harrelson opened the volume to the page, and with his light found the watermark.

"Do you see the difference?"

"No, I don't see any difference."

"The bar. It's under the t. Not under the c."

"What does that mean?"

"The bars in the substituted pages are all the same. The bar on all of the rest of the thesis is under the c."

"But why would they be different?" asked Power.

"Because the two sheets were part of a lot manufactured early last year and in the shops now."

"What?"

"Paper manufacturers commonly use this method for inventory control, to identify lot numbers and for many other purposes. I've checked with the Ashcroft people in Birmingham. The bar wasn't put under the t until last year."

"Are you certain?"

"Positive. The two pages had to have been inserted later. *They weren't even manufactured until 1964.*"

"But why would anyone want to do that?" asked Power, dumbfounded.

"To make it look like this young man had copied his essay. And there's even more."

"And what's that?" inquired Denning.

"Look at the letter e in the two forged pages. Gentlemen, the e is the most commonly used letter in the alphabet. Here, notice the e's." The two men gathered close to the volume. Harrelson was shining his light downward this time.

"What's so special about the e's?" asked Denning.

"They're clogged. Clogged with ink. Frequently the e's get clogged from the ribbon. They were typed with a different typewriter. There's no doubt about it."

"What does that prove?"

"Notice, if you will, the e's in the legitimate pages are relatively clean. It is very unlikely that the thesis writer would type away with unclogged e's, then suddenly type two pages with clogged e's, and then type the rest of his thesis back with unclogged e's."

"Incredible!" exclaimed Denning.

"Both typewriters were the same model of Olivetti. Our forger thought he was being very careful. He probably found his Olivetti in a secondhand shop, but he didn't know about the e's, did he?"

"Evidently not," said Denning. "But how did he get the pages into the book?"

"Obviously, he somehow managed to sneak out the bound volume we have here and then return it. I want to show the binding to you. I'm sure there are many tests that could be performed. I did just one. Here, let me show you."

Harrelson stood the book upright, while the proctors crowded around.

"This is my ultraviolet light." He shone the bluish light down onto the binding. "With this you can see much better than with the naked eye. See, there are two entirely different types of glue that have been used. A very clever job, but two different glues."

"How could any forger have managed the binding?" Denning inquired.

"I'm sure he didn't do it himself. No doubt it cost him several hundred quid to persuade some journeyman book binder to work late one night."

"It's hard to believe."

"Then there is the anonymous letter. I'm positive that it was typed by the same typist who did the two pages, although on a different typewriter. Harrelson showed the anonymous letter to the judges. "Notice how the writer has the habit of hitting the space bar only once after he finishes a sentence with a period, instead of twice, as most typists do? He did it on his anonymous letter too." Harrelson paused to be sure the judges had absorbed his point, then continued. "But the check-out slips presented the most interesting challenge."

"Yes, what about the check-out slips?" asked Denning.

Mark, along with everyone else, leaned forward, also silently asking the same question.

"Forged. Very carefully done, to be sure, but clearly forged." Everyone watched intently while the old man set up his overhead projector. "Could I have the room darkened, please?"

"Yes, would someone turn off the lights, please?" asked Denning. They all could see by the light from the windows as Harrelson projected several copies of Mark's signature onto the back wall.

"Let's take a look at Mr. Stevens's signature." He pointed to the first signature. "This is taken from a sign-up sheet for a bus trip to Stratford-upon-Avon. A sign-up sheet that, by the way, hung in full view of all Worcester students for several days. I'll put these other samples of Mr. Stevens's signature next to the first one. See how they are all slightly different? We call these 'natural variations.' One seldom signs his name exactly the same way." Harrelson pointed out the differences with his marker.

"Now, I want you to notice that the three check-out slips don't show any such variances. They are all too much alike. No natural variations. They're made with a very careful hand." Harrelson put copies of the three check-out slips on the projector. The differences he was referring to became clear.

"Next, I want you to notice the pen lifts. Gentlemen, a forger has to work very slowly and carefully. See, there, how he lifts his pen very frequently, compared to what would be natural."

"Yes, indeed, I do see," said Denning.

"There are several other points that I will not bother you with. Gentlemen, it is absolutely clear that Mr. Stevens is not your forger." Harrelson dramatically flipped off the projector. "May I have the lights, please," he asked. "I have other matters in London that require my attention."

The people in the room whispered in amazement.

"Certainly," said Denning deferentially. "The lights, please."

The lights were turned on and Harrelson continued, "I made one last observation in my laboratory that I think conclusively shows these slips are forgeries."

"What is that Mr. Harrelson?" asked Denning, still looking amazed by all that was happening.

"If you look at the last two of the check-out slips, you see that they have indentations on them from other writing. Here, let's look at them one at a time." Harrelson held his side light to the slips, showing the judges what he was talking about.

"But what is the significance of that? asked Power warily.

"The first slip must have been the top slip on the pad. If you'll look, you'll see that it has no markings from writings done on top of it.

"Now, let's look at the second slip. The side light clearly shows indentations from the writing of the first slip." Harrelson pointed out the indentations. "You can make out some of the writing from the first check-out slip. Can you see it?" Harrelson waited until the proctors confirmed his observation. "Now, bear with me, and take a look at the second slip. Notice it has indentations from *both* of the other slips."

"And what do you conclude from that?" asked Power who seemed at this point willing to accept anything Harrelson might say.

"The forged slips were written one after the other on a blank pad of check-out slips."

"How could anyone do that?" Power asked.

"I'm sure that our forger simply stole a pad of slips, made out the forgeries in private and then used them to check out the bound volume. Oh, he probably signed a different slip in front of the clerk all right, but he could easily manage to trade the forgeries when he wasn't being watched."

"I must confess, I'm absolutely stunned by what you have told us here today. I'm afraid we have all been duped into falsely accusing Mr. Stevens," said Denning.

"I have no doubt that the forger thought he was being very clever, but he left a rather amateurish trail. And for that I say thank God," said Harrelson.

Yes, thank God, Mark thought. He was every bit as astonished as Denning.

"Good Lord, how could the forger have accomplished all this?" queried Denning, still amazed.

"I have a theory that appears to be well supported by the facts, if you care to hear it."

"By all means, Mr. Harrelson," said Denning.

"Very well. Mr. Stevens finishes his essay at the end of the Michaelmas term. He is called suddenly to Paris and leaves it in his desk. The forger manages to steal the essay, get it photocopied and return it to the desk, before Mr. Stevens returns from France."

"But he couldn't know the essay was going to be submitted for the Linde-Ewell Prize," said Power.

"I don't think he knows what he will use his copy for. When he picks the lock to Stevens's door, he simply wants to see what mischief he can cause."

"What came next?" asked Denning.

"He realizes he can make it look as if Mr. Stevens has copied his last economics essay of the term and hatches this scheme to cause him trouble. The prize is purely fortuitous. Finally, he sends the anonymous letter when he thinks it will cause the most harm, just before graduation."

"Mr. Stevens, I'm afraid I owe you the deepest of apologies," said Denning. Mark stood, facing the judges. "It is obvious that we were being too quick to judge you. We should have thought of the possibility of forgery ourselves. Perhaps conducted our own investigation. I don't know."

"There are many more people than you realize who are falsely accused," said Harrelson.

"I'm afraid I, too, owe you an apology, Mr. Stevens," said Power. "I hope that you will accept the prize despite this perfectly awkward situation. Frankly, we all are very embarrassed."

"Of course, I'll accept the prize," said Mark. "With honor." He turned to J. J. Harrelson. "Mr. Harrelson, I owe you everything."

Before Harrelson could respond, they were startled by loud applause that suddenly filled the room. Mark turned and looked. He had been so intent on listening, he had not noticed the 10 or 15 students, who had crowded into the room. "What is everyone doing here?" he asked Rodney.

"The list is up. They must have come to find out about their grades and heard what was happening here in Clarendon."

John, Rodney and Mark ran down Catte Street to the Examination Schools, where the grade list had been posted. Scrambling, they found their names. John and Rodney had each received second class honors. Then, under "First Class Honors," Mark saw "M. Stevens."

The others caught up with them and joined in congratulating Mark.

"What a triumph!" said Rodney.

"Where's Mr. Harrelson?" shouted Mark. "I want to thank him."

With Rodney and John close behind, Mark ran back to the Clarendon Building. The old man was putting away his equipment with Mavis's help.

"Mr. Harrelson, I apologize for rushing off like that without properly thanking you, but the list was up."

"And how did you do?"

"I won a first."

"Congratulations! This has been quite a day for you."

"And I owe it all to you. How can I ever repay you?"

"You can buy me a beer," Harrelson smiled. "That's what you can do."

-20-

Mavis ignored every speed law on the 50 mile trip from Oxford to Castle Enfield. Mark had persuaded J. J. Harrelson and Dawbarn to join them in the cramped Aston Martin. Packed into the sports car, the celebrants had the time of their lives, laughing and joking as they darted past traffic on the narrow country roads.

"Did you see the look on the face of the Junior Proctor when Mr. Harrelson was testifying?" Rodney asked.

"I surely did. He couldn't believe it," answered John.

"I can tell you I was never so relieved in my life," said Dawbarn. "Mr. Harrelson, when did you find out you could prove Mark innocent?"

"I didn't have it right until late last night." The old man was crowded into the back seat, joining in the fun with everyone else.

"I thought you'd never get to Oxford in time. You surely had me worried," said Mark.

Mavis joyously tooted the horn, as she pulled the car to a stop in front of Castle Enfield.

Rodney's fiancee, Rebecca, burst out of the door and rushed to the car.

"What happened? How did it turn out?"

"Mark won!" shouted Rodney, picking her up with a hug and swinging her around. "Mr. Harrelson made them look like a bunch of bloody fools."

Henry Enfield and his daughter Priscilla rushed out of the house. "What happened?" Priscilla asked.

"I won!" answered Mark. "Priscilla, I didn't know you were in England. It's good to see you."

"I got here only yesterday. Mark, that's simply wonderful news. My congratulations to you."

"Mr. Harrelson proved someone else had forged the papers," said Mavis excitedly.

"And Mark got a first too," added John.

"I'm so happy for you," said Rebecca, enthusiastically kissing Mark on the cheek.

Mark held her affectionately for a moment. "Thanks, Rebecca. I don't mind telling you, I was awfully worried."

"Did they find out who it was that committed the forgery?" Rebecca asked.

"They're pretty sure it was Derek Harden," said Rodney.

"And who's Derek Harden?" Priscilla asked.

"A bloody troublemaker, that's who," answered Rodney.

"He was one of my tutorial partners," Mark explained. "There's been bad blood from the beginning, but I never imagined it would come to anything like this."

"It's of no matter now," said Henry. "I'm very pleased with the outcome, my boy, very pleased indeed," said Henry, offering his hand to Mark. "And a first too! My congratulations to you, young man."

"Shall I tell the servants to set out the drinks?" asked Rodney.

"Of course, and prepare a feast," cried Mavis. "The biggest feast Castle Enfield has ever seen."

When they finished dinner in the French Dining Room, Mark rose to his feet. "I propose a toast—a toast to J. J. Harrelson. Without him this would be a wake and not a party. Here's to you Mr. Harrelson."

"Hear, hear," they all said in unison, raising their wine glasses.

Smiling mischievously, Harrelson rose to his feet. "I had to win this one. You see today is my birthday." Everyone offered him congratulations. "I can't think of a nicer birthday present than to see this young man graduate from Oxford with first class honors."

"That day in your office I wasn't at all sure of my future," said Mark.

"Frankly, young man, you were so convincing I knew there must be a forgery someplace."

"What do you think is going to happen to Derek?" asked Rodney.

"I'm bloody well going to look into it," said Dawbarn. "If Mr. Harrelson thinks we can prove that Derek is the culprit, then he shouldn't get away with it at all."

"I remind you, it's one thing to show that a document is forged, but quite another to prove who did it, even when we bloody well know who," said Harrelson.

"I think he should be given the boot right out of Oxford," said Rebecca.

"Head first!" Rodney added.

"I'm all for that," said John. "He tried to ruin Mark."

"Wouldn't that be sweet justice?" said Mark.

"Derek kicked out!"

"I can assure you, we shall at least look into it," said Dawbarn.

"One thing, at least I'm through with Derek Harden forever."

"I have a toast of my own." Henry Enfield stood, holding his glass. A fortnight ago, I offered this young man a position with Enfield & Co. I still have your acceptance, don't I Mark?"

"You certainly do. The only reason I was at all hesitant, sir, was that I was concerned about today."

"We were all concerned, but all's well that ends well."

Dawbarn rose to give the next toast. "I propose a toast to one of the best students I ever had. I only wish I could persuade him to follow me into teaching. I remember years ago a senior faculty member telling me, 'A teacher's reward is the occasional student whose life you affect and who goes on to have an impact on the world.'" Moved, Dawbarn was having difficulty holding back his emotions. "Mark, I have no doubt that we shall read about you in the financial pages one day."

It was Mark's time to respond. He stood in his place at the head of the long table, looking at Dawbarn and the others. At the other end of the table he saw Mavis, smiling her Gene Tierney smile. These people all meant so much to him.

"Two years ago when I came to Oxford, I wasn't certain I could succeed . . ."

"What? You—not succeed?" interrupted Rodney. Everyone laughed.

Mark looked down, embarrassed. "I have gained a great deal more than success here in England. I have gained the friendship of all of you." Mark's expression grew mischievous. "However, I must admit, while I knew I had your *friendship*, there was a time this morning when I wondered if I had your *confidence*." They all laughed again.

"But the truth was I knew that no matter what happened today you would be behind me." Mark shifted nervously. His mouth felt as if it were full of cotton. He had to force himself to continue. "With the exception of my mother, you are the only people in the whole world who would've stood by me. And I appreciate it . . ." The others, seeing Mark falter, came around the table and began shaking his hand.

"Thank you," said Rodney.

"Congratulations," repeated Dawbarn.

Mavis and Rebecca kissed him on his cheek.

"All right everyone. Finish your dessert," concluded Mark. "I want to talk to you all night long."

As the evening progressed, Mark took each of them aside for a few private minutes.

When he chatted with Rebecca, she reiterated her offer that he stay with them whenever he was in London. "We'll be married next summer. Rodney's father is buying us a flat in Knightsbridge."

Priscilla was enthusiastic about Mark's joining her father's firm. "I knew that I liked you the night we met. Perhaps you'll join us for dinner again before the fall term starts at Wellesley."

"I'd like that," Mark answered. He was reminded how they had joked that if they were ever to have dinner together, it would have to be without Henry's knowing.

"How are we going to get everyone home?" asked Rodney, when the evening was drawing to a close.

"I want to drive them back to Oxford. I don't want to say good-bye yet," said Mark. Harrelson, Dawbarn and John were the ones needing rides to Oxford.

"Take the Aston Martin," volunteered Mavis. She gave Mark the keys from the table. "But you've never driven it. Come, I need to explain the shift to you."

While the others were saying good night to each other, Mavis took Mark to her car. They sat in the front seats while she explained the gear shift to him. "Mark, I want to congratulate you on today."

"Thank you, Mavis. I couldn't have done it without you."

"I want to thank you for something too. Thank you for our night together. I shall never forget it."

"Nor shall I, Mavis."

"And thank you, too, for not pressing me again as some other men might have done."

"There's no need to thank me. It's the way it has to be." He hesitated for a moment before reaching over to her. Quickly, they kissed and got out of the car before the others came out of the house.

On the return trip to Oxford the four laughed and reminisced about the day's events. "Did you see Power's face when Harrelson was testifying?" asked John.

"He probably looked as surprised as I did," laughed Dawbarn.

Mark dropped off John at the bed and breakfast, from where he would return to Yorkshire in the morning.

"See you at Rodney's wedding," John said.

"Good luck."

Next, Mark let Harrelson out at his car for his drive back to London. "I can never thank you enough. I owe everything to you." Mark would never forget what the old man had done today.

"Mark, I need to talk to you seriously for a moment," said Dawbarn, as they sat in the idling Aston Martin in the college car park, where Dawbarn had left his car. "I owe you an apology of the deepest sort. I don't know if you can forgive me."

"Don't blame yourself. I know how it must have looked." Mark put his hand on Dawbarn's shoulder. "You were the greatest teacher I ever had and I thank you. I'll drop by and see you when I come back for Rodney's wedding."

"I'd like that very much, and many thanks for including me in tonight's celebration," said Dawbarn as he closed the car door. "Good luck."

Mark stopped the car as he drove by the entrance to Worcester. He remembered that first day, struggling with his baggage and entering what then seemed to be an unwelcome fortress. Impulsively, he pulled the two left wheels over the curb onto the sidewalk so as not to block traffic, and turned off the ignition. He walked into the quad, as he had that first day. He looked up at his window in the Terrace. This fall a whole new batch of students would take over where he left off.

He walked through the passageway under the Cottages, as he had done the day of his first tutorial. He remembered how apprehensive he had been and how difficult Derek had proved to be. He was so happy to be acquitted of the plagiarism charges that he felt little anger. He was simply grateful that he would never see Derek again.

He walked back to the pond. The moon was rising, but the ducks were nowhere to be seen. It was different now, with the tensions of those days resolved. "Good-bye, ducks. You'll remember me, won't you?" he said aloud and tossed a pebble into the water.

Mark returned to the car and drove by the hotel where the blonde and her student friend had stayed. As he sat in the car for a moment, looking at the hotel, he knew what he wanted even now was to return to the Montmartre Hotel on the Rue Caulaincourt. It was not the blond woman that was still in his system, despite everything, it was still Christina. However, he knew he would never see Christina again.

As he left Oxford he had reached a new stage in his life. He was the holder of a B.A. from Oxford with first class honors. He was the 1965 winner of the Linde-Ewell Prize. He had a new job and his future waited for him in San Francisco.

Except for the entry lights, Castle Enfield was totally dark as he stopped in front of the vast house. He found the house key on the ring of keys that Mavis had given him. In his room he found a note.

> *Mark.*
> *Please come to the music room. I would like to talk some more.*
> *Mavis.*

Mavis had fallen asleep on the music room couch. The record player was endlessly rotating. He put the arm in the off position and removed the record. It was the new Beatles record "Help." Mavis stirred at the slight sound he had made.

"Mark, is that you?"

"Yes, Mavis, it's me," he whispered.

"Mmmm. I must have fallen asleep." She stretched her arms high above her head. She had changed into a light cotton dress. No matter what Mavis wore she looked beautiful.

"I spent some extra time wandering around Oxford."

"It's a sentimental time for you, isn't it?"

"I guess it is."

"You deserve it. After all you've been through."

"I never would have made it without you," he said gently grasping her hands.

"Do you remember that night in St. James's church?"

"Of course I do," he answered.

"Remember how I told you, even though we couldn't see a way out of the plagiarism charges, I knew in my heart there had to be a way?"

"Yes, I remember."

"I told you there was a force in the universe that had the answer."

"You said it was just that we couldn't see the answer from our perspective."

"Well, there was an answer wasn't there?" Mavis asked.

"There sure was. It was J. J. Harrelson."

"Yes, but why do you suppose I ever thought of seeing my solicitor? Without him we'd never have heard of J. J. Harrelson."

"And you think there was some sort of a divine connection?"

"All I know is, when I was quiet there in the church, I was trying to connect to that power. The same power I have used so often before. Then the next morning I knew I should see my solicitor. It was that simple."

"But that was pure coincidence. It was only logical to see your solicitor." Mark wanted to respect her beliefs, but he thought there was an easier explanation to what had happened than God.

"If it was only logical, then why didn't either one of us think of it before? No, Mark I think there's more to it than my poor ability."

"Yes, but . . ."

"It's all right, Mark," she interrupted. "I'm not trying to convince you of anything. I'm just telling you what I believe."

"Okay, Mavis. It just doesn't seem logical to me."

"Much of life is not logical, but no matter. That's enough of that for one night. Let's go for a walk. It's too beautiful a night to discuss religion. How does that sound?"

"Sure. Let's go," he said. "You're right, this is a sentimental night." It was well past midnight, but he was wide awake, stimulated by the events of the day.

A beautiful full moon was now high in the sky above Castle Enfield. Mavis and Mark could plainly see each other by its light as they approached the woods. He felt awkward with her in this romantic setting. It seemed to him that whatever he did or said could be interpreted as breaking their agreement. What was more, he knew that part of him wanted to break the agreement and make love one last time.

They reached the gazebo at the edge of the woods. Mavis turned to him. "I want you to know that I'm happy I met you. You have been a very important part of my life. I don't regret anything."

"I thought perhaps you felt guilty. I know I do, sometimes." They sat next to one another in the gazebo, looking at the moon over the woods.

"It's odd, but I don't feel guilty at all. Stanley will never know how much I've given to keep our life together."

They talked for another half-hour, then began walking back toward the mansion, silhouetted against the moonlight.

"What will happen to you?" Mark asked. "Do you think you'll go on the same as before?"

"You know about smiling Cheshire cats?"

"Yes."

"And the cat that swallowed the canary?"

"Yes."

"Well, that's me." She laughed her throaty, earthy laugh again. "I'll be the smiling Cheshire cat that swallowed the canary. Everyone will wonder why I'm always so happy."

That was what it was about Mavis's laugh, he thought. It was the cat-that-swallowed-the-canary laugh.

He put his arms around her. She returned his long kiss. She leaned back. "I love you, Mark Stevens. I hope you will be happy in your new life."

"I love you too, Violin Lady. May we both be happy with whatever the future brings."

Mark knew they were doing the right thing in honoring their contract.

As they had in December, Rodney and Mark sped along the A4 in the luggage-filled Aston Martin. This time, however, they were headed in the opposite direction, toward Heathrow. It was a windy, clear day with the clouds racing across the blue sky. They were talking about Mark's job with Enfield & Co.

"When do you start work?" asked Rodney.

"In three weeks. Henry and Priscilla won't be back from the continent until then."

"What sort of work will you do?"

"Underwriting new stock issues, I suppose. Whatever gets me on the fast track to a partnership."

"But Uncle Henry owns the entire business. I don't think he ever makes anyone a partner."

"Oh, really? He told me we would discuss finances in San Francisco."

"That's what I've always understood. No partners."

"I'll tell you one thing, he's going to make me a partner one day or I'll go someplace else, after I get some experience."

"Of course, he might change his mind for you."

"Well, if he doesn't, I'm out. To make real money you have to have a piece of the action. I may even start my own company after a while."

Heathrow was only a few miles away. They could see the planes landing.

"Father and I were talking a few days ago. He wants me to learn more about the family capital. He was saying I'll have to manage the family investments one day when he dies."

"I suppose that's true," Mark agreed.

"After all, he is so much older than Mother. We spoke very frankly."

"I wish I could have been that way with my father."

"I asked him how much he and Mother were worth. Do you know what he told me?"

"I don't know. Several million I suppose. No, it must be a hundred million, maybe more."

Rodney laughed. "Father said he didn't know. Can you imagine that? My father has no idea what Mother and he are worth."

"It must be too vast to count."

"No, I don't think that's it. I think he's indifferent when it comes to money."

"Amazing!"

"I feel quite inadequate to managing everything. Frankly, I'm frightened by the whole idea."

"Anyone would be. It would be very intimidating."

"When father dies, Mother and I may need your help. I know very well how much you mean to my mother and I know she'll want your advice."

"Your mother is a wonderful lady. The way she found Mr. Harrelson! She even took me to her church in the middle of all the trouble, all because of my friendship with you."

"There's more to it than that. Mother likes you quite apart from your being my friend."

Before Mark could answer, they were at the airline terminal. The time for parting had come upon them too quickly.

As Rodney pulled the car to a stop, he shifted to a falsely cheery attitude. "Good-bye old chap," he said loudly, as if wanting everyone to hear. "Happy to give you a lift. Anytime, just ring me."

Mark joined in the game. It was a good way to deal with saying good-bye. "Thanks, old boy. Good to bump into you," he joked. He shook Rodney's hand briefly. "I'll see you at the wedding." Without another word he removed his luggage from the Aston Martin and went inside the terminal as Rodney sped off.

Mark was pleased that the check-in line was so long. He needed time to collect himself. He was going to miss Rodney. He was going to miss Mavis. He was going to miss them very much.

"Ladies and gentlemen, due to the winds today we are going to take off in an easterly direction. Our expected time of arrival in Montreal for refueling will be 2:00 p.m., local time."

During takeoff Mark pressed as close to the window as possible to get a last look at England. Most of the clouds were gone now. He recognized Big Ben and Parliament. In a moment he saw the Tower Bridge and next to it, London Bridge. London gave him the same thrill as it had that day in the taxi from Paddington two years ago

Next to him was an American couple returning after their first visit to Europe.

"Wonderful place, England," the man said to him.

"It certainly is. It certainly is."

Part Four

-21-

San Francisco's Financial District

Friday, January 10, 1969

In the three and one-half years that had passed, Mark had never forgotten Rodney's warning that Henry Enfield had never made anyone his partner. Upon graduation from Oxford in 1965, Mark had taken the position he had been offered with Enfield & Co. A few months after starting, he had sized up the situation at the investment banking firm. Henry's no-partner policy had resulted in all the bright young men's leaving Enfield & Co. after a few years. The result was an ultra-conservative staff, afraid to take prudent business risks. Old men at 40, they were content to earn a gentleman's living from selling bonds and preferred stocks to the gentry of San Francisco.

Despite these facts, Mark had formulated a plan to succeed. He had spent the past three years making himself financially indispensable. Henry would have no alternative but to make him a partner.

From the beginning, Mark had carefully monitored Great Britain's worsening fiscal situation, constantly analyzing whether the government would be forced to devalue the pound. Devaluation could present an unparalleled opportunity to make a great deal of money. He watched as Prime Minister Harold Wilson unsuccessfully attempted to deal with the monetary crisis. Mark had participated in several panel discussions, and had written a Sunday newspaper article warning of impending international monetary problems.

On November 10, 1967 Mark had delivered a brilliant speech before San Francisco's prestigious World Affairs Council. He urged that the Bretton Woods system be abandoned, as he had in his prize winning essay at Oxford. He said that Britain had little choice but to devalue the pound. He predicted a swift devaluation from $2.80 to $2.50. After the speech many San Francisco investors gathered around, asking questions. In the ensuing few days, several of them placed very significant guarantees with Enfield & Co. for speculation in the pound. Seeing what was happening, Henry Enfield himself had asked Mark to sell short £10,000,000 for the firm's own account. On his modest salary Mark had only been able to save $10,000, but he risked it all.

Eight days later, on Friday November 18, 1967, Mark's prognostication proved brilliantly accurate. After the banks in Britain had closed, the government devalued the pound from $2.80 to $2.40, even more than Mark had predicted. Mark's clients made a great deal of money—Henry alone had made $4,000,000 profit—all with very little risk, because there had been virtually no chance at all that the pound would move in the other direction.

Mark's ingenious prediction made him a hero to his clients. Though he had made it clear that such results were not an everyday event, he experienced a flood of new clients wanting to use the other facets of the firm's business, such as underwriting new stock issues, obtaining venture capital, and the like.

Henry Enfield had rewarded Mark with a $150,000 bonus at Christmas, and had assigned him to the large, corner office overlooking the city. In all, his income for 1967 was over $250,000, with a promise of at least as much in 1968. Mark made the down payment on a luxurious condominium on Nob Hill and ordered a red Aston Martin. He was succeeding in his plan to get a partnership.

Some months after the devaluation coup, Mark had approached Henry, in the latter's office, about becoming a partner.

"Henry, I appreciate everything you've done for me, but you must know that a partnership in the firm is what I really want."

"Now, Mark, you've not been with me very long. I think it's much too early to be talking about such things. How old are you now?"

"I admit I'm only 27, but I don't think age should have anything to do with it."

"I agree you're doing marvelous work." Pondering, Henry turned and looked out at the Bay Bridge for a moment. "I tell you what. We'll talk again at year's end. Let's take a look at the whole situation then."

While Henry had promised nothing, Mark was very encouraged. He was responsible for much of the money the firm was earning, and had come a long way toward his goal of being indispensable to Henry. Furthermore, he had become an Enfield family friend. On several occasions Henry had invited Mark to the opera along with his daughter, Priscilla. Mark attended two or three art shows with the red-haired Priscilla, and had gone to dinner with her crowd afterward. Mark knew Henry was reluctant, but a partnership had seemed only a matter of time.

As 1968 turned into 1969, there had been no repeat of the currency speculation killing, but Mark had led the way to a very profitable year for the firm.

Henry called Mark into his office this Friday morning and handed Mark his bonus check.

"Thank you very much, Henry. It's very generous."

"You're welcome. You've earned it. What's more, next year your base salary will be $30,000 a month. That's $360,000 a year." Henry was smiling broadly. "What do you think of that?" Henry came around his desk and patted Mark on the back.

"You're very generous, Henry, but . . ."

"But what, Mark?"

"I don't want to seem ungrateful, but you promised we'd talk about a partnership."

"Mark, you are still very young. A partnership would be a big step for me to take. Don't you see? I've never made anyone a partner before. I really believe you need more seasoning."

"You don't understand. It's very important to me to be your partner."

"But I pay you over twice as much as anyone else here at the firm."

"That's just it Henry, it's still *you* paying *me*. I'm still only an employee. Henry I don't know how to say this without offending you, but I think I've earned a partnership."

"It's too soon, Mark."

"But, Henry . . ."

"I don't want to talk about it any more. Besides, I'm late for lunch. I'm seeing Bernie Allard at the Olympic Club. It's about their new stock issue."

"Henry, we've got to talk about this."

"Bernie will take up my whole afternoon. You know how he is. He'll want to play gin rummy."

"I'll come by your house this weekend, if you want."

"You know I don't like to talk business at home."

"What about Monday then? It's very important to me, Henry."

"All right. We'll talk more Monday, if that's what you want."

Mark stormed to the elevator. He knew that making anyone a partner was a big step for Henry, but he had earned it. He had assumed Henry was going to tell him the good news about the partnership today. He had imagined the scene in his mind many times. Henry would say, "My boy, I thought perhaps last year had been a fluke, but this year you have done even better. Congratulations, my good man. I am proud to call you my partner."

What the hell was wrong with the old man? Didn't he realize Mark was responsible for over 75% of the firm's profits? Enfield & Co. was the toast of the town. The firm would sink back to nothing without him. Surely, Henry could see that.

Mark had a lunch appointment himself with Rolf Williams, his old high school friend and Cal fraternity brother. They had been meeting regularly for lunch since Rolf had finished law school. He wanted to tell Rolf about Henry.

Mark's taxi pulled up to the Pacific Union Club, atop Nob Hill, where he was to meet Rolf Williams. Last year Henry had proposed Mark as a member to the prestigious club, located in the old brown mansion across from the Fairmont Hotel. When Mark arrived, Rolf was already waiting in the paneled lounge, reading Herb Caen's column in the *Chronicle*.

"I'm sorry I'm late, but I've been having a rather heated discussion with Henry."

"I can see you're upset. Sit down. Let's talk about it."

Mark saw that Rolf already had his martini. He turned and beckoned to the waiter, who had been waiting at a discreet distance." I'll have my usual gin and tonic please, Joseph."

"Yes, sir."

Both men were dressed very conservatively in the tradition of San Francisco business. Mark had much more gray in his hair now. It probably would be all white by the time he was 30. Since graduation Rolf had been an associate in Kellogg and Proctor, a large downtown law firm. Their friendship had deepened in the past two years and they had become confidants to each other.

"Why don't you tell me what happened today?" Rolf asked.

"I pressed him again about the partnership."

"And what did he say?"

"He tried to put me off again, but I wouldn't have it."

"Don't you think you're pushing things a bit? You're already making as much money as the senior partners in my law firm."

"I guess I don't have your patience, Rolf."

"You sure don't. It would drive you nuts if you had to do what I do for a living."

"Still taking depositions on that big anti-trust case?"

"Hell, I don't even *take* the depos. I just sit there and summarize them for the partner who takes them. I've been doing that for two years now. I'm the one who should be unhappy with my firm, not you."

"That's the way I am Rolf. Ever since I can remember, I've wanted to get ahead."

"As if I didn't already know that! Remember me—Rolf? I'm the guy who grew up with you."

They both laughed, looked at each other, and then laughed again.

"Have you talked to those New York people?" Rolf asked.

"Dufton and Watts. I'm going to see them the week after next unless I get that promise from Henry. They put a good chunk of their profits in a pool for the producers. That would mean a lot more money than with Henry."

"What about a partnership with them?"

"They're a corporation, so they don't have partners. The best I could get would be a vice-presidency with a piece of the action."

"That doesn't sound like it's for you."

"I'm really just testing the waters. If I left Henry, I'd probably, start my own firm right here in San Francisco."

"Henry would fight like a tiger to keep his clients. You could bet on that."

"It would be an unknown, all right."

"And wouldn't it take considerable start-up capital?"

"I figure at least a million."

"One million bucks! You don't have that kind of money."

"It wouldn't be easy, but maybe I could borrow it from the bank."

"A million dollars! You've got more nerve than I have. It would take me forever to pay back $1,000,000."

"I'm playing golf with Don Willets tomorrow. Don's bank is involved in the Dictor Electronics deal. Maybe I'll talk to him. Goddammit, Rolf, I don't like being under somebody else's thumb!"

As they ordered lunch they could see the flags on the front of the Fairmont, vigorously flapping in the wind swirling around Nob Hill. Mark felt a sense of resolve. It was clear that now was the time really to push Henry. He had to convince Henry that making him a partner was the smart thing to do.

When they finished lunch, Rolf lit a cigarette. "You never talk about the women in your life. Are you still seeing Priscilla?"

"We're just friends. I only see her occasionally, except with Henry. The old man would throw a fit if he thought we might get serious." The waiter came with their clam chowder, and left. "It's one thing to be nice to the bright young man from the office, but the idea of my even thinking about marrying his daughter—forget it. Maybe it's that English class thing. There's a certain line you don't dare cross."

"Remember the time we all went to the Beatles concert at Candlestick?"

"I sure do. We were lucky we went. It turned out to be their last concert." The waiter brought the rest of their food and Mark continued, "I really don't have much interest in dating. Maybe I've not met the right woman yet."

"Maybe you already have met the right woman," Rolf observed.

"What do you mean, I already have?"

"I'm talking about Christina Movelli."

Mark smiled wanly. "Christina's in the past. It was mostly sex anyway."

"Mostly sex? What's wrong with 'mostly sex.' My God, man, there wasn't a man in the Sonoma Valley who wouldn't have died for her! I still remember that day she came to the fraternity to see you—that new red Thunderbird. Don't give me that 'mostly sex' stuff."

Mark smiled again. "I admit there was a time I would have given up everything for her, but I've learned my lesson."

"Well, I know this. I've never seen anyone like Christina Movelli. I mean, I love Melinda, but . . ."

"Yes. I know what you mean. Remember that woman I dated for a while there?"

"Sure. Joanne," said Rolf.

"She was every bit as good-looking as Christina."

"Yes, but what about in bed?"

"I didn't have any complaints. No complaints at all," Mark sipped his coffee. "But it wasn't the same as with Christina."

"Listen, you don't have to explain Christina to me."

"When I left her in Paris, I thought I'd never want to see another woman like her as long as I lived."

"But you were pissed off then."

"I still don't think a man can marry a Christina in real life."

"I don't know, I never had the chance," replied Rolf wistfully.

When they came out of the club a cable car was in sight near Grace Cathedral, and so they rode together down the steep hill to the financial district.

"Good luck with Henry on Monday," said Rolf as they said good-bye.

"Thanks, Rolf. I'm not sure who needs the luck more—Henry or me."

-22-

It was seven o'clock the following Monday morning. Mark walked toward his Aston Martin convertible in the garage of his Nob Hill condominium. Last April when Mark was in London, Rodney had gone with him when he ordered the shiny red sports car. Two months later, when they had called his office to tell him the car was arriving at the Oakland pier, he had dropped everything and excitedly watched as it was hoisted from the freighter. The stevedores, who had never seen a car like it, crowded around, asking him questions. Since then the automobile had come to symbolize his new affluence and freedom from the poverty of his student days. This morning his heart danced at the sleek beauty of the little car, parked in a remote, ding-proof corner of the garage. Sitting in the bucket seat, Mark slipped his hand over the rich, tan leather, which reminded him of the aroma and touch of the saddles in the Movelli horse barn.

He put the car in gear and pulled out of the garage onto Sacramento Street. The small size of the car always reminded him of that last night in Oxford, when they had all piled into Mavis's Aston Martin. To this day, he could not imagine how they had all managed to fit in. What a wonderful night that had been. He waited for the cable car and turned toward his office.

As he drove down Nob Hill, he thought about today's important meeting with Henry. Indeed, he had been thinking about it incessantly all weekend. Logically, he thought, Henry had no choice but to make him a partner. What he had to do was be careful of the old man's ego, so that it did not appear that Mark was pushing him. He would have preferred to have finished their discussion Friday, but Henry had insisted on keeping that lunch date with Bernie Allard.

Mark turned the car into the garage of the ornate '20s building where Enfield & Co. officed. Bernie was one of Henry's old cronies. They had been talking for months about that stock issue. Bernard's son, Jack, who ran Swiss Allard, had recently confided to Mark that he intended to scuttle the deal, because it was ill-advised. Mark had always been suspicious that the stock issue was nothing more than a pipe dream. The two old men were only using it to delude themselves into thinking they were still in the thick of things. Mark knew very well that the two had played gin rummy, and then Henry had probably slipped home for a nap.

"Good morning, Mr. Stevens," said the garage attendant, opening the car door for Mark.

"Good morning, Rudy," answered Mark, getting out of the car. "It'll need gas. I'm going to Sonoma to see my mother Thursday night." Rudy would park the Aston Martin next to Henry's empty stall and carefully dust the prized automobile.

Mark left the elevator on the penthouse floor and walked to the prestigious corner office that Henry had assigned him despite the flurry of complaints from the firm's more senior men. Two Enfield & Co. associates were already at their desks in the bull pen, checking out the opening transactions on the New York Stock Exchange.

"Good morning, Charlie," he said to one of them. "How's the market?"

"Up two points," the young man answered. "Say hello for me to your man in London." Everyone knew that every morning Mark called Harold Smith-Browning, his trader on the London foreign exchange market.

"I'll do that, Charlie," said Mark.

Mark's office was on the opposite side of the building from Henry's, with a view back toward Nob Hill and the City. This was one of those bright, clear mornings that made everyone want to move from the East to California. The gleaming morning sun reflected off the windows of the Fairmont Hotel Tower, and bathed with gold all of the buildings that marched up the hill. Mark reflected as he looked out his window. He was looking forward to his day. After calling London and studying some reports, he had a conference on the Dictor matter, and would meet with Henry when he came in at eleven. He felt so good today. Surely, he would be successful with Henry.

Mark dialed the international operator. The market would be closed in London. He would find out what had happened to his foreign currency positions and see what new developments might bear on his decisions today. Until Mark's recent trip to London, Harold Smith-Browning had been only a telephone voice.

Mark thought back on that meeting. It had been the day he had ordered the Aston Martin. Rodney had accompanied him to Smith-Browning's Threadneedle Street office in London's financial district, where they had discussed Mark's ideas about controlled risk-taking in the currency market.

"I remember, at Cal, studying the 1949 devaluation of the pound," Mark had told them. "After that happened, everyone was kicking themselves. Suddenly, it was all so obvious there really had been no choice, for the government, but devaluation."

"But what if it hadn't happened?" Rodney had asked.

"Then the speculators wouldn't have made money, but they wouldn't have lost either," Smith-Browning explained.

"Those are the situations I try to find. In 1949 there was no way the pound was going to go *up* in value," Mark said. "And you could see it might very well go down."

"Of course. That's what you did last November," Smith-Browning commented.

"Exactly. Of course, it wasn't that easy. What I was actually looking for was a situation where I could say the market was *more apt* to go one way than another," Mark observed. "Last November I didn't see how the pound could go up, and I thought it was apt to go down."

Indeed, it had been that very method of analyzing the risks that had led Mark to his spectacular success last November.

Mark stopped thinking about that first meeting with Smith-Browning and concentrated on the ring-ring of the telephone.

Smith-Browning answered his telephone. "Harold Smith-Browning here."

"Hello, Harold, how's the weather in London today?" Mark asked. "The newspaper said you had rain over the weekend."

"It's finally stopped. Everyone on the Tube was carrying his umbrella, but it's cleared up."

"What happened to the franc today?"

"It's as you thought. It slipped a little."

"I want to watch the franc especially carefully. I have very little doubt that the French are going to have to devalue one day. After one currency is devalued, it's always the next-weakest currency that goes."

"That may well be," answered Smith-Browning, "but the question is: when?"

"If there's the slightest hint of De Gaulle's resigning, then I want you to sell the franc short immediately."

"All 100,000,000?"

"All 100,000,000. I checked with the bank this weekend and our line of credit is all set."

"Very well."

"I'll call again tomorrow. You go head now and catch your train."

"By the way, I had lunch with your friend, Rodney, last week. He asked me to recommend a share advisor."

"A share advisor? Rodney?"

"It seems Lord Ashley has put him in charge of some family money. Rodney wanted an advisor less conservative than the man his father has always used. He said you've been urging him to break out of his father's conservative mold."

"Well, I'm sure you recommended someone sensible."

"Oh, I did. I wouldn't worry. Well, good morning. We'll talk tomorrow." When Smith-Browning hung up his telephone, he reflected for a moment. Mark Stevens certainly had nerves of steel. As the Americans say, Mark puts his money where his mouth is. Mark was prepared to invest 100,000,000 francs as if it were a pocket money wager on a horse race.

Bette, Mark's secretary, buzzed on the intercom. "Mr. Stevens, Mr. Dictor and the others are here for their nine o'clock meeting. And I remind you of your meeting with Mr. Enfield at eleven."

Nearly two hours later the meeting with Paul Dictor and Donald Willets, Mark's golfing partner of last Saturday, was nearing its conclusion.

"So you agree with me then. Dictor Electronics will not go public, until next year," Mark said.

"I agree. The bank will increase its line of credit to $50,000,000," said Willets.

"At one half below prime," added Paul Dictor.

"But with Enfield & Co.'s guarantee," added Willets.

"Yes, but remember, the guarantee applies only to the portion of the loan above $20,000,000," Mark reminded him.

"Right," answered Willets.

"This way, you can handle the new Lockheed Missiles and Hewlett-Packard orders without issuing stock now," said Mark, rising to his feet to signify an end to the meeting.

"Gentlemen, I think we should celebrate our transaction on the golf course Thursday," said Don Willets as they left Mark's office.

"That sounds good. Mark has been after me to improve my image," laughed Dictor.

"I keep telling him he has to give up bowling. He's in the big time now," laughed Mark. Dictor had become Mark's client after hearing him speak at a business forum at the St. Francis Hotel.

"It's a date, then. Eleven forty-five for lunch at the club Thursday," said Willets.

Mark turned to his secretary. "Put down Thursday afternoon at the Olympic Club." He accompanied them to the elevators. "See you Thursday."

This deal would impress Henry in today's meeting, Mark thought. With next year's profits, Dictor's stock ought to bring triple the eight dollars a share it would bring on today's market. Enfield & Co. would get a healthy fee now, and the underwriting fee next year when it went public. The capper was that Dictor would give the firm an option at eight dollars on 100,000 shares. If the stock went to twenty-four dollars, the firm stood to pick up a neat $1,600,000, and maybe at capital gains tax rates. That would buy a lot of Aston Martins and more than pay his share of the partnership profits.

"Is Henry in yet?" he asked Bette as he returned to his office."

"Yes. Julie called. Mr. Enfield is waiting for you in his office."

The morning had been so fast-moving that the full impact of the impending conference with Henry had not yet struck Mark. However, as he walked around the bull pen toward Henry's side of the penthouse floor, he was suddenly jolted with self-doubt. Without warning, he was nervous, his lips were dry and his hands were invisibly shaking. The Mark that had calmly committed to 100,000,000 francs and advised Paul Dictor to borrow $50,000,000 was a long way from the Mark who had been so nervous that first day at Oxford. Increasingly, he had been able to decide what course of action he should follow and simply do it—do it without fear, without self-doubt and without sweating out what he should do. But now, as he approached Henry's secretary, his confidence faltered. What if Henry said no? Was he an idiot for risking everything like this? His father would have said so. Self-doubts or not, he knocked on Henry's door. It did not matter that he was trembling inside, he was going to see this out with Henry.

"How was your weekend?" asked Henry. He was smiling and bright-eyed. "I thought a great deal about our relationship this weekend."

"I did too, Henry. Our relationship is very important to me."

"Very important to me too. Very important."

"I hope I'm not saying anything I shouldn't, but in many ways I feel as if I am part of your family," said Mark.

"Exactly. Part of my family. You put it very well." Henry walked to his wet bar. "Would you join me in a drink?"

"Thank you, Henry. Perhaps one of your gin and tonics—you make them so well." Mark had no intention of actually drinking more than a sip or two, at least until the meeting was over.

Glass in hand, Henry stood behind his desk, looking over the Embarcadero and the Bay. Mark walked up to the window and stood next to him, looking outside. A gold sight-seeing boat was overtaking a large freighter. Although the passengers were bathed in the midday sunlight, they nevertheless sought protection from the chilling wind, behind the glass.

"Do you remember that afternoon, when I first met you in this very office?" asked Mark. Standing there with Henry calmed Mark's apprehension. Perhaps he was being silly to be so nervous.

"I certainly do," Henry said. "You were in from Oxford. We looked at the sunlight on the windows over in Berkeley." Henry pointed across the bay. "How many years has that been, now?"

"Four years ago last month, Henry."

"It seems like yesterday."

Mark sat opposite Henry's desk and they continued exchanging pleasantries. He took a really good look at Henry against the light from the Bay. Odd, he had seen Henry nearly every day for almost four years now, but he could not remember the last time he had ever really looked at him. He was an old man now. He felt apologetic for belittling Henry's meetings with Bernie Allard, and his frequent naps—after all the man was in his 70s now. Mark would be pleased if he could just get to the office at that age, let alone accomplish anything. He realized he felt affection for the old man. He would be proud if Henry Enfield made him a partner.

"You asked about my morning. Well, this has been quite a morning." With pride, Mark told Henry in detail about plans for the French franc and about the Dictor Electronics deal. "Paul Dictor was so happy. I had no trouble getting us an option on 100,000 shares." Mark beamed when he was finished, and sat back, eagerly anticipating Henry's reaction.

"Congratulations, my boy. Wonderful work! I've been working on a new underwriting myself with Bernard Allard, so I know how you feel. For months now I've been currying the old boy's favor. He's a terrible gin player, you know. If he can get rid of his son's objections, we're going to take their company public."

"Yes, you've told me about it," Mark said, resisting reminding Henry that this was the thousandth time he'd heard about the stock issue that would never happen. "You know Henry, my deal this morning—the Dictor deal—could mean $2,000,000 for the firm."

"Two million dollars. That's a great deal of money. My congratulations to you. That leads me to what I decided to tell you this morning."

Mark's pulse raced. In a moment he would know if Henry had changed his mind.

Henry continued, "I've decided to give you a whole new compensation package." He waited a moment to see Mark's reaction, but seeing none, went on. "I'll give you one half of the pre-tax profits you generate, against a guarantee of half a million."

"That's very generous, Henry."

"What's more, I want you to accept my check for an additional $100,000 for last year. I've been thinking it over, and perhaps your year-end bonus didn't truly reflect how I feel about you."

"Henry, I don't know what to say."

"Shall I have the lawyers draw up the contract?" Henry puffed as he lit his pipe.

"Henry, I don't think you understand. It's not just the money."

"Good for you, Mark. Good for you. It takes most men years to learn money isn't everything." Henry puffed on his pipe and leaned back with a look of satisfaction on his face. "Do you want more time off? Perhaps you've been thinking about marriage and a family?"

"No, it's not that. It's what I was talking to you about Friday."

"Not that damn fool notion about a partnership?"

"It's exactly that—a partnership. I think I've earned it. It would be good for the firm—good for you. I wish you could understand what being a partner means to me. It would mean being an owner. It would mean the respect of my colleagues. Don't you see it would mean a new relationship between the two of us? It's not a matter of how much you pay me, it's a matter of self-respect."

"Good God, man, you're asking more than I can give." Henry's voice was a combination of anger and conciliation.

"Henry, I'm sorry. Perhaps you don't mean it that way, but I don't think you're leaving me any alternative but to leave the firm. I don't want to, but . . ."

"Are you threatening me?" Henry raised his voice.

"No, Henry, I don't mean to threaten you, but you are leaving me no alternative."

"No alternative? *I'm* the one who is leaving *you* no alternative?" Henry nearly dropped his pipe.

Mark started to speak, but Henry held up his hand, stopping him.

"Never mind." Henry abruptly got up from his leather chair and looked out at the tourist ship making its way back toward Fisherman's Wharf, as if collecting himself. Finally, he turned and slowly took his seat again. His ruddy complexion had become pale and he looked grim. He pointed the bit of his pipe at Mark and spoke: "You listen to me, young man. I was shocked Friday and I'm shocked today." He thought for a moment more. "Your greed astounds me! Everyone at Enfield & Co. knows I never make anyone a partner."

"But you've always had such enthusiasm for me. I always thought . . ."

"I've never said anything to make you think you'd have the slightest chance to be my partner."

"Yes, you have. Last year you were very clear."

"What is clear is that I don't have partners."

Mark realized that Henry's remarks that had seemed so important to him, had meant nothing at all to Henry. "But look at what I've produced."

"Your production has nothing to do with your being a partner." Henry was very angry. He was emphasizing every word. "Your production has only to do with money and how much *I* choose to pay you. This is *my* firm and it's going to stay that way." Henry spoke with a disdain that he had never before used with Mark.

"But, Henry, this year alone I'll personally account for well over half the firm's profits. I'm not asking to be an equal partner. I know it's your firm, but the big law firms make their good men partners, even when they're young." Mark knew his pleas were futile, but nevertheless, he found himself stumbling forward with his arguments. He simply had not expected Henry's blunt rejection.

"Enfield & Co. isn't a bloody law firm."

"You must have known I expected a partnership."

"I've offered you an extremely generous compensation package."

"I've told you a thousand times, it isn't the money, it's being a partner."

"I'd have stayed in England if I wanted partners watching my every move. No one is ever going to tell Henry Enfield what to do. I told them I'd leave England and start my own firm, and I bloody well did." Henry's story had always been that he had left to start a branch office. This sounded as if he had left under a cloud, Mark thought. "After all these years, I'll not let some smart know-it-all shove me aside."

"Henry, nobody wants to shove you aside." Mark was dismayed at the way the conversation was going. He had thought he had been prepared to leave the firm, but now that it was actually happening, he was not sure at all.

"You're bloody right about that. I've got all the money I'll ever need, even if I don't make another dollar. Try $50,000,000 in gilt-edged securities on for size. You'll never top that, no matter what sort of tricky deals you make."

"Jesus Christ, Henry you're twisting things! I haven't done anything tricky—and I don't give a damn how much money you've got." Mark never used profanity around Henry, but his anger had gotten the best of him.

"You've been angling for a partnership for a long time, haven't you? I see now why you've been seeing my daughter. Stay away from Priscilla. You're not going to get my money by marrying my daughter and you're not going to get it by being my partner!"

"You listen to me. I'm not interested in your money or your daughter. As of right now, I'm not interested in your goddamned firm!" Mark's anger exploded at Henry's outrageous charges. He did not give a damn what happened now.

"That suits me just fine, young man. When San Francisco thinks of Enfield & Co., it thinks of Henry Enfield and it will always be that way. I'll never share that with you or anyone else!"

"Believe me, you'll have to pump every cent of that 50 million into your precious Enfield & Co., just to keep it going. Don't you think I know you goof off all day? Nobody runs this firm, including you. Your whole staff is a bunch of fuddy-duddies, selling rich old widows stupid investments. Take away my business and it won't be three years before you'll be in the red—if you're lucky!"

"I got along just fine before you came begging for a job!"

"Begging for a job? You're the one who asked me!"

"I only offered you a job because of my sister. I stuck with you through that whole bloody cheating scandal at Oxford, only because of Mavis. I still think you were guilty."

"And you pretended to stick by me!"

"I don't know what sort of hold you've got on my sister. I've wondered why she was always talking about you." Henry glared at Mark, but Mark knew Mavis would not have told anyone about their night together. "It's best I never find out anyway."

"You leave Mavis out of this. I don't know what you're implying, but she's the finest woman I've ever known."

"Well, yes, of course she is," Henry sputtered. "But you stay away from my Priscilla, do you hear me?" Henry was nearly shouting.

"Priscilla can see who she damned well wants. And I'll tell you this much. Don't expect her to be your little virgin princess, just to make you happy. You can kill off Enfield & Co., but Priscilla is going to live her own life!"

"My daughter will live the way I raised her, do you understand? I don't want you in her life and I don't want you in my office!"

"That suits me just fine, you pompous stuffed shirt! I'm getting out of here right now!"

"Good! It can't be too soon for me!"

"And I'll tell you something else. I'll be able to buy and sell Enfield & Co. one day!" Mark was shouting.

"No one will ever buy Enfield & Co. No one, ever!" Henry shouted back.

"That's all right, Henry," Mark said sarcastically, his voice suddenly lowered as if to prove he wasn't speaking from emotion. "I don't know of anyone who would want to buy it. Least of all me."

Mark did not return to his office, but strode rapidly and purposefully toward the elevators.

"Are you all right?" said Bette, pad in hand, running to the elevator to intercept him. "Julie said you had a terrible argument with Mr. Enfield."

"She was right about that. It was a beaut all right." Mark repeatedly jabbed at the elevator button and paced up and down looking at the green arrow. "I'm getting out of here as fast as I can." He was speaking angrily.

"You mean you're leaving?"

"I'm leaving as soon as this damned elevator gets here, and I'm not coming back."

"But what about that letter I'm typing? What about your things? Aren't you going to take your things?"

"To hell with them! To hell with everything about Henry Enfield!" The elevator dinged and the door opened.

"What about the taping on KQED? Don't forget the KQED interview at five o'clock."

"I may make it and I may not."

"But you can't miss it, Mark. What will they do?"

"They can interview Henry. He knows everything there is to know about investment banking."

"But where are you going?" she wailed. "What will . . ."

The elevator closed cutting her off. He did not know where the hell he was going. All he knew was that he wanted to get out of here as soon as he could.

"I just filled your gas tank, Mr. Stevens," said Rudy. "That sure is a sweet little car."

"Thanks, Rudy." Mark threw his suit jacket in the back seat, loosened his tie and stomped hard on the accelerator. Tires squealing, the Aston Martin leaped out of the garage onto Montgomery Street. He had no idea where he wanted to go, but wherever it was, he wanted to go in a hurry. That son of a bitch! After all he had done for Henry! He ignored the light, which had just changed to red, and in a minute was on the freeway. He wanted to be as far away from Henry Enfield as possible. Berkeley—he would go to Berkeley. He had been happy at Berkeley.

On the Bay Bridge the little red car darted quickly in and out of traffic. He didn't give a damn if he got a ticket. Can you imagine that bastard? It was all so obvious now. The son of a bitch never had any intention of making him a partner, ever. There was nothing that Mark could have done to make things different. He could have earned $100,000,000 for the son of a bitch, and all Henry would have said is, "Good job, Mark. Here's another bonus. You should be so grateful for whatever bonus I decide to give you. I'm only giving it to you because I think you were fucking my sister. But one thing I want to make clear to you, young man, is that you're not good enough to be my partner, and you're certainly not good enough to fuck my wonderful daughter."

On the Oakland side, he could not find the exact change and so he impatiently waited to pay the toll. Yes, he could see things clearly now. Enfield & Co. was nothing but a plaything for Henry. He had inherited so goddammed much money he didn't care whether the firm made a penny. Why had he not realized that from the beginning? Of course, now he could see it all. Henry must have inherited as much money as Mavis, so he did not need to earn money, he did not need a partner and he did not need anything else, except to feel important around San Francisco.

Mark turned off the freeway and made his way though the traffic up to the Cal campus. How this would help his anger he had no idea, except that the campus seemed far away from Henry Enfield. He drove by his old fraternity house, but the students were all different now. Everything was different. Nothing ever stayed the same. He really had no safe harbor anywhere in the world. Helter-skelter thoughts flooded his mind. Without thinking, he turned toward the Durant Hotel. He remembered that weekend with Christina. He had not cared about anything except being with her. His problems with his father and with Antonio had seemed miles away. What he would not give if his problems with Henry did not matter. Goddamn that ungrateful son of a bitch! Didn't that old bastard know that Mark would have made Enfield & Co. into the greatest investment banking firm on either coast?

He pulled into a parking place around the corner from the hotel, and went into the hotel restaurant for a hamburger. How wonderful it had been to be there with Christina. In some ways it was too bad he had ever seen her again after their night in the hotel. If their love affair had ended right here, it would have been better than what had happened in Paris. He remembered how they had loved each other so much as they had eaten by this same window. They had hardly been able to wait to get back to their room that day. He finished the hamburger and coffee. The moment Henry came back to his thoughts his anger returned. It was one o'clock. The KQED program was at five. He didn't want to return to San Francisco, but he knew he should. No! What he wanted to do was go back to Sonoma—to the place where he was born. In a few minutes he was on the freeway again, speeding north. He remembered the many times he had driven back and forth. Wouldn't it have been something if he had had the Aston Martin when he was at Cal? He remembered how fast he had driven this same route the time when he thought his father had stolen the letter from Oxford. On a two lane portion of the road near Sonoma, he ducked back in line just in time to avoid an oncoming car that blasted its horn at him.

He avoided driving up to the compound, because he didn't want to be involved in talking to his mother. "Mark, are you sure you know what you're doing? You should go back and apologize to Mr. Enfield," she would say. She would not understand why he felt the way he did.

He drove the back road to Jack London Park, still driving too fast. Maybe he would find that quiet place by Wolf House and think for a while. But as he drove by the corner where his father had thrown him from the tractor, he suddenly knew where he wanted to be. He shifted to second gear, turned around and accelerated for the cemetery. He wanted to look at Jonah's grave.

Jonah Stevens
1910-1964

Amanda Stevens
1914-

Mark had never seen the tombstone. His mother must have had it put there. It bothered him to think that one day she would be lying under this ground. He had expected to continue with his orgy of anger and hatred, this time at Jonah, but as he stood there his feelings were different. His father had been dead some five years now. The undertaker had said bodies usually rotted away in three or four years. So now there was nothing remaining in the buried casket to hate. The hostility he had felt for so long had mellowed into an intense resolve: *He would never, ever be like his father. He would do everything in his power to rise above the muck of what his father had been.*

One day he would have a son of his own, or maybe a daughter. When that happened, he would be a good father. He would never be the terrible father that Jonah had been. As he sat on the grave, he seriously thought for the first time about having a family. He would like to get married some day, and show the world what a good father was like. He ran his fingers over the soil, remembering his emotions that day after the funeral, when the earth had been so freshly barren. He stayed there for over an hour, thinking, pondering his future. Finally he stood, resolved. He had reached an inner decision.

He looked at his watch. He would be going against the traffic, so if he hurried he could make it in time for the five o'clock television show.

"Our featured guest today is Mr. Mark Stevens," said the television moderator, reading from the teleprompter. "Mr. Stevens is a graduate of the School of Economics at the University of California at Berkeley. He was a Rhodes Scholar at Oxford, where he won the highest honors. His paper on Bretton Woods was awarded Oxford's coveted Linde-Ewell Prize. Mr. Stevens is an associate with the established San Francisco Investment banking firm, Enfield & Co."

"Thank you, Mr. Simnat," said Mark as the red light blinked on the guest's television camera. "But first, I have an announcement. Henry Enfield is a fine gentlemen and I remain very fond of him, but at a meeting earlier today we mutually decided that it would be best if I formed my own firm where I could continue with my unique investment strategies. Effective immediately, I am no longer associated with Enfield & Co., but am chairman of my own firm, 'The Stevens Group.'"

-23-

It was September, 1969. Eight months had passed. Mark had borrowed $1,750,000 from Don Willets's bank, for working capital, and had begun business as The Stevens Group in a small suite of offices three blocks from Enfield & Co. The new firm consisted of himself, his secretary, Bette, and the two young men from Enfield & Co. who had always arrived in the bull pen early. In June he hired two bright new graduates recommended by his Cal professor, Dr. Hall, to assist him. He made an arrangement with Dufton and Watts of New York to assist him with underwriting and other very large matters.

The San Francisco financial community was abuzz over The Stevens Group's fast start. The Dictor Electronics deal was hailed for its brilliance. Several large stock issues and a bond issue had come to the new firm.

The biggest success story had been Mark's early August killing in the French franc. Continuing to keep his finger on the pulse of foreign currencies, he felt strongly that the franc was now the currency most likely to be devalued. The official line of the French government was that the franc would be defended to the death, but Mark thought otherwise. Wage negotiations and strike threats foreboded more inflation, he thought. Continuing balance-of-payment deficits were eroding French reserves. De Gaulle, with his pride in the franc, was the main bastion against devaluation, but if Mark waited until De Gaulle resigned to enter the currency markets it would be too late. He made the decision, selling short 200,000,000 francs. Two weeks later, as he had thought inevitable, De Gaulle resigned, touching off a flurry of increased speculation that the franc would be devalued. Mark sold off half his position at a very sizable profit. Then on August 8, the franc was devalued 12.5%.

In all Mark had cleared approximately $5,000,000, after interest and expenses. His clients had made even more. He paid off his loan with the bank, keeping the rest for expansion and reserves.

Next, he decided it would be the Deutsche mark that was apt to be devalued. He now was watching that situation carefully, in order to decide when to enter the market again.

Mark was in his condominium watching television, when he decided to telephone Rodney. He had not talked to his friend since he had told him he was leaving Henry's firm.

"Hello, Rodney. It's me. Mark."

"Good Lord, Mark!" Rodney shouted. "Rebecca, it's Mark calling!"

"I was watching an English movie on television and it made me homesick for England. I had an impulse to call you."

"I'm glad you did. I was reading my paper before breakfast."

"Have you ever yet found a paper that doesn't make you angry?" asked Mark, referring to Rodney's old habit of cursing at newspapers.

Rodney laughed robustly. "There's little chance of that."

"I wish I were there having breakfast with you right now. I really miss London."

"Well, dammit, you should come over. Just get on a plane and you'll be here before you know it!"

"You're right, I should. The problem is I've been so busy since I left Henry."

"From what I hear, Henry is still very upset with you."

"No more upset than I am with him, I'll tell you."

"Henry can be such a pompous ass. Remember, I told you he never made anyone a partner."

"Yes, but I think it was Noel Coward, or was it William Saroyan, who said that he knew everyone had to die, but he thought God would make an exception for him."

Rodney laughed heartily.

"I guess I always thought Henry would make an exception for me, and make me a partner."

Rodney laughed again. To Mark it was worth calling, just to hear Rodney's hearty laugh. "I'm bloody happy you left him. How is your new business coming along?"

"I've been very busy. Can you imagine it, Rodney? I've already made more money than all last year with Henry."

"I surely can. I knew you were making the right move."

"Here I was, worried that business might be coming to me because of Enfield & Co., but when I left every one of my accounts stayed with me."

"Super! That's wonderful."

"And you know what?"

"What?"

"For years Henry has had this client, Smith Allard Company. Old man Allard has been Henry's gin rummy buddy since Year One. Henry was trying to get him to go public. Well, you'll never guess what happened."

"Don't tell me you got that customer too?" Rodney asked excitedly.

"That's right. The week after I open up my new office, Allard's son comes to me. Seems he never trusted Henry's judgment, but didn't want to consult with me while I was with Enfield & Co. Can you imagine that?"

"You must have been on top of the world."

"I was. It was a real coup. I told him he shouldn't go public until his father gifted him more of the company's stock. Saves them millions in estate taxes. So now I'm arranging private financing for him."

"You're definitely on your way. Come on, now, tell me when are you going to get on that plane to London?"

"Maybe we should think about the holidays. Am I invited to the New Year's weekend?"

"Of course you are. Christmas, too, if you like. Mother would love to see you."

"I'd love to see her, too. What are you doing, besides bouncing little Allison on your knee?"

"I've persuaded Father to let me invest some family money in an office block—against his better judgment."

"Good for you!"

"It's with a chap at the Blue Sheep Club. He's had successful projects before."

"You're sure about him, are you?"

"Oh, yes. He's quite all right."

"Well, give my best to Rebecca—and to Mavis when you see her."

"I will. Oh, Mark, you'll never guess who made the news."

"Who?"

"Derek Harden."

"You're joking!"

"His father died. Left him a fortune."

"Really? That lucky bastard."

"According to the newspaper, their import-export company is quite vast."

"I'll be damned! Derek Harden!"

"I'll send you the newspaper clipping."

"Okay. By the way, I'm seeing your cousin tomorrow."

"Priscilla? You're seeing Priscilla?"

"Yes. I'm looking at a house at Monterey for weekends. She's going with me."

"Monterey? Isn't that where Uncle Henry has a place?"

"Yes. Pebble Beach. That's why she's going with me. I want her advice on this house I've been looking at."

"It sounds like a little bit of a romance to me," Rodney teased, "but then, I'll wager you have plenty of women."

"Don't I wish. I've been much too busy for women. We're staying at Henry's house, but it's all very proper. Separate bedrooms and all."

Rodney laughed. "Does Uncle Henry know?"

"Of course not. He'd have a fit. I think maybe that's half the attraction of taking her with me."

When they finished talking, Mark flipped off the T.V. The movie had ended. It made him feel good to talk with his old friend. Rodney's spontaneous invitation for the holidays sounded wonderful. He could use a chat with Mavis, too. He missed their talks about the deeper things of life. He wished he had more time for that type of thing.

Mark began packing a few things for tomorrow's trip to Pebble Beach. Priscilla was planning to come to his condominium at 8:30 in the morning. Every time he had seen her since leaving the firm, she had insisted she meet him at a restaurant or bar, rather than be picked up at the house. She knew that Henry would be upset if he knew she were still seeing Mark. As for tomorrow, Henry would be furious if he knew Mark were staying at the Pebble Beach house, separate bedrooms or not. The truth was, Mark was beginning to have more than just a friendship interest in Priscilla. He remembered Henry's shouting at him the day he quit. "You stay away from my daughter." Mark smiled to himself. He wondered what the old bastard would say if he took his daughter to bed one of these times?

It was foggy in San Francisco, but by the time Mark and Priscilla reached the turnoff below San Jose, the sun was shining brightly. Mark pulled the Aston Martin to the side of the road and lowered the convertible top. It was a delightful day.

"I appreciate your coming with me, Priscilla. I value your opinion."

"I think it would be wonderful for you to have a place on the peninsula. I can't remember when Mom and Dad didn't have our house at Pebble. Before she died, we went there all the time. That's where I learned to ride horses."

"I'm anxious to see what you think of the house. The owner made a counter-offer and I've got to make a decision."

"I can't picture which house it is."

"It's just after where Padres Lane goes off the Seventeen Mile Drive. Maybe half a mile from the Lodge."

"That's a beautiful area. Do you have a view of the ocean?"

"I don't think so, but the day I was there it was too foggy to tell. The owners live in the East someplace. He died a while back, and she hasn't been there since."

"It sounds wonderful."

"It's too big for me, really, but I couldn't resist. Wait until you see it."

Priscilla happily stretched her arms above the windshield into the wind. "What an absolutely gorgeous day. I've really been looking forward to this. Bob and Lorraine were so happy I was coming down."

"Bob and Lorraine?"

"The caretakers. They've lived in the guest cottage for years. They're like family."

"Sounds more like they're chaperones than caretakers," Mark joked.

"I told Lorraine to make up a guest room for a friend."

"Will she tell your father it's me?"

"No, I swore her to secrecy. I told her we were just friends, but Father would be upset. She won't tell. I've known them since I was a child"

They drove for a while before she spoke. "Mark, do you think you could ever get over being so angry with my father?"

"Not a chance. He said some pretty awful things to me that day—things he'd been holding back for years."

"Until you had that big fight, I thought you were going to be the son father always wanted."

"If that was the way he felt, he sure as hell didn't show it."

"You know, Mark, I'd try to get Father to forgive you, if I thought you'd do the same."

"Him forgive me? What the hell did I ever do to him?" Mark spoke angrily.

"I'm sorry, Mark. That wasn't a good choice of words."

"It sure wasn't."

"It's just that it would be very important to me if you'd try to be friends with him again."

"I've been that route before, Priscilla. I know it very well."

"I don't understand."

"Antonio, my dad's boss." Mark choked on his words and had to stop talking for a moment. He was surprised at his emotions. He thought he had gotten over Antonio.

"I've never heard you speak of Antonio before."

"I was like a son to him. He was far more important to me than my own father, and then he cut me off." Mark took one hand off the wheel and made a motion across his throat. "Just like that."

"What happened?"

"He got mad at me for something I did. Something bad. Right then and there all those good years came to a screeching halt."

"And he stayed angry?"

"Damned right. No matter how often I apologized, he stayed mad at me. As far as Antonio is concerned, I'm dead—as simple as that."

"But now you're doing what he did to you. Staying angry."

"It's not that easy. Don't try to make things sound so damned simple." Mark's temper flared. "He's your father. That makes it hard for me to say what I want. Suffice it to say, I'm not exactly in the mood to forgive."

"Okay, Mark, okay." Priscilla held up her hands helplessly.

"Priscilla, listen to me. Let me explain. Your father never even *considered* making me a goddammed partner. Can you imagine how that made me feel? No matter what I did, I wasn't going to be his partner. Not *ever!*

"On top of that, he told me in no uncertain words to stay away from you. First, I'm not good enough for his firm, then I'm not good enough for his daughter."

"Mark, he was angry. He says things when he gets angry."

"Oh, he meant it all right."

"Well, promise me one thing at least."

"What?"

"Promise me you'll think about giving him a chance. Just a small chance that you might change your mind."

"I can't promise that, Priscilla. I just can't."

"Okay, Mark. I'll never bring it up again."

They did not talk for several miles. There was nothing further to say about Henry, yet neither could think of anything else they wanted to talk about. Finally, they passed the Army artillery range on Monterey Bay. "THRUMPTH! THRUMPTH!," sounded the big guns.

In another 15 minutes, they identified themselves at the Del Monte Forest gate house. A short drive later, through the tall pines and redwoods, the red Aston Martin pulled up to the large gate in front of a magnificent two-story house.

"Is this it?" she asked excitedly.

"Yes. They gave me a key," said Mark, leaning out and inserting the card into the gate opener.

"My Lord! What a house! It's larger than Daddy's place. It's every bit as large as our San Francisco house."

Mark was happy that he had impressed Priscilla. The house was a reward of his success. He was certain his stature had suddenly expanded in her eyes.

"I fell in love with the place the minute I saw it," he told her enthusiastically.

"I don't blame you," she bubbled. "I would have too. The front approach is magnificent."

Mark zipped right on past the front entry and, suddenly tooting his horn, continued right around the circular driveway, making a complete circle before stopping. They broke into laughter at his boyish enthusiasm. "I hope you like my new house, because I think I'm going to buy it, no matter what."

The magnificent house could have passed for a Frank Lloyd Wright creation. The structure appeared to be low and a part of the gentle hill, in the style of the famous architect. It looked like only two stories, but on closer inspection the horizontal windows actually belonged to a third story. Mark opened the magnificent, inlaid paneled front door. The house had been left unfurnished. The entry was on split levels, with a short flight of stairs leading up to the living room, and another flight leading down to a billiard room, an indoor-outdoor pool, and so much else that he could not even remember. He was as excited as he had been the day he picked up the Aston Martin at the dock.

"Today's such a gorgeous day, I'm anxious to see what the view is," he said, leading her upstairs to the living room with its large redwood deck.

"Look," she enthused. "You can see the ocean through the trees."

"What do you think? Should I buy it?"

"It's a marvelous house. It has 'Mark Stevens' written all over it. It's so wonderful you've been this successful."

"Come on. Let me show you the rest."

He grabbed her by the hand, pulling her after him, as he ran through the house.

"This is the dining room," he said, and excitedly took her into the next room. "And this is the kitchen. But, hell, Priscilla, I'll bet you've never even been in a kitchen in your life."

"Oh, I have too!" she laughed, trying to keep up with him without falling down. "Wait a minute, Mark." She stopped to pull off her high heels. Holding his hand with one hand and her shoes in the other, she continued through the house in her stocking feet.

"And this will be my study. Look, it's got a view of the ocean, too." They paused, looking at the blue water through the pine trees.

"I can just see you while you're making your millions—holding your phone and looking out this window."

"Not me. There'll be no business in this house."

"I wouldn't bet on that," she laughed. "The day you don't use your house for business, will be the day you stop using it altogether."

"*My* house. That sounds very good. Then you think I should buy it?"

"I don't know of anyone who would enjoy this house more, and I don't know of anyone, who has earned it more than you."

"I never, ever, thought I'd ever have a house like this. Priscilla, I'm going to buy it." Mark did not think he had ever been happier in his life.

That afternoon they decided to play golf at the famous Pebble Beach golf links, not far from Mark's new house. When they had finished their round, they sat in the Tap Room in the Lodge. "I didn't know you were such a good golfer," Mark said. "The course certainly got the best of me."

"It does that to everyone who plays it the first time," she said. "Besides the ladies' tees give the women a huge advantage at Pebble."

"Not on the seventh hole. For a minute there I thought you had a hole in one," he exclaimed.

"It did look like it, didn't it?"

"It sure did." The waiter came with the two beers they had ordered. "What's the matter Priscilla?" he asked. Suddenly she looked apprehensive.

"That couple at that table." She pointed with her head at a table behind Mark. He started to turn around. "No, don't look."

"Why, what's the matter?"

"They're friends of my father. I don't want them to see me." She partially hid her face with the menu."

"Come on Priscilla, you're 23 years old. So what if he does find out we're here?"

"Don't say that, Mark. I can't handle it when he gets angry with me."

Mark was both annoyed and mystified. He could not under-stand why Priscilla feared her father so.

After a minute or two she peered around her menu. "There, they're leaving. I don't think they saw me."

Mark sighed and blew some air through his pursed lips, show-ing his displeasure.

"I'm sorry, Mark. I just can't help it."

"I'm sorry, too. I shouldn't criticize you. It's just when it comes to your father . . ."

"I know." Priscilla reached across the table and squeezed his hand. "Let's forget Father. Okay?"

"Believe me, I'm all for that."

They were quiet for a minute. "Mark, I have an idea. Let's have something to eat here and then go riding, while there's still light. I really would like that."

With an hour of daylight left, they had saddled two of Priscilla's horses and were riding. They left the forest and rode around the sand dunes to the ocean, from where they followed the Seventeen Mile Drive along the magnificent shore.

"Let's stop and watch the sunset," she said. "Come on, I'll show you the secret place I had as a child."

"I'd love to see it."

They walked the horses into the trees and tied them where they could not be seen from the road.

"This is Cypress Point Golf Club. They'd kick us out if they found us," she said as they walked through the trees to the golf course.

"Have you ever been caught?"

"No, the golfers are through by sunset. My secret place is behind those trees on the other side of the fairway," she pointed.

"Priscilla, look at the deer. Shush. Be quiet or we'll scare them." There were a dozen deer grazing on the fairway of the short hole.

She laughed. "You don't need to be quiet, silly. They won't move unless you try to touch them."

"I had no idea there were so many deer in the forest." Mark was spellbound by the sight as they walked across the fairway to the trees and the cliff beyond, where Priscilla had pointed to one large buck and two younger males. The rest were fawns and does. They neared the edge of the high cliff and sat in the tall grass. The lower edge of the huge, oversized sun was about to touch the ho-rizon.

"That last summer, when Mother was so ill, I'd come here every night at sunset," Priscilla said as they watched the sun steadily sinking.

"It's amazing how large the sun gets when it's setting."

"When I was little, I thought people who didn't live near the ocean didn't have sunsets," she said.

Mark smiled. "I've never thought of you as being a child. What were you like?"

"Innocent," she said and thought for a moment. "Yes, innocent is the perfect word."

"When did you lose your innocence?"

She thought for a moment. "A long time ago."

"Really?" Mark was puzzled.

"Maybe someday, I'll tell you about it."

"Okay." Mark took her hand.

They watched as the sun disappeared from view, casting its brilliant hues of color across the sky. They could hear the sea lions from around the bend making their barking noises. Finally she spoke again. "Then, when I was a teenager, after my mother died, I had to grow up in a hurry."

Priscilla had never talked so openly to Mark before. He had never really gotten to know her.

"We all have to find ourselves when we're that age. Losing your mother must have made it doubly tough."

"My way was to learn what people wanted from me and to do it."

"Isn't that what happens to all of us? We do what gets us strokes from other people."

"After Mother died, Daddy wanted a daughter who could play the piano, be properly dressed and be the head of his house. I was still only 15 and there I was, arranging for caterers and being the hostess at his parties. He didn't want to come to Pebble Beach any more, so I gave up riding." Priscilla paused. She was fighting back tears. "All I really wanted to do was keep on being a girl in jodhpurs, riding my horse." When her tears came, she turned from Mark, fishing in her pocket for a tissue.

"I'm sorry. I can't remember the last time I cried."

Until now Mark was unaware of the impact Henry had on his daughter. It saddened him. "Don't we all cry sometimes?" he comforted.

"You? I can't imagine you crying."

"The last time I cried was on my father's grave, but I've cried plenty inside."

"Really?"

"You won't believe this, but the night after your father and I quarreled . . ."

"Yes?"

"I felt like crying."

"I thought you were angry with father."

"I was angry, but I was sad also. Do you realize Henry is the third father I've lost?"

"No, I didn't. The third father?" She looked up at Mark, her tears drying.

"Sure. There was my own father; then there was Antonio—I've told you about him; and then there was Henry."

"I didn't know you felt that way about Father."

"Well, I did at the beginning. You were my real family for a long time there. He was the closest I had to a father. I didn't do anything to deserve the way he treated me," said Mark, grim-faced.

"I know."

"I dreamed of the day when I could be his partner. 'Enfield, Stevens & Co.' God, how I wanted that on the door."

"But look at you now. The Stevens Group! You don't have to share it with anyone."

"I *wanted* to share it. Don't you see? I *wanted* him to want me for a partner."

"I can see how you felt rejected."

"But I didn't wallow in it. I did something about it."

"Maybe the argument with Father was the best thing that ever happened to you."

"I've thought about that. I used to think the only way I could make it as an investment banker was to be Henry Enfield's partner."

"You know what I think would have happened, if you'd become a partner?"

"What?"

"Before long, you'd have resented Father's not making you a 50-50 partner, when you were bringing in a lot more than half."

"Maybe," he agreed, reluctantly.

"And knowing Father, he'd always keep control. You're both a lot alike that way, you know. Wanting control."

"I guess you're right."

"And now look at you. You did it on your own. You don't have to depend on anybody."

"You're right. I've got my own business and now I'll have my house at Pebble Beach."

"Bigger and better than my father's."

"But there's one other thing I want."

"Oh, really? What's that?"

"I want to kiss his daughter."

At first Priscilla held herself back, but then she placed her arm around his neck. He had kissed her before, but not like this, on the lips. It had always been a peck on the cheek. This kiss was born from the closeness they had experienced all day, especially in the last few minutes. The rules of this weekend in Henry's house were clear. He would sleep alone in a guest room, he knew that, but this moment called for a kiss. And there was nothing Henry could do about that.

"Mark, you surprise me."

"I surprise myself, but it was something I wanted to do."

"I'm glad you did."

He knew if he kissed her again, the excuse of spontaneity would be absent. Part of him wanted to hold her and maybe even make love right there on the cliff, but another part was stunned by the kiss and the feelings that had led up to it. Priscilla was a very attractive woman, but as Henry's daughter she had always been off-limits to him. As the brilliant light from the vanished sun reflected off the glassy sea, he knew that that had all changed.

-24-

The herd of deer was still grazing on the fairway as Priscilla and Mark returned to their horses, tied to the tree near the road. Silently they rode through the near darkness, each keeping to his own thoughts.

At the barn the caretaker took the horses. "I'll come by later to lock up. I've put wood in the fireplace," he said.

"Thank you, Bob," said Priscilla. "Big Red seemed a wee bit logy to me. Have you noticed anything?"

"You don't come down often enough any more to suit him. That's what Big Red's problem is, Miss Priscilla."

"I'll try to do better. Good night, Bob."

"Good night," Mark added as they entered the main house.

"I'd like to change out of my riding clothes," Priscilla said. "I'll be only a minute,"

"Okay. I'll fix drinks and wait for you."

Priscilla went to the back of the house, while Mark sat on the large couch next to the stone fireplace. The growing flame crackled, as it jumped from the kindling to the logs. Although the living room was very large, a small grouping of furniture provided intimacy near the huge freestanding fireplace. It was dark outside now, so the view was of total blackness. Mark took off his shoes and stretched out on the couch. He would have to buy riding boots if he were going to have a weekend house at Pebble Beach. The golf and riding today had been great fun. He had some pain in his bad leg, but he knew it would be gone by morning. Staring at the burning wood, he fell deep into thought.

Why had he kissed Christina? he asked himself. Now that was odd—he had slipped and said 'Christina' to himself when he had meant Priscilla. Now why would he do that? The two women were so very different. Christina, with her wildness and sexuality and Priscilla, with her conservative well-bred ways. He realized that it had been some time since he had even thought about Christina.

The logs were crackling with flame, as he reflected on their conversation by the cliff. Priscilla's vulnerability had stirred something inside him. She had never exposed her feelings that way before. Always so reserved, always showing her pleasant side. If she ever had a problem, she never mentioned it. Although he had liked her from the beginning, he had often wondered what she was really like. There on the bluff Priscilla had poked her head out of her protective shell, but why had she burst into tears when she had told him about having to grow up so fast? There was something she was holding back, even as they talked so intimately.

"I can practically touch your brain waves," said Priscilla, who had walked into the darkened room. "Is my genius house guest going to tell me what is on his mind?" she teased. She had taken her long, red hair down from the riding cap she had been wearing. Mark looked at Priscilla in a closer light. He could see the family resemblance to Mavis. She did not have the high cheekbones, but her skin had the same English purity. Mark could smell a distinctive feminine, after-the-bath fragrance about her. She had changed to a black button-up-the-back sweater, a conservative gray skirt and black flats. Her clothes looked left over from her Wellesley years. She looked fresh and very appealing, even naive.

Mark laughed at her question and walked to the bar. "I'll tell what I'm thinking, but on one condition."

"And what's that?"

"If you tell me what Priscilla Enfield is really like."

"That's not fair," she laughed, teasingly. "Not fair at all. No lady would tell a man what she's really like, just to learn his thoughts."

"Okay, then, I suggest a compromise. All you have to tell me is what you want to tell me." Mark fixed her the vodka and tonic she customarily drank.

"I can't lose on that one, can I?" Drink in hand, she laughed again and sat in the big chair opposite him.

"That's all you'd tell me anyway. After all, you're a woman," he kidded.

"You're too smart for me," she laughed in return. "Come on, tell me what you were thinking when I came in."

"Okay. Well, I was wondering what you thought of my kissing you?"

Priscilla grinned and went to the record player. "Would you like me to put on a Beatles record?"

"You're stalling me, Priscilla. Come on, I can tell when you're stalling. I don't care what record you play," he said light-heartedly, enjoying their banter.

She pulled a record from the shelf and removed it from its cover. "You're right. I am stalling. I haven't decided what I'm going to say yet." It was a Mancini album. She waited for the record to drop down. "How's that?" she asked after the music started.

"It's fine. Sort of romantic."

Priscilla walked around the bar from the record player and flirtatiously sat down next to him on the couch. "How did I feel about your kissing me? Is that your question, sir?"

Mark laughed. "That's the question, madam, but the real question is whether the lady will ever give me an answer?"

"Oh, I will all right. It's just that it takes a little courage." She gathered herself together and sighed. "Let me see, what did I think when you kissed me?"

They were quiet for a moment. Both knew that their little game had become serious now. Finally she spoke. "I liked it. I really liked it, but I was surprised."

"Okay. Fair enough. I guess that was true of me, too. I liked it, but I was surprised."

"I never expected you'd be interested in me. Not that way."

"You've always been so . . . well, so unapproachable. I didn't dare be interested in you. What I mean is, I've always felt our relationship could never change from what it always has been. You know, friends."

"But it felt special, Mark. You've always been very special to me."

"You know what I think, Priscilla?"

"No."

"I think we're talking too damned much."

He took her in his arms and kissed her. At first she was tense. He could feel her wanting to pull back, although she did not actually do so. Then she was released from whatever invisible hand held her back, and participated in their embrace. They held each other for a long time in the light of the fire.

"It seems so strange, after all these years," she said, her voice barely above a whisper.

"I know. I feel strange, too. There's always been this wall." They sat for a long time holding hands, saying nothing and looking into the flames.

"When we were talking at sunset, that wall between us came crashing down. Suddenly I saw you as a beautiful woman."

"You did?"

"Yes, and I had feelings for you—feelings that I've never felt before."

Mark kissed her again. This time he put his hand gently on her breast.

Quickly, she pulled back from him. "Mark, please."

"I'm sorry. It's just . . . well, I thought it was all right."

"It's not you, it's me. I just can't. Not with you." She got up suddenly and ran to the window. She stared off into the blackness, through the reflection of the flames from the fireplace. Suddenly, she held her hands to her face, bursting into tears.

Mark stood behind her. "I'm sorry I upset you." He softly stroked her hair and gently put his hands on her shoulders.

Her sobs lessened. "You didn't do anything wrong. This is the sort of evening every woman dreams of. It's not your fault, but it's you."

"It's me? I don't understand."

"I don't understand myself. If you were one of those silly young men I meet all the time, I wouldn't be this way."

Mark didn't understand what she was talking about. Tonight he was seeing a troubled side of Priscilla he had never seen before. He was concerned about her. "Let me fix us another drink and we can talk." He made another Rob Roy, and a vodka and tonic. He sipped his drink, chose several more records from the shelf and put them on the turntable.

"Do you think you can tell me what's bothering you?"

"I doubt it." Having collected herself, she dried her eyes with a tissue. "You see, I'm not sure myself what it is." She chuckled at her plight and blew her nose. "You'd better stay away from me, Mark. I'm nothing but trouble."

"Dammit, Priscilla! You've dated lots of guys. Every time you talk about a date, it's with a different man."

"But I care about *you*. Don't you see I never cared about *them*?"

"I didn't know," he murmured.

"You're different. I've never known anyone like you."

"How am I so different from anyone else?" He took the cushions from the couch and put them in front of the fireplace.

"Well, for one thing, you've made your own way. All the men I know were born with silver spoons in their mouths."

"And you don't like men who are born rich?"

"It's not that. My father was born rich, but there's a difference."

"What difference?"

"You got there by yourself, not from some rich father. What you've become is really you." She faltered, trying to find the words. "Do you know what I mean? I respect you. I can't respect the

others. It's as if they're playing at what they do. Yes, that's it.
They're playing at what they do."

Mark felt drawn to her. He wanted to kiss her again, to hold
her. Reluctant to encounter whatever it was that had caused her
crying spell, he held back.

"When Mother died, Father was very upset. You have no idea
how much he depended on her. From then on, I had to go everywhere with him. It was me he depended on. He'd never go alone—
to the opera—to dinner at friends' houses—to England."

"Didn't he ever date other women?"

"Twice that I remember. Friends fixed him up with rich widows. I don't know what happened, but he never went out again.
So I had to do everything mother used to do."

"But you had a life anyone would envy."

"Only from the outside. Until I went away to Wellesley, I didn't
have a life of my own. You don't know it, but he didn't want me to
go to Wellesley."

"He didn't? But he always acted as if he were so proud of your
being at Wellesley."

"'Acted' is the operative word. He always acted in front of others. Whenever I came home, he tried to persuade me not to go
back. He even threatened to cut off my tuition once."

"Jesus! I'm amazed."

"Oh, I love him. Don't get the wrong idea. He's my father and
I love him, but my life was no piece of cake."

"Do you think you'll ever move out of his house?"

"I don't think I could hurt him that way."

"Oh, come on now. I can't buy that."

"I don't expect you to understand, when I don't understand
myself."

"I sure as hell left him, didn't I?"

"Maybe that's why I admire you. You did what I'd like to do."

"Priscilla, you've got to start leading your own life. The sooner
the better."

"I want to. I really want to."

He took her in his arms again. "Then I'd suggest you start
right now." He had felt protective, but now he felt passion—strong,
growing passion for her. Right now he didn't give a damn about
the stupid separate bedroom rule. Eagerly, they embraced. This
time she did not stop him, as he began to unbutton her sweater.

"I want to make love with you, Priscilla," he whispered.

"But what about Bob?" She said, referring to the caretaker.
"He said he was going to lock up."

"All right, let's go to your bedroom. That would be even better."

Mark's heart was beating rapidly as they walked down the long hallway to the master bedroom.

"It's Father's bedroom. I've been using it since he stopped coming down here." She closed the drapes of the dimly lit, luxurious room. When she pulled back the bedspread, he took hold of her.

"I feel funny, being here like this in Father's room."

"Not me. I think it's great." He was engulfed by desire for her as he took her in his arms. Being in Henry's bedroom added all the more spice. He finished unbuttoning her sweater and gently pulled it off over her arms. He was amazed at the turn of events. How ironic was Henry's impassioned warning, "Stay away from my daughter!" Here he was about to defy the warning, in Henry's own bed.

No sooner had they commenced to make love, than he could tell something was wrong. "What's the matter Priscilla, you seem frightened." She looked as she did in the Tap Room, when she was afraid she would be recognized by her father's friends.

"Oh, Mark, I'm so sorry. I don't know what's the matter with me." She was nearly crying.

He sat on the bed looking intently at her.

In anguish she continued, "I want to make love, but I don't think I can."

He stifled his impulse to throw up his hands in dismay, and instead spoke soothingly: "What's making you so upset? There's nothing to be frightened of. This is Mark Stevens, remember?

"What if Bob or Lorraine come in the house? They'll know we're in the bedroom. I can't have them know I'm in Father's bedroom with you."

As absurd as he thought it was, Mark knew her apprehension was very real to her. He suspected that it had a lot more to do with Henry than with Bob and Lorraine. "Well, I could tack up a 'Do Not Disturb' sign on the front door. Then they'd stay out."

He had gotten her to laugh. "I can just see Bob now, telling Lorraine about your sign."

He laughed too. "But I've got a better idea to solve the Bob and Lorraine problem."

"What?"

"It's time for my new bachelor pad to have its baptism." Mark put on his trousers, without bothering with his underwear, his shirt or even his shoes. "You're coming with me. We're getting the hell out of this place."

As he had done earlier in the day, he started to lead her by the arm. "Wait!" she shouted. She grabbed her purse and playfully allowed him to pull her along the hallway and out the door, toward his Aston Martin.

They laughed like two children playing a Halloween prank as he fished the car keys from his pocket. Top still down, the car roared down the driveway with its two giggling, half-naked passengers. He gunned his engine while waiting for Henry's automatic gate to open. Suddenly, a light went on in the caretaker's cottage and, as they zoomed though the open gate, the yard light burst into life. "At least Bob and Lorraine know we aren't in bed together," he laughed.

"Do you suppose they'll think we're going dancing at the Casa Munras?" she laughed. At least for now she seemed to have had thrown her fears to the winds.

In the blackness, Mark made a wrong turn, but finally found Padres Lane and his house. He struggled with his plastic key card. "If you aren't a sight!" she joked. "San Francisco's rich young investment banker, with no shirt and no shoes, trying to break into a house he doesn't even own."

"You're quite a sight yourself. 'Heiress to San Francisco fortune assists bathrobe-clad burglar. Jury rejects claim she was being chased by notorious Bob and Lorraine mob.'" Both laughed uproariously at the imagined headline.

Finally his card went in and the big gate creaked open.

"Ouch, ouch," he complained, as he pranced barefooted on the driveway stones, searching for the front door key."

He took a blanket from the back seat and, to her surprise, picked her up to carry her across the offending stones. "Don't hurt your leg," she cautioned, laughing at the same time.

"Tonight me Tarzan," he laughed.

"Yes, I see. You're dressed like Tarzan of Pebble Beach."

To Mark's annoyance, thoughts of Christina kept popping into his mind as he made love with Priscilla. Was he to be forever plagued by memories of Christina? He thought of how daring she had been that night at the Movelli mansion. He remembered the time at the Durant Hotel and then how she had so desperately wanted him in Paris. The last thing in the world he intended was to compare Priscilla to Christina, but despite himself, the thoughts kept invading his mind.

He could tell that Priscilla wanted to please him, but she did not seem emotionally present. She was like an actress trying to give a good performance. She was so different from Christina, and even from other women he had known. It was as if part of her did not really want to be in bed with him.

"I wish they'd left some vodka here," she whispered when they had finished. "I was still nervous."

They were lying on the car blanket he had hastily spread on the carpet of his unfurnished living room.

"I was a little nervous, too. After all it was our first time. I guess we were both still virgins," he wisecracked.

"That must have been it," she chuckled.

Soon they began to shiver. Priscilla tried to cover them both with the blanket, but they were still cold.

"This place is like a barn in winter," he said. "Let's go back before we freeze to death. I want to be in bed with you all night."

"Are you going to hang up that 'Do Not Disturb' sign?"

"Yes, as soon as I pour you that vodka."

When they got back to Henry's house, Mark began making drinks while Priscilla went for their robes. When she returned, they huddled by the fireplace. She quickly downed her vodka as he sipped his Scotch. She poured herself another, without adding more ice, and sat on the floor by his knees, looking at him.

"I'm sorry, Mark. It's all happened too fast, I guess. I'll be all right in a minute."

When they had sex again, Priscilla was much more relaxed, even though they were in Henry's bedroom. This time Mark did not once think of Christina.

"You know what, Mark dear? I think the vodka helped. I didn't think of Bob and Lorraine once. I couldn't care less if they know about us."

"And what about your father?"

She laughed. "I don't care if he knows either."

He wondered if she were telling the truth, or if it were the vodka.

He looked at his watch when he woke up the next morning. It was just after six, but Priscilla was not next to him. He sat up on the edge of the bed, reaching for his trousers, when she returned with a tray of toast and coffee.

"Good morning, darling," she said cheerily.

"Did Bob and Lorraine make the coffee for you?" he joked.

"Oh, stop. If you'll forget about them, I will."

"Okay, I'll try."

"Actually, I really meant it, when I said I didn't care what they or Father thought. If Father had walked in on us, I might have just said, 'Why, hello there, Father. How are things at the office?'"

"I can't believe that."

"No, really. I'm glad we made love right here in his bedroom."

"I am, too." He reached for her hand as she put the tray on the foot of the bed.

"For the first time since Mother died, I felt free."

They sipped their coffee, sitting on the bed.

"You look very beautiful today," he said.

"I cheated. I combed my hair before I went to the kitchen."

"But I want you to do something for me," he said.

"Yes?" she asked provocatively.

"I want you to take off your robe while we have our coffee. It's always been so dark, I haven't had a good look at you. Besides, it's not fair for me to be the only one sitting here stark-naked."

She gaily tossed her robe aside and stood naked, her legs tightly together and arms raised, like a Las Vegas showgirl. "There you are! And what's the verdict? Do you approve?"

Priscilla had a much more beautiful body than he would have imagined. "You are one gorgeous lady. If I'd known what was under those clothes, it wouldn't have taken me so long to seduce you."

Naked, they sat cross-legged opposite one another on the large bed while they finished their toast and coffee. They did not say a word, but simply grinned continuously, looking at each other's bodies.

"Do you remember what I said when I first met you that December?" he asked.

"Every word."

"No, really. I asked you if you had a nickname."

"I do remember that. I always wished I had a nickname."

"Well I have finally thought of one for you."

"You have."

"Yes. It's Pris. I want to call you Pris."

-25-

Mark settled back in his seat as the New York bound 747 lumbered toward its cruising altitude. He was deep in thought about the events of the four months that had passed since the Pebble Beach weekend. Pris had told him about Henry's confronting her when he heard gossip about their romance.

"I forbid you to see Mark Stevens! Do you understand me? You have your pick of any man in San Francisco. Why in God's name are you seeing him?" Henry had shouted.

"Father, I will see any man I choose. I'm a grown woman now."

"Of all the men in San Francisco. You know how I feel about him. If you have any respect whatsoever for me, you will stop this sordid affair at once."

"Father, I'm going to do what I should have done a long time ago. I'm moving out."

"Move out? But where will you go?"

"I'll get an apartment of my own."

"What will you do for money?"

"I'll get a job. Will that be so awful?"

"But you aren't fit to earn any money on your own."

"We'll see about that!" she had shouted. "The money from Grandfather's trust comes in at year's end. I think I'll just start that art gallery I've been dreaming about."

"A pipe dream! You—an art gallery—of all things!"

To her credit, Pris had followed Mark's advice and rented a modest one bedroom apartment across Powell Street from Nob Hill's Stanford Court Hotel. A short time later, with Mark's encouragement, she had rented a storefront two blocks down Powell. Last month she had proudly opened her own art gallery, "The Enfield Galleries."

Tonight the first class seat next to Mark was vacant. He spread out his work papers for tomorrow's meeting at Silverton, Budd, the New York investment house. This was his fourth trip to see

Nat Silverton. Last October 24, the Deutsche mark had been re-valued and Mark had made another killing, this time in excess of $5,000,000. In all, 1969 had been a phenomenal year for The Stevens Group. Mark had been exploring with Silverton, Budd the possibility of taking his new company public. At the last meeting in New York, the decision had been made. He would go public with Silverton, Budd as lead underwriter. Tomorrow they planned to discuss the price of the stock and the problems involved in Mark's retaining control.

His thoughts returned to Pris as the stewardess brought him a Rob Roy. He could not honestly say he loved Pris, but the truth was he had been thinking about asking her to marry him if this deal with Silverton, Budd went through. He could be worth $100,000,000, perhaps more. One hundred million dollars! That would be incredible. With a fortune of that size and a woman like Pris Enfield for his wife, he would be the king of the hill.

Pris was the epitome of what a man in his position would want in a wife. Mark had never felt as accepted by San Francisco society, as when he was with Pris. She knew everyone who was anyone in San Francisco. She was one of the inner circle. Money alone would never put him in that group, but with Pris as his wife they would be the movers and shakers of San Francisco. He could see this happening already, and they were merely dating. At the opera, at benefits and at parties, Pris opened doors for him that would otherwise be closed to the new rich. Then too, he was not unmindful of what being married to Priscilla Enfield would do for him in business. Nor was he unmindful of the sweet revenge that would be his if Henry Enfield's daughter became his wife.

No, he did not love Pris yet, at least not in the same way he had once loved Christina. Certainly there was not the sexual passion he had known with Christina. Pris wanted to be a good sex partner, but she was simply unable to let go, to really participate. Quite the opposite of Christina, Pris never had orgasms. She did not seem even to expect them. Once he had suggested oral sex, but, although she had gone through with it, she seemed nearly repulsed by the idea. He had never approached her again. He had decided that the sex was not that important. After all, Pris was nearly always willing, and if Christina had proved anything to him, it was that love based on sex was disastrous. He would learn to love Pris.

He wanted a big house. One that would dwarf Antonio's. He even had bought a five acre homesite in prestigious Hillsborough. He wanted an attractive wife. Pris was certainly attractive. He wanted to be prominent, to be respected, even envied. He wanted

San Francisco's inner circle to eagerly await invitations to grand parties at his mansion. With Pris, that would happen.

Mark also wanted children—children whom he could love as his father had never loved him. Pris could give him children. It was true she had some sort of problem with sex, but who didn't have some problem or another? Perhaps with marriage and time she would change; and, if not, it was not that important.

"Mr. Stevens, would you like to move your papers, so that I can serve you?" Mark looked up. It was Vicki, the brunette stewardess who had introduced herself earlier.

"Sure, I've done enough work for one day." He put his papers in the empty seat, making room for the tablecloth. "Tell me Vicki, are you based in San Francisco or New York?" Mark had noticed that she was attractive.

"Actually, I live in Redondo Beach," Mr. Stevens. Vicki did not mind showing off her well-endowed body, as she fussed over him excessively. Earlier it had occurred to him to ask her out, but he had thought better of it in view of Pris.

After dinner, the lights were turned down for the movie. "We have a variety of cheeses, grapes and this wonderful German chocolate cake," said Vicki.

"I'll indulge myself with the cake; thanks, Vicki."

"Do you live in New York?" she asked.

"No, I'm from San Francisco. I'll probably stay in New York only one night."

"Me, too. It's back to San Francisco tomorrow."

"Maybe I'll see you again on one of these flights," he suggested. "I go to New York often."

"That would be nice."

When Vicki cleared the dishes, he took out his yellow pad. He reveled in financial figures. He loved to let his mind wander while he made notes, tracking his thinking. So often, while sitting in a meeting or talking on the telephone, he would find himself jotting down figures about something else altogether. How much he owed the bank—the price of the dollar in pounds or of marks in dollars—his profit on an anticipated deal. He wondered how long Nixon would stick to Bretton Woods. It couldn't be forever and there was plenty of money to be made if Bretton Woods were finally abandoned. In the dim light, the passengers laughed about something funny that happened in the movie. He looked at his watch. It was nine o'clock San Francisco time. He'd be in New York in three hours.

"Would you like more coffee, Mr. Stevens?" asked Vicki.

"No, I've had enough." She took his dishes and tablecloth. He noticed again how very attractive Vicki was.

In an hour Mark put away his papers and flipped off his light. He knew he was too excited about the stock deal to sleep, but he closed his eyes and tilted the seat back, thinking about the deal.

The next he knew, Vicki was sitting next to him. They chatted until they were nearing New York. Vicki had been a stewardess since she had graduated from Redondo Beach High School. She shared her apartment with two other young women, and had her own sailboat.

"Well, I've got to get back to my duties," she said. "It's been nice talking to you."

"Vicki," he said impulsively. "Would you like to come to my hotel for a drink?"

It was seven-thirty the next morning in Mark's hotel suite. Vicki quickly kissed him on the cheek and climbed out of bed. "I'd better go. You've got to get ready for your meeting," she said as she dressed.

"Wait, I'll order some breakfast."

"No, thanks, Mark. I don't eat breakfast."

"I'm glad I was on your flight."

"Me, too. It was a stroke of good fortune."

Mark had wrapped himself in the thick hotel robe. He watched her as she put on her heels. What a lovely creature, he thought. Her body was every bit as sensual in her short-skirted uniform as it was when they made love.

He walked with her through the living room. As she reached the door, she turned and kissed him again on the cheek. "I don't do this all the time. It was very special for me."

"Me, too, Vicki. The limo driver will drop you off wherever you want," he said.

"You have my number in Redondo Beach."

"If a man answers hang up?" he joked.

"Right," she laughed delightfully, and was out the door.

Mark felt ill at ease as he shaved and dressed. Vicki's unique fragrance was still in the air. The memory of how uninhibited she had been stuck in his mind as he tried to shift his thinking to the meeting. He went to the window and looked down to see if by any chance he could get a last look at her. Vicki had the same reckless abandon as Christina. He had almost forgotten what it was like. As he was leaving the suite, he saw that Vicki had dropped an earring. He scooped it up and dropped into his pocket. The earring had a delightful feminine quality about it.

.   .   .

The hotel doorman hailed a free-lance limousine and gave Silverton, Budd's Wall Street address to the driver. As the long black limo worked its way down Fifth Avenue, Mark remembered his first trip across Manhattan on his way to the *Ile de France* in 1963. He wondered what would have happened if Mavis hadn't suggested he see Henry. He realized he would probably be a partner in a New York firm by now and would never have considered starting his own company. Now he was *hiring* a New York investment banking firm. If this deal went through, he should consider buying a co-op here in New York. Perhaps he would look at some likely neighborhoods before going home. Everybody seemed to think the upper East Side was the place to be, but he would like to look around. The U.N. area was interesting, and hadn't John Lennon bought up on Central Park West? The driver pointed out the Flatiron building and some other points of interest and let him out in front of the Silverton, Budd building on Wall Street. He took out Vicki's earring and felt it in his hand.

Nat Silverton was a sixtyish, short, Jewish man, who smoked a fat cigar and had a pot belly. He looked for all the world as if he were the stereotypical Hollywood movie producer. He was the senior partner in Silverton, Budd, and looked totally out of place in the Brooks Brothers, button-down world of investment banking. Mark and he had co-underwritten several stock issues. Silverton had earned Mark's respect as a shrewd judge of what stocks, and at what price, investors would buy. Mark met Silverton alone in his corner office before the meeting with the others. Although they were on the 40th floor, Silverton had a fireplace in his office, with a view of the harbor and the Statue of Liberty.

"You know Nat, when I sailed out of that harbor for Oxford seven years ago, I thought I'd end up in New York. That's where all the action was then."

"It still is, but you're a major exception. What you've done in San Francisco has been sensational."

"Thank you, Nat, but the question is, do you still think investors will buy the stock?"

"Oh, yes, I do. Especially if we price it right. What have your earnings come in at for the last half?"

"Between eleven and twelve million before my salary."

"Absolutely spectacular! I've never seen anything like it in such a short time."

"I've been very fortunate."

"Okay, then. I think the whole company should bring at least $200,000,000 minimum." Silverman punched his calculator. "If we got 20 times earnings, the value of the whole company could be $400,000,000. Of course $400,000,000 would be unrealistic, but it would set an upper limit. I'd say $200,000,000 is the right number.

"I've been thinking. Given say a $200,000,000 valuation, and my keeping 51%, I'd have $100,000,000 in cash for myself."

"That would be true, but if you keep 51%, you're going to have trouble getting the $15 a share price. People don't like buying minority interests."

"I don't like giving up control. I don't like it at all. It's my company and I don't like the idea of someone telling me what to do."

"Dammit, Mark, how are you going to get a decent price if investors know you can tell them to go fuck themselves? I think you've got to sell about 75% of the stock." Silverton's cigar had burned out and he reached for another.

"But, Nat, when Ford Motor Company went public, the family kept control."

"But that was different. Everyone had wanted to buy Ford for years."

"I don't know, Nat. My company is my whole life."

"Look, Mark, with 25% you'll be able to get enough other votes to keep control, unless you've been an absolute asshole. We're talking about one hell of a lot of money here."

"I suppose I could always take my money and do whatever I wanted."

"Now you're talking!"

Waiting in the conference room was William Crosslander, another partner in Silverton, Budd; and Joseph Backman, a well known securities lawyer and partner in a big Wall Street law firm. Mark was astonished at the conversation that ensued.

"I think the price should be 20 times earnings. That would be $400,000,000 for all the stock," said Crosslander. "That way, if Mark keeps 25% back, and I agree he should, he would have $300,000,000 worth of stock to sell in the market. That would be $30 per share."

"That's pretty ambitious, Bill," said Silverton. I told Mark I thought the price should be 10 times earnings. That's $200,000,000, with the market paying $150,000,000 for Mark's shares, and him keeping 25%."

"I'll tell you what," said Crosslander. "We could start out with an issue price of $30 and shift lower if the price goes soft."

Silverton addressed Mark, "That way you'd have a shot at the 300 mill."

"But I think the offering would have to specify that Mark would have to market at least, say, 60%, because of the control issue," said Backman, the lawyer.

"Then we try for $30?" asked Mark.

"That's what I say," said Crosslander.

"Thirty dollars a share it is," said Silverton.

Mark was amazed. If the plan worked, they had decided as with a snap of their fingers that Mark would realize about $300,000,000 in cash, before underwriters' profits and expenses, when he would have been willing to settle for a third of that.

"A major point, however Mr. Stevens," said Backman, "is your new employment contract with the corporation."

"What about it?" asked Mark.

"Its length. I don't see any problem with the million a year you've been taking as salary or even the bonuses, but the contract has got to have a long enough term. I'd say seven years."

"Of course," said Nat Silverman. "You're the kingpin Mark. If it weren't for you, The Stevens Group would be just another investment banking company. If you took a walk, the investors would be up shit's creek."

"What if I lost control?" Mark protested. "For seven years I'd be working in an intolerable situation. I don't like it."

"Everybody knows you built this company because you know monetary exchange," said Crosslander. "The stock isn't worth a damn if you could take a walk."

"Seven years! I don't like it! Could I quit?"

"Well, technically, yes, but they couldn't force you to work against your will. There would have to be a covenant not to compete, if the contract is to mean anything."

"What sort of covenant not to compete?"

"If you did quit, you couldn't go into the investment banking business with a competitor or for yourself," Backman explained.

"What the hell are you talking about? The investment banking business is my whole life."

"Nobody in his right mind will buy stock in The Stevens Group if you could quit. And to make it stick, there has to be a covenant," Backman asserted.

"So you mean, if somebody gets control of the company, I'd have to keep working or get out of the business?"

"Well, technically, yes," said Backman.

"What the hell do you mean *technically?* I am right, aren't I? I'd be stopped from working someplace else, wouldn't I?"

"Well, yes."

"Screw the deal then. Who needs it? Christ, I'm making 20 million this year! That'll buy a lot of houses and cars. Dammit, Nat, I don't like it."

"Come on, Mark," said Nat. "We're talking $300,000,000 at capital gains rates, and you keep $100,000,000 in stock."

"You'd be one of the richest men in the world," said Crosslander.

"Look at it this way. You'd never advise a client to have his entire $400,000,000 portfolio in one stock, would you?" asked Backman. "Well, that's what you'd be doing if you blow this deal. Everything you own would be in one company."

"Mark, you're blowing at a straw man," said Silverton. "Nobody but you is going to get control, with you holding 25% of the stock and having an employment contract."

"Anybody would be nuts to want to take over the company with you having a seven year contract," said Crosslander.

Mark thought about the $300,000,000 in cash. That was one hell of a lot of money! He guessed Nat was right. He was being spooked over nothing.

"Listen, with $200,000,000 or $300,000,000 in the bank, I think you'd manage to play for a few years. Don't you?" asked Silverton.

"I suppose I could."

Mark was eager to share his good fortune with Pris. He had tried twice to telephone her at his Pebble Beach house, where she was meeting with the interior decorator, but she had not answered. He called again from a phone at the club room at Kennedy Airport.

"Pris. They decided to go for it."

"That's wonderful!"

"We go public sometime in the fall."

"Did everything work out the way you wanted?"

"Better than I ever expected."

"That's wonderful!"

"If it works, I could get as much as $250,000,000, maybe more."

"Two hundred and fifty *million* dollars?"

"That's more than Henry ever dreamed of having."

"Amazing! Congratulations! Where are you now?"

"Kennedy."

"Shall I pick you up at the airport?"

"That would be wonderful."

"I've missed you."

"I've missed you too."

"Pris, listen to me."

"Yes, I'm listening."

"If this works out, will you marry me?"

"What did you say?"

"I said 'Will you marry me, if this deal works out?'"

"What do you mean 'if it works out?' Don't you know, I'd marry you if you were a pauper?"

Mark was excited, as he handed his ticket to the stewardess and boarded the plane. He was delighted that Pris had accepted his proposal. This was his day.

He wondered if she really would have married him, if he were a pauper. Anyway, he was going to wait to get married until the deal went through. He could see the look on Henry's face when he found out about the stock issue. The greatest pleasure of all would be in the church, when Henry gave Pris away.

"May I offer you a cocktail before we leave the gate?" asked the stewardess.

"Yes, I'd love a Rob Roy."

He checked his pockets before giving his suit jacket to the stewardess, and found Vicki's earring. He'd have to mail it to her. He had no regrets about Vicki. Their night together had reminded him so vividly of Christina. However, he had gotten where he was today by using his mind and he was not going to let his emotions run his life, as had happened with Christina. He was contented with his decision to marry Pris. Perhaps he had needed the brief affair with Vicki to get something out of his system, but that was all over now.

-26-

Mark had followed Nat Silverton's advice and waited another year before taking The Stevens Group public. Silverton's advice had been sound. The year 1970 had proved to be an excellent one for earnings. Currency trading profits had been modest because there had been no major revaluations, but the other aspects of the business had grown at a phenomenal pace.

To insure continuity of management, Mark had hired an Executive Vice-President, Steve Baumgartner. Mark continued to make the final decisions, but Baumgartner had put in place a staff that not only carried out Mark's decisions, but came up with excellent ideas of its own.

Armed with these developments, Silverton, Budd took The Stevens Group public in April, 1971. Investors had oversubscribed the stock at $30 per share and, after all expenses, Mark had received over $250,000,000 for 75% of his stock.

Mark had commenced construction on his dream house in the affluent suburb of Hillsborough. He and Pris set a June date for their wedding in San Francisco's Grace Cathedral. Pris had told him that Henry was enraged, and vowed that he would not attend the wedding. For the first time Mark began reading the society pages. The idea of rich, young Mark Stevens marrying the socially prominent Priscilla Enfield had San Francisco in a state of excitement. San Francisco had not known a social event like this in years. Henry's attitude had only added spice to the anticipated festivities. Mark did not know whether he preferred the old man to stay away, or that he come to the wedding and face the humiliation.

Mark was in his office when Rodney's telephone call came. They talked frequently, so at first Mark did not anticipate that Rodney was in trouble. However, as they exchanged pleasantries, Mark thought he detected depression in his friend's voice.

"Rodney, if something is wrong, you'd better come out with it."

"You're right. Something is wrong. Very wrong."

"I'm listening. You'd better tell me about it."

"It's business, this joint venture I'm in—the one to renovate the office block."

"I remember."

"Father warned me, but I thought he was just being conservative."

"All right, now. What has happened?"

"It took more money than we had calculated. I thought Billings knew what he was doing."

"Who is Billings?"

"The managing partner. That friend from the Blue Sheep Club. I'm afraid we have already used our entire overdraft commitment."

"They won't extend it?"

"No, and father won't loan any money. I've used up the money he entrusted to me to invest. He says he advised me against it and I've got to learn my lesson."

"Christ, Rodney! You're 30 years old. You don't need him to teach you any lessons."

"That's not the worst of it."

"You'd better tell me."

"We signed a lease with a large tenant for most of the block."

"Yes."

"They're threatening to take me to court—breach of promise, all because the building wasn't finished in time."

"Jesus!"

"What's more, they've filed foreclosure on the block."

"Can . . ."

"They want to own our bloody building."

" . . . they do that?"

"They're trying to get a large court judgment against me as well." Rodney sounded as if he might burst into tears.

"Don't you have any contacts at the bank?"

"It's not a bank. The overdraft is with some venture capital group Billings knew about. I guess they'd give us a larger loan than the banks would."

"How much is the mortgage?"

"Nine hundred fifty thousand pounds. We used what Father advanced and some of the overdraft money to buy the ground lease. We thought the rest would be more than enough to renovate the block. I feel awful. Father won't even speak to me."

"What about Mavis?"

"Father hasn't told her."

"And Rebecca? Does she know?"

"No. I'm so ashamed. I wanted to prove that I was as bright as Father."

"Listen to me. You're every bit as smart as your father. He inherited everything he ever had. All he did was sit on his hands."

"That's what I should have done—not done anything. Father says he may put everything in some trust so I can't get at it. I don't know what to do next." Rodney sounded as if he were in great anguish.

"Do you want me to come over to London?"

"Oh, Mark. Could you? I'd really appreciate that."

"I'll be there Thursday morning. I think we should talk with a solicitor. See if you can get an appointment for Friday."

"You're the only one I can talk to. I don't want to tell Mother or Rebecca, and Father won't talk to me." Rodney's voice was shaking. "I haven't slept since all this happened."

"Listen, you've got to get hold of yourself. There isn't any problem too big to solve. You'd better get that solicitor's appointment."

"I'll ring him right now. And Mark . . ." Rodney's voice had trailed off.

"Yes?"

"Thanks for coming . . ."

As many times as Mark had flown to England, he still marveled at the sight of the verdant green English countryside that came into view as the plane popped through the rain clouds. He was stirred as he peered through the rain-streaked plane window. The lush green of the wet fields and gardens was so very different from the dry hills of California. The overnight flight thrust him into a totally different world. The farm buildings and unique villages could have been from a travel brochure. He loved England. It was as simple as that.

At the airport, Mark found the Daimler limousine that his secretary had ordered waiting. Rodney had wanted to meet him, but Mark had insisted on the limousine. He would be at the Knightsbridge flat in a little over half an hour. Poor Rodney, trying to prove himself to his father, Mark thought as the car turned onto the highway to London. It had always been clear to Mark that, given some experience, Rodney was perfectly capable of handling the Ashley holdings. Apparently in his anxiety to prove himself, Rodney had gotten in over his head.

Mark looked outside the limousine window at the familiar route into the West End from Heathrow. The rain had stopped, at least for a while. They passed Albert Hall, then Harrod's department store; finally they were in Cadogan Square, and arrived at Rodney's flat. Ever since they were married, Rodney and Rebecca had lived in this fashionable part of Knightsbridge, not far from Mavis's Chelsea home. As he tipped the driver and turned to the door of the flat, the warm glow he had felt upon landing in England changed to apprehension about Rodney.

When he rang the doorbell, it was Rebecca who answered.

"Mark, I'm so pleased you're here." Then she did something she had never done before. She surprised Mark with a hug. It was a quick, tentative hug, but a hug nevertheless. She released him before he could hug her in return.

"Rodney told you about the office block, didn't he?" he asked.

But before she could answer, the chauffeur came with the luggage. "Right inside, driver. Please put Mr. Stevens's cases in the lift."

"It's all right driver, I'll take care of it," Mark said. He knew they couldn't talk until the driver left.

"Yes, he finally did tell me. Those awful people!"

Mark pushed the button. "Third floor, isn't it, Rebecca?"

She nodded. "Rodney isn't here yet. He went to a meeting, and I made him promise to see the doctor before he came home."

"Is he all right?"

"No, he's not. He's perfectly awful. At first, he wouldn't tell me why he has been so nervous and upset. I actually imagined he was involved with some woman."

"Not Rodney. He loves you and the baby."

"I know. It was perfectly silly of me. The dear—he's actually been trying to protect me from this bad news. I'm a lot stronger than he thinks."

"That's the way he is. Wanting to spare his family."

"I want to help him, the poor man! He hasn't slept in a fortnight. He thinks he let me down somehow. It's all so ridiculous. We're going to be perfectly all right."

"Of course you are."

"You know what I think it is?"

"No. What?"

"I think it's his pride," she replied. Mark sat on the couch by the fireplace and she sat opposite him. "Would you like a drink?"

"Actually, I would, but I'm afraid it would put me to sleep. I'm really tired."

"That's all right. I told Rodney you'd want your usual bit of sleep. Otherwise I never could have persuaded him to see Dr. Oliver this afternoon. Did you sleep at all on the plane?"

"Not very much."

She fixed a Rob Roy for Mark and poured herself a glass of

wine. Contrary to English taste, she had ice cubes ready for his drink.

"Thanks Rebecca. It's so good to be here." He leaned back and took a sip of his drink. "So you think it's Rodney's pride, do you?"

"Yes, I do. He wanted so desperately to do well with the money his father entrusted to him. I assume you knew about that."

"Yes."

"Now he feels he's a total failure, you see."

"But couldn't he get help from Mavis, or perhaps from your father? I mean surely . . ."

"Of course he could. They'd help in a minute, but he won't ask. He won't even let me tell them about the trouble. I don't know what we're going to do." She held her wine glass nervously in both hands.

"Does he have any plan to save the office building project?"

"He says he's tried everything he knows. Mark, he's even been cross with me and the baby. That isn't like Rodney at all. He's always so happy and so much fun. If he'd only ask my father for help."

"Rebecca, he can't. Don't you see how that could destroy him?"

"I know you're right, but I don't know what to do."

Mark was surprised at the compassion Rebecca had for her husband. Although she was very pleasant and he liked her, he had always thought of her as a rich girl whose most serious problem was which dress to wear to the party.

"Mark, he trusts your judgment. He always talks about you. He thinks perhaps you will see something he's overlooked."

"That's why I'm here. I'm sure there's something I can do."

Rebecca was right about the nap. He had learned that the way to cope with jet lag after the 10 hour flight to London was to have a short nap—no longer than 2 hours. Then he'd have dinner, and after a few hours would be ready for a full night's sleep about midnight. The next day he would be adjusted to European time.

What Rebecca had said about Rodney was true. At dinner Mark had never seen him this way. Rodney picked nervously at his food and looked as if he had not slept in days. To Mark, the dinner conversation had an unrealistic quality. Although his friends were in great distress, they talked only of such things as the weather and Mark's flight from San Francisco. Clearly they did not wish to discuss Rodney's financial problems in the presence of the servants.

Once, when both servants were in the kitchen, Rebecca quickly whispered to Rodney, "What did Dr. Oliver say?" Before he could answer, one of the servants returned to the dining room and the conversation reverted to form.

A minute later, when both servants were again absent, Rodney muttered a reply to her. "He says it's nerves. I'm to get some tablets from the chemist."

At last, the painfully long dinner was completed. "I know you and Rodney want to talk," said Rebecca. "I'll fetch Allison so you can say good night to her."

Rebecca joined Mark and Rodney in the study, carrying the toddler. "Here's Uncle Mark," Rebecca said to her daughter. "Uncle Mark has come all the way from America to see us."

Mark took the child in his lap. "My, what a young lady you are! I'll bet you're the apple of your daddy's eye, aren't you?" Allison looked more like Rebecca than she did Rodney. Mark knew it pleasured his friends to have him dote on their daughter.

"All right, Allison, say good night to Uncle Mark," said Rodney.

The toddler managed some words that Mark took to be "Good night, Uncle Mark," and Rebecca took the child from him.

"I'll put her to bed while you two chat," said Rebecca. "With all that's happened, I'm sure you have a lot to talk about."

"It's perfectly all right if you stay," said Mark.

"No, it's best if it's only you men," she said and left them alone.

Rodney made after-dinner drinks, and lit up his cigar. He seemed calmer now, eager to confide in his friend, perhaps somehow to find a solution to the difficulty that was tormenting him.

"Father and I had this long discussion perhaps a year ago. I wanted to start choosing some of the family investments. After all, Mother totally relies on him, and he is getting on in years."

"How old is he now?"

"Seventy-three. Seventy-four next month."

"He never has really known much about investments himself. So he's always taken the easy way out. He chooses the most conservative advisors in all of London and then does what they tell him."

"If you don't take any risks, you're safe from criticism."

"Anyway he agreed to set aside £250,000. I was to have the complete say."

"Very nice."

"Your man, Smith-Browning, put me in touch with a share advisor and I did quite well."

"Smith-Browning told me something about it."

"Then, through the club, I heard about this office block opportunity."

"Where?"

"In the City—beyond the Bank of England. I think there's
going to be a need for office space as the City expands." Mark
knew London's financial district was called the 'City.'"

"So I asked Father to advance me more capital. Another
£700,000. I wanted to invest £1,000,000 in all."

"And he agreed? I'm surprised."

"Not until after we had a very nasty row."

"About the money?"

"Yes, about the money, but mostly we argued about the office
block. He thought it too risky."

"Right in character, wasn't he?" Mark dourly commented.

"I told him that it was about time we took a few calculated
risks. I told him how well you were doing."

"What did he say to that?"

"For some reason, he doesn't like you very well. Mother's always talking about you, and when I told him you'd left Henry and
were doing very well, he said some . . ."

"Some what?"

"Well, some rather nasty things. You know, I think my father's
jealous of younger people's success. Sometimes I think he doesn't
want me to outdo him."

"Maybe he took lessons from my father. Do you suppose?"

Rodney smiled grimly. "I know Father loves me. It's just that
he wants me to be conservative about money, the way he is."

"So you bought the office building?"

"Yes with the £1,000,000 and part of the overdraft. In actual
fact, we don't own the building itself. It's a ground lease you see."

"I assume it's renewable for that kind of money."

"I don't know. I think it expires in the 1980s sometime. I left
all that up to Billings, as the managing partner."

"Billings didn't negotiate an extension of the ground lease?"

"I don't think so. We have an appointment with Mother's solicitor tomorrow afternoon. I gave all the papers to him."

"I'm astonished. I can't imagine not having a freehold, or at
least a 99 year lease."

"Damnation, Mark! Billings has done projects like this before.
That sort of thing was his responsibility."

"Sounds like he let you down."

"I should have paid more attention to what he was doing."

"I suppose so, but after all, it was his responsibility."

Rodney reiterated what he had said on the telephone. The property was in foreclosure. The lending syndicate refused to grant a delay, and a disgusted Lord Ashley had refused to help his son.

"It's too late to pay off the mortgage. The date has come and gone. There's nothing to stop the syndicate from taking over. What I'm hoping for is to avoid having a large judgment against me. I'm in trouble enough with Father as it is."

"There has to be a way out of this," said Mark as the clock on the mantle neared midnight. "That's why we're seeing the solicitor tomorrow."

"I hope you're right. If Father carries through on his threat to put everything in a trust after he and Mother are gone, all I'll be able to do is sit back and collect on his bloody government bonds."

"He wouldn't do that to you, would he? And what about your mother's money?"

"I don't know. I don't bloody know anything." Rodney crushed the remains of his cigar into the ashtray. "Well, we can't solve all my problems tonight. It's time to go to bed anyway. You must be exhausted."

"Actually I'm not. It's the time change. If you don't mind, I think I'll go for a walk down Kings Road as we used to do."

"I don't mind at all, but I've got to go to bed. I think maybe I'll get some sleep for a change, with your being here."

"I hope so."

Rodney got up and stretched. "It's like old times talking with you this way. Your key is there on the table."

"Thanks—and Rodney?"

"Yes?"

Mark put his hand on Rodney's shoulder. "We'll find a way out of this."

Mark walked the few blocks to Sloane Square and began walking down Kings Road, as they had done after the Beatles concert years ago. A group of young people were coming out of the Tube station. They were laughing and joking as he walked behind them down Kings Road. A woman's shoe shop was still open, with a miniskirted customer trying on a pair of boots. The young people chatting on the street corners and outside the restaurants had a different look now. Some even had spiked hair, and wild designs painted on their faces. Punkers, he thought they were called. As before, the traffic on Kings Road was heavy with young people jammed into cars.

When he was at Oxford, he had wondered at the happiness of the Kings Road people. He had come a long way since then. He was glad he had worked his butt off at Oxford while this crowd had played away their nights. Now that he had his $250,000,000, it was time for him to have some fun of his own. He hadn't told Rodney, but he intended to order himself a Rolls-Royce on this trip. It would look great next to the Aston Martin in the garage of the new Hillsborough house. Most of all, if there were any way that money could get Rodney out of this jam, he wanted to do it.

Mark and Rodney gave their wet umbrellas to the solicitor's receptionist. They were ushered into the small, cluttered office of Adam Hawkes, and sat on the edge of their chairs, hoping to find some way to extricate Rodney from his difficulties.

"I had my clerk look up the court records," said Adam Hawkes. "He tells me the foreclosure is well along."

"Is it too late to stop it?" asked Rodney.

"The time for paying the mortgage has expired, but I can appeal to the court's equity power. Can you raise the money to pay off the loan?"

"I'm afraid that is impossible."

"I'd like to ask a few questions, if I may," said Mark.

"Certainly, Mr. Stevens, I'll do my best to answer." Hawkes and his father had been legal advisors to Mavis and Lord Ashley for many years.

"I don't see how a building could be worth over a million pounds, when the ground lease has only 10 or 15 years left. I mean, the building will belong to the landlord then," asserted Mark

"That's simple enough. You see, the lease must be renewed."

"Must be renewed? You mean the owner of the land can't just take over the building when the lease expires?" asked Mark.

"That's right. The law is clear."

"But how could that be?"

The solicitor laughed." I've seen other Americans puzzled by our law in that regard. Apparently American law is quite different. In London a commercial lease must be renewed by the landlord, even if the document doesn't provide for it."

Mark laughed with him. "They don't go that far, even at home in Berkeley. So the landlord must renew the lease, eh?"

"Yes, at an adjusted rental rate of course, but the increase is normally fairly modest."

"I'm amazed," said Mark.

"Yes, it's a relief to hear that," commented Rodney.

"This equity power of the court to extend the foreclosure time, I assume the borrower would have to show he had the money to pay the mortgage," Mark inquired.

"Of course. Absolutely."

"All right now, what about the economic viability of the project, assuming the mortgage could be rearranged somehow?" asked Mark. "After all, there would be no point in paying off the mortgage unless the project is a good one."

"I'm convinced it's an excellent project," said Rodney.

"I wouldn't venture a guess about that," said Adam Hawkes. "That's not my department."

"If we could still get the tenant, the one that's angry because of the delay, we'd be all right. Look I have my financial scheme here in my case." Rodney rifled through his brief case, and showed Mark a *pro forma* cash flow statement. "That top figure represents the gross income from rents when the block is fully leased. The net after operating expense leaves enough for the mortgage payments, and gives us a return of 4.75 % on our capital."

"Four point seven-five. Isn't that pitifully small, especially given the risk?" Hawkes asked.

"Not when you consider that the restaurant and the shops on the ground floor would have percentage leases, giving us a very nice upside," countered Rodney.

"I assume there would be appreciation," Mark asserted.

"Of course, that's the whole point. If I'm right about the growth in demand in the City, it's a bloody terrific investment for the long run."

"I do know something about that," commented Hawkes. "We've several clients taking office space there."

Rodney looked pleased at Hawkes's expression of confidence. "The way I have it analyzed is: the return is only, perhaps, two points below what father would get on some of his investments, but the long term growth potential is tremendous. Here, let me fetch some more figures I've worked out." Rodney took more papers from his brief case, and handed them to Mark, who studied them carefully.

"Yes," said Mark after finishing with the sheets. "Your chart says if rents go up 3% a year, after five years you'd be earning 20% on your original investment."

"That's right. I'm anticipating a tremendous escalation in rental rates and property values in the City. That's where the big profit will be," said Rodney.

Mark read through both sets of papers a second time. He was very impressed with the way Rodney had analyzed the project. He turned to the solicitor. "Mr. Hawkes, I think Rodney has a well-thought-out concept. I've made a decision."

"What decision?" asked Hawkes.

"I want you to offer to pay off the loan in full, with interest and penalties."

"But I doubt if they'll accept. They've made it clear they want the block."

"Then I want you to go to the court and prove that Rodney has the money in hand to pay off the mortgage. You said the court would call off the foreclosure."

"Well, yes," Hawkes stammered slightly. "There's an old maxim: 'Equity abhors a forfeiture.'"

"But, Mark, how can Mr. Hawkes prove I have the money to pay off the mortgage? I told you father won't loan it to me."

"Can you get rid of Billings's interest in the project?"

"I'm sure I can, but . . ." Rodney was puzzled.

"Then you're looking at your new partner," Mark grinned.

"My new partner?" Rodney was startled.

"Yes, you've convinced me your project will fly. I'd like a piece of the action, if you're willing."

"Willing? Of course I'm willing." Rodney's brow furrowed. "But I don't want you doing this because we're friends."

"Listen Rodney, I know a good business proposition when I see it. Am I in the deal or not?"

"I'm flabbergasted. I didn't know you had that kind of money. Are you sure? Nine hundred fifty-thousand pounds?"

"Do I have it right?" Hawkes asked, astonished. "You intend to advance 950,000 pounds to Mr. Ashley?"

"Yes, you have it right. Plus whatever amount is necessary to finish the renovation in time to save that tenant. I'll have my bank make the transfer any time you say." Mark turned to Rodney. "If that's all right with you?"

"Mark, I don't know how to thank you. I don't know what to say!"

"Just say it's okay."

"I didn't know you had that much money", Rodney repeated.

"I told you, I took my company public."

"Yes, but I didn't realize . . ."

"Come on, old friend," said Mark. "Are we going to be partners?"

"Of course we are." Rodney was smiling broadly.

"Then, come on. Let's not sit around looking at each other. Let's go tell Rebecca."

-27-

That night Rebecca, Rodney and Mark celebrated with dinner at the Quo Vadis restaurant in London's Soho district.

"Here's to our partnership," said Rodney, raising his glass.

"Yes, here's to our partnership," Mark responded.

"Here's to you, Mark," said Rebecca. We both thank you from the bottoms of our hearts."

All three joyously sipped their drinks. "I don't think I ever told you, Rodney, your mother took me to dinner here one night. Remember when they brought those plagiarism charges against me at Oxford?"

"How could I ever forget?"

"Mavis knew how upset I was, so she invited me to dinner to try to help. It's been my favorite restaurant ever since."

"And did she help?" Rebecca asked.

"Oh, yes. After dinner we took a taxi to her church. The one on Piccadilly. I'll never forget it as long as I live."

"It sounds like something Mother would do."

"I don't know what would have happened to me if she hadn't been there."

"Well, I don't know what would have happened to us if you hadn't been there for Rodney today," said Rebecca.

"Listen, I know a good business proposition when I see one. I could see Rodney had done his homework."

"All the same, I've never seen Rodney as happy as he is tonight. It's as if a weight had been lifted from him."

"Hawkes says when we offer to pay off the mortgage it will eliminate the chance of a judgment against me. The worst that could happen is we'll lose the office block," said Rodney.

"Hawkes is filing some papers to make them accept the late payment. I thought he seemed optimistic, didn't you Rodney?"

"Yes, I did."

"Rodney, do you know what I'd like you to do tomorrow?" Mark asked.

"I don't care what it is, I'll do it," Rodney laughed.

"I'd like you to go with me to the car exhibition at Earl's Court."

"I'd love to."

"I've been thinking about buying a Rolls-Royce."

"A Rolls!" exclaimed Rebecca. "That would be marvelous."

"Do you remember when you showed me London the first time?"

"Of course I do. We saw the Beatles."

"You had the taxi take us by Buckingham Palace."

"I remember," said Rodney. "We saw the Queen and Prince Philip in the Rolls."

"Ever since that night I've dreamed of having a Rolls-Royce someday."

"I hope not like the Queen's," laughed Rebecca.

"No, not like the Queen's," Mark laughed. "What do you say Rodney? Will you go to Earl's Court?"

"Here's to my partner's new Rolls," laughed Rodney, raising his glass in another toast.

"By all means. Here's to Mark's Rolls," said Rebecca, joining in the toast. "And here's to my husband's being happy once again."

Joining them, Mark raised his glass. It was going to be fun having money.

That night, after Rebecca had gone to bed, Mark and Rodney chatted over after-dinner drinks in the library of the flat. Their mood was entirely different from last night's, when Rodney's troubles had dominated the conversation.

"I feel like a different man," said Rodney.

"Don't forget, the lawyers have to find some way to stave off the foreclosure before we're completely out of the woods."

"That's true, of course, but I feel as if I've turned an important corner. I have my energy again. I'm fighting back."

"I was impressed with your analysis of the office project. I think the mistake you made was in your choice of partners."

"I'm afraid I was a bit impulsive."

"If this all works out, perhaps we should take a look at some other London projects together. What with the money from going public, I've got to begin looking for investments."

"When you made that offer in Hawkes' office today, I figured you'd done very well for yourself."

"Can you imagine—Mark Stevens, the chap who had to borrow a jacket from you, having more money than he knows what to do with?" Mark laughed. There wasn't anyone else on earth who could understand more than Rodney what Mark's success meant to him.

"I never doubted you'd do it." Rodney got a cigar from the box on the table and carefully lit it. Suddenly, he began laughing.

"What is it?"

"I was thinking about Uncle Henry. I'd love to see his face when you marry Priscilla."

"He says he won't come to the wedding."

"Do you think the old boy will change his mind?" Rodney asked.

"I sure hope not."

"I'll tell you one thing, I've known Priscilla all my life, and you're a fortunate man."

Mark stood, staring at the logs in the fireplace. "Rodney, let me ask you something."

"Yes?"

"Did Pris change a whole lot after her mother died?"

"I didn't notice anything much. She was extraordinarily close to Henry in those years. Why do you ask?"

"Oh, no reason." Mark turned from the fireplace and looked intently at Rodney. "You know, there was a time when I never thought I'd get Christina out of my system, but now I know you're right. I am a fortunate man to have Pris."

"Time to settle down, is it?"

"I often think of that Oxford waitress of yours. What was her name?"

"Madeline. The fact is, I often think of her, too. Especially when I'm randy."

Mark laughed. "Randy" was British for horny. "I don't suppose you ever have any regrets about marrying Rebecca instead of Madeline, do you?"

"Regrets?" Rodney reflected briefly. "Heavens, no. I don't have any regrets. I'm very fortunate that Rebecca loves a fat, not-so-bright fellow like me. Madeline was a long time ago. Like you with Christina, she's out of my system. However, that doesn't keep me from wondering what it would have been like with her."

"Rodney, I'd like to ask you something." Mark swallowed nervously.

"Of course my friend. What is it?"

"I'd like you to be my best man at my wedding."

"You would?"

"You're my best friend."

"I'd be very honored to be your best man. You're my best friend, too."

.   .   .

That night Mark lay in bed, thinking. He was glad he had asked Rodney to be his best man. It would be wonderful to have Rodney there when he took the big step.

Earl's Court was a huge hall where each year the various manufacturers displayed their automobiles. Rodney and Mark looked at the various brightly lighted displays of the latest models. Finally, they came to the Rolls-Royce exhibit.

"I would be pleased to answer any questions you might have about our motor cars." The salesman was a dignified white-haired man of 65, who looked as if had driven his own Rolls into London that morning from his country house.

"My friend, here, is from America. He's been thinking about a Rolls for some time," said Rodney.

"We have here examples of all of our models." The salesman unlocked the car Mark was looking at. "Would you like to sit behind the wheel?" He lowered the red cordon that kept the public from the cars. Mark sat in the magnificent automobile on the driver's side, while Rodney took the passenger's seat.

"It seems strange, having the steering wheel on the right." Mark put his hands on the wheel, and inspected the beautiful polished wood which decorated the dashboard.

"I've never been in a Rolls-Royce before," said Rodney. "It's stunning."

"This is the Silver Shadow," said the salesman.

"Don't you have a limousine?" Mark asked.

"Many of our customers who prefer a chauffeur use the long wheelbase model. It's four inches longer in the rear seat."

"No, I mean a real limousine. Haven't I seen a long limousine model?"

"Yes, sir. That would be our Phantom VI. They are made to special order. We don't have one here. May I show you an illustration?"

Mark looked at the offered brochure. "Is this the one the Queen drives?"

"Oh, no, sir. We build very special cars for the royal family. No one else can have them."

"She drives a Phantom, did you say?"

"Yes, sir. The royal family had been driven in Rolls-Royce Phantoms for many years."

"In 1963, would she have been driving a Phantom?"

"In 1963? Why, yes sir. That would have been her special Phantom V."

"And the one you make now is called the Phantom VI?"

"They're made just outside London. Wellesden, in actual fact."

"I'd like to buy one of your Phantoms VIs. A black one. I'll write out the check now if you like."

"You'd like to buy one? Now? Right now, sir?" The salesman was trying not to show his astonishment. "But, don't you want to see one first, sir? See an actual car?"

"Oh, I saw one once."

"You did, sir?"

"Yes, I noticed one on the street one day. Don't you remember, Rodney?" Mark smiled knowingly at Rodney.

"Oh, yes, I think I do." Rodney grinned in return, enjoying the little joke they were playing on the salesman. "A man and woman were inside."

"You'll have to pardon me, sir," said the salesman. "It's just that I didn't expect anyone to be ready to buy a Phantom so quickly."

"I understand. Tell me how long before it would be ready?" Mark asked.

"That would depend on whether they could commence immediately. However six months' time would be a proper estimate."

Rodney laughed uproariously as their taxi made its way along Old Brompton Road toward his flat. "Did you see his face when you said you'd buy it without even asking the price?"

Mark laughed in return. "The poor man! I think I was the last person he ever expected to buy a Phantom."

"You're so bloody young, and you don't look like one of those oil sheiks."

Mark was reminded of the time in Paddington they had climbed into the taxi, so filled with luggage they couldn't put their legs on the floor. Now, one day soon, he would be picked up in his own Rolls-Royce Phantom.

Three days later Mark had completed the transfer of £1,000,000 to Hawkes's trust account, and signed the papers for the Rolls. Baumgartner had called yesterday, urging Mark to return to San Francisco. The telephone company planned to issue $750,000,000 in convertible debentures. The company's chairman was insisting that Mark give the underwriting his personal attention. Consequently, he had decided he must return to San Francisco, and this morning Rodney was driving him to Heathrow.

"Mark, old friend, I don't know what to say."

"Don't say anything."

"Everything seemed so desperate last week when I called you."

"Look. I have confidence in you." I know your—I should say *our*—project will be successful."

"I don't know how I can thank you."

"You can make our project successful; that's how you can thank me. I know you've got what it takes."

"I wish Father felt that way."

"Don't worry what your father thinks. I want to be there when you tell him that the building is finished and completely rented."

Rodney pulled up next to the curb to drop Mark off at the terminal. "I'll see you at the wedding, but if you want me to come over in the meantime I'll be on the first plane. Besides, I'd love to watch my Rolls-Royce being built."

Mark waived good-bye to Rodney and pushed his luggage cart into the terminal.

Pris was to pick him up at the airport. Their wedding date was getting closer. Next week the invitations would be mailed, and in another month they would be standing in the front of Grace Cathedral. He thought of Rodney's confession that he still often thought about his Oxford waitress. He had lied when he had told Rodney he had forgotten Christina. In fact, he wondered if he would ever forget her. As his marriage day drew nearer, Christina had been on his mind more and more. He had gone over his decision to marry, a thousand times. Maybe that was the way of the world. Maybe, like Rodney and his waitress, he was destined to remember Christina always, to wonder what it would have been like if things had been different.

At the counter, he checked his luggage to San Francisco. He had over an hour to spare, and decided to wait in the V.I.P. lounge. He leafed idly through a magazine. He was sorry he had agreed to return to San Francisco so soon. He was not at all in the mood for a dull securities issue, even if there were a lot of money involved. He tossed the magazine into the empty chair beside him, and went to the bar. He sipped his Rob Roy, and looked at the gold watch he had bought on New Bond Street yesterday. Another 45 minutes to wait. Restlessly, he decided to go for a walk in the main concourse.

"*FLIGHT 901, NON-STOP TO ROME, NOW BOARDING AT GATE 34, CONCOURSE D,*" said the public address system.

Suddenly, he knew what until now had been buried deep within him. *He wanted to go Rome. He had to be on that plane to Rome.*

His mind raced in confusion. What a ridiculous impulse. He couldn't go to Rome, for Christ's sake. He had to be in San Francisco tomorrow for the stupid telephone company underwriting. Besides, his luggage was already on the plane to San Francisco.

He had no idea where Christina was anyway. How could he ever find her in a city as huge as Rome?

But, then and there, he made his decision. *No matter how irrational it was, he was going to get on that flight to Rome.*

-28-

"You've got to get me on that plane to Rome!" Mark commanded the bewildered airline clerk. He didn't know what he would do in Rome. He had no idea how to find Christina, nor what he would do if he found her. But he was overcome with a compulsive urge to go to Rome right now.

"But sir, the flight to Rome departs in two minutes time!"

"Then write that ticket as if your life depended on it." It was out of character for Mark to behave so impulsively. He was badly needed in San Francisco. It would cost millions if the telephone company underwriting were lost. To hell with it! He was going to Rome no matter what!

As the clerk hurriedly finished his ticket, Mark handed her a hundred pound note, along with his credit card and passport. "The hundred pounds is for you."

"That's not necessary, sir."

"It's my apology for shouting at you."

"Why, thank you very much, sir," she said, taking the money, "but where is your luggage?"

"It's headed for San Francisco. I'll have to manage without it."

Mark dashed through the labyrinth of Heathrow corridors, clutching his briefcase. Intent on catching the flight to Rome, he raced around the slow people-moving ramps. He rushed to the gate and handed his ticket to the uniformed man, who was holding the door open for him. "Welcome on board Mr. Stevens. The ticket clerk told us you were on your way."

"Thank you," Mark puffed. "I was afraid I wouldn't make it."

The instant he took his seat, the airplane began backing from the gate. As he buckled his seat belt and caught his breath, his mind unexpectedly flashed back to the blond woman at Oxford's Eagle and Child pub. Whatever it was within him that had made him return so many times to the pub, hoping to catch another glimpse of her, was the same force that was driving him to make this irrational trip to Rome. Perhaps all he wanted before he got married was to see Christina one more time from a distance, or maybe only see where she lived. He would find that out when he got there.

At the Rome airport, Mark bought several daily newspapers at the newsstand near the foreign exchange booth. He remembered that Christina was marrying a man who owned a string of newspapers. He sat on the bench, searching for the mastheads of the newspapers and casting them aside when he failed to recognize the publisher's name. Wasn't his name Otello? Yes. Finally he found the name Otello. There it was. Otello Bagliani, publisher. The newspaper was *La Verita*.

Mark hailed a taxi. He leaned forward to the driver and pointed to the address of the newspaper on the *La Verita* masthead, "*Piazza di Spagna.*" As the little black Fiat lurched forward into the airport traffic, Mark hoped the driver had understood where he wanted to go.

They drove through the countryside to Rome, and in 45 minutes were in a mass of traffic. The taxi driver said something in Italian and pointed to a huge white marble monument they were passing. Mark recognized it, from a picture in the airplane magazine, as the Victor Emanuel monument. Shortly, the taxi came to a stop in front of a prestigious building on a large square. The driver pointed to the name *"La Verita"* carved in the stone above the building's marble pillars. Mark paid the driver, and went up the steps into the vast ornate reception hall of the newspaper.

"I would like to see Mr. Bagliani, please," he said to the pretty, dark-haired receptionist.

She said something in Italian and then said "No English," as she shrugged her shoulders in a gesture of helplessness.

Trying to communicate somehow, Mark spotted a stack of *La Verita* newspapers on the marble counter next to the receptionist. "If I could borrow one of your papers," he said to the uncomprehending young woman, pointing to the newspapers. He opened a copy to the masthead and pointed to Bagliani's name. "Could I speak to Otello Bagliani?," he asked, pointing first to himself and then to the name on the masthead.

The receptionist shrugged, said something to him in Italian, then picked up the telephone. After a short conversation with someone on the line, she handed him the telephone. "May I help you?" said the English-speaking male voice on the other end of the line.

"Yes, I've come from America to see Mr. Bagliani. May I see him?"

"I'm sorry, but he's in *Milano* today."

"May I see him tomorrow? It's very important."

"I'm sorry, but Mr. Bagliani never sees strangers."

"I'm an American businessman. I wanted to interview him," Mark said." Could you find out if he would see me tomorrow?"

"I'll ask him, but his schedule is completely full for several weeks. What is your hotel? I'll telephone you tomorrow."

"Actually, I don't have a hotel yet. Could you recommend one?"

"Certainly. There's a very fine hotel right here on the *Piazza di Spagna*. Americans seem to like it. The *Albergo delle Scale*, 'The Hotel of the Steps.' It's opposite the Spanish steps."

"Thank you; I'll call tomorrow." Mark doubted if he'd ever get a chance to talk to Bagliani; besides it was Christina he so desperately wanted to find. He would have to figure out some other way to find her.

The personnel at the *Albergo delle Scale* hotel spoke good English. Within a short time Mark had a suite in the front of the hotel, overlooking the *La Verita* building. Soon the hotel operator had Baumgartner on the line. "This problem with Rodney is talking longer than I expected," Mark told him.

"But Mark, Andrews says he'll only do business with you."

"You'll have to handle it, Steve. Tell him I'll be home in a couple of days. Steve, I want you to call Priscilla at Pebble Beach right away. You've got to catch her before she leaves for the airport. Tell her I'm sorry, but Rodney needs me." He didn't like lying, but if he were going to marry Pris, he had to do something about this obsession for Christina.

He dialed the hotel's assistant manager and asked him to come up to the suite. "Get me a driver. I need a chauffeur who speaks good English."

"Yes, sir. I know of several."

"I want the best. I'll need him to do some detective work. I need to find an old friend."

"I have just the person for you. He used to be, as you say it, a detective. He was with the *Roma* police."

"Good, have him call me as soon as possible." Mark gave the assistant manager two £100 notes. "I'm sorry for giving you British money, but I don't have much lira."

"Thank you, Mr. Stevens. You are very generous. My friend's name is Mario. Mario Cappucci. He'll be here in less than an hour."

.   .   .

In half an hour, Mario Cappucci was in Mark's hotel suite. A good-looking man of 50, with black hair having no hint of gray, Cappucci was dressed conservatively in a dark, double-breasted suit.

"I don't know how long I'll need you for. Maybe a day, maybe a week. If you get the results I want, I'll pay you $20,000 including expenses. Let's see, in lira that would be . . ."

"I believe that would be over 12,000,000 lira, Mr. Stevens." Mario did not bat an eye at the large sum. "What do you want done?" He spoke English with a heavy accent, but Mark understood him well.

"I'll pay you half tomorrow morning when I can get to a bank, the rest when we're through."

"That would be well. When do I start?"

"Do you know Otello Bagliani?"

"The newspaper man?"

"What do you know about him?"

"He's very wealthy. He's a very prominent person, although not so much in the last five or six years."

"What do you know about his family? His wife?"

"He got a divorce from his first wife a few years back. She went someplace for the divorce. Monaco, I think. There wasn't much about it in the newspapers. He's a very powerful man, and the newspapers wouldn't print much."

"Another woman was involved, no doubt?"

"Oh, certainly. The one he's married to now. The story was, she wouldn't be just his mistress. That meant he had to get a divorce, even if it were against Italian law."

"Can you get me some sort of report about the new Mrs. Bagliani by tomorrow? I've got to find out where she is. I can't tell you how important it is."

"Bagliani probably keeps his address very secret. They all do. Kidnapers, you know. But don't worry. I have sources. You'll have a full report by tomorrow morning."

Mark was having breakfast in his hotel suite the next morning when the telephone rang. It was Mario.

"Yes, Mario. What did you find out?"

"I have a full report for you. My friends with the police were very helpful."

"Wonderful!" Mark reached for the pad and pen. "Go ahead."

"Mrs. Bagliani's name is *Cristina*. Is that the correct person?"

"Yes. That's right." So she had indeed married Otello. Christina had made her "bargain with the devil," as he had angrily called it that day in Paris.

"They live in *Parioli.* That's a wealthy section of *Roma.* I have the address."

"Could you get a phone number?"

"No, not yet. My contact at the telephone company won't be in until later this morning."

"Do you know if she or her husband is at home?"

"No."

"I want you to go out there now. Follow her if she leaves."

"I'll be there in 20 minutes."

"I'll be out of the hotel for a while. I'm going to a bank, and then buy a few clothes. Listen carefully, Mario. I want you to call me even if you haven't found out anything. Do you understand?" He still had no idea what he would do if Mario found Christina, but he had to find her and get on with his life.

When Mark returned to his suite, the telephone was ringing. It was Mario. "I'm at *Il Ristorante Giuseppe.* I followed her." In his excitement, he was not speaking English clearly.

"Slow down, Mario. You've found her?"

"Yes, Mr. Stevens. She was driving very fast, but I was able to stay with her."

"Where are you again?"

"At *Il Ristorante Giuseppe,*" Mario repeated. "You can be here in 10 minutes by taxi."

"I'll be there."

"And Mr. Stevens."

"Yes?"

"She's having lunch with Mr. Bagliani."

Mark paid the taxi driver in front of *Il Ristorante Giuseppe.* Mario was waiting outside in a long, black Mercedes. "They're at the corner table in the main dining room, the far corner" he said. "They drove separately."

"Good job, Mario. Have your car ready when they come out. I may want to follow her."

The maitre d' approached Mark in the reception room. "Do you speak English?" Mark asked.

"A little sir," the maitre d' answered.

"There's a couple at the corner table. Otello Bagliani and his wife. It's important that they not see me. Can you arrange it?" Mark gave the maitre d' a 50,000 lira note.

The maitre d' glanced at the money without seeming to look at the denomination. "Of course, sir. Mr. and Mrs. Bagliani are at their regular table. I have a little table near a post, where you will be safe."

"Good." Head down, Mark followed the maitre d' and sat at the offered table. He peered around the post.

There was Christina!

She was sitting with her profile to Mark. He was at a perfect table to avoid being seen by her. Bagliani sat opposite her in full view of Mark.

My God, Christina was beautiful! Much more beautiful than he remembered. As he looked at her hair, he recalled the sensuous, long, blond locks tumbling across his naked body, as they lay in bed. Christina was talking animatedly with both hands. He had all but forgotten how she talked with her hands.

"Would you like a menu, sir?" asked Mark's waiter in acceptable English as he placed a basket of bread on the table.

"No, no need." Mark realized he was whispering and raised his voice to a normal tone. "I'll have pasta. Whatever you consider your speciality."

"We are very proud of our *Linguine Giuseppe*, sir. And to drink?"

"Mineral water would be fine."

"With or without gas, sir?"

"With, please. Bring it now, before the meal, if you please."

My God, there before his eyes was Christina! So many years had passed, and there she was. Think of all that had happened since that hotel room in Paris. The reality of her being across the room had not sunk in yet.

Christina looked beautiful, as if no time at all had passed. She had lowered her hands to the table, and Bagliani was talking now. For a moment Bagliani looked directly at him. Nervously, Mark looked away, moving out of the line of sight, while keeping his eyes on Christina's profile.

Mark did not know what he had expected from seeing Christina, but he had not expected the impact he now felt. A chill ran up and down his entire body. A rush of emotion ran up the outside of his little fingers and the hair on the back of his neck. The sudden feeling was so intense that a noise from somewhere deep within him nearly escaped his lips. It was some sort of animal noise he had to consciously bottle up, lest it come forth. There was an element of the terrifying. It was a deep-seated yearning that had been struggling to escape and he had been struggling to contain. In that moment, he knew he should not have come to Rome.

If he could have fled the restaurant without risking being seen, he would have done so that instant. He would have been on the first plane to America, and back to his life in America. Instead, he sat at his table, his gaze fixed on Christina, waiting for his meal to come. Waiting for them to finish and leave the restaurant. Waiting for anything that would make these longing feelings go away, so that he could return to some semblance of normalcy. Mark was accustomed to being in charge, but now he felt helpless in the grip of his emotions. He did not like it at all.

At last, Christina got to her feet. Mark pushed himself backward, to be out of her line of sight. He was terrified at the thought of Christina's seeing him. Bagliani got to his feet also as Christina left the room, no doubt to go the ladies' room. The skirt of her outfit was well below the knee, so that with her high boots, it covered all but a glimpse of her legs as she moved down the hall. Knowing the feminine flesh that was concealed under the sensuous black cloth of her skirt brought another rush of emotion, a compulsion to own her, a desire to make whatever it was about Christina a part of him again.

She disappeared down the hall. Here was his chance. He got to his feet and quickly left the restaurant, mumbling apologies and pushing currency into the hand of the maitre d'. There was Mario, standing by his limousine at the corner. Mark ran toward the haven that the car represented. He sat in the back seat, breathing hard and trying to get his bearings. What sort of grip did she have on him? He could never explain what he had felt in the restaurant.

"Where do you want me to go, Mr. Stevens?" asked Mario.

"Stay here at the curb as long as the police will let you. I want to think."

It was five minutes or more before he calmed down. There had to be some explanation for what had happened, besides merely seeing Christina. Certainly she was beautiful and exciting, but after all, she was only a mortal woman. It had been a mistake to follow whatever impulse had made him want to see her. He had thought that an advantage of having money would be that he could act more impulsively—the way he had as a boy. He had been wrong thinking that. He was not going to let whatever happened in that restaurant screw him up. He definitely would be on that plane to America tomorrow.

Mark was about to tell Mario to drive him back to the hotel when he looked out of the car window at the restaurant. The maitre d' held the door open as Christina and Otello came out. Otello stood to his full height as he took her hand. He looked as if he were the proudest man in Italy to have a wife he knew to be the envy of all. Around the corner came a red Ferrari. A uniformed valet got out of the Ferrari and held the door open for Christina. He could see her provocatively pull her long skirt well above her knees as she got into the low-slung sports car, indifferent to the valet, and wave good-bye to her husband.

"Mario, follow her. I want to see where she's going."

"Yes, Mr. Stevens."

Mario was able to keep up with her for several blocks through the heavy traffic, but then Christina accelerated through an intersection just as the light turned red.

"Run the red light!" shouted Mark. "I don't care if you get a ticket! Run the goddammed light!"

Mario obeyed, and plunged into the intersection sounding his horn.

Mario cursed in Italian. A car had entered the intersection and blocked his intended path.

"We've got to catch her. I want to talk to her!" shouted Mark.

Mario tried to back his Mercedes, but could only move a few feet. He was hopelessly caught between two other cars. "I'm sorry, sir. We've lost her. We'll never catch her."

Mark sat slumped into the back of his seat. He was a fool to think Mario could have caught her. He should not have followed her, anyway. She was obviously very happy with her life. There was nothing to say to her. No point.

"Let's go back to the hotel, Mario. I'll get ready to go to the airport. I want to get out of Rome this afternoon. I'm sure I can get on a plane to somewhere that will get me to San Francisco."

"We can put you on Flight 4576 to New York. You can connect to United Flight 301 to San Francisco," said the Alitalia telephone voice.

"Good. Make the reservations. My car is waiting. I'll leave the hotel now."

Mark packed into his new overnight bag the few things he had bought this morning. He went to the window and glanced down at Mario's waiting Mercedes. Across *Piazza de Spanga* he took one last look at the imposing *La Verita* building. The likelihood was that Otello Bagliani had returned to his office after lunch with his wife. Impulsively, Mark turned from the window and reached for the paper on which Mario had written Christina's address and her phone number that he had obtained: 119 *Corso Mediterraneo. Parioli.* 987-123. "The telephone number is Mrs. Bagliani's private line," Mario had said.

Mark knew that if he reflected on it he would not dare telephone Christina, and so, without hesitating, he dialed the number on the pad. He listened as the connection was made and the phone rang. One ring, then a second ring. At the third ring, his resolve weakened. When the fourth ring also went unanswered, he felt relief that Christina was not at home. But as he took the phone from his ear to hang up, someone answered.

"*Pronto*," said the young female voice that was not Christina's. Mark hesitated. Christ, he wished he had hung up before there had been an answer!

"*Pronto*," said the female voice again, in consternation.

"Mrs. Bagliani, please. Christina Bagliani. *Grazie*," he mumbled.

"*Un momento, per favore*," said the voice. He assumed it was the maid and that she was getting Christina.

Mark's hand shook. The logical part of his mind wanted to hang up, but he sat on the edge of the bed waiting, nervously wiping his forehead with his other hand.

"*Pronto*," said another voice. It was Christina's voice.

"Christina?" asked Mark.

"*Sì*," Christina answered inquisitively.

"This is Mark. Mark Stevens."

"Mark! Mark! Is it really you?" she shouted.

"I've been wondering how you've been."

"After all these years, you're wondering how I've been?"

"Yes, all these years I've been wondering about you, and I finally called."

"I've wondered about you, too, but I didn't dare contact you. I knew you'd never forgive me."

Mark hesitated. "So, Christina. Did you ever actually marry him? What was his name?"

"Otello. Yes, I did."

"I'm getting married soon, too," he blurted out.

"Oh, you are?"

"Yes. We haven't set the date yet, but it won't be too long."

"Is that why you're calling me, to tell me you're getting married?"

"Well, yes. I wanted you to know." He knew that was not the real reason he had called, but he wasn't sure himself what it was.

"How did you get this number?"

"I don't know. I just asked my secretary to get it. I told her your husband owned some newspapers."

"Where do you live now?"

"In San Francisco."

"Remember Anna? My maid in Sonoma?"

"Yes, of course I remember Anna."

"We wrote for a while. She told me your father died."

"Yes, I was still at Oxford."

"I know you hated your father, but he had many good qualities."

"Yeah, like he was good in bed", Mark wanted to shout into the phone, but did not. He had not called her to get even. "I suppose so," Mark quietly agreed.

"It's very wonderful of you to call me all the way from California. It must cost an absolute fortune."

Call from California? Good God, Christina thought he was calling from California! What should he say? Should he tell her the truth? Should he tell her that he was in Rome—that he could be with her in half an hour? Should he tell her that if Otello were home she could drive her Ferrari to his hotel, and that they could be in each others arms? Impulsively, he decided not to correct her false assumption. "I don't have to worry about the cost of telephone calls any more, Christina," he said. "I just wanted to see how you are before I got married."

"I had lunch in Rome today. You'll never believe it was actually with my husband."

"Are you happy with him?"

"Oh, yes. Otello gives me everything I could possibly want."

"I don't mean does he give you everything, Christina. I mean, are you really happy with your husband?"

"Well, Otello is too old now to have a mistress," Christina laughed, "so at least he's faithful to me."

"The trouble with that is, it doesn't give you an excuse," Mark teased.

Christina laughed in response. "Tell me about your wife-to-be," she said, changing the subject.

"She's very pretty. The life of San Francisco."

"Do you love her as much as you once loved me?"

"That's not fair. Do you love your husband as much as you loved me?"

"I have you on that one," she laughed. "You've forgotten—Otello knew from the beginning I didn't love him."

She was right. Otello did know she was in Paris with him. Talking to her this way diffused the mysterious energy he had felt when he saw her at the restaurant. It also diffused the old negative aspects of their relationship—the betrayals—the pain of her deception—her rejection of him because he was poor. All were in the dim past and were unimportant now. As they chatted even the passion of their nights together was faded and distant. His reasons for coming to Rome were no longer as compelling.

"Otello must have loved you very much to let you come to me in Paris like that," he said.

"Love? I don't deceive myself Mark. It's the same love he has for his newspapers. The same as for this beautiful Villa or the one at Lake Como. I'm just something that makes him feel good. But I've always known that."

"I could never do that."

"Do what?"

"Marry to have a possession. Just for a woman who was like an ornament."

"Oh, really? I'll bet you could."

"I love Priscilla. She'll make a fantastic wife."

"That's wonderful, Mark." The tone in her voice indicated a weariness of the conversation, or at least that she was weary of talking about Priscilla.

"I'd better say good-bye now, Christina. I'm glad you're happy. I'm really pleased it's worked out for both of us."

"Thank you for calling, Mark. Will you call me again? I can't call you without Otello's finding out."

"Of course, I'll call."

"Mark?"

She hesitated before continuing.

"I loved you," she said.

Mark did not answer her.

"I loved you very much," she said. Then she hung up.

Mark would have been all right, if she hadn't made that last statement. Their conversation had been stilted and banal until then. He would have gone to the airport, gotten on his Alitalia flight, been satisfied that Christina properly belonged in his past, and returned to his life in America. The trip to Rome would have been an aberration. But as Mario drove the Mercedes toward the airport, Mark could not get Christina out of his mind. He knew they were not for one another, but his heart rebelled against his mind. He wished he had told her he was rich. Probably richer than Otello. He wished he had told her he still loved her, though he loved Pris and was still resolved to marry her. He wished they could make love once again, without its being clouded by the specter of betrayal and anger, as it had their last time together. He got the beginning of an erection, just thinking about Christina. He would never have the same pure sexual excitement with Pris or with any other woman on the face of the earth.

"Mario."

"Yes, Mr. Stevens?"

"Turn the car around."

"Turn around, sir? But the airport! Your plane!"

"I want you to go the Bagliani Villa!"

"But sir, Parioli is on the other side of Rome. You'll miss your plane."

"Do it! Just do as I say, dammit, Mario! I want to see Mrs. Bagliani."

Mario did an excellent job of avoiding the city congestion. Soon they were in the exclusive section of Rome called Parioli. It was possible that Christina had left, and of course she might not want to see him at all, but he didn't care. He could not go home without trying.

Mario stopped outside the imposing gate bearing the number 112.

"It's all right Mario. See if they'll let us in."

Mario pushed the buzzer at the gate. Mark heard him say something in Italian, and the gate slowly opened. Mario turned to Mark in the back seat. "I told the stupid maid I was a new driver for Mr. Bagliani. I could be a kidnaper." Mario guided the Mercedes up the long driveway to the front of the house. Mark could see Christina's Ferrari parked in the courtyard.

"Mario. Somehow you've got to get the maid to have Christina come to the car."

"Don't worry, Mr. Stevens. I'm sure I can manage it." Mark sat deep in the back seat while Mario rang the bell of the huge Mediterranean-style residence. He could see a uniformed maid open the door and talk animatedly with Mario. Mario gestured and stepped inside the house. Mark waited impatiently as the minutes slowly passed. He did not know what he would say to Christina if she came to the car, but he wanted to see her once more, if only to touch her hand.

Mario stood inside the entry hall while the maid disappeared up the stairway. In a few moments Christina appeared at the top of the stairway. "I'm Cristina Bagliani. What is it you want?" she asked Mario in Italian.

"I'm the chauffeur for an American gentleman. He wants to see you."

"There is no one from America whom I want to see. Tell him to go away."

"But he has come all the way from California just to see you."

"It must be Antonio. He tried this a few years ago. I don't want to see him. It's Antonio Movelli, isn't it?"

"No, it's not Antonio Movelli," Mario answered. "The gentleman's name is Mark Stevens.

With those words, Christina suddenly grabbed the railing and shouted at Mario. "Mark? What craziness is this? Mark couldn't possibly be here! He's in California."

"Mrs. Bagliani, I'm only a chauffeur. All I know is that for the past two days I've been driving for an American who says his name is Mark Stevens. We were going to the airport when he ordered me to come here. He wants to see you. He's in the car right now."

"In the car now? Mark is in the car now? How could that be? I just talked to him on the telephone in the United States." Christina raced down the stairs, brushed Mario aside and ran to the open car door. "Mark, is it you?" she shouted in English. "How could you be here?"

"I had to see you once more, but I knew I shouldn't."

She stood breathless outside the car. "Mark, dear, I don't know what to say! I've wanted to see you every day of my life, since we were in Paris."

"And I've wanted to see you!"

Mark reached out and took Christina's hand, gently pulling her into the car. Mario and the maid appeared at the door. The maid shrugged her shoulders and closed the door, as Mario discreetly closed the car door and walked away.

"Mark, why did you play such a trick on me?" she said, sitting in the plush back seat of the Mercedes and putting her arms around him.

"I thought it was best if I never saw you again."

"But you had to see Christina again, didn't you?"

She kissed him passionately. He responded, holding her tightly. "We are impossible for one another," he said. "I guess we always have been, but I had to see you again before I got married. I didn't want to, but I had to."

Mark drew her to himself and put his hands under her sweater. Christina pulled up her skirt and impatiently yanked at her undergarments.

Over the years, when he had fantasized about making love with Christina, he had often recreated their first night in Antonio's bedroom. Sometimes, he would think of their last time together, the time he had taken out his anger on her with his love-making. But this afternoon was like none other. Never before had they reached this level of passion. It was not only the erotic desire that they had temporarily satiated so many times before, it was deeper. The erotic was present, as with lovers seeing each other after years of absence in the war, but there was more. There was a deep knowing that they would have only a short time together. An understanding that they were committed to others, and that their passion for each other would have only this brief time. They knew they could never again have an experience such as this. For the moment, Mark was able to satisfy the longing, the desire to own her and be one with her, that he had felt at the restaurant. It did not matter that their time together would be brief.

When they made love the first time, Mark could not wait for her, but Christina did not need him erect to have her climax. In a short time, they made love again, and this time he was able to be more considerate.

When they were finished, they sat back in the seat, rearranging their clothes. As he watched her combing her long blond hair with his pocket comb, he could not believe that he had made love to the seemingly happy woman he had seen at the restaurant a few hours ago. It was as if he finally had made love to the mysterious blonde in the Oxford restaurant.

Christina handed back his comb and finished straightening her clothes. Mark felt he should say something, but perhaps their bodies had spoken better than any words.

"I don't know what to say," he finally said. "We can't just say good-bye as if nothing had happened."

"The same old Mark, aren't you?"

"What do you mean?"

"My dear one." She looked at his face and ran her fingers through his white hair. "You always thought that because we loved one another, we should be married. Remember?"

She was right. They'd had this discussion before.

"We had today," she continued. "Tomorrow will take care of itself. You'll soon have your wife and I'll still be married to Otello."

"I still don't see how you can be so blase about such things."

"That last time in Paris—when you looked back at me in the window of the hotel . . ."

"Yes?"

"I ran after you."

"You did?"

"I would've married you even though you had no money."

"You would have?"

"At least in that moment I would have." She turned and looked into his eyes. "It was fate that I couldn't find you on the street. You can only bend fate a little bit, like we did this afternoon. In the end, fate is the master of us all."

"You know, I have money now. A very great deal of money."

"I know. You wouldn't have come here, if it were otherwise."

"I suppose you're right."

"Can you accept our fate, my dear Mark?"

"I really don't believe in fate, Christina."

"I do. We'll each be very happy. I'll be with my husband and you'll be with your new wife."

Mark knew she was right. He would be happy with Pris now. Being with Christina this last time had been everything he could possibly have imagined, but now the compulsion that brought him to Rome had ended. It did not really matter that Pris was not the spectacular beauty that Christina was. Nor did it matter that Pris did not have the same lust for love-making as Christina.

"Would you like me to come inside and talk?" said Mark.

"No, Mark. Otello might come home any moment."

"Would you like to ride with me to the airport?"

"No, there is no more that we can do. I shall never forget that you came to see me and that we made love one last time and that you are being polite to me now, but there is nothing more to be said, is there?" She opened the car door and got out.

"No, Christina, there isn't. I guess I'll always be sentimental about you."

Mario approached the car.

"Sentimental? The truth is, Mark, I shall always love you. I'll love you until I die."

Mark had never understood how Christina could admit her love and yet walk away from it. As for himself, he could already feel his feelings for her retreating into himself. He hoped that was where they would stay, because, unlike Christina, he doubted if he could love someone and be married to another. From now on, he had to concentrate only on his love for Pris.

Mark rolled down the window as Mario began to drive away. "Good-bye, Christina. I don't know what else to say."

"*Arrivederci*, Mark. *Arrivederci.*"

As the Mercedes rolled down the driveway, Mark turned and looked back. Christina was already inside the mansion.

Part Five

-29-

The wedding of Priscilla Enfield and Mark Stevens had been the sensation of San Francisco's social season. Nob Hill's Grace Cathedral was completely filled that Saturday afternoon in June. Pris wanted the press excluded, but despite their efforts it was obvious from the next day's newspapers that reporters had been in the church. Photographers had swarmed around the happy couple and the guests, as Mark and Pris ran under a hail of rice to the reception at the Pacific Union Club, half a block away.

Pris was radiantly beautiful in the white lace wedding gown that had belonged to her mother. At the end of the ceremony, Mark had lifted her veil. Before the traditional kiss, he had framed her face in his hands, drinking in her exquisite skin and long, red hair. "I love you Pris," he had said, and meant it.

Mavis had accompanied Rebecca and Rodney to San Francisco for the wedding, with Mavis staying with Henry in Pacific Heights, and the younger Enfields staying with Mark. Rolf Williams had driven Amanda to the wedding. The day before, Henry had changed his mind and told Pris he would attend the wedding. He gave Pris away at the altar and attended the reception. Although he was pleasant, even charming, to Amanda and the others, he never once looked at Mark.

The Hillsborough mansion was completed, but Pris and Mark had decided not to move in until after their honeymoon. They had walked from the Pacific Union club to Mark's Nob Hill condominium, with the crowd again tossing rice and wishing them well. The next day they had left for their honeymoon in Hawaii.

They had been in their new house less than a week when Mark telephoned Rolf Williams. Newly divorced, Rolf had quit the prestigious San Francisco law firm, and had returned to Sonoma and opened a modest law office.

"I'm giving a speech at the Bohemian Club's Grove tomorrow," he told Rolf. "How about if I swing by Sonoma on the way? I want to check on my mother, and I thought we could have lunch."

It was noon and raining very hard in Sonoma. Rolf Williams stood looking for Mark as the rain pounded on the sidewalk in front of the storefront that had "Rolf Williams—Lawyer" painted on the window. Rolf looked across the grassy town square at a man and a woman dashing through the sudden downpour toward the Chamber of Commerce office. It had been too long since Rolf and Mark had had one of their long talks.

"Freakish weather," Rolf told his secretary. "Imagine a storm like this in summer,"

"I've never seen anything like it. The radio says the storm's hanging off the coast," she answered.

"Just look at it come down!"

They stood together looking through the window at the pelting rain.

"How long have you known Mr. Stevens?"

"Oh, we go way back. We went to high school and Cal together. He was raised a few miles up the road, on the Movelli Vineyard. Almost to Jack London Park." Rolf pointed northward. "We've been friends all these years."

Mark pulled his Aston Martin into the parking space in front of the office. Rolf opened his umbrella and dashed to the car, trying to protect them both from the rain.

"Thanks, Rolf," Mark laughed, huddling under the umbrella with his friend. "Where are we going for lunch?"

The umbrella was not large enough for both of them and they were getting wet.

"Sally's, of course," Rolf said. Trying to stay under the umbrella, they rushed across the square.

"It's not big enough. There's no use both of us getting soaked," Mark shouted. "I'm going to make a run for it." He raced across the grassy square toward Sally's restaurant, outdistancing Rolf.

When Rolf caught up with him inside Sally's, both were soaked. Sally, a large jovial woman in her 60s, handed them some towels. "You boys dry yourselves," said Sally. Rolf and Mark had habitually stopped by Sally's after they had double-dated at the movies, when they were in Sonoma High School. To Sally, they would always be boys. The two laughed at their predicament, as they wiped their faces and patted their clothes.

"What will you boys have?" Sally asked when they settled into a booth. Mark ran a comb through his soaking hair. They laughed as the water flew off his hair as it would from a dog after a bath.

"A hamburger and a coffee," Mark told Sally.

"I'll have the same."

"With everything?" asked Sally.

"With everything," both answered simultaneously.

"This is like it was in high school," said Mark. "I haven't had this much fun in years."

"Me, neither," said Rolf. "We should run through the rain like this every day. We'd live to be a hundred."

Mark was more relaxed than he had been in a long time. He had forgotten how carefree they had been in high school

"Tomorrow I'm going to speak at The Grove at the Bohemian Club."

As Rolf knew, the Bohemian Club was the most prestigious businessman's club in San Francisco. It maintained a campground in the midst of a giant grove of redwood trees along the Russian River, a few miles northwest of the Sonoma Valley. Many prominent visitors were invited by members to attend The Grove. Private jets flew into the Santa Rosa airport from all over. Governors, senators, industry leaders, even cabinet members converged on the prestigious annual event.

"Speak? I didn't know they had speeches at The Grove. I've heard they have plays and entertainment, but not speeches."

"Yes. Some of the speeches sound a little dull. I'm told a lot of guys don't show up to listen, but it's quite an honor to be asked."

"I see you on television all the time," said Rolf. "You're very effective." Mark was a frequent guest on the news. He was in the stable of prominent businessmen questioned by television reporters when business stories broke.

"You do one decent interview and you get to be a regular."

"And it all started with that KQED program a couple of years ago, didn't it?"

"That was the day I quit Enfield & Co. I almost canceled the show."

"You're always saying that Bretton Woods should be dropped. Do you think it'll ever happen?"

"We're headed for real trouble, if we don't. You mark my words, Rolf, there's going to be a run on Fort Knox if Nixon doesn't do something and do it soon."

"Is your speech going to be about that?"

"Some of it." Mark wiped his wet hair with a paper napkin. "You know what I realized last night, when I was working on my talk?"

"No, what?"

"When it comes down to it, I'll be making damned near the very same points I made in my Oxford essay. You know the one they almost kicked me out of Oxford over?"

"Yes, I remember your telling me." Rolf sipped his coffee. "Mark, I'm damned proud of you. Imagine one of us speaking to the Bohemian Club."

"It's a long way from Sonoma High School, isn't it?"

"One hell of a long way!"

"Boy, Sally's hamburgers are as good as ever," Mark said as he munched on his lunch.

"Yes," Rolf agreed. "By the way, I had a nice talk with your mother when we were driving to the wedding. She's very proud of you, you know."

"I appreciate your taking her."

"I got a kick out of her at the wedding. You'd have thought you were marrying Princess Anne."

Mark laughed. "I swear Mom thinks Pris is heir to the throne, at least if San Francisco had a throne."

"I see she still lives in your old house."

"I'd buy her a house of her own, but she won't hear of it. When Antonio's housekeeper retired, he practically begged Mom to take over. She's as happy as a clam, taking care of him. He's almost 80 now."

They finished their hamburgers and Sally offered them coffee refills.

"How was the honeymoon?" Rolf asked.

"Hawaii drove me nuts. Nothing to do but play golf."

"Nothing to do but play golf? On your honeymoon? You've got to be kidding!"

Mark smiled. "I got restless. I even found myself calling the office."

"You did? How did Pris go for that?"

"She didn't seem to mind. At least she didn't complain."

"I was glad to see she persuaded Henry to come to the wedding," Rolf said.

"There was no persuading involved. The old boy decided to come on his own."

"Oh?"

"I'm sure it was humiliating for him to have to give Pris away there in front of his whole crowd, but he couldn't stand the idea of not coming to his only child's wedding."

"So, are the old wounds finally beginning to be healed?"

"Not a chance," Mark said grim-faced. "Henry may have forgiven Pris for marrying me, but talk to his no good son-in-law? That'll never happen."

"I thought it was as if there were two separate receptions. One for Pris and you, and the other for Henry," Rolf remarked. He was referring to the incongruous sight at the Pacific Union Club, where guests greeted Henry at one end of the reception hall and Mark at the other, with Pris flitting between the two.

"That's the way I want it. As separate as possible. Pris says she wants to have dinner at his house once a week. But as for me, I'll be happy if I never see him again."

"Come on, you'll get over it. I thought I'd never speak to Melinda again, but we had to. We have children together. You and Henry have Pris together, you know."

"Henry's the loser, not me."

Rolf shrugged his shoulders. It was obvious that he could not change Mark's mind. "It looks like you and I have traded places," Rolf smiled, changing the subject.

"What do you mean?"

Rolf laughed. "I was always the marriage enthusiast and you were always the bachelor."

Mark laughed, too. "You're right. I never in the world expected you and Melinda to get divorced."

"And I never expected you, of all people, to get married."

"I thought it was time to get married, that's all."

"You never told me much about Pris. I danced with her a couple of times at the reception. She's a super gal."

"There's not much to know, really. You know, I didn't want to marry her until my stock deal went through."

"You mean she wouldn't have married you if you hadn't been rich?"

Mark smiled sadly. "That's what I thought once, then she said it didn't matter to her."

"You sound like you didn't believe her."

"I don't know. I'm not sure. I've always thought I had to have money to get what I want."

"Even a wife?"

Mark hesitated thoughtfully, thinking first of Christina and then of Pris. "Yes, even a wife."

Rolf did not respond, as they sipped their coffee.

"You know, having all that money doesn't make me feel as different . . . you know . . . as different as I always thought I would."

"No, I don't suppose it would. You're still Mark Stevens, whether you're rich or poor. All that's happened, as far as I can see, is that you're Mark Stevens rich, instead of Mark Stevens poor."

"Maybe that's what it is about Pris."

"What?"

"Pris makes me feel like I'm not just Mark Stevens poor, who got rich." Mark thought carefully as he spoke, feeling his way along, then he spoke in a burst of words, as if he'd had an insight. "You know, Rolf, I think I can put my finger on it."

"What?"

"When I was waiting for her to come down the aisle . . . at the church."

"It was a fantastic wedding."

"I don't mind telling you, until then I had some doubts about getting married. Some serious doubts. But when she came down that aisle, I felt like I'd never felt before in my life."

"Sure, it was a big moment in your life—a very big moment."

"All those society types were there. And here I was marrying the prettiest damn one of them all!"

"I envy you, Mark. I remember how I felt when I married Melinda. I wish . . . "

"I was really surprised when you told me Melinda fell in love with her doctor."

"Yeah, her gynecologist, for Christ's sake."

"Are they actually married yet?" Mark inquired.

"Not yet. Still just living together. His wife is dragging out the property settlement."

"That's one thing about Pris."

"What?"

"Well, Pris would never cheat on me like Melinda did on you. I don't think I could handle it, worrying about my wife while I'm involved in my work."

"I don't think Melinda would have gotten involved with that guy if our marriage had been different."

"You don't?"

"Let me tell you, my friend, marriage needs attention. I know you've been very successful in business, but take it from me, there's one hell of a lot more to life than business. I was working every damn night, even weekends. I found out it wasn't worth it, but it was too late."

"I don't think I could slow down." Mark paused, thoughtfully. "Speaking of slowing down, how's the law practice?"

"Mark, I'll never be able to thank you enough for sending me that business. If it hadn't been for you, I'd never have made it."

"You don't need to thank me. I knew you'd do a good job."

"Well, I do thank you. I simply couldn't handle that pressure cooker at the big firm. I had to get out. Everyone trying to get in more chargeable hours than the next guy. Melinda wanting to get a big house and private schools for the kids. It was nothing but status, that's what it was! And all for what? Hell, I'm happier now than I've ever been."

"Well, that's all that counts, I guess."

Rolf smiled. He knew Mark could never understand how anyone could be happy with a simple, small-town law practice. "I don't have your drive for success. Basically, I'm contented practicing law right here in Sonoma. Sometimes I think I would have been better off getting lousy grades in law school."

"Oh, come on now!"

"No, I mean it. Back at Cal I never in the world expected to make law review, but when I did I thought I had to take a shot at the big time."

"I guess we were different. I always wanted a shot at the big time. That's why I went to Oxford."

"I was lucky, though."

"Lucky?"

"I didn't make the big time. I was never really cut out for the fast lane. I'm a totally different person from you, Mark."

"I suppose you are."

"Finally, I'm here where I really want to be."

"I guess we both got what we wanted, eh?"

"I guess so."

"More coffee?" Sally asked. "It sure is like old times, having you boys around here again."

"Sure, I've got time for more coffee. How about you?" Mark asked.

"Sure. My conference with the judge isn't until four. See, it isn't so bad to slow down for a change. Besides, I see it's raining out again."

"Rolf, I'm going to make this marriage work." Mark had a look of determination. "It's very important to me. I want a wife and a family. We're going to have children right away."

"Children—that would be wonderful. But remember, marriage isn't like some securities underwriting. You can think you've got a perfectly good marriage and find out that you're wrong. Dead wrong!"

They talked for another hour. Rolf admired his friend. At 30 he was on top of the world. Mark was one of the richest men in San Francisco and now he was married to the most eligible socialite in the City. His friend seemed to have everything he could ever want.

The rain had stopped and the sky was clearing as they walked toward Mark's Aston Martin. Mark started the engine and rolled down the window to bid Rolf good-bye. Rolf was struck with an unpleasant foreboding. Where would all Mark's drive ultimately lead? Rolf recalled the story of King Alexander. When he had conquered the entire ancient world, he had cried because there were no more worlds to conquer. As Mark's little red car sped off, Rolf silently wished him well, but he wondered what would happen to his old friend now that he had conquered his world.

-30-

Mark was nervous. He would meet many prominent men here at The Grove. He wished his suit were not so rumpled from the rainstorm in Sonoma. He parked in the main parking lot, and a young man took his suitcase. Cars were not allowed inside the grounds at The Grove. The area was divided into separate sections or camps, enabling the men to get to know one another better. Mark followed the young man on the long walk through the gigantic redwood trees to his particular camp. As the path led through the majestic trees, they passed several other camps with groups of men sitting at tables drinking and laughing. Mark saw that the men were all casually dressed, and chuckled at himself for worrying about his wrinkled suit. What a contrast between today and his first day at Oxford years ago, when he had to borrow Rodney's tie and oversized jacket to meet the dining hall rules. Today in his rumpled suit, he was overdressed. It was ironic that these men from the upper echelons were so casually dressed, while the Oxford students, who were nothing but students starting out, wore jackets and ties. Perhaps the more important you were, the less you cared about the so-called proper way to dress. On the other hand, maybe it was just a case of conforming to different uniforms.

Mark's host at The Grove was Donald Willets, a member of the Bohemian Club. It was Don Willets whose bank had loaned Dictor Electronics the needed expansion money, and who had been Mark's sponsor for membership at San Francisco's Olympic Club, where Mark usually golfed. He had had Don and his wife to the Pebble Beach house a couple of months ago. They had been drinking beer in the Tap Room at Pebble Beach after a round of golf.

"Mark, how about coming with me to the Russian River?" Don had asked. "The Bohemian Club is having The Grove in a couple of months. You'd have a wonderful time."

Mark knew about the Bohemian Club and hoped to be invited to join the prestigious organization someday. "Sounds great! I know a few members already. Mostly from the P.U. Club." He was referring to the Pacific Union Club.

"There's a catch, though." Don had a twinkle in his eye.

"A catch. What catch?"

"Would you be willing to give a short talk? I've heard you on television and I think you'd go over big. Most of them will be business leaders."

"A talk? They have talks there?"

"Oh, yes. Nearly every day. On some topic of interest."

"Well I . . ."

"We aren't supposed to invite California residents to The Grove, but they'll make an exception if you'll be a speaker."

Mark was taken aback by the unexpected invitation to speak before such an imposing group. "Well, sure, Don, I can come up with something to talk about. I'd be very flattered to do it." It was also an opportunity to make himself known to some very influential leaders from across the country. It could do nothing but help business.

"Then it's all settled," Willets said. "I'm the committee chairman, so you can consider it a done deed."

"Here you are, sir. Here's your camp," said the young man carrying Mark's luggage, when they had arrived at the shady setting in the midst of the huge Sequoia trees.

"Mark. Over here, over here." Drink in hand, Don Willets left his group of men and greeted Mark. "How was the drive up?"

"I got caught in a rainstorm. Soaked clear through."

"A rainstorm? Rain in summer? We didn't have any rain here."

Mark laughed. "I hadn't expected any rain either, but I went by way of Sonoma to see my mother, and it was raining like hell."

Don turned to the group. "Mark, I'd like to you meet some very fine gentlemen who are joining us at our 'summer boys camp' this year."

All the dozen or so men at the table stood as, one by one, Don introduced them. Don remembered all their names and occupations without a hitch, as if he had known them all his life. One was the president of a New York bank, another the head of a New Jersey electric company, still another was a college president. They all held prominent positions across the country. Mark knew most of the San Francisco men who were Bohemian Club members, but he did not know their guests. When the introductions were completed, he sat at the table with the others.

As Mark listened to the conversations, he recalled that his father always called such important people "big shots." To Jonah "big shots" were "them." Jonah thought it was always "them", the "big shots," and "us," the "workers." Big shots had the power and "us" were controlled by them. When Jonah was angry with Mark, he often shouted, "What are ya trying to be—a big shot or something?" Even as a young boy, Mark knew something was wrong with his father's belief. Jonah always called Antonio a big shot, but to Mark, Antonio was not some distant, formidable giant, even though he had money and was the boss. For years now Mark had been doing business with men his father would have labeled big shots. He was accustomed to them and knew they were simply men, just as he was. But at a deeper level the lessons of the father were not lost on the son, especially when he was with a group of men such as these. Deep in his gut, it was still as if they were "them" and he were an outsider. He drank with them, laughed and joked with them, but he did not feel he was one of them.

"What about those Giants?" asked Charlie Mitchell. Charlie was a senior partner in a large San Francisco law firm.

"I think they're going to win it all—four games ahead at the All Star break," another man, an insurance company president, answered.

"They may win the West, but the Yanks will knock them off in the World Series," said Maurice from Chase Manhattan Bank.

"You've got to be kidding, Mauri. Baltimore is way ahead of the Yankees. The Yanks will never see the playoffs, let alone the series." The man who spoke was John Martin, a prominent lobbyist from Washington, D.C. Washington did not have a major league baseball team, and so most Washingtonians rooted for the Baltimore Orioles.

The conversation drifted into a debate as to whether the top baseball teams of today could compare with the great Yankee teams under Casey Stengel after World War II. Mark was surprised. Here the leaders of American industry were, debating whether the Giants of '71 could defeat the Yankees of '48 in a mythical series, as if it were the most pressing issue of their time. Although Mark knew very little about baseball, he soon joined in the discussion, with opinions every bit as strong as the others. "What the hell," he thought. "I don't think they know much more about it than I do, anyway."

After an hour it was time for dinner. The different camps at The Grove ate at a vast, central, outdoor eating area, seating 600 or 700 men. The men from Mark's camp walked to dinner together, but broke up to find places at the partially filled tables. Don and Mark found two spaces at a table and introduced themselves to the others. As before, many of the diners were heads of giant corporations from around the nation. The man next to Mark was Bill Monahan, a senior partner in a big accounting firm. Across from Mark was Knute Lockman. He was a U.S. senator on the select Lockheed loan committee that had just recommended the government loan guarantee. As he had at cocktails, Mark felt the same uneasy nervousness. The silent voice of Jonah yelled that these were big shots and he was not one of them. But as Mark had always done in his drive to success, he ignored his nervousness and plunged into the conversation as if he had not a self-doubt in the world. He exhibited no clue that he was not completely at ease.

The conversation at dinner was little different from that at cocktails. No great issues of the day were discussed. It shifted from baseball to Lee Trevino's win in the British Open, then away from sports altogether.

"I see that the Manson trial is still dragging on. That son of a bitch should get the gas chamber," said Al Webster from Detroit. He was a vice-president of Ford.

"He's just one of the million kooks they have down in L.A.," added a man Mark recognized, Bill Sander from the gas company.

When Don had first told him of the names of some of the accomplished men who would be at The Grove, Mark expected the conversations to be about weighty matters of the day. "What do you think about the prime rate going to six percent?" or "Nixon had better get off the dime and do something about the balance of payments," was what he had imagined he would hear. But now he was worried whether anyone would be interested in the speech he had planned for tomorrow. Maybe they were talking about inconsequential matters because they were on vacation. Or perhaps when people didn't know each other very well, they talked about things they knew they had in common. Suddenly, he was worried that the speech he had prepared was far too serious for the occasion. He doubted they would understand or care about what he had planned to say. He decided he had to put in more work tonight on his speech.

When dinner was over, Mark turned to his host. "Don, I've got some new ideas for my talk tomorrow. Would you mind if I skip tonight's entertainment? I've got to rework my speech."

"Come on, Mark, I've seen you on television a million times. You don't need to prepare."

"No, I've got to spruce it up a little bit. You go on." The Bohemian Club had three or four bowls carved out of the wilderness, where each night there was some sort of entertainment. Members and guests would sit on rows of logs around campfires and watch the entertainment. Except for the occasional guest who might be a professional, the entertainment was put on by amateurs attending The Grove. Mark was disappointed to miss it, but he wanted to perfect his talk.

"Well, all right, but I think you'll do just fine."

"Save me a seat. If I finish early, I'll join you."

Mark returned to the sleeping quarters of his camp and took out his speech. He'd go over it again and again if he had to. He wanted this to be the best talk he had ever given.

Don stood to introduce Mark to the audience. About 75 casually attired men sat in a semi-circle on the slope that rose gently from a large pond. The spot was known as "Lakeside."

"Mark Stevens was born in nearby Sonoma," said Don. "He graduated with honors from the University of California at Berkeley. He was awarded a Rhodes Scholarship to Oxford, where he studied economics and won the highest honors. He is the founder of The Stevens Group, investment banking firm in San Francisco. He was recently married to the former Priscilla Enfield, a well known name in San Francisco.

"Mark has an uncanny ability to see the essence of a complex problem and then to make the solution seem simple.

"I only see Mark on the golf course these days. He has so much money he doesn't need a banker any more. As a matter of fact, only yesterday I asked him if he would make our bank a loan." The group chuckled mildly at the joke.

"Gentlemen, I present to you Mr. Mark Stevens."

There was polite applause as Mark walked forward. Carefully, deliberately, he put his notes on the lectern and intently looked at the group. Mark had spoken many times around San Francisco. He had learned that he was less nervous if he carefully thought through what he intended to say. As he had done last night, he often wrote down his speech word for word, and by the time he spoke had it virtually memorized. Television was a piece of cake. Since he could not prepare for the question-and-answer format of the news shows, his answers had to be spontaneous.

He was especially tense this morning. He had worked very late last night, rewriting every word. The idea of speaking to this group frightened him half to death. As he stood before them, throat dry and hands shaking, he remembered the Blue Sheep Club. The thought relaxed him. If he had survived giving that speech, he could survive anything. He finished scanning the audience and began speaking.

"What a wonderful spot to listen to a speech, here at Lakeside. This beautiful river and these wonderful sequoias, hundreds of years old! My talk is on economics, but remember if you find it boring, you can just look at the scenery." A few in the audience chuckled. "But, please, do me a favor will you? At least pretend you're listening." A few more laughed.

At that moment a group of three men walked from the redwood trees, and prepared to sit down on the slope. Mark recognized the first man. He was John Connally, the new Secretary of the Treasury of the United States.

Mark was astonished. There was no mistaking the tall, trim figure of the former Governor of Texas, who had been shot in the Kennedy assassination limousine. In a surprise move a few months ago, President Nixon, a Republican, had appointed Connally, a lifelong Democrat, to his new post. Whenever Mark had seen famous people, they had seemed smaller in real life, but not Connally. Even as he sat on the ground, he seemed larger than those around him. Handsome and rugged, Connally smiled broadly as he saw that Mark had recognized him.

"Gentlemen, I see that we are privileged to have amongst us our new Secretary of the Treasury, John Connally."

Mark pointed as he spoke. The small crowd broke into applause, as they turned their heads toward the prominent guest. Connally nodded his gray-haired head at Mark and waved his hand at the group.

"Secretary Connally and gentlemen," Mark began. Strangely, the unexpected appearance of Connally and the crowd's response relaxed Mark, and his nervousness eased. "With Secretary Connally present, I'm really going to have to watch what I say. I feel like I did when my old professor asked me to come back to Cal to lecture to his economics class."

Mark departed from his script. "How many of you thought when you were students that you knew all there was to know?"

"Come on! Certainly I'm not the only one. Let's see a show of hands." The crowd laughed, as nearly everyone joined Mark in raising their hands.

"Well, when I was in the School of Economics at Cal, I certainly thought I knew it all. Fortunately I had a professor—Dr. John Hall was his name—he still teaches there—who understood this about students. Instead of telling me I was an idiot, he encouraged me. I still remember his saying. 'If you feel you're on to something, don't let the experts discourage you.' I was still at Cal when it first occurred to me it was bad policy for a country to determine the value of its currency. If the free market should set the price of a car or a loaf of bread, why shouldn't it determine the price of the dollar or the pound on the foreign exchange markets, instead of the government?

"I remember once, in class, debating the subject with Dr. Hall. He disagreed with me. In fact, I think he still disagrees with me,"

Mark smiled impishly, causing the audience to smile with him. "I don't remember for sure what he said, but I imagine he said something like, 'Now, Mr. Stevens, money is a medium of exchange, not a product. It doesn't hurt competition to fix the price.'" Mark imitated a stern professorial voice. "In fact Dr. Hall would have argued it is necessary to fix the value of the dollar to have a stable economy."

Mark paused and looked at John Connally. He felt confident now. His nervousness and self-doubt had vanished. "Sound like some of the advice you've been getting lately, Mr. Secretary?" The big Texan grinned.

"One day Dr. Hall invited me to drop by his office. I remember it like yesterday. The second floor of Wheeler. We argued about Bretton Woods and the narrow trading band it imposed. To tell you the truth, I think I was just being bull-headed. You know, at that age I had to be right about something." The audience laughed again. Mark had created a rapport with his listeners.

"Years later, when I was at Oxford, my old idea stuck with me. I felt at Oxford and I feel now that Bretton Woods must go—the gold window must be closed.

"Do you know that our negative balance of payments in the first quarter was over 34 billion dollars? We have to do something about it! The rest of the world isn't stupid, you know. Remember the United States promised at Bretton Woods that it would sell an ounce of gold to anyone who paid $35 in U.S. currency.

"The rest of the world is saying the dollar isn't worth that much. Thirty-five dollars for an ounce of gold is a bargain. They're lining up to buy our gold for that ridiculous price. It's a situation made for speculation."

Mark spoke for only 30 minutes. He wanted to keep it simple. He always had been amazed at how difficult international economics was for most leaders to understand.

"The logic of ending Bretton Woods is no different today from what it was when I was a student at Oxford," he concluded. "Except now we have more experience. Interest rates and inflation are rising, the balance of payments deficit is huge and the administration is not acting. I don't intend to take this occasion in this wonderful setting to be argumentative, but only last month the distinguished guest, Mr. Connally, reaffirmed official U.S. economic policy. And I quote you, sir." Mark read from his notes. "We should ride it out. We've done everything we should do. Give our policies time to work." As he spoke, Mark watched Connally intently, but the big Texan gave no hint of reaction.

"As I said, I'm not talking politics now—that's for the politicians. I'm talking economics. I say we must change our thinking or this country will have the biggest depression since the '30s. We must change our policies, or we're all going to be fighting to keep our businesses above water." Mark concluded his speech: "Surely a President who chooses his Secretary of Treasury from the opposition party and who promises to go to China, can meet this challenge and change his mind. We need action and we need it now!"

Mark was discouraged by the polite, but brief applause he received. Perhaps his speech had been over the audience's head. Perhaps it was in bad taste to disagree openly with Connally in such a forum. He did not have long to ponder. John Connally was the first to reach him at the lectern.

"Young man, I want to have a drink with you."

In his early 60s, the handsome Connally was strikingly dressed in the finest western casual clothes. He wore expensive, lizard-skin boots. His pale blue western shirt and tan western trousers were elegant. A glittering silver belt buckle announced a man used to center stage.

"You sound like you know what the hell you're talkin' about— at least you damn well think you do. I want to hear some more."

Mark accompanied the fast-paced Connally through the giant trees to the Texan's quarters. Connally's aide appeared with a bottle of bourbon and two glasses.

"Bourbon all right with you, Mark?"

"Sure. Bourbon's fine." Mark was taken aback by Connally, and by the fact that the Secretary of the Treasury of the United States cared about what he had to say. Awe-struck, he felt as if his mouth were hanging wide open.

"Ice?" asked Connally, removing the cap from the whiskey bottle.

"Yes, lots," said Mark.

Connally put ice cubes in Mark's glass and poured himself some bourbon. Mark intended to let the ice melt a bit before sipping his drink, but Connally immediately started on his.

"You had some pretty strong criticism for the President's policy."

"I don't mean to be rude, Mr. Connally, but . . . "

"Mark, I wish you'd call me John, dammit."

"All right, John. What I mean to say is: I don't think the administration has much of a policy."

"Oh, is that so?"

"Only the other day I read something that you said—or at least you were supposed to have said."

"And what was that?"

"Something along the lines that the administration doesn't intend to do anything. 'The natural resiliency of the economy will bail us out of our trouble'. Something like that. I don't agree with you at all." Mark leaned back in his chair, sipping his drink. What they said about Connally was true. He had a commanding presence. Supreme self-confidence.

"I'll tell you something, if you'll keep it to yourself." Connally grinned and looked around out of the corners of his eyes, pretending to be sure no one could overhear him."

Mark laughed. "I'm used to keeping confidences, John." Mark forced himself to use the first name.

"What I tell the newspapers is for public consumption. The fact of the matter is, the President has already asked me to come up with a new economic plan. We've got ourselves a mighty fine president. He doesn't want to sit still, any more than I do. Whatever plan I come up with, I have to do it fast. It's supposed to be on his desk in early August."

Mark had read that President Nixon had supreme confidence in Connally. Recently, Nixon's other economic advisors had been effectively demoted, when the President appointed Connally his Chief Economic Spokesman.

"I'm happy to hear that John. What is your plan going to propose?"

"I don't really know yet. I've been doing one hell of a lot of reading, and talkin' to a lot of mighty wise folks, but I haven't decided yet. One thing, though, I know a lot more than when I started." Mark liked Connally for admitting he didn't have the answer to the mess the country was in. "I'd like to get your ideas," Connally finished.

"As I said in my talk, I've thought for a long time we'd have to abandon Bretton Woods someday. Frankly, I think that day has come."

"Well, you've got to tell me why you think that way, without giving me a bunch of technical crap."

"Okay, I'll try." Mark liked the way Connally got to the point. "What do you know about Bretton Woods?"

"Damned little! Oh, I took some econ courses when I was at U.T. By the way, I liked what you said about debating your old professor. I had my special professor, too. Old Robert H. Montgomery. Everybody at U.T. called him 'the Doctor.' Quite a man, I'll tell you. But to be honest with you, Mark, when I first took this job, I knew as much about foreign exchange as a chicken knows about swimmin' in a gravel pit pond, which isn't very damned much. So treat me as if I don't know a thing."

"To start at the beginning, they held a big international conference in 1944. It was supposed to set up a whole new international monetary system. They called it Bretton Woods."

Connally laughed. "That much I know already. You don't have to go back that far. When the President nominated me six months ago, they got me a tutor to teach me stuff like that."

"You're kidding."

"No, I wanted to learn all I could. You've heard of William McChesney Martin?"

"Sure."

"Martin tutored me for days on end."

"Then, you understand what the problems are."

"Hell, I know this: we're the greatest damn country in the world, but the dollar isn't going to be worth a good shit if we don't do somethin' quick. Everybody's sellin' dollars. Inflation's running damned near four percent. As you said, the foreigners all want gold for their dollars. We're going to run out of gold if we don't stop the damned bleeding." Connally had finished his drink. "Do you want another?"

"Sure."

As they talked about the problems of the economy, Mark was very excited. Here was his chance to have input into the very formulation of a new national policy. He'd talk as long as John Connally would listen. As the afternoon went by, neither was conscious of the passing of time.

"I've always believed someday we'd be forced to abandon Bretton Woods and stop selling our gold."

"I don't like it," Connally said. "This country has always prided itself in the strong dollar. Politically, it would smell."

"Not if it were done right."

"What do you mean?"

"Nixon likes to be a bold President, right?"

"Right."

"He could say he thinks the nation has to pay the price of Viet Nam and take its medicine. Voters would like that."

"There don't seem to be one hell of a lot of choices."

"I'm afraid not."

They walked over to dinner together, continuing their discussion while they dined. The others at the table listened respectfully as Mark kept driving home his points about the crisis. When the black-trousered waiters began clearing the dishes, Connally and Mark were talking as vigorously as when they had begun.

"Governor, the entertainment starts in half an hour," an aide told Connally.

Mark sat with Connally's group to watch the entertainment, which took place in a natural hillside bowl in a small clearing in the redwood forest. The entertainment was more professional than

Mark had expected. Members played both the male and female parts in a hilarious one act play, which, although placed in San Francisco, had all the elements of a British farce. The audience had the most fun with an amateur jazz band that called themselves the "Firehouse Four Plus One." Mark had heard them perform once before, with Pris, at a charity event in San Francisco, but hadn't known they were Bohemian Club members. The jazz group that had performed before the play was called back afterwards for another half-hour, while the exuberant audience clapped and joined in singing songs.

"Mark, how about you and I having a little nightcap," said Connally when the show was over. "I'm leavin' early in the mornin' for Washington and we need to talk some more."

They returned to Connally's camp and sat alone again, talking economic policy. Mark was oblivious to anything else as they talked on and on.

"I'm mighty impressed with what you've been telling me. Shutting the gold window makes plenty of sense to me. You aren't the first one to tell me that's what we should do, but you're the first one to explain it so that I could understand it."

"I can't tell you how happy that makes me, John. When I was at Oxford, I could see that international economics was a mystery to almost every political leader in the world. It always seemed to me that if a politician came along who could get a feel for the subject, he'd have a leg up on everybody else. I think that man could be you."

"Maybe so, maybe so. You know when The Volcker Group first started working on this problem a few months ago, I told them I wanted some action. Hell, back then I didn't know what we should do, but I wanted to do something besides sitting around on our collective asses while the country went to hell in a hand-basket."

"Volcker would have a tough time abandoning Bretton Woods. He's a traditionalist."

"Yeah, well, he finally gave me a draft memo. He thinks a devaluation is going to happen, but I don't think he much likes it."

"At least that is a first step."

"I showed Volcker's memo to the President."

"What did he think?"

"The President isn't much interested in that sort of thing. He's a hell of a lot better president than most people give him credit for, but his mind is on other things. China and Russia for example—not foreign economic policy."

"What do you think is going to happen now, John? There's going to be one hell of a big run on Fort Knox if something isn't done soon."

"The fact of the matter is the President has pretty much left the problem up to me."

"I envy you, then."

"Envy me?"

"Yes. I wish I had power like that. I'd shut the gold window so fast it would make your head swim."

"Mark, I've an idea. One hell of an idea, if I do say so myself."

"What?"

"Have you ever been to the White House?"

"Sure, as a tourist."

"I want you to meet the President." Connally turned to his aide. "Get me my date book." He spoke to Mark again, "Would you come to Washington, say about August 10th?"

"Of course I would."

"I'll see to it then. I want the President to meet you. I think he should hear what you've been telling me."

When Mark went to bed that night, he just lay on the blanket, his hands clasped behind his neck and his clothes on. His mind was racing. Never could he have imagined a day like today. John Connally, the architect of a new economic order, had invited him to the White House to advise the President of the United States. He could hardly wait to tell Pris. He would like her to go to Washington with him. This was inconceivable. Connally had soaked up every word of what he had said.

He got up and put on a sweater. He knew very well he was not going to sleep. He walked through the hush of the giant redwoods until he came to Lakeside. He grasped the lectern with his two hands, facing where the audience had been. "Good to see you here, Mr. Connally," he said very softly, although no one was around.

"Oh, why, yes, I'd be very happy to tell you about Bretton Woods." He paused in the darkness, waiting for the absent Connally to ask another question.

"I see. You've read my Linde-Ewell essay, but you'd like me to explain it? Why, certainly, sir. Anything to help you and the President decide what to do."

Mark turned from the lectern and walked to the edge of the water. It was very calm. The small crescent of a moon could be seen through the trees in the western sky. He found a log and sat down, thinking. He wished the pond had ducks on it as had the lake at Worcester College. He missed those ducks. He would like to tell them what he had done today. They would be proud of him.

Suddenly, he was seized with an impulse. He stripped off his clothes and plunged naked into the water. With strong strides, he swam until his feet touched down on the far side and then, without stopping, swam back. The water was cold, and as he dressed again the night air felt warm on his body.

He walked back thinking about his father. If only Jonah could be here and know about his triumph. If only he could tell him about the White House invitation. Even Jonah would have to admit that Mark was part of "them" now. Even Jonah would have to admit that his son had arrived, and that he was a "big shot."

-31-

It was late afternoon when Mark sped up the circular driveway of his newly completed Hillsborough mansion. His red Aston Martin braked to a stop behind the staked truck that blocked the driveway. "Milton Landscape Services," read the lettering. Mark tooted his horn and waved his hand at the workers, who were planting shrubs and finishing the sprinkler system. He and Pris had moved from his Nob Hill condominium after returning from their honeymoon. They had spent just five nights in their new home.

Two days ago when Mark mentioned he planned to keep the condo even though they were married, they had argued vociferously:

"I don't see why you want to keep it. I just don't like the idea. It's as if we weren't married."

Mark had never seen Pris so angry.

"It's not that at all. I might need it. The company could use it for visitors, and maybe we'll stay there sometimes, like after the opera. I just don't want to sell it. Not yet, anyway." Mark was angry, too. Keeping his condo was his business. He didn't like Pris telling him what to do.

It had been their first argument. He could not understand her viewpoint, nor could she understand his. In the end, Pris had no alternative but to accept his decision, but she made it clear that she did not like it.

Pris had agreed with Mark that the mansion should be in the manner of Castle Enfield. He had been largely in charge of the exterior design and she the interior layout and appointments. Mark had the architect design a small lake near the property entry. Mature eucalyptus trees had been brought in to provide a dramatic border to the edge of the lake and the driveway. A dozen ducks paddled in the lake. Although much smaller, the house, with its lake and English look, held the same special feeling for Mark as did Castle Enfield. The mansion was two stories high with a steeply peaked slate roof and a series of old-fashioned-looking chimneys. Mark was particularly proud of the stonework that decorated the house and gardens. The driveway was paved with cobblestones, as he remembered from the Ashley Chelsea house.

While the house was magnificent, it carefully drew short of being ostentatious. What Mark wanted, and what the architect achieved, was a look of understated elegance. The observer would know that the owner was a man of great wealth, but would also see he was a person of good taste. When the landscaping was completed, the house would look as if it had been built many years ago.

The house was everything Mark had ever wanted. He got out of his car and looked carefully at the masterpiece. He took a deep breath of pride and satisfaction. Here was the house of his dreams! This was where Pris and he would spend the rest of their lives and where they would raise their family.

He had stayed for lunch at The Grove and had driven straight through to Hillsborough without stopping at the office. He was anxious to tell Pris about Connally and the invitation to see the President. He inserted his key and let himself into the house, which still smelled of fresh paint.

"Pris! Pris!" he shouted.

He looked first in the study and then in the unfurnished living room, where she might be talking to the decorator. He walked to the bedroom suite. Pris was not to be found. He decided to look for the maid.

"Zeldah! Zeldah!" he called without success, searching in the kitchen and the servants' quarters. He entered the garage through the house calling, "Pris!" and then "Zeldah!", but there was no answer and there were no cars in the garage.

Damn, he was disappointed! He was so excited about Connally, he had wanted to tell Pris right away. He wished now he had called to be sure she would be home, but she knew he would be back about now. He had assumed she would be waiting for him, after his first trip away since their marriage. He flipped on the T.V. in the den and idly watched the soap opera that popped into view. Damn, he wished she were home!

"We're going to Washington!" he would have shouted. "Connally wants me to advise the President!"

"How wonderful, sweetheart!" Pris would have excitedly gushed. "I have the brightest, most wonderful husband in the whole world."

Mark sat in his favorite red leather chair that he had brought from the condo. Without really seeing, he watched the television.

When he heard the grinding of the garage door's opening, he walked quickly to the garage to greet Pris, but it was Zeldah.

"Oh, I'm sorry, Mr. Stevens. Mrs. Stevens is with Mrs. McCartney from the opera committee. They're golfing at the club. She said she'd be playing cards and would be late."

"I thought she knew I was coming home. Did she say anything?"

"Oh, she knew you'd be back this afternoon. She said to remind you about the art exhibit this evening. You're supposed to have dinner at Ernie's with some folks from the art group."

"I don't remember her telling me about any art exhibit." He flipped off the television. "I'm going to the office. Tell her I'll meet her at the exhibit."

It was late afternoon when Mark arrived at the office. After the firm had gone public, Mark had moved it to a new building on Montgomery Street. He had a special penthouse suite constructed for himself and Steve Baumgartner, his executive vice-president. Mark was dressed in a dark suit for the art show and dinner tonight. He was disappointed, but it wasn't Pris's fault, he supposed. She could not have known about Connally. He would tell her the exciting news tonight.

Holding his message slips, Mark swiveled in his red leather chair so that he could see the activity on the Bay. He had carefully chosen a building with a view the same as Henry Enfield's and several stories taller. The first message he saw indicated that Rodney's solicitor, Adam Hawkes, had called from London. It was urgent. He left his home telephone number. Mark was to call him at any time of night or day. He checked the international clock on his desk. It was two-thirty in the morning in London, but he dialed the number. It must be important.

"Sorry to ring you up at this ungodly hour," Mark told Hawkes, "but your message said I should."

"Yes, indeed. It's urgent I speak to you. I'm afraid it will be necessary for you to come to London."

"What's the problem?"

"Trafalgar Financial won't agree to abandon the foreclosure. I've told them Rodney would pay off the loan in full, but they're still trying to seize the office block."

"That's ridiculous! Can they do that?"

"The managing director of the mortgage company is a very determined man. He's fighting like a tiger."

"Two can play that game. When do you want me in London?"

"The case has been set down for trial next Thursday. Can you come?"

"I've got to be in Washington the next week after, but I can fly directly from London to Washington after the trial."

When Mark arrived at the Enfield Galleries, it was already filled with San Francisco art patrons and collectors, there to see the new collection of Samuel Wade, an artist who had recently moved from New York. A white-gloved waiter offered him a glass of champagne. The room buzzed with the conversation of the well-dressed crowd. Several people congratulated him on his marriage. He spotted Pris in the back of the room. At moments like this Pris was at her best, Mark thought. Young, attractive, vital, she was dressed in a teal dress that went well with her red hair. She wore a single string of pearls, and pearl earrings. Her skirt was shorter than the other women's, but then she was younger and better-looking than most. Her new, black leather pumps caught Mark's eye. She was talking animatedly to the honored artist and the enthusiastic group that surrounded them as they studied one of his paintings. It was Pris, not the painting, that was the center of attention. A strong feeling of love and admiration for her passed through Mark. He had really struck gold when Pris had agreed to marry him. For the moment at least, he forgot about being angry when she had not been home.

"Mark, sweetheart, I see you found us all right." Pris turned her head to receive his kiss on her cheek. "Mark, I'd like you to meet Samuel Wade. Samuel is the one who created these wonderful paintings. Samuel, I'd like you to meet my husband, Mark Stevens." In situations such as this, one would never suspect that Pris had a vulnerable bone in her body. In her element, she was very different from the confused, uncertain woman that finally went to bed with him that night at Pebble Beach.

"How do you do, Mr. Wade," said Mark. Pris frequently sponsored new artists. Single-handedly, she had arranged for this showing. The blessing of Priscilla Enfield, now Pris Stevens, assured Wade of immediate acceptance in San Francisco society.

"How was your trip, sweetheart?"

"Very successful. You'll never guess who was in the audience for my speech."

"Speech? I didn't know you were going to give a speech."

"Yes, I . . . "

A blond woman took Pris's hand, gaining her attention. "I'm sorry for interrupting, Mark, dear. Excuse me, but one of life's little emergencies has come up." As Pris went with the blond woman through the crowd, leaving Mark with the small group, she turned briefly back toward him. "I want to hear more about your speech. I'll return when I can."

"Well, Mr. Stevens, you certainly have a busy wife," said the man standing next to the artist. "I don't know what San Francisco would ever do without Priscilla. My wife is one of her biggest fans."

Mark remembered the man's name—Elwood Sheppard. He had been stuck with sitting next to Sheppard's wife at a fundraising dinner. Mark and Sheppard idly exchanged pleasantries about tonight's art exhibit, and about the Giants' leading their division.

"And what is your profession, Elwood?"

"I'm President of my father-in-law's company. He's a publisher, you know. And what do you do, Mark?"

"I'm an investment banker." Mark had expected Sheppard would already know that, since he said he knew Pris so well.

"Oh, the same as Priscilla's father. You must be in business with him."

"No, I have my own firm. Montgomery Street. We have several hundred employees."

"Henry used to squire Priscilla to these occasions. You have such a successful father-in-law."

"Yes, Henry's quite a man," Mark said, looking desperately around the room for a way to escape his companion. "Excuse me, Elwood. I've got to find my wife. She must be somewhere in this mob."

"Well, good to see you again, Mark. Good luck with your company. If ever I need an investment banker and old Henry Enfield is on the golf course, I'll look you up," he laughed heartily, thinking he was being funny.

Mark could hardly wait to get out of the art gallery. The summer fog had rolled in, and it was getting nippy as he walked down the hill to Union Square. He walked around the square, looking in the department store windows. He could not stand people like Elwood Sheppard, he thought. The jerk probably showed up for work about ten and left before the day was half over. Hell, Sheppard was only 40 years old and was wasting his life.

Mark felt a little better as he finished walking around Union Square. He paused to look in the window of the men's clothing shop in the St. Francis Hotel. "I don't know why I'm so damned irritable tonight," he said to himself. "I'd better get back to the art gallery before Pris misses me."

By the time he climbed the hill and returned to the art show, the crowd had thinned out considerably.

"Mark, where on earth have you been? People were asking for you," said Pris.

"Oh, did Elwood-what's-his-name want to float a bond issue?"

"What on earth are you talking about?"

"I don't know. I guess I'm in a lousy mood."

"What's the matter? Didn't your speech go well?"

"It went very well."

"I'm sorry. I didn't have time for you to tell me about your speech. The show has been so hectic."

"John Connally was there . . . "

"Good night, thanks for coming," Pris said to a couple as they left the show.

He could see that Pris was only half listening, as she waved goodbye to a departing couple. "Do you know who John Connally is?"

"I'm sorry, dear. John Connally? Why of course I remember John Connally. He was shot with Kennedy, wasn't he?"

"Yes, that's the one."

"What was he doing there?"

"He's Secretary of the Treasury now."

"He is?"

"Yes, Nixon has asked Connally to come up with a whole new international monetary plan."

"It sounds very impressive, dear."

"Yes, and he liked my speech."

"That's wonderful, dear."

"Do you know what happened?"

"No, but it must have been very important."

"It was. We talked for hours about . . . "

"Good night, Larry," Pris interrupted. "If I were you, Larry, I'd put down a deposit. If that painting sells to someone else, Alicia will never forgive you." She turned her attention to Mark. "I'm sorry, darling."

Mark grimaced. "Connally and I talked for hours."

"Goodness, what about?"

"He wanted my ideas about Bretton Woods."

"Oh, darling, that must have been great fun for you."

"Yes. And do you know what happened when we finished talking?"

"No, dear."

"He wants me to come to the White House in two weeks to explain my ideas to President Nixon. Can you imagine that?"

"President Nixon! That awful man! Surely you're not going are you? I've hated him since the Kennedy debates."

"Pris! He's the President of the goddammed country!"

"All right, you don't have to raise your voice! I know Nixon is President. That's what makes me so unhappy."

"Priscilla! John Connally, the Secretary of the United States Treasury, wants me to go to the White House and advise the President of the United States and all you can say is that you hate him!"

"Mark," she whispered taking him by the arm and pushing him toward the door. "People are listening. Please lower your voice." Once outside on the sidewalk, she stopped whispering. "I think it's a great honor, I really do."

Mark lowered his voice. "Well, goddammit, Pris. You aren't home when you're supposed to be, and now this! Don't you understand a man wants to share these things with his wife? Not have her on the golf course all the time?"

"Come on now, Mark. Take it easy." A clanging cable car going up Powell interrupted their conversation.

"Well dammit, Pris . . . "

She quickly hugged him. "Let's have a good time at dinner tonight. Can't we talk about this later?"

"Okay," said Mark, mollified at having spoken his mind.

There were nine in their group for dinner at Ernie's restaurant. Mark was seated next to Jane Traggert, a woman of 45 whom he had met before. Pris didn't like Jane, but tolerated her because her husband, Wayne, was a large contributor to the opera. As Mark talked to Jane, he was still annoyed with Pris.

Pris sat at the other end of the table, making her usual sparkling conversation with Samuel Wade, the artist, and Wayne Traggert. The food and wine were excellent, making the evening passable. Jane Traggert drank too much and ended up the evening making suggestive remarks to Mark. It was probably because he knew that Pris didn't like Jane that Mark subtly egged her on. Finally, the dinner was over. Mark signed for the bill for the entire group, and they all got up to leave. Jane took Mark by the arm, walking with him to the foyer.

"Let's have lunch next week," Jane whispered. "May I call you on Monday?" she said, not quietly enough to suit Mark.

"I'm in London next week." He very nearly added, "But call me after that," but decided not to.

As the group stood on the curb waiting for the valets to bring their cars, Pris spoke to Mark: "I left my car at the art gallery. Samuel will drop me off. Do you want us to drop you at your office for your car?"

"No, I'll walk." It was only a short walk to his garage.

"Suit yourself, sweetheart. I'll see you at home."

"Sure, I'll see you at home," he said and started down Montgomery Street.

Pris turned to talk to her friends, who were chatting as they waited for the valets. Suddenly, she thought better of it and ran down the sloping street after Mark. Hearing the sound of high heels on the concrete, he turned toward her.

"Sweetheart," she said. "I'm sorry we quarreled." She kissed him on the cheek and, looking into his eyes, held his hands. "I'll see you at home. Don't be late. Okay?"

"Okay," he responded, still not yet ready to totally give up his anger.

As the light turned amber, Mark ran across the intersection, rather than wait for the red. In was cold in the San Francisco fog. He hated the way tonight had gone. If it hadn't been for all the other people at the art gallery, he would never have come back after he stormed out. Then at dinner, did you see the way Pris talked to that damned fool artist? She treated him as if he were some long lost king. I'll bet if Samuel Wade had told Pris that something great had happened to him, it would have been a different story:

"Hello Priscilla, I just won the Zabowitz Prize for Nearly Broke Painters," went the imagined telephone conversation between Wade and Pris. Mark could see Pris sitting at the desk in her study when Wade called.

"Oh, Samuel, how very marvelous. Tell me all about it," she would say.

"The prize is $200; can you imagine that, Priscilla?"

"That's wonderful Samuel. Imagine $200 whole dollars."

"Yes, and next week I go to the White House. President Nixon is giving me the Prize."

"President Nixon! How wonderful. Samuel, I'm so proud of you."

Walking quickly, Mark reached the garage in his building.

"Hello, Mr. Stevens. Working late?" said Bob, the attendant. "The keys are in your car."

"Good night, Bob." Mark said as he drove off.

Instead of heading for the freeway, he drove up California Street to Nob Hill and his condominium. He had no intention of going in, but there was a certain reassurance in driving by. He didn't like Jane Traggert very much, but she was certainly sexy enough. Maybe he should really have lunch with her and then, who knows, perhaps it wouldn't be a bad idea to spend a couple of hours in the condo.

He got on the freeway at Gough, and headed for Hillsborough. By the time he passed Candlestick Park, lighted for the Giants' game, his anger had nearly cooled off. After all, Pris's kiss outside

of Ernie's was her way of apologizing. He supposed marriage included getting angry and compromising.

Pris's Jaguar was already there, as he pulled in. to the garage.
He felt vaguely apprehensive as he entered the house. "Pris! Pris!"
he called out. He saw a note on the table.

Sweetheart, I'm in the bedroom. Please come back.

The bedroom suite was at the far end of the house. As he
approached, he could smell wood burning in the bedroom fireplace. Pris was lying on the fully made bed, watching the Johnny
Carson show. The drapes were open, showing the lighted back
yard and swimming pool. She was dressed in a provocative negligee. "Sweetheart, I'm sorry I hurt your feelings," she said. "Will
you forgive me?"

"Of course I will," he said.

"Do you want to talk about things?" she asked.

"Maybe sometime," he said. "But right now I've got other things
on my mind."

Pris's being the first one to want sex aroused Mark. He slipped
off the straps of her negligee and kissed between her breasts. He
had intended to totally remove the garment before making love,
but suddenly he could not wait.

"Mark, wait. Please, the drapes," Pris whispered.

"To hell with the drapes. Let them watch. They might learn
something." He began making love, but he could feel the old
resistance in her.

"Please, Mark," she asked, almost begging, "I just can't—not
with the drapes open."

Mark got up from the bed and walked to the drape pull. "Hey,
out there! Did you ever see an erection as big as this?" he shouted
as he closed the drapes.

Priscilla laughed. "Come on and get back in bed with me."

It wasn't long before he wanted to make love again. Not since
their honeymoon had they made love twice in one night, but tonight he was stimulated by their quarrel and by her invitation to
sex. When they finished, he said, "I love you Pris."

"I love you, too," she said.

Mark could not sleep after Pris had fallen asleep. An old movie
was on the television. Still naked, he got up and turned it off,
being careful not to wake her. The embers in the fireplace cast the
only light in the room as he walked around the corner into the
special den-alcove they had built off their bedroom. Mark made

himself a Rob Roy in the small bar, and sat naked on the love seat, his body dimly lighted by the outdoor lights. He marveled at the beauty of his house. It was the fulfillment of every dream he had ever had. He had nearly everything he had ever wanted. Money, a wonderful business, recognition, two perfect homes, nearly everything. And, as lousy as tonight with Pris had started out, things were better now than they ever had been. He really loved Pris. In time there would be children, and he would be completely happy.

He finished his drink and decided to talk to the ducks. His impulse was to walk by the lake naked, but he decided to put on his robe and slippers. He turned on the front yard lights and stood at the edge of the lake.

"Hey, there, ducks! Are you related to the ducks at Worcester?"

The ducks, who had apparently been sleeping, were startled by the lights, and began swimming and occasionally quacking.

"Sorry, I can't understand you. I can only understand quacking with an English accent."

He walked around to the other side of the lake to be closer to the ducks. "What do you think of this house, eh? It has to be the best house for ducks in the whole damn world."

The ducks swam across the lake, away from him.

"What's the matter? Oh, I know—you *are* English. It's your English reserve. We haven't been properly introduced, have we? I'm Mark Stevens. I own this place. I'm the guy who pays the bills around here. But you're welcome to stay if you want. The only thing I ask is a little companionship and some occasional advice."

After a while Mark decided to go inside.

"Okay, guys. I'm going back to bed now. I've got to go to work in the morning."

Pris stirred when he went back to bed. "Is everything all right with us?" she asked.

"Everything's fine," he said, sure he was telling her the truth.

-32-

Although Pris was very busy at her gallery and decorating the Hillsborough house, she had decided she should take the time to accompany Mark to London for Rodney's court proceedings.

"I wish I could explain how I feel when I come to London," Mark told Pris. They were riding in from Heathrow in a hired Daimler limousine. "Maybe it sounds silly," he continued, "but the ride into town from the airport is always my favorite part of coming to London."

"I was so young, I don't even remember my first time in England," Pris said.

"I'm still every bit as excited as the first time Rodney showed me around London in a taxi."

"What I remember the most is Castle Enfield. Before Mother died, we spent every Christmas there with Aunt Mavis and the whole family."

"Castle Enfield is magnificent, all right. I'll never forget the first time I saw it. Was I impressed!"

"And was I impressed when I met cousin Rodney's American friend." She lovingly squeezed her husband's arm. Pris was referring to meeting Mark at the New Year's Eve party, when she was 17. Recently, she had confessed to Mark that she had a crush on him the first time she met him. Mark affectionately patted her arm in return. Their relationship was much improved since their argument at the art gallery last week. Mark was pleased that Pris had volunteered to cancel her busy schedule to join him on this trip.

As they neared Knightsbridge, the chauffeur slowed for the heavier traffic. "Aren't these buildings wonderful? They've been here for centuries," Mark marveled. "London gives me a sense of adventure. When I feel this way I wish I lived here."

"How come you didn't settle in England? You like it so much."

"Well, you know California was always home . . . there was my mother . . . then your father offered me the job."

"I could never live anyplace else but the Bay Area," said Pris. "Besides, London is a man's town."

After a good night's sleep, Mark woke up in Rodney's Knightsbridge flat. Rodney's trial was not scheduled until tomorrow, and so Mark had planned to visit the Rolls-Royce factory today. Pris and Mark were finishing breakfast with Rodney and Rebecca in the breakfast room overlooking Cadogan Square.

"I'm sorry, Mark," said Rodney. "I thought I'd be able to go with you to see your Rolls being built, but I've got another bloody meeting with the contractor." Rodney had completely recovered from his near nervous breakdown of a few months ago and was his old, happy self again.

"Why don't you come with me, Pris?" asked Mark. "I'd love to have you see my new car."

"Oh, sweetheart, I don't want to go to a factory."

Mark's face showed his disappointment. He wished Pris would show more enthusiasm about his Rolls.

"I'll see your car often enough after it's been delivered," she continued. "Rebecca is going to show me a marvelous art gallery she found off New Bond Street."

"It can wait until tomorrow if you want to go with Mark," said Rebecca.

"Oh, no. Let's go today. I've planned to shop here in Knightsbridge tomorrow."

"I just thought you might want to keep me company," said Mark.

"I'll go, if you want."

There was no point in pressuring her, he decided. "No, you go with Rebecca. That way I can spend all afternoon at the factory if I want."

Mark walked the two blocks to Sloane Avenue and caught a taxi for the Rolls-Royce factory. As he looked from the cab at the buildings and pedestrians, he thought about his life with Pris. He would have to adjust to a different kind of marriage than he had imagined. Pris had led an independent life before they married. He had been naive in thinking she would want to be his constant companion. He had been single a long time before getting married and he had gotten along just fine. Maybe being married wouldn't be so different from before. But Mark was not being honest with himself. The truth was that he wanted Pris to share his life with him. He wished she understood how important his business was to him, what this Rolls-Royce meant to him, and the many other things he had always kept inside himself.

With typical expertise, Mark's cab driver found the factory in the remote industrial section without a wrong turn. "Rolls-Royce. Mulliner, Park Ward," said the small sign on the vast, old, brick factory building. The receptionist asked Mark to wait, as he was early for his appointment. Mark idly looked in the display cases. There were photographs of Charles Stewart Rolls and Frederick Henry Royce, the co-founders of the Company. Mark read the material on display with curiosity. In bygone years, Rolls-Royce did not make bodies for its cars, only the engine and the chassis. In the old days, if you wanted a Rolls-Royce, you went to one of the several independent coach builders who offered choices of different hand-crafted bodies. In the post-war years, the coach builders could not compete with machine production, so in order to keep alive the custom-body-building craft, Rolls-Royce had bought two of the companies and made them into a subsidiary. Here, near London, Mulliner, Park Ward hand-made the Corniche convertibles and the Phantom VI limousines. The other Rolls-Royces were made in Crewe, many miles to the north.

Mark looked up from the photographs in the display case, at the smiling, cheerful, white-haired man who entered the room. "Hello, my name is Kent Newsom. I've been assigned to show you around the works this afternoon." Mark shook hands. Newsom was 70, slim and the same height as Mark's six feet. He wore a white lab coat with the "RR" symbol embroidered above the breast pocket. "Your Phantom is nearly finished. Shall we go up and have a look?"

They walked through the ground floor, where men were busy working on various stages of the convertibles. Some were readying the shiny aluminum and steel bodies for painting, while in another area upholsterers prepared the leather seats for installation into more nearly finished cars. Newsom punched the elevator button. "You'll find your motor car to be a beauty Mr. Stevens. They're finishing up with the upholstery now."

"I can't tell you how excited I am. This has been a dream of mine since the first time I saw a Rolls, years ago."

The old elevator, which was large enough to hold a car, clanked open and they got on. Newsom pushed the button and the elevator jerked upward. "When we finished the body on your car, we sent it north for its chassis. It's back here now for finishing touches. It should be ready in one week's time." The elevator opened, and Newsom led Mark around busy workmen, toward the area devoted to making the limousines. "We only make one Phantom body at a time. You see, there? Those men are starting another body on the buck." Newsom pointed at two craftsmen fitting pieces of sheet metal around a wooden skeleton, called a buck.

Mark was excited when he glimpsed the bright, shiny, black metal of his car, partially hidden by some machinery. Suddenly, there it was in full view.

"Congratulations, Mr. Stevens. Here is your Phantom VI."

"My God, it's so beautiful!" shouted Mark. Excitedly, he ran up to the car and grabbed the driver's door handle. "I've never seen anything so beautiful in my life!"

Several men working nearby looked up. They smiled at Mark's exuberance. Still holding their tools, they walked nearer to the sight of the enthusiastic visitor.

Mark started to open the car door. Then, remembering that he had not taken a good look at the outside of the car, he stood back in awe of the graceful, sculpted lines. An upholsterer got out of the other side of the car and joined his amused coworkers.

His gaze fixed on the car, Mark slowly walked around to the front. The grill, reminiscent of an ancient Greek temple, proclaimed that this was a Rolls-Royce. Mark reached forward and touched the hood ornament.

"That's the 'Spirit of Ecstasy', Mr. Stevens," said the grinning Newsom. "Sometimes it's called the 'Flying Lady'. She's been on our radiators more than 60 years."

Mark admiringly stroked the delicate silver statue. "For a such a nice lady, she doesn't seem to mind my feeling her," Mark laughed.

Newsom laughed, too. "Perhaps that's because you're her owner now, Mr. Stevens." The workers, whose ranks had grown, politely chuckled at Mark's infectious enthusiasm.

Mark continued circling his prized car. "Elegant! There's only one word for it and that's 'elegant.'"

Mark sat in the driver's seat, looking over the long hood, and took the wheel as if he were driving. He inspected and worked the various controls and knobs, until he hit upon the control for the glass dividing the chauffeur from the back seat. Slowly, the glass rose into place. Impulsively, he turned the key, starting the engine. After a short idling period, the engine quieted, and was absolutely silent.

"We always say that at 60 miles per hour, the loudest noise is the sound of the ticking of the clock."

"Amazing," said Mark. He got out of the car and cocked his ear, listening for a sound from the engine. "I can't hear a thing."

Leaving the engine running, Mark got into the gigantic rear seat. He felt the smooth, luxurious cloth. An upholsterer's tool still lay on the seat. Mark looked about him at the lavishly lacquered wood. He opened up the two picnic tables, and then the bar.

"We don't put the crystal in the bar until the very last thing," explained Newsom.

"Kent," said Mark, "I have one hell of an idea."

"Yes?" said Newsom, with the air of a man apprehensive of what Mark would do next.

"Let's go for a ride."

"Oh, no, sir, I couldn't do that."

"What do you mean, you couldn't do that? It's my car, isn't it? It's all paid for, isn't it? Come on, Kent, let's go for a spin."

Newsom blushed. He stood there, not knowing quite what to do. Mark approached the group of workmen. "Which one of you would like to chauffeur us around for a while?" They all grinned and laughed, but no one stepped forward. Mark spoke to the youngest, an apprentice of about 25. "I'm Mark Stevens. What's your name?"

"Kevin, Kevin O' Donnell."

"A little Irish in you, Kevin?"

"From away back, sir."

"How about it Kevin? How about taking me my friend and me for a ride in my new Phantom VI? Come on now. Haven't you always wanted to do that?"

"All right, sir. If you don't think I'd lose my job."

"They wouldn't dare fire you, Kevin. Come on, take the wheel," said Mark, gesturing toward the chauffeur's seat.

Uncertainly, Kevin sat down and took the wheel. Apprehensive, yet grinning at his coworkers, who were now cheering, Kevin slowly guided the car forward. Mark zipped down the division window. "Wait, Kevin," he shouted. He opened the big, back seat door, and pointed to Newsom. "Mr. Kent Newsom, by order of the Royal Family of San Francisco, I command you to sit in the back seat with me."

Shy, but not able to resist, Newsom got into the car, as the group cheered. "Any of the rest of you chaps want to come with us?" cried Mark.

"Me, I will!" shouted one.

With that the reserve of the rest of the men collapsed. Laughing and joking, they all piled into the car. Two sat in front with Kevin, their grinning chauffeur. Two more unfolded the jump seats and sat in the back. The final two joined Newsom and Mark in the back seat. In all, eight people crammed into the big car. Kevin slowly drove it to the large elevator. "I haven't had so many people in a car since I was in Oxford," Mark merrily shouted.

One of the men opened the elevator door, and Kevin drove the long Phantom inside. Once on the ground floor, the car and its waving occupants left the elevator and made its way past the stunned workers toward the outside door. When the workmen realized what was happening, they dropped their work. They followed the slowly moving limousine, cheering as it disappeared around the corner.

Even though laden with eight fully grown men, the big Phantom lost none of its dignity as it waited for a traffic signal. Passing drivers rolled down their windows to get a closer look. As the signal changed and the Phantom drove off, pedestrians looked up at the waving limousine passengers and began to wave in return.

"Wait, O'Connell, wait!" shouted Mark. "There's a pub. Let's all have a pint." The car stopped in front of the pub and the men, one by one, disembarked from the Phantom and walked through the door, anticipating a beer or two.

As Mark rode in the taxi returning to Knightsbridge, he thought about the afternoon. He had certainly come a long way, since he had first seen the Queen's Rolls-Royce. He wished it were possible for his father to know about his Phantom. How sweet that would be!

Mark had been afraid the Rolls-Royce people would be upset with the men, so when they had returned to the factory he had apologized. "Oh, that's quite all right," the executive had said. "My only regret is I wasn't invited along." Mark never ceased to be amazed that so many seemingly withdrawn and conservative Englishmen were in fact quite the opposite.

Mark paid the taxi driver in front of Rodney's flat. He decided he would not tell Pris about the test drive. She probably would not think it was very much fun anyway. It was too bad, he thought, but she would never know the side of him that would pile a bunch of workmen into his Rolls-Royce, she would never know that he talked to ducks late at night and she would never understand the relentless drive deep inside him.

-33-

Adam Hawkes, Rodney's solicitor, had retained the highly reputed London barrister, William Thackery Scott, Queen's Counsel, to defend Rodney against the foreclosure court action. This
morning the trial was to commence, and Mark and Rodney were
meeting for final preparation with Hawkes and Scott in Scott's
paper-strewn chambers in Number Eight, Old Square, Lincoln's
Inn, WE 2. Lincoln's Inn was one of the four surviving historic
Inns of Court, where barristers had their chambers. Because fore-
closures were "equity" cases, and since the barristers who specialized in equity cases had chambers in Lincoln's Inn, Adam
Hawkes had selected William Thackery Scott, Lincoln's Inn's most
noted barrister.

"Our case has been delayed until eleven o'clock," said Scott.
"So we have more time to chat." Scott, who was in his mid 60s,
tossed his feet across the top of his battered and unpretentious
desk, and leaned back in his chair. Mark noticed the beginnings
of a hole in the sole of the great barrister's shoe. Scott lit his pipe,
shook out the match and threw it, still smoking, in the general
direction of the paper-filled waste basket. It completely missed
the basket, just missed the carpet and lay smoldering on the
wooden floor. Mark wondered how the ancient building had stood
unscathed all these years, with such careless barristers. Scott
brushed some still-smoking ash off his vest and continued. "If
you have any questions, Mark, we should go over them now. Once
you take the witness box, I can't talk to you until you've finished
your testimony. Unethical, you see—would be influencing a witness."

"No, I don't think there's much more to it. I'm prepared to put
up the money to pay the mortgage. Rodney has taken me on as
his new partner."

"You'll remember that since I first instructed you in this case,"
Adam Hawkes said, "Rodney's partner, Billings, has signed the
proper papers. Mark has replaced him as Rodney's partner."

"Yes, I recall," said Scott, sucking life into his pipe. "Do you have any further questions, Rodney?"

"Well, yes, I do," Rodney answered hesitantly. "Do they have any chance at all of winning?"

"Their barrister certainly thinks so," answered Scott gruffly. "I learned a long time ago that, in trial work, even the best of cases are won only 75% of the time."

"Perhaps less than that," Adam Hawkes joined in.

"That unpredictable!" exclaimed Mark.

"There's always some bloody unexpected problem that comes up. If not that, the judge may be out of sorts that day," said Scott, satisfied his pipe was burning properly.

"That doesn't help my nerves much," said Rodney anxiously. Rodney had been eating and sleeping much better, but in the last few days he had become very apprehensive again.

"I've found it serves little purpose to fret about these things," said Scott. "Remember, the opponent always faces just as many uncertainties."

Mark had stood and was looking out the window. The buildings of Old Square, Lincoln's Inn formed a quadrangle surrounding a beautiful green grass field, not unlike the colleges at Oxford. Robed and wigged barristers hurried from their chambers and scurried along the sidewalks bordering the field, towards the nearby Royal Courts of Justice. Barristers from the other Inns of Court used robing rooms in the court building to change into their traditional costumes. But Lincoln's Inn was close to the back entrance of the courts, and many barristers donned their robes and wigs in their chambers before dashing off to do battle.

Scott sprang to his feet as the teakettle clicked its signal that the water was boiling. He began serving tea to his guests. Mark smiled to himself. He doubted if he'd ever see a Montgomery Street, San Francisco lawyer making his own tea. The teakettle stirred memories of the many times Dick Dawbarn had made tea at Worcester College.

"How many days do you think the case will take?" Mark asked.

"Days!" exclaimed William Thackery Scott. "Even starting at eleven, we should finish by mid-afternoon."

"In America a case like this would take several days," rejoined Mark.

"So I've heard," said Adam Hawkes, chuckling.

"It's a matter of proving you have the ability to pay the mortgage," said Scott, "then persuading the judge not to make an order of foreclosure. The master has decided that we raised a proper issue on the affidavits. I'm arguing that a forfeiture would be unconscionable. That's the key issue. Foreclosure wouldn't be just under the circumstances of this case." He had put on his robe and was adjusting his wig. The wig was yellowed and tattered. Probably the only wig Scott had ever possessed, Mark thought.

Scott was emotionally worked up, as he spoke. "But then I'd better save my little speech for the judge, hadn't I?" He motioned that it was time to go. "We're in for a fight to the finish," said Scott, knocking the tobacco residue from his pipe. Some went into the big ashtray, but some scattered onto his desk. "The owner of the mortgage company is a very difficult person," Scott continued. "His barrister told me, at the appointment before the master, that his client is always embroiled in some sort of litigation or another—never settles out of court."

As the conference ended, Mark marveled at William Thackery Scott's calmness. The case, which was vitally important to Rodney, seemed just another case to Scott. Tomorrow, no doubt, there would be another case just as important to still another litigant, and Scott would be just as cool.

As with all Queen's Counsels, Scott was joined by a junior barrister, who carried some of the books and papers as they left the chambers for the brisk one block walk to Carey Street and the rear entrance to the courts. Scott, however, carried his briefs in a special velvet bag. They entered the rear entrance to the massive Victorian building, and the troop marched down a narrow flight of stairs and out into a huge hall. The room was four or five stories in height, and was large enough to hold a thousand armored knights. It echoed with the footsteps of barristers and others who had business in the courts. Some paused to read posted lists telling where the day's cases would be heard. William Thackery Scott had no need to read the notices. He purposefully led his procession across the great hall and through one of the many small vaulted archways leading to various courts. Followed by the others, Scott climbed the short flight of stairs that led to court number 15.

It was Rodney who first saw the familiar well-dressed figure talking with his barrister in the narrow stone corridor outside court.

"My God, Mark, look!" exclaimed Rodney.

"What?" asked Mark.

"Do you see who that is?"

"Where?"

"There, talking with that barrister."

"Good lord! It's—It's Derek, isn't it?"

"You're bloody right, it's Derek. What the hell is Derek Harden doing at my trial?"

"Harden?" asked William Thackery Scott. "Do you know Derek Harden?"

"Yes, we knew him at Oxford, the bloody bastard!" said Rodney. "Don't tell me you know him, too?"

"He's the one I was just talking about. He's the one who owns the mortgage company," said Scott.

"He's what?" asked Mark.

"He's the one who is foreclosing." Scott nodded acknowledgment to the other barrister. "His company is the plaintiff."

"But he's Derek Harden! He's been nothing but trouble since my first day at Oxford," said Mark incredulously.

"That's strange," said Scott. "The first time I saw him was at the master's appointment. His name is Derek Harden, all right. He's the same chap I said is so litigious."

"This is the first I've heard anything about Derek," said Rodney.

"How the hell did Derek ever get a mortgage on your office building?" Mark was astounded.

"I don't know," said Rodney. "I never was at the bloody mortgage company. Billings did all the paper work. I don't understand it. Derek! I just don't understand."

William Thackery Scott directed Rodney and Mark to enter the courtroom by a rear door, while he went in an adjacent door leading to the front benches.

To Mark, the old courtroom was breath taking. It was not an especially large room, having only about half a dozen benches for the lawyers, witnesses and spectators. The court personnel were already in their places, sitting in two separate levels below where the judge would soon sit. Some wore wigs as well as robes, others only robes. The room had an extremely high, domed ceiling. The total impression was of fine old wood everywhere. Carved wood decorated the walls, carved wood formed the judge's massive bench, even the witness box was made of carved wood.

William Thackery Scott entered the room and sat in the first bench, facing the judge's bench. The junior barrister sat in the bench behind Scott. Adam Hawkes and Rodney sat in the next bench, and Mark sat in still another bench.

"I can't get over Derek's being here," said Rodney turning to Mark. "He must be the one behind all of this." Mark could see Rodney nervously twisting his hands.

"Try and relax. You've got a damn good barrister."

Just then, Derek's barrister, his junior, and Derek's solicitor entered the room, and began taking their places across from their opposite numbers.

At that moment, Derek entered the courtroom and sat on the other end of the very same bench on which Rodney sat, not 15 feet away.

"Bloody hell!" Rodney whispered to Mark. "Look at the bastard!"

As at Worcester, Derek was very well dressed. His suit was made from a rich small patterned material. His plain conservative tie toned down the bold stripes of his shirt. He looked straight ahead, avoiding looking at them. His head was held the same arrogant and disdainful way that Mark remembered.

Then the judge entered the courtroom. "Court rise," said the usher. The frail, aging usher, the English equivalent of a bailiff, could not have quelled a courtroom disturbance if his life had depended on it. He looked as if his most difficult task of the day were to stay on his feet until the judge took his place.

Then the associate, a young woman wearing a black judicial robe but no wig, spoke: "Trafalgar Financial Limited vs. Ashley."

"Mr. Tudor," said the judge to Derek's barrister. The judge was The Honorable Mr. Justice Percival Thompson, a businesslike man with sharp features. His wig was tilted forward so that it nearly touched his round glasses. The man seemed to be very young to be a judge. Mr. Justice Thompson wore a bright red sash over the shoulder of his robe.

Derek's barrister rose and addressed the court. "My Lord, in this case I represent Trafalgar Financial Limited, the plaintiff." Ramsey Tudor, the barrister, reminded Mark of the Lord that Mark had heard speaking before the House of Lords, when Rodney had once taken him there to hear his father debate—so stuffy and proper that his mouth barely moved as he spoke. Only because of the microphone system could Mark hear Tudor. "My learned friend represents the defendant." Ramsey Tudor nodded acknowledgment toward his opponent, William Thackery Scott. There seemed to be no need for the barristers to identify themselves to the judge. "If I may direct your Lordship's attention to the pleadings, you will see that this is a straightforward action in equity to foreclose the plaintiff's mortgage." Tudor, who looked in his 50s, also wore a wig and robe. "The plaintiff loaned Mr. Ashley, the defendant, and his partner the sum of £950,000 that was secured by a mortgage on a certain office block in London. Whilst certain interest payments were indeed made, the obligation soon fell into arrears and remains unpaid. Therefore an order of foreclosure and a judgment against Mr. Ashley would appear to be routine."

Tudor poked at his wig with a pen in an attempt to scratch his head, and then adjusted his wig as he continued. "My learned friend contends however, that your Lordship should not issue a foreclosure order because he will attempt to prove that an offer to pay the obligation in full was made. While it is the case that such an offer was made, I contend that the so-called offer fails on two counts, my Lord. First it was made well after the due date, and after the plaintiff's rights to foreclose had vested. Second, and of even greater importance, the offer of payment was not made in good faith. The defendant never had the actual means to pay the obligation. As you will see, the bundle of evidence contains all the requisite documents."

"Very well," said the judge, peering at the documents that he held close to his glasses. "I see from the witness list that you have only one witness." The judge, who had been sipping from a tall water glass as Tudor spoke, took another sip.

"Yes, my Lord. My witness is Derek Harden, the majority share-holder of the plaintiff corporation."

As Derek was escorted to the witness box to take the oath, Mark still could not believe his old enemy was the one behind all this. How in the hell had Derek managed to worm his way into holding the mortgage on Rodney's property? Just the sight of him stirred up the hatred Mark had felt when he had hit Derek the night of the Kennedy assassination. The same hatred as when Mark had learned it was Derek behind the plagiarism charges.

While the witness box was to one side of the judge, it was forward and turned, so that the witness's facial expression and demeanor were in full view.

"Mr. Harden, you are the Managing Director of Trafalgar Financial Limited?" asked Tudor.

"Yes, its one of my ventures. I don't attend to the day-to-day activities of the business."

"But in this case you did?"

"Yes. I had a special interest in this case."

"Why is that?"

"I recognized the name when the Loan Committee reviewed the loan application. I recognized Rodney Ashley's name on the application."

"You knew Mr. Ashley, then?"

"Yes, I knew him at Oxford. He lived across the hall from me at Worcester College."

"Did he know that you controlled Trafalgar Financial Limited?"

"I doubt it very much. Very few know that fact. Besides, it was his partner, Billings, who dealt with my company."

"Did the Loan Committee approve the loan application?"

"Yes, it did. I told them I knew Mr. Ashley very well, and that his organization should be granted whatever loan he wanted."

Rodney turned, skeptically looking at Mark.

"Now then, did the loan ultimately go into default?"

"I followed it very closely because of my ties with Mr. Ashley. At first we were paid interest payments, but then it went into default. Finally, the principal became due and wasn't paid."

"What did you do then?"

"We were very concerned about the arrearage, and so all the proper notices were sent, and that sort of thing."

"My Lord, if you will look in the bundle of evidence, you will find the notices."

"There is no disagreement on that point, my Lord," said William Thackery Scott, rising to his feet. "The notices were sent and received."

"Very well," said the judge.

"And so you commenced foreclosure proceedings," Tudor resumed. "To this day has the mortgage been paid?"

"No," Derek answered. "It has not."

"I have no further questions."

"Mr. Scott," said the judge. "Do you wish to cross-examine Mr. Harden?"

William Thackery Scott stood. "I have just a few short questions, my Lord."

"Very well, please ask them," said the judge impatiently. One suspected that the judge knew very well that Scott's questions would be neither few nor short.

"Mr. Harden, you say that nothing has been paid on the mortgage?" asked Scott.

"Except for the first few interest payments, you are correct," answered Derek warily.

"Isn't it true that within 10 or 12 days after the letter of demand, an offer was made to pay the entire loan?"

"Well, yes, if you can call it an offer. No one at Trafalgar took it seriously," said Derek flippantly.

"Was the 'no one' in fact you, Mr. Harden?"

"I had a full credit report on Rodney, Mr. Ashley, that is, and another credit report on Billings, his partner. Their resources were pitifully small compared to what they owed my company."

"That may be true, Mr. Harden, but did you ever think that Mr. Ashley might have other resources at his command? Family or friends, for example?"

"I had heard that Lord Ashley was adamant in not paying his son's debts."

"And where did you hear that?"

"With respect, my Lord, I object," droned Tudor, rising routinely to his feet as if he had done so thousands of times before. "It is totally immaterial in the first place, as to where, or even whether, Mr. Harden heard that Lord Ashley thought his son's venture ill-advised."

"Now, Mr. Tudor," said the judge. "You may or may not be technically correct, but I think we should hear his answer. Please answer the question, Mr. Harden."

"I'm not sure where I heard it. One of my people is a member at the Blue Sheep Club. I think he was the one who first told me that Lord Ashley was angry with his son. There was talk at the club that Lord Ashley didn't want Rodney to invest in the office block, let alone borrow money for the project."

"So that is why you thought Mr. Ashley would not be able to raise the necessary money—because of his father's attitude?" asked Scott.

"Yes, that is correct."

"Mr. Scott, it's one o'clock and time for lunch adjournment," said the judge. "We shall commence at two o'clock." Everyone in the courtroom stood while the judge left the courtroom.

Mark, Rodney, and William Thackery Scott chatted in the hallway outside the courtroom. "Mr. Scott, Derek is implying he and I were friends at Worcester. We were no such thing. In fact, we were the opposite," Rodney pointed out.

"Yes," said Mark. "Derek and I were mortal enemies. I wouldn't put it past him to try to get even with me by foreclosing on Rodney. He knows we're the best of friends."

"There's more to this than meets the eye," said Scott. "After lunch I think I'll go on a little fishing expedition with our friend, Mr. Harden."

After lunch, with Derek again in the witness box, William Thackery Scott resumed cross-examination. "Mr. Harden, tell us when you first knew that Mr. Ashley was one of the principals?"

"As I said this morning, I just happened to notice his name on the papers when the Loan Committee met."

"And not before?"

"No."

"But before the loan was finally approved, you knew it was Ashley?"

"Oh, yes, I knew by then."

"Did the fact that Rodney Ashley was involved affect your decision in any way? Your decision to approve the loan?"

"Well, I suppose it did."

"And in what way?"

"I suggested we loan the full amount originally requested. I wanted to help out Rodney, if I could. We had been friends you see—Oxford together—same college and all of that."

"The amount originally requested?"

"Yes, you see the original request had been reduced by our loan manager. As I remember, Mr. Ashley's partner had requested £950,000. My loan manager thought that was too much—too risky. He recommended a loan of £650,000."

"And so, what amount did the committee finally approve?"

"I insisted on the full £950,000."

"Despite the loan manager's reservations?"

"Yes. As I say, I wanted to do Mr. Ashley a favor if I could."

"And so, the committee did what you wanted and approved the original £950,000."

"Eventually, yes."

"Eventually?"

"Yes, the loan manager wanted to wait a week to look into the matter further."

"What did he intend to do?"

"I really can't recall. Get some more credit reports, I suspect."

"What is the loan manager's name? Perhaps if he is subpoenaed he'll be able to recall."

"I can't recall his name, but as I think about it . . . yes, I remember now. He wanted to get Lord Ashley to guarantee his son's note, if we were to go to £950,000. We postponed the matter a week to see if he could get the guarantee.

"And did he get Lord Ashley's guarantee?"

"No, he didn't. I remember now. He told us at the next meeting that he couldn't get the guarantee. As a matter of fact, I believe that is where I first heard that Lord Ashley disapproved of the whole venture." As he testified, Derek looked directly at Tudor, never looking at the judge, or at Rodney or Mark.

"So, at the next meeting, the Loan Committee approved the loan for the full £950,000, even without Lord Ashley's guarantee?"

"Yes."

"Why was that?"

"That's what I recommended to the committee. I was willing to take a chance on my old friend."

"You said, I believe, that the loan manager recommended only £650,000. I'd like to be sure we all understand his reasons. My Lord, may I have the shorthand writer read back Mr. Harden's previous testimony on that point?"

"Very well," said the judge. "But I fail to see the relevance."

"Nor do I," said Tudor. "I should have objected long ago, but I did not out, of deference to my learned friend."

"But, my Lord, in fact my learned friend failed to object. We are into it too far now to go back."

"Yes. Yes. Read the testimony. Let's be on with it."

The shorthand writer looked up from her notes. "I believe I've found the proper place, my Lord."

"Please read it, then," said Scott impatiently, "with my Lord's permission."

The court reporter began reading aloud. *"Yes, you see the original request was reduced by our loan manager. As I remember, Mr. Ashley's partner had requested £950,000. My loan manager thought that was too much—too much, too risky. He recommended a loan of £650,000."* The reporter put down her notes and readied herself for further testimony.

"The loan manager thought it much too risky," repeated Scott. "Exactly what was the risk, Mr. Harden?"

"Well, the risk was as with any loan. If you loan too much compared to the worth of the underlying security and the ability of the borrower to pay, you might have to seek an order of foreclosure, even ultimately seek a personal judgment, if the security doesn't fetch enough."

"And the underlying security in this case was the office block?"

"Yes, it was."

"So you knew at the meeting that by loaning the full £950,000, it was more likely that the loan wouldn't be paid off and you'd bring foreclosure against your old friend? Isn't that right?"

Tudor jumped to his feet. "My Lord, I take objection to the question. My learned friend is trying to put words in Mr. Harden's mouth. Why would anyone deliberately make a loan that would lead to foreclosure?"

"Indeed, why?" said Judge Thompson. "I was wondering the same thing."

"My Lord, I submit that Harden, here, saw an opportunity to kill two birds with one stone," asserted Scott, pointing at Derek. "He could get a valuable office block for less than it was worth. Secondly, he could get revenge against Mr. Ashley, whom he never liked, and who was the loyal friend of his old Oxford enemy, Mark Stevens, who now sits in this courtroom."

"Now, just a minute!" said Derek from the witness box.

"Then answer the question I put to you a moment ago. Didn't you deliberately make the loan in an amount that was likely to lead to foreclosure?"

"My Lord," said Derek, for the first time turning to the judge. "I did not approve the loan so that I could foreclose."

"Oh, no?" asked Scott. "Did you not see an opportunity to acquire a building for substantially less than it was worth?"

"That's not what happened."

"Let's stand back and take a look at the situation. You tell me that quite by coincidence Mr. Ashley's partner, Billings, applied for a loan with Trafalgar. Is that right so far?"

"It's not so much a coincidence. Trafalgar's business is making loans that banks have rejected. Banks refer many such cases to us."

"But you didn't know about this loan until the Loan Committee met?"

"Correct."

"Nor did you know that Mr. Ashley would be one of the borrowers?"

"Correct."

"Then you pushed through the loan, knowing that Mr. Ashley did not have the funds and might lose the property to you, did you not? You already knew that Lord Ashley would not assist his son."

"What you're implying is not true. I did not want to foreclose. We make loans to get repaid, not to foreclose on properties."

"Even if foreclosure would give you a chance to settle an old score?" pressed Scott.

"I don't know what you're talking about." This time Derek looked questioningly at his own barrister.

"Isn't it true that at Oxford Mr. Ashley was very good friends with one Mr. Mark Stevens?"

"Yes, Mr. Ashley had many friends at Oxford."

"And isn't it true that you were mortal enemies with Mark Stevens?"

"My Lord, I must object," said Tudor rising to his feet. "My learned friend knows very well that Mr. Harden's college relationship to this man, Mark Stevens, is quite irrelevant to this case."

"Yes, I quite agree," said the judge. "The objection is allowed."

"Very well, my Lord," said Scott. "Then, Mr. Harden, going back to what you said before, I'll ask this question. Since you did not make the loan with an intention to foreclose, you would have gladly accepted repayment, if it had been made?"

"Of course I would."

"Repayment was all you ever had in mind?"

"Yes. Of course."

"Even if the mortgage were overdue by a few days?"

"Well, yes. I suppose so."

"Loans are frequently paid late, aren't they?"

"Not frequently. No."

"But often late. Isn't that true, Mr. Harden? Often late?"

"Well, yes. I suppose so."

"Say 10 or 12 days late?"

"Yes, I suppose so."

"All the more reason to be glad to get payment—if it were late?"

"Yes. I suppose so."

"Then you would have accepted payment in this case, too, wouldn't you?"

Ramsey Tudor rose to make an objection, but he was too late.

"Yes," Derek answered.

"Even if it were 10 or 12 days late?"

"Yes."

"As a matter of fact, even it were, say, four months late—isn't that so?"

"But Rodney doesn't have the money. From the very start he didn't have the money. His father wouldn't loan it to him—not in a thousand years."

"Yes, and you knew all that from the very beginning, did you not?"

"So what if I did? The fact is, I haven't been paid."

"Maybe you haven't been paid, Mr. Harden, but an offer was made to you on Mr. Ashley's behalf, was it not?"

"Hah! Some offer! He didn't have the money, and to this day he doesn't have the money. It was a sham offer."

"Is that so?"

"Yes, that's so, Mr. Scott," said Derek sarcastically. "I've had him checked out very thoroughly."

"So that you could count on foreclosing. Is that not correct, Mr. Harden?"

"No, that's not correct, Mr. Scott. I only wanted to know if he could repay the loan."

"So you got credit reports to see if Mr. Ashley could repay the loan. Then, if I understand you, when the reports showed that he could not repay the loan, you gave him an even larger loan than your own loan manager wanted! Isn't that what you've testified to, here, this afternoon?"

Tudor rose to his feet more quickly than he had all day. "My Lord, I object to this question! Mr. Scott is attempting to put words in Mr. Harden's mouth."

"The objection is allowed. I think Mr. Harden's prior testimony speaks for itself," said the judge. "There's no need for the witness to summarize his own testimony."

"Thank you, my Lord," said Tudor smugly.

"Mr. Tudor," replied the judge. "I remind you that in my court I do not want the barristers to thank me for doing my job."

"Sorry, my Lord," said the reproved Tudor.

"Well, now, Mr. Harden," continued William Thackery Scott. "What if I told you that my client has a backer? A new partner. That his money was available four months ago, when this offer that you call a sham was made?"

"I didn't believe it then, and I wouldn't believe it now."

"What if I told you that Mr. Mark Stevens, here in this courtroom," Scott pointed toward Mark, "was that new partner? What if I told you that Mr. Mark Stevens is willing to advance the necessary funds right now?"

"Over £1,000,000? Mark Stevens? Don't make me laugh!" Derek gloated.

"We'll see who does the laughing. I have no more questions of this witness."

"My Lord, I have no further witnesses," said Tudor. "Despite all the thunder from my learned friend, I have completely proved my prima facie case. Simply put, the mortgage was made, it has not been repaid and my client is entitled to an order of foreclosure. Even imprudent lenders are entitled to their remedy."

"Mr. Scott?" said the judge, raising his eyebrows at Scott as if asking him to commence his defense.

"Thank you, my Lord. The defense has but one witness to call. The defense will show quite simply that at the time of the offer to pay the mortgage, Mr. Mark Stevens had become a backer with Mr. Ashley. That, with the help of Mr. Stevens, Mr. Ashley had sufficient funds to pay the mortgage obligation, and that therefore no order of foreclosure should be made. I call Mr. Mark Stevens as a witness."

Mark was ushered to the witness box and given the oath. For the first time during the trial, he was nervous. Rodney's whole future depended on his testimony. His lips were dry, and he could feel his heart beating fast as he waited for the first question.

Head tilted down, William Thackery Scott peered over his half-glasses at Mark. "Mr. Stevens, you are friends with Rodney Ashley?"

"Yes. I consider Rodney Ashley to be my best friend."

"You knew him at Oxford?"

"I was a Rhodes Scholar at Oxford. Mr. Ashley lived across the hall at Worcester College."

"You now live in America, I believe. What is the nature of your business?"

"I'm an investment banker." Now that Mark had answered a few questions, he was more calm. He was barely aware of anyone in the courtroom except Scott.

"Have you become a partner with Mr. Ashley in the matter before this court? That is, the office block development?"

"Yes, I have. Subject of course to being able to stop this bedamnable foreclosure. Sorry, my Lord."

Tudor had stood to object to the use of the offending word 'bedamnable', but as a barely perceptible smile passed across the face of the judge, Tudor sat down without making the objection.

"Do you have an opinion as to the proper value of the office block?"

"My Lord," said Tudor, slowly getting again to his feet. "The witness is not an expert on the value of London real estate."

"My Lord," said Scott. "Mr. Stevens may not be experienced in the London property market, but if your Lordship will permit him to answer the question, subject to the objection of my learned friend, I will justify its relevance in a few moments."

"Very well, Mr. Scott," said the judge. "The witness will answer the question on Mr. Scott's assurances as to relevance."

"Go ahead, Mr. Stevens, you may answer the question," said Scott.

"When the project is finished and fully leased up, it will be worth perhaps £2,000,000."

"Why do you say that?"

"Mr. Ashley showed me his financial projections for the building. He had worked out what the probable earnings would be after two or three years.

"And how does that affect value?" interrupted the judge.

"If I'm given the R.O.I., I can tell you the value."

"What's R.O.I.?," asked the judge.

"Return On Investment," said Mark. "From the return that Rodney projected, I estimated the value of the building at £2,000,000 minimum."

"But this building is in London, not America," the judge asserted.

"That wouldn't matter to the sophisticated investor. He's interested in R.O.I., no matter where the income comes from."

"I see," said the judge.

It's rather like the international money market, where I have more experience," elaborated Mark. "U.K. government bonds are worth about the same as U.S. government bonds, if they have the same yield."

"I see," the judge repeated. "You have some experience in international monetary matters?"

"Yes, my Lord. That's how I make my living."

Judge Thompson leaned back, apparently satisfied.

"So you think the building will be worth over £2,000,000 in two to three years?" asked Scott.

"Yes, that's why I'm putting up the necessary money to rescue the project."

"Don't you think it rather inequitable for Mr. Harden to foreclose on a two million pound building, when he is only owed half that?" Scott asked.

"My Lord," said Tudor, this time jumping to his feet. "My learned friend knows full well that we are not interested in what Mr. Stevens thinks is fair or unfair."

"My learned colleague is quite right," said Scott. "I withdraw the question."

"Gentlemen," said the judge. "This is a court of equity. There are no juries to impress in courts of equity. As for the judge, I can assure you that this is one judge who is quite capable of seeing the issues without help from you learned gentlemen."

"I'm quite sorry, my Lord," said Scott. "Shall I proceed?"

"Please do, Mr. Scott, and with dispatch, if you please," the judge gruffly responded.

"Mr. Stevens, I have only one or two more questions," said Scott. "Are you quite willing to advance funds sufficient to pay the delinquent principal and interest, even though they may amount to 1.1 million pounds, or even more?"

"Yes, I am."

"Then, to my last question, Mr. Stevens. Do you have sufficient funds to do this?"

"Not in cash. Not on my person—but I have it available."

"Quite, Mr. Stevens. That's what I meant. I have no further questions." With that, William Thackery Scott sat down. Mark turned and looked at the others. Rodney was smiling broadly, but Derek glared straight ahead, avoiding eye contact.

"Do you wish to cross-examine this witness, Mr. Tudor?" asked the judge.

Tudor stood, shuffled his notes for a few moments and began with an expression of disdain. "Mr. Stevens, do I correctly understand you claim to have the means to pay over 1.1 million pounds?

"Yes, I do sir."

"How old are you Mr. Stevens?"

"Thirty years old."

"Have you inherited money? Is that it?"

"No, my father died without any money, and my mother is still alive."

"Well then, what proof can you offer of the financial means you claim?"

"I have a financial statement in my brief case."

"Very well. May we have it, please?" asked Tudor confidently.

Mark opened his briefcase and handed the old usher a copy of the financial statement. The usher shuffled over to Ramsey Tudor and handed him the document. Still standing, Tudor studied the paper. His look changed to one of puzzlement. "I'm not sure that I understand what you have shown me."

"My assets are worth approximately 400 million dollars."

"Yes I see that figure, but certainly you mean 400 thousand dollars, don't you?"

"No, Mr. Tudor. I mean *million!* My net worth is four hundred *million* dollars."

"But . . . " Tudor sputtered, obviously taken back.

"My bank accounts add up to about 40 million. I keep about 10% in cash for safety and unexpected needs. Some of the rest is in real estate, but most of it is stock.

"Do you expect me to believe that you, at 30 years of age, have over . . . let me see . . . some 150 million pounds? Do you have any proof of such an astounding contention?"

"Actually, I think it's closer to *200* million pounds. Let's see, I have the statement of my company, The Stevens Group, with our London brokers. We do a lot of trading in currency here in London." Mark found another paper in his briefcase and held it out toward the usher. "It shows a credit balance of over £10,000,000 with our currency brokers."

"But you don't *own* The Stevens Group do you?"

"No. You're right about that. I'm the president, and I only own 25%. The rest is publicly traded."

"So this balance with your London brokers is not yours, but only that of your employer. Is that correct?" Ramsey Tudor asked with a triumphant tone.

Mark hesitated. "Yes. It belongs to The Stevens Group. I agree on that."

"Well, then, except for this financial statement, which you yourself prepared, you don't have any proof at all of what you are claiming."

"No, I don't. Not written proof, today." Mark nervously brushed back his gray hair. "But I do have my Nat West statement of account."

"You have what?"

"My National Westminster Bank statement and my check book. I've kept an account at the Oxford office since student days." Mark reached into his briefcase and offered the bank book to the usher.

"Yes, but how much do you have on deposit in this student account?"

"About £1,500,000,"

"What?"

"One million, five hundred thousand pounds. I transferred most of it from America last month, when I told Adam Hawkes I would make the investment with Rodney."

Ramsey Tudor stared at the bank statement for what seemed like an eternity. Everyone in the courtroom was silent as he finally turned the paper over and inspected the reverse side, before once again turning it and staring at the front.

"Well, Mr. Tudor, do you have any more questions?" asked the judge.

Ramsey Tudor did not respond, but dumbfounded, continued staring at the bank statement, saying nothing.

"Mr. Tudor, I asked you if you had any more questions," the judge repeated, again sipping from his glass of water.

"Er, no, my Lord. I have no more questions."

"Very well," said the judge. "Unless you gentlemen have further witnesses or wish to make a further submission, I am ready to give my judgment."

"Nothing further, my Lord," said William Thackery Scott.

Tudor had sat down, but was still looking at the bank statement.

"Mr. Tudor," said the judge. "Do you have anything more to say?"

"No, my Lord," said Ramsey Tudor, forgetting to rise before he spoke.

"Very well, then, I shall rule on the matter. I grant relief against the plaintiff and in favor of the defendant, conditioned upon payment of the outstanding obligation, plus interest, within 10 business days." The attention of everyone in the courtroom was riveted on the judge as he spoke. "To allow foreclosure would be to allow an unconscionable forfeiture. Furthermore, it has been clearly established that Mr. Stevens has the financial ability to pay the obligation. My judgment is conditioned upon the obligation's being paid in 10 days." The judge sipped from his water glass, gathered his papers and stood to leave the court. He then turned to Mark. "By the way, Mr. Stevens, do you think my investments should be in pounds or dollars?"

Mark wasn't sure whether the judge was joking or seriously asking for advice. "Most Englishmen, in reality, have all their assets in pounds, because everything they own is in England," Mark answered. "I would say that in the present climate, that's a wise place to be, your Lordship."

"I see," said the judge. "I hope you're right." Again, the faintest of smiles crossed his face.

.   .   .

Outside the courtroom, Derek stopped in front of Mark, and glared. "As for you, Stevens, don't expect this is the last time you will hear from Derek Harden. If it's the last thing I do, I'm going to get even. I'm not just bluffing, either. You can count on that."

Before Mark could respond, Derek stalked down the hallway to the stairs, leaving Ramsey Tudor struggling to pursue him.

That evening, London suffered a fierce storm. As the rain poured down, Rodney, Rebecca, Pris and Mark piled out of their taxi in front of the Quo Vadis restaurant. They had aperitifs in the foyer while they waited for their table.

"Celebrating like this has become a tradition with us," said Rodney.

"Except that Pris is with us now," said Mark.

"Yes, here's to Pris's being with us," added Rebecca, raising her glass.

"May we ever remain good friends," said Rodney, raising his glass also.

"And partners, too. It's a wonderful feeling, owning a part of London," said Mark, joining the toast by raising his Rob Roy glass.

The rainstorm had let up, and Mark was in a euphoric mood as the four returned to the Ashley flat after dinner. Pris had tenderly taken his hand in the taxi. He was eager to make love with her as soon as they could make their excuses to their friends and retire to their bedroom.

Mark was vigorous in his love-making that night. These last two days—buying the Rolls-Royce, winning the trial, and now Pris's reaching out to him—made any disappointments in his marriage seem very unimportant.

Meanwhile, across rain-soaked London, Derek Harden's top advisors gathered in the richly paneled conference room of his headquarters.

"I wonder what he wants," one nervously inquired of another as they waited for Derek to arrive.

"He lost the lawsuit today."

"I understand he was very upset."

"That's a bloody understatement."

"I've never seen him so angry."

At exactly midnight, Derek entered the room from his office. He was impeccably dressed in a fresh suit. Although his several business enterprises were located elsewhere, they were controlled by him from these offices.

"Gentlemen, I do not like what happened to me today. I was humiliated. I do not like being humiliated." No one spoke, waiting for Derek to continue. "My plan is to get even. I have been reading the information about Mark Stevens that I ordered you to assemble." Derek began pacing at the head of the large conference table. He held the dossier on Mark that his staff had prepared after the trial. "I think I've found Stevens's weak link. He owns only 25% of his company. The remainder is publicly held."

"What is your plan, Mr. Harden?"

"It's that 75%. All I need is control of two-thirds of that 75%, and I will control his company."

"What should we do?"

"Begin buying up the stock tomorrow morning. Buy it quietly. Buy it slowly. Buy it under assumed names. Do not attract any attention. I don't care if it takes years."

"What will you do then?"

"I will get even with him. That's what I'll do."

-34-

Wednesday, August 11, 1971

Mark had taken the Concorde from London to Washington for his meeting with the President of the United States. In the taxi from Dulles Airport he was brooding about yesterday's argument with Pris. Without warning, she had changed her plans and was going to fly directly to San Francisco, instead of accompanying him to Washington.

"You'll be in the meeting with Nixon and there won't be anything for me to do but stay at the hotel," she had complained. "I'd be bored silly."

"For Christ's sake Pris, I'm going to see the President of the United States! A man wants his wife with him at times like that."

"You forget that it's you who are going to the White House, not I." Pris had angrily gestured, while standing in front of the fireplace in Rodney's and Rebecca's guest room. "And keep your voice down. I don't want them to hear your every word."

"There would be plenty for you to do. There's that art gallery on the Mall. I forget the name of it."

"The National Gallery of Art." Her tone made it obvious that she was disgusted that he didn't know the gallery's name. "I've already seen it a million times."

"There are lots of other galleries in Washington."

"Mark, you don't understand—or you don't want to. I want to get home. I've got things to do."

"Dammit, Pris!" Mark had grumbled. "If that's what you want, but you don't give me much choice."

"After all, Mark, I came to London in the first place just to please you. You don't seem to appreciate that."

"Of course I appreciate it, but I wanted you in Washington."

"Don't be so upset, sweetheart." Pris walked over to Mark, reached up and kissed him on the check. "After all it's only *one day.*"

"Yes, and it's only *one day* that you could be with me," Mark had wanted to retort, but did not. There was no point in arguing any more. Pris had her mind made up and there would be no changing it.

The taxi pulled to a stop in front of the Washington's Mayflower Hotel. Connally's secretary had called Mark in London, telling him that reservations had been made and that he would be contacted upon his arrival.

"Ah, Mr. Stevens," said the desk clerk. "We've been expecting you."

"Thank you. Do you want my credit card?"

"Oh, no, sir. You are a guest of the White House. Everything has been attended to by the government."

The porter wheeled his luggage down the wide main hall of the grand old hotel to the elevators. The suite was beautiful, with a lovely view of Connecticut Avenue and the many full trees. As he looked at the scene, he was disappointed that Pris was not standing beside him, sharing his excitement at being invited to dine with the President of the United States.

Despite the air conditioning, the air was humid. The humidity in the East always bothered him. After he showered, he made himself a drink and sat on the sofa, contemplating. It had been his first trip on the Concorde. It was amazing how quickly he had been transported from one world to the other. He had hardly had time to savor yesterday's victory over Derek, and now he was in Washington going to the White House. He turned on the television and found a mid-afternoon news program. The T.V. weatherman predicted thunder showers for this evening. He listened anxiously to see if there were any more large demands for gold from foreign governments. A few more like last week and the crisis would be out of hand.

The telephone on the mantle interrupted him. "Mr. Stevens. My name is John Fellows. I'm an usher at the White House. How was your flight?"

"Fine. Thank you. Just fine. I came on the Concorde."

"I hear it's really a quick trip."

"Amazing, really amazing."

"Dinner will be at six o'clock tonight, sir. Everyone will be arriving at that time."

"That's fine."

"The car will be in front of the Mayflower exactly at 5:45. Can you be there?"

"Yes."

"Look for a black Cadillac limousine with government plates."

"I'll be there. By the way, can you tell me who the other guests will be?"

"I'm sorry, sir. I hope you will understand, but I'm not allowed to give out that information on the phone."

Mark looked at his watch. In two hours the White House limousine would be waiting. He looked at the television.

Today Congressional leaders met with President Nixon about the stalemate on the minimum wage bill," said the news anchor man. The television showed Nixon conferring with some Congressmen. Suddenly, Mark was nervous. Like the Congressmen, Mark, too, would soon be in the presence of the most powerful man on earth. He was struck by the awesome reality of his situation. Suddenly, the whiskey glass felt clammy. This would be a lot different from writing a paper on Bretton Woods, or giving a speech to businessmen about the monetary crisis. This was the big time. This was not academic theory. This counted.

Mark swallowed hard as the guard at the White House guard shack waved his limousine through and they drove up the driveway to the entrance of the famous building.

"How do you do, Mr. Stevens?" asked the tall good-looking man of 35 who came out of the entrance. "I'm John Fellows. We spoke on the telephone. Welcome to the White House."

"Thank you, John. This is quite an experience. I'm sorry, if I'm gawking a bit."

"They all do that, Mr. Stevens. Except most won't admit it," Fellows smiled.

"I can't imagine any American not being a bit awe-struck."

"Nor can I, Mr. Stevens," said Fellows, guiding Mark inside. "The dinner tonight is in the East Room."

The historic room had a bar set up on the left side of the room. The bartender was mixing a drink for a man standing at the bar. Mark's eye quickly took in the sparsely furnished room, with its bare wooden floor. He recognized the full-length painting of George Washington. It was a Gainsborough, wasn't it? Or was it a Stuart? Pris would be upset that he didn't know. On another wall was a similar portrait of Martha Washington. Huge ornate chandeliers hung from the fancy ceiling. The impact of the well-known paintings made him realize he was actually in the White House.

"Would you care for a drink?" asked Fellows, gesturing toward the bar.

"Yes, I would," said Mark.

"Why, it's Mark Stevens!" said a booming Texas voice from the group chatting around the unlit fireplace. It was John Connally. "How the hell are you Mark?"

"I'm fine. I came in from London this morning." The two men shook hands.

"Mighty glad you came." Tonight Connally's clothes carried no hint of the western style he had worn at The Grove. They were conservative, in the Washington mode. "When I told the President I wanted him to hear your ideas, he suggested I call in a few other experts and make a dinner of it."

"Yes, your secretary told me. I'm sure the others will have some good ideas."

"Some of them are academic types," said Connally, "although the tall fellow over there is a banker. Here, let me introduce you around."

Mark hadn't known what to wear, but Connally's secretary had suggested a business suit, rather than the tuxedo Mark had presumed would be required. The hotel valet had pressed the same dark suit Mark had worn in court in London.

John Connally introduced Mark to William Wirt, an economic theorist from N.Y.U., whose recent article urging return to the gold standard Mark had read. The next man was Harvard professor Nathaniel Rittman, followed by Nancy Albaum from the American Economics Institution. As the conversation progressed, Mark realized that, as at The Grove, no one was talking about the economic crisis. Instead, the subject of conversation was where they each lived, and whether or not their flights to Washington had been troubled by the storms across the country. It was the same as The Grove, where the conversation had been so mundane.

The conversation shifted to "credentials." Subtly, each participant wanted to be very sure the others knew that he belonged in the august group.

"Did you read my article in *The Economist*?" Ritterman worked into the conversation. As with all articles in *The Economist*, his was anonymous. It was titled "Balance of Payments—1971."

"Oh, was that article yours?" asked Jonathan James from Yale, who had joined them.

"I thought it sounded like you," laughed Albaum.

"My bank is financing over 10 billion in Europe," said Stuart Trapp, an economist from a giant New York bank. Trapp had carefully slipped his comment into the conversation, so that his one-upmanship was not obtrusive.

"Oh, I don't teach any more. I hated to give up the classroom, but the university feels my time is better spent elsewhere," Yale's Professor Wirt brought into the conversation.

While Mark was amused by the credential game, he nevertheless was ill at ease. The age differences made him feel as if he were a college student among a group of eminent professors; Nancy Albaum, the next youngest person, was at least 20 years his senior.

Suddenly, Richard Nixon entered the room. Mark was stunned by the appearance of the man. He wore a blue-gray single-breasted suit, with a lighter blue tie and a white shirt. His dark eyes radiated power. Mark had not thought of Nixon as a good-looking man. In the flesh, however, he was striking. As with Connally, his very presence in the room commanded attention. When Nixon approached the group, Fellows brought him a drink from the bar.

"Ladies and gentlemen," said Connally. "I would like to introduce you to the President of the United States."

Mark was the first to meet Nixon.

"Mr. President, this is Mark Stevens, from San Francisco."

"Yes, you're the one who gave us the idea for this dinner, aren't you? Your speech out there certainly impressed John."

"Mark is my whiz kid," laughed Connally.

Connally introduced all the others, telling the President the occupation of each and where they lived. Ritterman was the last. "Mr. Ritterman is on the faculty at Harvard."

"Let's see," said Nixon. "That's one professor from Harvard, one from Yale and another from N.Y.U. Three academics from the East should just about balance off our young investment banker from San Francisco."

Nixon's witticism drew laughter. Mark had not expected him to show any humor. He was pleased that Connally had told the President about him, and that Nixon remembered he was an investment banker.

As the group began to talk, there was a curious occurrence. They all formed a horseshoe, with Connally and Nixon at the head and the others fanning out slightly. The conversation emanated from the two leaders, with the others reacting to what they said. The President did not talk about the grave issues that had brought them together. Instead, he spoke about the baseball standings, and about the fact that his daughter, Julie, and he could hardly wait to see the Washington Redskins' football exhibition games.

"How would you like a mini-tour of the White House?" asked Nixon suddenly.

The group enthusiastically responded and moved into the main entry hall, with the 37th President of the United States acting as a tour guide. He showed them the Blue Room, the State Dining Room and the other famous rooms on the main floor. Mark was surprised at the President's knowledge of the history of the mansion. Nixon frequently commented on events that had occurred in the various rooms.

"And of course the East Room is where Abigail Adams is supposed to have hung her laundry," said Nixon as they returned. "I haven't been able to get Pat to cut down on expenses by hanging our laundry here, even though I told her it would help me politically." Mark joined everyone else in laughing politely. "The East Room is one of my favorite rooms," the President continued. "A great deal of history has occurred here. All seven Presidents who died in office lay in state in this very room. This is where the White House weddings are usually held. And remember, when you see a concert on television, it's in the East Room." Everyone listened attentively to the President.

Connally spoke up. "Mr. President, I'm told dinner can be served whenever you are ready."

"I'd say we're ready right now. These good people look hungry to me."

There were no name tags on the table. Surprisingly, Connally sat at the head of the table, while Nixon sat in the middle. Mark took a chair opposite the President.

The servants stepped forward to begin serving the first course and the wine. Until now Mark had not noticed what evidently were Secret Service men in plain-clothes. It struck him as odd that the two by the door looked Vietnamese.

Nixon began talking to Nancy Albaum, who sat next to him, giving Mark a moment to reflect. He could not get over what was happening. He was dining in the East Room of the White House, opposite the President of the United States. As keyed up and excited as he was, a calm came over him as he ate his salad. In his heart he knew he was capable of presenting his views to the President, and that those views were correct. He reflected that only eight years ago, when he was at Oxford, President Kennedy's casket had been only a few feet from where they were now eating. Dolley Madison had risked being captured by the invading British to save that very painting of George Washington from burning. He hoped the President would make the correct decision about the economic mess. Imagine, the person opposite him had received the torch of power that had been passed from such presidents as Washington, Lincoln and F.D.R.

While the group waited for dessert to be served, Connally, with his booming voice, called for attention. "Ladies and gentlemen. The President and I thank you for being here with us tonight.

Your country thanks you for sharing your expertise. It is greatly appreciated."

"Before making important decisions I try to get as much input as possible from experts," said Nixon. The man came across as a vital and strong leader. Much stronger than on television, Mark thought.

"I'd like to call on you, one by one, to state your views," said Connally. "There are five of you, so I ask that you limit your initial remarks to five minutes. But don't worry, there will be plenty of time for discussion later.

"I'd like to call on Mark Stevens first," Connally continued. "Recently, I spent a few days at the Bohemian Club out in California. They have a tradition of giving speeches—right in the middle of those gorgeous redwoods. Frankly, I'd heard the speeches were pretty dull. Rather like a professor's lecture." His remark brought snickers. "But someone told me that Mark, here, was going to speak on the international monetary crisis, so I thought I'd better listen. To tell you the truth, I'd rather have spent the time chewing the fat with my friends over a little bourbon, but it turned out to be quite a speech. He got me to thinking in a new direction. So, I've asked him to join us tonight." Connally indicated with his hand that he wanted Mark to speak.

While Mark was nervous, he felt resolute and confidant. He did not know for sure what the advice of the others would be, but from who they were, he had guessed that they were unlikely to agree with him. Perhaps, speaking first, he had a better chance of influencing the President.

Thank you, John." The word "John" rang awkwardly, but after all, Connally had invited its use at The Grove, and using Connally's first name could have an effect on the President and the others.

"When I was thinking about what advice to give you tonight, Mr. President, I remembered my tutor at Oxford and how simply he could explain things," continued Mark. "He was the best tutor at Oxford. His name was Richard Dawbarn. I still often see him when I'm in England."

"I know that feeling," said Nixon. "I had a professor like that at Whittier College—Paul Smith. As a matter of fact, he gave me the only B I ever got in a history course. Except for that B, I would've gotten all As in history." He laughed as he spoke. "I'll never forget it. We had to read *The Economic Interpretation of the Constitution*. What a mouthful! Maybe that's why, to this day, I need help from people like you when it comes to economics." The others joined in laughing at the President's recollection.

"Certain teachers have a remarkable impact on our lives, don't they?" continued Mark. "Dawbarn had the uncanny ability to make even very complicated subjects seem simple. Tonight, I'd thought I'd try to explain myself the way Dick Dawbarn would."

"Okay, Mark. Fire away," said Nixon. "Dawbarn style."

"Mark wrote a paper on Bretton Woods when he was at Oxford," Connally interjected. "Didn't you win a prize for it?"

Mark was glad for Connally's remark. Perhaps that would impress the academic types around the table. "Yes, it's true. As a matter of fact, my paper wasn't all that different from what I'm going to tell you tonight. You see, we've stuck to Bretton Woods as if it were the gospel all these years. I think we've just been lucky, and have gotten away with it until now."

Mark briskly explained why he thought Bretton Woods should be abandoned. "The seeds of its own destruction were inherent in the design of the system in the first place. If the American economy, or more precisely if the dollar, faltered, the system would be in trouble. To me it was always obvious that one day we'd see a run on our gold supply like the one we're having right now." Mark looked across the table at Nixon. "Mr. President, I'm afraid you've got no choice but to close the gold window. It never should have been opened in the first place. We must develop a new system. A system tied to market forces. If we don't, everyone will want our gold as soon as they get worried about the dollar, and who can blame them?"

"John, I think you should tell everyone. Don't you?"

"About the British, you mean?" asked Connally.

"Yes, the British."

"The President is referring to the fact that this morning Great Britain notified us that it wanted our assurance that we'd continue selling our gold for $35 an ounce. They said if we wouldn't make that guarantee, they'd want to convert three billion in dollar reserves to gold right now."

That was what Mark had feared as he had watched the news this afternoon. The British were saying they might follow the other countries in demanding gold. A run on our gold was imminent. "That proves all the more what I'm saying, don't you see?" Mark continued. "The British are saying they're going to do what everyone else has already started to do. They want gold before it's too late."

Mark continued on for more than his allotted five minutes, but Connally made no effort to cut him off. In fact, it was the questioning from the President that took much time. "I'll be the first to admit that stable exchange rates are important to the international scene," concluded Mark. "But using the dollar as the centerpiece is not the way to go. Again, I think that we shouldn't be so frightened of market forces. I say shut the gold window— worry about solving the other problems later."

Connally then called on Nathaniel Ritterman, the dignified fiftyish man from Harvard. Mark knew of Ritterman, and that he disagreed with him, but he had not expected the disdain that the academician displayed.

"Thank you, Mr. President," Ritterman began. "Without the Bretton Woods System, the world could never have sustained the remarkable economic recovery we have known since World War ll. Despite very great difficulties, Europe has been rebuilt. Even Japan is fast becoming a major economic force. No doubt our friend here is too young to remember the state of the world at the end of the war." Ritterman, who sat next to Mark, turned and looked at him. "And that may have affected his judgment. The world's economic system was in shambles. The capital stock had been depleted. The means of production largely destroyed." Ritterman directed himself back to Nixon. "I know, sir, how strongly you have always felt about the communist menace. Without Bretton Woods, surely the communists would have taken over all Europe."

To Mark, it was obvious that Ritterman was appealing to the strong anti-communist stance that had propelled Nixon to national attention. Mark knew that, as with so many intellectuals, Ritterman had disliked Nixon for his tactics. Ritterman was being two-faced.

"But Professor, why is Bretton Woods so important?" the President asked Ritterman.

"Fixed exchange rates. The cornerstone of the Bretton Woods system is that exchange rates cannot have major fluctuations. It is absolutely essential for effective trade that business be able to rely on predictable exchange rates. That they not fluctuate as widely as Stevens would have."

Without speaking, the President turned his attention to Mark, inviting him to respond. When writing his essay on Bretton Woods, Mark had debated his views on Bretton Woods with Dawbarn. Dawbarn could, and frequently did, take the opposite position on any issue under discussion. But those discussions were academic and friendly. This was different. This debate was for the mind of the President. The economic policy of the United States and the whole world could depend on his effectiveness. There was no time to get nervous. By the time the sweat appeared on his palms, he was well into his response.

"I was only three years old in 1944, but I'm sure the professor's recollection about what the founders of Bretton Woods had in mind is totally correct. I agree they believed fixed exchange rates were

essential. I agree also that they felt the tremendous growth in
trade in the last century was due to fixed rates and that they had
seen how disastrous it was for Great Britain to abandon the gold
standard in 1931." Ritterman looked curiously at Mark, with a
slight hint of satisfaction on his face. "But they made a fatal error." Ritterman's expression abruptly changed to feigned indiffer-
ence as to what Mark would say next.

"A fatal error? What was that?" asked Connally.

"For one thing, they didn't adequately forecast the need for
vastly increased amounts of what I'll call 'international money.' I
don't intend to lecture you on the difference between outside money
and inside money."

"Thank God for that," laughed Connally. "You're already way
over my head."

"I'm with John on that one," said the President.

"Bretton Woods assumed there would be enough gold mined
to handle increased international trade," Mark continued, "but
the price has never been high enough to encourage enough min-
ing."

"I don't agree," said Nancy Albaum, the woman from the American Economics Institute. "I think the dollar, in effect, replaces
gold under Bretton Woods. Certainly even you have to agree there
are plenty of dollars."

Mark laughed. "In one sense you're correct, Miss Albaum.
There are too many dollars. That's what's causing our inflation.
But there can never be enough of the kind of dollars I'm talking
about. In international terms, you can't have a growth in the
number of dollars held abroad without the United States owing
more in dollars. It's the nature of the beast." Mark sipped his
wine confidently. He was on his home turf now. By the look on
Albaum's face, he could tell that she did not understand his point,
but did not want to admit to it. Mark half-expected Ritterman or
one of the others to attempt to rebut him, but the President spoke
up.

"You economists can debate that stuff all night long," Nixon
said with a weary expression. "I'm the one who has to decide what
to do."

"You've got to strengthen the dollar," said Professor Jonathan
James of Yale, who had not yet spoken. "It's the weak dollar that
has caused the problem. No one wants a dollar being eroded by
inflation. They'd rather have gold. My advice is to take every step
you can to cut down on inflation." James went on for several
minutes. He allied himself with the others in opposing abandoning Bretton Woods. "I've noticed for years, young bright students
want to free up exchange rates the way Mark, here, does. They

don't see the bigger picture. Mr. President, the monetary system isn't something to tinker with. It's not the Bretton Woods System that is undermining the dollar. It's the dollar that is undermining Bretton Woods."

"I agree, Professor James. We should not tinker with it. What we should do is *change* it completely," responded Mark.

"Then, if you were president, you would shut the gold window," said the President. "Is that your advice?"

"Yes, and let a free exchange system develop."

"I agree with James, here," said William Wirt of N.Y.U. "It was Johnson's guns-and-butter policy that gave us this rip-roaring inflation in the first place. You should go ahead with your plan to stop the war, as soon as you can. It's inflation and the trade deficit that is wrecking our economy. That's what you have to stop, Mr. President." Wirt ground out his cigar in the ashtray. "Closing the gold window would be a disaster to the monetary markets."

"Mark?" said the President, turning his attention to Mark.

"And we don't have a near-disaster now?" asked Mark rhetorically. "I say we do! How long will it take to end the war? How long will it take to stop inflation, if it ever is? By the time that's all accomplished, we won't have any gold left, and the system will be in total shambles." Mark knew he was on a roll. "Certainly there will be dislocation in the monetary market—I don't deny that—but markets are resilient. There will be new devices, market-created devices, to hedge against large changes in exchange rates. The same way there are now in wheat futures or pork bellies. I already have several new ideas my company expects to try."

In another half-hour, they all had finished. Nixon excused himself. "I want to thank you all for so freely giving me your opinions and advice. You can rest assured that what you have told me will go into the decision-making process." Everyone stood. The President walked around the table, shaking hands. "I'd love to stay longer with you, but I have some work to finish up this evening. You've given me a lot to think about." He turned to Connally. "John, could I have a word with you?"

The two walked to the door together. Nixon said something to the big Treasury Secretary, then turned toward the group. "I want all of you to stay as long as you like. I've asked John to see to it that you have a good time. Remember, it isn't often you get free drinks on the government."

For more than an hour, the group stayed at the table talking. Finally, Connally indicated the evening had ended. "I want to thank you all for accepting the President's invitation to be here. You have served your country well tonight."

Connally stood and began opening the package which Fellows had handed him. "As a memento of your visit tonight, the President would like you each to have one of these." Mark looked at what Connally had presented him. It was a small pad of note paper with "The White House" embossed at the top of each sheet. The evening was over. Mark and the others had had the ear of the most powerful man on earth. It had happened so fast that he needed time to reflect. He was anxious to show the note pad to Pris and to his mother. How incredible to think that the views he had given to the President might result in a change of national policy!

As he walked with the others to the front door of the White House for the waiting limousines, Connally took him by the arm. "Mark, could I talk to you privately for a moment?"

"Of course."

Mark and Connally stood alone by a portrait in the main entry hall. "The President told me he was very impressed with you. He respects, and I have always respected, men who have been out there in the real business world. It hasn't escaped our attention that you have been very successful—financially, I mean."

"Thank you, John. I appreciate that."

"There's more. The President wants to meet with you privately. He wants to talk some more."

"Privately? When? Tomorrow? I can arrange . . . "

"No." Connally smiled. "He wants to meet with you now. He's in his office."

"He wants to see me? In the oval office? Now?" Mark was flabbergasted.

"No, he's in his hideaway office across the street. He often goes there when he wants to think."

"I see."

"He told me he wants to talk to you. He asked that I have you escorted there."

"Of course, John. Anything the President wants."

"I'm catching a plane for Texas in a couple of hours, but one of the Secret Service men will take you over."

Mark was bowled over. He thought the evening had ended. He had intended to return to the hotel and call Pris. That the President wanted to see him privately was difficult for him to absorb. What on earth did the President want to see him for? For a moment, ridiculous thoughts raced through his brain. Had the Internal Revenue Service given Nixon an audit report on Mark's taxes? Was he going to criticize his past currency speculation?

He knew such thoughts were preposterous, but he couldn't imagine why he was being summoned.

Mark walked through the little-known tunnel to the Executive Office Building, escorted by a Secret Service man. The noise of their shoes echoed in the tunnel. The events of tonight had been far beyond his imagination. The White House, with all its awesome history—dinner with the President of the United States—advocating his views about Bretton Woods to the President—now this! The President actually wanted to see him in his hideaway office. As he walked, he had a sense of unreality.

They passed a Secret Service man at the E.O.B. end of the tunnel, and waited for the elevator. Another agent was in the hall as they left the elevator, and still another was in the hall outside the Nixon suite. The last was posted inside the reception room. This expense-be-damned protection given the President contributed to the feeling of power surrounding the President. No wonder it was called the "Imperial Presidency."

Mark's escort opened the door to the inner office. "Thank you for coming, Mark," the President said, smiling. The President shut the dark wooden door to his inner office, and they were alone. "Please sit down." At Nixon's invitation, Mark sat in a side chair, while the President sat behind his desk in his leather swivel chair. The long office had a high ceiling, in the style of the old building that had once housed the State Department. Mark noticed the three framed photographs of Mrs. Nixon and their two daughters on a glass rack. On the wall was a giant map of the world with Washington at its center.

"I never knew this office existed," said Mark.

"Oh, yes. This is where I do my best work. Here and Camp David."

"I always picture a President's being in the oval office."

"I'll show it to you sometime, if you like." Mark was beginning to relax, although he still couldn't believe he was talking with the President of the United States this way.

"Mark, have you ever thought of getting into politics?" Mark looked intently at Nixon to see if he were serious.

"No, I haven't Mr. President. I guess I've been too busy building my company."

"John tells me you've been extremely successful in your business. I admire that in a man."

"Thank you, sir." Mark wished Jonah could hear the President.

"Like your Oxford professor, you have a gift for explaining complicated subjects."

"I appreciate your saying that, Mr. President."

"That's an ability that could take you a long way in politics. I was watching you very carefully at dinner tonight. You know how to conduct yourself."

"I'm flattered. I don't know what to say."

"Here, how about a drink? Let's have a drink together." Nixon reached for a buzzer on his desk. "What would you like?"

"Scotch—Scotch on the rocks would be fine."

A man came in. "Manolo, Mr. Stevens would like a Scotch on the rocks. I'll have the usual." The man, the presidential valet, nodded and left the office.

"I know what it is about you. I think I've put my finger on it."

"What is that, sir?"

"It's the way you express yourself. You say it well and you say it simply. But the main thing is the way you say it."

"The way I say it?"

"Yes, as if you really know what you are talking about. You see, even if I didn't completely understand you tonight, I would accept what you said because you speak as if you are correct. Do you know what I mean?"

"I know I've always felt I was right about Bretton Woods."

"That's it! That's exactly what I mean. Keep it up, Mark." The President spoke with the same familiar gestures Mark knew from television.

"I'll try."

"I really think you ought to be in politics one day. As a matter of fact, I'm sure John can use you at Treasury, if you want."

"Thank you, sir. I've never even thought about such a thing."

"Or here in the White House, when something opens up. Yes, I could use you in the White House." Now Mark knew why men could not resist doing whatever the President asked. In that moment, if the President had asked him to take a job, damned near any job, he would have accepted despite himself. The power of the Presidency clouded the senses.

The valet returned, with the drinks on a tray.

"Anyway," the President took a sip of his drink. "I didn't ask you over here tonight to offer you a job."

Mark didn't respond, but wanted to scream, "Come on, then, tell me why you asked me here!" The anticipation was nearly unbearable.

"I was very impressed by your views on Bretton Woods. You have really felt that way since you were a student at Oxford, eh?"

"Yes, I have. Now that this crisis is on us, I feel even more strongly."

"The arguments that the others made at dinner tonight. What did you think of them?"

"Traditional—they were the traditional arguments. The ones I've heard all my adult life. I simply don't agree."

"The fact of the matter is, I've never much been interested in theoretical economics. There are no votes in that." Nixon laughed. "What you said made a lot of sense to me."

The President stood up and walked to the fireplace, cogitating. Then he turned to Mark, as if a brainstorm had struck him.

"How about a meeting? A meeting at Camp David?" The President was thinking as he talked. "I'm very concerned about this three billion dollar request by the British. I told John to call them when he gets to Texas, and tell them we can't give them any guarantees."

"Good!"

"Yes, I agree with what you said on that. We've got to stop the run on Fort Knox." The President walked to a window and looked out into the night. "But that's only short term. We've got to do something for the long haul."

"I'm glad to hear you say that, sir." Mark sipped his Scotch as he listened to Nixon.

"I've always tried to be a President who acts for the long haul."

Mark nodded his understanding.

"I don't want to be putting out fires all the time. Too many leaders are always putting out fires—they don't lead."

"I always go to my place at Pebble Beach. I don't seem to be able to think about the big issues when I'm at my office. Too many interruptions."

"Camp David. Yes, that's what I'll do. I'll call a meeting at Camp David. I'll invite all my financial people. The upper level. We'll brainstorm the various solutions. I'd like to hear what the others think."

"That's a good idea. John Connally, Burns, Volcker. Everybody."

"Yes, that's right. John leaves for Texas tonight, but as soon as he gets back, we'll go to Camp David and hammer out a solution to this thing. I want to do something bold, like you suggest."

"That's good, but I think you're running out of time, sir. I think you should consider calling the meeting right away before things get worse."

"You're right. Of course you're right. It's settled. The meeting will start Friday. Friday at Camp David. John will just have to turn around and come back." Having made up his mind, Nixon stood up. The meeting was over. "Thanks for acting as my sounding board."

"Thank you, sir. I'm glad, if I helped you."

"You did. You have no idea how much you've helped me." The two shook hands. The President's face brightened. "Mark, could you be there Friday? Could you come to Camp David with the others?"

"Friday? Why, of course I could."

"I'd like you to make the same arguments you did tonight."

"I'll be glad to be there, sir."

"It will probably take the whole weekend."

"That's okay."

"One of the Secret Service men will show you back to the White House. They'll get you a car."

"Good night, sir."

"And Mark?"

"Yes, sir?"

"I'm sure I don't need to remind you. You can't tell anyone about the meeting—not even your wife."

"Of course not, Mr. President."

As he walked back through the tunnel, he was astounded at what had happened. He wished he could telephone Pris with the news. He wished he could tell her he would be at Camp David with practically the whole damned government of the United States.

Mark waved aside the limousine in the White House drive. "I'd rather walk," he said to the chauffeur. The pavement was dark with rain from an earlier shower. The air was heavy, presaging more rain. He didn't care. The way he felt it would be fun if another storm would let loose while he walked to the hotel. As soon as he was out of sight of the guard station, he began running through the park. Can you imagine the President's inviting him to the meeting at Camp David? He couldn't think of a single person who would believe him. Rodney would think he had gone totally cuckoo. Even Pris might say something like, "Mark, sweetheart, you don't have to make up these wild stories just to impress me. This is no way to solve our problems."

"Wahoo!" he shouted, throwing his folded umbrella into the air. As he left the park he noticed a vagrant sleeping on the park bench. The man raised his head, looking at him with bewilderment. "No, I'm not crazy," Mark said to the vagrant, who shook his head as if Mark were indeed crazy.

"I wish to hell they had some ducks around here," thought Mark. "I'd rather talk to a duck or two than a bum."

At the hotel, Mark dialed Pris.

"Pris, I've got to stay over for the weekend."

"Oh? What's going on, Mark?" she asked a little warily.

"I've been invited to play golf," he lied. "I hope you won't be upset."

"Golf? With whom?"

"Connally. He wants me to fill out his foursome at Congressional Country Club."

"But I was counting on you for the Fillmore party!"

"I know," Mark paused. He wished he could tell her the truth. "It might be very good for business to play with Connally."

"Sweetheart, you already have all the business anyone could ever want."

"It's a big opportunity for me—golf with the Secretary of the Treasury."

"All right. You have a good time. I'll go to the party with Maggie and Jim."

"Thanks, Pris."

Over and over again, as he lay in bed, he reviewed what had happened tonight. His mind kept coming back to one thing. Power. The awesome power of the Presidency. Tonight he had influenced that power. He hoped he could do the same this weekend at Camp David.

-35-

Friday, August 13, 1971

Mark looked down on Washington from the helicopter as it left for Camp David. The flight along the Potomac Valley to the Presidential retreat in Maryland's Catoctin Mountains would take only 30 minutes. The racket of the helicopter made it difficult to converse with his fellow passengers: Presidential Assistant Robert Haldeman, Budget Director George Shultz and John Connally. At Nixon's behest, Connally had returned from his aborted Texas trip to attend the Camp David conference. Connally's long legs made it awkward for him to sit in the small seat next to Mark.

"Bob, this is Mark Stevens," shouted Connally over the helicopter noise. "When I was in California, I heard his speech on reforming the foreign exchange system." Connally was trying to make himself heard by Robert Haldeman, who sat behind him. "Mark was one of the international economists who met with the President and me at dinner Wednesday."

"Yes," said Haldeman, also nearly shouting over the noise. "The President told me you were coming. Happy to meet you. Shake hands with George Shultz. He's from northern California, too."

Mark reached over the back of the seat and shook hands with Shultz. "You must teach at Cal or Stanford," Shultz said.

"No, I'm not a professor, Mr. Shultz. I'm in investment banking in San Francisco. We do a lot of currency trading." Mark knew of Shultz from his success with a giant construction company in the Bay area, before Nixon had appointed him Budget Director. The noise made it difficult to be heard, but the four managed a certain amount of small talk. Shultz and Mark learned both were golfers.

"We must get together when I'm at home in California. I'm not a very good golfer, but I play whenever I can," Shultz said.

"If you'd like to play Pebble Beach, I'll have you and your wife down to my weekend place," said Mark.

"Give me a call. I'm sure we'll get back home for a few days after this mess is straightened out."

The whirring copter prepared for its landing on the Camp David helipad in the midst of the forest. Mark again thought about the "big shot" ideas that his father had implanted in him. At The Grove he had come a long way toward shedding the false image that big shots were aloof, god-like people. The White House dinner Wednesday, and now the chitchat on the helicopter trip, were further demonstrations that Jonah was wrong. Even the President had proved to be very human, and now at Camp David he would be meeting the financial elite of the administration.

As they disembarked, two helicopters were already parked in the clearing. One bore the distinctive white top and painted U.S. flag of the President's chopper. Mark accompanied the others in his group to the special Camp David limousine for the short ride that remained.

"I'm Al Benson. Welcome to Camp David." Benson, a Camp David staffer, took Mark's suitcase. "You're staying at Woodlawn. I think you'll find it very comfortable."

"I'm surprised at how much cooler it is than in Washington," Mark said.

"It can be 20 degrees cooler here. Everyone notices it."

"What a beautiful place," Mark said enthusiastically as they rode an electric golf cart.

"President Roosevelt used to call it Shangri-La. The name certainly fits. How about a quick tour?"

"I'd love it."

"The meeting doesn't start until three, so we have some time."

"The President comes here a lot," said Benson, as they walked around the Camp David grounds. I started here when Kennedy was President. It was too peaceful for both Kennedy and Johnson. They didn't use it much. But it's different with Nixon."

They saw the President's swimming pool and the various buildings. Ten or 12 "cabins" as they were called. In actuality, the President's cabin, Aspen Cottage, was a spacious and beautiful home, not a cottage at all.

"We have about 200 acres of forest, surrounded by a double steel fence. These trails you see go all over the place. The Secret Service try to stay behind bushes and trees, so you seldom see them," said Benson.

"The air is so invigorating. I see why the President likes it so much"

"We have a three hole golf course, bowling, the works. The outside perimeter is constantly guarded by the United States Marines. We don't want any more assassinations."

The expense involved must be beyond belief, thought Mark. This, the White House, San Clemente and Nixon's Florida place. No one would be able to earn the kind of money that it must take to operate all these places. You'd have to be the Queen of England to live this way! What it added up to, Mark thought, was the tremendous power of the Presidency. It was impossible to fully comprehend anyone having the power to summon all these people to a remote spot in the woods, by expensive helicopters, and the power to make the momentous decisions that lay ahead this weekend.

The meeting was convened by the President in the living room of his residence, Aspen Cottage. The room was comfortably furnished. A gentle fireplace fire contributed to the relaxed atmosphere. Extra chairs had been brought in to accommodate all those present. Only Haldeman sat out of the circle, in the back of the room.

"Gentlemen," said Nixon. When the President spoke, all side chatter immediately stopped. "This is a historic occasion. What we decide here will affect the people of the United States and of the world for many years to come."

Mark counted the participants. Including himself and the President, there were 17. He was thrilled to be one of the circle that was going to help the President decide such important matters. He thought again of Jonah, and how he wished his father could see that he was no longer on the outside looking in.

"I want you all to sign the Camp David guest book," said Nixon. "I know in future years each of you will remember this weekend and what you contributed to your country." The President's valet handed Nixon the Camp David guest book. He carefully signed his name to a fresh sheet. "I've asked John to sit at my right. John, I'd like you to sign after me, if you would."

"Thank you very much." Connally took the guest book and wrote his name. The book was then passed from one man to the next.

"It gets cold at Camp David," said the President. "So I've had special Camp David jackets made for each of you." An aide began passing out the windbreakers. Each had the words "Camp David" printed on it. In addition, each person's name and the date, August 13, 1971, were sewn in. There was considerable buzzing and chatting as each examined his jacket. Mark knew he would keep his forever.

When the guest book came to him, Mark looked at the signatures. Under Connally's name, Shultz and then Ehrlichman had signed. There were several names that Mark did not recognize, but he did know Caspar Weinberger, and Herbert Stein, whose book he had read. Paul Volcker was also on the list, as was William Safire, the President's speech writer, along with Paul McCracken, Chairman of President Nixon's Council of Economic Advisors and former advisor to Presidents Eisenhower and Kennedy. Mark had also heard of Peter Petersen, head of the Council on International Economic Policy.

"Gentlemen, I apologize for the short notice I gave you for this meeting, but I only just decided on this meeting. I also must warn you that secrecy is of the utmost importance. In the wrong hands, speculators could make billions. I'm asking that you make no phone calls. Is that perfectly clear?"

The President then continued. "I'm asking John to throw out the first pitch. I want John to tell you as a group what we have been discussing individually with many of you."

"As I see it," said Connally, his Texas accent vividly contrasting with Nixon, "We have three main areas we should tackle. First, there's the problem of inflation. Four percent inflation is just too damned high. Now, I'm thinking about a freeze of some sort." A price freeze had not come up at all the other night. Mark knew Nixon had frequently said in speeches that he was deathly opposed to wage or price controls. "Next, we've got to do something to stimulate the economy. We've got to create new jobs. We've been talking about repealing the automobile excise tax and maybe reinstating the investment credit. Last, and maybe the most urgent," continued Connally, "we've got to stop the hemorrhaging of this golldang balance of payments deficit. We're losing too much gold.

"There are some pretty good men out there who think the whole damned international monetary system should have been changed a long time ago. One's here right now," Connally nodded his head in Mark's direction. "Mark Stevens is an investment banker from San Francisco. Mark was a Rhodes Scholar at Oxford. At Oxford he won a prize for his studies on the international monetary system. Mark, would you mind repeating what you told the President the other night?"

Mark had not expected to be called on in this manner, but before he had a chance to be nervous, he simply began talking as he had at the White House. "Gentlemen, I've been convinced for a long time that the Bretton Woods system needs reform. The dollar has to be able to fluctuate. With our present system, just as soon as the U.S. economy falters, what else could you expect but a run on gold?"

Mark continued on for some time, methodically making the points he had made at the White House dinner. Everyone in the room listened attentively. As he spoke, he remembered the President's comment that he was convincing because he spoke as if he knew what he was talking about. Well, he did know what he was talking about! He knew he was right about Bretton Woods, and he intended to convince the others. He finished making his points and began drawing to a conclusion.

"After the gold window has been shut, I think we should invite all the countries with modern economies to a conference. Its purpose would be the same as the Bretton Woods conference. To devise a new international economic system."

"But what about stability?" It was Treasury Undersecretary Paul Volcker, a highly respected member of Connally's inner circle, who was speaking. "International trade is absolutely dependent on stable exchange rates."

"I understand the dilemma very well," said Mark, "but we can't continue the way we have. If the United States gold supply disappears, we certainly won't have stable exchange rates. We'll have no system at all. Whenever we get government trying to ignore the forces of supply and demand, we get ourselves into the same old fix. It can't be done. When we try it, we get economic stagnation. You cannot ignore natural economic forces, any more than a mountain climber can ignore gravity."

"Well, I'm not in favor of shutting the gold window, at least for now," said Arthur Burns, Chairman of the Federal Reserve. "We've got several other options we should give a try first."

"But Arthur, what would you have me do?" asked the President.

"The British have asked for a guarantee of three billion in gold," interjected Connally. "We're damn well runnin' out of time!"

"We *have* time, John," answered Burns. "If the other things we've been discussing don't work, *then* we close the gold window." Burns was talking about wage and price controls, border taxes and other actions to make the dollar more attractive to the markets.

The President let the group fully speak their minds about closing the gold window, then shifted to wage and price controls. "I've always been opposed to controls, but we have to do something to stop inflation."

In his heart, Mark knew that as a freshman in the group, he should hold his tongue, but he had to speak his mind on wage and price controls. "Mr. President, may I speak to that issue?" he asked.

"Certainly."

"I've always thought you were a free enterprise man, sir. The economy can't function if we put it in a strait jacket. Wage and price controls are that very strait jacket. You'll stop business expansion in its tracks. Business expansion is your way out of this crisis."

George Shultz spoke up. "I don't think the President is talking about permanent controls. The freeze is only to slow inflation down a bit."

"Mark is fundamentally correct. I am opposed to wage and price controls, and for exactly the reasons you state. I'm only talking about a 90 day freeze. Any more than that, and I admit we'd stop the economy dead in its tracks."

"But then, why do it at all?" asked Mark, perplexed. "I don't understand."

"I've got to send a message," explained the President. "The administration is serious about fighting inflation. Everyone knows I oppose controls, so when Dick Nixon puts on controls the message is doubly strong. It's not that different from a conservative Republican's going to China."

Mark could think of several reasons why even temporary controls would do more harm than good, but he could see that no one in the room had serious opposition to the idea, so he decided he had said enough on the subject. The meeting lasted four hours, until seven that evening. But for Mark, time stood still. On the surface the meeting was not much different from meetings in his conference room in San Francisco, discussing an underwriting or some other business matter. Here, however, the stakes were vastly different. Here were the leaders of the greatest power on earth. After his experience this week, he doubted that any of his decisions would again assume the same large proportions.

After the meeting, Nixon wanted to meet further with what was called the Quadriad. John Connally, George Shultz, Arthur Burns and Paul McCracken. The President also asked Paul Volcker to stay. "Gentlemen, I want to address Arthur's objections to shutting the gold window," the President told the group. "We'll see the rest of you in Laurel Cabin for dinner about eight-thirty."

Mark decided he would use the time to go for a walk on the Camp David trails. Because the night air was quite cold even in August, he wore his new Camp David windbreaker. As he walked, he reflected further on the day's meetings. Although it was true that there had been plenty of give and take and ample free discussion, it seemed to him that the President had been strongly leaning toward shutting the gold window at the beginning of the meeting. Only Volcker and Burns had offered serious opposition. Volcker had finally given up his reservations, and it looked as if the President were at work on Burns in Aspen Cottage right now. Perhaps it was the President's style to use the conference process to make his aides feel they were involved in the decision. Or maybe he wanted to see if anyone would come up with an overwhelming reason to change his thinking. But if Mark were right, it was clear that he had had an important impact on the President the other night, for it looked as if it was then that the President had begun to make up his mind.

Dinner was served at the big table in Laurel cabin. The President had decided to remain in Aspen Cottage and dine alone. The atmosphere at the dinner was one of relaxation. Word had gotten around at cocktails that Burns had reluctantly given in to Connally's position that the gold window be closed immediately. As it turned out, Arthur Burns sat on Mark's left and Paul Volcker on Mark's right at dinner.

"It's been a very difficult day for me," said Volcker, a 6-feet-8-inch giant of a man, who was Connally's Undersecretary of the Treasury. Volcker had more formal education in international economics than Connally and most others at the meeting. "As you perhaps know, Mark, I've always been a believer in Bretton Woods. I've always believed in fixed exchange rates. I don't mind telling you, it has been hard for me to give it up."

"I think your back was against the wall," said Mark.

"You're right. In the end I had no real choice. We have to close the gold window or we'll be in no end of trouble. I do think we've got to negotiate new fixed rates as soon as possible."

Mark disagreed with Volcker on that, too, but decided not to press the point. "One thing we agree on is the need for absolute secrecy," said Mark.

"Certainly. If the word gets out, the speculators will have a field day," Volcker replied. "The President is right about that."

Burns talked candidly with both Mark, and William Safire, the Presidential speech writer, who sat on Burns's other side. "I had no objection to the rest of the program," Burns told them, "but I couldn't agree on closing the gold window now. We should have waited until there wasn't anything else to try. Obviously, in the end, I had no choice but to support the President." Burns turned to Mark, "I guess you convinced him, Mark, but you didn't convince me."

"It wasn't just me," said Mark. "There were Connally and the others."

The rest of the conversation on Mark's side of the table had to do with tomorrow's agenda, which was to refine the ideas agreed upon today. Safire suggested the need for a press conference after the President made his speech, a speech that Safire would commence work on right after dinner.

As the dinner ended, Mark knew that a series of momentous decisions had been made by the President today. Although tomorrow would be a full day, it could never compare to what had already happened.

Saturday, August 14, 1971

Mark slept well, and awoke exhilarated by yesterday's events. Before breakfast, he took a long walk on the trails of Camp David. Many others had also awakened early, and they, too, were walking. Both on the trails and later at breakfast, everyone cheerfully greeted one another and was in upbeat moods. Mark detected no indication of disappointment in yesterday's decisions. Everyone was enthusiastic about having decided on a course of action, and now wanted to get on with its implementation.

The excitement of yesterday did not diminish the importance of today. The group again gathered in the President's Aspen Cottage living room, but this time the President was absent, and Budget Director George Shultz started the meeting.

"Gentlemen, the President isn't here this morning because he's sleeping. Rosemary tells me the President got up in the middle of the night and wrote a draft of his speech. He didn't finish until after daybreak and just went to bed." The "Rosemary" Shultz was referring to was the President's long-time secretary, Rosemary Woods. As Shultz spoke, she was busy in another cabin, typing the draft Nixon had written on a yellow pad.

"I'd like us to divide into smaller groups to implement yesterday's decisions," Shultz continued. "The President has decided he'll address the nation on television Sunday night and not Monday, as we were thinking."

One group was to make decisions about the President's temporary wage and price control plan, another about the budget cuts, still another about the new tax proposals and lastly, the group to which Mark was assigned, about the international monetary plan group.

The work pace throughout the day was frenetic. The groups conferred in different rooms, but the interplay between groups was constant. Connally was nominally assigned to Mark's monetary exchange group, but the big Texan's voice could be heard throughout the cabin, as he was called from one room to another to assist in making decisions. Connally's frequent absence left Mark in charge of his group, for all practical purposes. The President's decision to close the gold window immediately, meant the end of currency trading in the manner previously known.

"Gentlemen," Mark said, "the President's decision will create absolute chaos in the exchange markets. That's an inevitable fact. Of course, we can't shut the markets the way Roosevelt shut down the banks, but I think the markets will shut themselves down by simply refusing to open until the dust settles."

"We can't go on without some kind an exchange system. What do you suggest we do?" asked Rob Martin, Connally's Assistant Secretary of the Treasury, who had agreed with Mark yesterday.

"Safire told me the President doesn't want to make it complicated in his speech. That should be left for later," replied Mark. William Safire, the Presidential speech writer whose job it was to develop the President's draft into final form for tomorrow's television address, had given Mark a copy of the President's draft. Mark continued: "Here's part of what the President plans to say." Mark read from the draft: '*Let me lay to rest the bugaboo of devaluation. Will this action reduce the value of the dollar? The long term purpose . . .*' Here I can't quite make out the President's handwriting," Mark interjected. "'*The long term purpose will be to strengthen the dollar, not to weaken it. But if you're one of the overwhelming . . .*" I'm sure what he means is: '*one of the overwhelming number of Americans who . . .*' yes . . . '*who buy American, your dollar will be worth the same tomorrow as it is today . . .*' That's the President's idea," Mark continued.

"I think his speech should point out that Americans won't be hurt by devaluation," said Martin.

"Sure. Only the speculators will get hurt," added William Speck, Treasury Department expert in Mark's group.

"Well, I'm not so sure about that," laughed Mark. "Anyone who has dollars will be hurt, because his dollar will be worth less. But I have to agree, the perception is different, because after all domestic prices will remain the same."

"I'm still concerned about developing a new monetary system," said Rob Martin.

"You think the speech should say something about it, Rob?" asked Mark.

"I sure do."

"All right," said Mark. "Let's give it a shot."

The rest of the day was spent developing recommendations as to what should be done to assuage the anticipated worry of other governments as to the future, now that gold convertibility had ceased. When they finally finished, they had agreed on specific language for the speech.

Similarly, the other groups spent the day developing policies and plans that might have taken days in the everyday Washington process. But today, the miraculous had occurred. The complicated agreement had been hammered out and presented to the President.

After dinner a few key figures such as Connally and McCracken were still conferring with one another. Safire and the President worked on the speech, but most of the participants were celebrating completion of the historic meeting. Each knew the tension would not totally be released until the President had finished with his speech tomorrow night, but from here on out it was downhill.

Sunday, August 15, 1971

Mark was in his suite at the Mayflower at eight p.m. The President would speak in an hour. The President had thanked him this afternoon when he had left Camp David on the helicopter to Washington. Nixon stayed on, as he wanted to polish his speech until the last minute.

"Don't forget what I said about politics someday," the President had said as he shook Mark's hand. "Remember, my offer still stands if you'd like to join the administration."

"You flatter me, Mr. President." Mark had said. "But I think I'd better stick to what I know."

Mark dialed Amanda's number. "Mom, I'm in Washington, D.C."

"What are you doing there?" she asked.

"I've been meeting with the President."

"You mean President Nixon?"

"Yes. *The* President Nixon. I had dinner at the White House and then went to Camp David. Listen, Mom. I want you to turn on your T.V. At nine. The President is giving a speech."

"What about? Why do you want me to watch?"

"It's a speech about the economy. And Mom, *your son* had a lot to do with it."

"You did? What do you mean?" Her voice was incredulous.

"Just watch, Mom, just watch. It's the stuff I studied at Cal and Oxford. The President asked for my advice about it."

"I don't know what to say. I'm so proud of you!"

"You said it all just then, Mom. Sorry, I've got to hang up now. I've got to tell Pris."

"Mark?"

"Yes, Mom?"

"Is everything all right with you and Pris?"

"Yes, Mom. Everything's all right."

He was sure everything would be all right as soon as Pris heard the news.

"Pris. Listen, I don't have time to explain, but I want you to watch television at nine. The President is speaking."

"What channel?"

"Any channel. He's talking to the nation. Please don't ask the details. I had to lie to you about playing golf. President Nixon invited me to a secret conference at Camp David. He told me I couldn't tell."

"You didn't play golf?"

"I had to make that up. If word had gotten out that there was a meeting, it would have been hell to pay."

Pris was still not completely understanding what he was telling her. "But why should I watch television?"

"The speech. He's taken my advice. I was at Camp David with all the experts, and he took my advice. You'll see on T.V."

"Really?"

"Yes, I'll be home tomorrow. I'll tell you all about it."

"I wish you hadn't lied to me."

"But I had to!"

"Mark?"

"Yes?"

"I'll have some people for dinner tomorrow. I want everybody to know about your advising the President."

Mark turned the knob at five minutes to nine, and the television flickered to life. The Ed Sullivan show was just ending. He stared at the screen until it showed the Presidential Seal.

"Ladies and gentlemen, the President of the United States," said the off-camera voice. Then Nixon appeared. The vigor and color Mark had seen in the President was replaced by the familiar, uninspiring television image.

I have addressed the nation a number of times over the past two years on the problems of ending a war. Because of the progress we have made toward achieving that goal, this Sunday evening is an appropriate time for us to turn our attention to the challenges of peace.

A hard lump came into Mark's throat. He had actually worked with this man only a few hours ago. Now here he was addressing the entire nation.

The image continued: *"America today has the best opportunity in this century to achieve two of its greatest ideals: to bring about a full generation of peace, and to create a new prosperity without war."*

Mark sat glued to his chair. His drink remained untouched as he stared at Nixon. *"We are going to take action, not timidly, not half-heartedly, and not in piecemeal fashion. We are going to move forward to the new prosperity without war as befits a great people, all together, and along a broad front."*

The President was right, Mark thought. Normally he would have passed off Nixon's introductory words as pseudo-patriotic bullshit, but not this time. He had been there and he knew that was not so.

' *"The time has come for a new economic policy for the United States . . . "*

The President then spoke about his plan for a Job Development Act with its investment credit. He had heard the President's concern that his opponents would criticize a tax break for business. It was good politics to frame it as a "Job Development" measure.

Next, the President addressed the problem of inflation. *"I am today ordering a freeze on all prices and wages throughout the United States for a period of ninety days."* Although he knew it had been decided, Mark winced. He was still sorry the President had done that. It seemed contradictory to freeze prices and wages and to expect the economy to grow. Maybe that was politics, but Mark wished he had not done it.

"Let me lay to rest the bugaboo of what is called devaluation . . . " Mark's excitement grew. The President was coming to the international monetary crisis. Mark sat up straight in his chair without moving his eyes from the screen. *"I have directed Secretary Connally to suspend temporarily the convertibility of the dollar into gold . . . "* That was it! What he had wanted for years! What he had urged to Connally and the President was actually done!

" . . . If you are among the overwhelming majority of Americans who buy American-made products in America, your dollar will be worth just as much tomorrow as it is today." It was the same language his group had reviewed yesterday.

"To our friends abroad, let me assure you that the United States will continue to be a forward-looking, trustworthy trading partner . . . " The President was addressing Rob Martin's concern about developing a new system, and was using the language Mark's group had worked on yesterday.

" . . . we will press for the necessary reforms to set up an urgently needed new international monetary system . . . " The Presi-

dent promised there would be meetings to set up a new system, but the Bretton Woods system was as dead as a dodo bird.

"Let us invest in our nation's future, and let us revitalize that faith in ourselves that built a great nation in the past and that will shape the world of the future.

"Thank you and good evening."

The screen flashed back to the Presidential Seal, and the voice of the announcer said. "You have been listening to an address to the nation by the President of the United States."

Mark walked down Connecticut Avenue and through the park to the White House. The mansion was bathed in its usual evening lights. He walked by the guard house, where his limousine had passed Wednesday night. He looked out the corner of his eye at the guard, half hoping that the guard would recognize him. "Aren't you Mark Stevens, who came here the other night and advised the President how to clean up this mess?" the guard might ask. "Yes, I recognize you. I just saw on television that he followed your advice. Thank you very much, Mr. Stevens." But it was a different guard anyway.

Mark walked around the ornate old Executive Office Building, where he had conferred with Nixon in his hideaway office. It was warm and humid. The dim twilight was now totally gone, and a group of young men who had been playing baseball walked from the Ellipse. Mark stood at the wrought-iron fence across the south lawn, and stared at the other side of the White House. Magnificent. All the more magnificent, now that he knew what went on inside and had touched the skirts of power.

As Mark stood there, he was at the pinnacle of his success. From that terrible night that Jonah had ordered him out of the house, from his struggles at Oxford and from his confrontation with Henry Enfield, he had become the richest man for his age in America—and now the achievements of this week.

As he stood staring at the distant light-bathed mansion, he knew that life could not get better than this.

Part Six

-36-

Nine years had passed. Mark's business success had progressed at a breathless pace. A year ago, in 1979, he had opened new offices in Hong Kong and Tokyo. The year before that, it had been a new office in New York, and the year before that, in London. The Stevens Group had added a second business jet, which could fly from San Francisco to London with only two refueling stops. Mark had put the first jet completely at the disposal of Steve Baumgartner and his staff. He had made Steve president, while remaining Chairman of the Board. Originally, he had hired Steve so that he could work less and devote himself to the larger picture; instead, he was working as much as ever. While he had never been bothered by the stress of business, his drive to expand had become increasingly compulsive. He wanted The Stevens Group to be larger than any of the New York investment banking firms, and to have a world-wide network of offices.

The prestige Mark had obtained from the Camp David episode had contributed heavily to the firm's phenomenal growth. John Connally had left as Treasury Secretary, to be replaced by George Shultz. Shultz, who had also attended the Camp David meeting, often invited Mark to policy meetings in Washington. Several times Schultz had been Mark's guest at the exclusive Cypress Point Golf Club, near Pebble Beach. Once Schultz had offered Mark a position as Undersecretary of the Treasury, but he had respectfully declined. While Mark's direct influence on government under Presidents Ford and Carter was smaller, he was nevertheless frequently consulted on financial policy.

Lord Ashley had been incapacitated by a serious stroke, and Rodney was now in charge of all Ashley family investments. Rodney had invested 33% of the family assets in various London real estate investments, mostly in the City. In addition, through their partnership, Mark and Rodney had bought up 14 smaller hotels in the West End, totally renovated them, and formed a hotel group that they named "Worcester Hotels." Worcester Hotels now showed a net worth in excess of £100,000,000. Mark had bought a large flat of his own in the Belgravia section of London, and had purchased another Rolls-Royce limousine for use in England.

Despite these successes, Mark had experienced unexplained bouts of depression. Confiding in no one, he had sought relief only by pouring himself into his business. In the last year he had begun to stay overnight three, even four nights a week in his Nob Hill condominium. When Pris complained, he explained that he needed more time to study the new projects Baumgartner's staff had worked up. Lately, it was not unusual for him to sleep only four or five hours on week nights.

Over the years Pris and Mark remained shinning stars of San Francisco society. Pris had become an important leader in the San Francisco Opera, and was largely responsible for bringing good theater to the city. She had expanded Enfield Galleries, adding branches in Carmel and Beverly Hills. This week she was in New York with one of her proteges, looking into opening still another gallery.

However, in the past two years their marriage had deteriorated. Mark wished he and Pris were closer. She never traveled with him any more, preferring her life in San Francisco. He was lonely, especially when he was away on business. For a while, he had tried curtailing business travel to spend more time with Pris. One summer they had tried playing golf together two times a week, but soon it became evident each would rather do their own things. Even at the grand parties at the Hillsborough mansion, there were two separate groups of people—Mark's group and Pris's group. Without planning it, or even realizing it, their lives had become separate.

Lately, his depression had been getting worse and he did not know why. What was more, he had not been feeling physically well for a long time. Yesterday, before she left for New York, Pris pointed out that he had been complaining of being tired all the time. He canceled a meeting and saw the doctor.

"Mark, your electrocardiogram is fine. I can't find anything wrong," the doctor told him after a rigorous two hour examination.

"But I've been feeling so depressed and tired."

"I think you've been working too hard. I know I couldn't keep up your kind of pace."

"I've been working hard all my, life and it's never bothered me."

"I'm sorry, but I can't find any trouble physically. Have you given any thought to seeing a psychiatrist?"

"No, it's nothing I can't handle myself."

The next morning at his office, Mark impulsively called Rolf Williams in Sonoma. "Rolf, can you get away from the office? I'd like you to come down to Monterey for some golf. Besides it's been six months since I've seen you."

"You mean today, right now?"

"If you can. Frankly, I need someone to talk to."

"I'll have to cancel a few things . . ."

"Pris is in New York. We could play golf every day through the weekend, if you want."

"All right. I could leave in an hour."

"Don't you drive. I'll send Alex in the Rolls for you. If we can tee off by four, we can still get in 18 holes."

Rolf was shocked at Mark's appearance as they sat in the back seat of the luxurious Rolls-Royce, headed down the Bayshore Freeway towards Pebble Beach. Mark's hair was whiter than when they had last seen each other. The circles under his eyes were more pronounced.

"Are you all right?" Rolf asked.

"Nothing a little golf won't cure."

"Every time I call the office you're away someplace."

"I know. I haven't been to Pebble in nearly a year."

The Cypress Point golf course was deserted when they teed off. They were the only golfers on the exclusive course. It was after four o'clock, but with the long summer days, they figured to finish the full 18 holes before dark.

A herd of deer grazed nonchalantly in the the fairway on the first hole. Rolf's shot had landed near the herd, which barely moved as he made his second shot. It was extremely peaceful on the course, with the white-capped Pacific in the distance. Tall redwood trees bordered the course, waiting to catch their errant shots.

"Good shot," Rolf shouted across the fairway after Mark hit his second shot. Mark was the better golfer. His shot reached the green for a likely par.

Happily, Mark waved his club in response to Rolf as he and his caddie briskly walked toward the green.

But despite his low handicap, Mark did not par another hole. He was not concentrating, and the game was a struggle for him. When he took a horrible seven on the 13th hole, he disgustedly tossed his putter to his caddie.

"I can't remember playing so badly."

The caddies handed the players their drivers and walked up the fairway, while the golfers made their way up to the next tee. Rolf hit his drive and waited for Mark to step up to the tee, but Mark continued to sit on the bench, staring off at the ocean.

"Come on, hot shot," Rolf teased. "Only five more miserable holes and we can start drinking."

But Mark did not get up. He continued to look off into the distance.

Rolf sat down next to Mark. "Come on, Mark, you'd better get it off your chest."

"Tell me, Rolf. Do you think I'm a failure?"

"A failure?" Rolf asked, incredulously. "Hell, Mark! If anyone is a success, you're it."

"I'm not so sure any more. I've got plenty of money, but things aren't what they should be."

"In what way?"

Instead of answering, Mark made his shot, and they walked down the fairway. They did not resume their discussion, because the caddies were near. They finished the hole and crossed the Seventeen Mile Drive toward the 15th, their spikes crunching on the asphalt.

"Here's where Pris and I tied our horses one time before we were married," Mark said wistfully, the caddies having gone ahead. "It was about this same time of night, too—twilight."

"It's a romantic spot, all right."

"I had just bought my house. I wasn't a member of Cypress Point in those days," he laughed. "So I thought we might get arrested for trespassing on the course."

"That would have been a laugh," Rolf said.

The view was breathtaking, as they stood on the tee above the ocean at the edge of the cliff.

"Pris and I sat over there," Mark said, pointing to the edge of the cliff where he and Pris had talked. "I think it was then I fell in love with her."

"I've never seen a sight as beautiful as this. I can see how you could fall in love."

The two friends stood, golf clubs in hand, taking in the breathtaking view of the setting sun and the wild waves smashing over the rocks below.

Both men hit their shots toward the green. Avoiding the deer, they walked toward the green. Impulsively, Mark changed directions and walked toward the edge of the cliff. "Come on, I'll show you where Pris and I were."

They looked over the edge of the cliff to the surf and rocks below. The enlarged sun was very low in the sky. "I hope you don't mind," Mark said. "This place has a very special meaning for me."

"I can see that it does."

"I've been doing a lot of thinking lately."

Rolf waited for Mark to continue.

"I'm not sure I'm on the right path."

"I'm not sure we humans have right paths."

"I never had any doubts until lately."

"It's strange to hear you say that," Rolf said. "You always knew exactly where you were headed."

"You're right about that," Mark smiled wistfully. "Especially since my last year at Cal." He paused, thinking. "You remember that time my father ordered me out of the house?"

"Sure, I remember. That was the time your dad caught you with Mr. Movelli's wife."

"You know what I found out after that?" Mark asked wistfully.

"No, what?"

"He'd been screwing Christina himself."

"What? Who?" At first Rolf did not absorb what Mark meant.

"My dad—he'd been screwing Christina before I did. Of course I didn't know it."

"My God! That explains why he was so angry." Rolf was astonished.

"That man was angry with me from the day I was born."

"Incredible! The same woman!"

"I think he did me a favor really—kicking me out that night." Mark picked up a pebble and threw it to the sea below. "From that moment on, I knew I wanted to be rich. I wanted to be somebody. Somebody he never could be."

"Yes, and look at you now. I don't know anybody any richer."

"Yes, but . . ."

"Jesus, Mark! You've got everything anyone could ever want. You've got money. You've got Pris . . ."

The lower edge of the sun met the horizon. Mark looked off at the ocean that had become calm. Tears were trickling down his cheeks.

"What's the trouble, Mark?"

"I'm not sure."

"I say we quit the golf game," suggested Rolf. "After all, we came to talk didn't we?"

Mark wiped off the tears with his hand. "Yeah," he sighed. "Let's talk."

"I'll tell the caddies to go on in."

.   .   .

The two friends sat near the cliff, watching the sun begin its descent below the far-off horizon. They said nothing for several minutes.

Finally, Mark spoke: "It's very hard for me to tell anyone, but the truth is Pris and I aren't what we should be." He dug in the dirt with a stick he had picked up.

"Listen, Mark, there's a problem with any marriage. I speak first-hand."

"I know. Pris is a great lady. We hardly ever argue. It's just that we don't offer much to each other any more. It's so different from the time she and I sat here together."

"What would you say a man and woman are supposed to offer each other, anyway?"

"Companionship, I suppose, for one thing."

"I agree, companionship is important."

"We have damn little of that any more. Of course sex is important, too."

"It sure is. Is sex a problem?"

"No, sex is . . . not the problem. It's okay." Mark looked away, avoiding his friend's eyes. "Sure it gets a little routine sometimes, but that's my fault as much as hers." Again, he dug with the stick. "I have to admit she's got a few hang-ups, but I knew that before we got married."

Rolf waited patiently, as if expecting Mark to tell him more, but when he did not, Rolf changed the subject. "What about kids? A man wants a family, especially when he reaches your age."

"Sure, I want kids."

"You've said you did."

"To be honest, Pris didn't want kids at first."

"I didn't know."

"She didn't want to be tied down. She's been trying to get pregnant this last year. Pris is past 35, you know."

"Kids are damned important. I still see mine every week."

"Talking about purpose in life," Mark said. "I think that's what kids are about. What's the point in building up a huge estate, if a man can't leave it to someone? Someone who is a part of him."

"Maybe that's our shot at immortality. Maybe that's what it's about."

"If I had kids, I'd teach them to run the business. That would be important to me." Mark spoke thoughtfully. "I'll tell you one thing. I'd be a real father, not hand out all the shit my old man always gave me."

Darkness approached and they started for the club house. Mark looked very depressed—as if the talk had not helped at all.

That night they had dinner at an elegant French restaurant in Carmel. "It's good to see you again, Mr. Stevens. We haven't seen much of you lately," said the maitre d'.

"I've been traveling, Paul. Unfortunately, I've been too busy to get down as much as I should."

The wine was excellent, and the introspective conversation continued over dinner. "I never thought I would tire of business, but lately there's begun to be a certain sameness about it," Mark said.

"Sameness?" Rolf was astounded. "How on earth can you say that about million dollar deals?"

"I know, but I just don't get the same satisfaction I used to."

"Have you ever thought of seeing a psychiatrist?"

"No, and I don't want to see one. Half of them can't handle their own problems. It's nothing I can't deal with myself."

"You ought to think about it. I saw one when I was getting a divorce. He helped me a lot."

"No, I'll work it out myself."

Silently, they watched the sun disappear.

Mark broke the silence. "Something strange has been going on with my business. Baumgartner told me last week that one of the London investment houses has accumulated almost 11% of The Stevens Group stock. Can you imagine that?"

"Probably because you opened your office there."

"That's what I thought, too, but we checked it out. They started to buy long before we opened in London."

"Pretty flattering. England is a long way off for investors to be interested in you."

"I don't know, Rolf. I don't like it. I don't like it at all."

"You don't think there's a takeover possibility, do you?"

"I don't know. I just don't like it. I'm not sure . . ."

"Maybe you should find out who's behind it."

"Maybe I should."

"Do you think anyone could really be trying a takeover?"

"I own 25%. I don't see how anyone could get 51%. The price has gone way up. It closed yesterday at 105.

"One hundred and five dollars a share! At that price it would take a fortune for someone to get control. Wasn't it $30 when you started?"

"Yes, 30. I signed an extension of my employment contract— another seven years. I figured I had to support the price of the stock."

"Good idea."

"I'll have Baumgartner find out who really owns the stock."

Alex was waiting with the Phantom outside the restaurant, when they finished eating.

"I saw your mother in Sonoma the other day," Rolf said. The guard waved the big Rolls through the Carmel Gate to the Forest.

"It's been months since I've seen her. I can't get her to come into San Francisco, so we talk on the telephone."

"She said Antonio was getting more feeble. I never see him in town any more. Your mother does all the shopping and cooking for him."

"I don't know what I'm going to do with her when Antonio dies."

"Maybe you should buy her a house in Sonoma. Do you think she'd like that?"

"I don't know. She's lived on the compound so long. I know it's something I'll have to face someday."

"And Antonio? Any chance of your ever reconciling with him after all these years?"

"I never tried it again after the funeral. That's all history. I haven't spoken to him since."

"Same thing with Henry?"

"I know what you're thinking. Two old guys who were very important, and now they both hate me. I've thought about that. I've wondered if it's something with me."

"As a matter of fact, that wasn't what I was thinking."

"No, it's still the same with Henry, too. I know Pris would like things to be different, but as far as I'm concerned it'll be the same until the old guy finally kicks off one day."

The cold fog had closed in on the Padres Lane house. Alex lighted the fireplace in the den, and Mark put on a Beatles album. The friends sat down, determined to put a good-sized dent in the brandy bottle.

"I'll never forget the time I saw the Beatles in London," Mark reminisced.

The phonograph played "Love Me Do."

"God, what a racket that crowd made—and then actually meeting them!" Mark continued.

"That had to be a thrill. That time at Candlestick, we couldn't get within a mile of the stage. Remember?" Rolf was referring to the last concert the Beatles had ever given. "That was 1967, wasn't it?"

"No, 1966. I remember, I couldn't understand why the Beatles broke up. They really had a good thing going for them."

Rolf nodded his agreement.

"But now I think maybe I do," Mark said

"How do you mean?"

"The sameness. Not boredom mind you. How could you ever get bored, performing in front of 100,000 screaming fans? It's sort of analogous to my situation. Making money can never be boring, but it just isn't enough. It's not satisfying any more."

"Are you sure anything is ever going to be enough for you?" Rolf asked.

"I don't know. All I can say is, I sure hope so."

Mark was already at the breakfast table the next morning when Rolf came out at six-thirty.

"You're an early bird," Rolf said.

"I never got to sleep. I've been up all night."

"You look terrible. Are you all right?"

"Rolf, would you mind if we went back today instead of playing golf?"

"No, to be frank with you, I almost expected it. You never could sit still for long."

"You can stay here at the house if you want—I can make arrangements at Cypress for you to play—but I've got to get back."

"It's all right, Mark. Don't worry about it. I've got some stuff I should do anyway."

"I made a decision this morning."

"Tell me, what?"

"I've decided to get even more involved in the business. I've had this idea about buying up companies in trouble, and keeping them until I've turned them around."

"You think that's going to solve your problems? Even more business?"

"I don't know, but what the hell else am I supposed to do? Business is the only thing that's ever worked for me."

-37-

It had been less than a month since Mark's golf game with Rolf at Pebble Beach. He had returned to San Francisco with a resolve to ignore his nagging self-doubt and to further expand The Stevens Group. He had asked Steve Baumgartner, who was doing an excellent job as president, to get the word out that they were in the market for troubled companies. Steve had recommended Erie Steering Corporation as a good candidate. This afternoon's meeting was to talk with Erie's owner, Jack Langdon.

Under Langdon, Erie Steering had become an important supplier of steering units to Detroit's automobile industry. When Langdon had retired, he had handed the business to his two sons, who had virtually ruined the business. Jack Langdon had raced back to Cleveland from his Florida retirement, but it was too late. He was now looking to The Stevens Group for a heavy capital infusion, in an attempt to save the company.

Baumgartner had warned Mark that Langdon would resist giving up control, but that new management was absolutely essential if The Stevens Group were to get involved.

Mark's intercom buzzed. It was Bette, his secretary. "Mr. Baumgartner is in the conference room. He has Mr. Langdon and his sons. They brought their attorney with them."

Steve Baumgartner had reported that he was enthusiastic about the possibilities of turning Erie around. The situation sounded perfect for the new direction Mark had decided upon that sleepless night in Pebble Beach. Nevertheless, for reasons he did not understand, Mark dreaded today's meeting. He had developed a severe headache and wished he were someplace else.

Pris was in Beverly Hills. Samuel Wade, Pris's protege, was showing the unsold paintings from his New York show. Wade was the same artist Pris had been helping for so long. Mark had not liked him since their first meeting at the gallery, years ago. He had even wondered if Pris might be having an affair with the man.

Mark supposed he should not keep the Erie Steering people waiting. He forced himself up from his desk. He sure as hell would rather be in London, chatting with Rodney, he thought, or in Sonoma having lunch with Rolf.

Steve introduced Mark to the Langdons and to Earl Beekman, their attorney. Mark asked Steve to summarize the facts, while he leaned back in his big chair at the head of the long wooden table. The paneled room was decorated with a set of leather-bound classics. A painting of a traditional English fox hunt hung on one wall. He had chosen it because it reminded him of Castle Enfield.

When Steve finished, Langdon's attorney, Earl Beekman spoke. "I've represented Erie Steering for many years and I think I can speak for them." Beekman was a man of nearly 70. No doubt he once had been a handsome man, but the years, and too much alcohol, had left him paunchy and tired looking. He held a cigarette in his hand. "As I told Mr. Baumgartner when I was here last week, my clients have several offers from others, but they like the approach of your company, Mr. Stevens. I've advised my clients . . ."

"Mr. Beekman," Mark interrupted. "I would suggest if Mr. Langdon has a better offer, he should take it. I wouldn't want him to do anything else." Mark did not see the need for a lawyer's being present, and now Beekman apparently intended to run the negotiations.

"Of course, Mr. Stevens, but the point of this meeting is to find out what are the best terms you will offer my client and whether they're acceptable."

"Acceptable to whom, Mr. Beekman? Acceptable to Mr. Langdon or acceptable to his lawyer?" Mark did not care that he was being rude.

"Acceptable to the Langdon family. As their lawyer, I'm not the ultimate decision maker, but I think you'll find that the Langdons pay a great deal of attention to my opinions."

Suddenly, Mark had a very strong compulsion to leave the room. There was a strong voice inside him telling him: "Mark you have to get the hell out of here. Get out of this place and leave these people." He felt extremely dizzy. He wondered if there was an earthquake, and put his hand on the edge of the table. He had felt this way a couple of times lately.

He had been in a thousand such negotiating sessions before. There was nothing special about this presumptuous lawyer that was any different than he had endured before. In fact, in former days he had enjoyed dealing with difficult people. However, today it was all he could do to force himself not to leave the meeting.

"Steve," he said. "Perhaps I missed something in your report. Would you tell me again the terms on which we should be involved with Mr. Langdon and his family here?" The dizziness left, but his hand was sweaty as he took it from the table. The immediacy of having to leave the room eased, although he still wanted to be elsewhere.

"Of course," said Steve, "It is my opinion that $20,000,000 in new capital will be needed. I feel that we should commit to another $10,000,000 if necessary. Mr. Langdon doesn't think that much is needed, and wants to give up a smaller share of the company.

"I remember the figures very well."

"The company would double its common stock plus one share, giving The Stevens Group 51% and the family 49%. All stock now held by the public would be retired," Steve continued.

"In addition a new class of stock, Class B, would be issued to The Stevens Group. Class B would have total voting power until it was redeemed. There would be no dividends on any stock until the Class B was retired.

"Very well," said Mark.

"We can't agree to that," said Beekman, self-righteously. "We must retain control. Right, Jack?"

The senior Langdon blew a puff of smoke from his cigar. "That's right. I must have control."

It happened again. The impulse to leave the room. To "get the hell out of here." What was he doing sitting here with these assholes and their lawyer, anyway? He must be worth over a billion dollars. Here he was, talking to these idiots over a $20,000,000 deal.

Mark got up and looked out the window. He felt faint and wobbly. Wiping his forehead, he looked at the tourist boat circling the Bay Bridge. Maybe the same boat as the day he had quit his job with Henry. That's what he felt like now—quitting everything and getting the hell out.

As he stared out the window, the others fell silent. Finally, he felt a little better. This was ridiculous. He shouldn't feel like this. Surely he could spend half an hour with these guys for $20,000,000. Look at Rolf Williams. How many times did Rolf have to listen to some idiot judge make a stupid ruling? Rolf couldn't go stomping out of the courtroom every time he felt an urge to dump everything. Mark could take the profit from this deal and give it to charity if he wanted. He would be stupid to walk away from millions in profits. Maybe he should see a psychiatrist, he thought. Maybe there was some tranquilizer he could take and everything would be okay.

Mark grimly turned back to the group. "Mr. Langdon, I must speak very frankly."

"I thought we were being frank."

"I don't think so. I think what we've been saying has been so much bullshit."

"What?" said Beekman, but Langdon held up his hand, quieting the lawyer.

Mark took a deep breath. The only way he could get through this meeting this was to say exactly how he felt.

"Jack, it's obvious you're a bright man. You've got more than your share of guts, too. If that weren't so, you never could have built such a business—such a damned good business that we still want it, even after all that's happened. But you've got a blind spot, Jack. A big weakness." Mark paused for a moment. "Jack, you're a lousy judge of executive talent."

"What?" said Beekman, but Langdon held up his hand again.

"Be quiet, Earl," Langdon interrupted. "Let him have his say."

"Why on earth did you choose your sons to run the business?" continued Mark. "A man's loving his sons is admirable; I'll give you that. But Jack, there are better ways to love your sons than to give them a business they don't know how to run."

The younger Langdons did not say a word of protest. They had never heard their father spoken to this way before.

"Another thing Jack, you use lousy judgment when you let Beekman, here, tell you what to do. You've got to exercise your own judgment, not Beekman's. You duck your responsibilities when you make your kids try to run a company that's too much for them. When it comes right down to it, the failure of your company is Jack Langdon's fault—not your sons'—not Beekman's and certainly not the competition's."

"Listen Stevens . . ." Once again, Beekman started to speak, but Langdon waved his cigar.

"Now, Jack," Mark continued. "Perhaps you can see why Steve and I don't want you to have control of our new company."

"Go on," said Langdon.

"I know you're talented. I'm asking Steve to offer you a contract as a consultant—an active consultant. I want the manufacturing expertise of the same man who could build up a company like this in the first place. I want you and Steve to agree on a figure."

Jack Langdon looked at Mark in noncommittal silence.

"Another thing, Beekman can get you other offers. I'm sure of that. Just as we have the choice of many companies. You're the one that has to choose. Do you want The Stevens Group, or do you want someone who will let you control the company? If you choose us, your sons will have to develop careers of their own. I might also add that if you choose us, the new company will have a new lawyer—a man who knows that he is only a lawyer and nothing more."

"Well I . . .," said Jack Langdon.

Mark shook his head, interrupting him. "No, I don't want your answer now. You think about it and tell Steve. I'm sorry, but I have to leave now."

All but the attorney rose to their feet as Mark left the room without saying another word.

"Bette, tell Alex, to have the car ready," said Mark, as he headed for his private elevator without returning to his office.

"But you aren't finished with the meeting yet, are you?"

"I'm getting out of here as fast as I can."

"Are you all right, Mark?" said Steve Baumgartner, who had followed Mark.

"No, I'm not all right. I just want to leave."

The elevator door closed, and he was gone.

"What's the trouble with Mark?" asked Steve. "He's been looking terrible."

"He wasn't feeling well this morning." A worried Bette picked up the telephone to call the chauffeur. "I hope he's going to be all right."

Mark got into the back seat of the Phantom. "Where should I drive, Mr. Stevens?" asked Alex.

"I don't know. Just get me away from the financial district. I'm feeling lousy." Although the Rolls was cool inside, Mark took off his suit jacket and wiped the perspiration from his forehead. He still had feelings of dizziness. It was as if the ground were quaking under the car. He knew it was irrational, but he felt he had escaped from the building not a moment too soon. He put the handkerchief back in his jacket breast pocket, and looked at his shaking hand. Maybe he should have Alex drive to the doctor's office. What was the matter with him, anyway?

Alex drove the Phantom up California toward Nob Hill.

"Where should I go? The club? Your apartment?" the chauffeur asked with concern.

"No, neither one. Just keep driving." Mark zipped up the divider glass and sat back in the deep seat. He wanted to get away from his condo as much as from the office. His mind was whirring for some explanation, some way to stop what was happening, but the intense pressure inside remained. All he knew was that he wanted Alex to get him away from everything he knew in San Francisco—and to do it fast.

Alex took Van Ness toward the Civic Center. Soon they passed the Opera. He felt the same way about the Opera. Never again would he set foot in that place. When he went to the Opera, he was phony, unreal. He had never liked the Opera. Sure, he had felt good that everyone knew Pris and that everyone admired him for being the top contributor, but he had never liked the goddammed Opera!

Maybe he should go to Sonoma. He could see the compound, talk to his mother, maybe have dinner with Rolf. He pushed the button and lowered the divider window to tell Alex to head for the Golden Gate Bridge and Sonoma, but he knew that was not what he wanted either. He felt sentimental about Sonoma, but there were no answers there.

"Shouldn't I take you home?" Alex asked.

"No—thanks, Alex. I'm feeling a little better." The last place he wanted to go was Hillsborough—that meant Pris. He wanted to get away from her, too.

London. How about going to London? He remembered the time he and Rodney had walked Kings Road. He remembered the young people, hanging out on Kings Road. What had ever happened to them? Were they all in offices now, feeling that they too "had to get the hell out"?

"Alex! Take me to the Haight-Ashbury District," he shouted.

"Haight-Ashbury? I haven't been there since the '60s."

"I've never been there. Let's go." He did not know why he wanted to go to Haight-Ashbury—only that he might feel better there.

When Rolf Williams was getting divorced in the '60s, he had hung around the Haight-Ashbury District of San Francisco. In those years Rolf had been into the hippy, easy sex and marijuana scene that Haight-Ashbury offered. Rolf had often discussed his experiences with Mark. Other than that, Mark knew nothing of Haight-Ashbury.

"It's a lot different from what it was in the old days," said Alex as he steered the imposing Rolls along Haight Street. "The place was really jumping then. I used to hang out in a little bar that was right there." He pointed to a book store, with tables laden with books on the sidewalk.

There was a considerable number of pedestrians on the street. Alex drove for several blocks, until they were through the commercial area, and the street had become another San Francisco apartment house street.

"I'm getting out. I want to walk." Perhaps walking might make him feel better.

He left his suit jacket in the car, and began strolling along the street. He shoved his hands deep into his pockets, and looked in the storefront windows. The first was a lawyer's office. "Frederick J. McClintock. Lawyer." He wondered what kind of a man would have a law office in this area. Probably sued the government to make sure it gave away his tax money to everyone equally. He had half-expected Rolf to open a law office like this when he left the big firm.

Next was a flower shop. There couldn't be any flower children left. Through the glass he watched a woman buying flowers. She was about 30, wearing a summery dress with a short skirt, and thongs. Her legs were tanned. That meant she probably was not from San Francisco. He wondered what she was doing in Haight-Ashbury, and whether she had a husband. He stood, watching, until she completed her purchase. She smiled at him as she passed him, and walked down the street ahead of him, carrying her flowers. They were yellow daisies.

Next was a used-furniture store. He had forgotten what it was like to be poor and to buy used furniture. A bedroom mirror was angled, so that he got a good look at his reflection through the window. Funny, he looked at his face every morning when he shaved, but it had been a long time since he saw himself as others saw him. God, he looked tired—tired and old. Pris said he looked distinguished with his white hair, but he thought he simply looked old. There were lines in his face and circles under his eyes. Only 39 years, and he looked so damned old! He sighed solemnly. Inside too, he felt old—very old and very tired.

For another 15 minutes Mark peered into windows, thinking and wondering. As he walked, Alex followed in the Rolls, periodically changing parking places. Everyone seemed happy enough, going about their business—taking in dry cleaning, greeting customers, buying vegetables. He wondered if they had ever been forced to deal with any idiotic lawyers from Cleveland.

He came to a restaurant with outdoor tables, and could see they served beer. He would like a beer. He had not drunk much beer since his Oxford days. He sat down at a table to wait for the waiter. For the first time, he realized he felt better. His giddiness was gone. He was no longer perspiring. The need to run away had left him. He decided it had not been a heart attack.

Only one other table was occupied. It was a lady by herself, drinking tea and reading a book. A bunch of flowers wrapped in green paper lay on her table. They were yellow daisies. He looked carefully at the woman. It was the same woman he had watched in the flower shop.

Her dress was in a yellow daisy pattern, like her bunch of flowers. She was prettier than he had noticed before. The waiter came with his beer. He took a sip and looked at the woman again. She was lanky, and almost as tall as Mark. Her medium-long hair was black, yet was streaked with very dark red. The streaks looked as if her hair had been hastily dyed. However, he could see that her shoulders and face were tanned, so perhaps the uneven hair color had been caused by the sun. Her book was something about human potential. The beer relaxed him. He no longer worried about the terrible feelings that had plagued him half an hour ago. The woman looked up from her book, and saw that he was looking at her. She smiled briefly.

"I apologize, if I was staring", he said. "I was noticing your beautiful flowers. I've always liked daisies."

"Thank you. I find it's impossible to be blue with daisies around." Her engaging smile was her most attractive feature. Except for very red lipstick, she wore no make up over her slightly freckled face.

"I was making a bet with myself," he said. "You're not from San Francisco, are you?"

She smiled again. "How did you know that?"

"You're so tanned. You've been in the sun."

She laughed. "You must be from San Francisco, yourself."

"Yes, I am. Please, may I introduce myself? I'm Mark. Mark Stevens."

"I'm Diane Chandler. You were right about the sun. I live near Concord now. I take care of people's flowers. I'm always in the sun."

"You're a gardener, but you're buying flowers in Haight-Ashbury?"

"I used to live here, before I got . . . before I got married. I'm divorced now. I come back every once in a while."

"Reminiscing a bit?"

"Exactly. I lived here in the '60s. I used to buy daisies at that flower shop whenever I had a little money."

Mark noticed that Alex had parked the Phantom across the street and was reading something.

"Do you ever think of moving back here? To Haight-Ashbury, I mean. Now that you're divorced."

"I do, but it's not the same any more. Besides, I have two children. It could never be the same."

Mark took his beer to Diane's table. "May I sit down?"

"Sure, if you'd like."

"What was it like here?" he asked, intently leaning toward her. "In the '60s?"

"We thought we had all the answers. Naive flower children, that's what we were. I never found answers. Then I got married and moved to the suburbs."

"But you got divorced?"

"I didn't like that life, either. My husband turned into a square, overnight. He became a banker of all things. Home every night at 6:45. Left for work at 7:15 in the morning."

"So you got out?"

"No. Actually, I would have stuck it out. He was the one who wanted the divorce."

"Really?"

"He fell in love with one of our friends. How very middle class! They live within two blocks of me, so he can see the kids."

"So you became a gardener?"

"I like gardening a lot. With that and what Harold gives me, I'm doing okay."

"But what about the future?"

"I don't know. As far as the future is concerned, it's right now anyway. You have to live right now."

Mark wanted to keep talking with Diane. She was refreshing. He glanced at Alex, still reading in the Rolls. He could ask Diane to go with him to the condo, but he did not want her to know he had money. Surely Diane would interpret the condo as an invitation to sex. Maybe she would be right, too. He wasn't prepared to be unfaithful to Pris, not now.

"Actually, I'm in banking, too. I had to get away from the office this afternoon, so I ended up here."

"I know how that is, Mark," she laughed. "That's why I come here. This is my respite from reality."

He enjoyed the openness of their conversation. He wished Pris and he could talk this way. He was thinking about ordering a third beer and more tea for her, when she glanced at her watch.

"Mark, I have to go. I have to be home at six."

"Because of your children? I'm disappointed." He wanted to keep talking with Diane. She was like a tonic.

"May I tell you the truth?"

"The truth? You don't have to tell me anything. I'm a perfect stranger."

"I'm really not divorced. Harold did have an affair—as a matter of fact, I think he still sees her once in a while—but we didn't get a divorce."

"But why did you tell me . . .?"

"I don't know. I come here almost every week. When anyone asks, I tell them I'm divorced. Sort of a fantasy."

"You wish you were divorced, is that it?"

She laughed. "At least this way, I'm divorced one day a week."

"And what do you do in your other fantasies?"

"A handsome man on a white horse takes me to his castle."

"What do you do in the castle?"

"We smoke a joint and have sex, like in the old days."

Mark put his head back and laughed. "Really? Does your fantasy ever happen?"

"Never a white horse, but the truth is the joint and sex happens once in a while."

Diane's frankness struck a responsive cord, and he knew he wanted to take her to the condo. Her situation was not dissimilar from his own. Locked into a life that had betrayed her, she was trying to find some happiness, even if it were in unreality.

"Diane, would you like to ride on my white horse?"

"Your white horse?"

"It's a modern day white horse." He turned and looked at the Rolls.

She turned, too. "What?"

"See that limousine across the street?"

"Sure, the one with the chauffeur. I noticed it."

"It's my white horse."

"It's yours? You're kidding me! The Rolls?"

"Let's take a ride to my castle."

His first thought had been to take her to the Hillsborough house since Pris was away. He would love to have a one-time screw with her on Pris's and his bed. Like Diane, he would like to get away from marriage for a day. But as he rolled down the window to speak to Alex, he knew he could not take her to Hillsborough.

"To Nob Hill," he told Alex.

-38-

The next morning Mark drove his red Aston Martin up the Bayshore Freeway from Hillsborough. Last night Diane had not wanted him to drive her home in the Rolls, so he had dropped her off at the BART station on his way to the Hillsborough house. He kept waking up in the night, thinking about what had happened. Diane was attractive enough, but their sex had been loveless and uninspired. Little different from with Pris these past years—there had been no lust, no passion.

The San Francisco skyline came into view as the freeway curved around the hill. He had always loved his life in San Francisco. He felt fine this morning, and was mystified by the terrifying feelings that had compelled him to leave his office yesterday. Surely it had been a fluke. His work had been his whole life. He lived for it. What had happened yesterday was ridiculous. He was eager to leap into today's schedule.

He drew the sports car to a stop at Market Street. Where had his feelings for Pris gone? Their marriage had started out with such promise, but now it was largely empty. There were still the parties, the opera and the whole social scene, but there was no passion between them. Perhaps he had been a fool to imagine their early problems with sex were not important. Lately, he had been thinking a lot about Christina.

He turned the Aston Martin over to John, the parking attendant in his building. He stood in the lobby, waiting for his private elevator and thinking about his schedule. Suddenly, with no warning he was attacked by the same feelings as yesterday. His knees nearly gave way. Again, it felt as if there were an earthquake. He began to sweat. His elevator arrived, but he could not bring himself to get in. He steadied himself with his hand on the cold marble wall. "Jesus," he mumbled. He knew he had to go up to his office. He had a conference call with Hong Kong and London. He had meetings all day long. Goddamn! What was he going to do? Should he see Doctor Mangoles? What was happening anyway?

Suddenly his ears began to ring. He covered them with his perspiring hands, but the ringing continued. He grabbed his brief case and rushed back to the garage.

"John, get me the car." He wiped his forehead with the silk handkerchief from his breast pocket, and straightened his tie. He did not want John to see him like this.

The Oakland airport flashed through his mind. Pris had taken his jet to Los Angeles, but Steve and the others were flying to New York in the other plane. Suddenly, he wanted to be on that plane.

The tires squealed as the car was delivered. "John, call my secretary. I'm going to New York. Tell her to hold Steve's plane."

"Yes, sir."

Mark was driving far too fast as he raced across the Bay Bridge. He had no idea what he would do in New York. He had to get away—away from his office, away from Pris, away from everything. The ringing in his ears had stopped and he felt a little better, but his hands remained cold and clammy.

Christina came to his mind once again. He must have thought about her a dozen times since last night with Diane. He wondered what it would have been like if he had married Christina instead of Pris.

His symptoms disappeared as soon as the flight gained altitude out of Oakland. He sat by himself in the rear of the plane, trying to figure out what to do. He was devastated. Perhaps he should order the plane turned around, so he could see Dr. Mangoles. Maybe he needed a vacation. He had been tired for such a long time. His friends had been asking him if he felt all right, and then yesterday he had seen himself in that mirror. No, it was not a vacation he needed. At least not hotels, golf and the beach. What he needed was to be by himself for a few days. He needed a chance to figure things out.

By the time the jet landed at La Guardia, Mark had decided to go on to London. Perhaps he would not even see Rodney. He always kept fresh clothes in the company flat. Maybe he would just walk around London and think things through. Yes, he would stroll down Kings Road, watching the young people. Perhaps he would go to that church on Piccadilly, where Mavis had taken him.

As the plane landed, he felt wonderful about being in London again. It was five in the morning, and the old city was not yet awake. He had called from La Guardia to be met by the Rolls-Royce Phantom he had bought for the London office. The feeling of being crushed had left him. The chauffeur guided the big car into town from Heathrow. If he lived to be a hundred, he would feel wonderful about arriving in London.

His flat overlooked Belgrave Square. It was within walking distance of Rodney and Rebecca in Knightsbridge. When he had remodeled, he had installed a lavish tiled shower with an American-style shower head. He hated those small hand-held showers so common in England. After he showered, he sat at the desk overlooking the square, wearing his heavy terry cloth robe and holding an orange juice in his hand. It was good to be in London. It was so wonderful to feel good again.

Once again Christina came to his mind. Idly, he thumbed through the cards in his wallet. As he had done a thousand times over the years, he looked at the ragged business card. *Ristorante Giuseppe.* Long ago, he had written Christina's address and telephone number. "987-123. 119 *Corsa Mediterraneo.*"

My God, how he had loved her. What passion she had stirred within him. He recalled the first time they had had sex, in Antonio's mansion. He thought about that time in the car in Rome when he saw her last. How often he had thought about these things over the years.

He decided he would call her. Was she even still alive? Was she still married to that old publisher? Did she ever think of him?

Christina's telephone rang several times before the maid answered. "Pronto," she said.

"May I speak to Mrs. Bagliani, please. Christina Bagliani?"

The maid said something in Italian, then left the telephone. In two or three minutes a male voice too young to be Otello Bagliani's spoke in an Italian accent. "Yes, may I help you?"

"I'm . . . I'm an old friend of Mrs. Bagliani. May I speak to her?"

"I'm sorry, Mrs. Bagliani is on her way to America. Her former husband died yesterday. She's going to the funeral. Who did you say this was?"

The news stunned Mark. Antonio was dead! How would he ever be able to think of him as dead? It was strange that Christina would want to attend the funeral. Who would be there? His mother, the vineyard employees, a few neighbors, probably Rolf.

"Sir?," said the voice.

"Oh, I'm sorry. I'm an old friend from America—I didn't know—I hadn't heard that Mr. Movelli had died."

"May I have your name, sir?"
"That's all right. I'll call again."

Perhaps he should attend the funeral. His mother would need him. Besides, it would be his chance to see Christina.

Suddenly, he was very weary. He set the alarm for three hours later, and pulled the bed covers over himself. He wondered if the funeral would be like his father's. Now his mother was the only member of her generation living on the compound. A voice inside him said he should attend the funeral, but he wrestled with the painful memory of Antonio's refusing to speak to him.

As he slept, he dreamed of Antonio in his open coffin at the funeral. In the dream, he looked at the faces of the mourners as they filed by. The workmen, followed by Christina and then his mother. Behind Amanda there was a gap in the line. A gap just large enough for one person. After the gap came Rolf Williams, dressed in a black suit.

Suddenly he woke up with the realization that it was a dream. The image of the open coffin would not leave. In the bathroom he splashed water on his face. He had to wake up. He had to get the dream out of his mind. He sat in the chair in the dimly lighted bedroom, refusing to return to bed until he was fully awake and he could be sure the dream would not return. Then he made a decision. It would be much too painful to go to the funeral.

-39-

When Mark woke up, he thought he was in Hillsborough. He was immediately filled with fear and tension about getting on his elevator at the office. Then he realized he was still in London, and was able to relax.

He thought about his dream of Antonio's funeral. His mother would expect him at the funeral, but he did not want to go. No one at home knew he was in London, so his excuse to Amanda would be that he had not heard about Antonio. As for Christina, it was just as well he did not see her. Perhaps he would call her when she had returned to Italy. He would be better off using the time in England to think and get his bearings.

He peered outdoors, past the curtains of his flat. He felt free. Free of the emotions that had gripped him since meeting with the Cleveland people Tuesday. The sun reflected off the leaves of the large trees in Belgrave Square. San Francisco and its problems were thousands of miles away. He supposed he should let Pris and the office know he was in England, but part of the feeling of being free was that no one knew where he was.

But an hour later, he felt the need of human contact, and telephoned Rodney. The maid said Rodney and Rebecca were in the country for the weekend. He called Castle Enfield, knowing that Rodney would invite him to join them in the country.

"Mark, when did you arrive?" asked Rodney.

"Just a few hours ago. I came on an impulse."

"I insist you join us at Castle Enfield. Mother is having a party. It will be wonderful to see you."

"And how is Mavis?" Mark asked.

"She's super. She often asks about you."

Mark was glad he called. It would be wonderful seeing them all again. He hoped Mavis and he could have one of their chats, such as the time in St. James's Piccadilly church. Mavis was always there to help when he was in difficulty.

. . .

There were 30 or 40 cars parked at the edge of the Castle Enfield driveway where it skirted the lake. Mavis's party was large, with her usual list of guests. Mark's chauffeur drove very slowly, so that the tires would not kick up the gravel against the car's paint. What a contrast, arriving in his majestic Rolls-Royce compared to his first visit to Castle Enfield, when he had to borrow Lord Ashley's tuxedo.

"Mark, old boy! I'm so glad you came," said Rodney. "Rebecca," he called, "Mark's here!"

Rebecca kissed Mark on the cheek and impulsively hugged him. Since the trial with Derek, she had always been affectionate toward him.

"I'm so happy you're staying the night," she exclaimed.

"I am too. I feel right at home."

Together, they walked to the crowded ballroom, where Rodney introduced Mark to a group of guests.

Across the room, another small group noticed Mark's entrance. Jacqueline Abshire, a good-looking blonde about Mark's age, took Mavis by the hand, asking:

"Tell me," who is that white-haired chap with your son? He's a handsome one." Jacqueline's short turquoise cocktail dress made her stand out from the other women at the party.

"Why that's Mark—Mark Stevens. I didn't see him come in. He went to Oxford with Rodney. Pardon me while I say hello to him." Mavis gracefully moved across the ballroom.

"My, he is handsome," said the woman who stood next to Jacqueline.

"And rich, too," said the woman's husband. "Rumor is he's one of the richest men in America."

"Really?," said Jacqueline. "I wonder if he's married."

"I hope, for your sake, he isn't," laughed the woman.

"Isn't he the one who was an advisor to Nixon?" asked the man. "Rodney talks about him all the time. I'm sure he's the one. The expert in international economics."

Mavis held out her hand. "Mark, dear, I'm so glad you've come."

Mark kissed her on the cheek. "It looks like a wonderful party. No one can put on a party like you, Mavis."

"Have you been well?" she asked.

"Pretty well."

"And Priscilla. Is she with you?"

"She couldn't make it this trip. She's awfully busy at home."

"Pardon me, Lady Ashley," interrupted a manservant. "Lord and Lady Stiffel have just arrived."

"I'm sorry, Mark, but I must greet them. Has Rodney asked you to stay for the weekend?"

"Yes, he has."

"Then we can chat later." Mavis left to see to her guests.

Mark felt let down. He had felt a sense of urgency about wanting to talk with Mavis. When she had asked if he was well, he had wanted to tell her the truth: that his life had become unraveled, that Pris was not busy at home at all, but was at an art show with another man. He desperately needed to unburden himself.

Mark was pleasant to the guests as the evening progressed. Drink in hand, he amiably chatted and joked, but his mind was not on the party. Frequently, he glanced in Mavis's direction as she moved about the house talking with the guests, but she was too busy to talk with him. Finally, he asked Rebecca to dance.

"How has Rodney been?" Mark asked.

"He's his old self. Thanks to you."

"He's doing a magnificent job on our various ventures—becoming quite the mogul."

"We'll never forget what you did for him." Rebecca danced well to the fast-paced music.

"Where's Lord Ashley? I haven't seen him all night."

"Upstairs. His stroke, you know."

"I didn't realize it was that bad."

"It was much worse than we all thought."

"How's his father's stroke affecting Rodney?"

"The two of them are getting on quite well. Rodney has completely taken over the family finances."

When the dance ended, Rebecca's attention was distracted by another guest, and Mark stood alone, albeit momentarily.

"Hello. I'm Jacqueline Abshire," said the attractive woman, extending her hand to Mark. "I told Mavis that I wanted to meet you, but she's so busy. Well, you know how Mavis is."

"Yes, ever the perfect hostess. I'm Mark Stevens. An old family friend." Mark shook her hand gently.

"I know very well who you are. Everyone has been telling me all about you."

Jacqueline Abshire was a very pretty woman. Vivacious, her blond hair was cut short. Her smile was her most predominant feature. She was a refreshing change from the other women at the party, who were dowdy by comparison.

As they spoke, the band began playing. It was John Lennon's "She Loves You."

"Would you like to dance?" he asked.

"Of course," she said, and they moved into the fast-forming group of dancing couples.

"Are you married?" she asked after they had danced for a minute.

"Why, yes," he answered. "My wife's in California." He was surprised by her question.

"I was married once," she said. They were dancing apart, but came together with the music.

"What happened? Divorced or widowed?" he asked.

"Oh, divorced. Andrew would never have done me the favor of dying."

Mark laughed at her directness.

"Dying would have been out of character for Andrew."

Mark continued to laugh. "What was poor Andrew's problem?"

"Never bold enough to try something new. Same old job. Same old house. Same old car."

"I gather you weren't willing to be the same old wife."

"That's right. One night I had an extra drink, and had it out with him. Do you know what he said when I told him I wanted a divorce?"

"No, what?"

"'Well, I'd better get some sleep', he said. Can you imagine that? 'Well, I'd better get some sleep.'"

"Sounds like a dull fellow to me."

Mark was interrupted by a tap on the shoulder.

"Pardon me, old man, but may I cut in?" It was a tall, tanned, athletic man in a double-breasted blazer.

"Certainly," Mark replied. He watched the man dance off with Jacqueline. For a few minutes, she had helped him forget the problems that had driven him from San Francisco.

Mark noticed that Jacqueline danced every remaining dance that evening, each with a different partner. Even when the band was not playing, she was in conversation with one, and sometimes several, admirers. Finally, as the evening neared its end, Mark interrupted and asked her to dance once again.

"My, you are a very popular lady," he told her as they stepped onto the floor.

"Thank you very much, but I don't know that it's much of a compliment."

"Why do you say that?"

"After I was divorced, I learned the rest of the men were no different from my husband."

"What do you mean?"

"They all ask me to lunch. Always someplace where we'd not be seen."

Mark laughed.

"Most of them would have a heart attack if I accepted."

"Have you? Accepted, that is."

Jacqueline laughed. "Of course I have. Usually they make an excuse at the last minute."

"But not always?"

"I'm guessing you want to know if there's more to it than lunch."

Just then a man tried to cut in. "James, dear. I was just telling Mark here about a new novel that I'm reading. Would you be a dear and let me finish telling him?"

The man nodded his assent.

"Thank you, James," she said, as the man retreated from the dance floor.

"You mean what you were telling me is only from some novel," Mark teased, "and not about you at all?"

"No, my little story wouldn't sell more than a hundred copies. Only our group would be interested."

Mark spun her away from himself as the music grew faster. Soon the dance was over.

"You see, Mark, we are all really very dull people. I do what I can to stir up a little excitement. It's the only way I can keep alive."

"I wouldn't have thought that."

"It's quite true." She glanced from the dance floor. "Oh, oh, here comes James again. Tell me, Mark, are you staying over tonight?"

"Why, yes, I am."

"I am too. Mavis always gives me the George V room. She knows how I love it. Do you know the room?"

"No, I don't."

"It's at the head of the stairs on the second floor. Oh, here's James now."

She turned to James as the band commenced what was the final number of the evening.

As he watched them dance, Mark remembered how thrilled he had been with all the guests on New Year's Eve at Castle Enfield that first visit. Tonight, however, with the exception of Jacqueline, they all seemed uninspiring, even dreary. It was he who had changed. He was no longer dazzled by parties with prominent guests. Perhaps there was nothing left any more that could dazzle him.

It was twelve-thirty. After more chatter, the guests walked down the drive to their cars, laughing and talking. Mavis, Rebecca and Rodney walked from one automobile to the other, bidding guests good night. Several of those who were staying over, including Jacqueline, stood under the lighted entry waving good-bye to the others.

Mark lingered in the Great Hall, knowing Mavis would pass him on the way to the library, where the overnight guests had assembled to play a board game. As the evening had progressed, he had become more anxious to speak with her.

When she came by, he took her gently by the arm, "Mavis, I need to talk to you. I've been having a great deal of trouble lately."

Mavis turned to him. "You having trouble? Forgive me, but that's hard to believe. I mean that kindly. It's that you've been so self-confident these past years. With your success, you've seemed such a different person."

"I have?"

"Perhaps we can talk tomorrow. I have my guests."

"I was hoping tonight."

Just then a male guest came into the Great Hall. "Come on, Mavis, we're all waiting for you. You're holding up the game."

Mavis looked helplessly at Mark. "Come, sit and watch the game. We can talk afterward, as we used to."

Mark sat on a chair next to the fireplace in the library, watching the group play a board game. The game, "Sherlock," challenged the players to solve a crime. It was obvious that the group had played together many times and were experts. They were laughing and joking, but still taking the game quite seriously.

Mark was not yet accustomed to European time and was tired. However, he was determined to wait for the game to end, hoping to see Mavis. He watched her carefully as the contest unfolded. Mavis must be nearly 60 now. He thought of the portrait that had hung in the Chelsea House. She still looked much like Gene Tierney. Her black hair was held severely back, making no effort to hide the wrinkles that crept across her face and neck. She was still a very beautiful woman.

Jacqueline played opposite Mavis. James, the man from the last dance, stood behind her, watching her play. Mark wondered if Jacqueline had told James she was sleeping in the George V bedroom.

Mavis drew a card from the deck. "I've just got to show my card to all of you," she laughed, putting the card face up on the board. "Surely, Dr. Watson is the murderer." The group laughed heartily. Mavis's personality was the same. She could be 90 years old, and, with her laugh and charm, still be fetching.

As he watched the game, Mark wondered whether any other men had come into Mavis's life. He hoped so.

Several times he glanced at Jacqueline. James had excused himself and gone off to bed.

Finally, after an hour, "Sherlock" was finished. Mavis, who had a replete knowledge of the Sherlock Holmes stories, had won.

"I knew it couldn't be Moriarty all along," she joked, as the group broke up for the evening. Mavis was radiant from the fun of the party and her success at the game.

"Well, Mark," she said when the other guests, including Jacqueline, had gone upstairs. "I'm sorry to have taken so long, but that silly game has become a tradition with us at parties."

"I can see that it has. Perhaps next time I could play."

"You'd win every time," she laughed.

"I know it's late. Perhaps you're too tired to have that talk."

"I'm wide awake. Where should we go?"

"Perhaps the music room. I have fond memories of the music room," he said.

"So do I, but I think with all the guests, we'd better stay on the ground floor."

"You're right, of course."

"How about the blue room?"

Mark had remembered the blue room. The blue room, which looked over the gardens, was small and lined with bookcases and a corner fireplace. Except for a chair in front of the small writing desk against the wall, the only seating in the room was a green leather couch, and, at each end, green leather chairs facing one another but turned slightly toward the unlit fireplace.

"Has anyone ever explained why we call it the blue room?" she asked.

"No. Come to think of it, there isn't any blue to be seen."

"Not a bit."

"I suppose it was originally blue, or had blue wallpaper."

"No—not that. Grandmother named it the blue room. She used to come here when her mood was blue."

"I never would've guessed that."

"I remember we children weren't allowed to come in when she wasn't feeling well." Mavis had gone to the liquor cabinet. "Looking back on it, I think she was having migraine headaches."

"Could be."

"I'm afraid we don't have any sweet vermouth here. Would straight Scotch whiskey be all right?"

"I'm flattered you remember, Mavis."

"Of course, I remember." She handed him the whiskey in an old crystal glass, and sat on the leather chair opposite Mark, holding her own drink. She curled her legs under herself, and looked expectantly at Mark. "What shall we talk about?"

Mavis was certainly a good-looking woman. She was indifferent to the fact that her skirt had ridden well above her knees. Mark began to feel the same stirrings that had once led him to her bedroom door. For a moment, as he sipped his Scotch, he wanted to act on those feelings. Instead, he spoke to her about his recent problems. He told her of his unhappiness, and about his terrible panic seizures.

"Since I've been in England, I've been okay," he said.

"Exactly what happens?"

"It's as if I couldn't stand being at the office another minute. I've just got to get out of there, no matter what."

"And when you leave?"

"When I leave, I'm all right again. That's what's so puzzling. I'll be perfectly fine, and then, when I get near the office, comes this feeling. Mavis, it's driving me crazy."

She was watching him intently. When he finished, she leaned far back in her chair. "May I ask why you're coming to me? Of course, I'll do what I can, but I wondered."

"I'll never forget, when I was so distraught about those plagiarism charges. I met you at the restaurant."

"Yes the *Quo Vadis*. I'll never forget either."

"You took me to the church. The one on Piccadilly."

"St. James's."

"Do you remember what you said?"

"I can guess. Did I tell you there was a power that could help you?"

"That's right. I remember how close I was to you then. I'd never had someone help me that way before. Except for then, I've always been alone. To this very day, I'm alone."

Mavis's eyes glistened with tears at Mark's confession. She kneeled in front of him, taking his hand. "You are not alone, Mark. As long as I'm alive, you'll never be alone." She stopped, as if gathering her courage. "You say that you can never forget what I did for you. Well, I'll never forget what you did for me."

"What I did for you?"

"You'll never know what you did for me, when we made love upstairs."

"Mavis, I don't know what to say. I didn't know it was that important to you."

"I was so closed up then. Without realizing it, I had turned away from life. With Jimmy dead, the joy in my life was completely gone. I was just living it out to the end—just finding things to do."

Mark tightened his grip on her hand, and slowly stroked her hair with his other hand. "You were very important to me, too, Mavis. I'd never known anyone like you before, or since for that matter."

She turned and sat looking at the empty fireplace. "I think about you all the time, Mark. I've always been half-afraid to see you again. I'll wager you didn't know that."

"Afraid to see me?"

"I've often wondered what would have happened to us if we'd been from the same generation."

"I know, me too, but I think it was our very age difference that appealed to me. Your years have made you a very wise person, you know."

"I wasn't being very wise about my own life. I'll say that. It was only after our night together that I finally came alive."

"Really?"

"My life had no passion. No real purpose."

"But you've stayed married to Lord Ashley all these years."

"And I've been faithful to him too."

"I . . ."

"You're surprised?"

"I'll admit, I have wondered."

"You see, when I say passion, I don't mean mere sexual passion. I mean passion for life. Passion for what I do. For what I am."

Mark nodded his understanding.

"I won't pretend I didn't think about having a love affair a time or two. With the group here tonight there's always some man on the loose, but I knew it was more than sex."

"You sound like you're happy now."

"I am," she paused for a moment. "When I think about it, I'm very happy. I'm giving lectures and teaching classes. I'm involved with my family."

"And that's enough for you?"

"It is for this moment in time. This moment is all there is, you know. All any of us have."

"I thought keeping busy would be the answer for me."

"And you've found it isn't?"

"I guess not. Last month I was feeling really lousy about things. I decided to expand my business."

"Why do that?"

"It's the only thing I knew to do. Business has always worked for me before."

"But not this time?"

"No. That's when everything got so much worse."

"What about Priscilla? How's your marriage working?"

"Pretty well, I guess."

"Pretty well?"

"Mavis, the truth is, she's never there for me. Always traveling. Never interested in what I do."

"And that's not what you want?"

"No, dammit, I don't. I understand she needs her own life, but even when we talk she doesn't really care. Everybody I know admires me except Priscilla Enfield Stevens."

"Forgive me, but why ever did you marry her? I've always wondered."

"Believe me, I've thought about that plenty."

"And what are your conclusions?"

Agitated, he stood up and walked to the fireplace. "I don't know. Love. Companionship. Sex. The usual reasons a man marries." He avoided looking at Mavis.

"How about money? Position? You know, Mark, those are quite legitimate reasons to marry. People do it all the time."

"I'll admit, looking back on it, I was pretty impressed with who Pris was. I was awfully damned young in those days. She was something I could only dream of being, but I didn't marry her for money."

"A lot of people do marry for money. I see it all the time."

"Well, I never wanted Henry Enfield's money. You can count on that." He threw his hands up as he spoke.

"How is Henry, anyway?"

"I never see him. I couldn't care less about Henry Enfield."

"Rodney tells me you've never forgiven Henry."

"Forgiveness doesn't work in the real world. What's the point of it, anyway?"

"Even though he's my brother, I'll be the first to admit Henry can be difficult at times."

"Pris still sees him all the time, but I don't."

"There was something about the way Henry treated Pris after her mother died, that I didn't like," said Mavis.

"Oh?"

"It was as if he insisted she replace her mother. She always had to be the grown-up hostess. That sort of thing. I didn't like it at all."

"I always thought one reason she married me was to defy Henry, but for years now she has had dinner with him every Thursday evening at six-thirty."

"Something was wrong. Whenever they were here at Christmas, I felt she hated him, even though she didn't dare show it."

"Strange."

"What about Priscilla? Do you think she's happy?"

Mark was standing by the fireplace in the book lined room. "Mmmm. I hate to say it, but I don't think I've ever asked myself that question."

"It's a question you'd better ask, my dear friend."

Mark sat down in the leather chair. Pondering, he tapped the fingers of his hands together. "I suppose the correct answer is that she's happy, but not with me."

"Fair enough. And what about you, Mark, are you happy?"

"I thought I was happy, but I guess the truth is I'm not."

"And your feelings for Priscilla?"

"I still love her . . ."

"But what? I hear doubt in your voice."

"You spoke about how you didn't have passion in your life?"

"Yes."

"I don't feel any passion for Pris any more."

"And you did once?"

Mark fidgeted. "You're asking some tough questions."

Mavis laughed, showing her extremely white teeth.

"If I'm honest, not even in the beginning. I never really felt passion, real passion for Pris," Mark continued.

"But you must have felt something."

"Sure I did."

Mavis waited, saying nothing.

"I felt sex—she was attractive. I wanted her."

"Of course. What else?"

"I admired her. Her background. Being part of your family. She was the kind of wife I wanted."

"But no passion. Is that what you're saying?"

"I've known plenty of what we've been calling passion, but listen, I was burned by it once. I would have gone to the end of the world for Christina. Given up everything. My career—everything—but she didn't want me."

"It's a very good thing you didn't give up your career. You've been terribly successful."

"That I have. Beyond my fondest expectations." Mark chuckled momentarily.

Mavis smiled. "What are you laughing at?"

"You wouldn't believe this, Mavis, but I've built my own Castle Enfield in California."

"Rodney tells me you have a lake like ours." She was pouring him another Scotch.

"In my Oxford days, I never would have imagined I would have all the material things I have now."

"And how has all this success affected you? I mean deep inside."

"Another tough question." He accepted the Scotch from her. "Money hasn't affected me as much as I would have thought. Oh, I love all the things money buys—my way of life and all—but really it's been a letdown."

"A letdown?"

"I thought it would mean more to me. To have money."

"I see."

"I know this. I know I don't want to spend the rest of my life making more deals, piling up more money. That doesn't do it for me any more. Trouble is, I don't know what to do."

"The thrill has gone? Is that it?"

"As I say, it's like you said about your own life before. There wasn't any passion any more."

"It sounds as if you've never had much passion in the first place."

"Oh, no. I did for my work. In the beginning I wanted to be the richest and the most famous investment banker in the world."

"But it wasn't enough?"

"I guess not."

"You know, Mark, you're facing a tough question. A question most people don't ever even get to."

"What do you mean? What question?"

"'Where do you go when you've got it all?' That question."

"You think my problem is as simple as that?"

"The question is simple enough, but for those of us who finally ask it, it's the answer that isn't easy. I wouldn't pretend to know the answer for you, but I've told you what has become important for me."

"What? Teaching and so on?"

"No, I mean passion for life, zest. It isn't what one is doing. It's the way one *feels* about it. From what you've said, you've lost it."

Much later, Mark lay awake in bed. Mavis was right. He had no passion for life any more. Nothing stirred his soul. His enthusiasm for work was gone. What was the point in making another deal? What was the point in expanding or buying up more companies?

He got up and turned on the light. He was so agitated—he would never get to sleep. The same thing was true about his marriage. Mavis's prodding questions had made it clear to him he had never had passion for Pris. It wasn't Pris's fault, but the reasons for their marriage no longer existed.

He paced the floor and thought of Diane, from Haight-Ashbury. He thought of Jacqueline in her room down the hall. He thought of Christina, who was in California for the funeral by now. Then he thought of Mavis in her bedroom. He wondered if she would still be awake.

There was no sign of anyone else, as he quietly made his way along the dimly lit hallway to the head of the stairs. His heart pounded as he looked around to be positive that no one had seen him. There was a dim light from under the bedroom door. Jacqueline had said that her room was at the top of the stairs. The light must be hers. Jacqueline was a tempting woman. He wondered if James was with her. His heart continued to race as he slipped by Jacqueline's door. God, wouldn't it be awful if James came out right now, and saw him creeping down the hall?

Finally, he reached Mavis's room, at the far end of the hallway.

There was no light from under her door. His heart quickened more as he gently knocked.

"Oh, you've come," Mavis said as she opened her door. He could see the outline of her slim body through her thin silk robe.

"I had to see you," Mark told her. His voice was tentative.

"I had just turned off the light. I was reading." She pointed toward a book on the table by her bed.

"I've been thinking about what you said."

"Yes. And I about what you said."

"I know I shouldn't come here like this. With so many guests."

She nodded slightly.

"But I had to come."

"Oh . . ."

"You're right about me, Mavis. I can't get along any more without feelings. I can't get along without the passion."

"Mark . . . I." She put her hands behind her so that Mark wouldn't see they were shaking.

"I thought I could, when I married Pris, but I was wrong."

"Would you like to sit down?" Her voice was unsteady. "It's so late . . ."

"I've called for them to get my plane ready. I'm going to California," Mark plunged on, not realizing the effect of his words on Mavis.

"To California?" Mavis put her hand to her necklace, and sat on the edge of her bed.

He sat on the chair at her desk. "Yes. I've got to find Christina. I can't ignore how I feel about her. I've loved her all this time."

"You can love more than one person, you know," she said softly, her face devoid of expression.

"I'm sure you can. I'd never pretend I haven't loved Pris. It's the lack of passion, the zest, you talked about." Mark gestured vigorously.

"I can see how strongly you feel."

"Mavis, I came here to thank you for our talk. It's been a long time, but I'm finally doing the right thing."

"Good luck, Mark," she said weakly.

"I don't even know if I'll find her, but I've got to try."

"Will I see you?"

"Of course. Soon. But I'll be leaving right away. Mark kissed her on the cheek. When he started to back away, she pulled him closer and put her arms around him. He could feel her warm body next to his. It was only then he knew that she had wanted to make love.

"It was wonderful to be with you tonight," she said. "I felt so close."

He walked quickly to the door. Before leaving, he looked back at her, so desirable in her thin robe. Perhaps he was a fool for wanting only Christina.

He returned to Mavis, and kissed her on the lips.

"I know you're right when you say you can love more than one person at once," he said.

"You do?" She whispered

"Yes, you see I love you, too."

Before she could respond Mark opened the door and was gone.

It was barely daybreak. Mavis stood watching from her open bedroom window. The gravel crunched under the tires of the Rolls-Royce as the chauffeur pulled up to the front of Castle Enfield. For a moment, Mark looked up at the mansion, as if looking for her window. She watched as he got in and the car slowly followed the driveway around the lake toward London.

"And I love you, too, Mark," she said. "I love you, too."

-40-

In San Francisco, Priscilla and Henry Enfield were having cocktails in the study of his Pacific Heights mansion.

"Frankly, Father, I don't know whether to be angry or worried about Mark." Pris was nervously pacing in front of the fireplace.

"Why should you worry? This certainly isn't the first time he's disappeared without showing you the simple courtesy of telling you where he is."

"I know, but its always been because of some pressure-packed business matter. Bette said he got upset and just walked out of a meeting. He didn't show up to work the next day."

Henry Enfield was in his 80s now. His red hair had gone completely white, but was still very full and bushy. He moved more slowly and was slightly bent over, but still radiated considerable strength and power.

"I still think you should get a divorce," said Henry. "You're an Enfield. You don't have to put up with his nonsense."

"Something's the matter with Mark. He's not been himself for over a year."

"Rubbish! Mark Stevens is a self-centered egotist. As soon as I realized that, I fired him."

"Father! I don't want to quarrel with you again. Sometimes I think you're jealous because he's been so successful without you."

"That's absolutely untrue. He may have made a lot of money, but he's nothing but a ruthless speculator. He's always been able to fool people. He fooled Oxford, he fooled me, he even fooled Nixon. This country would be a whole lot better off today if Nixon had never heard of Mark Stevens."

"He's been very depressed. He looks awful."

"That's no excuse."

"Something has to be wrong for him to leave a meeting like that. Bette said he even insulted the client."

"He probably went off with another woman."

"This isn't working, Father. I thought we had an understanding that we wouldn't talk about my marriage."

"I'm sorry, Priscilla, I have to break that understanding. You're my only daughter. I can't stand to see this man make you so miserable."

"You didn't care much about my happiness when I was growing up."

"All right, you win. We won't talk about any of it. The past is past."

"Good. You've got to let me live my own life."

They sipped their drinks for a minute in silence, each avoiding eye contact with the other. Finally, Henry stood next to the painting of Castle Enfield, that hung over the fireplace. "Priscilla, my dear. I know we agreed, but I must say something."

"Father," she said with a warning tone in her voice.

"I want you to see Jack Conlan tomorrow. He'll assign you to one of his divorce partners. I've already talked to him about it." Henry was referring to a senior partner in the law firm he regularly used.

"Father! I'm very annoyed with you! This is my life. I'll talk to a lawyer when I'm ready, in my own time, not a moment before. Now I must insist that you not bring it up again."

Henry lit a cigar from the box on the coffee table, and waited until his daughter's anger had cooled.

"Very well," he said. "I suggest that we have our dinner now."

They talked very little as they dined, looking out on San Francisco Bay. As the evening passed, Priscilla's resentment toward Henry's interference eased. She knew that he was right. It was only a matter of time until she would have to see a divorce lawyer.

-41-

Despite his misgivings, Mark decided he should go to Antonio's funeral. After his talk with Mavis, he wanted desperately to see Christina. His Rolls-Royce pulled up to the Spanish-style Catholic church in Sonoma. Despite ordering Alex, his chauffeur, to ignore the speed limit from the Oakland airport, he was late.

Father Polifrone was droning his eulogy for Antonio when Mark took a seat on the center aisle, alone in the last pew.

"And so this man, who had nothing except his desire to succeed, came to America . . ."

Mark looked at the backs of the mourners. The front row was vacant. In the second row, listening intently, was Amanda. In his hurried journey from London to Oakland, he had found no time to call his mother. Next to Amanda sat her church friend, Beth Markey. There were two or three empty rows, then a scattering of townspeople and several rough-hewn vineyard workers, looking uncomfortable in their suits.

He felt panic when he could not find Christina in the congregation. Again, he carefully checked everyone in front of him. He had not been mistaken. Christina was not there. My God, he thought, had he traveled all this way for nothing?

The priest continued. " . . . Antonio Movelli always made his presence known in Sonoma. He loved us and we loved him."

Antonio's flower-covered coffin rested on the undertaker's cart, near the priest. A shudder went through Mark as he saw that the coffin was open. He could not see Antonio's body, but the thought of him lying dead sent waves of emotion through him. Part of his life was forever gone with Antonio. There had always been the faint hope that one day Antonio would have called him to his death bed. In his mind he had rehearsed the conversation a thousand times.

Mark would have leaned down, embraced him and said: "I never should have allowed myself to be beguiled by Christina. I was betrayed by my own lust. Can't we be friends again, like in the old days?"

"Mark", Antonio would have whispered in his Italian accent. "I'm so happy you came. I'm so sorry for all these wasted years."

"Can you ever forgive me?" Mark would have asked.

"Of course I forgive you. I was such a fool for not accepting your apology."

"No, you weren't a fool. I was so very wrong."

"I'm so proud of you. You've accomplished far more than I ever have. It is good that you have made so much money. I was so proud of you when you helped the President. I'd like to call you, 'my son.'"

Mark hoped the others would not hear as he softly cried. My God, if only the scene with Antonio could have actually happened. If only Antonio had accepted his apology. If only he had somehow forced Antonio to accept. Now it was too late.

Suddenly, Mark saw Christina. She had come in, and was sitting by herself at the other side of the church in the same row as he. She must have been lingering in the foyer to avoid being seen by the others.

Without turning his head, he could see the bright afternoon sunlight stream through the stained window and reflect brilliantly off her blond hair. The sight of her deeply excited him. All thoughts of Antonio evaporated. The words of Father Polifrone went unheard. He knew he had not made a mistake in coming home.

She wore an expensive black dress and a black hat that were out of place in this church of plainly dressed simple folk. By turning very slightly, he could see her sleek black stockings. She had crossed her legs, showing several inches of her thigh. The white of her bent knee sensuously showed through her hose. His tear for Antonio quickly dried on his face.

"And especially to Amanda Stevens, who attended to him in his last years, may God be with you," continued the priest.

While Mark faced forward he could see Christina peripherally. She wore black gloves that only partially covered her glittering diamond bracelet. He could see her hips, and by turning his head a little bit more, he caught a glimpse of the rest of her body. He was suddenly deluged with a rush of forgotten feelings. What had taken him so long to recognize that Christina was essential to his life? His feelings were beyond sexual. He was connected to Christina in an inexplicable way. She was part of him, as no other woman had ever been. He hungered to be with her, to posses her, to make her one with him. He would love her forever.

Father Polifrone finally finished. "You are all invited to the cemetery, where we will say our final good-byes."

The undertaker went down the aisle to close the casket. The mourners began to rise. Mark wanted to rush over to Christina, but knew that he should not. Instead he went forward toward Amanda. "Mom. Are you all right?" He kissed her.

"Mark! Where have you been? Nobody knew where you were. How did you find out about Antonio?"

"I called the office," he lied. "I was shocked."

"Antonio's time had come. He was very sick at the end."

Mark shook hands with Beth Markey, his mother's friend.

"Your mother's been worried sick about you, you know. Even your wife has been calling her."

"Now, Beth," Amanda answered. "Mark is a very busy person. The important thing is that he's here now."

They all gathered on the church lawn before the drive to the cemetery.

Suddenly, for the first time, Amanda saw Christina standing by herself. "Good Lord, it's Christina Movelli!" Amanda nearly shouted.

In all these years Amanda had avoided Christina's name.

"The nerve of her, being here," said Mrs. Markey. "After what she did to Antonio."

"Now, Beth, I know how you feel, but it took courage for Christina to be here. It's the Christian thing to make her welcome. After all, this is a funeral."

"Humpth," rejoined Mrs. Markey. "It's a good thing Antonio's coffin is shut. That's all I can say."

"Well, I'm going to speak to her, no matter what she's done," said Amanda, and walked over to Christina.

"Alex," said Mark to his chauffeur, who was standing by the Rolls. "Do you see that woman talking to my mother?"

"The pretty one?"

"That's Mrs. Bagliani. I want you to offer her a ride to the cemetery. I'm going with my mother in the funeral car."

"Yes, sir."

"And lag behind. Don't get in the procession."

"Yes, sir."

The mourners were going to their cars to form the funeral procession. Mark stood watching Christina talk with his mother. The feelings he had felt in the church persisted. Impulsively, he wanted to interrupt their conversation right now. To hell with the funeral. He wanted to spirit her away in his Phantom. He only hoped

Christina was as unhappy in her marriage as he was miserable in his.

At Mountain Cemetery, the somber group gathered around Jonah's grave for the burial services.

"And so we are gathered here in final remembrance of our friend, Antonio," intoned Father Polifrone.

Mark stood on one side of the coffin with his mother and Mrs. Markey. On the other side stood the vineyard workers and the townspeople. Floral displays surrounded them. Some distance away, down the hill, Christina stood by the Rolls, watching the ceremony.

Mark looked down at the gravestone near his feet. It was Anna Movelli's marker. He remembered the good times they had all had together.

As the priest continued, Mark thought back to his father's burial service on the hill only a short distance away. The anger he had felt for his father was in the distant past now. Even the once-stunning news that Christina had been sleeping with Jonah was an old wound. It was like a scar carried from childhood that one could scarcely remember. As he looked at Antonio's coffin, he recalled how Antonio had rebuffed his apology. He thought of Henry Enfield. He would never give Henry the chance to refuse him the way Antonio had.

Soon, the ceremony was over, and people were leaving for their cars to return to Amanda's house.

"Mom, I'd like to see Dad's grave. Do you want to come with me?"

"No, go ahead. I don't go to your father's grave any more. I've got to be home for the guests. I'll go on ahead."

Mark shook hands with the others and walked to his father's grave.

Jonah Stevens 1907-1965

The headstone on the next grave said,

Amanda Stevens 1912-

Mark wondered what year of death would be on his own marker. "Mark Stevens 1941-19??" or perhaps "1941-20??."

This was 1980. Jonah had been dead 15 years. Mark doubted if there was a single soul who ever remembered his father except for his mother and himself. By God, when he died, he wanted more than that. He wanted there to be headlines in the papers. He wanted to have made an impact on the world. He did not want to die in some long-forgotten bar fight about some woman whose name no one could recall.

"What are you thinking?"

Mark jumped in surprise.

Christina was standing next to him, her high heels digging in the ubiquitous gravel, characteristic of the old cemetery.

She looked at the headstone. "That was a long time ago—1965."

"Yes, it was," he said. "In 1965 I thought my success was the most important thing in the world."

"We were both very young."

"What about you, Christina? If I recall, you wanted money pretty badly yourself."

"If you remember, it wasn't so much money as it was security." She was looking down at the grave markers.

"Aren't they one and the same?"

"Perhaps you're right, but you see, I never really needed the big house and all. What I wanted was to be safe."

Mark looked up, away from the granite stone and off into the distance. "What do you do after you have it all?"

"What?"

"It's the question."

"The question?"

"Yes," he said gently. "That's the big question in life. 'What do you do when you have it all?'"

"I don't know," she said, turning toward Mark. "Do you have an answer to your question?"

He turned, facing her. "Perhaps. Perhaps I have part of the answer."

Neither spoke as they looked down on the grave. "Are you going to share your 'part of an answer' with me?"

"Yes, sometime. But it will cost you," he kidded.

"Cost me?" she smiled. "I hope I have enough money to pay."

"It'll be expensive."

Mark looked around to be certain they were alone and took Christina into his arms. "I've wanted to kiss you from the moment I saw you in the church."

As Mark kissed her, he felt her resist at first. Then she put her hands on the back of his suit coat, returning his kiss.

Some distance away an old woman sat in front of her husband's marker. She looked over at the embracing couple and smiled wistfully.

"We'd better go to the reception. Your mother will be upset if you're late," said Christina.

"You're right," Mark answered.

The old woman watched the striking couple as they walked down the slope to the parking area. The blond woman was beautiful with her long hair and sensuous high-heeled walk. The good-looking young man with thick white hair guided the blonde around the tombstones, toward the Rolls-Royce limousine. "How romantic," the old woman thought. "They make such a wonderful couple."

But the old woman could not know that each of them was married to another. She could not guess that the handsome man was dismayed with his life, nor that the funeral was that of the woman's former husband, that the grave they had been standing on was that of the man's father as well as the woman's former lover.

-42-

Priscilla Enfield squealed the tires of her green Jaguar as she drove into the subterranean garage of the San Francisco office building. She turned the car over to the valet, and waited impatiently for the elevator. She was dressed in black high heels, smart, gray pin-striped trousers, and a red blouse. As she waited, she nervously twisted a tissue and punched the elevator button again. When the elevator door opened, she quickly entered and punched the third floor button several times until the door finally closed.

"Suite 306-Van A. Goodwill, Ph. D.-Psychologist."

Pris pushed open the door, entered the reception room and pushed the buzzer under the sign that said, "Please announce your presence."

Pris sat down in the small reception room, looking at her watch. Almost ten o'clock. She took a fashion magazine from the table and quickly flipped its pages. She tossed it aside and looked at her watch again.

"Priscilla," said Dr. Goodwill sticking his head into the tiny room. "You sounded so desperate. Come in please." Goodwill, 40, wore a haphazardly trimmed beard that looked as if it had been stuck on his chin with glue. His thick glasses made his eyes look bulging.

"You're right, doctor. I'm desperate. I don't know what to do."

Goodwill followed Pris to his room. "What's the problem, Priscilla?"

"It's Mark, as usual—and my father, as usual."

"Suppose you sit down and tell me about it."

From the window behind Goodwill, his patients could see Coit Tower. Half a dozen framed certificates decorated one wall. Shelves with imposing and learned books covered another.

"Mark has gone away," she began.

"That's not unusual, is it?" He looked intently at her, holding his hands together.

"He hasn't told a soul where he is. His secretary says he might have gone to New York, but she doesn't know."

"Could he be ill?"

"Mark? Mark's never ill." She uncrossed her legs, then nervously crossed them again, tapping her fingers on her leg. "Even his mother can't find him. An old family friend died, and nobody knows where Mark is. I came home from L.A. totally resolved to give our marriage another try, and now look at this."

"Do you think he's with another woman? Is that why you're so upset?"

"That's what Father thinks. He thinks I should see a divorce lawyer. He even has one picked out for me."

"And what about you? What do you think?"

"I don't know what to do. I'm so tired of Father's trying to tell me what to do, I don't even know my own mind." Pris stood up and began pacing.

"Remember what you said a few sessions ago? About your father?" Dr. Goodwill's eyes followed his distraught patient as she nervously walked back and forth.

"No, I guess I don't. Not specifically."

"You said you wished there were a way to divorce your father."

Pris laughed. The tension in her face eased a bit. "That's right. I did."

"That always gives you conflict, doesn't it? When your father wants you to do one thing and you really want to do another."

"You mean like when I married Mark?"

"Well, Priscilla, you yourself said a few sessions ago that defying your father had a lot to do with marrying Mark in the first place."

"That's true, but I really thought I loved Mark."

"I'm sure you thought you did. Remember a whole lot of people get married for the wrong reasons. That doesn't mean you can't have a good marriage."

"But I'm sick and tired of Mark's always being gone someplace. He never invites me along any more. He's so wrapped up in his business. If I'd wanted to be alone all the time, I'd have stayed single." She sat down again. "If it weren't for my art gallery, I'd go crazy."

"In the beginning Mark used to ask you to go along on his trips, didn't he?

"Yes, but I knew he didn't mean it. I'd just sit around hotel rooms while he went to meetings."

"Did he stop asking you?"

"Oh, he always asks, but I could tell that he was tired of having me along." She hesitated and avoided looking at Dr. Goodwill. "The truth is he hardly ever even asks for sex any more."

"And you? How do you feel about sex?"

"I've never refused him. He knows that."

"I see."

"Doctor. You've got to help me decide what to do. Should I do what my father wants, or what? I'm so nervous, I don't think I can stand this indecision another day."

"I can't tell you what to do. It sounds to me as if you're caught between two very powerful men."

"I don't know what to do."

"I have a suggestion, if you're ready."

"What is it?" She hesitated, as if fearing to ask. "What's that?"

"I've made it before."

"Not hypnosis again?"

"Yes, hypnosis. You've been seeing me for nearly three years now, and we still don't understand why your father has such a hold on you. I think you should try hypnosis."

"You keep coming back to that," she said angrily. "My father is a very intelligent man. I would be stupid if I ignored his advice. Why do you keep saying something's wrong?"

Impatiently, Goodwill put his hands up in dismay. "I'm sorry if I seem to be pushing you, Priscilla. It's just that . . ." He looked at his watch. "Well, I see our time's up." He slowly stood up. "Please remember, if and when you're ever ready for hypnosis, I'm here to help."

Priscilla left through Dr. Goodwill's side door. Damn him, she thought, as she walked down the hall. Three years of therapy. He was of absolutely no help at all. She had come to get help in deciding what to do about Mark, and all Dr. Goodwill did was tell her she should go into hypnosis about her father.

She walked along the hall towards the elevators, as she had once a week for three years. Out of the corner of her eye she saw the lettering on the door. It must have been there for a long time, but she had never noticed it before. "Suite 304-Thomas T. Wahl-Attorney-Certified Family Law Specialist."

She continued on and pressed the button for the elevator. Strange that today was the first time she had ever noticed the lettering on that door. She got on the elevator.

"The green Jaguar," she told the attendant, giving him her parking ticket.

The attendant pulled up in her car, and opened the driver's door for her. She got in, but did not close the door.

"I'm sorry, but I forgot something," she said, getting out of the car. You'll have to park it again," she said. I'll show Dr. Goodwill, she thought, that I can make up my own mind.

Pris opened the door to Suite 304 and strode in.

"May I help you?" said the young receptionist.

"Yes. I believe you can. My name is Priscilla Stevens. I'd like very much to see Mr. Wahl. I'd like to see him right now. I've decided I need to talk to a divorce lawyer."

-43-

The afternoon at his mother's home was slow torment for Mark. Amanda had invited everyone from the funeral to the buffet. Mark stood in the living room, coffee cup in hand, talking to Mona, the retired Movelli cook. Christina stood across the room, talking with Father Polifrone, the priest. Any other time Mark would love talking to Mona, who had been such a friend in his childhood, but with Christina present it was not at all what he wanted. He wanted to be with her. He yearned to find out how she felt about him. Did their embrace at the cemetery cause the same riptide of emotion in her as it did in him? He knew he must persuade her to delay her trip to Rome.

"Remember how you used to have dinner with Mr. Antonio and Mrs. Anna every Friday night?" asked Mona.

"Ah, Mona, you used to cook such wonderful food. I still can't believe you aren't Italian," laughed Mark.

Mona was an old woman now, living with her daughter on the Mendocino coast. They enthusiastically hugged and touched one another as they talked, but Mark's eyes always returned to Christina.

Mark realized that everyone in the house was keenly aware of their old love affair and the explosion that it had let loose on Sonoma. He knew that Christina must be thinking the same thing, for she had been avoiding him—to do otherwise would be to revive the old gossip.

Father Polifrone left Christina alone to say good-bye to Amanda. It was dark outside now, and many of the guests had left. Mark glanced away from Mona and caught Christina's eyes. She returned his look as she refilled her wine glass. Mark wanted to be with her as soon as he could.

"Mother, we need to leave soon. We've got a long drive ahead, and Johnny's getting antsy." It was Mona's daughter.

"All right, Jean," said Mona. "It's been wonderful seeing you again, Mark. Everyone's so proud of you."

"Thank you, Mona," Mark said. "I always knew you were in my corner." He kissed Mona warmly on the cheek. Christina had left the rear of the house, with her glass of wine. He waited to be sure no one would see him leaving, then he followed her.

The bright quarter moon was already high in the November sky. It provided considerable moonlight, but he could not find Christina. Thinking that she may have left for Italy, he was filled with panic. He raced around the house to where he had seen her rental car. Ignoring his fine suit and calfskin leather shoes, he plunged through Amanda's flower garden. She must not get away. He was relieved when he found that her white Lincoln was still there. Perhaps she had walked up the hill to the mansion.

Thinking that Christina might have gone to the Movelli mansion, he raced up the hill to the quiet, unlighted villa, but there was no sign of her. Apprehensively, he circled the big house, looking for her. He tried the front door, but it was locked. Nervously, he felt behind the drainpipe for the hidden key.

"Christina?" he said from the dark foyer. There was no answer. "Christina, are you there?" he shouted. Still there was no answer.

Could something have happened to her? Where had she gone? The barn—perhaps she had gone to the horse barn. He ran down the slope until he neared his mother's house. He wanted to avoid the chance of anyone's seeing him running, so he slowed until he passed the cottage, then resumed running. He stumbled over something and stretched out his hand to break his fall. "Damn!" He had cut his hand. As he ran on toward the barn, he put his hand to his mouth and tasted the warmth of his blood.

Christina was nowhere to be seen as he neared the barn. Then he saw a dim light. The top of the stable's split door was open. His heart was pounding. He grasped the bottom half of the door, and stood peering into the dimly lighted stable. There in a stall with a black horse was Christina.

"Christina!" he shouted. "What the hell are you doing?" Winded, he gasped for breath.

"Mark?"

"Yes. It's me. Are you all right?"

"Of course I'm all right." She was strapping a saddle to the horse.

"What are you doing?"

"I'm going riding."

"Riding? In the dark? Tonight?"

"Yes. Like I used to. I thought this horse might be Madera's son. It's so black."

"It might be." Mark recalled that Christina's favorite horse had been named Madera.

"I think those might have been the happiest times of my life—riding on Madera."

"But you can't go riding in your good dress."

"I don't care about my dress." She had finished with the saddle, and was preparing to lead the horse outside. "It's Antonio's funeral dress. I'll never wear it again, anyway." She kicked off her shoes. "What about you?"

"What about me?"

"Why don't you come riding with me," she laughed. "When you were young and poor, you'd go riding with me."

Mark laughed, too. "You know very well I was only invited to ride with Mrs. Antonio Movelli that one time."

She tossed her head and gestured with her hand. "That wasn't Mrs. Antonio Movelli who invited you. That was a young woman named Christina."

"Yes, but Christina who?" he teased.

"Christina with no last name," she grinned. "I don't like last names. I have a history of paying much too dearly for my last names."

They rode through the cool night air—sometimes walking the horses and sometimes galloping. Mark was more cautious and less expert than Christina. She had ridden ahead too far for him to see.

"Come on!" she shouted back. "I don't see how you've gotten so rich, lagging behind that way."

"One thing. I don't fall in a lot of holes," he shouted ahead, laughing. My God, he was enjoying being with her. For the first time in a long time there was life flowing through his veins. He didn't give a damn if he fell in a hundred holes.

After a bit they were on the old gravel road. Christina prodded her horse, and again raced ahead of Mark. She stopped at the corner, and they let the horses rest.

"This is where my father threw me from the tractor."

"When you hurt your leg?"

"Yes."

She reached over and took him by the hand.

They rode together for another half-hour. The night was getting colder, but the air felt good on his face. They pulled up where the road was on a rise. They could see the lights of the compound through the trees a half-mile from them.

"Would you like to be getting back?" he asked.

"Whatever you say."

"I don't care."

"I don't either."

"Christina?"

"Yes?"

"I haven't been so happy in a long time." He realized he had been totally free from the nervousness and the feelings of panic he had felt in San Francisco. "You're good for me."

"You think it's me and not just the idea of me?"

He laughed. "Maybe it's both. I sure do have an idea about you."

"Oh, you do, do you?"

With that, she galloped off toward the compound.

"Hold on there, woman!" he shouted, urging his horse to gallop after her.

Even in the dark the horses knew the way. He nearly caught her as they neared the barn, but she quickly dismounted and touched the door as he pulled up. "I'm the winner!" she shouted.

"No way you're the winner." He, too, jumped from his horse and, holding the reins, held her with his other arm. He kissed her quickly, and then whispered. "I'm the one who's the winner."

They found an empty horse stall freshly bedded with yellow straw. What a fool he had been! In Paris he should have refused to accept Christina's decision to marry Otello. In the car outside her Roman villa, he should have told his driver to head for the airport while they made love in the back seat, and then taken her with him to America. So often over the years he had relived in his mind the eroticism he had known with her. He knew that she was a part of him. A racy, feminine creature that he had to possess.

He kissed her tenderly, and began to unbutton her dress. She returned his kiss, and with her hand felt his erection through his trousers. Inflamed by a wave of excitement, he abandoned the idea of proceeding slowly. He took the hem of her dress, and with her help, lifted it off over her head. Passionately, they helped each other remove their clothes, until the perspiration on their bodies glistened in the light of the lone light bulb. He kissed her again, and slowly eased her down into the straw. He glimpsed her pubic hair, and put himself on top of her. He was so eager for her, he thought he could not wait for her to climax. But quickly, he could feel her coming, and exploded within her just as she finished.

Catching their breath, they lay on their backs in the straw.

"You were so anxious," she teased when she had caught her breath. "Did you think I was going to run away from you?"

He laughed. "Maybe that was it." He waited, and then added. "I know I don't want to lose you again."

They said nothing for several minutes.

"I can't tell where your hair leaves off, and the straw begins," he whispered, propping himself on one elbow and gently stroking her blond hair.

"I hadn't expected we'd end up like this when I saw you at the church."

"Didn't you feel what I felt at the church?"

She laughed. "How do I know what you felt?"

"For one thing, I knew I wanted you. I knew I wanted you in my life. You're a part of me, Christina. We belong together."

Abruptly she sat up in the straw, her breasts outlined against the light. "Those are very nice things that you say, but please don't forget that we are both married to other people."

"Good Lord, how could I forget? Marrying Pris was the biggest mistake of my life."

She put her finger to her lips. "You shouldn't say that. I'm sure she is a very nice woman."

"But it's the truth. I should have married you."

Christina reached for her clothes, and began putting on her dress. "You're forgetting, my darling Mark. The timing always made marriage impossible for us."

She knelt and kissed him on the lips. He began to become erect again. He pulled her on top of him and returned her kiss. "The timing may have been wrong once, but not any more."

"Mark!" she spoke sharply. "What are you saying?"

"I'm saying I love you more than anything in the world. I think we should get divorces and be married."

"You're dreaming," she sighed. "You know very well that's impossible."

"But I'm used to having the impossible."

She had gathered her hose, shoes and undergarments together, and held them in her lap. "Oh, my dear Mark! My dear, precious Mark. The timing still is never right for us, is it?"

"We'll make it right."

"Mark?" she said softly.

"Yes?"

"Can we stop talking of such things, at least for a while?" she whispered. "Please. It upsets me."

"All right."

He kissed her again, and they sat together.

She stroked his hair. "It's nearly all white now."

"I'm getting to be an old man, Christina," he smiled.

"You weren't very old a few minutes ago. In fact you were very young."

Again, he kissed her.

"I have an idea," he said.

"Yes, Mister Idea Man! What's your idea?"

"Let's go up to the mansion."

"You are a devil," she said, apparently understanding the full implication of what that meant. "An absolute devil!"

"I learned how to be a devil from you, my dear Christina. You're the one who taught me."

As they left the horse barn for the Movelli mansion, he was a different man from the Mark Stevens of 1963. He was no longer the uncertain youth, seduced by Antonio's wife. This time he was very certain of what he wanted. He was determined that Christina be with him always. Determined that no matter how reluctant she might be, he would have her as his wife.

-44-

The office of Thomas T. Wahl, attorney-at-law, had the same view of Coit Tower as did Pris's psychologist's. Wahl sat behind a large, ornate, Louis XIV desk. His desk was covered with stacks of files and papers. On the wall behind him were perhaps 20 framed photographs of himself with well-dressed, smiling women. Pris recognized some of them as movie and television stars.

"I want to tell you right up front that the State Bar doesn't like me very well, Mrs. Stevens," said Wahl gruffly. "Some of my esteemed colleagues hate losing to me, so they sic the State Bar on me." Wahl sucked on a pipe stem, attached to a long cord that disappeared somewhere behind him. He blew out a drag of smoke. "You'll have to pardon me, but I can't give up smoking. My doctor got me this damned contraption from Hong Kong. The smoke passes through water somehow."

Pris was nonplused. Wahl was a heavy, clean-shaven man with bushy eyebrows. He wore an expensive, camel-hair sport jacket over a silk, print, double-breasted vest. A white carnation protruded from his button hole. She thought he looked a little like Jackie Gleason.

"My dear lady, I hope I haven't offended you. Sometimes I come on a little strong."

"Oh, no." Pris had been more amazed than offended by Wahl.

Suddenly, Pris realized that she had heard of Thomas T. Wahl, but had just not put together that this was the same man. Wahl had represented many Bay area women in cases that had made headlines. Hollywood stars frequently consulted him. If she were not mistaken, Wahl had established an office in Beverly Hills.

"I've found that when my clients see the results I can get for them, they are only too happy to put up with what I'll call my eccentricities."

"I see you have some famous clients." Wahl was a pushy man, but he must be all right if so many well known people retained him.

"Yes, I have." Wahl turned his chair, and pointed to a photograph. "I know you're a San Franciscan. Perhaps you recognize that woman, Mrs. Rider."

"Yes. I do." Pris was flattered that Wahl evidently knew who she was. Indeed Pris did recognize Angela Rider. Timothy Rider was a friend of Mark's. Mark had taken Rider's corporation public."

"Old man Rider found this dolly that he simply couldn't live without."

Pris smiled at Wahl's language. "Yes. I read about it. I didn't know you were the lawyer."

"Rider got to live with his new young whore—pardon the expression—but it cost him an absolute bundle."

"Didn't the Riders reconcile later?"

"Sure did." Wahl took another drag on his pipe. "He came crawling back. The dumb shit didn't have a premarital agreement with his new pride and joy. She took him to the cleaners, too. Then he decided he wanted to go back to Angela." He laughed, as if he had told a very funny joke.

Pris faked laughing along with him, although she was appalled by the story. "Did you represent the second wife in her divorce?"

"Heavens, no! Although she did try to hire me. I figured the State Bar might think I had a conflict of interest. I didn't want to give them any more ammunition, so I turned her down. Believe me, Angela had me tie him up good before she took him back."

"But doesn't Mrs. Rider mind? I mean your telling everyone?"

"Good God, no. Angela tells everyone. She's proud of it all. I never get my picture taken with a client without a proper release. I'm not a fool, my dear Mrs. Stevens."

"I'm sure you aren't." Pris hoped he would not ask her for her photograph.

"You don't need to worry about publicity unless you want it."

"That's good. I'm sure you're a very good lawyer, but if I actually decide on a divorce, I'd want everything to be kept quiet."

"Of course. I understand. I'll do everything to keep your divorce out of the newspapers. You must understand, the press has its own ways." Wahl placed a long yellow pad in front of him. "Now, I assume you're here because you've decided on a divorce, or as we call it now, a dissolution. Is that right?"

"Well, no. Not exactly. I just thought I should discuss my whole situation with an attorney. You see my therapist's office is right down the hall and I . . ."

"Mrs. Stevens, may I call you Priscilla?"

"Well, yes, certainly."

"Priscilla, I'm not a psychologist. Thank God for that. We've had no-fault dissolution now for over 10 years."

"But doesn't it matter that he's gone all the time? All he ever cares about is his business."

"Priscilla. My job is to get dissolutions. I leave all whys and wherefores to the psychologists."

"I see." Pris looked disappointed.

"Oh, let me take that back a wee bit. Tell me, has he got another woman?"

"I don't know. My father thinks he has."

"Another woman can make a hell of a difference in settlement negotiations. Like our friend, Rider, usually the man wants out fast."

"There's no one Mark would want to marry. A long time ago, years before we met, there was a woman, but she married someone else."

"How about you, Mrs. Stevens?"

"What do you mean?"

"Let's be frank. Is there anyone you want to marry?"

"No. Mark has always been suspicious of Samuel, but I'm positive Samuel's gay."

"Who's Samuel?"

"Samuel Wade. He's an artist—works in oils. Samuel's sort of my protege. I have an art gallery.."

"Yes, on Powell isn't it? But what about Mark? Does he know this Samuel is gay?"

"I doubt it," she laughed. "Mark is oblivious to things like that. He's very smart in business, but very unobservant."

"What I'm trying to find out is whether Mark thinks you want to marry someone else."

"Oh, no, Mr. Wahl. Mark knows I'd never leave him."

"All right then." Wahl took another drag on his pipe and blew out the smoke. "I want to explain something. These days what lawyers and courts do is divide up the community property. It may sound simple, but it isn't. It can get very tricky, valuing things."

"If I decided to go ahead with it, would I get to keep the house?"

"Priscilla, I'll tell you one thing. I can stake my reputation on getting you your house."

"What about alimony?"

"Spousal support. We call it spousal support."

"Oh."

"What I'm going to do for you, Priscilla, is get you so damned much community property that you won't need spousal support. Oh, maybe a dollar a month, so that, if worst comes to worst, you can tie him up later. But believe me, you'll have so much income from your property that you won't need spousal support."

"I see."

"If you can stay and work through lunch time, I'll send out for sandwiches."

"But I'll need some time to think about all this."

"Of course you do, Priscilla. I'd be the last one to push you. However, I would suggest I get the necessary information from you, in case you decide to go ahead."

"Well, if you think it's a good idea."

"You can always call me, and I'll cancel everything. Happens all the time. Some women see me three or four times before they finally go ahead."

"I really should ask you—this is very embarrassing."

"My dear Priscilla, tell me what is on your mind."

"I need to ask you about your fees."

"Now don't you worry about my fees. In cases like these we get our fees from the community property. If you've heard of me, you know that Thomas T. Wahl charges very substantial fees, but it's a very small percentage of the property involved." He laughed. "I've never had a complaint yet, except of course from the husbands."

"I don't want to be unfair to Mark. You see, when father dies I'll inherit a substantial fortune."

"Of course you don't want to be unfair to your husband. I'm sure you loved him very much once, but I insist that you let me get everything you are entitled to. What is fair is what the judge says is fair. By the way, who do you think your husband's lawyer will be?"

"I don't know. He uses a couple of big firms."

"Hah! Those big firms. They don't know a damned thing about a good divorce fight." Wahl took a pen. "Can your husband's lawyers claim any separate property?"

"Separate property?"

"Yes. What did Mark own when you married him?"

"Well, there was his bachelor condominium on Nob Hill."

"Oh, he kept that, eh?" Wahl wrote on his yellow pad. "Anything else when you got married?"

"His car."

"He still has the same car?"

"Yes, his Aston Martin. He loves it."

"Anything else? Had he started his business when you married him?"

"Yes, he had."

"Tell me about that."

"He had broken away from my father's business. He didn't want to get married until he had enough to stand on his own. I don't want to take Mark's business away from him."

"We wouldn't take his business, Priscilla. But if the business, or even some of it, is community property, I can use it as a lever to get you a better settlement. Maybe more cash—whatever."

"But I'm not even sure I want a divorce, and here you're talking as if I'm a greedy woman!"

"Look, Priscilla. I want to get you everything you're entitled to. I wouldn't represent you if I thought you were greedy, but I'm not going to let you throw your future away."

"I don't know about Mark's business. It would kill him."

"I'm going to look into this separate property angle. I'll take on the responsibility. There may not be anything to it, but I don't want you to worry about it. Do you hear me?"

"Yes," she sighed. "I guess I do."

"Good. Now let me ask a few questions. Has he always worked for his company? I mean since you were married? I want to examine a theory or two."

"Yes. He has an employment contract with The Stevens Group. He told me he signed it to keep up the value of the stock."

"You see, there's one of my theories, right there."

"How do you mean?"

"You see, under the law his efforts, his work, after marriage are community property. I'll argue that your husband's efforts have made the stock more valuable, and that value is community property."

"But that would make Mark very angry."

"That's his problem, not yours or mine."

"Would I have to face him in court? I don't think I could stand that."

"You're looking at a man who's not afraid of going to court. I don't want you being afraid either. Half the goddammed judges will be mad that Mark is getting a divorce while they have to stay married to the same old fat wives. No judge will be very sympathetic to Mark."

"I want to settle out of court."

"We will, we will, but never be afraid of going to court. When Mark's fancy lawyers realize that, believe me, they'll settle."

"I'm not sure about this—I want to be fair."

"Priscilla, I take that for granted." Wahl turned a sheet on his yellow pad. "Before we get into listing your community property, I need to ask you about your will."

"My will?"

"Yes, you'll need a new will, Priscilla. What does your present will provide?"

"It leaves everything to Mark, unless we have children."

"I assume you don't have children."

"No, we don't. That may be one of the things he'll complain about. He's always wanted children."

"And you don't?"

"At first, I wasn't ready. Later, our marriage was getting so very bad."

"That's very good thinking. Too many children are brought into lousy marriages. But we need to change your will."

"Why?"

"If something happens to you before you're divorced, everything would go to Mark. You wouldn't want that, would you?"

"I guess not. I hadn't thought about it. I just came here to talk."

"Who would you want to get your property if you, God forbid, passed away suddenly?"

"Father, I guess. In my present will, Father would inherit if Mark should die, but . . ."

"All right, then. I'm going to call in my secretary right now. It's only temporary, you know. When you want a more permanent estate plan, we'll refer you to a specialist. But ex-husbands shouldn't stand to inherit everything."

Wahl's secretary took the chair next to Pris.

"Kathy, Mrs. Stevens needs a new will. I'll be dictating the divorce papers later this afternoon, but I'd like you to type up a new will while we're working."

Kathy Connors was a businesslike young woman with a steno pad. "Yes, sir. I'll do it right away."

There are no children. No specific bequests. Just leave the entire estate, real and personal wherever situated, including her share of the community property, to her father, Henry Enfield. Put in that clause that specifically excludes her husband, Mark Stevens. All right? Do you have that?"

"Yes, sir." Miss Connors turned to Pris. "You spell your name 'P-r-i-s-c-i-l-l-a S-t-e-v-e-n-s'?"

"Yes, I do."

"Who should be the executor, Mr. Wahl?" asked the secretary.

"Would you say your father should be the executor?" Wahl asked of Pris.

"I suppose so. What would he have to do?"

"The executor manages the estate while its being probated—that sort of thing."

"Well, Father's in his 80s."

"How about me? I'll be the executor if you want. Isn't apt to happen anyway, you know."

"All right. I can change it at any time. That's right, isn't it?"

"Of course you can. It's only temporary. Even if we file for dissolution, it's only temporary."

"Should I bring in a blank dissolution petition when I've finished the will?" Kathy asked.

"Yes, Kathy. I'm sure Mrs. Stevens will sign a blank petition."

"What does that mean?" asked Pris.

"It saves a second trip, Mrs. Stevens," explained Kathy.

"It's common practice," said Wahl. "Kathy will type in, over your signature, the information I give her. That way my court service can file the papers with the County Clerk without your coming back. Saves a trip."

"But what if I change my mind? I want to think about it."

"I'll tell you what. We won't actually file the case until you call Kathy," Wahl responded.

"All right. I'll sign, then."

It was past three o'clock when Pris left the attorney's office. She had signed her will and the blank dissolution forms. Slowly, she walked down the hall and pressed the elevator button. Nervously, she stood waiting for the elevator. When it arrived, instead of getting on, she turned and walked purposefully past Thomas T. Wahl's office to Dr. Goodwill's office. She opened the door and pushed the buzzer. She knew Dr. Goodwill was probably in session, but in few moments the bearded psychologist opened the door.

"Priscilla. I'm surprised to see you."

"I'm sorry to interrupt you, Dr. Goodwill, but I've decided that you're right."

"Right? Right about what?"

"About hypnosis. I've just seen a lawyer. I've signed divorce papers."

"I see. Very well. But what's that got to do with your deciding about hypnosis?"

"I'm miserable, Dr. Goodwill. Signing those papers didn't help me at all. The lawyer isn't going ahead unless I call him. Can I see you tomorrow? Please?"

"Of course you can. I'll make time. Can you come at two o'clock? It's my afternoon off, but I can see you then."

"Thank you, doctor. I really appreciate all you do for me."

.   .   .

The parking attendant brought Pris her Jaguar. She entered the freeway and soon was in the fast lane, headed for home. Suddenly she burst forth with tears. "Oh, my God," she said aloud. "What's happening to me?" She sobbed uncontrollably. "Why did I sign those papers? Mark, you're the only good thing that's ever happened to me."

Pris put on her blinker, and got off at the first exit. It was a bad neighborhood, but she was sobbing so that she could drive no further. A man in tattered clothes sat on a box in front of a seedy bar. Pris pulled her Jaguar to the curb and parked at the curb in front of him. The man stared at the costly car with its blinking tail light and attractive occupant, sobbing into her handkerchief. A man sure sees all sorts of strange things in San Francisco, he thought.

-45-

Giggling like a teenager, Christina hurried up the main staircase of the Movelli mansion, still carrying her shoes and undergarments. Mark caught her from behind and playfully ran his
hand up her dress, along the inside of her leg.

"You are a devil, all right," she laughed. "A very anxious devil."
Her Italian accent added to her sensuality.

Mark pushed her long hair aside and kissed the back of her
neck.

"I want tonight to last forever." He held her tightly from behind. "I want to savor every moment."

Playfully, she took his hands from her waist. "You'll have to
catch me first." She ran up the stairs, laughing.

Still clutching her things, she turned at the top of the dark
stairs and ran to the bedroom where they had spent the night long
ago. He caught her, and they embraced once again, he wearing
only his white dress shirt, and suit trousers, and she only her
black dress.

Christina turned on the bedside lamp, while Mark lay on the
canopied bed, propping his head on his hand, looking at her. "I
can't tell you how many times I've thought of us and this room,"
he said.

She pulled one of the pillows from under the bedspread. Putting it under his head, she gently kissed him on the forehead.
"And what do you think about when you think about us in this
room?"

"What we did together. How I felt about you."

"That was a long time ago."

"Let me tell you about the fantasy I've had all these years."

She leaned back to listen. "All right."

"In my fantasy, we do everything the way we did that first night."

"Exactly the same? I'm surprised you remember."

"Well, I do." He got out of bed, and took her by the hand.
"Come with me. I'll show you how well I remember."

Smiling, he pulled her into the elegantly marbled bathroom. "First, we're going to have a bath together."

Christina laughed at Mark's exuberance, as he turned the old-fashioned bathtub water handles. As in the barn, with her help he slipped her dress over her head. The hot water mixing with the cold was steaming the mirrors as he started to unzip his trousers.

"Here, let me do it," she said. She undid his trousers, unbuttoned his shirt, then buried her head in his chest.

"The hair on your chest isn't white," she said, feeling it with her fingers.

"It's not as old as I am," he responded, putting his arms around her naked shoulders, and stroking her back with his fingers.

The water level in the tub was high as they bathed. She sat with her back to him, between his long, soap-covered legs. Reaching around her, Mark covered her breasts with soapy water. "I see you want every part of me to be clean," she said.

Still holding her breasts, he kissed her on the back of her neck. "Every part. Every single part."

She reached forward and pulled the lever to empty the tub. Without speaking, she faced him and began pulling on his body until he realized she wanted him to slide down in the tub, on his back. As the water drained, she worked his penis with her hand, until he was fully erect, then took it in her mouth.

She nearly brought him to climax, but stopped at the last moment. "I want to save you," she said smiling.

"And you said you didn't remember what we did before!" he teased.

"Did I say that?" she laughed. "I couldn't have said that."

While Christina finished drying herself in the bathroom, Mark found her high-heeled shoes and mischievously slipped them under her pillow. He lay waiting expectantly when she slipped off her huge bath towel and put her head on the pillow. "I'm cold!" she exclaimed, putting the sheet over them. "That bathroom was steamy."

"The steam was probably from me," he laughed, "I was breathing pretty heavily."

She moved closer to him, but then abruptly felt under her pillow. "What's this?" she said, pulling out the offending shoes.

"I'm a shoe man," he said. "Don't you remember? I want to make love with your shoes on."

She laughed. "In all my life, I've never heard of a man who wants his women to wear shoes in bed."

"Women? You're the only woman I want with her shoes on."

"Oh, all right," she said, pretending to complain. One at a time, she put her shoes on, while still lying in bed.

"That really turns me on," he said.

"Me or the shoes?" she teased.

"Both."

Gently, he spread her legs and began to make love to her with his tongue. As he did, he took her breasts. He had never felt so totally unified with any other woman. When he had seen her at the church this afternoon, he had wanted so much to be one with her. It was as if Christina's femininity was his own. He wanted to feel this way forever.

She quietly moaned as she had her orgasm. Lovingly, he watched the spasm of her abdominal muscles. He had never forgotten the way she had been in Paris. All these years, he had stifled his yearning to make love to her like this again, but now she was with him.

Mark was about to put himself inside her, when she slipped her hand over his penis.

"No, wait. It's your turn," she whispered. "I want to suck you until you can't stand it any more."

It was exciting for Mark to see her lascivious side.

As she pleasured him, he watched the exciting sight of her high-heeled shoes and her smooth outstretched legs. He looked at her pubic hair, then her breasts. As he watched her making love to him, he tried to hold himself back, to make the idyllic pleasure last, but suddenly he lost control, let out a cry and was finished.

As they lay together, there was nothing more to say or do. If she had experienced even half the pleasure he had, she would want to be with him forever. She pulled the sheet over them and soon he saw that she was fast asleep.

He tried to sleep, but his mind was too busy. His thoughts turned involuntarily to Antonio. He could understand how Antonio had coveted Christina. It was no wonder that the old man had been so upset over Mark's affair with her that he exorcised them both from his life.

He got out of bed, being careful not to disturb her. He opened the closet, looking for Antonio's bathrobe. He found it, but no sooner had he touched the cloth than he knew it would be wrong to put it on. Instead, he put on his trousers and shirt and made his way down the stairs.

He looked through a window. The moon had set and the night was very dark. Mark turned on a light in the ghostly living room and sat down. Even though he, too, would have been angry with Christina if he had been Antonio, he knew he would have taken her back. Antonio had been a fool to let his pride stand in the way of having such a woman.

Mark went into the den where he had played chess with Antonio so many evenings. The table and chessmen were set up as if a game would soon be played. Mark sat in his old chair opposite Antonio's, but, with Antonio's death, the imagined game would never happen.

An uncomfortable thought came to Mark as he contemplated. He had finally bested Antonio. He was not proud of such a thought, but it was true—an untellable part of the pleasure in winning Christina.

Idly, he moved his pawn. Then he moved Antonio's pawn to the opposite position. Playing both sides, he made several more moves, and then, with his queen, made the key move, checkmating Antonio's king. He remembered the first time Antonio had pulled the Scholar's Mate on him. Antonio had laughed at the embarrassed young man, but today it was different, wasn't it? Today, Mark was the winner.

Mark smiled grimly. He had to stop thinking in terms of winners and losers. He thought of Mavis's big question: "What do you do when you have it all?"

"Mark? Mark, where are you?"

"Here, in the den."

"What are you doing?" Christina had wrapped herself in the sheet.

"I couldn't sleep. I was reminiscing."

She pulled his legs away from the table to sit on his lap. "Who's winning the chess game?"

"I am, of course. I always win at solitaire."

"I didn't know you could play solitaire in chess."

"I used to do it all the time. It was the only way I could beat Antonio."

Christina laughed. "Were you playing him just now?"

"No, I was just fooling around," he lied.

Sitting on his lap, she bent forward to return the chess pieces to their starting positions. The sheet opened up, showing her breast. He slipped his hand over her. "But I'd rather fool around with you." He kissed her and, under the sheet, ran his hands over her body.

"Mark! Be careful!"

It was too late. Accidentally, he had forced her to bump against the table. It tipped, spilling the chess pieces. She attempted to keep the pieces from falling, but she herself fell to the carpeted floor. She laughed heartily. Her sheet had fallen off, exposing her body.

"Are you all right?"

"Yes, but these men are attacking me." She picked a chessman off her breast, and held it up.

Mark was aroused. He put himself on top of her, both of them partially under the table.

"Careful Mark—the table."

"To hell with the table!"

"Don't you think we should go back upstairs?"

"No, I want you right now." He kicked off his trousers as she unbuttoned his shirt.

This time they were slower and more methodical in their love-making. His urgency had been dissipated.

He thought she was finished and was about to reach his own climax when he could feel her body trying to roll them both over. "I want to be on top," she said.

They giggled as they became further entangled in the legs of the table, and finally rolled free with Christina on top. In the new position her emotions were different.

"Don't move," she urgently commanded, just before she had her orgasm.

When they finished they lay on the floor, totally spent. Finally, she managed the effort of covering them both with her sheet, and they fell asleep among the chessmen.

-46-

It was nine o'clock in the morning in London. Derek Harden's black Daimler limousine let him out at the curb. This late November morning, the London weather was chilly. Many of the pedestrians carried umbrellas as protection from the predicted cold rain. Indifferent to the weather, Derek carried no umbrella and wore no top coat.

"Wait for me, Harold," he told his chauffeur. "I'll be less than an hour."

Derek made a striking figure as he entered the granite building in London's financial district. The uniformed doorman briskly opened the door for him.

"Good morning, sir."

Derek brushed by the doorman into the lobby without a response. The brass plate near the entrance bore the lettering "Harden Capital Investments."

Derek burst into his paneled conference room, where three of his staff nervously waited. When Derek's secretary had told them of the meeting, she had warned them that he was extremely angry. All three stood while he seated himself in the leather chair at the head of the long table.

"Gentlemen, I want to get to the bottom of this Stevens Group problem." Derek waved at them to sit down. "I've had quite enough of your excuses." As usual, he was dressed impeccably. His dark lightly striped suit was from the same Saville Row bespoke tailor he had used since his Oxford days. He inserted a king-sized cigarette into his long silver holder. Richard Green, his financial officer, leaped to his feet to light his boss's cigarette. Derek had developed considerable gray in his hair, and had gained 5 or 10 pounds, since losing the foreclosure lawsuit . He looked even more formidable than then. When they had all seated themselves, Derek continued, "This whole episode has proven to be unduly troublesome."

"I regret to report that we've met with very little success since our last meeting," said Albert Sleeter, a thin, nervous man, who was Derek's assistant.

"How much stock do I control now?"

"Our goal was two thirds of the 75% Stevens doesn't already own. That would be 50% plus one," said Richard Green.

"But we've all agreed that realistically 40%, perhaps 41%, would get control," interjected the third man, Robert Thom, another executive. "A certain percentage of the stockholders won't turn in proxies, and there always will be some who will vote against Stevens."

"How much do I have?" asked Derek. "Last time it was 26%."

"You have a little over 27% right now," Thom answered.

"But Mark has 25% to start with. We'll never get enough of the others to throw him out." In disgust Derek crushed out his cigarette.

"We paid $1,000 a share for the last block. There's absolutely nothing being traded now," said Sleeter. "The market knows very well that someone is attempting a takeover."

"Yes, and we have to worry about the American securities laws," said Green. "We've been buying mostly through your various foreign associates, trying to keep the whole matter quiet."

Sleeter added, "In actual fact, we're in violation of their law as it is."

"Our New York lawyers tell us you can't get around the reporting rules by having others buy for you," said Thom.

"How much money have I put in, to date?"

"Almost a billion, I'm afraid, sir," answered Green.

"Dollars or pounds?"

"Oh, pounds, sir."

"There must be something we can do," said Thom.

"Of course we can make an effort to buy even more, but . . .," said Sleeter.

"That's perfectly obvious, Sleeter," Derek interrupted. "We've got to find a way without paying those ridiculous prices." Derek had opened the paneled bar and, despite the early hour, began pouring himself a large brandy.

"Yes, sir. I'm very sorry, sir."

"Tell me, if we liquidated our position, what would we realize?" Derek was looking at Green.

"Perhaps two thirds of what you have in it."

"A loss of a third of a bloody billion?" Derek jumped to his feet and began pacing at his end of the large room.

"I'm afraid so, sir."

"Damn you! Damn you all! You should have stopped me before I got in so deeply."

"But, sir," dared Richard Green.

"Don't you 'but, sir' me. Part of your job is to tell me when I'm wrong." He gulped down his brandy.

They all watched without answering him.

"Have you all got that through your heads? Well, have you?"

"Yes, sir. I'll remember," said Green.

"I intend to think about this over the weekend. I'm going to the country. When we meet on Monday, I expect each of you to offer something constructive. I don't want to be the only person around here who can think."

"Pardon me, sir," said Thom, "but before you leave, sir, I have some rather puzzling news to report."

"What?"

"We have learned that Stevens was in London yesterday."

"What has that got to do with anything? He comes to London all the time, doesn't he?"

"Yes, sir, but he didn't tell anyone this time. No one in his company knew where he was."

"Maybe he's cheating on his wife. How do I know what he was doing here? Why do you bother me with such rubbish?"

"It seems he was behaving very mysteriously. Left a conference abruptly. Not like him at all."

"He's probably secretly buying up some company in England."

"I don't think so, sir. His secretary thinks he may very well be ill. Perhaps a breakdown of some sort."

"Very interesting." Suddenly Derek showed interest. "Do we know if it's serious?"

"Not yet, sir."

"What would happen if Stevens died or went to the hospital?" asked Sleeter.

"The stock would drop in price and Mr. Harden could get control," said Green.

"Of course I could, you idiot. But why on earth would I want control then?"

"But sir, it could be a very valuable company, even without Stevens."

"Green, you miss the whole point."

"I'm sorry, sir, but I don't understand."

"There's no point in buying the bloody company if Stevens doesn't know I bought it," said Derek disgustedly. "When I take control, I want him to know that it is *Derek Harden* who is his new boss." He spoke very deliberately. "Now, I want you all here Monday at nine o'clock and I want some of those clever ideas I'm supposedly paying you for." Abruptly he left the room, closing the door loudly behind him.

All three had stood as Derek stormed out. Green looked at Thom. "How did we get that information about Stevens?"

"I have a woman on his San Francisco staff. She's the secretary to Stevens's right-hand man."

"We pay her for information?"

"Of course we do."

"My God, man, isn't that illegal? What would Mr. Harden say if he found out?"

"My good fellow. You are very naive, indeed."

"What do you mean?"

"It was Derek Harden who told me to do it in the first place."

-47-

Mark awakened to the rich aroma of coffee. He lay alone under the sheet he had shared with Christina on the carpet near the chess table. Several times during the night, he had snuggled close to her back, feeling her breasts with his hand. Christina's coffee smelled so good this morning. He had never been so happy in his life.

"Hello, there, my beautiful young lady. Do you have another cup of coffee for a half-asleep fellow?" Holding the sheet over him, Mark leaned against the door casing connecting the den with the morning room. Christina sat at the breakfast table, looking out, sipping her coffee. The view was of the heavily flowered slope rising up from the grounds at the rear of the mansion, toward the mountain.

"You certainly didn't act half-asleep last night," she laughed.

Christina wore a pale orchid robe. As she stood to get Mark's coffee, he could see the outline of her beautiful figure against the morning light. How fortunate he was to be with her; he loved her deeply.

"Where did you find your robe?" he asked.

"Antonio must have kept it all these years. I was looking in my old closet this morning. Can you imagine that?" She felt the delicate fancy work on the front of the robe. "Here, I found this, too." She held out a man's robe." It was the same robe he had seen in Antonio's closet.

"Oh, so you don't like me wrapped in a sheet?" he teased, taking the offered robe.

He stood naked, putting it on. "The truth is, I like you best when you are with nothing." Leaning over, she put Mark's hot coffee on the table.

Mark put his hand around her waist, and drew her to his lap. "Christina, you make me so happy."

She gave him a long, gentle kiss, framing his face with her hands. "I'm happy to be with you, too."

He thought she seemed slightly remote, perhaps apprehensive.

"I love you, Christina. The truth is I've never stopped loving you."

Christina drew his face to her breast. "Why is it the timing has never been right for us?"

"So often I've wished we could be together." His lips pressed against her through her robe.

"When you left me in Rome, I was sad for many days. I wished you had asked me to run away with you."

"I tried to get you out of my system so I could marry Pris."

"I would have left Otello. I really would have, if you had asked. It all happened so fast. There you were in the limousine, then suddenly you were gone."

Christina went to the kitchen and started preparing sausage and eggs, while Mark stood, watching.

"I've never cooked for you before." The frying pan sizzled as she dropped the eggs into it.

"You're the most elegant cook that I've ever seen."

Christina took two plates from a cupboard. She was remembering the kitchen very well. "Here, waiter, put these on the table for us."

As they ate breakfast, they sat side by side, looking at the view.

"It's so very peaceful here. I used to love this place," she said.

Mark paused before answering her. "Now that Antonio is dead, I want to buy this mansion for us."

"Please don't say such things," she said urgently.

"Don't you see? Everything is different now."

Stunned, she suddenly put down her fork and got up. "But you know I can't." Nervously, she went to the kitchen for more coffee.

"Can't you see it? You and I living here. Running the vineyard. I'd never go into San Francisco. I would never look at another business deal in my life. We could make love any time we wanted."

Her hand was shaking as she poured more coffee.

"Mark, you upset me when you talk that way." She sat down opposite him.

"I'll find out who Antonio's executor is, and buy the compound."

Christina looked incredulous.

"I'll make an offer they can't turn down. You can divorce Otello and move in. I'll get my divorce as soon as possible."

"Mark, it's all very romantic." She took a deep breath and blurted out: "But I can't divorce Otello."

"What?" he exclaimed. "Why not? Italy has a divorce law now."

"I can't just walk away from Otello like that. He's a sick man. He's done everything he promised me. He's been a good husband."

"You have your own happiness to think about. You have me to think about."

"No, Mark. I can't do it."

"Goddammit, Christina! If it's money he's promised you, I have plenty of money." He banged down his coffee cup. Despite his love for her, he was very angry.

"It has nothing to do with money." She was dismayed.

"I'll give you all you want before we're married. You can have anything you want."

"I knew you'd say that. Don't you know you cannot buy me?" She stood, glaring out the window. She, too, was angry.

"No, I don't think I can buy you." Sorry he had been angry, he put his arms around her from behind, carefully avoiding her breasts. He could feel her bristle. "I just felt you should be independent of me, that's all," he said soothingly. "That way you could leave me anytime you wanted."

Abruptly, she turned, breaking from his grasp. "If I were married to you, *I would never leave you.* I'm not that kind of woman."

"I'm sorry. I didn't mean to insult you."

"I won't leave Otello, either. I won't divorce him just because I'd be happier with you."

"Christina, I'm not a college kid any more. This time I'm not going to let you get away from me. You belong with me. Do you hear me? You belong with me."

"I can't do it. I won't do it for anyone—not even you."

She suddenly burst into tears. He held her gently while she sobbed. "It's all right, Christina. It's all right." She continued with sobs that wrenched her deeply.

He had never seen her cry before. She had always been so much in control. "You can love more than one person, you know," she had once said so coolly. "You can love a person, and not marry him," she had said without shedding a tear. Obviously she had changed now.

Finally, she stopped. "Mark, I do love you, don't you know? I've loved you from the very beginning."

He took a napkin from the table, and wiped the tears from her face.

"Mark?" she asked.

"Yes."

"Would you please take me upstairs and love me? I need you to love me. Please—love me."

They kept their robes on as they lay on the bed.

"Hold me," she asked. "I need you to hold me."

Her body was shaking. He put a blanket over them and held her tightly. "Everything will be all right," he said softly. "We'll find an answer to this. There has to be an answer somehow."

He made no move to press her sexually. He loved her, and it was all right if she was never ready.

Finally, her shaking subsided. The minutes ticked by as they remained still, with him holding her tightly. Then she reached for him. "I'd like for us to take our robes off now," she said.

They had never made love as tenderly. Christina's orgasm was very different, very gentle. She was completely quiet, yet he could feel her coming. When she was through, he asked: "Have you had all you want?"

"Yes, it was very nice. You can go ahead."

Mark had caught her mood. He, too, was very quiet as he finished.

After they had rested a few minutes, she turned and ran her hands across the hair on his chest. "Mark, I love you."

"I love you too, you know."

"I'll meet you anytime you ask." She said. "I can always get away for a while."

He gently ran his finger over her breast, ending with her nipple.

"You could come to Rome all the time," she continued.

He kissed her nipple, and ran his hand to her navel.

"You could send your plane for me, and we could meet in London."

Even though what she was saying pleased him, he was very sad.

"But you won't divorce Otello, will you?"

"Don't you see? That's the one thing I can't do."

He abruptly sat on the edge of the bed. "I don't understand. You do all those things with me behind his back, and yet you can't divorce him—or I should say, you won't divorce him."

"I know I can't possibly make you understand."

"That's very sad, Christina. I know I'd divorce Pris to marry you. I'd do anything to marry you." He wanted to be angry, but he could not.

A tear formed in her eye, and flowed down her face. "Mark, dear, I wasn't go to tell you this. But Otello is very ill."

"Oh?"

"He has cancer."

"I didn't know."

"Cancer of the prostate."

"That's often not fatal." For a moment he wondered if she were telling the truth.

"I know."

"Is it going to be fatal with him?"

"I don't know. He had an operation and some difficult radiation."

"Can he . . ." Mark thought better of his question.

"No, he can't have sex," she said. "He hasn't for a very long time anyway."

"I see."

"Mark, I've done some pretty awful things in my time, I know"

"Going to bed with my father was one of them." He was sorry the minute he had spoken.

"You're right it was."

"I'm sorry, Christina. I shouldn't have said that."

"I've hurt you, haven't I?"

"Yes, you have. I thought you'd want to be with me."

"Don't you see? I do want to be with you, but I've got to do this. I've got to be his wife to the end. I promised him. Don't you see? I'd never be able to respect myself if I deserted him."

"Dammit, Christina! Where does this leave me?" He felt bleak, desolate. Mavis had said he should get more passion into his life. He had done that, and where had it gotten him?

"I'm sorry. I'll come to you any time you say."

He got out of bed and put on his robe.

"Where are you going?" she asked with panic in her voice.

"I want to think. I want to be alone for a while."

Mark sat at the chess table, straightening out the chessmen and repeating the Scholar's Mate moves; only this time, it was the opponent's, Antonio's, side of the game who first moved its pawn. This time he played the victim.

On the fifth move, Antonio had mated his king and he was defeated.

"You win, Antonio," Mark said aloud. "You have beaten me again." He tipped his king over on its side. "I can see now that you were right," he continued out loud. "If you couldn't have her all to yourself, you didn't want her at all." He knew he would reject Christina's offer to be lovers while she remained with Otello.

Mark realigned the chess pieces, setting them up in their starting positions. "You were right, old fellow, but there's a big difference between you and me, Antonio. I'm not going to keep her robe in my closet forever. I'm going to get out there and find a new woman. My own woman—a woman who loves me and nobody else."

-48-

Pris was early for her appointment with Dr. Goodwill. She hesitated as she walked past Thomas T. Wahl's office. Perhaps she should stop and tell Wahl to hold off indefinitely on the divorce, but she shied away from confronting the gruff lawyer. After all, Wahl was not going to file the case until she gave the go-ahead.

She entered the familiar small reception room, and pushed Dr. Goodwill's buzzer. Last night, she had bought her first package of cigarettes since her Wellesley days. Nervously, she lit the first cigarette of this morning. She looked at the package before putting it back in her purse. It was half gone. Disgusted with herself, she took a second quick drag and crushed out the cigarette in the ashtray. She was wound tight as a drum this morning. Her sleep had been very fitful.

One part of Pris was glad she had signed her new will and the divorce papers. Her father was right: Mark must have a girl friend. He had not wanted sex with her for so long now. The divorce had been building up for years—his long absences—his preoccupation with business—his utter lack of interest in her. Surely she was entitled to more than this in a marriage. After all, she was attractive, well-educated and moneyed. She was the daughter of Henry Enfield.

But there was another part of Pris. The part that knew her unhappiness was not wholly Mark's fault. Because of her therapy, she was beginning to realize that long before Mark she had been only pretending to be happy. That when she had gone to the opera and acted as her father's hostess, it was pretense. She saw now that she had always held herself back with Mark. Even with her friends in the art community, where she was her happiest, she could see that she was not genuine. Nobody really knew Priscilla Enfield, not even herself. However, the fact was that she never would have been motivated to see Dr. Goodwill in the first place, if it had not been that her marriage was in serious trouble.

Appearances to the contrary, Pris's marriage was vitally important to her. She loved Mark, and she knew if she did not do something she would lose him. She felt that she could never again find a man as right for her. She was ready to face up to the fact that if she didn't do something her life would be destroyed. While she had grown during these years with Dr. Goodwill, it was not enough. She had to stop being this phony, plastic woman, and be real; but she did not know how. For these reasons, she had finally decided to try hypnosis, no matter how frightening it was to her. As she nervously waited, she longed to light another cigarette, but resisted. She recalled how she had admired Mark when she first met him at her Aunt Mavis's house when he was at Oxford. By the time Mark was working for her father, she knew that she wanted to marry him. She was thrilled when Mark was finally romantically attracted to her that night in her father's Pebble Beach house. Frozen by inexplicable terror, she had panicked when he wanted to make love. She had desperately wanted to please him, but the thought of being in bed with a man in her father's house was too much for her.

During her college years, she had had sex many times. Being sexually active was sophisticated, and put her in the midst of the sexual revolution. If her father had known, he would have made her return at once to San Francisco. That pleased her, made her feel smugly superior to him. But Pris had never actually liked having sex, even looking upon it as somewhat repugnant.

She pulled another cigarette from her purse, put it in her mouth, but did not light it. After college, sex was something she often did on dates, but she still never enjoyed it. That she did not have orgasms, bothered her at first, but then she read that that was true of many women. Eventually, she accepted that she could reach a climax only when she masturbated, and put the whole matter out of her mind.

That first time in Mark's empty Pebble Beach house she had desperately wanted to avoid losing him. She knew that men wanted a woman to like sex, so she had tried to pretended to be eager. In the past she had even tried to be seductive and earthy for men. She remembered Carla, her sorority sister at Wellesley, telling her, "They all like a blow job. Christ, they even want you to like doing it."

She never had the nerve to tell all this to Dr. Goodwill. Maybe she could tell him about some of her feelings, but certainly not about the lack of orgasms, and about sleeping with so many men. That was why she had resisted hypnosis. Dr. Goodwill seemed obsessed with talking about her father. To Pris, her father was not the problem at all. Goodwill was wasting his time there. It was disclosing all these other things that scared her half to death.

"You look deep in thought, Priscilla." Dr. Goodwill stood, smiling, at the door. "Why don't you come in now?"

"I'm sorry you had to give up your day off. I really appreciate your seeing me."

"It's a big step for you to go into hypnosis. Nothing I was planning is as important as that."

They walked into his office. "I'm very nervous about this whole thing. I'm really frightened."

"Don't be nervous. For three years now, you've been telling me your most intimate thoughts."

"Maybe that's it. Maybe I haven't had the guts to tell you what I really should have."

"Priscilla, sit down a minute. I want to explain some things to you before we start." Priscilla sat in her usual chair, opposite the psychologist's desk. Behind her was a tufted leather couch that she had never used. Again, Priscilla started to reach for a cigarette, but changed her mind. She didn't want Dr. Goodwill to know she was smoking.

"When you get into the hypnotic state, you will be fully conscious"

"Really? I thought I'd be blacked out."

"No, that never happens. You'll be aware of everything that's said, everything that happens."

"What's the point of hypnosis, then?"

"In the hypnotic state, your conscious mind tends to stop censoring out unpleasant and unremembered data. Material you may have repressed for many years."

"So, then I can see what I've refused to remember?"

"Yes, many of our memories are so unhappy that the conscious mind protects us from recalling them. There's another point, also. Many times we remember things perfectly well, but don't connect it to our problems. We don't have the insight consciously."

"And we do under hypnosis?"

"Often we do, yes."

"So if we can recall a painful memory, we'll be all right?"

Dr. Goodwill smiled. "Unfortunately, it's not that simple, but it's a beginning—an essential beginning. Once hypnosis helps us find out what's at the core of the problem, we try to reprogram ourselves, regroove our thought patterns. For example, I remember the case of a young minister I had once as a patient. He would get these panic attacks before every sermon."

"A minister? How awful for him."

"Yes, it was awful. He would be filled with panic and nervousness all through his Sunday morning talks."

"What happened."

"Finally, under hypnosis, he discovered that when he was a child, at the dinner table . . ."

"Yes?"

"Whenever he would express his opinion about something, his mother would scold him—tell him to shut up. 'Children should be seen, not heard.' That sort of thing."

"And that was why he had those attacks?"

"Yes, the old patterns surfaced again, whenever he would speak. This inner voice, implanted there by his mother, would scold him for expressing himself."

"A minister—of all things!"

"Of course a minister's job is to give his opinions about things—to be outspoken."

"Did he ever get over it?"

"Yes, he did. Remarkably fast, too."

"How did he do that?"

"In his case, we suggested a thought pattern of helping people that he really cared about. Giving them good advice. Then, whenever he was about to speak, he would think of the good he was doing. He would have a good feeling, instead of fear. You might say, he was successful in not listening to his mother within."

"And you think something like that would work for me?"

"I do. Priscilla, there's too much in your past, your childhood, that simply doesn't add up. I believe it likely you're repressing some early memories—memories that are too painful for you. I'd like to uncover them." Dr. Goodwill left his chair, and walked over to the couch. "So, if you're ready, I think we should get started. I'd like you to lie down on the couch."

Still apprehensive, Pris lay down on the couch, taking the pillow Dr. Goodwill offered.

"Would you like me to put this blanket over you?"

"All right," Pris said, nervously.

"I suggest you take off your shoes, so that you can relax."

Pris slipped off her shoes, spread the blanket over herself and lay back.

"Now, do you have any questions before we begin?"

"I don't have any questions, but I don't mind telling you, I'm frightened."

"Do you want to tell me about it?"

"I guess I'm scared of what I might say—of what you might find out—or really, what I might find out."

"That's an excellent insight Priscilla." Dr. Goodwill grinned. "I want you to know something. The unconscious never reveals anything you're not ready to know. The reason the mind represses things in the first place is that the conscious mind can't deal with it. Your mind will continue to protect you in the same way until you are ready to reveal it."

"All right. I guess I'm ready."

Sitting on a chair beside her, Dr. Goodwill started the ticking of his metronome while Pris, less fearful, closed her eyes.

"Now, Priscilla, I want you to relax your left big toe. Make it very relaxed." He gave her time to do as he asked, and then did the same with all of her toes.

"Now, I want you to concentrate on your entire left foot. I want you to make it relaxed . . . very relaxed," he intoned as the metronome ticked.

As Pris followed his continuing suggestions, various parts of her body went into a state of deep relaxation. She was aware of opposing sensations. She felt wide awake and perfectly in control, yet she seemed drowsy, as if she were in a state of deep sleep. She knew that at any time she chose, she could refuse Dr. Goodwill's instructions and pull away from the trance, yet she knew she would choose not to stop. She trusted him and what he was doing.

"I'd like you to choose either an escalator or an elevator."

Pris paused. "All right."

"Now choose a floor number."

"All right."

"What do you see?"

"It's an escalator."

"All right Priscilla, let me know when you're on the escalator."

"I'm on it now—going up." She was aware that she was in a state of hypnosis, yet she was choosing everything she was doing.

"I would like you to get off the escalator on the floor you chose."

"I'm getting off at the fifth floor."

"Tell me what happens next."

"It's my mother. I see my mother."

"Is your mother doing anything?"

"She's taking me into one of the shops."

"How old are you?"

"Ten years old."

"What is happening in the shop?"

"She's buying me something."

"What is it?"

"It's a new dress. It's for me." Pris could clearly see her smiling mother.

"Is it some special occasion?"

"No, it's just because I'm her little girl."

"What does the dress look like?"

"It has polka dots. Big polka dots. I like it a lot." Although her voice was not that of a child, Pris felt as if she were 10 years old again.

"What happens?"

"I try it on. Mother buys it for me."

"What happens next?"

"Mother lets me wear the dress home. She loves me. I'm very happy." Pris found herself wondering whether the scene had actually ever happened; yet it was so real.

"Now, Priscilla, I'd like you to tell me when you are back on the escalator."

Pris did not respond for a few moments. "I'm on it now."

"Now choose a floor."

"All right."

"As you travel on the escalator, I want you to go more deeply asleep."

Pris did not say anything.

"Where are you now, Priscilla?"

"I'm going down the escalator. Very far down."

"Where are you?"

"I'm getting off on the next floor."

"All right."

"Here I am."

"Good. What do you see?"

"I'm in Boston."

"What happens in Boston?"

"I'm with a man. He's taken me to his room."

"What's his name?"

"Donald Brats."

"Who is he?"

"He's my boyfriend."

"What is happening?"

"Donald wants to have sex with me."

"What happens now?"

"We did it. He's through now."

"I see. What is happening now?"

"I'm upset."

"I see."

"I thought I was supposed to enjoy this, but I hated it."

"What happens next?"

"Donald calls me a cold fish."

"How do you feel about that?"

"I don't like it. He says I didn't do anything." Pris started to cry gently. "He says I didn't do anything but lie there."

"What happens next?"

"He asks me to put his penis in my mouth."

"Do you answer him?"

"I tell him I wouldn't do that for anyone." She stopped crying, and said firmly: "His penis is smelly. It's awful!"

"Is there anything else you want to tell me?"

"No."

"Very well, Priscilla. I want you to choose another floor and get on the escalator again."

"All right."

"Tell me when you are on the escalator."

"I'm on it. I'm going down, very far down."

"All right."

Pris was silent.

"Where are you now?"

"Still going down."

"Tell me when you get off."

"I'm off now."

"What is it like?"

"It's very dark."

"What do you see?"

"I can't tell who it is."

"Can you see who it is?"

"I can't see."

"Priscilla," Dr. Goodwill raised his voice slightly. "Is there some-one with you?"

"Yes."

"Who is it?"

"It's my father."

"How old are you?

"Fourteen. Mother is dead."

"Is your father talking to you?"

"Yes."

"Tell me what happens."

She raised her voice suddenly. "He's saying awful things."

"What is he saying, Priscilla?"

"He says I have nice breasts. He puts his hand on my breast." She spoke as if she were repulsed.

"What is happening now?"

"He says no one will know."

"No one will know what?"

"No one will know if . . ."

"If what, Priscilla?"

"He says no one will know, if we have sex together."

"Do you say anything?"

"I tell him I don't want to."

"Does he answer you?"

"He says he's very lonely without Mother. He wants to know if I love him."

"What is happening now?"

"I'm running away from him. He's caught me. The door is locked."

"What happens next?"

"He puts his hand on my behind."

"Yes."

"I take it off, and shove him. Hard."

"What does he do?"

"He is arguing with me. He says a lot of fathers and daughters have sex when they love each other. He says there's nothing wrong with it. He says everybody is a bunch of hypocrites." Pris's voice was cracking, but she was not crying.

"Does he say anything else?"

"Yes."

"What does he say, Priscilla?"

"I can't hear him. He's saying something, but I can't hear what he's saying." Pris fidgeted anxiously.

"Tell me what happens."

"I'm very angry with him. I tell him to get away from me. I tell him if he ever touches me again, I'll tell everybody in San Francisco about him."

"Does he say anything?"

"Yes."

"What does he say?"

"I can't hear him. He's saying something, but I can't hear him."

"Does he do anything?"

"He stomps out of the room."

"How do you feel about that?"

"I'm so angry with him, I could kill him. I shout after him."

"What do you shout?"

"If he ever tries that again, I'll run away. I'll hitchhike to Pebble Beach and ride my horse."

"Is there anything more you want to tell me now?"

"No."

"Priscilla, I want you to choose another floor and get on the escalator again."

"All right."

"Where are you now?"

"I'm going down the escalator."

"What's happening now?"

"Its very, very dark."

"Yes."

"I'm getting off the escalator."

"Give me a report, please."

"I'm in my bed." Suddenly Pris's voice took on the characteristics of a youngster.

"Is it day or night?"

"Night."

"Are you at home or away?"

"Home."

"How old are you?"

"I'm six." Pris continued to speak in the manner of a child.

"What happens next?"

"Mother finishes reading to me, and tells me good night."

"What happens now?"

"Mother puts out the light, and I'm going to sleep now." Suddenly Pris's body began to shake under the blanket.

"Tell me what happens next, Priscilla."

"I don't know"

"Priscilla?"

"Yes."

"Tell me what happens next."

"The door—my bedroom door is opening."

"What do you see?"

"I can see the light in the hall. I can see him standing there."

"Who, Pris, who is standing there?'

"Daddy? Is that you, Daddy?" Pris's voice continued with the characteristics of a six-year-old.

"Is your father doing anything?"

"Yes."

"What?"

"He's coming into my bedroom."

"Is he doing anything?"

"Yes."

"What?"

"He's smiling at me."

Dr. Goodwill's pulse quickened. He felt a hint of perspiration on his palms. At last, he said to himself, momentarily pondering what he expected to be an important discovery for Pris, we're getting to the bottom of all this.

-49-

Mark walked from the mansion into the bright morning. He was taking Christina's rejection of marriage better than he would have imagined. He felt more anger than anything else. He knew she loved him, yet she was throwing it all away because of her exaggerated loyalty to Otello. He grabbed a pebble from the walk, and flung it as high as he could. Some loyalty, he thought. She was willing to screw him behind Otello's back. Before the pebble landed, he threw another. This time, the stone smacked against the house, just missing the bedroom window.

What he ought to do is go back upstairs and make her change her mind, but what could he do? He could fuck her again. He could argue with her. He could tell her how much her needed her. He could take her flowers. He could give her ten million dollars, even a hundred million dollars. There must be something he could do to make her change her mind.

She was being absolutely stupid. Shit, the more he thought about it the less he wanted her anyway! She probably had played around on Otello with lots of men. A man never could be sure about Christina Movelli.

"Mark, where have you been?" Amanda called out. She was taking out the trash from her kitchen when she saw her son wandering down the slope from the mansion. "Are you all right?"

Mark was embarrassed. His clothes were rumpled, and he was unshaven. He had been oblivious to the effect of his unexplained overnight absence. He avoided looking at his mother as he answered her. "I'm sorry, Mother. I slept at the big house. I should have told you."

"I was worried sick. You were out all night."

"I know it was thoughtless of me. I'm sorry."

"I'm worried about you. You've not been your old self at all." She nearly burst into tears. He could see she was troubled.

"I'm sorry you're so upset. I'll be all right." He put his arms around her. "Let's go inside and talk."

Mark sat at the kitchen table, but his mother busily went to the stove. "Would you like some coffee?" He assumed she knew he had been with Christina

"No, I've already had some. On second thought, I wouldn't mind if you'd heat up what you've got there."

"I'll make some fresh. It'll only take a minute. After all, it's not very often I get to see my son."

Mark knew better than to stop her from going to the trouble. As she fussed over the coffee, he took a close look at her. She still had less gray in her hair than he had white. She had to wear her glasses all the time now. She had always refused financial help from him, although she had consented to his giving her a new car. Even with the Social Security she would get on her next birthday, there would be no way she could be self-supporting now that Antonio was dead. Perhaps she finally would let him help her.

He loved his mother dearly. She had always stood by him, always believed in him. She seldom interfered in his life, but he knew that she did not approve of his being with Christina last night.

"Let me fix you some breakfast," Amanda said.

"Mother, please sit down. I'm just fine. I can see how upset you are. We need to talk."

Amanda poured coffee for both of both of them. "I'm sorry I'm this way. Antonio was such an important part of my life—especially these past years. I haven't been myself."

"Don't apologize, Mom. Now sit down, please, and tell me what's really bothering you. Let's get to the bottom of this."

"You want the truth?"

"Yes, I want the truth."

"It's you, Mark. It's everything. I try not to interfere, but I'm so worried."

"What, Mom. What about?"

"You've not looked well for over a year now."

"Don't worry. I'll be all right. I'm not going to work as hard any more."

"And you should be having children by now. A woman my age wants grandchildren, you know. And here you are, seeing Christina again! You were with her last night, weren't you?" She spoke rapidly, getting it all out before she lost her nerve. "Aren't you ever going to get her out of your system?"

"She is out of my system. I don't ever expect to see her again."

Amanda looked surprised. "My goodness! Really? You don't know how happy that makes me. I'm so glad you've decided to leave her alone."

"No, Mom."

"No, what?"

"Never mind, Mom." He decided against telling her it was Christina who had broken it off—that he had been willing to divorce Pris.

"Well, I'm glad it's over with Christina." She poured more coffee. "I was afraid you and Priscilla might get a divorce."

"It's not up to me alone, you know. Pris isn't very happy with me."

"Priscilla would never divorce you. Every woman in the world would give up her eye teeth to be married to a man like you."

"Yeah, a man who sleeps with his old girl friends. The truth is, Pris and I would probably both be better off divorced. As for grandchildren, Pris isn't very excited about having a baby."

"Well, I certainly can't imagine a woman like Christina wanting children." Mark knew she was right. The thought of Christina raising children was absurd, but he would have readily abandoned having children if Christina had consented to marry him.

"Don't worry, Priscilla will change her mind," Amanda continued. "You mark my words. She'll want someone to carry on the family line." She got up and poured more coffee. "Now, young man, no matter what you say, I'm going to fix you some breakfast."

"All right, Mom," he smiled.

"How about your usual?"

"Of course."

It was a good feeling to have his mother cook for him. In his haste to get ahead in life, he had lost such simple pleasures.

In a few minutes Amanda put bacon and two easy-over eggs in front of her son, and sat down with her coffee to watch him eat.

"It's so wonderful to have you here."

"It's wonderful being here, Mom."

"Mark?"

"Yes?"

"Are you happy? Are you going to be all right?"

"Happy is a big word, Mom. It's mixed up with a lot of other things."

"Like what?"

"Like satisfaction. Pride. Reaching goals."

"How about just being happy, without all those worldly things?"

"You remind me of a friend of mine, Rodney's mother."

"Mavis. I remember her from the wedding."

"She's a very wise woman. She told me about the 'big question.'"

"The big question?"

"Yes. 'What do you do when you have it all?'"

"I don't know. What do you do?"

"No, Mom, that's just it. 'What do you do?' That's the question."

"Well, I know one thing. I've never 'had it all,' as you put it, but I didn't much care that I didn't."

"Do you know what I think, Mom?"

"No," she answered.

"I think you're a lot wiser than I am."

When Mark finished his breakfast, he began to carry his dishes to the sink. "Here, let me do that," said Amanda. "You're a guest in my house."

"Speaking of houses, Mom, have you thought about what you're going to do now that Antonio is dead?"

"He and I talked about it quite a lot. Especially in this past year."

"Really?"

"I doubt if things will change all that much, except . . ."

"Except what?"

"Except that I won't have to take care of him any more."

"But you'll have to move out now that Antonio's gone. I'd like to buy you a house closer to me."

"Oh, no. I couldn't do that. I've lived here practically all my life."

"Then you want to live in Sonoma someplace? I could buy you a house there."

"No, I'd prefer here, on the compound."

"But Antonio's heirs . . ."

"No, son. Antonio has seen to it that I won't have to move."

"That's great. What did he do, make some arrangement where you can stay in your house for the rest of your life? You never told me."

"No, it's more than that. He swore me to secrecy. He didn't want you to know."

"Know what?"

"Antonio's will leaves me everything he owns."

"What? What do you mean 'leaves you everything'?"

"Antonio appreciated my taking care of him all these years. He left me everything."

"You mean the mansion, the compound? He left you everything?"

"Yes. The vineyard, the winery, even his stocks and bonds."

"Are you serious? Antonio left you everything he had?"

"He really didn't have anybody in this country, you know. And his relatives in Italy died years ago."

"Mom, that's wonderful. It's hard for me to believe. Don't get me wrong. You deserve it. It's just hard to believe that Antonio Movelli would do something like that."

"He was a very generous man."

Mark was amazed by his mother's news. He remembered when he was a teenager, his father's telling him if he played his cards right Antonio and Anna would will everything to him. "That's the only way you're ever going to get rich," his father had said. And now here it was his mother who had everything! He still could not absorb it all. A dark thought flashed through his mind. Had Antonio and his mother had a secret romance? He pushed the thought away. If it were true, it was none of his business. Perhaps they had found some happiness in these last years.

"Are you going to move into the mansion?" he asked.

"No, I don't think so. I wouldn't be happy there. I think I'll stay right here in my house."

"What will you do with the big house, then?"

"Do you know what I've been thinking?"

"No, what?"

"I think I might make it into a home of some sort."

"A home?"

"Yes, at first I thought of a bed and breakfast, but then I thought about a home for children, maybe handicapped children. Something like that. My church has been thinking of a project like that."

"That would be a good idea. You know, I've always had a daydream of owning the mansion one day myself."

"What would you have done with it? You have a big house already."

"Oh, I don't know. But your idea is better than anything I would have done." He would never tell her he had dreamed of living there with Christina.

"Someday you'll inherit it from me."

"I just can't get over it—Antonio willing you all his property."

"Do you know who was getting everything under his old will?"

"No."

"Until five years ago, he had never changed his will. Christina was still going to get everything."

"Christina? My God, he was a sentimental old man, wasn't he? Never changing his will." Mark got up from the table and moved toward the door. "Wouldn't it have been something, if Christina lived in the mansion?"

"Where are you going?" Amanda asked.

"I want to talk with Christina. It's important that I talk to her." As he walked back toward the mansion, all his feelings for Christina were gone. His anger of half an hour ago had disappeared, but nothing had come in to replace it. His emotions had been so intense, he felt completely spent. Still he wanted to make one last attempt to persuade her.

"Christina? Christina? Are you there?" He climbed the stairs to the bedroom. There was no answer. The bed was neatly made, but she was not there. She must have gone already.

Not wanting her to get away without saying good-bye, he turned to dash downstairs, but saw an envelope on the nightstand. Hesitantly, he picked it up. *"Mark"* was in her handwriting on the envelope.

He ripped it open, yanked out the letter and raced through the words. The letter in his hand, he slowly walked downstairs. There was no use looking for her now. Stunned, he sat down at the chess table. He placed the chessmen in their starting positions, and reread the letter.

> *Thursday*
> *20 November, 1980*
> *My Darling Mark,*
>
> *How can I ever explain myself to you? When I left for Antonio's funeral, I didn't know if I would see you. In truth, that was the main reason I went. I tried to find out if you were attending, but no one knew, so I went anyway, hoping I might see you.*
>
> *These past few years have been very bad for me. Otello has been so ill and demanding. I want to tell you that ever since you were with me in Rome, I have not had sex with any other man, even my husband. It is not that I am such a moral person—I am not. It is more because no man has interested me.*
>
> *This last day you have brought me alive again. I will always be happy for that. It was as if I were dead before yesterday. Maybe that is why I came to Sonoma. To be alive for one day.*
>
> *I used to fall in love so easily that it didn't mean much to me, but we all change. I am very flattered that you loved me and wanted to marry me. But you must try to understand why I cannot do this. Otello would*

understand if I had a lover, but he would not understand divorce. I think he might even have both of us killed, but that is not my reason.

I wish I had married you when you asked me in Paris. We must profit from our mistakes.

I love you.
Cristina

Tears came to his eyes. For at least a minute, he sat silently staring at the letter. Then he put it on the table, and idly began the first moves of the Scholar's Mate. Having no heart to go on, he soon stopped. Sadly, he tipped over each of the kings. "Stalemate," he muttered.

Head down, he stuffed the letter into his pocket, and walked to where her rental car had been parked. As he expected, it was gone. She must have left while he was talking to his mother.

So what would he do with himself now? He did not want to go back to the office. He was fearful that his panic attacks might return. Burying himself in more work was futile.

"Mr. Stevens? Mr. Mark Stevens?"

Mark turned to see who was there. It was a young man in jeans and an old shirt.

"Yes?" Mark answered.

"I have something here for you," the young man said.

"What is it? Mark asked warily.

"Papers, sir." The man handed Mark some legal-looking papers. "I'm afraid your wife has sued you for divorce, sir."

-50-

Dr. Goodwill continued with the hypnosis session. "All right, Priscilla, you're six years old. Your father is in your bedroom. What is happening now?"

"He is sitting on my bed."

"All right."

"He acts kind of funny—like he does after parties." Pris's voice still took on the characteristics of a child.

"Yes."

"He is kissing me now."

"Yes."

"His breath smells funny."

"What is happening now?"

"He says he loves me. I like that."

"What happens now?"

"He says I'm his little girl."

"All right."

"Oh, dear."

"What is happening, Priscilla?"

"Father is putting his hand under the covers. He's feeling me under my nightie." Her tone was one of amazement and anxiety.

"Tell me, what happens now."

"I'm a little scared."

"What do you do?"

"Nothing. I don't do anything. I'm scared."

Neither said anything for a time.

"It's all right, Priscilla. When you're ready, I want you to tell me what happens next."

Pris twisted and turned under her blanket.

"What is happening now, Priscilla?"

"Father is putting his finger in me—you know—down there."

"In your private parts?"

"Private parts, yes."

Dr. Goodwill paused momentarily, before going on. "Tell me what is happening now."

"It's scary."

"I see."

"Oh, dear! Oh, dear!"

"What is it, Pris?"

"I don't know what to do."

"What do you want to do?"

"I don't know."

"Do you want him to stop or to keep on?"

"I don't know! I don't know!" she agonized.

"What are you feeling?"

"It feels good. It feels good to be close to my father."

"Does he stop?"

"No, he asked me to put my arms around him."

"How does that feel?"

"It feels very warm and nice."

"What happens next?"

Pris pulled back, as if recoiling. "He's taking my hand. He's putting my hand on his . . ."

"On what, Pris?"

"On his . . . you know . . . through his pants."

"On his penis?"

"Yes."

"And what do you think?"

"I let him do it."

"What then, Priscilla?"

"He takes himself out of his pants. He's so big!"

"And then what?"

"He tells me to put my hand on him."

"And do you?"

"Yes. I do what he wants me to."

"How do you feel about that?"

"It's so big and hard."

"What happens next?"

"I can hear the front door opening, downstairs."

"Is somebody coming in?"

"It's Mother. She is calling upstairs. She says her meeting has been canceled."

"All right."

"I can hear her talking. She's coming upstairs."

"Yes. What next?"

"Father is standing up tall. He is zipping up his pants."

"Yes"

"He's hollering at me. He's mad at me. I don't like him being mad at me."

"What is he saying?"

"You naughty girl! Don't you dare tell your mother. I'll tell her you're lying if you do.' He's mad at me."

"Then what happens?"

"I'm crying."

"Does your father say anything more?"

"He is telling me to be quiet. He says something very bad will happen to me, if I tell Mother what I've been doing."

"I see."

"Mother is at my door now."

"What is happening now?"

"She's asking me, why I'm crying. Father tells her he came in because I was crying." Pris was gently crying.

"What happens next?"

"Mother is holding me."

"Does your father do anything?"

"He leaves."

"Does anything else happen?"

"She asks me why I'm crying. I tell her I've had a bad dream. I've lied to her."

"All right, Priscilla. Does anything else happen?"

"No, that's all." Pris sobbed, one very large sob.

The session lasted nearly an additional 30 minutes. Dr. Goodwill made hypnotic suggestions, designed to assist Priscilla in changing the psychological reactions implanted by her early traumatic experiences. After that, he slowly and methodically began to bring Priscilla out of hypnosis.

"On the count of three, I'm going to snap my fingers and you will be awake. You will remember everything you have told me. You will have a feeling of well-being. All right, now. One. Two. Three." At three, Goodwill made a loud *snap* with his fingers. Pris opened her eyes and rubbed her face, as if waking up from a nap. She stretched and when she was ready, they resumed sitting at the desk.

"Amazing," said Pris.

"That's a good word for the process."

"My father. My own father. He's a very evil, sick man. I had no recollection of any of that, except the time after Mother died when I was a teenager.

"Do you think he's sorry?"

"I doubt that. I doubt that very much."

"I see."

"The dirty old fool! I remember now. He fondled me whenever Mother went away. I remember very well now."

"Some in his position deny such things really happened, even to themselves."

"It happened all right."

"I believe they know very well what happened."

"This is all so incredible," she said.

"When did he begin leaving you alone?"

"I'm not sure. It went on a long time. He always warned me not to tell. Finally one time when I was older, I told him if he didn't stop, I'd tell Mother myself."

"Did you ever tell her?"

"No. The poor soul never dreamed what he was doing."

"What do you think of when you think of what your father did?"

"I feel dirty. It was disgusting. I worry that I seem to have liked it. I feel awful about that. My God, Doctor, I feel disgusting!

"You see, *that* is the problem."

"What do you mean?"

"From the viewpoint of an innocent child, Priscilla, it isn't disgusting at all. It was quite natural for you to feel good about it. Even to feel good sexually. A young child doesn't know it's bad, even with her own father. That's all learned behavior, don't you see? Some scholars debate whether incest is inherently evil, but the fact is that our society labels it bad, evil."

Pris sighed. "Oh, Jesus!"

"But you, as a six-year-old child, couldn't possibly understand any of this. So when your father tells you bad things will happen to you if anyone finds out—that you were doing awful things—it's very natural for your unconscious to get the message: 'Sex is evil. You'll be punished, if you enjoy sex. You can please men, but you dare not enjoy sex.' Don't you see?"

"How does all this fit into the Donald Brats situation? It was funny that my mind would bring him up."

"The unconscious works in unusual ways."

"Donald Brats was a real nothing."

"The problem is that you may be reacting to all men as if they were Donald Brats, or as if they were your father."

Pris sighed. "I'm really screwed up, aren't I?"

"I think you're on your way to recovery."

"I certainly can't be cured by one session, can I?"

"There are many cases where a phobia, for example, can disappear after one session. What it takes is the courage to go through the fear—experience the fear."

"Whew," she said blowing air out through her mouth. "I see. Do you think I can do it?"

"Yes, I do, Priscilla. You may need some reinforcing by another session. Many people do."

"Do you think I would have a chance with Mark?"

"You could give it a try, if you wanted."

"Oh, my God, the divorce papers!" Pris jumped up from the chair.

"What about them?"

"I've got to stop them. I can't let Mark see them."

Hurriedly, Pris put on her shoes. Without combing her hair or fixing her make-up, she dashed down the hall to Thomas T. Wahl's offices.

"Cathy," Pris said frantically.

"Oh, hello, Mrs. Stevens."

"I've got to stop those divorce papers from being filed!"

"I'm afraid it's too late, Mrs. Stevens."

"What do you mean, 'too late'? Mr. Wahl said he wouldn't file them without my okay."

"Mr. Wahl told me to go ahead. I'm sorry, I gave them to the court service last night. They would've been filed this morning."

"Oh, my God!" Pris reached into her purse for her package of cigarettes.

"Now, don't worry, Mrs. Stevens, the court service wouldn't know where he is. They wouldn't have been able to serve the papers yet. Here, I'll call them."

"I can't believe he filed those papers." Pris fidgeted in the chair, while Kathy O'Connor hurriedly dialed the attorney's court service.

"This is Mr. Wahl's office. I want you to hold off on serving the Stevens dissolution papers."
     ***

"You did?" said Cathy.
     ***

"I see."
     ***

"How did you manage that?"
     ***

"I see."
     ***

"No, it isn't all right. Not all right at all."
     ***

"Well, normally it would be a good job, but not this time."

***

"When did it happen?"

***

"All right. Good-bye."

Pris had been frantically pacing up and down during the conversation. Kathy hung up the phone.

"I'm very sorry, Mrs. Stevens. Your husband was served with papers this morning. Unfortunately, our process server was too efficient for his own good."

"Where was he? Where was my husband? My God, you've destroyed my marriage!"

"In Sonoma. At his mother's. They found out he was at some funeral yesterday and was at his mother's."

"A phone. Where's there a telephone I can use?"

Kathy ushered Pris into Wahl's empty office and left her alone with his telephone.

Pris found Amanda's number in her address book and frantically dialed. A woman speaking an oriental language answered the phone. Pris had misdialed. She slammed down the phone and dialed again. This time Amanda answered.

"Mrs. Stevens. This is Priscilla."

"Priscilla, how are you, dear?"

"I'm fine, thank you. Please, is Mark there? I've got to talk to him. It's urgent."

She held the phone, waiting for Mark.

"Hello, Pris?"

"Mark, they just told me they had made a mistake, and served you with divorce papers."

"You're damned right. I just read them. Pris, you're asking for the moon. Your attorney must be some egomaniac."

"I'm sorry. It's all been a mistake. I only meant to ask him a few questions, and I ended up signing everything in blank. He told me he wouldn't use the papers without my okay. Oh, Mark, I'm so sorry."

"Jesus, Pris, what am I supposed to think? I knew you were unhappy, and now these papers."

"I don't want a divorce. Not at all. I just didn't know what to do, so I saw the lawyer."

"But these goddammed papers. They're so ridiculous."

"Mark, please believe me, when I say I'm sorry. I should have discussed things with you first, but I've been so upset. I've learned so much about myself lately. I'd like to try again, if you would be willing."

"Try again? Pris do you have any idea what he asks for in these papers?"

"I'm sorry, Mark. I haven't read them. They weren't supposed to be filed. I'll tell him to cancel them."

"Good Lord, Pris!"

"Honey, please won't you accept my apology? I didn't mean for them to go ahead like that. You've got to believe me."

It had been years since Pris had called him 'Honey'. Mark was beginning to calm down. "All right. All right. I believe you."

"Mark, I want to try again. I want our marriage to be a good one."

Mark was surprised. This was not like Pris.

"Mark, dear, let's go away someplace, even if it's just for the weekend. What harm could that possibly do?"

"Pris, we both deserve better than we've been together—a lot better."

"I know, I know." She nervously stroked her hair.

They were silent for a moment.

"Mark, I have an idea."

"What?" He was skeptical. His better judgment told him it was probably best if she just went ahead with the divorce. After all, only a few hours ago he had been ready to file himself."

"Let's run away. Have a wild time together. Go some place we'd never go."

"A fling?" asked Mark, surprised by her suggestion. Pris was not the type to go on a fling.

"Yes, darling just a fling, like with some woman you met at a bar."

"Picking you up at a bar, eh? I kind of like the idea." Although it was difficult to imagine with Pris, he was intrigued.

"I like the idea, too."

"But where would we go?" he asked.

"I don't know. Someplace fun."

Mark thought for a minute. "How about Puerto Vallarta? I've got a friend with a villa at Puerto Vallarta."

"I'm all for it," she said excitedly. "Do you want to come home and pack?"

"I don't think that would be such a good idea."

"Why not?"

"You don't pick up a lady at a bar, and go to her house to pack."

"You're right about that," she laughed.

"Tell you what."

"What?" she asked.

"I'll send Alex down with the Rolls to get you. I'll meet you at the plane."

"When?"

"He'll be there in an hour and a half."

"Mark?"

"Yes?"

"I'm very excited about our fling."

-51-

Mark's jet was at 32,000 feet headed for Puerto Vallarta. The early evening was bright and clear.

Even though the chances of a reconciliation with Pris were slim, Mark was glad he had taken her up on the fling. Being rejected by Christina hurt badly, and the weekend trip would divert his mind. Besides he owed it to Pris. As soon as the plane had taken off from Oakland, he had poured himself an extra stiff Scotch, and had begun to relax a bit. He had done without Christina for a long time, and he could get on with his life without her.

"Sir, that's Las Vegas to the left," said the pilot on the intercom.

"Look, Pris. Off in the distance." The lights of the Nevada city sparkled in the clear, dark sky.

Pris leaned over Mark, and peered out the window. "Mark," she said excitedly. "Could we have our fling in Las Vegas? That would be a lot more exciting than Mexico."

Mark grinned happily. "Why not? Your wish is my command. Las Vegas it is!" Mark picked up the microphone. "Charlie, the lady has changed her mind. We want to land at Las Vegas."

"Yes, sir, Mr. Stevens. We'll head for Vegas."

Pris hugged Mark's arm. "Thank you, Mark. You have made me very happy."

They could see the signs on big hotels sparkle as the plane came in for its landing.

"I've never been to Las Vegas before. It's very exciting," she exclaimed as the wheels touched the runway.

Ever since Pris had met him at the Oakland airport, Mark had observed a clear difference in her. She was more alive, more vital and especially more attentive to him. He was intrigued by the sudden change. To suggest spontaneously that they go away together was totally unlike Pris—and now Las Vegas. A remarkable change had occurred.

Mark rented a limousine at McCarran Airport, and directed the driver to the strip. "What would you like to do first?" he asked Pris.

"I've always wanted to see one of the those big gambling casinos." Again, she took him by the arm. "I've always wondered what it would be like to gamble." The lights of the nearby strip hotels glistened in the clear desert air.

"Driver, drive down the strip. We'll tell you where to stop."

"Yes, sir."

Pris was very excited as they turned onto Las Vegas Boulevard at the Tropicana Hotel. The thousands of lights made the busy street as bright as daytime.

Just look at those signs," Pris exclaimed, referring to the gigantic, lighted hotel signs announcing their entertainment.

"Look, there's Caesar's Palace," Mark said. He had been to Las Vegas three or four times before, for meetings, but he was seeing it anew through Pris's enthusiastic eyes.

"It's spectacular," Pris said. "Can we stop there?"

"Driver, let us out at Caesar's. The lady wants to try her luck."

They piled out of the limousine. "Welcome to Caesar's Palace, and good luck to you," said the grandly uniformed doorman as he opened the car door for them.

"Wait here, driver," Mark ordered as he and Pris entered the opulent hotel.

Slowed by the crowd, they found their way past the banks of slot machines, with their players so intent.

"Good Lord, look at all the gambling tables," exclaimed Pris. Though the night had barely begun, Caesar's Palace's vast circular casino was already crowded. Only a few of the gaming tables were empty.

"Do you know how to gamble?" Pris asked him.

"A little. Shall we give it a try?"

"Yes, if you'll tell me what to do."

They found an empty blackjack table. "You try to get as close to 21 as you can. Here, I'll bet five bucks to start. You can watch me."

"Good luck, sir," said the dealer.

He dealt Mark's cards. "You see, I have a queen and a five. I have to decide whether or not to take a hit. If he deals me a six or less, I'm all right, but if it's a seven or more, I'm over 21, and I lose. So I'll probably stay."

"Oh come on, Mark. Be a sport—draw a card."

"Okay, give me a card."

The dealer dealt Mark another card, face up. It was a four of hearts.

"There, that gives me 19. We'll stay with that."

The dealer turned his original two cards over. "He's got a jack and a six," Mark explained. "That's 16."

"You've got that beat, don't you?"

"Yes, but the dealer will draw another card. He could still get a 20 or a 21 and win."

The dealer drew another card—a face card.

"So, what does that mean?" asked Pris.

"It means he's broke. He's over 21 and I win."

"You mean you made five dollars, just like that?"

"Just like that." Mark snapped his fingers.

"I like Las Vegas already. I want to play now." Mark could not remember seeing Pris so happy. He gave her a five dollar chip, which she put on the table. The dealer smiled slightly at Pris's enthusiasm, as he dealt their cards.

She was dealt an ace and a king. "What does this mean, Honey?"

"It's a blackjack. You stand to win an extra $2.50."

"You mean I win $7.50 for drawing a blackjack?" She excitedly grabbed Mark by the arm as the dealer handed her winnings to her. Mark grinned. He was having fun just being with her.

Pris won five straight hands before her luck turned. Then, time after time, she took chancy hits. Each hit put her over 21, and soon she had lost her winnings.

"Could I bet some more money?"

"Sure." Mark gave the dealer a hundred dollar bill for more chips.

Again, Pris started out winning. But, as before, her luck soon turned, and she ran through the $100.

"I don't like this game any more." Good-naturedly, Pris pretended to pout.

"Maybe you take a few too many chances."

"It's about time Priscilla Stevens took a few chances!"

"Let's try a different table," he suggested.

"No, let's try a different game. Isn't that a crap table over there? Let's try that."

Mark tipped the dealer, and they went to the crap table. It was crowded, so they stood at the edge of the gamblers while Mark explained the action. When the players had placed their bets, the croupier passed the dice to a gambler in shirt sleeves at the end of the table. "The man with the dice is trying to throw a seven the first time out," Mark explained. The thrower stuffed his cigar in his mouth, and tossed the dice across the table.

"Six," announced the croupier. He held the dice with his stick while the players began placing various bets.

"There are a million ways to bet," said Mark, "but basically the thrower keeps trying for his point, a six. If he gets it, he wins; but if he throws a seven before he gets his six, he loses."

"I thought a seven was good."

"Not unless you throw it the very first time out."

They stood watching until the man finally crapped out and it was the next player's turn with the dice.

"I want to try it. Can I?" asked Pris enthusiastically.

"Sure, let's find a table with a place open."

They found a place at the next table. "Here, you do the betting," suggested Mark, handing her his left-over chips. "I'll coach you."

"Would you care for drinks, sir?" asked the cocktail waitress, who was dressed in a short Roman garment.

"Sure. A gin and tonic for the lady, and I'll have a Rob Roy."

Tentatively, Pris placed various bets at Mark's suggestion. But after several throws of the dice, she became more confident. He bought her a small stack of chips, and watched with amusement as she played. The change in her tonight was remarkable, he thought.

She won a little more than she lost. When it was her turn with the dice, she put down three chips and took the dice. "Come on," she said, tossing them against the inside of the table.

"Seven," said the croupier in his monotone.

Pris jumped up and down excitedly. "I've won! I've won!" The attendant standing across from her pushed over her winnings.

She left the winnings and her original bet on the table, hoping to double it all. Mark was tempted to caution her that, as before, Lady Luck might desert her at any moment.

When the others had placed their bets, the croupier raked the dice to Pris. To Mark's amazement, she added four more chips, making her total bet $50.

"Coming out," cried the croupier.

"Come on, you little sweethearts, do it again for your Priscilla," she cried, flinging the dice across the table with the air of a professional gambler.

"Six," said the croupier. "The point is six."

"Nuts!" exclaimed Pris. "Now what do I do? I've got to throw a six, right?"

Mark could barely keep himself from laughing at her enthusiasm. "Right, but rolling a six isn't so tough."

"Can I up my bet?"

"Up your bet?"

"Yes. I feel lucky."

"Sure you can, if you want."

Pris tossed down nearly all her remaining chips. "Mark, I love this. It's more fun than I've had in years."

She shook the dice and threw them.

"Eight," said the croupier.

"What do I do now? I just keep throwing them, right?"

"Right."

Pris threw the dice four more times without getting her six, but avoiding the fateful seven.

"Seven," droned the croupier after her next toss.

Several players moaned at the loss. The attendant took away Pris's chips. "Damn!" she said, fingering the rest of her chips.

As the dice were being readied for the next player, Pris put all her remaining chips on the pass line.

"Going for broke, are you?" asked Mark.

"Might as well."

With three tosses by the thrower, Pris had lost her stake, "I don't like this game any more," she said disgustedly.

"Come on, Pris. What do you say we try another hotel? Maybe that will change your luck."

Pris gathered her purse. "That's a very good idea. I'd rather blame it on the hotel than on me."

"Spoken like a true gambler."

As they left Caesar's Palace, their waiting limousine pulled up and the Caesar's doorman opened the car door.

"Look," Pris said excitedly. "There's the MGM Grand Hotel over there." She pointed across the corner to the gargantuan sign announcing singer Mac Davis and the upcoming attractions.

"Yes. It was almost ready to open when I was here for that banker's convention."

"Can we go over there?"

"Of course we can. We could walk if we want. They have this moving sidewalk." Mark pointed to the covered moving walk that went to the street corner.

"No, let's arrive in style in the limo."

Pris plunked herself down in the back seat of the car, and Mark joined her as the limousine pulled away.

"I like Las Vegas," she enthused. "Could we come here more often? That is, whenever you're in town, sailor."

Mark laughed. "What on earth has happened to you, Pris?"

"Nothing," she said impishly. "I'm on a fling with my handsome husband."

"Well, I like it, whatever it is." Spontaneously, he kissed her. "This is fun isn't it?"

Pris looked at him attentively. "Yes, darling, it's more fun than I've had in a long time."

The limousine driver opened the door for them, and they stood under the magnificent Grand Portal of the MGM Grand Hotel. "My God, Mark, what a beautiful place! Let's stay here tonight."

"That's a good idea. Looks to me like it would be a good place for a fling. Driver, have our luggage sent in. We're staying."

"Yes, sir."

"You're fortunate, Mr. Stevens. There's a computer convention in town, but we have a couple of cancellations," said the desk clerk. He placed a hotel key in front of Mark. "Room 345, sir. Will that be all right?"

"Mark, can we have a room higher up? I'd like to see the view."

"Yes, Ma'am. We have one on the 19th floor. Room 1916. Would that be all right?"

"Perfect," said Mark, taking the key and returning the first one.

"Can I see the key?" Pris asked.

Mark handed her the key as he filled out the room registration form.

Pris fingered the key. "Look Mark, it has a fancy lion on it— the MGM lion. We're going to have a wonderful time, I just know it."

The bellman took their luggage and led them to the bank of elevators. They got off on the 19th. The hallways leading to room 1916 were lined with enlarged photographs of old-time Metro Goldwyn Mayer movie stars. Periodically placed along the halls were attractive pillars that, together with the rich carpeting and fancy ceilings, gave the hotel a feeling of grand elegance.

"Thank you sir," said the bellman as Mark tipped him. Before leaving, he arranged their bags at the foot of each bed, and explained the air conditioning controls.

"I'd like to put on a dress and freshen up before we try the crap tables," said Pris.

"Good idea." Mark kicked off his shoes and lay back on one of the double beds as he watched Pris get ready for her bath. When she went into the bathroom, he rubbed his eyes soothingly. What an amazing two days this had been, he thought. Yesterday morning he had flown from London for Antonio's funeral, and had spent the night with Christina. Today, Christina had exploded his dream, and he had been served with divorce papers. Who would have ever thought that now he would be in a Las Vegas hotel room with his wife, of all people? He needed a chance to catch his breath.

·   ·   ·

When Pris had finished her bath, Mark took the bathroom for his shower. Each carefully avoided appearing naked in front of the other. When he came out from his bath, she was wearing a beautiful new black dress that contrasted with her red hair. It had a low-cut bodice and a skirt cut sightly above the knee. She wore very dark hosiery. Shoes off, she stood in front of the mirror, putting on long diamond earrings that he did not remember seeing before. Pris was a very attractive woman, especially when she dressed in something a little more daring.

"My, you look very beautiful," he complimented.

"Thank you, Mr. Stevens. I thought this would be a good dress for our fling."

Mark smiled. It was fun having her talk about their fling. "Do you want to have dinner before you hit the crap tables?" he asked.

"Oh, I don't know. I'm pretty anxious to get even."

"We could go to a show later. We could see Mac Davis."

"Yes, or Ann-Margret at Caesar's. I've always wanted to see Ann-Margret."

"Well let's decide that later, after you've broken the bank."

"It must be as long as a football field," Pris said incredulously, as they entered the vast casino at the MGM Grand.

Mark took her by the hand through the crowds of intense gamblers and onlookers toward the cashiers. In a city known for superlatives, the casino was the largest, with its numerous tables and endless slot machines.

At the cashier's window, Mark bought a stack of five dollar chips. He realized he had less than $2,000 in his wallet. Because of Pris's happy mood, he, too, was ready to try his luck in a bigger way.

"I'd like to arrange a line of credit," he asked the woman who waited on him.

"How much would you like, sir?"

"Oh, I don't know . . ." Mark hesitated. He felt in a rare mood. Maybe whatever had happened to Pris was contagious. "Would $100,000 be all right?" He certainly did not plan to gamble $100,000, but it gave him a good feeling to know that he could go that high, if he wanted.

"One moment, sir, I'll call the manager."

"Here, Pris, take these chips and find a place for us at a table while I see the manager."

"Mark, we don't need to bet that much."

"It's all right, Pris. It won't hurt to have our credit established."

Taking the chips, Pris disappeared into the crowded casino.

The tuxedo-dressed manager took Mark to his small office. Mark identified himself as owner of The Stevens Group, and gave the names of two of his banks.

"Would it be all right, sir, if we limited your line to $10,000 for now? It takes a bit of time to check out our new customers for the higher amount."

"Certainly, I don't blame you a bit. After all, you've never heard of me."

"Oh, I recognize who you are, Mr. Stevens. If you had been able to give us notice, we would have arranged a suite for you. Perhaps next time."

"Of course."

"I'm sure the credit approval will be a matter of routine."

Escorted by the manager, Mark found Pris already betting at a crap table. Twisting his body to get next to the crowded table, Mark took his position next to her. "Okay, my dear, in a little while we're going to own a piece of this hotel." Until now, Mark had gambled very little. He had preferred the more favorable odds of currency speculation and corporate takeovers, but tonight his mood was different. He wanted to have fun, matching wits with the hotel. He knew the odds always favored the house, but he was caught up in Pris's idea of a fling. Why not? he thought. What was a few thousand dollars?

A tall, well-dressed blonde at the other end of the table was the thrower. Happily, Pris squeezed Mark's arm while they each put down $1,000 on various bets.

Consistently, Mark placed his bets "behind the line," where the house got as poor odds as possible. Pris, on the other hand, craved more action. When the croupier raked the dice to her, everyone at the table reflected her enthusiasm by placing their bets with her. "Go, baby, go!" a gambler at the end of the table shouted.

Just then the credit manager approached Mark. "Your credit has been approved, Mr. Stevens. Good luck." He then whispered to the pit boss, who nodded his understanding. With that, Mark felt more venturesome.

"Give me 10,000," Mark asked the attendant, who looked to the pit boss for permission. Mark signed his marker as the chips were handed to him.

"Let's each bet $2,000," he said to Pris. The pit boss nodded, indicating the limit had been raised for them.

"Coming out," said the croupier.

Immediately, Pris threw a seven. The bettors, all of whom had won, cheered and began placing their money on the pass line for her next roll. Mark took his winnings, leaving only the original

$2,000; but seeing Pris letting it all ride, he put his own chips back. Together they were betting $8,000.

"Coming out," repeated the croupier

"Come on, you little babies!" cried Pris, throwing the dice against the table. It was another seven, a one and a six.

"Seven," said the croupier. The group cheered again, and the personnel began paying off the bets. More people joined the crowd at the table.

Enthusiastically, everyone placed new bets. Again both Pris and Mark let it all ride. This time the total was $16,000. It seemed to take forever until all of the betting around the table was finally completed, and the dice had been returned to her. They looked at each other and smiled nervously.

"How do you like the MGM Grand?" he laughed.

"So far, it's just fine," she answered, and shook the dice.

This time she threw a four.

The crowd groaned. "Four is a difficult point to make," Mark said. The croupier held the dice with his stick, waiting for more bets to be placed.

"I'm with you all the way," cried the man at the end of the table, putting a sizable additional bet on four.

"Here we go!" exclaimed Pris, and tossed the dice. It was a six.

She threw several more times, not getting her four, and yet not crapping out with a seven. No more bets were being placed. Everyone was intently watching and, for the moment, not interested in more bets.

Then she did it.

With one more fling of the dice, she made her four.

"A four," said the croupier, departing slightly from his monotone. The crowd went wild.

"Whoopee!" shouted Pris, nearly leaving her feet. She turned to Mark, and they hugged one another. "Oh, my God, we're rich!" she cried, not caring that the money they had won was less than one one-thousandth of one percent of their net worth. Several people gathered around, excitedly extending congratulations

"They're still your dice, Ma'am," said the croupier, when the table had quieted down.

"Don't tell me I have to roll again!" she complained. "I want to celebrate with my husband."

"You'd better do it, Pris," cautioned Mark. "It's bad luck to quit when they're your dice."

"All right. All right. But I'll only bet one chip." Smiling, Pris gathered all her winnings close to her, and put down a five dollar chip. It took her less than a minute to lose. Her point was a six, and she quickly threw a seven for craps.

"I don't want to cash them in yet," said Pris, gathering up her chips. "I just want to hold them in my hands for a while."

"Why don't we have a drink to celebrate?" Mark asked.

"Better yet, let's have dinner. I'm famished."

Mark put the chips that Pris could not hold in his pockets, and they walked toward the restaurant area. He looked at his watch. "It's too late to go to a dinner show."

"What are you in the mood to eat?" Pris asked. They walked past the deli, and Pris, holding her chips, began reading the menus of the various restaurants: Barrymore's, Caruso's and the Orleans Room.

"I don't care. You're the one who's so hungry. You choose."

Pris decided on the elegant Caruso's. They sat next to one another at a corner booth. Pris arranged their chips, and began counting as they were served cocktails.

"Thirty-two thousand dollars," she exclaimed, when she finished counting.

"Here's to the richest woman in Vegas." Mark raised his glass in a toast.

"And here's to the most handsome man." She squeezed his hand under the table.

"Pris, may I say something?"

"What?" she smiled.

"I've never seen you like you've been tonight. I like it."

"And I like it, too." She looked serious for a moment. "Mark?"

"Yes, Pris?"

"Please help me to stay this way."

Indeed, Mark thought, he hoped she would stay that way. She was far more genuine than he had ever seen her. It occurred to him that perhaps getting a divorce was not inevitable after all.

-52-

"The lady will have the chocolate mousse and, let's see—I'll have a strawberry tart," Mark told the waiter at Caruso's restaurant. He and Pris had laughed and talked endlessly about her winning streak. They were having the time of their lives, and planned to return to the gambling tables after dinner.

"When the waiter comes back with the dessert, would you like a Black Russian?" Mark asked.

"No, I think I've had about enough to drink. A Black Russian might wipe me out."

"Want to be sharp for the crap table, eh?"

"No, that's not it. Actually I feel quite mellow." She slid comfortably back in the booth. In stretching she bumped her leg against Mark. "I'm just happy to be here with you. I'm enjoying our fling."

"Me, too." Impulsively, Mark put his hand on her knee under the table. It had been a very long time since he felt romantic towards her.

"Mmmm, I like that," she said.

Mark laughed. "Perhaps you'll like this even better." He ran his fingers under her dress to the top of her leg.

"You're right about that, sailor. I do like it even better."

When the waiter came with the desserts, Mark did not remove his hand. "Chocolate mousse for the lady," the waiter said, putting the mousse before Pris. "And the tart for the gentleman."

"Thank you," said Mark.

Pris smiled as the waiter left. "You should have told him you already have a tart, and that tart is me." She laughed and leaned forward, running her own hand up Mark's leg. With that, he was aroused.

"Pris?"

"Yes?"

"Do you really want dessert?"

"Yes, I really want dessert, but this isn't the dessert I want."

Mark hurriedly signed the bill as Pris waited for him by the door.

Pris held Mark's arm tightly as they exited the elevator on the 19th floor. They followed the several turns of the hallway to their room. As he searched his pockets for the key, Pris noticed the large photograph on the nearby wall. "Look, sweetheart, it's Spencer Tracy. Do you think he's wondering what we're up to?"

"Oh, I think Spencer would approve, all right."

As he closed the door to their room and unzipped the back of Pris's dress, he was reminded of the first time they had made love. He had wanted her very badly that night, as he did now. She stepped out of the dress, and stood before him as he sat on the bed. He felt a brief twinge of apprehension. He hoped she did not take this as a sign that everything was all right between them. Their marriage had been too unhappy these past years for one night to change everything.

"Let me help you, darling." Pris unbuttoned his shirt as he took off his tie.

With her back to him, he undid her bra, putting his hands on her breasts and kissing the back of her neck. She turned and opened his belt. His desire for her mounted. She undid his trousers and pulled down his zipper. Their whole married life had been burdened by her hang-ups about sex, but tonight she was so different.

"My, but you're ready," said Pris putting her hand on the bulge in his briefs.

"It's all your fault," he whispered.

Mark felt strange making love. Pris was like some other woman, the impulsive woman wanting to land at Las Vegas, the Pris at the crap table, doubling her bets on her wild winning streak.

He was surprised when he felt her moving, as if to have an orgasm. When it happened, it was gentle and she made no sound.

When both had finished, she looked up at him. "Mark, I came. Did you realize I came?"

"I thought you had."

"It was my first time."

"I know, baby. I know."

"You were so quiet," he said, as they lay naked facing one another.

"I was embarrassed," she giggled. "I didn't know how to behave."

He kissed her gently. "Don't be embarrassed. I'm happy for you." He was happy for himself, too. Now he could be through with his old false rationalization that it did not matter to him.

"Have you had enough gambling for one night?" he asked.

"Yes, I'm tired."

"Me, too."

"It's been quite a day."

"Yes, quite a day." He pulled the covers over them and they each turned to go to sleep.

"Mark?"

"Yes?"

"I'm sorry about the divorce papers. I didn't mean for it to happen."

"I know."

They were silent for a while.

"Mark?"

"Yes?"

"I love you."

Mark knew if he thought about it too long, he might not be able to give her the answer she wanted. "I love you, too, Pris."

"Good night."

"Good night."

He was exhausted. He had been on an emotional roller coaster and wanted to sleep the clock around. In a short time he could tell from her breathing that she was asleep.

He lay there for over an hour, thinking. Last night he thought he could never live without Christina, but now he felt love for Pris. It did not seem possible that he could love two women on the very same day.

He turned over in bed again and again. He realized something very important. His feelings of love, his feelings of passion, belonged to him. The deep emotions he had so long reserved for Christina were his own. Christina could not take his ability to love away from him, even though it had always seemed that way.

He need not have hesitated in telling Pris he loved her. The truth was he really did love her. It was Christina who had told him a long time ago that a man could love more than one woman. Tonight, he realized he could choose which love he wanted to follow, which woman he wanted to make part of his life.

Finally, he gave up trying to sleep. He was careful not to wake Pris as he got up. Pris had thoughtfully packed leisure clothes for him. He put on a pair of slacks and a casual shirt, and quietly slipped from the room.

.   .   .

It was after three in the morning, and the action in the casino was relatively quiet. He watched the gamblers at the crap table. Idly, he tried the door to the Ziegfeld Theater, off the casino. *Jubilee*, the new spectacular replacing *Hallelujah Hollywood*, had finished its final rehearsal and would open shortly. Two lighting technicians had lingered after the rehearsal, and were tinkering with the lighting arrangements in the big showroom. Still thinking about today's events, Mark took a seat in one of the back booths, listening to the technicians chatter. Perhaps he should bring Pris to Las Vegas over the holidays. She enjoyed herself so much—but that smacked of commitment, and he was not ready for that.

He still was not sleepy. It was 3:30, and the entertainment in the Club Bar had wrapped up. A few late-night gamblers were taking a break in the deli. He decided to eat something. Maybe that would help him sleep. He ordered a plate of lox and scrambled eggs. When he was finished, he felt more relaxed, and decided to return to the room. Maybe at last he could sleep.

Unbeknownst to anyone, serious trouble was present. In the deli, where Mark was eating, an electrical short had occurred. Defective electrical wires had made unseen, dangerous contact. The condition could lead to live sparks, and even worse.

Pris stirred as he got back into bed. He lightly kissed her back through her nightgown, and soon was fast asleep.

Mark's first thought upon awakening was to glance at the clock. It was a little after 7:30 in the morning. He was still tired, and was surprised he had awakened so early. Then he felt Pris running her hand over his shoulder.

"Honey," she said. "I'm very happy to be here with you."

He turned over with a mild groan of protest, and put his arm around her. "Me, too," he muttered.

"I'm sorry. I shouldn't have disturbed you."

"That's all right. There's lots of time to sleep."

"Last night was very special for me."

"I know."

"It was my first time . . ."

"Yes. I know, sweetheart."

"I'm sorry I never did before."

"That's all right, Pris. It never bothered me. You shouldn't let it get to you."

"Well, it did." She slid her hand under him.

Aroused by her, he was no longer tired. She kept her hand on him until he was erect. Silently, he slid her nightgown above her hips, and kissed her patch of pubic hair. He began making love to her with his tongue. They had had oral sex only that one time before they were married, but now she was eager and responsive. To his surprise, he felt the same emotions of unity and oneness as he had with Christina. After a short time, he realized she was nearing a climax again.

"Oh, my God, Mark, it's happening."

She moaned and shuddered several times as she came. Then they both lay still catching their breath.

"Look what I've been missing all these years," she laughed, good-naturedly.

Still lying between her legs, Mark softly put the side of his head on her stomach. They rested for a minute or two more, reveling in their emotions.

Suddenly, the flames burst through the ceiling in front of the deli, chasing back the newly arrived firemen. The ball of fire raced from the restaurant area to the casino. The inferno quickly raged the length of the 400-foot casino, destroying everything in its path—slot machines, plastic furniture, gaming tables, as well as human beings running to get away.

The ball of heat and flames burst through the hotel's front door and incinerated an automobile parked under the Grand Portal, where Pris and Mark had arrived in their limousine. Huge amounts of poisonous smoke were immediately formed by the combustion of the tons of plastic material in the casino. The super-heated smoke sought a way to rise, and poured into the elevators and air conditioning system. The smoke quickly shot up the elevator shafts and air conditioning vents to the upper floors of the hotel, before settling back down again in an ever-thickening nightmare.

"Mark?"

"Yes?"

"I'd like to 'do' you now."

"Are you sure, baby? You don't have to. I did that because I wanted to."

"No. It's all right. I want to. I really want to."

He turned over onto his back while she sat upright for a moment stroking his erection. My God, she was beautiful, he thought. It was amazing. Yesterday he had been angry as hell when she had served him with divorce papers and today—well, today, he loved her.

Pris began to lower her head, when they heard the loud knocking on the door and the shouting:

"FIRE!!! FIRE!!! THE HOTEL IS ON FIRE!!!"

-53-

"What the hell is that?" Mark exclaimed.

"I don't know," said Pris. "Something about fire."

"Stupid jerks! Don't they know it's dangerous to go around yelling fire?" Mark quickly put on his robe and went to the door.

"Careful, Honey, she warned. "They're probably drunk."

Mark opened the door and looked into the hallway. There was smoke coming from the direction of the elevators. "What the hell is going on?"

Running down the hall was a hotel waiter, knocking on doors and shouting "FIRE!" All the while, the waiter was unthinkingly being careful not to spill the breakfast tray he was holding above his head. "It's fire, sir!" the waiter shouted back. "The hotel is on fire!"

Mark ducked back into the room. "Pris, it's for real! The whole damned place is on fire. We've got to get the hell out of here."

"My God, Mark, are we going to die?"

"No, we're not going to die." Mark started putting on the clothes he had tossed on the chair last night. "Get some clothes on!" he cried. "Quick, Pris! Quick! Your clothes!"

Jolted into action, Pris got up and raced to the closet for her clothes. "I'm frightened Mark! I'm frightened. What's going to happen to us?"

Mark hurriedly put on his shoes, and opened the drapes. He looked down on the roofs of two big MGM Grand showrooms. He could see no sign of flame, but a huge amount of smoke was escaping from the Grand Portal and partially obscuring the addition under construction across the way.

To his left, he could see smoke gathering around another wing of the hotel. A naked man and woman appeared briefly on an upper floor balcony, and quickly disappeared.

"We'll be all right," Mark assured Pris, "but we must keep our heads. We've got to keep calm. We've got to think."

Pris had put on slacks and a blouse, but was scurrying to find her flat shoes. She found them in the suitcase, and quickly put them on. "Look, Mark, there's smoke coming through the air conditioning vent."

"Yeah, around the door, too. Pris! The bathroom! Soak the towels in the bathroom! Quickly!" he commanded. He put his hand on the hall door to be sure it was not hot. He peered down the hallway. He could not see very far to his right because of the jog in the hallway. The smoke was thicker in that direction, but he could make out the exit sign. He raced to the window again. There would be no way they could get down the 19 stories without being killed. He struggled to open the window to get fresh air, but it was shut tight. The thing to do was to break the window. Heavier smoke was coming into the room now. He knew it would kill them unless he broke the window. His mind raced, trying to think logically. Maybe they should make a break for the stairs instead. No, he decided, the stairs might be engulfed in flames.

Pris came with the dripping towels. "What should I do with these?"

"Stuff them around the door while I smash this window."

Furiously, Pris rolled up one of the wet towels and stuffed it along the bottom of the door, but the smoke was seeping around the top of the door. She reached up as far as she could with the other towel, but it was no use. It mattered little anyway, because more smoke was coming through the air conditioning vent. Then, both began coughing.

Mark had grabbed the lamp to smash it against the window, but it was bolted to the table. He tried to lift the whole table, but it was too bulky and heavy. He grabbed at the hotel radio, but it was also bolted to the table. He pawed at the television. Again, it was bolted down.

"We'd better make a run for it! Take that towel. You can use it as a mask." He grabbed the other towel, felt the door again, and carefully opened it.

The smoke in the hallway was thicker. The flames must be getting closer, he thought. A man and woman were coughing as they groped through the smoke. Mark took Pris by the hand and tried to make his voice reassuring. "Come on, Pris, we'll make it. Come on, sweetheart."

Pris held her towel to her mouth and nervously followed her husband. The photograph of Spencer Tracy was still visible through the smoke. In a few steps they came to the large mirror at the jog in the hallway. Not realizing it was a mirror, at first Mark thought their reflection was another couple. In the mirror he saw the terror of a cornered animal in Pris's eyes. The smoke down the hall behind them was thickening, and people were sticking their heads out from doors.

"Keep your head down." They fumbled their way along the hallway, struggling to keep their eyes open in the stinging smoke. "I think the fire stairs are right around the corner."

Crouching, they felt along the walls. He touched one of those fancy pillars on his left, and then spotted the emergency exit. Two other couples were close behind and followed them into the stairwell. The smoke was better here. They started down the stairs as fast as they could move.

On the 20th floor, five people rushed for the elevators. The cables had melted and the elevators never came. It mattered little, however. The elevators would have taken them to certain death on the ground floor. The five inhaled too much of the deadly smoke, and would be dead in a short time.

Mark, Pris and the others from the 19th floor saw little smoke as they made their way down two, then three, then four floors. Surely they were going to make it, Mark thought. At each floor they were joined by others who had decided to make a run for it, and at each floor the smoke got worse.

At the foot of the next flight, Mark could see the body of a woman in her nightgown, lying on the landing, propped against the bottom step. A weeping man was bent over her. "I think my wife is dead," the man told Mark. "Next year we would have been married 20 years."

Mark was filled with dismay. The smoke in the stairwell did not seem thick enough to kill someone. Realizing the danger, he slowed down letting those behind push on by. They all began coughing and holding their fists to their mouths. Suddenly ahead a few more steps, he could see through the smoke what looked like half a dozen bodies.

The iron workers, who had watched with horror from their construction jobs on the hotel addition, rushed to help the victims. One picked up a woman who was lying in a hallway and carried her down the far staircase. Partway down, he realized she was dead. Another was more successful. He carried one victim and led several others to safety down a fire stair. It was a different stairwell from where Mark and Pris were struggling with smoke.

Mark could tell that Pris was light-headed from the carbon monoxide. "Come on, Pris. We've got to go back up. It's sure death to go down any more."

She turned to do as he asked. "I can't, Mark! I can't! I'm so tired."

"You listen to me, Priscilla Stevens! I love you. We're going to get out of here alive. Do you understand me?"

"Yes, Mark, I understand." But her eyes glazed over and she collapsed into his arms.

On another floor a desperate hotel guest had tied several bed sheets together and was lowering himself, but when he reached the second sheet, it let go under his weight. As he fell, his body caromed off a balcony railing. His wife, who had been watching the desperate attempt, turned back in anguish, her hands covering her eyes. Even if the bed sheets had held together, the man would have been left dangling hundreds of feet in the air.

Mark picked up Pris in his arms, and began the long ascent up the gray stairwell. He thought they had come down about five floors, and he had no idea how much higher the hotel went past the 19th. He knew their only hope was to get to the roof—they must get to the roof.

He wrapped his towel around his lower face. As he carried Pris, he replaced her towel whenever it slipped off. He did not know whether she was alive or dead, but he was determined they both would get upstairs to the roof. He tried the door leading from the stairway to the hallway. It was locked. All the doors were locked tight. There was no chance to do anything but climb. He must climb as far as he could force his body to go.

A young man, holding a handkerchief over his mouth and nose, and climbing upward, caught and passed them.

Mark had climbed up two or three floors when Pris's towel slipped off. My God, there was an ugly black fluid draining from her nose and the edges of her mouth!

Mark began to cry. Two, then three great sobs, followed by tears.

He put Pris down on the landing, and gently wiped away the black matter. He thought of the man downstairs, who would have been married 20 years. The man was lucky. It looked as if Pris and he would never get close to that. "I'm sorry, Pris," he sobbed. "I'm sorry for the times I didn't love you."

He felt himself getting light-headed, and put his head down as low as he could. He looked up the stairs and saw that the young man who had passed him had collapsed. He must not panic. He must not panic, even though he knew it was likely that he would die in this Godforsaken place.

Downstairs, the fire department was frantically training water on the elevator shafts, trying to keep them cool so as to keep the flames themselves from spreading into the hotel towers.

The clouds of smoke still enveloped the upper floors of the hotel as the first helicopters arrived. They had no way to get close enough to rescue the victims, who were waving frantically at them from windows and balconies. The helicopter pilots were forced to confine themselves to lowering people from the roof.

Suddenly, a group of giant military helicopters arrived. These 'copters, which had been engaged in a nearby Army training mission, were equipped with special rescue chairs and winches that enabled them to commence rescue operations as they hovered dangerously close to the structure, their blades beating the smoky air.

Tears for Pris streaming down his face, Mark realized that to stay on the landing would mean death. Whether Pris was dead or not, he would not leave her. Despite the smoke and his giddiness, he wrenched himself to his feet and picked her up. He made it up two more floors before he collapsed. He lost consciousness and tumbled on top of Pris.

They were four steps short of the 19th floor, where they had started a lifetime ago.

The two firemen, equipped with oxygen, came down the emergency stairway from the roof.

"Look, there. Just below the landing. Two of them."

"Yeah, the poor devils. They're probably gone."

One fireman turned Mark's body, so that it was off Pris. He took the towel from Mark's face and held out his hand for signs of breath. Then he felt for a pulse. "This one's still alive. He's lucky."

"Not the woman, I'm afraid. She's dead."

Part Seven

-54-

Henry Enfield's butler handed him the Saturday morning *San Francisco Chronicle*, as he sat down to his English breakfast. The morning fog obscured his view of the Bay. He noticed the headline:

PROMINENT SAN FRANCISCAN KILLED IN HOTEL FIRE

Henry had seen the tragic Las Vegas MGM Grand fire on the television news last night, but nothing had been said about a San Francisco resident. He wondered who it was. If he were 'prominent' as the newspaper said, Henry probably knew him.

Civic Leader perishes with over 80 others in tragic Las Vegas Fire. Husband missing.

A woman, Henry thought. Who could she be? He reached for his spectacles. Without them, he could read only the headlines. Putting the paper down, he slipped on his glasses and drank his orange juice. He took a piece of sausage with his fork. No matter what the doctor said, his morning sausage was one thing he would never give up. For 60 years he had eaten his first link of sausage before his eggs, his toast or his muffins, and he didn't intend to change because of some doctor.

Priscilla Enfield Stevens, San Francisco civic leader and art expert, died yesterday in the tragic blaze that engulfed the . . .

Henry choked on his sausage. "What?" a voice that seemed to come from someone else shouted. When he recovered from his coughing spell, he picked up the paper from the floor where it had fallen. Stupid bloody newspaper, he thought. They should be more careful about making mistakes like that. Priscilla was in

Beverly Hills. She had left a message canceling Thursday's dinner. She would never go to Las Vegas. Wait a moment, he thought, could she have gone there to file for divorce?

Priscilla Enfield Stevens, San Francisco civic leader and art expert, perished yesterday, he read again, *in the tragic blaze that engulfed the MGM Grand Hotel yesterday killing over 80 victims.*

According to wire services, the body of Mrs. Stevens, the wife of Mark Stevens, prominent San Francisco financier, was identified by the pilot of their private jet. Mark Stevens, who was known to have accompanied his wife to Las Vegas, has not been located, and is feared dead, although Las Vegas authorities said the body count was in a state of confusion . . .

In shock, Henry's mind rebelled against the truth of the awful intrusion. Henry automatically reached for a piece of toast, as if the news were about a remote acquaintance who lived in London. He chewed the tasteless toast, and stared into the cold fog, uncomprehending. Once again, he read the newspaper item. Preposterous, he thought. Priscilla would be at home in Hillsborough. He would telephone her, that is what he would do. Yes, that was the way to end this stupid mistake. As if sleepwalking, he went to the phone and dialed Pris's number.

"This is Henry Enfield," he told Zeldah, Pris's maid. "I'd like to speak to my daughter, please, that is, if she is up and about yet this morning."

"Oh, Mr. Enfield! Haven't they told you yet, sir?" Zeldah was crying.

"Told me what?" he asked, annoyed. "I read some rot in the newspaper about Priscilla's being in Las Vegas. I want to speak to her. Will you please put her on the line? Right now, if you please."

"I'm sorry Mr. Enfield, sir, but she's dead. Someone from Las Vegas called late last night. I told him we hadn't heard from Mr. Stevens. I'm sorry you weren't told, sir."

Without answering, Henry lowered the phone. He sank into his battered red leather chair, putting his hands to his face. One part of him knew very well the news was true, but the main part of Henry Enfield would not accept that his daughter was dead. Numb, his mind returned to many years ago, when his friend Bob Hillard had lost his son in a Lake Tahoe boating accident. He had seen how Hillard had been decimated, and, even then, knew it would be the same for him if Priscilla died before him. The dreaded thought had never since returned to trouble him. But now, at 82, it had happened. Henry Enfield was prepared for his own death, but never for the death of his only child.

.   .   .

Disconsolate, Mark sat alone in the passenger compartment of his company jet. He was returning to Oakland from Las Vegas. The hospital had been in confusion. He had simply ripped off his pulmonary equipment, and walked out. Grimy and still dazed, he had walked all the way to McCarran Airport. Breathing was difficult, but he wanted to get out of Las Vegas as fast as he could.

From the window of the plane Mark stared down at the Sierra Nevada mountains, reflecting on the terrible events of the last 24 hours. He had not yet absorbed what had happened. It was as if he were awakening from a deep sleep. Pris was dead. He was alive. He knew that. But the enormity of what had happened escaped him. The awful struggle in the stairway came to his mind. He had thought they were going to make it. He had been so determined. All his life his strong will had made things happen, but not this time.

As his plane landed, it occurred to Mark. What about Pris's body? What should he do about her? Pris should not be left all alone in Las Vegas.

Derek Harden was seated in his office. It was late Saturday afternoon in London. He did not plan to make his final decision about The Stevens Group takeover until Monday at nine, but his mind was constantly returning to the problem he faced. Finally, he gave up working on other matters, and again went over the familiar Stevens takeover figures. Should he put good money after bad? Even if he paid exorbitant prices for more stock in The Stevens Group, it did not look like he could buy enough to gain control.

Alex, Mark's chauffeur, met Mark's plane at the Oakland Airport, wearing his customary dark suit.

"I'm very sorry, sir. You have my deepest sympathy," said Alex, holding open the door of the Rolls-Royce Phantom. "Is there anything I can do for you? Anything at all?"

"I wish there were, Alex. There's nothing any human can do."

"Where would you like me to drive you, Mr. Stevens?"

"Home, I guess. I don't know where else to go." Mark had shaved and washed on the cramped plane, but he still looked bedraggled, wearing the same smoke-covered clothes.

The big car swiftly pulled away from the plane, whose engines had not yet been shut off. Mark had directed the pilot to return to Las Vegas to see about bringing back Pris's body for burial.

.   .   .

"Stop!" shouted Mark, as Alex steered the limousine through the gate of the Hillsborough mansion. "I want to get out here."

Mark sat on the stone wall near his lake, and looked at the beautiful home he had built with such love and pride. Once it had symbolized everything he had ever wanted in life. It had been all that he had striven for.

He picked up a pebble and flung it to the far edge of the lake, where it splashed. This week had been more than he could bear. It had begun with his compulsion to flee his office for Haight-Asbury. How he dreaded the thought of going back to that office. He recalled his one-night stand with the former flower child. Her name was Diane, wasn't it? He hoped Diane was doing a better job at finding herself than he was. He flung a second pebble into the water.

He stood at the edge of the lake, hands on his sides, and took a deep breath. There had been the emotional roller coaster of finding and losing Christina, and now the agony of the fire. He would never know if Pris and he would have had a chance together, but, looking at their house like this, he already missed her terribly. Pris had been no different in struggling to find her way than he or anyone else, and now she was dead. Her life had ended with a snap of the fingers. Poor poor Pris would never have a chance to find her happiness. Gone, too, were the children they might have had.

"Oh, God Pris!" he said aloud, throwing another stone into the lake as hard as he could. "I tried to save you. I did everything I could." Tears streamed down his face as he sat down again on the wall, feeling totally desolated. The stones had frightened the ducks. Quacking, they left the water and scurried up the slope. Would this time in his life ever pass? he thought. What more could he have done to save her? If she had only had more strength. If only he had gone up the stairs in the first place, instead of down.

Mark returned to the Phantom. "I can't go in the house, Alex. Let's go."

"Yes, sir. I understand." Alex opened the car door for him. "Where would you like me to drive you?"

"I don't know, Alex. I can't stay here. San Francisco, I guess."

It was Saturday evening in Rodney's Knightsbridge flat. He was on the telephone to Mavis, who was at Castle Enfield for the weekend.

"Mother, I just received a call from Mark's secretary in San Francisco. I'm afraid I have terrible news."

"What is it?"

"That horrible hotel fire in Las Vegas?"

"Yes? It was in the newspaper this morning."

"Priscilla and Mark were in it."

"Oh, my God, Rodney, you're not going to tell me they've been killed?"

"No, not both of them. Mark is all right."

"You mean Priscilla is dead?"

"I'm afraid so. They don't have any details yet."

"Little Priscilla dead! It's hard to believe."

"At first, they thought Mark had died too, but his pilot took him to San Francisco. They don't know where he is, but he's alive."

"Thank God for that!"

"Mother, I'm going to San Francisco. Mark will need me. I want to help."

"Of course. Poor Henry! Poor Mark!"

"I'll let you know as soon as I know more. I know how much Mark means to you."

"Yes."

"Well, good-bye. I'll ring you when I can."

"Rodney?"

"Yes?"

"I want to go with you. I'll be ready in an hour. Get me a ticket, too."

Mark had never ceased to be excited at the San Francisco skyline, but today, as downtown came into view, he was very depressed. Would the city ever be the same to him? Nothing much mattered any more.

The Rolls was nearing downtown. He didn't know where he wanted to go. He thought of his office. Good God, no! He did not want to go there. What about his Nob Hill condo? No, not there either. He could try Haight-Ashbury. Where he really wanted to be was London. He wished he were talking with Mavis. Maybe at the *Quo Vadis* restaurant. Mavis would understand. Mavis would have some wise advice. He wished she were here.

"Alex?" Mark had rolled down the chauffeur's divider window.

"Yes, Mr. Stevens."

"I want you to take me to Sonoma. I want to see my mother."

Derek Harden's idea of dressing casually for Saturday afternoon at the office was to wear his Daks sport jacket with an open shirt and a silk scarf around his neck. Whenever Derek worked off hours, he required his secretary and his assistant to work also. His intercom buzzed.

"Mr. Sleeter would like to speak to you, sir," said his secretary. "He says it's very important."

"Very well," replied Derek. "Send him in."

Albert Sleeter, Derek's assistant, was a few years older than Derek. Sleeter's notion of independence from his employer was to wear a bright red sweater and no jacket. He was obviously very excited, but was waiting for his superior to invite him to speak.

"Yes, Albert, what is it?"

"Something of great significance to the Stevens matter has happened, sir."

"All right. What is it?"

"You remember sir, that we have a contact in The Stevens Group's executive offices?"

"Of course I do. She's the secretary to Steven Baumgartner. What's her name?"

"Susan. Susan Waite. She just telephoned me with some very important news."

"Yes, Albert," until now Derek hadn't looked up from his papers. "Well, let's have your news."

"Susan thinks Mark Stevens may be dead."

"May be dead?" Derek's pen fell from his hand. His mouth dropped open. "What on earth do you mean, dead?"

"Did you see the news reports about that hotel fire in Las Vegas?"

"I heard something about it, yes."

"Stevens's wife was killed in the fire. It seems Stevens himself is missing. He may very well be dead."

"Of all the bad luck! Mark Stevens dead!"

"Sir? Bad luck?"

"Weren't you listening the other day when Green asked his stupid question?"

"Yes, sir I believe I was. If I remember, you felt there was no point in taking over the company if Stevens should die."

"Well, I'm glad I got the point across. The whole idea is to get control of Mark Stevens himself."

"But how could you do that sir?"

"First of all I want him to know it's I who has done it."

"Yes, sir. I understood that."

"Second. I would want him to know he would have to be working for me. Don't you see? I could destroy the man if he had to work for me."

"But wouldn't he just resign from the company?

"No, he couldn't resign."

"Couldn't resign? Oh, I see sir. If he resigned, the company's stock would fall. His stock along with yours. He'd lose his whole fortune, wouldn't he?"

"That's not it at all Albert. Legally he can't resign from The Stevens Group—that's the point."

"What you mean, he legally couldn't resign?"

"His contract. He has signed an employment contract with the Stevens Group. Don't you see? For the next five years he's legally bound to continue with the company."

"I didn't know that."

"Well, it's true. I read it in the annual report and checked up on it. Our American lawyers say that if he quit, we could get a court order keeping him out of the financial world. He'd probably be liable to me for millions if he quit and the stock went down."

"My compliments to you, sir. I think I see your plan now."

"There isn't anything in the world that would hurt Mark Stevens more than to have to work for a company I control—unless it would be not to work at all—and, on top of all that, to risk losing his money."

"What would happen if this report is correct sir—that he's been killed?"

"It would be a disaster as far as I'm concerned. An absolute disaster. Ironic, isn't it, Albert?"

"Ironic?"

"Yes. I never thought I'd see the day I would want to see Mark Stevens escape from a hotel fire."

In his Telegraph Hill flat Thomas T. Wahl, noted divorce attorney, had returned home from a day of sailing in San Francisco Bay. He poured a glass of his expensive Scotch and unfolded the morning's *Chronicle*.

PROMINENT SAN FRANCISCAN KILLED IN HOTEL FIRE

He wondered who it could be. Like Henry Enfield this morning, there was a good chance he would know the person.

Priscilla Enfield Stevens, San Francisco civic leader and art expert, died yesterday in the tragic blaze that engulfed the MGM Grand Hotel.

Wahl spilled Scotch over the front of his robe. My God, Priscilla Enfield, he thought. Life always had its surprises. He hastily finished the article, then slowly reread the part about Pris.

What should he do? Wahl wondered. He had lost a fat divorce fee, that was true, but, as executor of her will, he would be in for an executor's commission. That could be a lot more than the divorce fee. What was more, there might be a chance to make one hell of a lot more somehow. As executor, he would be in control of her estate, and that would be a powerful position.

The first thing was to find out whether Mark Stevens had in fact died. If he had, perhaps Wahl could figure out a way to control both estates. Even if Stevens were alive, Wahl thought, he might somehow be able to get control of The Stevens Group. Either way, dead or alive, he knew that somehow, some way, Thomas T. Wahl was going to be a very rich man.

Wahl dialed the telephone number of his private investigator, Tom Maxwell.

"Charlie?"

"Tom? Is that you?" asked the investigator.

"I've got a job for you. That hotel fire in Las Vegas?"

"Yeah?"

"I want you to find out whether a certain person was killed, and let me know right away."

"Okay. Who?"

"Mark Stevens."

Maxwell whistled. "*The* Mark Stevens?"

"You're damn right *the* Mark Stevens! And one other thing."

"Yeah?"

"Get me the telephone number of his father-in-law, Henry Enfield. I'm sure it's unlisted. I may wish to ring him."

"Drive in here. I want to see the cemetery," said Mark. The big Rolls-Royce had just passed through Sonoma.

Alex stopped the car in the cemetery parking area, and watched as a weary and bedraggled Mark trudged up the hill to Antonio's grave. From the fresh flowers, Mark knew that his mother had been there. A few days ago, he never would have dreamed he would return so soon.

He turned to Anna Movelli's grave and stood, alone with his thoughts, for a minute. When Anna had first died, he thought of her often, but with the passing of the years, she had become a distant memory.

Then he walked to Jonah's grave.

Here were three people who had once been so vitally important in his life, and now there was a fourth, soon to be buried. It was nearly dark, and he was not dressed for the cold. Nevertheless, head down, he started walking amongst the tombstones. From the car, Alex could see him occasionally disappearing behind a large monument, then reappearing. In passing, he read the many chiseled names and dates. It was hard to imagine seeing: "Priscilla Enfield Stevens 1945-1980."

Finally, Mark came to a small grove of trees in a newer section near the edge of the cemetery. There was only one grave marker. Mark looked down. "Baby Philman - 1980. She never knew life."

At the sight, Mark began to cry softly. He knelt on one knee. That was Pris. She had been struck down just when she was starting to really know life.

He looked around at the trees. This was the place, he thought. This is where he wanted Pris to be buried.

"Baby Philman," he said aloud. "How would you like a neighbor?"

"Mark, I'm so happy to see you!" Amanda shouted. "They thought you might be dead."

As he recounted the story of the fire, Amanda repeatedly touched her son, as if to verify that he was still alive.

"I thought I could make it to the roof. I must have passed out, because the next thing I knew, I was in the hospital."

It took nearly an hour until he finally wound down a bit. Amanda listened to him, fussed over him and insisted that he eat some food. When he had finished, she drew a hot bath for him, and turned down the bed in his old room.

Mark fell asleep instantly. At least while he slept he would be insulated from the events of this past week.

-55-

Mark mustered his courage and telephoned Henry from Amanda's house.

"Henry?"

"Yes?"

"This is Mark. I thought I should talk to you."

"I don't think there's anything to talk about."

"Look, Henry, Pris is dead. There's nothing anyone can do. Henry, I'm asking you to listen to me. Pris would have wanted us to get along."

"You've taken my daughter, my only child, from me, and you expect me to get along with you? You must be mad."

"Look, Henry, what happened between us was a long time ago."

"What happened between us happened again in Las Vegas two bloody days ago—that's when it happened."

"Henry, you're not making sense. I did everything I could to save her. They thought I was dead, too."

"There's nothing for us to talk about. You just tell me where you've got her body. I'll take care of the rest."

"What are you talking about? I'm the one who is her husband. That's why I called you. I wanted to give you the courtesy of discussing the arrangements."

"Well, Mister Know-it-all, it so happens that you're mistaken. Very much mistaken."

"What do you mean?"

"Pris left a will."

"A new will?"

"Yes, and you're not her executor. I got a telephone call from her lawyer. The lawyer who drew her will. The will makes him her executor, and he's already told me he'll do what I want about the arrangements."

"A new will! I didn't know anything about a new will. When did she do that?"

"The day before she died. In case you didn't know it, she had filed for divorce against you."

"But that was all a mistake. She didn't mean to. The lawyer did it, not her."

"The funeral will be Wednesday at Grace Cathedral. I'd prefer if you didn't come, but I suppose I can't stop you."

"Henry, don't talk crazy—I'm Pris's husband! You can't just go off on your own like this."

"Oh, you don't think so? I would suggest you see a good lawyer. Have him call my lawyer, not me. Thomas T. Wahl, W-a-h-l. He's in San Francisco."

"But, Henry . . . "

"Yes?"

"What about the burial?"

"England."

"England?"

"Yes. I want her to be buried next to me—and her mother."

Henry was right. Mark should talk to a lawyer. He dialed Rolf Williams and spilled out the story of the MGM fire and his conversation with Henry. "Rolf, I've got to see you right away. I know it's Sunday, but I've got to see you. Can I meet you at your office?"

"Can he do that? Can he get this executor, Wahl, whoever he is, to completely ignore my wishes for the funeral?" Mark was sitting opposite Rolf Williams's desk.

"I don't know the answer to that one, Mark. I've never had it come up before," answered Rolf. "Did her will have any burial instructions?"

"I don't know. I don't think her old will did. Who is this Wahl guy, anyway? Have you ever heard of him?"

"Sure, I've heard of him. Thomas T. Wahl? Everybody knows Wahl. He gives sleazy attorneys a bad name—represents mostly women—celebrities, money. Here, come on into the library with me," Rolf motioned. "I'll see if I can find a quick answer." Mark followed his old friend into the conference room that doubled as a library. "Everybody thinks attorneys are supposed to know all the law, but we don't. That's why we need all these law books. Sometimes I find the answer right away, and sometimes I look for hours and don't find anything."

Rolf made some instant coffee, and started looking through the law books. He looked at Mark out of the corner of his eye as he selected one of the books. God, Mark looked awful, he thought. He had heard about soldiers aging 10 years during a battle. That's how Mark looked. He looked shell-shocked, just like those soldiers after a battle. His eyes did not have their normal vitality, and he was stooped over with his head hanging. "Mark, are you feeling all right?"

"Don't worry, I'm going to make it."

Rolf opened a book. "One of the first cases we read at Boalt was about who owns dead bodies," he told Mark. "Not a very pleasant subject. I'll always remember those early cases from law school." He took down another volume, looked at the index and took down still another book.

"There it is," Rolf exclaimed. "I got lucky. 'Enos v. Snyder 131 Cal. 68: An executor or administrator has no rights to the burial as opposed to the surviving spouse. Health and Safety Code section 7100.'" Mark looked on pensively as his friend went to another shelf and pulled a blue volume from a set of statutes.

"You mean Henry was wrong?" Mark asked.

"More than likely Wahl told him wrong—probably didn't look it up—just shot from the hip." Rolf found his place. "Here it is. 'Section 7100: The right to control the disposition of the remains of a deceased person vests in the surviving spouse.'" Rolf put the book down. "Well, that settles that. You're right. Henry is wrong."

"Could there be any mistake?"

"No, no mistake," Rolf said, putting his arm on Mark's shoulder. "What do you say we have a hamburger over at Sally's?"

Mark smiled faintly. "Okay," he answered. "Might as well."

"I found a spot for Pris at the cemetery," Mark told Rolf as they took a booth at Sally's. "It's near a little baby's grave. Except for that, she'll be all by herself. The trees are very pretty."

"You think she's better off there than with her parents? You know, Mark, if you should ever marry again, you might wish you'd have buried Pris with her mother and father."

Mark managed a tiny smile. "Me? Getting married again? Not very likely. Besides, England is so far away."

"But you go to England all the time."

"I'd hate to give that old bastard the satisfaction. He wasn't going to let me have any say at all. What a relief to know he was full of shit!"

"Yes, but you have to decide what's best for Pris, regardless of him."

"Rolf, I nearly died with her in that damned hotel! She was a California woman. I want her here, not in England, for Christ's sake!"

"Okay, okay."

"Henry's having the funeral at Grace Cathedral and that's fine with me, but I'll decide on the cemetery, not him."

.   .   .

"Sally's hamburgers are always so damned good. The same as they were in high school," Rolf said.

"Yeah," muttered Mark.

But Rolf had nearly finished his hamburger when he saw that Mark had only taken a bite or two.

"Are you all right?" he asked.

"Oh, sure, I'll be all right."

"You've been through a lot."

"That I have Rolf," he said vacantly. "That I have."

"What do you think you'll do afterwards? After all this is over, I mean."

"I'm not sure."

"When I saw you at Pebble Beach, you were anxious to get started on some new acquisitions."

"Yeah, that's what I was planning then."

"And it didn't happen?"

"No. Actually, Rolf, I ran into some problems."

"Some problems?"

"I just seem to be fed up with business. It doesn't do it for me any more. What's the point, anyway?"

"I remember our talk on the golf course."

"It hasn't changed since then. If anything, it's worse."

"You boys want something else?" asked Sally. She reached for Rolf's empty dish. "Say, you aren't eating, Mark. I heard about your wife. I'm very sorry."

"Thanks, Sally. Just leave my hamburger here. I might want it a little later. Say, I know! How about a milk shake? That would taste good—a milk shake."

"One shake, coming up. Chocolate?"

"Yes. Chocolate." Mark turned to Rolf. "Can you imagine Pris's having a new will? This guy, Wahl, conned her into signing the divorce papers. He wasn't supposed to file them in court, but the next thing I know, some process server hands me the papers."

"Sounds like Wahl."

"I wonder what the will says."

"I don't know," Rolf answered. But Rolf did know. There could be only one reason for a divorce lawyer to have a woman sign a new will, and that would be to cut off her husband.

-56-

In many ways Pris's funeral was like their marriage ceremony 10 years earlier. Nob Hill's Grace Cathedral was filled to capacity. People had begun arriving at nine o'clock for the ten o'clock service. The crowd was so large that the church doors had not been closed until half an hour late. Somber mourners gathered in the outside courtyard to listen over the hastily arranged loudspeakers. The cool fog nearly obscured the American flag on top of the Mark Hopkins Hotel a block away. A Pacific storm was predicted for this afternoon.

Henry sat in the second row on the left side, as he had at the wedding. Mavis, who had arrived the day before yesterday, sat with her brother. "Mark, I hope you don't mind, but I really should be with him until after the funeral. He's so very alone." Mark had no alternative but to assent to her request.

While the organist played, Mark sat on the opposite side of the cathedral with Amanda, Rodney and Rolf.

As at the wedding, Mark and Henry had not acknowledged each other's presence. Steve Baumgartner and his secretary, Susan Waite, sat behind Mark. Prominent figures from San Francisco society and the arts dotted the crowd. Most were dressed in black. A few women wore veils.

Mark had planned to have Pris's body remain at the mortuary until burial this afternoon in Sonoma, but Mavis had approached him yesterday. "Henry says he can't bear to go the cemetery. He wonders if you would change your mind and have the casket brought to the church."

"And you think I should?" responded Mark.

"Yes, I think you should."

And so Pris's closed casket now rested in the church. It was covered with but one large arrangement of flowers—the flowers Mark had given.

It had been barely a week since Antonio's funeral, thought Mark, as he listened to the dreary music. Life had its unexpected turns. Antonio had led a full life—his death was expected—but Pris was barely in the middle of life, looking forward to many more years. But for a matter of luck, it could easily be a double funeral this morning. He could be lying in his own coffin, next to her. He wondered what would have happened if there had been no fire. If there had been no pounding on their hotel door. "Fire! Fire! The hotel is on fire!" They would have finished making love, returned to San Francisco, and then what? Or what if, instead of choosing to go down the emergency stairs, he had led Pris to the roof and the fresh air? What would have happened to their marriage?

The soloist, Annie, Pris's Wellesley classmate, was singing. Mark did not know any religious songs, and so he told Annie to ask Henry for a suggestion. Henry went to church here every Sunday. He would know. She was singing "Nearer My God to Thee."

Mark's thoughts drifted to Christina. What if she had agreed to marry him? Pris would still be alive and they would be headed for a bitter divorce—especially with an attorney like Wahl.

Morosely, he jerked his attention back to the funeral. Pris was lying in that coffin a few feet away. In a few hours she would be in the ground. There was no use speculating on what might have been, what might have happened. His life would change now. Unlike Pris, he had an opportunity to make his life different if he wanted.

"Priscilla Enfield Stevens, 1945 to 1980." The minister began his eulogy. It was Reverend Yarrick, the same man who had married them. "Like most of us here, I had never expected to outlive Priscilla. I knew Priscilla when I first moved to San Francisco. She was away at college then, and I would see her in the church at vacation time. I watched with great joy as she became a leader in our city, contributing her many talents to our cultural enrichment . . ."

Perhaps that was the way with funerals, Mark thought. He had always considered Pris's art shows a pain in the ass, a waste of time when he could have been at the office. He wished he had paid more attention to her and her world.

The minister was finishing his tribute. "And now I have been given a special request." What special request? Mark wondered. "Our hearts have gone out to Henry Enfield since we heard the horrible news. Our city was indeed blessed many years ago when Mr. Enfield chose to make San Francisco his permanent home. This morning he asked me to come to his beautiful home over-looking the Bay where Priscilla grew up. Mr. Enfield told me he wanted to speak here this morning. So now I ask Henry Enfield to come forward."

A gasp came from the congregation. Without assistance, the old man strode toward the pulpit. Mark could not believe what he was seeing. The sight upset him. He had not been consulted about this. He had no idea that Henry wanted to speak. There was nothing he could do but sit back and listen.

Determined, Henry made it to the pulpit, and after a long pause while he composed himself, began: "Like Reverend Yarrick I never expected to outlive Priscilla. I have heard people say over the years that there is no pain deeper than the death of a child. I know now that it's true. There will be no seeing Priscilla for dinner on Thursday nights. There will no longer be the joy of seeing her bring pleasure to all of you, her friends. No longer will I hear her piano playing. I will never have grandchildren."

The old man's voice was quaking, but otherwise he was steady. Mark had to give him credit. It was obvious that Henry had truly loved Pris. But he never had doubted that love. It was the clinging, demanding nature that he hated. Henry was speaking without notes and gave no sign of breaking down.

"As a child, Priscilla brought joy to me, and when her mother passed away she was my crutch, my salvation. You people out there, my friends, my business associates, those of you who don't know me very well, you think of me, I am sure, as a strong man, a powerful man." Henry gulped and continued. "Well, those things might be true, but you don't really know me. Without Priscilla, I don't know what would have become of me. She was . . ." Henry's emotions began to get the better of him. He stopped talking and put his shaking hand to his throat. He looked around, as if looking for a glass of water. "You'll have to excuse me. This is very difficult." Mark swallowed hard. He had never seen Henry like this. As far as he knew, Henry had no soft or tender side. Henry's words sounded sincere, but Mark wondered if it were an act. "Priscilla and I never quarreled," Henry continued. "Oh, I admit when she was a teenager, like teenagers everywhere, she had a mind of her own, but she was an unusual daughter. We never quarreled . . ."

As Henry spoke, a man seated in the center of a pew got up and, excusing himself, began to leave. The man wore a beard and thick glasses. He nearly tripped over another person as he hurriedly stepped into the side aisle and walked to the back of the church. He worked his way through the people outside of the church, and rushed down the steps to the little park across the street. He sat on a bench taking deep breaths, trying to compose himself. For a moment in the church, listening to Henry Enfield, the man had become sick to his stomach and thought he was going to vomit. Such a hypocrite, the man had thought. Those sanctimonious lies about loving Priscilla and never arguing. He wished there were something he could do to punish Henry Enfield, but now no one but he would ever know the old man's awful secret. The bearded man with the thick glasses was Van A. Goodwill, Ph. D., Pris's psychologist.

The business day was nearly over in London. Derek Harden's assistant, Albert Sleeter, was reporting.

"We know that Stevens's wife had seen a divorce lawyer before they left for Las Vegas."

"How odd," Derek responded.

"Yes, and that's not all. Our contact, Susan Waite . . ."

"Baumgartner's P.A."

"Yes. Miss Waite listened in when Stevens rang up Baumgartner. It seems the lawyer had Mrs. Stevens sign a new will shortly before her death."

"A new will? What do you make of that?"

"I don't really know."

"One would think it would not have been to Stevens's benefit."

"Apparently, Stevens thinks as much, as well. He's already consulted a lawyer."

"I want to know what's in that will. Get me the name of that divorce lawyer."

"Of course, Mr. Harden. Right away."

"And one other thing."

"Yes?"

"I'd suggest you reach Henry Enfield, the father-in-law."

"Yes."

"I think he could turn out to be very useful to me, especially if I'm correct about that new will."

It was late in the afternoon at Sonoma's Mountain Cemetery. Only a few mourners had come from Grace Cathedral. After the graveside service, most of the others had extended their sympathies to Mark, and had returned to the city. Despite Mavis's urging, Henry Enfield had refused to make the trip. Mark now stood by Pris's casket and her open grave. Amanda, Rolf, Mavis and Rodney were with him.

"What a beautiful place, Mark," said Mavis.

"Yes, the trees. All by herself," commented Rolf.

"I was struck by this grave over here," said Mark. "Did you see it? It's the only one in this newer section." All four of them walked to the infant's grave that Mark had seen the other day.

"She never knew life," said Rodney, reading the grave marker.

"Yes. It was that inscription that appealed to me about this little place. As soon as I saw it, I knew this was where Pris should be. She had changed, radically changed. She was just beginning a whole new phase of her life, and then . . ." His voice trailed off.

"Shall we go back to the house now? Amanda softly inquired. "I started some things for dinner last night."

"If you don't mind, I'd like to be alone with Pris for a while. Why don't you all wait in the car? I won't be long."

"Are you sure you'll be okay?" Rolf asked solicitously.

"Don't worry. I just want to be with her."

The three walked toward the Phantom, which Alex had parked nearby.

Head bowed, Mark stood alone by Pris's coffin. During these few days, he had forced himself to remain emotionally aloof. He had cried only once, when he had first viewed Pris's body at the mortuary. She had looked so beautiful. The terror was gone from her face, as was the ugly black fluid that had drained from her nose. She looked so peaceful, as if she might wake up and want to try the crap table again, to try out her new life again.

Now, alone at the cemetery beside Pris's flower-covered coffin, the bottled-up emotions burst forth. Tears streamed down his face. His heart ached terribly. Vivid recollections of his struggle in the hotel staircase flooded him. The people dying. Pris passing out. Struggling to carry her body up the stairs. Great sobs escaped from deep inside him as he put his hand on her coffin. The pain, the tears went on and on. His soul needed to exorcise itself.

Finally, he was aware of another voice inside himself—another part of him that was at peace. Empathetically, the part watched as his sobs lessened and finally ceased.

"Oh, Pris," Mark said aloud. "I'm so sorry for everything. I wish I could have saved you. I think we finally could have been happy together. Don't you think so, too? Don't you, Pris?"

He knelt down on the green carpet with his hand on the coffin. A yellow rose tumbled to his feet. He picked it up and held it tightly. "I'm going to miss you, Pris. I'm going to miss you very much." His voice faltered as he finished, and the tears came again. He knew it appeared hypocritical for him to feel so strongly for Pris only a few days after wanting to marry Christina, but his feelings came from his heart.

As he stood to join the others in the limousine, a powerful realization came to him. As Pris had changed in Las Vegas and had become another woman, so too, he had to change. He could go on with this way of life no longer. He had to do more than just idly talk with Rolf about changing. He had to do something real and he had to do it now.

-57-

For a week after the funeral, Rodney and Mavis stayed with Mark at the Movelli compound. Every night after dinner they had long chats, usually at Amanda's kitchen table. Mark reveled in their companionship. He would miss them when they returned to England.

One night Mavis played the piano in the living room of the mansion. After the others retired for the evening, she lingered on.

"Are you going to be all right?" she inquired.

"I'll be okay."

"You look better. I quite despaired for you for a time there."

"It was an ordeal I wouldn't want to go through again."

Mavis looked up from her liqueur glass. "I've decided you look more distinguished with your hair nearly all white. How old are you now, Mark?"

Mark smiled. "Almost 40."

"They say 40 is the start of the second half of your life." Mavis, who was nearly 60 now, still reminded Mark of Gene Tierney in her prime.

"One thing I know is that I can't spend the rest of my life the way it's been so far."

Mavis left her chair to sit on the sofa next to Mark. She kissed him lightly on the cheek, and took his hand. "Just look what you've accomplished in your 40 years."

"Yes, but I'm not happy at all. The fact is, I'm at a complete dead end."

"Listen to me. Everybody has to constantly rethink what they want out of life."

Mark got up and stood by the piano. "When I was in Oxford, I wanted a first. When I came home, I wanted to get rich. For 20 years I wanted Christina." Still standing, he picked out a little tune on the piano—one Anna Movelli had taught him.

"Would you have been happy if Christina had married you?"

Mark looked up from the piano and gave a soft laugh. "I've thought about that a lot the last few days."

"And do you have an answer?"

"No, I don't think I would have been. There would have been a messy divorce from Pris. It would have kept me occupied like some business deal for a while, you know, distracted. But then . . ." He sat down on the piano bench as if to continue with the one-finger tune, but changed his mind and closed the keyboard cover. "No, the truth of the matter is that Christina wouldn't have made me happy. I'm afraid no woman could do that. I have this restlessness in me."

"You know what I think, Mark?"

"No, what?"

"I don't think you're ever going to get rid of that restlessness. Furthermore, why should you? It's part of you. It would be like trying to get rid of Mark Stevens himself."

As Mark readied for bed, he recalled a feeling that had moved through him when Christina said she would not divorce Otello. He had felt a strange sense of relief. A feeling that having Christina was not the answer.

That night he had a vivid dream. He was in Grace Cathedral. Pris's funeral was going on. Organ music was playing. In the remote distance, Reverend Yarrick was speaking. Mark got up from his pew and walked forward to the casket. In the dream itself he knew that he must be dreaming, because the casket was open, where in fact it had been closed at the funeral. He fought to awaken as he turned to look at Pris. He did not want to look, but as he did, it was not her at all. It was a blond woman. He forced himself to look more closely, but he could not tell if it were Christina.

The dream dissolved as Mark awoke. He went to the window. What a horrible dream, he thought. He must try to remember it and tell it to Mavis. Perhaps she could make some sense of it. But later in the morning, try as he might, the memory of the dream had slipped away.

Two days later, Mark took Mavis and Rodney to the San Francisco airport for their return to London. He had asked Rolf Williams to go along so that he would have company on the return trip.

"Then you'll visit us in the spring," said Rodney, as they said good-bye at the gate.

"Maybe sooner," said Mark, shaking hands. "I may decide to do that lecture series at Oxford. I haven't decided what I'm going to do."

"Rebecca and I will not have you staying alone when you're in London. Do we have that clear?"

"Of course we do." Still speaking to Rodney, Mark winked at Mavis. "I'll really be coming to England to see your mother, you know."

"You want to hear more of my piano playing, is that it?" Mavis joked.

They kissed each other on the cheek. "Actually, Mavis it's your violin playing I can't resist." And then he whispered so that the others could not hear. "Good-bye, Violin Lady. And thank you for all you've done for me."

They showed their tickets to the agent, and disappeared down the ramp. Mark felt a lump in his throat. "Come on, Rolf. Let's go."

Leaving the airport, the Phantom had entered the Bayshore Freeway going north, when Alex lowered the chauffeur's window. "Mr. Stevens, I've just heard some very bad news on the radio."

"What's that, Alex?"

"John Lennon has been shot. They say he's dead—assassinated."

"My God!" Mark exclaimed. "What next?"

"Assassinated? Who would want to assassinate John Lennon?" exclaimed Rolf.

Mark often repeated how he had seen the Beatles in 1963, and had actually talked to John Lennon. He had a great deal of admiration for Lennon's success at such a young age.

"Here's Candlestick now," Mark said, nodding to the right as the Rolls neared the huge stadium.

"I'll never forget that night." Rolf was alluding to the Beatles concert they had attended at Candlestick Park in 1967. "What a mob scene."

"Their last concert ever."

As they continued up the freeway, Mark turned the back seat radio on, to see if he could get any further news. "John Lennon, dead. I don't know what to think . . ."

"Yeah. The poor guy is on top of the world one minute, and the next minute he's flat dead," Rolf added.

"My mother always says bad news comes in threes. First Antonio, then Pris and now Lennon."

"You're right. It is three."

"You know Rolf, there's a tendency to think we have all the time in the world."

"True."

"But we don't."

"It can end at any time," Rolf agreed.

"Some jealous bastard could shoot us because of my Rolls-Royce."

Mark switched radio stations, but when Lennon's death came up again, there were no new details.

They were silent, as Alex made their way through San Francisco and across the Golden Gate Bridge. Finally, Rolf spoke:

"He must have had millions."

"I'm sure he did." Mark mused: "I wonder if he was happy."

"From what I've read, he was on kind of a back-to-nature kick. No more music. Taking care of his kid. Stuff like that."

"Searching for a new direction, too, I guess."

For the rest of the way they spoke very little. Mark's mind was churning. Alex stopped in front of Rolf's law office to let him out.

"I've made a decision, Rolf."

"What?"

"I'm going to New York."

"New York? You mean because of Lennon?"

"Yes, I want to be there."

"I'm a little surprised, Mark."

"The poor son of a bitch, he didn't have a chance."

"You want me to go with you?" Rolf asked.

"Sure, if you want. It'll be the end of an era. Yes, why don't we both go? The plane can be ready in no time. I really want to be there."

It was still dark in New York when they arrived, early in the morning of December 9th. The cab radio had reported that crowds were gathering near the assassination scene at the Dakota Apartments. They checked in at the Plaza Hotel, and gave their small amount of luggage to the bellman. Without going to their rooms, they headed for the Dakota.

The sidewalks on Central Park East were filled with silent people funereally walking north toward the scene of the murder. There were thousands of people who felt deeply about Lennon and his times. At Amanda's suggestion, the two friends had brought their heavy jackets. Many in the crowd were wrapped in blankets as they walked. Most of the mourners were considerably younger than Mark and Rolf.

At the Tavern on the Green the crowd was backing up although the Dakota was still many blocks away, so they cut into Central

Park where the crowd was thinner. As they neared 74th and the Dakota, they could see a throng of grieving young people who were singing—more of a chant: "Give peace a chance . . ." They worked their way to a knoll where, through the barren trees, they could glimpse the building where Lennon had lived and been cut down by the madman.

Many in the vast sea of people who flooded the streets and the park were crying. A few television cameras were recording the event. Thousands were holding lighted candles. "Would you like this candle?" offered a young woman. "I'm sorry I have only one extra." Mark accepted the candle and, together with Rolf, held it.

Their jackets were not enough protection against the cold, and they were shivering. A young man and a young woman were huddled in a blanket next to Mark and Rolf. "Would you like to share our blanket?" asked the man. They gratefully accepted the offer and joined the couple inside the blanket, where their body heat made them warmer.

Without any apparent cue, the singing of the crowd shifted from one song to another. Sometimes different parts of the vast, mournful crowd would be singing songs different from each other. Then the lyrics would invade an area, and suddenly both groups would be singing the same song. "Imagine there's no heaven. It isn't hard to do. No need for greed or hunger . . . You may say I'm a dreamer . . ." No matter which song was being sung, there was a distinctly mournful, moaning quality that hung like fog over the assembled singers.

Mark and Rolf stood with the others in the cold for two, perhaps three hours. What had brought out such a vast crowd in such cold weather? Perhaps each mourner had his own reason, but they also had reasons in common. For some, the last element of their youth was gone, their connection with the '60s ended. For others, it was simple sadness, and tribute to a man they thought great. For Mark, it was a more complex reason.

"I'm ready to go, if you are," Mark finally suggested. Even though Rolf was deeply chilled, he had waited for his friend to suggest leaving. Between them, Mark had the deeper reason to be there that night.

As they returned down Central Park East, they passed many others who, despite the cold, were headed for the Dakota. "Let's not go to the hotel yet," Mark suggested. "Let's have some breakfast. There's a 24-hour deli down Seventh Avenue."

There weren't many in the deli. Mark ordered lox and eggs. Rolf wanted only a Danish and coffee. "For me, it really drives home the point," Rolf said. "I mean it's the '80s now. The '60s are long gone."

"What I can't get over is the suddenness," Mark said, his voice nearly inaudible.

"Yes," Rolf agreed. "You've seen enough of that these past couple of weeks."

Looking out the window, Mark didn't answer.

"It makes you think, doesn't it?" Rolf mumbled.

"I knew when Pris died, I wanted to make some serious changes."

"Right."

"There has to be more than money."

"Apparently that's what John Lennon had decided."

"And then some ass puts a bunch of bullets in him."

"Makes you think all right."

"You may not have all the time you think."

The waiter came with their food. They talked very little about Lennon while they ate. Mark had the same stunned look that he had had since the MGM fire. When he finished, he wiped his mouth with his napkin and leaned back in the booth.

"I've decided to have Baumgartner take over the business. I'm going to have as little to do with it as possible."

"What are you going to do?"

"I don't know. Maybe I'll go back to England. Leave San Francisco. There isn't much for me there any more. You know what I think I might do?"

"No."

"Go back to Oxford. Maybe teach. I don't know."

Thomas T. Wahl, Esquire, never went to see a client. It was part of his strategy to insist that the client, however wealthy, come to him. It was a matter of power. But today he made an exception for Henry Enfield. Henry had telephoned, saying that the Englishman, Derek Harden, had flown in from London yesterday with an important proposition. Earlier Harden had called Wahl, asking about Priscilla's will. Henry wanted the three of them to meet in his office at Enfield & Co. Wahl agreed, but had come to Henry's office a few minutes early so as to talk privately with Henry. The two sat in Henry's office overlooking San Francisco Bay.

Since Wahl had drawn Pris's will, he knew that nothing could keep him from earning a fat fee as executor. He ought to be able to work that up to at least $250,000. As executor, he would have control over the assets of the estate and, if he handled the situation correctly, there could be one hell of a lot more for him than a lousy quarter of a million.

"Harden wants control of The Stevens Group," Henry said firmly. "He knows very well he has to deal with both of us. He already knows you're the executor and I'm the sole heir."

"That's what I told him when he called from London."

"You had no business telling him what was in Pris's will. That was confidential information."

"Now, Henry, don't go flying off the handle. I figured he'd find out soon enough anyway."

They were in the very same office where Henry had humiliated Mark so many years earlier.

"Harden says he already owns enough stock so that with Priscilla's share he'd have control."

The intercom sounded and Henry was informed that Derek was in the reception room.

"Harden's here now. Let's hear what he has to say for himself."

Elegantly dressed as usual, Derek made a striking figure. Not bothering with pleasantries, he stood by the large window as if contemplating buying all San Francisco. Suddenly he turned to the other two.

"I think the best way to appeal to you, Mr. Enfield, is to go directly to the truth. I've made a great deal of money in my life, but I'm not interested in The Stevens Group for money alone."

"What is your interest then, Mr. Harden?" asked Henry.

"I don't like your son-in-law, Mr. Enfield. It's as simple as that. It would not be incorrect to say I despise him."

Wahl laughed. "We may all have something in common, eh, Mr. Enfield?"

Ignoring Wahl, Derek directed his remarks to Henry. "My staff tells me you are not exactly fond of Mr. Mark Stevens, yourself. Tell me, Mr. Enfield, is my information correct?"

"You wouldn't need much of a spy network to know that is the case. You say you don't like him either?"

"Mr. Enfield, from the time Mark Stevens and I were tutorial partners at Worcester College, I've hated him and his insufferable superior attitude."

"So you've known the man since Oxford?"

"Indeed I have. We've had many a run-in over the years, but this time, I'm going to win—that is with your cooperation, sir."

"And what exactly do you expect us to do?" inquired Wahl, who had gotten to his feet so as to be more the equal of Derek.

"I propose that we enter into a joint venture to control The Stevens Group. We can share the profits according to our percentage of stock."

"Mr. Harden," said Henry. "It is very likely that I despise Mark Stevens even more than you do, entirely for my own reasons, you see. But we should not let our dislike for him interfere with our good judgment."

"Of course not. What is it that you mean?"

"Stevens is a brilliant trader. Without him, The Stevens Group is just another company. Surely, he would quit the company if we took over."

"He can't."

"What do you mean, he can't?" asked Wahl.

"He's signed a long term contract with the company."

"I didn't know that," said Henry.

"More than that, his contract has recently been renewed. It assures the value of the stock."

"But, surely, you can't keep a man from quitting," suggested Henry.

"You're right. He could quit, but we could get an injunction keeping him from working for another company," contributed Wahl. "He'd have to retire, or go into a totally different business."

Henry smiled. He had stood, too. All three were looking out the window at the shipping as they talked. "Mark would never do that. He's too much of a compulsive worker."

"Don't forget," said Derek. "If he left the company his own stock would go down in value, too. Besides, he makes a very large salary. Almost ten million last year with his percentage."

"But why do you want to control the company, with or without him?" asked Wahl.

"You don't understand, do you, Wahl?" Henry asked.

"There's nothing in the world I would like more than to be able to order Mark Stevens about," said Derek.

"Yes," said Henry, "we would control the board. We could override his every decision. Run the company the way we want. Rub his nose in the dirt."

"We could make life miserable for him. Just knowing we controlled his company would drive him mad."

"But what about money?" asked Wahl. "Surely, you expect to make money out of this."

"Don't you understand, Mr. Wahl?" asked Henry. "I don't need any more money."

"Don't worry, counselor, there will be plenty of money for us all," said Derek.

"And how do you propose that?"

"I'm wagering he'll come to us, begging to buy us out for a huge profit. And—I think I see your concern, Mr. Wahl—we'll see to it that you'll participate in the profit. Won't we, Henry? After all, Wahl, here, is the one who drew up the will."

"Yes. And I control Priscilla's stock during the probate proceedings," Wahl pointed out.

"Indeed," said Henry. "I can assure you that that fact had not escaped my attention."

"I'm glad you understand," smiled Wahl.

"I do understand, Mr. Wahl. However, there's one thing I want you to understand."

"Oh?"

"When I spoke to my own lawyer yesterday, he told me that I stood a very good chance of removing you as executor. Something about a conflict of interest to get yourself named as executor."

"Now, you listen to me, Enfield!"

"No, you listen to me!" Henry exclaimed. "I told you, I'm not interested in the money. I don't care how big a fee you take, but there is one thing I will insist upon."

"And what is that?"

"That you do as I say."

Christina Bagliani sat in her dressing room in the Pariole district of Rome. She stared through her window across the lush grounds of her husband's villa, still holding the letter she had just read. The letter was from her old friend, Carol Ann Spagnola, who owned a gift shop in Sonoma. Her friend wrote about the MGM Grand Hotel fire, Pris's death and Mark's narrow escape.

Christina was dressed for riding, and had been about to leave for the stables when the letter arrived. She placed the letter in the lower drawer of her desk. Thoughtfully, she removed a large worn envelope from the drawer, and took out a newspaper clipping that Carol Ann had sent her some years ago. It was an article about Mark in *Fortune* magazine. She looked at the smiling photograph of Mark. His hair was not as white in the photo as it had been two weeks ago.

Christina was not one to second-guess herself, but today she found herself not sure of her decision to turn down Mark. In a way, she had been testing him. If Mark had really wanted her badly enough to turn his life—both of their lives—upside down, he would never have accepted her rejection. He would have pursued her, even if it meant coming to Italy and charging up the stairs after her. For a moment, it entered her mind that, with his wife now dead, that might be exactly what Mark would do. If he came after her again, she did not know what she would do, but there was no point thinking about it.

With resolve, Christina put the clipping back, locked the drawer and hid the key. She walked to the far end of the villa to see Otello. He was sitting in his pajamas, reading his newspaper, *La Verita*. His nurse was nearby.

"How are you this morning, my dear?" Christina inquired.

"I am much better today. I had a good night's sleep."

"Is the doctor coming to see you?"

"He's scheduled for this afternoon, but I may cancel him. I'm thinking of getting dressed and having Vito take me for a drive."

"That would be a good idea, my darling."

"Are you going for a drive?"

"Yes. Driving is about all that interests me any more. But don't worry my love, I enjoy it."

Christina bent down and kissed Otello on the cheek.

"I'll see you this evening," he said. "And please, do go for that drive. It will be good for you."

Christina backed her Ferrari out of the garage. She shifted into first gear and gunned the engine. The high mellow whine of the 12 cylinders excited her every bit as much as the gallop of her favorite horse. She eased out the clutch, and the blood-red car zipped down the long driveway. As the car gained speed, her long blond hair flowed in the wind. She was as desirable as she had ever been.

-58-

Steve Baumgartner had left word at New York's Plaza Hotel that he had to see Mark about the many pressing business problems that had cropped up. Returning to San Francisco, Mark had called Steve from the plane. He was fearful that if he went to the office he might have another panic attack, so he asked Steve to meet him at the Pacific Union Club. Steve ordered a martini, and went straight to the point.

"Mark, I'm very worried."

"What is it?" Mark asked. "The Edison underwriting? That Cleveland deal? What?"

"No, not any of that."

"What, then?"

"Frankly, Mark, it's you."

Mark swallowed. He wasn't used to having Steve or anyone speak to him this way. "What do you mean, me?"

"Mark, you're only human. Nobody can stand all you've been hit with."

"That may be, but I . . ."

"I've been doing my best, but the office is in chaos."

"I appreciate everything you've been doing, Steve. I'll be back in the office before long."

"When I couldn't find you, I had to make a decision on that Cleveland deal. I hope you don't mind."

"What decision? What did you decide?"

"It wasn't easy calming them down that day."

"Those assholes! Especially their lawyer."

"I know, Mark, but we could make one hell of a profit."

"So what did you do?"

"I told them we'd go for it. It took some talking, but they agreed. The papers are ready to sign."

"I suppose it's okay."

"They insisted on one thing, though."

"What's that."

"They want me on the deal, not you. They don't want to have to talk with you any more."

"*They* don't want to talk with *me*?"

"They were pretty upset that day."

"What I told them was perfectly true."

"I agree with you, Mark, but . . ."

"Go ahead, go ahead with the deal. I don't give a good goddamn. It's all right with me, just so I don't have to be involved with them either."

"Then I'll sign for the company?"

"Might as well."

Mark looked up, at the noise of a hard rain. The sudden December deluge was noisily flowing down the old windows of the club, as if someone had turned loose a garden hose. The rain fit his mood. Inside the cozy former mansion, he felt protected from the outside world. That was what he needed, at least for a while.

"But it's more than that. More than the Cleveland deal," Steve continued.

"What?"

"Mark, are you sure you're okay? You don't look well. You're as nervous as hell today."

"Listen, Steve, you'd be nervous too, if you—if you were me."

"I'm sure I would. I'd probably be in the booby hatch."

Mark finished his Rob Roy, and motioned to the waiter for another. Steve quickly finished the last of his martini. "I'll have another, too." Steve paused, as if gathering his nerve to go on speaking. "Mark, the company is like a ship in a storm, with the captain below decks."

"Come on, Steve. You're exaggerating."

"No, I'm not. Everybody is doing their best. But when it comes right down to it, you're the genius behind it all. You know that, don't you?"

"They can make decisions on their own."

"The little decisions, yes, but take for example your currency trading program. You've always been able to make the trades when you see the trends starting. Right?"

"Well, yes, that's true."

"But the others can't. They chicken out. They don't have the courage to risk millions, like you do."

Mark sipped his newly arrived drink, and shrugged his shoulders.

"You know very well if you're afraid to lose, you can't win," Steve added, "and they're afraid."

They stopped talking while the waiter put their lunches before them. Then Steve continued: "And what's more, the trading program needs updating. It's that way all through the whole company."

"Steve, I appreciate your worrying, but I've spent my whole life building up the organization. Believe me, they'll get along, at least until I'm back."

When they finished lunch, Mark stood to indicate that the meeting was over. "I'm going for a walk. The rain seems to have stopped."

"Then you're not coming in today?"

"No, Steve. Things will be all right."

Steve looked downcast. "Will I see you Monday?"

"I'm not sure about Monday, either."

Mark walked with Steve to the front of the Fairmont Hotel, where it would be easier for Steve to catch a cab back to the office.

"Mark. There's something else. I wasn't going to tell you until later."

"What?"

"Somebody is trying to take over the company."

"What do you mean, somebody is trying to take over the company? Who?"

"I don't know. At least not for sure. Either that or . . . Have you been thinking of selling out?"

"Certainly not. Why on earth do you ask that?"

"There's been a lot of activity in our stock."

"I'd never sell out. This company has been my whole life."

"Well, something is going on with our stock."

"It's not my doing, you can count on that. Steve, you're a good man, but I think you're worrying too much. You forget how much stock I own."

"Yeah," said Steve, as he got in the taxi. He closed the cab door. Shit! he said to himself, banging his fist into his hand. The captain is below decks all right. What's more, he doesn't want to know about any storms.

Saturday Mark listed the Hillsborough house with a real estate agent, and told Zeldah to move his things to the Nob Hill condo. He did not want to set foot inside the big house again. That part of his life was over. He did not want to look back at what he and Pris had so carefully built. He had no intention of buying a replacement house, at least until he had sorted out what he wanted to do with his life.

Mark did not sleep well Saturday night. What Steve had told him was on his mind. He supposed Steve was right, that he ought to go into the office if only to make an appearance. What was this about activity in the stock? Nobody would be crazy enough to try a takeover. But still, he wondered.

Sunday he mustered up his courage to go to the office. He did not want to wait until Monday to see if a panic attack would recur. It was quiet in San Francisco as he walked down the hill to the Financial District. He was nervous as he waited for the elevator. The suite was deserted as he went into his private office and took his big leather chair. It seemed like a year since he had sat here.

For now at least, the compulsion to flee did not return. Monday would be a greater test, because the office would be busy and he would be faced with decisions. Damn, he wished he did not have to come in at all tomorrow. He shook his head in dismay. He had devoted a lifetime to being in this office and now, for reasons he failed to understand, he no longer wanted to be here.

But on Monday morning Mark was in his office, listening to Steve outline the various problems that required immediate decisions. It was a strange experience. Mark heard himself making decisions, but it seemed as if a person other than himself were speaking. As they talked, he was relieved that the dreaded panic attack had not recurred. The meeting finished with his telling Steve: "I want you to find out who has been buying our stock. If somebody is trying a takeover, we'd better know who it is."

When Mark was alone, he stood looking out his office window at the activity on the Bay. He was relieved to have the meeting behind him. He wished he were someplace else. He was tired of being the captain. The gold tourist ship he had noticed so often over the years was plying its way towards the Bay Bridge. It looked chilly outside, but the morning fog had lifted and the sun was coming through. Mark pondered for a moment, then picked up his telephone. "Bette," he said, "I'm knocking off for the day. I've decided to take a boat ride."

If Derek Harden had looked out of his San Francisco lawyer's office that moment, he would have seen the same gold tourist boat that had attracted Mark. But the last thing that was on Derek's mind this morning was taking a boat ride. Derek loved the prospect of doing battle with his old nemesis, Mark Stevens.

Derek expected to spend a lot of time in San Francisco piloting his takeover of the Stevens Group. He fully intended to be soon running Mark's company. Consequently, this afternoon he expected to sign papers buying a penthouse in the new Embarcadero condominium project, a few blocks from here. Derek's lawyer's name was Joseph P. Raymer, Jr., a partner in the litigation department of one of the largest firms in the city.

"Tom Wahl? Sure I know Tom Wahl," said Raymer. "Every lawyer in San Francisco knows Tom Wahl. Tricky, but very bright." Raymer had joined Salisbury and Bush, then comprising 45 lawyers, right out of Boalt Law School. After only a few years of experience, he had been thrust into defending one of the firm's big oil company clients when the partner in charge had a nervous breakdown on the eve of trial. By the end of the trial, Raymer had the jury eating out of his hand—no small feat in an anti-trust case against a big oil company. In less than a year, Raymer had made partner.

"The way to keep Wahl on your side is to see to it he stands to make a sizable profit for it," Derek remarked.

"What have you promised him?"

"Nothing specific yet. I think Enfield will give him some of his shares. Whatever it is, I want both Wahl and Enfield out of the company when it's all over."

"That would certainly be best. Give them nothing permanent."

They had spent half an hour discussing the case when Raymer reached for the phone. "I'm going to call in one of my corporation partners, Bill Mickel. We need some corporate expertise."

Raymer dialed a number and waited. "Bill? Joe Raymer. Can you come over for a few minutes? I have an interesting new case. It's against Mark Stevens, of all people. I'd like to pick your brain."

Mark waved off his chauffer. He wanted to walk the mile to the wharf and the tourist ship. He was so happy not to be in the office. As often as he had looked at the ships from high up in his building, he had never taken the cruise around the Bay. The ticket line was short this time of year, and he took a seat on the top deck. He doubted he would be dressed warmly enough in his business suit, but he chose to be outside in the sea air rather than inside. He really felt good today, better than he had for months. He yanked off his striped tie and stuffed it into his suit jacket pocket. The captain blew the whistle, and Mark leaned forward with anticipation as the ship backed away from the pier.

Derek's meeting with the two lawyers was ending.

"So from the viewpoint of strict corporate law, the case would be straightforward," advised Raymer's partner. "I wouldn't foresee any problem. After all, it's the shareholders who elect the board of directors. If you don't want to wait for the annual share-holders' meeting, you'd have to have a special meeting."

"But as you say, we could have the shareholders enlarge the number of board members and get control that way," said Derek.

"I don't see that it requires a lawsuit," said Raymer. "At least not right away. We simply call for a shareholders' meeting to put our people on the new board. With Derek's shares, and Wahl voting Pris's shares, we have control."

"Gentlemen, I've known Mark Stevens for nearly 20 years," said Derek. "You can wager everything you own that he'll put up a bloody good fight."

"There's no doubt about it. The argument he'll be forced to make is the separate property argument," commented Raymer.

"I think you're right," agreed Mickel. "If I were his lawyer, I'd claim that The Stevens Group stock was all Stevens's separate property, and that Mrs. Stevens had no right to will it to her fa-ther; so he'd have no right to vote her share."

"But we'll argue, of course, that it was community property and that she had every right to do what she wished—as to her half."

"And who is right?" Derek asked.

"That, Mr. Harden, sir, is what makes for a lawsuit."

Mark could not remember when he had had such outright fun. The few other tourists who had braved the cold air to sit with him had given up and sought shelter behind the big glass win-dows.

The ship's bell clanged and the recorded voice announced: "There, in the tall buildings you see beyond the Embarcadero, is San Francisco's Financial District, where the City's business mo-guls have their offices."

Mark spotted his office building. "Hi, there, business moguls! I hope you're having one hell of a day," he shouted, raising his arm. The ships bell clanged loudly. God, he was having fun! For a fleeting moment he thought of Christina and what it would be like to have her next to him. He dismissed the thought and kept his eyes glued to the City. This was a trip he should have taken long ago. There were the Hyatt Hotel and the Ferry Building. On the top of Nob Hill, he could see the Fairmont Hotel tower and part of his condominium building. He was reminded of the excite-ment he had felt when Rodney had first showed him London.

The ship circled under the Bay Bridge, and headed back across the bay toward the Golden Gate Bridge. As they passed Alcatraz, he decided it was simply too cold, and retreated inside for the rest of the trip. In an hour the tour was completed, and he was disembarking near Pier 39. He would have to do that again soon, he decided. Disdaining the use of a taxi, he began the walk back to his office.

Before long, he passed by a bakery in the North Beach District. The smell of the freshly baked sourdough bread made him suddenly very hungry. He looked at his watch. It was nearly one o'clock. Soon he came upon a neighborhood restaurant, and asked for a window table. He munched on his sourdough bread as he waited for his pasta to be served. For the first time in a long time, he ordered a beer, and leaned back to watch the pedestrians. He noticed a couple several tables away. The woman was a blonde. Again, Christina flashed through his mind. He thought of the time he had spied on Christina and Otello in the Rome restaurant. He had thought Christina was totally out of his life, yet she had twice popped into his mind.

When Mark finished lunch, he again headed for the office. He passed the City Lights Bookstore on Columbus Street. He had noticed the shop many times, but had never gone in. He decided he would much rather poke around in the bookstore than go back to the office. The books were offbeat compared to what he saw at his usual bookstore in the Financial District. There were a great many paperbacks. They had in stock the complete works of many famous authors whose books he had not had time to read, such as Updike and Hemingway. Here was an Isherwood book. He had seen Isherwood interviewed by Dick Cavett, but had never read any of his books. By the time he finished browsing, he held half a dozen books and headed for the check-out counter. He was not sure when he would read them all, but it would be fun if he would just take his time, not push it. As he was about to leave, he noticed there was a downstairs to the bookstore.

"Would you keep these for me while I take a look downstairs?" he asked the clerk.

"Sure, be careful of the steps. They're steep."

Mark was amazed by what he found in the old basement. Small literary magazines, books on metaphysics and other esoteric subjects. He wandered around the alcoves, fascinated that such a place even existed.

In one corner was a used paperback section. He smiled at the thought that he, a billionaire, might save a couple of dollars by buying a used book, but found himself looking at the titles. Many of the used paperbacks were on various self-help subjects: *The Romance Factor. You Are Your Mind. Don't let Your Down Attitude Get You Down.* Mark thumbed through several of the books without finding any that interested him. Then a little book caught his eye. It was short, just over 100 pages, with a red cover: *Not By*

Bread Alone. Under the title was the legend—"When you've learned that money is not enough."

Mark smiled. He was reminded of Mavis and her "Big Ques-tion." "What do you do when you've got everything?" Was that not the way she had put it? He turned the book over to see who the author was. There was a photograph of a man about 60. "One of Great Britain's successful businessmen, Michael Hollingsworth, suffered a severe illness at the height of his career. He was forced to reexamine the premise of his life."

Fascinated, Mark flipped to the book's forward. *"And Jesus answered him, saying, It is written that man shall not live by bread alone . . . Luke, Ch. 4, Verse 4."* I'm certainly not excited about reading anything from the Bible, Mark said to himself. He turned to the first page.

"Not By Bread Alone," Hollingsworth began. *"That was the title of the sermon. Except for weddings and funerals, I had not been in church for 30 years, but I was desperate to find an answer. My life had gone all wrong. I had been diagnosed as having incur-able pancreatitis. My doctor told me I was going to die.*

"Walking along Piccadilly, I had seen the topic of next Sunday's talk, 'Not By Bread Alone.' Three months earlier, at 52, I was a wealthy man, on top of the world as I knew it, but material success had not saved me from illness. So the topic of Sunday's sermon portended a special meaning for me. The church was St. James's Piccadilly . . ."

St. James's Piccadilly, Mark nearly exclaimed aloud. That was Mavis's church! I'll be damned—St. James's Piccadilly. The church where Mavis had taken him, when he needed help.

Book in hand, Mark excitedly walked up the stairs. This was a book he wanted to read, for sure. It sounded as if Hollingsworth were a lot like himself. And can you imagine? He went to St. James's Piccadilly!

-59-

The prospect of reading *Not By Bread Alone* captured Mark's interest. As he stood on the curb looking for a taxi outside City Lights Bookstore, he thought about finding someplace to read it. The pyramid building down the street thrust into the December sky. Typical of San Francisco, across the street from this literate bookstore was a topless night club with a painted sign of a bare-breasted woman.

"Haight-Ashbury, please," Mark told the driver. Impulsively, he had decided to read his book at the same Haight Street restaurant where he had met Diane Chandler. He wanted to order a beer, put up his feet and read what the author had to say. Haight-Ashbury was totally outside of his day-to-day San Francisco life. That was what he wanted, different surroundings and a new mind-set while he searched for some answers.

Since it was mid-afternoon, the outdoor patio of the restaurant was deserted. Mark ordered a beer, and began reading. Hollingsworth had been born in the North of England to a middle-class family. His father was a shopkeeper who wanted his son to follow him in the business. More ambitious, Hollingsworth had left home and gone to London at the end of World War II. He worked his way up to be managing director of a manufacturing enterprise. Blocked from ownership in the company, he started his own business. Successful, he had expanded to the point of having manufacturing operations in Taiwan and offices through-out the world. At the pinnacle of success, he became mysteri-ously ill and was told he had only a few months to live. At the same time, his wife left him. Dismayed and depressed, Hollingsworth sold off his business, made a settlement with his wife and went to India, where he expected to die within the time allotted by the doctors.

Mark remained absorbed in the book the entire afternoon. Hollingsworth's desperate quest fascinated him. Living with an encampment of truth-seekers in the harsh mountains of India, Hollingsworth had studied various Eastern philosophies. Always retaining his skepticism, he had wandered from one guru to another, searching, and absorbing their teachings.

One sunrise while in meditation, Hollingsworth had a deep mystical insight. He had never believed in God or Jesus or any of the great religious figures, but there on the side of a mountain in the Himalayas—

"For the first time in my life, I experienced God. There is no way I can describe what I felt, for it is indescribable. Suddenly life seemed simple. In an instant, I saw that, while my ambition had brought me much of what life had to offer, it had become out-of-bounds and, like a cancer, had a life of its own. Early in my life, money and business success had become my measuring devices.

This was quite understandable given my background, but it wasn't enough. The money and material things brought me pleasure, but they weren't the stuff of life."

Mark looked up from the book. The parallels between Hollingsworth's life and his own startled him. He reflected on the times he had begun feeling dissatisfied with his life. He thought about that unhappy day on the golf course with Rolf. His life was not all that different from Hollingsworth's.

"Now, if you had sat down in my office and asked me," the book continued, *"if money and success were the most important things in my life, I would have responded, 'No, of course not.' I would have given you some socially acceptable answer that I thoroughly believed. I would have protested that my family was certainly more important. But that morning on the mountain in India, I realized that since I was a boy most of my energy and thought had been devoted to monetary success. Without realizing it, I had accepted the notion that if I got rich, I would be all right."*

"At the end of my meditation," the author continued, *"I had a second important realization. I had outlived the doctors' predictions of my imminent death. By then, I had been in India for four desperate months. During none of that time had I been pursuing money and success. Instead, I had been pursuing my spiritual enlightenment. I had shifted from my old way of thinking. To my surprise, I had not died. I had been forced to direct my attention elsewhere, and I did not even feel ill any longer. I had to face a serious question: Could it have been my old way of thinking that had threatened my life?"*

Mark ordered a second beer, and raced through the story of Hollingsworth's quest for spiritual development. From India, he had returned to England, then to a place called Findhorn, in Scotland, where many grew their own food. From Findhorn, he had gone to America, where he had involved himself with a wide range of metaphysical teachings.

To Mark's disappointment, the author offered no definitive recommendations. The upshot of the book seemed to be that the old way of living was a dead end. A man needed to get out of "self" and to find a way to serve mankind.

That was all well and good, Mark thought, but he already knew that his old way of living was not working. Besides, he already did a lot to serve mankind. Did he not regularly give to practically every charity in town? Last year alone, he gave over $2,000,000. True it was mostly in appreciated stock that helped on his taxes, but $2,000,000 was one hell of a lot of money!

When Mark finished the book, he realized it was dark and that the patio was filled with dinner patrons. He had totally lost track of time. He looked at his watch. It was nearly eight o' clock. Zeldah was expecting him at the condo for dinner at seven.

He took a deep breath. He was still absorbing the full impact of *Not By Bread Alone*. Hollingsworth had known the same heady success, followed by the same emptiness and unhappiness. Yet apparently Hollingsworth had found a solution. He wanted to know more. He wondered if Mavis had ever heard of the author. He looked at his watch again and calculated what time it would be in England. The earliest he dared call would be eight o'clock in the morning in England, which would be midnight here.

Mark looked up and down Haight Street, looking for a taxi. None was in sight, so he reached into his pocket for change to call Alex.

"Are you okay, Mr. Stevens?" asked the chauffer. "I was beginning to worry."

"I'm at that restaurant in Haight-Ashbury. You remember. The same one. I'll be out in front."

As Mark waited for Alex, a pretty, tanned woman carrying a bunch of flowers entered the patio, and started to walk by his table.

"Mark? Mark Stevens?" she called.

Mark looked up, not recognizing the woman.

"It's Diane Chandler. You remember me, don't you?"

"Oh, Diane," Mark fumbled. "I'm sorry. Of course I remember you. My mind was a million miles away. What are you doing here?"

"I always eat here on my day in the City," Diane laughed. "You know, my day off from my life."

"Sure. I guess we all need a day off now and then."

"May I sit down? I mean, are you with anyone?"

"No. Of course. Please sit down. I'm sorry if I was impolite. I was thinking about something else."

Mark held the chair for Diane.

"I'm so happy to bump into you Mark. I was hoping to see you again sometime."

"Yes. Well, me too," Mark stammered. Clearly Diane wanted to resume their brief relationship, but spending the night with her would not solve any of his problems. His mind was on telephoning Mavis. "How have you been?" he asked Diane.

"Oh it's the same old story with me. Unhappy, but afraid to do anything about it." She leaned forward inquisitively. "And how about you?"

"Not me."

"Not you?"

Mark stood up abruptly. "I'm not going to be afraid to do something about it." He took out his wallet to leave money for the waitress. "Diane, I'm afraid I'm being very rude, but I've got to go now. I'm sorry, but I've got something very important I must do."

Diane watched Mark get into his Rolls-Royce. She recalled how Mark had called his Rolls-Royce a magic carpet that might take her away, and how they had made love at his Nob Hill condo. Mark seemed so mysterious and unhappy. I wonder why a man like that comes to Haight-Ashbury, she thought as the big car turned the corner and disappeared from view.

Mark waited impatiently for midnight to pass so he could call Mavis. He realized now that part of his problem had been that he had not taken seriously the fact that he had been so unhappy. A chat with Rolf or Mavis, here and there, was all he had done. *Not By Bread Alone* had given him a sense he could do something about these feelings that had been plaguing him.

Finally, midnight came and he dialed Castle Enfield. "May I speak to Lady Ashley, please? If she's up and about that is. This is Mr. Stevens, Mark Stevens."

"She's having her breakfast, sir," said the male servant. "One moment."

Soon Mavis came on the line.

"Hello, Mark, dear."

"Mavis, I've come across the most amazing little book," he said enthusiastically. "It's by a man named Michael Hollingsworth. He may have something to do with St. James's Piccadilly. I thought you might know him."

"Michael Hollingsworth. I've heard of him. Why, I think—yes, of course. Hold on a moment, while I find that flyer." She left the phone. "Here it is. I thought so. Michael Hollingsworth is giving a lecture in two days, at the church. It's interesting that you should call."

"Are you're sure about that? Two days?"

"Yes, it's right here. Thursday night."

"What do you think of him, anyway? Hollingsworth?"

"I don't know much about him, really. From what I hear he's very good. He talks about our 'big question' you know."

"I know, I know." Mark laughed into the telephone. Of course Mavis would remember the "big question."

Mavis laughed too. "'What do you do, when you've got it all?' Right?"

"Yes," Mark chuckled. "Right."

He paused for a moment.

"Mavis?"

"Yes, what?"

"Would you think I was absolutely crazy if I flew all the way to London to hear one lecture?"

"Of course, my dear Mark, I would think you were crazy, absolutely mad," she laughed. "But you must promise that you will come to the country to see me while you're here. You will, won't you?"

-60-

It was very cold when Mark arrived in St. James's Piccadilly Church. He had gone first to his London condo from Heathrow this morning, where he had taken his usual jet-lag nap. Rodney and Rebecca were expecting him for dinner after Hollingsworth's talk. Londoners were preoccupied with Christmas, so the audience at the church numbered only about 50. It was so cold inside the old church that many had not removed their winter coats. Mark wore a sweater under his double-breasted blazer.

He had reread *Not By Bread Alone* on the company jet, and was eager to hear Michael Hollingsworth. The atmosphere in the Christopher Wren church tonight was more like a lecture hall's than a church's. After an introduction, Hollingsworth took the lectern to polite applause.

Hollingsworth looked the same as the photo on his book, except that he was now nearing 70. His wavy hair was completely white, and looked professionally styled. His suit was rumpled and old, but was expensive in its day. He began his talk in conversational tone, as if he were a businessman making a report, rather than a professional speaker.

Hollingsworth retold the story of how he had been an ambitious and successful businessman. How his life had fallen apart, and about his miraculous recovery from an apparently fatal illness. "As I traveled the world, I discovered that there are many people who have the same problem. I call it the 'empty lives syndrome.'" He turned and wrote "empty lives syndrome" on the chalkboard. "It is a syndrome much more likely to strike successful people."

"Most people in the world are struggling to make ends meet. When you are worried about where your next meal is coming from, you hardly are concerned with the meaning of life. To a hungry man, the meaning of life is simple: it's *food*. There is no 'empty lives syndrome' when you're hungry." Hollingsworth held the complete attention of his audience.

"But it's not just the hungry who avoid being stricken by the 'empty lives syndrome.' I call them 'the full, but still struggling.' They have good educations and good jobs. What they want is to get ahead. To have a large home, to have a fine motor car and all the rest. Often they are still under 50. Quite like those who are struggling merely to exist, they are not worrying about the meaning of life. For them, the meaning of life is still perfectly clear. It is success. 'Give me what I want and I'll be all right,' they say.

"Even when they don't achieve the success they envisioned, they remain fully convinced they are on the right track. They spend the whole of their lives seeking the elusive thing they are calling success. 'Oh, I'm all right,' they say. 'My life will be what I want when I get that promotion, or when the children are grown', or, more lately, 'when I lose some weight.'" The audience chuckled.

"The sad thing is if they do achieve success, they have to become *even more* successful. It is very frightening to them to have achieved their goals and to realize they aren't any happier than before. Oh, they enjoy the newly won comforts all right, but in fact they are even less happy, because in their souls the illusion has disappeared.

"So what do most successful people do? They create more and larger goals. 'My goals were too modest,' they say. 'My problem was my goals, so I'll change my goals. I'll be happy when I achieve these new goals. How silly of me to have thought I would be happy with only £30,000 per year.'" Again the audience chuckled knowingly.

Mark tried to apply to himself what the speaker was saying. It was true that from his earliest days, he had wanted to be successful, but that seemed perfectly natural. What was wrong with that?

"That was me. That was Michael Hollingsworth. I desperately wanted to be successful in business. I had no doubts about my goals. I never thought about the meaning of life. All my efforts were pointed in one direction, success. That is, until I got extremely ill and the doctors told me I was going to die. It was then I knew I had to do something different."

"Jesus," Mark muttered under his breath. Maybe he had not been told he was going to die, as Hollingsworth had; but he certainly had been unhappy, even though he had been successful beyond his wildest imagination. He had so many doubts and such haunting feelings of meaninglessness. And there had been those awful compulsions to run away. Like Hollingsworth he, too, knew he had to do something different.

Hollingsworth continued: "I think it was Oscar Wilde who said 'In this world there are only two tragedies. One is getting what one wants and the other is not getting it.'" The audience laughed. "Well, I've been in both situations. I've gotten what I wanted, and I have *not* gotten what I wanted. Frankly, I'm not sure which is best." Again the audience chuckled.

The room had gotten warmer and most people had removed their coats. "I know I was a lot happier as a young man, when I was under the delusion that I would be happy if only I could get what I wanted", said Hollingsworth. Mark thought about his Oxford days and his drive to get a first.

"All right, then. We have seen that many achievers remain fully convinced that if only they can achieve their goals, they will be happy. They seldom doubt this is so. They don't reach their goals, but they know they would be happy if only they could. The illusion is maintained.

"We have also seen that others need to keep changing and enlarging their goals when they find out their plan isn't working. They do this endlessly. Setting new goals, remaining unhappy, setting more goals, etcetera, etcetera, and etcetera, ad infinitum." Each time he spoke the word 'etcetera,' he slowed the cadence of his speech to illustrate the futility of all this goal-setting. Mark was reminded of his decision to begin buying up companies.

"But some are brighter than that. They begin to see the futility of it all. They see that all this goal-setting and achieving is not getting them happiness."

"So what do they do?" asked a fortyish, red-haired woman in the front row.

"Some drop out of the 'ambition' race. They change jobs. They buy Bed and Breakfasts in the country. They leave their spouses. But more often than not, they have solved very little, and remain unhappy. Perhaps all that is not too bad, though. At least they are no longer playing the game. Perhaps they are getting closer to their own truths.

"Then there are others. They know that ambition and goal-setting doesn't work, but they can't stand being unhappy. So, like dope addicts, they go back to setting even more goals and achieving more. They know it won't work, but they don't know what else to do. They remind me of the gambler. When someone asked him why he gambled at a dishonest table, he answered: 'I know I can't win, but it's the only game in town.'" Again the group chuckled. Hollingsworth had them all listening.

"Fortunately there are others. The only ones who at least have a chance. Perhaps a small chance, but at least a chance. Does anyone have any ideas about what they try?"

Again, no one in the audience spoke. Mark had no idea what Hollingsworth was leading up to.

"*They try to change their pattern.*" Hollingsworth wrote the word "CHANGE" in large letters on the board.

"That of course is the challenge for us. How do we change, and what do we do?

"I'm sorry, but you are all going to be very disappointed. Disappointed because I do not have an answer for you. Only some ideas.

"And now I want to ask you to pay special attention to me.

"The number one point I want you to remember is that the answer will be different for each one of you." He wrote the word "DIFFERENT" on the board. "What works for one person may not work for another."

"The second point I ask you to remember is equally simple. Each of us must find out for ourselves what that answer is. I cannot do it for you. No one can do it for you."

Hollingsworth turned and wrote the word "YOU". He paused and looked at his audience.

"As disappointing as that may be, I can assure you of one thing. At the end of your search, the answer for *you* will be much more meaningful, much more productive, much more apt to succeed than your old way of living."

Hollingsworth went on to make several other points. "In my view, the happiest people are those who seem to have nothing to prove about themselves. Often these are people who devote themselves to helping others: the sick, the troubled, the poor, those stuck in life. The happiest are often those who give to charitable causes, who teach others, who do in life what they really enjoy, and not what got them money and plaudits."

"Anything to give up those false goals of youth," he went on. "Anything to give up those erroneous beliefs—your old beliefs that you would be happy if only you were successful in your work, if only Susan would marry you, or a dozen other 'if onlys.'"

Mark raised his hand to ask a question. "Mr. Hollingsworth, I find that my ambitions, my goals, help me a great deal in life. As a matter of fact, they have brought me a very long way. You certainly don't expect me to give up all that, do you?"

"That's a very good question. I don't mean to embarrass you, but it is a question that a good many Americans might ask, given your culture. You see, it's not the ambition and the goals that make us unhappy." Hollingsworth paused, earnestly searching for words. "There is an old Zen saying. It goes something like this: 'Before enlightenment: Chopping wood. Carrying water. After enlightenment: Chopping wood. Carrying water.'"

Mark was puzzled. He did not know what Hollingsworth meant.

"It's difficult to explain. After a man has become enlightened, he may very well continue to do exactly the same thing as before. He may very well remain ambitious. You, sir, for example, I doubt very much if you would ever lose your ambition. Would you agree?"

"Why, yes, I think that's true," Mark answered.

A woman in the front row turned to look at Mark.

"But, you see, you'd be working and striving for different reasons, different motivations. In a nutshell, after enlightenment, as the Zen say, one's sense of self-esteem, one's opinion of oneself, is no longer dependent on achieving." Again, Hollingsworth was searching for words. "You'd be striving because you wanted to, not because you had to—I guess that's the best way I can put it. Not because you had to have success to be happy. Have I explained myself, sir?"

"I think so. I'm not sure," Mark answered hesitantly.

"The difficulty we all have is applying all this to our own lives. It's easier to see with others. You all laughed at the man who thought the secret to life was earning £75,000 a year. Thirty thousand is like a a million to one person, and a shilling to another. We all need to question our goals. Are you sure you are not deceiving yourself the same way that poor devil is about £75,000? The truth is the amount of money a person earns has little to do with his happiness. I know that may be difficult to accept, but it's true.

"I'm thinking of a man I once knew. This fellow—he had a very good education—truly believed that his life would be a success if he were admitted to a certain prestigious club here in St. James's. A club which I won't name. He never was admitted, but I feel certain that he would have felt just as badly about himself even if he had been admitted. Perhaps even worse, because his illusion would have been shattered. I haven't seen him in years, but to this day he may be thinking he has been unhappy because he was never admitted to that silly club.

"As I say, the solution for each of us is different." Hollingsworth was nearing the end of his lecture. "We must look ourselves squarely in the eye. We must honestly ask ourselves 'Is this really what I want? Am I doing with my life what I really want to do, or am I leading some sort of a false life?'"

Mark was eager to talk to Hollingsworth after the speech. This man had something. He wanted to know more.

"And after that, you must have the courage to change your life; for if you don't change, you will be doomed to spend the rest of your life worshiping a false god. The God of Success. The God of Ambition. And, yes, the God of Money."

Afterward, several of the group crowded around Hollingsworth, asking questions. Although he was very anxious to talk, Mark restrained himself until the others had finally finished. "Mr. Hollingsworth, my name is Mark Stevens. I've flown all the way from San Francisco to hear you tonight. There's a pub not far from here. I'd like very much to talk with you. Would that be all right with you?"

Michael Hollingsworth and Mark crossed Piccadilly and walked the long, darkened block to the pub. "Mr. Hollingsworth, I'm so glad to be able to meet you. I bought a copy of your book in San Francisco three days ago. It was so fascinating that I read it that very afternoon. I knew I had to talk to you."

"Ah yes, *Not By Bread Alone*. It seems a lifetime ago that I wrote that little book. And please, sir, won't you call me Michael?"

"Of course, and I'm Mark."

The pub was downstairs. Mark bought them each a pint of beer, which they took to a secluded table. "Did my book help you?"

"It certainly got me thinking. Your book and the talk tonight."

"Thinking about what? What's been your problem?"

"I don't know. I guess if I knew what the problem was, I would have solved it."

Hollingsworth smiled.

"But I'm a lot like what you described tonight," Mark said.

"What, a disillusioned rich man?"

"Not exactly disillusioned, Michael."

Hollingsworth sipped on his beer, waiting for Mark to continue.

"My story starts out a lot like yours. I have been very successful at business—very successful."

"Why?"

Mark looked puzzled. "I've worked very hard. I read economics at Oxford and . . ."

"No," Hollingsworth interrupted. "When I say 'why?' I mean what motivated you?"

"What motivated me?" Mark asked quizzically. "I've always wanted to have a lot of money. That's not so unusual, is it?"

"No, I suppose it isn't. But when it comes right down to it, most people aren't really motivated enough to become rich. What I mean is: what is there about Mark Stevens that made you so successful when most people aren't? Was your father successful?"

Mark smiled. "When I was a child, I always thought he was. He was a foreman. Hard-driving. Tough. All those things. It was only when I got older that I could see him more for what he was. Always drunk, whoring around, being mean to my mother and me."

"What was there about him that made you want to be so successful?"

Mark thought for a moment before answering. "I guess I wanted to show him up. Make him admit—make him admit something—I don't know what."

"You wanted to prove yourself to him?"

"I suppose so."

"That's true of most of us, anyway. It was certainly true of me."

"What, exactly?"

"Proving myself. I've spent years at it. Psychotherapy. Study in India. Well, you read my book."

"Sure."

"I had to prove to my parents—my father especially—that I was somebody special. I didn't know any way to do it except business success and money."

"Well, sure. That was certainly true of me. What other way would there be?" Mark asked.

"Tell me this. Did you ever actually prove anything to your father? Did he ever finally acknowledge that you were successful?"

"No. He died when I was at Oxford here—I went to Oxford."

"And you think it would have been different if he had lived?"

"My father? Are you kidding me? Jonah Stevens would never have admitted I was better than he, if he had lived a thousand years."

"You say 'better than him'?"

"Sure. That's it, when it comes right down to it. He was always putting me down."

"And so you wanted to be better than him? Even have him admit it?"

"I just wish he could have seen me get married to Priscilla Enfield. That would have showed him. His son marrying into the Enfield family. I wish he could have seen my big house in Hillsborough, the offices, the jet, the whole bit."

"Why? What would he have said?"

"Him? He wouldn't have said a goddamn thing."

"So your father would never have complimented you? Told you 'good show.' None of that?"

"Of course not."

"So how much money would you have had to make? How many houses? How many companies?"

"What? To please my father?"

"Yes."

"Hell. I could have owned the whole damned world, and he wouldn't have . . ." Mark stopped, as if searching for the right word.

"Wouldn't have told you he loved you? Right? Isn't that it?"

"No, not that. I never dared to expect him to say something like that."

"That's what you wanted, wasn't it?"

"Sure, as a kid—for a while there."

"And I'll wager as an adult. Even now. Today. How old are you Mark?"

"Forty."

Hollingsworth smiled. "So the point is no matter how much money you might make, no matter how successful you are, you can't please your father. He'll never love you, no matter what."

"Well, he's dead, of course."

"I don't mean your real father."

"What do you mean, not my real father?"

"I'm talking about that father inside of Mark Stevens. That big, bad, tough father inside you. Right now. Right this very minute."

"I see," Mark said hesitantly, not at all sure he was really seeing.

"He's in there right now, barking orders. 'Mark, do this. Mark, accomplish this. Mark, I won't love you unless you make even more millions.' Don't you see? That's what pushes you, that's what pushed me. That's what pushes us all so. Your father has become part of you. Don't you see?"

"It sounds hopeless. At least for me." Distress was in Mark's voice. "If that's what that is—my father within me—it will never let me go. Never in a thousand years let me go. Keeps pushing the hell out of me." He gestured with his arm, nearly knocking over his beer, and grabbing the glass to keep it from tumbling over.

"Yes, I know. It used to be that way with me, too."

"What did you do to change? I gather you did change."

"It's certainly not an overnight process. I'd say the most important single factor in changing is *awareness*." Hollingsworth spoke with vigor, as from personal conviction.

"Awareness?"

"Yes, it's absolutely amazing what simple awareness does." Hollingsworth tilted his head back and drained his beer. "If you can simply be *aware* that these inner forces are at work, you've come a long way. Being conscious of this demanding, inner father within you. This stupid father who would never love you, even if you owned the whole bloody world."

"You mean I can't get rid of it? Only become *aware* of it? What good would that do?"

"It loosens its grip on you. It doesn't have the same control over you when you are aware of the forces inside yourself." Hollingsworth stood. "Do you want another?" he asked, referring to another beer.

"Sure." The two walked over to the bar together to get more beer.

"I'm not sure I understand," said Mark. "What would I become aware of?"

"Take for example, your next business decision. Take some decision that involves a lot of money. It could be anything."

"Okay."

"When you're working through it, take a good look at what's happening inside you—what is really motivating you."

"Like, am I still trying to prove something to the father inside of me?"

"Yes—perfect—that's the idea! That's the way you can free yourself. 'Am I behaving the way I am because of some neurotic ambition?' If you find you are, then change—change your behavior. Only do things that are coming from your true self, not this old neurotic self."

"How about you, Michael? Have you changed?"

"I find change to be circular."

"Circular?"

"Yes, I find myself coming around to what seems to be at the exact same point in the circle. At first, I don't think anything is any different. But then I realize it *is* different. I'm in the same circle as before, but higher—a lot higher."

Mark looked at him, sipping his beer without commenting.

"It's like that Zen saying about carrying water and chopping wood. I'm doing the same thing, but not really the same thing. I'm different. I've changed."

"A different attitude?"

"That's part of it. A different way of seeing things. The first way is from the wrong direction and I'm unhappy."

"Well, I know this, I don't think I could live without being ambitious, without my business, without having money." I don't care what deep, dark psychological reason got me started."

"Of course not. No one would expect you to. However, you might very well end up by changing how you live—what's important to you. You know, it just might be that other things might become more important to you."

"But something inside me doesn't want to change."

"Of course, but there's also something inside you shouting at the top of its voice. It wants to be heard, to make things different. It's telling you to take boat rides instead of going to the office."

They took their fresh beer glasses back to their table.

"What about you, Michael? Have you found happiness?"

"Happiness? I don't know about 'happiness.' Satisfaction is a better word for me."

"What about money?"

"I don't care much about money any more. I've learned to trust that I'll be taken care of. If I do what I really want, the universe will see to it that I'm taken care of."

"I don't think I could do that."

"In the last analysis, no matter how much we struggle, it's really the universe that's fulfilling our needs, not us."

"I certainly don't intend to give away my money."

"Nor should you. I make a decent living from my writing and my lectures. That's the way the universe supplies my needs. My friend, you're the one who has to make those decisions for yourself. But you have to nourish your soul, not just your bank account."

"I've got a confession to make, Michael. When I found out you were speaking here tonight . . ."

"Yes."

"I thought I'd fly to London and get all the answers—that you would have all the answers."

"Did you?"

"And then I could go back to being the way I'd always been. You know, living the same way."

Hollingsworth laughed. "Did you really?"

"I have to confess, I did."

"I may not have the answers you wanted, but I do have a very strong suggestion for you."

"What's that?"

"It has to do with your father."

"Go ahead."

"It's forgiveness."

"Forgiveness?"

"You've got to forgive him."

"Me, forgive my father? You're not the first person to say that."

"I don't think you're ever going to find what you're seeking unless you do."

"Michael, you didn't know Jonah Stevens. He doesn't deserve forgiveness. Why on earth should I forgive him? Christ, to this day I walk with this goddammed limp, and he didn't even say he was sorry. You have to be kidding!" Mark was annoyed.

"Mark, it's for your own sake, not his. It has nothing to do with what he deserves. If you don't forgive him, you're going to be carrying this war around inside you for the rest of your life. Don't you see? You've got this father within you that you hate. You're hating part of yourself. You've got to start the healing process."

"Goddammit, Michael! You ask one hell of a lot of a man," Mark grimaced.

"I'm not asking anything of you. I'm just telling you what I think you've got to do for your own sake."

Mark was silent—pondering—thinking—not knowing what to say.

"Ever read the Bible?" asked Hollingsworth.

"The Bible?"

Hollingsworth laughed. "Don't looked so shocked."

"I can't remember ever reading the Bible."

"Do yourself a favor sometime."

"Okay."

"Read the book of Ecclesiastes."

"Sounds like the Old Testament."

"It is. It's about a man like you. And a man like me."

"Really, in the Bible?"

"Yes. Read it sometime."

They talked for another hour. Mark was questioning, probing, still hoping Hollingsworth might offer him some magic secret.

"Are you going to be in London for a while?" Mark asked. "I thought we might be able to chat again tomorrow."

"No. Tomorrow I leave on a tour of the continent. I'm going to be in California next September, though. Perhaps we can meet again there."

"I'll be there."

Mark's English chauffeur had been waiting with the Rolls-Royce on Jermyn Street, near the church. Mark dropped Hollingsworth off at his little hotel near Brompton Road. "I'll see you in September," said Hollingsworth.

"I'll be there. Many thanks to you. I've got a lot of thinking to do."

"Good night, Mark. And don't forget about Ecclesiastes."

"I won't. Maybe I'll read a little tonight." The chauffeur closed the car door, and Hollingsworth stepped toward his hotel.

.   .   .

It was past ten o'clock when Mark's Rolls-Royce arrived at Rodney's and Rebecca's Knightsbridge flat. It was like being home to be with them. Their daughter, little Allison, now 12, would be home from school for the holidays. Perhaps Mark should stay in London for Christmas. He would go to the country tomorrow and see Mavis. He might even spend Christmas at Castle Enfield.

He was excited by what he had learned tonight, and wanted to begin putting it to use in his everyday life.

Grim-faced, Rodney stood by the door. "Mark, there's been a call from your man in San Francisco, Baumgartner. There's some sort of very serious business problem at home. He wants you to call him immediately. Why don't you make the call in the library?"

Mark was on the telephone over 45 minutes before returning to the drawing room.

"You look awful," said Rodney. "What's wrong?"

"It's Derek. He's been the one buying our stock. He's trying to take over my company.

"Derek Harden?"

"The son of a bitch!"

"He doesn't have a chance, does he?" asked Rebecca

"I don't know. He's teamed up somehow with Henry."

"What, my Uncle Henry?" asked Rodney.

"What on earth does Uncle Henry have to do with this?" asked Rebecca.

"Pris left a will." Mark answered.

"But how would that change anything?" Rodney asked.

"Her will left everything to Henry."

"Yes, but how . . ." asked Rebecca.

"Their lawyers are saying Pris owned half my stock in the company. Now she's willed it to her father."

Rebecca and Rodney stood in amazement.

"If they're right . . ." Mark continued.

"Sit down, Mark. I'll get you a drink," said Rodney.

"If they're right, they'd control over half the stock. They'd take over my company. Don't you see? I'd be working for them."

Mark took the Scotch Rodney offered.

"Well, yes—but couldn't you just form another company?" inquired Rodney. "One you'd completely own yourself?"

"I can't do that. You see I have a contract. I can't work for anyone else."

Later, in his bed at his London flat, Mark tossed and turned. He hated to go back to San Francisco. He hated to get involved with courts and lawyers, but Derek had to be stopped. And Henry—

Henry teaming up with Derek! It was hard to believe. Son of a bitch! He wasn't going to let them get away with this.

Finally, he got up and turned on the television. There was nothing on. Ironic, wasn't it? he thought. With Hollingsworth's book and tonight's lecture, he was just beginning to understand he should see The Stevens Group in a new light. But suddenly now, here was this insidious threat to take it away from him. Yes, it was ironic, because right now the company seemed more important to him than ever.

-61-

Mark hastily returned from London to defend against Derek's takeover. The Stevens Group stockholders' annual meeting would be in five weeks. At that meeting, Derek and Henry would combine forces. Mark's position was desperate. If Henry could legally vote half Mark's shares on the theory that they were Pris's community property, Mark would lose control of his company.

The last places on earth Mark wanted to be was in attorneys' offices and courtrooms. He wanted to devote less time to the company, not more. He wanted to build a home near Sonoma, and venture into San Francisco only when Steve Baumgartner absolutely needed him. He yearned to go into seclusion and do some thinking about his life. He had planned to read Ecclesiastes as Hollingsworth suggested, and delve more into the spiritual life, but now he was trapped in this fight.

Steve met Mark's jet at the airport, and took him directly to The Stevens Group attorneys, Toler and McCarthy, for an emergency meeting.

"This couldn't possibly be more serious, Mark," Homer Toler sternly warned. "If they convince the court that your company stock was community property with Priscilla, you'll not only lose control of The Stevens Group, but half of everything else you own will be in jeopardy."

The thought of that propelled Mark into the thick of the fight. He had no alternative but to abandon the contemplative life. He was staying at his Nob Hill condominium, frenetically meeting with the lawyers. As Michael Hollingsworth had said in his London lecture, "A starving man does not worry about the meaning of life."

Two precious weeks had passed. Mark had grown extremely impatient with the slow pace of Toler and McCarthy. He had an appointment this morning with Homer Toler to discuss his dissatisfaction. His large law firm had the six top floors of an art deco office building in the Financial District. Mark had asked Rolf Williams to meet him there. Perhaps Rolf could get across to Homer that Mark wanted action.

Rolf was waiting in the staid, appropriately worn reception room. The old-line law firm had been founded by Homer Toler's father, Mann Toler. Homer Toler was Law Review, and Order of Coif, Harvard Law 1939. Mann Toler had insisted that Homer get his legal education from that prestigious eastern institution, where many established San Francisco lawyers also sent their sons. There was no question that Homer Toler was brilliant. His firm had been Mark's main law firm for eight years now and, as senior litigation partner, Homer would handle this case. But Mark had lost patience with Homer's conservative, plodding ways. He had tried to be diplomatic, but so far Homer had not gotten the message. Win or lose, Mark wanted to resolve the case as quickly as possible, but that was not Homer Toler's way. Today Mark intended to bring the matter to a head.

"Homer, meet my old friend Rolf Williams. Rolf and I grew up together."

"Mark and I went to Cal undergraduate together," said Rolf. I graduated from Boalt. I spent a few years with Kellogg and Jefferson, but I finally opted for the solo practice in Sonoma. I've been there over almost 10 years now."

"Kellogg and Jefferson. A fine firm," said Homer, motioning for them to sit in the conference area of his office. "My father used to tell me about his trials with old Anton Kellogg. A fine old firm." As senior partner, Homer commanded a large corner office with the same view of the Bay as Mark's. "Many a time I've dreamed of the small town practice, away from the pressures of the big firm and its big corporate clients."

"Don't let it fool you, Homer. May I call you Homer?" asked Rolf.

"Oh, of course. Please don't stand on formality."

"An important case for a small client has every bit as much pressure as for your large corporations—maybe more."

"I'm sure it seems that way. Everything depends on your perspective doesn't it?" said Homer condescendingly. "Well, Mark, what did you have in mind for this morning?"

Rolf spoke up. "I hope you won't be offended, Homer. My being here, I mean."

"Oh, of course not. Of course not." Homer lit a cigarette and leaned back.

"Mark thought maybe the three of us could figure out a strategy . . ."

"Yes," Mark interrupted, "there has to be some way to get this damned thing to trial—and soon."

"The courts are very congested. We intend to make a motion for an early trial as soon as the pleadings are at issue, but even then it would be at least a year, don't you think, Rolf?"

"I suppose so, but I haven't had a case in San Francisco for a long time."

"I'll need at least a year for preparation, anyway," Homer added. "There are nearly 50 depositions to be taken—interrogatories— I'm sure dozens of discovery motions. The usual thing. This is no simple case, Rolf."

"What's so complicated?" asked Mark. "Either the stock is community property, or it isn't."

"Just what do you see as the legal issues?" Rolf asked Homer.

"As Mark says, there is the question of whether Mark's stock was community property. If it wasn't community, she had no right to will it to her father, and Mark wins. Now of course that presents a plethora of sub-issues."

"I can imagine that it does." Rolf was conscious that it was a delicate matter to be second-guessing one of San Francisco's most prestigious attorneys.

"But I owned the company before we got married," Mark asserted.

"It goes beyond that," countered Homer. "Remember, if the court finds that the stock is community property, then most of the other assets will probably be community property, too."

"Jesus, Homer, there was no way Pris really wanted to will everything to her father."

"Don't forget, though, she did leave a will and did exactly that," Homer pointed out.

"That shyster, Thomas Wahl! She told me she never intended to file for divorce. He did it without her consent. How could a will like that be valid?" exclaimed Mark. "Wahl even made himself the goddammed administrator of her estate."

"Executor," corrected Homer. "That's why we have to take depositions. I want to take everybody's deposition, right down to the parking lot attendant. If I have to show Priscilla was crazy in order to upset that will, then I'll prove she was crazy."

"Pris wasn't crazy, Homer, for God's sake. You're barking up the wrong tree."

"Don't you think it's proper procedure to try to challenge the validity of Pris's will in a collateral action?" Rolf asked. "After all, the fight over who gets to vote the stock is a collateral action."

"I don't know the answer to that. You're right—we might have to contest the will in probate first. I've got a whole staff of our brightest associates working on that, and every other issue we can think of."

"Dammit, Homer!" interjected Mark. "At this rate, it will be years before we get a decision, won't it?"

"Maybe so, but I can't change the whole fucking judicial system, even if it's for you." Homer was testy. "It just doesn't work that fast."

"Have you thought about getting a TRO against their voting the stock?" Rolf asked.

"Of course we have. It wouldn't work."

"What the hell is a TRO?" asked Mark.

"Temporary Restraining Order," Rolf explained. "Usually to stop something from happening for a few days until a hearing can be held. A judge has the power to grant a TRO just on the plaintiff's affidavit, without the defendant's even having a chance to defend himself."

"We don't have a clear enough case yet to get a TRO," Homer said. "Maybe in Sonoma you could—no telling what some small town judge might do—but here in San Francisco we wouldn't have a chance."

"Well, what about a preliminary injunction?" Rolf asked hesitantly, not wanting to anger Toler.

"Of course that was one of the first options we considered," Homer answered. "We probably could get a hearing before the shareholders' meeting on the 29th."

"He means getting an injunction stopping them from voting Pris's shares on January 29th," Rolf explained to Mark. "It would stop them from voting the shares, at least until the trial."

"Why don't we go for that?" asked Mark.

"Because without proper depositions we wouldn't have a fat chance. I can't prove a prima facie case without depositions." Homer's face had reddened. He was clearly annoyed that his judgment was being questioned.

"But we would have a chance, wouldn't we?" Mark asked.

"Of course we'd have a chance. Christ, you always have a chance! Even the stupidest lawyer has a fucking chance."

"Why don't we go for it then? Homer, I'd like you to go for it," said Mark.

"Nothing doing!" Homer shot back. "This firm has a reputation to uphold. I'm not going into court shooting from the hip, and ask Judge Hopkins, or whoever the hell is sitting up there now, for a goddammed preliminary injunction. I'd get shot down. Jesus Christ, I wouldn't try a slip and fall case that way! You listen to me: Toler and McCarthy doesn't practice law that way."

"Couldn't you ask the judge to hear live testimony?" Rolf asked. "That way you would get to cross-examine Henry Enfield, or whoever else would testify. You'd have a better chance that way. Maybe with good cross-examination you could break them down."

"Goddammit, Mr. Williams! They aren't going to permit live testimony on a preliminary injunction. They always decide on affidavits, never live testimony. They simply don't do it."

Mark spoke up. "What difference does live testimony make, anyway?"

"With affidavits, you don't have a very good chance at proving they're lying," Rolf explained. "Live testimony is different. It's like a trial, only much earlier than a regular trial. With cross-examination, you'd have a shot at it."

"That's what I want—an early trial. That's what I want you to do, Homer. I want you to do what Rolf is saying."

"Listen to me, Mark," Homer said sternly. "You're talking about half of everything you own. Years ago you chose Toler and McCarthy for damned good reasons. You are one of the richest men in San Francisco. Maybe the richest."

"I don't give a damn, Homer. I'm not going to allow this case to consume three or four years of my life. Not even one year. I've got other things I want to do." Mark was very angry. "Depositions and all that crap! I want to get this over and done with."

"You can't treat this case like some small town case, and be taking your advice from some small town lawyer," Homer Toler said angrily.

"You listen to me, Homer," Mark responded. "I'm the client here. I'm the one who pays the bills, and I'm the one who's in charge."

Although still flushed, Homer Toler immediately calmed himself. He could see one of his firm's best clients stomping out his door, taking his business with him. "Now, Mark, of course you're the client. I'm sure Rolf and I can agree on the best strategy. And if I said anything in anger, I hope you'll accept my apology."

"It's too late for apologies, Homer. I've got to get this damned case on the road." Mark turned to Rolf. "You say we would have the right to cross-examination?"

"If the judge permitted live testimony, it would be just like a trial. Sure you'd have cross-examination."

"Then we need the best cross-examiner in the business. Tell me, Rolf, would I be allowed to bring in a lawyer from outside California?"

"Yes, lawyers from other states can be admitted to the bar for one particular case—at least if there's a California lawyer in the case, too."

"What about from another country? England? The best trial lawyer I ever heard was William Thackery Scott. He's the barrister who beat the shit out of Derek that time in London."

"William—Who?" asked Homer. "I've never heard of him."

"Thackery Scott. William Thackery Scott. You will have heard of him. Believe me, Homer, you will have heard of him."

"But Mark, you can't change attorneys in the middle of the case," pleaded Homer. "The firm has over 2,000 hours in time on this case. You can't throw all that away."

"Homer, you just watch me. I'm going to call Scott when I get back to the office." Mark looked at his watch.

"But Mark . . ." Homer sputtered.

"Let's see, it's early evening in London. I may not be able to reach him until tomorrow."

"What if he can't come over?" Rolf asked.

"Don't worry, he'll come over if he possibly can. He'll remember me from Rodney's case. Besides, I'll pay him whatever he asks."

"Where does that leave us?" asked a flustered Homer. "What do you want Toler and McCarthy to do?"

"I want you to send me a bill for the work you've done to date. Homer, you're off the case."

Mark turned to leave. "Come on Rolf, we've got our work cut out for us. William Thackery Scott is going to need help, and you're just the lawyer to do it."

-62-

Looking at the Bay from his office, Mark felt ambivalent. He did not want this takeover fight to turn into a monster that dominated him for months or years, yet he was stimulated by it. He had the same negative feelings as he had had with the Cleveland people. He was not going to allow himself to be dragged into that kind of crap. He wanted out. Yet this fight was exactly his cup of tea. He had gotten where he was today taking on challenges like this. In the lawyer's office he had felt like an old war horse who would spare nothing to grind Derek and Henry into the dirt.

He turned from the window and sat down. There seemed to be no reconciling these two parts of himself. He liked being ambitious and hard-driving, as he always had been, and yet he hated his predicament. He was trapped by Hollingsworth's "success syndrome."

Mark turned to the papers that Steve Baumgartner wanted him to read. He dreaded the detail. He felt the same as he had last month when he had impulsively left the office and gone for the boat ride. That was the day he had found Michael Hollingsworth's book. His mind recalled Hollingsworth's parting words: "Sometime you ought to read the book of Ecclesiastes."

Mark felt strange entering the religious bookstore. He had gone to the bookstore near his office, but it did not carry Bibles. "Sorry, nobody asks for them any more," the clerk had explained. "Try the religious bookstore over on Maiden Lane."

He had not read the Bible since he was nine or 10 years old. Confused by the many editions on display, he turned to the clerk.

"I want a Bible, but there are so many." He felt like a teenager buying a package of condoms.

"What kind of Bible do you want?"

"I want to read a particular book in the Bible—Ecclesiastes. It was recommended. Is there any such thing as a modern Bible?" The clerk smiled at Mark's discomfort.

"You want one without all the 'begats' and 'sayeths.'"

"That's what I'm looking for. One I can understand."

The clerk smiled again, taking a boxed Bible from the shelf. "This one's very good. It's published in England. Here, why don't you scan it a bit."

Mark's first impulse was to read his new purchase at the Haight Street restaurant. But he would feel strange reading the Bible in Haight-Ashbury, so he decided on his condominium. He walked to California, and boarded the cable car to go up the steep hill. He tucked the leather bound book under his arm, so that the other passengers would not see it was a Bible.

He put on his slippers and robe and, despite the voice within him that kept complaining he should be at the office in the middle of the day, flipped through the Bible until he found the book of Ecclesiastes. He wondered why Michael Hollingsworth had suggested it.

"Futility, utter futility . . . Everything is futile," Ecclesiastes began. *"What does anyone really profit from all his labor? All things are wearisome. Those who have lived and died are not remembered. Neither will those who follow them be remembered, nor those who in turn follow them."*

It was strange, Mark thought, to find such thoughts in the Bible. He had expected platitudes and some sayings with no modern-day relevance, yet it sounded as if whoever had written Ecclesiastes had felt some of what he had been feeling.

"I built palaces for myself, I planted vineyards, I made myself orchards and gardens. I acquired slaves. I owned more than any King before me. I amassed silver and gold. I obtained male and female singers. I obtained everything imaginable to delight my senses. They called me greater than any King before me. I did not deny myself any pleasure. All this I had well earned."

Mark was reminded of Alfred Hollingsworth's "success syndrome." The author of Ecclesiastes certainly had been ambitious. Like the people Hollingsworth was talking about, the author had kept setting more and more goals.

"Then having all this, I sat back and considered it all. I considered all of my work and all of my accomplishments. I considered all of the possessions and pleasure that they had wrought. I found it all futile. I found it all wanting. I found it to be like chasing the wind. I found it to be of no real profit to me."

Momentarily, he closed the Bible over his finger, holding his place and stared out at Alcatraz. The feeling was eerie. The author was so like himself. He wondered who he was and whether he had ever found any answers so many centuries ago.

"I realized the wise man is remembered no longer than the fool. Both will be forgotten. Both the wise man and fool are doomed to die.

"So I came to hate life. Everything was trouble to me. It is all futility and nothing but chasing after the wind. I came to hate my labor and my toil."

Mark thought about how he hated those Cleveland people. Even hated being in the office any more. How Baumgartner could not understand him. How he wanted to be free to go boat-riding, or read and think about other things.

"I considered all toil and all achievement. I saw that it all springs from rivalry between one person and another."

Perhaps Hollingsworth was right. Perhaps everything Mark had ever done was to prove himself to Jonah. If that were so, what a waste it all was!

"Better one hand full with peace of mind than two hands full with more toil. That too, is like chasing the wind."

Yes, Mark protested, but how to have peace of mind with one hand full, or even with a thousand hands full? That was the real question.

Mark turned the page.

"No one who loves wealth can enjoy any return from it. No one who loves money can ever have enough."

True, but with him it was not a case of not having enough money, it was a case of not knowing what else to do.

"The purpose of man's toil is to fill his belly, yet his appetite is never satisfied."

Mark checked to see how far he had to the end of Ecclesiastes. There were three pages left. The whole book was only 12 chapters long, not more than six pages in the Bible. He read of Ecclesiastes' journey. His search for satisfaction from wisdom, from knowl-

edge, from women, from power over his fellow man, from the writing of books and from education and study.

One sentence especially caught his attention.

" . . . *it is fools who nurse resentment.*"

The words stung him as he thought of his hatred for Jonah
and especially for Derek and Henry. He remembered Michael
Hollingsworth's advice: that he should forgive his father for his
own good.

As he neared the end of Ecclesiastes, he found himself reading
as if he were completing an exciting mystery. Before he knew it,
there were only two or three lines to the end.

*"This is the end of the matter. There is no more. Listen to God
and obey what he says. This is the answer. This is the salvation of
mankind. There is no more."*

He was disappointed. He had expected some answers, but
Ecclesiastes had provided no answers at all.

He made himself a drink and returned to the book. He read
the last part again.

*"Listen to God and obey what he says . This is the salvation of
mankind. There is no more."*

But he really did not believe in God. It was not that he was an
atheist, but the only thing he knew about religion was what his
mother had said, and he could never accept her simple beliefs. He
had planned one day to study religion, but that had always been a
long way off.

"Listen to God and obey what he says." There was no old man
in the sky to tell him what to do in life. He would like to discuss all
this with Mavis. He intended to ask Mavis and Rodney to come to
San Francisco for the trial anyway. Then something Hollingsworth
had written occurred to him. The answer lay in serving others,
Hollingsworth had written. Could that have been what Ecclesiastes
was driving at?

Mark's drink remained untouched as he read Ecclesiastes
again. His feelings of depression and melancholia heightened,
not lessened. He could see why Hollingsworth had recommended
that he read the book. The author of Ecclesiastes two to three
thousand years ago had faced the same problem that faced him
now.

He agreed that there was no point in piling up more wealth, but what was he supposed to do? It seemed to him that he was no better off than that morning in Pebble Beach when he had told Rolf he was going to expand his business because he knew nothing else to do. He had made no progress since he and Mavis had discussed the "big question" a thousand years ago.

He went for a long walk down to Fisherman's Wharf, around the Embarcadero and then back through Union Square to Nob Hill. When he returned, he had been gone over an hour and his mood had changed. He had no answers to Ecclesiastes, but one thing he knew for certain. As soon as it was daytime in London, he was going to telephone William Thackery Scott. He was not going to let Henry and Derek get control of his company.

-63-

Today was the day of the trial. Two weeks ago William Thackery Scott had canceled his schedule so he could try Mark's case. Mark had sent the company jet to London for him that very night. He provided Scott with a large suite in the tower of the Fairmont Hotel. There the barrister established command headquarters, where an entourage of secretaries, paralegals and an investigator constantly reported. Rolf Williams made arrangements for Scott to be admitted to the bar for this case. Rolf took a room in the Fairmont, and spent all his time on the case. His knowledge of California law was essential to Scott. They had filed for an injunction to prevent Thomas T. Wahl, as Pris's executor, from voting Pris's shares at the shareholders' meeting. Today's hearing would determine whether that injunction would be granted.

Throughout these past two weeks, Mark's ambivalent feelings toward the trial had persisted. At times he wanted no part of the tedious and demanding preparations. He would rather meet with Hollingsworth and discuss philosophical questions. Perhaps, like Hollingsworth, he would go to Findhorn or even to India. He was sick and tired of the world of lawyers. But he wanted desperately to win this fight, and would do whatever it took. The takeover attempt was serious, and he could not sit on a mountain top while all he had worked for was jeopardized. These past two weeks he had spent most of his time at William Thackery Scott's hotel suite preparing for the trial.

"All rise, please," commanded the beige-uniformed bailiff. "Department 'D' of the Superior Court in and for the County of San Francisco is now in session. The Honorable Otto Hammer, judge presiding. Be seated, please."

The black-robed Judge Hammer was unsmiling and stern. With a flourish of his judicial robes, he took his seat and opened the file of papers he had brought from his chambers.

"'The Stevens Group v. Thomas T. Wahl, Henry Enfield et al.' Gentlemen," said Hammer, "I've read the file. The first order of business is to decide whether I should begin by taking oral testimony, or follow the usual procedure of deciding the injunction on the written affidavits. I am ready for oral argument on that point."

Otto Hammer, who was just over 30, had been specially selected by the Presiding Judge for this case, which would have serious repercussions in the San Francisco business and social communities. At an extremely young age, Hammer had been appointed to the Municipal Court by California Governor Ronald Reagan, then elevated to the Superior Court during Reagan's second term as governor. Hammer had a brilliant law school record. From his law school days, his sole goal was to become a judge. He had never practiced law, but fresh from law school had attached himself to the Reagan campaign for governor. After Reagan's election, Hammer had worked in the California Attorney General's office, where he was when the Governor appointed him to the bench. Hammer's extreme confidence in himself was justified by his superior intelligence, but he had a reputation for being impatient and quick to judge.

William Thackery Scott rose to make his argument. He was flanked at the plaintiff's counsel table by Rolf Williams and Mark. Henry and Derek sat at the defendants' counsel table with their attorney, Joseph P. Raymer, Jr. Thomas T. Wahl sat with them.

Mark looked at the spectator section, which was filled with newspaper reporters. He had expected Mavis and Rodney to arrive from London, but they were not yet in the courtroom. The KRON television crew waited outside in the hall.

Surprisingly, William Thackery Scott wore his British wig and robe. Rolf had gently advised him that he would look strange, but Scott decided that it would be to his advantage to play to the hilt the role of visiting barrister. Majestically, Scott first turned toward Judge Hammer, then acknowledged his opposing counsel and began. "May it please the court. As your honor knows, I am a stranger to the American judiciary system. I apologize for the many errors I will undoubtedly make in protocol and courtesy. I assure you that the same are totally and completely unintentional and merely reflect the fact that I am a foreigner in your marvelous land."

"Mr. Scott," said Judge Hammer. "It is a pleasure to have you in my courtroom. Now if you would please proceed." If Otto Hammer was surprised at Scott's robe and wig, he concealed it.

"My case for using oral testimony is brief. A simple reading of the affidavits shows a conflict in the testimony. Much of it concerns alleged conversations with Priscilla Enfield Stevens, that poor dead woman whose presence will haunt us throughout this trial. Mr. Wahl will say she told him one thing and Mr. Stevens will say she told him something entirely different. Also we can expect conflicting testimony between Mr. Stevens and his father-in-law, Mr. Henry Enfield. How can your Lordship—pardon me, I mean your honor—how can your honor come to a proper decision as to who is telling the truth based on mere affidavits?"

When William Thackery Scott spoke, he assumed a manner not dissimilar to what one would expect if God were a lawyer who spoke with an English accent. He spoke as if there could be no question but what he said was correct, as if to disagree with him would be to betray the fact that one knew absolutely nothing about the law.

"Mr. Williams, here, assures me that in America, as indeed in England, affidavits are very carefully phrased and crafted by counsel before they are signed by the witnesses. All of us in this learned profession know that no witness would ever testify as smoothly or as convincingly as in an affidavit prepared by his own counsel in the privacy of his chambers." Hammer showed a bare trace of a smile at Scott's candor in stating the truth that lawyers found it easier to craft the testimony of their witnesses in affidavits rather than trust to live testimony from the witness stand.

"No judge, even one as wise as King Solomon himself, can ascertain which witness is telling the truth from slickly prepared affidavits—no, indeed. What is needed to serve the truth is testimony from the mouths of live, breathing witnesses. Where you, as the wise trier of fact, can see their faces. Where you, as a judge of human nature, can carefully watch their demeanor in the witness box." Scott grandly waved his hand in the direction of the witness stand. "And most of all, where in the great tradition of the common law, the tool of cross-examination is available—that ingenious creation of our forebears for getting at the truth."

Scott stepped back from the counsel table and began to pace as he made his points. Mark was pleased with his decision to replace Homer Toler with Scott. It was apparent that Scott would be every bit as effective in an American court as he had been in London. Best of all, here they were in trial only two weeks after he had fired Toler.

"Your Honor," Scott continued. "I have yet to figure out a way to cross-examine an affidavit. I have yet to figure out a way to wring the truth from a witness who is not even in the witness box. I . . ."

Judge Hammer held up his hand, stopping Scott. "Counsel. I am inclined to agree, but for reasons that you may not find too pleasing. If you would kindly be seated, I shall explain."

Mark was apprehensive. What did Hammer mean, "for reasons that you may not find too pleasing?"

"I have read the affidavits and the points and authorities submitted by counsel. It is clear to me, Mr. Scott, that you have an uphill fight. It seems to me that the stock in The Stevens Group, while it may once have been Mr. Stevens's separate property, has prima facie been transmuted to community property. If I am correct in that inclination, Priscilla Stevens had every right to will her half to whomever she pleased, and that certainly includes her own father."

Mark was shocked. He thought that the whole point of the trial was to find out if the stock were community property. That was what the trial was supposed to be about. Yet Judge Hammer was saying he had already made up his mind.

Scott rose to his feet with no more haste or dismay than if the judge had announced that it was time for the eleven o'clock recess. Again, Hammer raised his hand to stop Scott. "That is why I want to give you the benefit of the doubt, Mr. Scott. As you have argued, I believe that the witnesses should testify in person with, of course, the right of cross-examination. Mr. Raymer, I assume you have no objection."

Rolf Williams knew that Joseph Raymer, Jr. would be a fool to object. It was clear to Rolf that Hammer had made up his mind upon reading the affidavits and trial briefs. What the judge was doing was protecting himself from being reversed on appeal. To do this he was going to make all procedural rulings in favor of William Thackery Scott, including permitting live testimony. That way, there would be no prejudicial error justifying a reversal on appeal. It was a time-honored trick of trial judges. The only thing unusual was Hammer's announcing his inclination ahead of time. Rolf knew it. Joseph Raymer knew it. Scott knew it.

"No, of course I have no objection, Your Honor," Raymer said. "If the court feels it should make such a ruling in the interest of getting at the truth, then I certainly have no objection."

"Mr. Wahl?" Hammer asked. "Do you have any objection?"

"Oh, no, sir. I agree totally. We must get at the truth in this case." Like Raymer, Wahl was no fool. He knew very well that the judge was going to allow testimony no matter what protestations he might make. There was certainly no point in jeopardizing the victory that was right around the corner. If the takeover succeeded, and it looked as if it would, Wahl would be on easy street. During probate it was he as executor, and not Henry Enfield, who had the right to vote the disputed stock, and he intended to make the most of the opportunity.

"Very well, that will be my order," said Judge Hammer. "Mr. Scott, would you please call your first witness."

"I call Mr. Mark Stevens to the witness box."

Mark was angry with Judge Hammer. How could this person who was supposed to be impartial have the audacity to virtually make his decision before he had even heard him testify? Sensing his client's anger, William Thackery Scott put his hand on Mark's shoulder.

"An angry witness is a bad witness," Scott whispered. "You must cool your temper. There is still a chance."

Mark took the witness stand. "Do you swear to tell the truth, the whole truth, and nothing but the truth, so help you God?" intoned the bailiff.

"I do."

"Mr. Stevens, when were you married to Priscilla Enfield?" Scott asked.

"June 21, 1970. At Grace Cathedral here in San Francisco."

"And you loved you wife?"

"Yes, I certainly did."

"And she loved you?"

"Yes, she did."

"And when did your wife leave this earth?"

"November 21, 1980. Just last year. In Las Vegas, Nevada. She . . ." Mark choked on his words. For a moment he was unable to continue.

"And at that time, you still loved your wife?"

"Yes, I did." Mark barely managed to get the words out.

"And she loved you?"

"Yes—she said so just before the fire broke out."

"The fire?"

"Yes, we were trapped in a hotel fire—the MGM Grand Hotel."

Joseph Raymer got up as if to object, presumably on the grounds that how Priscilla Enfield had died had nothing to do with the issues, but sat down, thinking better of his idea.

"Tell me, Mr. Stevens. Did your wife ever indicate to you that she thought your stock in The Stevens Group was community property?"

"No, she didn't."

"Did you ever discuss it?"

"No, we didn't. We seldom discussed financial matters."

"You started your investment banking business before you married Priscilla Enfield?"

"Yes, I had worked for her father." Mark nodded his head toward Henry. "Henry Enfield."

"I see."

"I quit Enfield & Co.—Henry and I had a falling out—and I started my own company."

"And then you married Priscilla?"

"No, I knew Priscilla was a wealthy woman—stood to be a wealthy woman—and I wanted to be financially independent before I ever asked her to marry me."

"And did you accomplish that? Becoming financially independent?"

"Yes, I did. I eventually incorporated my business and then took it public."

"How much profit did you realize? By taking it public?"

"Over $250,000,000 in cash. Of course, I still owned 25% of The Stevens Group."

"The same 25% you still own today?"

"Objection," said Raymer. Whether Mr. Stevens owns 25%, or whether he and *Priscilla Enfield* owned 25% together, is the very question before this court."

"Go ahead and answer the question, Mr. Stevens," said Judge Hammer. "I'll be the one who decides the issues here—not the witnesses, and certainly not the lawyers."

Mark was confused. "I'm sorry. Would you ask the question again, please?"

"How much is the stock worth today? That 25%?" asked Scott.

"I don't really know. For some time now we have suspected that someone was secretly buying up all the shares he could get. It drove up the price. I guess we now know it was you, eh, Derek?" Mark turned his attention from Scott to Derek.

"Objection," said Raymer. "Mr. Stevens is the one being questioned here, not Mr. Harden."

"Objection sustained." Said the judge sternly. "Mr. Stevens this is my courtroom and not your boardroom. You will confine yourself to answering the questions posed to you. Is that clear?"

"Yes, it is. I . . ."

"Now," continued the judge, "what is the 25% worth if you use recent values?"

"Maybe a billion and a half—maybe less, if control of the company were in someone else. Could be more, if my shares are needed for control."

This time Otto Hammer's expression betrayed him. It was clear from his look of amazement that he was impressed by the sheer amount of wealth involved. "I see," he said, writing something on his yellow pad.

"So, Mr. Stevens," Scott continued, "you owned 25% of the stock before you were married, and that never changed until your wife's death?"

"That's correct"

"And it was your separate property before you ever married Priscilla Enfield?" Raymer started to object, but again thought better of it.

"That's correct."

"And the two of you never had any conversations, or documents for that matter, changing any of your holdings into community property?"

"That's true."

"Did Mrs. Stevens ever tell you that she thought The Stevens Group stock was community property, or even partially community property?"

"No. She would never make any claim like that. No."

"Your honor, I have no further questions of my client at this time. I believe I have made my point. The 25% is now, and always has been, the separate property of Mr. Stevens. I, of course, will have redirect examination after Mr. Raymer finishes with his cross-examination."

"Mr. Raymer, you may proceed," said the judge.

Joseph Raymer was an excellent lawyer. In the tradition of the large firms, he was not as flamboyant as William Thackery Scott, nor certainly Thomas T. Wahl, but he was smooth and extremely competent. Joseph Raymer seldom depended on chance. Raymer prepared his cases to a fault, and knew exactly what he was doing in a courtroom.

"Mr. Stevens, do you know what your net worth is?"

"Objection. Mr. Stevens's net worth is totally irrelevant to this case," said Scott, rising to make his objection as he did whenever addressing the court.

Mark remembered that Scott thought that this question would be asked in an attempt to show that he would be left with a huge fortune no matter the result of this lawsuit.

"Gentlemen, there is no jury here to impress. What is the purpose of this question?"

"Your honor, I wanted to show that Mr. Stevens is biased. He stands to lose as much as half of his entire net worth to Henry Enfield if his assets are held to be community property. I want to show what that half would be worth."

"Very well. Please answer the question."

The newspaper reporters in the audience leaned forward to hear Mark's answer, the bailiff was intently listening and one speculated that the judge was glad for a legal reason to know Mark Stevens's net worth.

"I don't really know," Mark answered.

"Come now, Mr. Stevens. Surely you've filled out financial statements for your bank. Surely you know what your net worth is?"

Mark was angry. It was none of Raymer's business. Furthermore he certainly did not want the whole world to know his net worth. Besides, he really was not sure how much he was worth.

"Mr. Raymer," Mark said sarcastically. "Do you know *your* net worth?" Instantly, Mark knew he had made a mistake by letting his anger get the best of him.

"I certainly do know my net worth, but my net worth is not an issue before this court. Yours is. Judge Hammer has ruled my question to be proper. Now, I'll ask you again. What is your net worth?"

"I do not know. I honestly do not know."

"Your best estimate, then. May I have your best estimate?"

Mark looked pleadingly at the judge.

"Answer the question, Mr. Stevens. Your best estimate."

"Somewhere between four and six billion, if you count the stock."

"Well, I am certainly counting the stock Mr. Stevens," said Raymer sarcastically. "Somewhere between four and six billion dollars," Raymer repeated, trusting that the message was not being lost on the judge, who earned somewhere in the range of $75,000 per year.

"All right, Mr. Stevens, isn't it true that when your company went public you signed an employment contract?" Raymer continued.

"Yes."

"What were the terms of the contract?"

"The main thing I remember is that it lasted seven years."

"And it's been renewed, hasn't it?"

"Yes. As a matter of policy, we renew it each year. It always has seven years to go."

"So right now, there are seven years remaining on your employment contract?"

"Six years and some months, yes."

"And how much are you paid? Per year?"

"Right now it's seven million."

"Seven million dollars?"

"Yes."

"That's a year?"

"Yes, a year."

"And how much salary were you being paid 10 years ago, when you were married?"

"I think it was $1,000,000 when I went public. Yes, $1,000,000."

"Where did all this money go?"

"We lived on it. That's before taxes, you know."

"You spent it all on living expenses?"

"We bought a house."

"*We* bought a house?"

"Well *I* did. I had some money for the down payment. I think I borrowed $2,000,000 from the bank. The house cost something like $2,500,000. Maybe $3,000,000, with the landscaping and the pool."

"What Mr. Stevens spent on his house has nothing to do with this case," the judge interrupted.

"It doesn't, Your Honor, but his employment contract does. Perhaps I was getting a little far afield."

"You were. Stick to the employment contract," said Judge Hammer.

"Very well, Your Honor." Raymer returned to his questioning. "And you entered into the seven-year contract while you still controlled the company?"

"I've always controlled the company."

"Well, before you sold to the public 75% of the stock, then. Have it your way, Mr. Stevens."

"Yes, I did."

"You wanted to be sure of a $1,000,000 a year job, then. You caused your company to enter into a $1,000,000-dollar-a-year, seven-year-contract, before you sold to the public."

"Yes I did, but not to insure me of a job."

"Why, then?"

It was at that instant that Rolf Williams saw where Raymer was headed. Mark had mentioned the employment contract in conversation years ago, but its relevance to this case had not occurred to Rolf until this moment.

"To protect the company," Mark answered.

"Why would that protect the company?"

"The investment bankers . . . Mr. Silverton advised it. He felt the market wouldn't pay the right price for the stock unless everyone knew that I'd continue to work for the company."

"Oh, I see. Even though you'd be paid $1,000,000 a year?"

Rolf cringed. He knew that Mark's answers were hanging him, but he was helpless to rescue him.

"A million dollars was not a problem. I had been making considerably more than that before I went public."

"I see. How much?"

"I don't really remember, but it was a great deal more than $1,000,000."

"Perhaps the $20,000,000 profit that was set forth in the offering prospectus?"

"I guess so. I don't remember exactly."

"Thank you, Mr. Stevens, I believe that I have proved my case. There is no need to ask you any further questions."

Mark was puzzled by Raymer's remark, but Rolf fully understood. In California, in the absence of a prenuptial agreement the earnings of the parties after marriage are community property. The rule was that while The Stevens Group stock was Mark's separate property when they married, any enhancement in value of the stock due to Mark's personal efforts after marriage would become community property; on the other hand, any increase in value due to general market forces would remain his separate property.

Raymer was attempting to make ingenious use of this rule. Raymer knew that Scott would argue that the increase in value was not due to Mark's efforts, since he had already been paid the huge salary of $1,000,000, more than enough to cover the value of his work. Ingeniously, Raymer had just destroyed Scott's argument by Mark's own testimony. Mark had testified that, huge as it was, his salary was inadequate to pay him for his real value to the company. That being the case, Mark's unpaid community efforts had increased the value of the stock, and Pris was entitled to her share.

"Ask the judge for a recess," Rolf whispered to Scott. "It's almost time anyway, but ask him now."

In the hallway, Rolf desperately explained Raymer's strategy to Mark and to William Thackery Scott. "The judge can award Henry almost any part of the stock he wants, all the way to a full one half. He's already tipped his hand, for Christ's sake. All he has to do is hold it was your efforts that made the stock so valuable."

"What about an appeal?" Mark asked.

"We wouldn't have a prayer on appeal. Hammer would be making a finding of fact. Appeal courts can't monkey with findings of fact. Rest assured, Hammer will protect his ass with his findings. He's good at that."

"What's more, they don't need *all* of Priscilla's shares to get control of the company," added Scott.

"You're right," Mark pointed out. "They only need another seven or eight percent for control." Mark was finding it difficult to control his anger at the circumstances that were closing in on him.

"We've got a problem," said Rolf, "a serious problem."

"Then we will simply have to overcome the problem," said Scott. "I have an idea or two. This old Englishman is not dead yet."

The bailiff came out of the courtroom. "Gentlemen, are you ready? The recess is over."

"Yes," said Rolf, "we'll be right there."

When they resumed their places, Judge Hammer reentered the courtroom. "The court is again in session," intoned the bailiff.

Just then the courtroom door opened. It was Rodney and Mavis, looking out of breath, but smiling at the sight of Mark. Because Judge Hammer was speaking, Mark was not able to greet them, except by nodding his head and smiling, albeit wanly.

"Mr. Scott, I've been thinking during the recess," said the judge. "I think it only fair to tell you that, based on your client's own testimony, it will be my inclination to hold that his post-marriage efforts, which are clearly community property, have not only added greatly to the value of Mr. Stevens's separate property, but that his separate property has become so intermixed with the community that it has lost its separate character and has become community property. I'm telling you this so that if you have any contradictory evidence you will present it."

Jesus, Mark thought. The judge was going to award a total victory to Henry. If Pris were alive, she would never have contended all this was community property.

Judge Hammer continued. "Mr. Raymer, were you through with your cross-examination of Mr. Stevens?"

"I do have one or two more questions, Your Honor."

As Mark took the witness stand, it seemed to him that the case was lost. Hammer was twisting the fact that he had worked brilliantly for The Stevens Group. Instead of his genius benefiting him or even Pris, this insane legal system was saying he had played into the hands of Henry Enfield. Mark was bewildered and angry. If he lost this lawsuit, he would quit the company despite the employment contract. Maybe he did not know what he would do with his life, but certainly he would not have anything to do with Derek or Henry. They could screw themselves.

"I remind you that you are still under oath," said the bailiff.

Mark grunted his acknowledgment. He did not need anyone to remind him of anything, let alone a bailiff who sat around all day in a court room doing nothing. He was seething inside.

"Earlier, I believe you said your investment banker recommended you have an employment contract in order to assure potential stockholders that you would remain with the company."

"Yes, that's what I said, Mr. Raymer. You heard me correctly." Mark barely concealed his contempt for the lawyer.

"And that worked, did it? The stock brought the price you had hoped for, did it not?"

"Yes, it did." Mark knew from what Rolf had explained that his answer would harm him, but there was nothing else he could do.

"And the employment contract made your 25% percent worth much more, did it not?"

"I take exception, Your Honor." interrupted William Thackery Scott. "How does this witness know the answer to that? It is pure speculation." Scott knew his objection would gain him nothing, but he too was frustrated.

"Mr. Scott, in this country a witness can testify as to the value of his own property. Your objection is not well taken," ruled Hammer.

"Please answer the question, Mr. Stevens," said Joseph Raymer, a verbal swagger in his voice.

"Yes, I suppose it did make my stock more valuable on the market."

"As a matter of fact, isn't it true that investors would pay a lot less if you were not bound by an employment contract that would keep you from quitting and forming a new company?"

"I already told you that that's what Nat Silverton advised me."

"And you followed his advice because you thought he was correct?"

The answer was obvious, and there was nothing Mark could do to change it. "I suppose I did."

"All right, then, I will move on to my last question," Raymer continued. "I believe you testified that your wife, Priscilla, had never told you she felt your stock was community property."

"That's right, she never did. You didn't know Pris. She was an independent woman. She would never have made a claim like that." At least here was a point that was to Mark's advantage.

"And she never did?"

"That's right. She never did."

"Mr. Stevens I show you a certified copy of a Petition for Dissolution, commonly called a divorce complaint. Your Honor, may I have this marked as an exhibit for identification?"

"That's not necessary, Mr. Raymer. The court can take judicial notice of a document filed in another of its proceedings. Go ahead with your question." Otto Hammer enjoyed showing attorneys in his court that he was one step ahead of them when it came to knowledge of the law.

"Do you recognize the signature on this petition?"

Mark looked at the document. It was a copy of the paper the process server had served on him at the Movelli compound. "Yes, I do."

"And . . ."

Mark hated it when a person said "and . . ." instead of asking a question, and he especially hated it coming from Raymer. "What do you mean . . . 'and?' Are you asking me another question?"

"Mr. Stevens, I understand that you have better things to do with your time. After all, there are only several *billion* dollars at stake here. To me that would be a great deal of money."

"It is a great deal of money to me, Mr. Raymer. After all, it is my money."

"Gentlemen," Hammer admonished. "I'll not have that sort of thing in my courtroom. Mr. Stevens, was it your wife who signed the Petition of Dissolution?"

"I'm sorry, Your Honor," Mark apologized. But the truth was he was not at all sorry. "That's Pris's signature, all right, but . . ."

"Thank you, Mr. Stevens. Your answer is quite sufficient," said Raymer. "Have you read the petition?"

"Yes, I read it after I was served with it that day."

"I would like to read a portion of it. 'Property claimed by the Petitioner,' that would be your wife, 'to be community property.' Now, would you read item two, please. Item two of the property your wife claims, under oath, to be community property."

Mark took the paper in his hand, read the language to himself, but said nothing. Christ, he had totally forgotten what the paper had said.

"Mr. Stevens, I mean for you to read item two aloud."

William Thackery Scott, who, with Rolf, was reading a copy of the document, stood up. "Your honor, Mr. Stevens is not required to read the document aloud. It speaks for itself. If my learned friend wants to make some special point about the paper, let him do so in argument, and not through the lips of my client."

"Very well, Your Honor, I shall read the language which counsel finds so offensive myself. Item two of assets Mrs. Stevens stated to be community property reads: '*Stock in The Stevens Group, a corporation.*' Mr. Stevens, do you wish to change your testimony that Priscilla Enfield Stevens never claimed the stock was community property?"

"No, I don't. She didn't mean to do that. She was tricked into signing that paper. That son of a bitch lawyer over there tricked her." Mark pointed a shaking finger at Thomas T. Wahl. "She told me so. She told me she never wanted to actually sue me for di-vorce. She was sorry she did. Pris loved me and I loved her."

"Oh, is that so?"

"Yes, that's so! We may have had our problems, but she didn't mean to sue me for divorce."

"Mr. Stevens, do you know someone named *Christina Bagliani*?"

Mark was stunned to hear Christina's name. It was as if Raymer had struck him in the face with his fist. What the hell was this man doing? Where did he find out about Christina? One look at Wahl gave Mark the answer. Wahl was grinning from ear to ear, taking delight in Mark's expression of surprise. It must have been the private detective that Wahl had hired to serve him with the divorce petition. How else would he have found out? Mark was perspiring, but he tried not to show how shocked he was. "Yes, I know Mrs. Bagliani," he answered, determined to sound matter-of-fact.

"Isn't it true, Mr. Stevens, that Christina Bagliani was your lover? That you slept with her in the very house where you were served with this paper?" Raymer was waving the petition excit-edly in front of Mark's face.

"Exception!" shouted William Thackery Scott, also surprised at the turn of events.

"And isn't it true that you have been carrying on with this Christina Bagliani for 20 years?"

My God, Mark thought, Wahl's investigator had left no ugly stone unturned!

"Exception. Whether Mr. Stevens was or was not carrying on with anyone for 20 years has no more relevance to this case than whether I, or even Mr. Raymer, have been carrying on with some-one not our wives. Are we to go into the sexual history of everyone in this courtroom because it appeals to the prurient interests of my learned friend?"

Nervous laughter swept the court room.

"Gentlemen, gentlemen," said Judge Hammer, "as interesting as Mr. Scott's proposal may be, he is quite right that it is not a proper subject of inquiry for this court."

"But Your Honor, he claims to have loved Priscilla Stevens up until the day she died, and I am prepared to prove otherwise." Raymer could hardly contain his self-satisfied grin.

"Love has nothing to do with this case," Hammer said, silenc-ing Raymer. "The issue is whether or not Mr. Wahl has the right to vote half of the stock, not whether Mr. and Mrs. Stevens loved one another."

"But, Your Honor," Mark protested, "I want to explain." The truth was he did not have the slightest idea what he would say.

"I'm not interested in your explanation, Mr. Stevens. Perhaps you will write a book one day, and perhaps I will even read it, but this is a court of law and your explanation has no bearing on this case. I've made my ruling and the objection will be sustained. There is no question pending for you to answer."

"Very well, your honor," said Raymer.

"Have you completed your questions, Mr. Raymer?" asked the judge.

"Yes, sir. I have nothing further at this time."

"Very well. Mr. Scott, please call your next witness."

"I call Thomas T. Wahl to the witness box." Scott's voice rang like a clarion, as if the calling of Wahl would end all the fuss in this case.

"Your Honor," Wahl protested, standing at the counsel table but angrily refusing to move toward the witness stand. "There is nothing in the pleadings to indicate that I would be a witness in this case. I am an attorney here, not a witness."

Rolf Williams stood to address the point raised. "Your Honor, the pleadings challenge Mr. Wahl's right as executor to vote the stock. There is no requirement that we state every theory upon which we claim we are entitled to an injunction."

"I don't know about that." Hammer authoritatively responded. "I remind you, this isn't the federal court. What is the plaintiff's theory this time, Mr. Williams?"

William Thackery Scott stood. "We would prefer not to state it in the presence of the witness."

"Very well. Gentlemen, approach the bench," said Judge Hammer. "Everyone except Mr. Wahl, that is."

"Your Honor, I protest!" said Wahl, shouting, "I'm here as an attorney. You can't exclude me."

"Mr. Wahl, you are excluded. I trust that is clear. You are being called as a witness. As a witness, you are excluded from this conference."

William Thackery Scott, Rolf Williams and Joseph Raymer huddled at the side of the bench to confer with the judge, while Thomas T. Wahl remained, fuming, at the counsel table. The court reporter moved closer in order to hear the low-voiced conversation.

It seemed to Mark that the conference took an interminable length of time. Although he could not hear, he could see Scott arguing animatedly. The judge listened intently as Raymer responded. Then Rolf returned to the table for a law book, which he opened for Hammer, who silently read a passage. Finally, the conference broke up, and the lawyers returned to their places.

From the look on the face of William Thackery Scott, he had prevailed.

"I am ruling that Thomas T. Wahl can be called, the same as any other person."

The bailiff stood and addressed Wahl. "Do you swear to tell the truth, the whole truth and nothing but the truth, so help you God?"

"I do," said Wahl, still flustered and displaying his displeasure at the whole business.

"Mr. Wahl, I'm ruling that you are an adverse witness. As such, Mr. Scott can cross-examine you under Section 776 of the Evidence Code," said the judge. "Is that clear?

"Yes, sir."

Scott began his questioning. "Was Mrs. Stevens distraught when she first saw you?"

"No, she seemed to me to be a perfectly calm, as well as a very determined, woman."

"Would you tell us what she said?"

"She told me her husband had been cheating on her. She wanted a divorce, and wanted me to bring an action right away."

"What did you do?"

"I asked her if she wanted to think about it, you know, have marriage counseling, wait a while. I always ask my clients that."

"I see. And what did she say to that?"

"She had been thinking about it a long time, and she wanted a divorce as quickly as possible. You see, this other woman, Christina someone . . ."

"What did she know about Christina?"

"She was afraid her husband, Mr. Stevens here, would run off with this woman, and would try to cheat her out of her community property. That's why she wanted me to sue right away—get a TRO against dissipating the community property—perhaps a receiver."

"And what else did she say?"

"She wanted me to file the case right away. So we worked through the lunch hour. I remember it very well. She told me what they had as community property. The stock in the company, the whole nine yards. They were very wealthy people. It took quite a bit of time to go through everything that she knew about."

"What did you do next?"

"She waited while I prepared the dissolution papers. Then she signed them. They were filed in court the next day morning, and my process server nailed the guy with his mistress. Pretty good timing, if I do say so."

"And the will, what about the will? You suggested a new will to her?"

"She was the one who brought up a new will—not me."

"So, out of the blue, Mrs. Stevens asked you to prepare a new will?"

"Not so much out of the blue. She asked me what would happen to her share of the community property, you know, The Stevens Group stock and all . . ."

"She specifically referred to the Stevens stock?"

"Yeah, she did. I remember, I was sort of surprised. I think she thought her husband might sell the company or something, I don't know. Anyway she was worried about an accident. What would happen if she got in an accident and got—got killed."

"And what did you say?"

"I told her her old will would control everything. They'd still be husband and wife after all. Legally, that is."

"Your memory seems quite clear."

"Oh, it is, very clear. It was very unusual for a woman to be so clear and farsighted on the first visit like that. Did you know Priscilla Stevens?

"No, I didn't." Scott answered.

"Too bad. Priscilla Stevens was a very determined woman, very beautiful I might add. A very unfortunate loss. Her death, I mean. Well, anyway, she wanted me to draw up a new will, so I did."

"And what did the new will say?"

"She wanted everything to go to her father, Henry Enfield." Something about the only reason that she had not always left everything to him in her old will was because her husband would get mad about it. She told me how much she loved her father. Respected him, you know. Well, Henry Enfield is an important name in San Francisco. I could see why. She must have told me two or three times how she loved her father. Very commendable, I thought."

"And what about the executor? She named you as executor— didn't you think that was a conflict of interest?"

"What, to be executor?"

"Yes. After all, you drew the will and recommended that she name you as executor."

"I didn't recommend anything. She was the one. She felt her father was pretty old, or at least might be by the time she might die. So she wanted me for the executor. There's nothing unethical about my being executor."

"You stand to make a very large fee as executor, isn't that correct?"

"Mr. Scott, I'm used to making very large fees. I don't need to be an executor to make large fees."

"That may be, but I remind you that your fees are based on the size of Mrs. Stevens's estate. You stand to make a great deal more money if you can convince this court that Mrs. Stevens's net worth was one or two *billion* dollars."

"My testimony is not for sale, Mr. Scott. I'm simply telling you what Mrs. Stevens said in my office that day."

"And you expect us to believe that Priscilla Stevens came to your office eager for a divorce, that it was she who brought up the topic of changing her will, that she wanted to leave everything to Henry Enfield, and that it was she who wanted to name you as executor?"

"That's exactly what happened. I'm not particularly interested in what you believe, Mr. Scott."

William Thackery Scott slowly walked from the counsel table to within a few feet of the witness stand. "Now Mr. Wahl, isn't it true that when Mrs. Stevens came to you, she was simply seeking legal advice as to the general nature of divorce proceedings? That she was not at all ready to commence proceedings?"

"It certainly is *not* true! She wanted me to file right away. We worked all through the lunch hour."

"Mr. Wahl, isn't it true that you asked Mrs. Stevens to sign a blank dissolution complaint, and that you had it filed without her consent?"

"It certainly is not true. I never do that. Some lawyers may, but I don't."

"Come, come, Mr. Wahl. What if I told you that Priscilla Enfield told her husband that she hadn't intended to file for divorce at all? That she had signed a blank petition, and that you told her you would not use it without her permission?"

"I would tell you that Mark Stevens is lying through his teeth. Mrs. Stevens would never tell anyone that. It simply is not true."

"Well, Mr. Wahl, it will be up to the court to tell who is lying and who is telling the truth. Tell me this. Is it not true that it was your idea that Mrs. Stevens make out a new will, not her idea at all?"

"That certainly is not true—not at all—it was her idea. She was very upset with her husband. She wanted to be sure her father got everything if she died prematurely."

Scott had not expected to get Wahl to admit anything. The purpose of the questioning had been to pin him down to his story so that he could not change it later. Now he had been pinned down.

Scott had not yet confided in anyone the fact that yesterday his investigator had finally found Cathy Connor, the former secretary to Thomas T. Wahl. The effort to prove Wahl to be a liar had struck pay dirt. The investigator reported that Miss Connor had become disenchanted with Wahl, and had quit her job. She was willing to testify to the truth of what had actually happened the day Pris signed her will.

"All right, Mr. Wahl, I have no further questions of you at this time. Your Honor, I would like to reserve the right to recall Mr. Wahl, if that should become necessary."

"Very well," Hammer responded. "As you gentlemen know, I have to take Judge Barlow's calendar this afternoon. This court will adjourn until tomorrow morning at ten o'clock."

After court, Mavis, Rodney, Rolf, William Thackery Scott and Mark met at the Pacific Union Club for lunch. The conversation was intense and cheerless.

"My God, how did they find out about Christina?" asked Rodney.

"Wahl hired an investigator in the divorce case," said Mark. "It must have been him. Pris didn't know about Christina. Jesus, I never saw Christina from the time we got married."

"I'm sure Wahl's lying about everything," Rolf said.

"I'm sure of it, too," commented Scott. "The problem is proving it. However fortune did smile on us yesterday. I think I have a witness."

"Who?" asked Rolf.

"Cathy Connor. Our investigator found her. She has agreed to come to the hotel suite when she gets off work."

"Cathy Connor?" asked Mark.

"Yes. She was Wahl's secretary when Priscilla signed her will."

"What is she going to say?" Rolf asked.

"I'm not completely certain," Scott answered. "But basically, she'll make out Wahl to be a liar about what actually happened."

"He looked as if he were lying," said Rodney.

"Yes, but the trouble is . . ." Scott's voice trailed off as his thoughts raced ahead.

"The trouble is," Rolf continued for him. "Proving Wahl a liar doesn't win the case for us."

"Exactly," said Scott. "Priscilla signed the bloody will. No matter what I say, that simple fact remains. I doubt very much that Wahl got her to sign something she didn't want to sign."

"What's the point then," Mark asked, "if we're going to lose anyway?"

"Maybe we'll lose and maybe we won't," Scott responded. "I learned a long time ago not to anticipate the outcome of a trial. If we can prove Wahl a liar, we'll have a chance. For all the talk about fairness and logic, when it comes right down to it, judges, like juries, are influenced by the personalities involved. It takes stern stuff to decide in favor of someone you dislike. When I get through, the judge isn't going to like Thomas T. Wahl very much."

"But it's Henry Enfield who stands to gain by all this," said Rolf. "And like it or not, Henry Enfield has an impeccable reputation."

"This lawsuit, this whole distasteful business, is ridiculous," said Mavis. "I'm going to speak to Henry tonight. He doesn't know it, but he's having dinner with his sister this evening. I'm going to tell him a thing or two."

"What exactly are you going to tell him?" Rodney asked.

"I'm going to tell him to drop this stupid scheme of his. Father would never have approved of all this. Enfields simply do not behave this way."

-64-

Mark and Rodney were dining in the Big Four Restaurant, one of the several elegant Nob Hill restaurants that Mark frequented. The Big Four referred to Messrs. Huntington, Hopkins, Crocker and Stanford, all San Francisco business barons of the 19th century. Early California was the theme of the richly paneled restaurant and its magnificent antique bar, where they were having cocktails before going into the dining room.

Mavis had not joined them because she was dining with Henry at his Pacific Heights mansion. William Thackery Scott and Rolf Williams were busy meeting with Thomas T. Wahl's former secretary, Cathy Connors, in the Fairmont Hotel.

"I wish it were tomorrow at this time," Mark told Rodney.

"You think the trial will be finished by then?"

"Scott thinks so. One way or the other." Mark looked depressed.

The waitress came with Rodney's sherry and Mark's customary Rob Roy. Photographs of the long-since demolished Nob Hill mansions of the Big Four, and other early California scenes, decorated the bar. Mark sipped his drink.

"I'll be glad when this damned case is over," Mark said. "I was just about ready to turn the business over to Steve Baumgartner, when Pris was killed. And now here's this crap about Henry taking half of everything."

Rodney could see Mark's hand shaking as he lifted his glass. "Yes, but look at it this way: Even if you lose you'll never have to work again in your entire life." Rodney sipped a little of his sherry, but Mark was well ahead with his drink.

"Jesus, Rodney, you've known me for over 20 years. Do you think I could just sit around collecting dividends? Come on!"

"Of course not. I'm just saying it wouldn't be the end of the world. You've been saying a long time how you're unhappy doing the same old thing. This may be the best thing that ever happened to you."

"I doubt that."

Rodney watched his friend take still another gulp of his drink. "Look at it this way. If you lose, you're going to have to figure out something to do with yourself. Right?"

"Sure, of course. I'm certainly not going to work for those bastards."

"And if you win? You see, it's the very same thing. Why not turn the whole bloody thing over to Baumgartner, win or lose? In the final analysis, it's really only money you're talking about. Money and nothing else."

"Yeah. A couple of *billion* dollars of *my* money that I'd have to give to Henry."

"But what I'm saying is that you would still have another two billion of your own left."

Mark did not answer, but smiled wistfully and took another swallow, nearly finishing his drink.

"When I first met you, who would have ever imagined that you would be unhappy about having two billion dollars?"

"Yeah." Mark managed another slight smile.

"Remember at Oxford, having to borrow a jacket and tie from me?"

"No, all I can remember is your belly and your cursing the newspaper." Playfully, Mark feigned slapping his friend's belly. He was feeling better.

The maitre d' approached their table. "Mr. Stevens, your table is ready. Shall I take your drinks in for you?"

"No, I'll finish mine. Bring another to the table, if you would. Bring another sherry for my friend, too."

William Thackery Scott was hosting Cathy Connor and Rolf Williams in his suite at the the Fairmont. Room service had served them an excellent dinner.

"Let's step into the living room and enjoy the view," suggested Scott. The winter sun had long since set, and the City's lights spread out below, showing the outline of the Bay.

"I've never been up high in the Fairmont before. You certainly have a wonderful view," enthused Cathy, looking out. She was an attractive young woman. She had been separated two years, and had finally divorced her husband, since he was still seeing the same other woman. Cathy had not liked the ethical standards of Thomas T. Wahl, and had quit as his secretary to work for less money for a young lawyer in The Cannery at the wharf, where the investigator had found her.

"We are grateful to you for being here," said Rolf. "We fully expect to reimburse you for your cab and your baby-sitting expense."

"Oh, thank you, but I really didn't expect anything. I remember Mrs. Stevens so well. When she came in, I knew right away who she was. She treated me so nicely, even though she was upset."

"You're doing the right thing," said Scott.

"I talked with my mother about it. We both agreed I should testify about what really happened. I don't know if it will make any difference, but I didn't like what Mr. Wahl did to her. I thought I should tell you."

Derek Harden was dining alone at an Embarcadero restaurant. Late this afternoon, he had met with Henry Enfield and Joseph Raymer in the lawyer's office. Raymer had expressed great confidence in the outcome of the case, which they expected to conclude tomorrow. Harden had just purchased a new condominium not far from the restaurant. He planned to rise early to make his many calls to London while businesses were still open there. At his restaurant table, overlooking the Bay, Derek was elated over how things had gone in court. He decided that after the takeover, he would stay in San Francisco for a few months. There was a lot of money to be made here; besides it would be a real pleasure see Mark squirm.

Henry had sent his limousine to the Stanford Court Hotel for Mavis. As the car pulled under the porte-cochere of Henry's magnificent Pacific Heights mansion, Mavis grew tense. She dreaded confronting her half brother, but she felt she must. Due to their substantial age difference, Mavis had known Henry very little as a child. During the war, he had been unable to return to England from San Francisco. However, upon the death of Lord Enfield, their father, they had come to know one another. They had evenly divided their father's estate, except for Castle Enfield, which Mavis bought from Henry. Mavis had known that there had been a scandal that had prompted Henry to move to America in 1937. Even though Lord Enfield had made it clear that it was not to be discussed, Mavis had a pretty good idea what it was about.

In her late father's safe, Mavis had discovered a 1937 promissory note from Henry to his father for £50,000. When Mavis asked Henry about it, he had dismissed the note, claiming it had been a loan to start his business in California and that it had been paid. Mavis had torn up the paper, choosing to accept Henry's explanation rather than risk an argument, although his explanation was suspect.

But this was different. Now Henry was trying to financially ruin Mark. She intended to stop him, if she possibly could.

Mavis felt sad for her brother. Henry was very much alone in the big house, with only his servants for company. He sat at the end of the 12-place dining room table with Mavis next to him. The unsmiling portrait of their ancestor looked down on them from over the fireplace.

"Priscilla used to dine with me nearly every Thursday evening. My God, Mavis, you can never know how much I miss her. She was such a sweet girl." As they dined, they made small talk, avoiding the trial that was on both their minds. Mavis saw her brother in a new light. He was a vindictive old man with not many years left. The realization shocked her, for she had never thought of Henry as dying. This trip might be the last time she would see him. She was not sure of her decision to confront him. When they had finished the main course and the servants had cleared the dishes for dessert, she took a deep breath.

"Henry, I must ask you something."

"Ah, so this occasion isn't to be completely social, after all!"

"Why are you doing this to Mark? I simply don't understand."

"Doing what? I'm merely insisting on my property rights." Henry contained his anger over his sister's impertinence.

"You certainly don't need the money, do you?" Mavis knew she was treading on dangerous ground in talking to him this way.

"That's not the point." His face reddened.

"Well, then, what is the point? At your age and with all your position, the last thing you should be doing is engaging in this unseemly lawsuit with a member of your own family."

Henry lost his temper and nearly screamed out his reply. "Member of my family? He's no member of my family! He took my Priscilla away from me. I thought she would stay with me for the rest of my life. And then, do you know what he did?"

Mavis could see she had said the wrong thing. "No, what did he do, Henry?" she said softly, hoping however vainly that his anger might lessen.

"He killed her—that's what he did." Suddenly the old man began to cry. "The bloody bastard! First he stole my daughter, then he killed her." He brushed the unwelcome tears from his face, and pushed on. "He killed her, and he wouldn't even let me bury her."

"You're wrong about Mark. He's a very kind man. He tried to save Priscilla's life."

"You listen to me. I don't know exactly what your relationship is with that man, but I'm telling you to keep out of my business, do you hear me?"

"Henry, I'm not trying . . ." It was apparent that she had failed. It had been a mistake coming this evening.

"That stock belonged to Priscilla. She left it to me in her will. I may give it away, I may even burn it, but he's not going to have it. Do you hear me?" Shouting, Henry was red-faced and very angry.

"Henry, you know very well that Priscilla only changed her will in case she got a divorce."

"Well, it was Mark Stevens who abandoned her to die in that terrible hotel. If she had lived, she would have gotten a divorce. She'd still be alive."

"Mark didn't abandon her. He risked his life to save her."

"I don't believe that for a bloody minute."

"I think it would be best if I leave. We're both going to end up saying things we will be sorry for."

"How right you are. We've already said everything that needs to be said."

"Isn't there anything I can say to change your mind?"

"Nothing can change my mind. I'd sleep with the devil himself to get even with that man. From the moment I saw him, he's been nothing but trouble."

After Mavis had left, Henry opened the library safe. He read the copy of his will that he had not changed for many years. In it he left all his assets to Priscilla. The will went on to provide: "If my daughter should predecease me, then I give, devise and bequeath the entire residue of my estate to my sister, Mavis Ashley of England." The original will was with the lawyer who had drawn it. I really should make an appointment to change my will, Henry thought. After tonight, I'm not too keen about Mavis's getting everything when I die.

At the Big Four restaurant the drinks had helped put Mark in a mellow mood. He was relaxed and enjoying his meal with Rodney. The couple at the next table in the Big Four had left, and with no one within ear shot the two friends were talking freely.

"The man I heard lecture in London, Hollingsworth?"

"Yes, I remember."

"I think he had a good handle on what makes people like me tick."

"You mean hard-driving people?"

"The more I think about it, the more I think he was right."

"Just what is his basic thesis?"

"I'll have to loan you my copy of his book. In a way, it's simple. What is difficult is actually living out his ideas."

Rodney looked up from his meal, waiting for Mark to go on with his explanation.

"Basically it's this: Money and the things money can buy are not enough to make us happy. It's true of ambition, too. The second you achieve one goal, you set another one. It goes on endlessly that way—setting new goals."

"But, look at you. Don't you think you're a happy person?"

"If you want the God's truth? The answer is 'no.' When I look back on it, I've just substituted one ambition for another. Hell, I never even stopped to take a deep breath."

"For such an unhappy person, you certainly enjoy what your money buys for you."

"Oh, sure. That I don't deny. But I'm talking deep down happiness. For example, I don't think I was really any happier after Pris and I built the big house in Hillsborough."

"It was a beautiful house."

"I thought it would make me happy, but it didn't. Oh, I enjoyed it immensely. But enjoyment is different from being happy." They finished their food and stopped talking for a minute while the dishes were being cleared.

"Have you ever read Ecclesiastes? You know, the book in the Old Testament?"

"No," Rodney laughed. "I haven't read the Bible since I was a lad."

"I just read it. Hollingsworth suggested it. It's all about this man—a king. He tries everything to make himself happy. Nothing works. He gets rich. He has wisdom. He has power. Everything. It makes for very depressing reading. You feel as if there's nothing you can do to be happy. Nothing really matters."

"And you want me to read something like that? I'm happy already, without reading something like that."

"That's what is so ironic about it all. You and I have been completely different from the very beginning."

"I quite agree. You've been the bright one and I've been the stupid one."

"Don't be ridiculous. That's the irony. I've always been trying to find something, and you—you chubby bastard—you had it from the very beginning," Mark laughed.

"And it had very little to do with my family's having money."

"Yes, that's the point. It didn't have anything to do with money."

The waiter came with tea and coffee. Rodney offered Mark a cigar. "Are you still smoking those things?" Mark asked.

"Sure, that's what makes me so bloody happy," Rodney chuckled. "A good cigar."

"Damn, Rodney! I should sell everything I've got and move to England, just to be near you. You're the wise old philosopher, not me."

They both laughed heartily, and lit their cigars.

Rodney exhaled the cigar smoke. "So what does this king do? Does he ever find happiness?"

"The way Ecclesiastes ends, I don't know if he does or not. He takes you through all this seeking of his, but then you find out it's fruitless. He ends up saying 'happiness is found in the works of the Lord.' Then he just stops—no other explanation whatsoever.

"I suppose the truth is, we each have to discover it for ourselves.

"It's pretty stupid of me, I know, but I've never thought much about such things."

"I keep telling you, that's because you already have the answer."

The evening over, William Thackery Scott was showing Cathy Connor to the door of his hotel suite.

"Thank you very much, Mrs. Connor. You can rest easy, knowing you will be serving justice. We shall see you at court tomorrow morning then?"

"Nine o'clock. I'll be there."

"I'll be putting you in the witness box right off."

"You aren't frightened, are you?" asked Rolf.

"I'm kind of nervous, but I'll be all right."

"Good girl. I shall see you in the morning," said Scott.

In his condominium Mark watched the Johnny Carson monologue before going to bed. He felt good about tonight's chat with Rodney. Perhaps, when this was all over, he would move to London. He would not do anything constructive at all. Just go to plays, good restaurants, maybe meet some women. Who was that woman at Mavis's party? Jacqueline was her name. He wondered if she were still single. Soon he turned off the television and was asleep.

Since Pris was killed, Mark had not had any dreams, but the dream tonight was startlingly realistic. As it unfolded, he had no sense of its being a dream, as he frequently did with others. Pris and Mark were in their room in the MGM Hotel. The waiter knocked on the door. They smelled smoke. Terror pervaded the entire dream. Suddenly they were in the emergency stairway. Pris was lying on the stairs. Smoke was everywhere. He knew he would die if he did not escape quickly. He bent down to pick Pris up, even though she appeared to be dead. Then he could see that her lips were moving. She was trying to tell him something. He bent down close to hear her. At first she could not make herself heard. Then he could hear her faintly say, "Mark, Mark."

He tried to ask her what she wanted, but he could not speak. Try as he might, words would not come out.

Then Pris spoke again. Her voice was stronger and louder. "Mark, *Don't be too busy to live.*"

Then her body went limp.

She died.

When he awoke he was covered with sweat, and crying. The terror was greater than it had been in the actual fire. It was as if he could smell the deadly smoke.

He got out of bed and looked out the window at the lights of the City.

Where did dreams come from? Had Pris somehow given him advice from the grave? Or was it some wise part of himself telling him he had been "too busy to live?"

At the Fairmont William Thackery Scott was awakened by the ringing of his telephone.

It was Hooper, his investigator, calling from London. "I think you will be most pleased with what we've discovered about Mr. Henry Enfield. It may be the break you've been looking for."

"Jolly good! And not an instant too soon."

"It is quite a long report," said Hooper. "The meat of the story begins in early 1937 . . ."

-65-

Mark lay sleepless after the dream. Pris's words continued to haunt him: "Don't be too busy to live."

Just before dawn, he decided to give up on getting to sleep, and go for a walk. He walked down Nob Hill and followed the cable car tracks. Except for an occasional jogger and a few vehicles, the City was deserted. The January fog penetrated his running suit.

He kept thinking about the dream. "Don't be too busy to live." It was true he had been too busy to live—at least to live the way he wanted to. For years he had concentrated on success and making money. In the early years that had been "living" for him, but not any longer. As he walked, he saw clearly the reason he had developed those dismaying feelings of having "to get the hell out" of his office. His soul wanted "to get the hell out" of the life he was living. The goals of success and money were no longer enough for him. He guessed he already knew this, but it had never hit him the way it had this morning.

By the time he had reached the end of the cable car tracks, near Ghiradelli Square, it was all clear to him. Being involved in this bedamnable litigation was not much different from dragging himself to the office when he no longer wanted to be there. Rodney was right. What the hell difference did it make whether he was worth $2 billion or $4 billion? Oh, certainly it mattered, but it was not a life-or-death issue. The world was going to go on whether or not he lost this case. He would be the same Mark Stevens. Even if something should happen and he lost everything, he could start all over again, and this time be happy while he was doing it.

Mark returned to Nob Hill by way of the more gradual slope on Powell Street. He decided to telephone William Thackery Scott. He would tell him, although the lawsuit did not look good, to simply do his best. He would accept any outcome that might happen. No longer was he going to be "too busy to live."

.   .   .

But Mark found that Scott's line was busy. Mavis Ashley had telephoned Scott, just seconds before.

"I thought I'd better ring you up," Mavis said. "I'm afraid I was totally unsuccessful in changing my brother's mind. He's determined to go on with this takeover. I'm terribly sorry."

"It's all right, Lady Ashley," Scott answered. "I thank you for doing what you could."

"Mark is going to lose to Henry, isn't he?"

"I wouldn't be too sure of that, Lady Ashley. I had a very interesting telephone call from London only a couple of hours ago. It may change things."

"All rise, please. This honorable court is again in session," cried the bailiff. "Otto Hammer, judge presiding."

Judge Hammer hurried to his seat, anxious to get started. "Mr. Scott, call your next witness, please."

"Your Honor, I call Mrs. Cathy Connor."

Thomas T. Wahl had not noticed his former secretary sitting in the back row. Taken by surprise, he quickly stood and began sputtering: "Objection, Your Honor. This woman worked for me as my secretary. I recently discharged her. Anything she might say would clearly be objectionable." It was legally a foolish thing to say, but Wahl was flustered.

"And why would that be?" asked the judge. "She hasn't even been asked a question yet."

"Anything she knows about Priscilla Stevens's affairs, she learned as my secretary," Gesturing, Wahl continued to sputter. "Attorney-client privilege. Anything a client says to a legal secretary is as privileged as if it were said to the attorney himself. The sanctity of the attorney-client relationship must be preserved."

Scott stood, knowing that Wahl's arguments were specious. "First of all, I have not asked a question yet. In England, and I would think in America, it is customary to object to a question *after* the question has been asked and not *before*." Judge Hammer barely concealed a smile at the obvious truth. "Secondly, if there is an attorney-client privilege, Mr. Wahl himself has waived it by not objecting yesterday when he testified at great length to his conversations with his client."

Unsettled, Wahl jumped up. "It's only the client who can waive the privilege, not the attorney. As the attorney I had no right to waive the privilege."

Judge Hammer spoke. "Do you mean to tell me that you are contending the attorney-client privilege was not effectively waived yesterday because you had no power to waive it?"

"Yes, your honor." Everyone in the courtroom knew Wahl's goose was cooked.

William Thackery Scott interjected. "Your honor, regardless of Mr. Wahl's rather ingenuous argument, it is clear that as executor of Mrs. Stevens's will he stands in the place and stead of Mrs. Stevens. He is acting as her executor. As executor, he obviously had the power to waive the privilege and he has effectively done so."

"No matter," said Hammer. "Young lady, will you please take the stand?" He was disregarding Wahl's objections.

Cathy Connors took the oath and sat in the witness stand. Although a legal secretary for several years, she had never been in a courtroom, and was nervous.

Thomas T. Wahl sat, fuming, at the counsel table. Joseph P. Raymer looked on apprehensively as Scott posed his questions.

"You were the legal secretary to Mr. Wahl on November 19th of last year when Priscilla Stevens was in his offices?" asked Scott.

"Yes, sir, Mrs. Stevens was very upset. She wanted to talk to Mr. Wahl about what she should do. We talked for a while there by my desk, before Mr. Wahl was ready to see her."

"Did she say anything else before she saw him?"

"No. Just that she was nervous and didn't know what to do."

"And afterwards?"

"I was in and out while they were talking. I took the petition forms in, to Mr. Wahl."

"Did you hear them talking?"

"He was telling her we would fill out the forms in case she decided to file for a dissolution. You know. In case she decided on a divorce, all she would have to do was call."

"Are you the one who typed the information in the forms?"

"Yes, I did. She had signed a blank petition before she left. Mr. Wahl gave me all the information to type in. After Mrs. Stevens left, I typed it all in, over her signature."

"Over her signature?"

"Yes. Mr. Wahl said he wouldn't file it with the court unless she told him to."

"You know that's a lie!" Wahl shouted. "A damned lie!"

"Mr. Wahl," Hammer said sternly. "You will be silent, do you understand me?"

Wahl looked down without answering.

"Thank you, Your Honor," said Scott. "And did she tell him to file the case? To your knowledge?"

"I don't think so. She never called the office again, to the best of my knowledge."

"And were the papers filed in court?"

"Oh, yes. The court service filed them the next morning, and they were served on Mr. Stevens."

"Did you tell them to do that?"

"No, sir. I was holding them on my desk. It was Mr. Wahl. He had written out the orders for the court service after I left. They followed his orders."

"About the will. Was it you who typed up the will?"

"Yes. Mr. Wahl called me into his office and dictated the will."

"While Mrs. Stevens was there?"

"Yes, she was there. He said Mrs. Stevens wanted to draw a will in case she went ahead."

"Went ahead?"

"Yes. Went ahead with the dissolution. You see, she was confused and hadn't decided for sure yet."

"Was Mrs. Stevens—was she the first divorce client that you typed up a will for?"

Thomas T. Wahl squirmed at the counsel table.

"Oh, no. Lots of clients decide on new wills when they file for divorce. It's Mr. Wahl's policy."

"His policy?"

"Yes, he's always afraid someone might die before they get their will changed."

"You're sure of all this? It's very important."

"I'm sure."

"Thank you, Mrs. Connor. I have no further questions."

Mark was pleased by Connor's testimony. Her story was entirely different from Wahl's. She had effectively demolished Wahl's credibility. Surely the judge would see that Wahl was a liar. Obviously, he had tricked Pris into signing the divorce paper and her will. She never meant them to be valid unless she filed for divorce.

Cathy started to get up from the witness chair, but Joseph Raymer stopped her. "Excuse me, Mrs. Connor, but I want to ask you a few questions. It will be only a few moments."

Cathy Connor sat back in the witness chair, apprehensively waiting for Raymer's cross-examination.

"Miss Connor. It is *Miss* Connor, isn't it?"

"*Mrs.* Mrs. Connor."

"Tell me, Mrs. Connor, from the time Mrs. Stevens first came into the offices until she left, were you with her all the time?"

"Oh, no. I didn't mean to give *that* impression."

"So, you weren't with her *all* the time?"

"No."

"When you weren't with her, who was she with then?"

"Mr. Wahl."

"Was Mr. Wahl with her alone a lot?"

"Yes."

"Most of the time?"

"Yes, I suppose so."

"Mrs. Connor, was he or was he not alone with her alone most of the time?"

"He was."

"So Mrs. Stevens could have said things to Mr. Wahl that you didn't hear? Is that correct?"

"Yes."

"Lots of things. She could have told him lots of things?"

"Well, yes . . ."

"Did she tell you that Mr. Stevens was cheating on her with a Christina . . ." Raymer looked at his yellow pad. ". . . Christina Bagliani, and she wanted a divorce?"

"No, she didn't."

"But she could have told Mr. Wahl that? Could she not?"

"Yes. She could have. I—as I said, I wasn't with them all the time."

"No, that's right, you did say that. Did Mrs. Stevens tell you that she was worried that Mr. Stevens might dispose of all the community property because he was in love with another woman?"

"No, not while I was there."

"But again, even though she didn't see fit to tell a legal secretary, she might have told Mr. Wahl, her *attorney*? Might she not?"

"Yes, that's true."

"And Mr. Wahl might have told her that in order to get a restraining order against the disposition of community property, the papers had to be filed?"

"Well, yes. I didn't hear that either, but he might have, of course."

"Mrs. Connor, did Mrs. Stevens ever tell you that she wanted to draw up a new will, cutting out her husband?"

"No, she never said that."

"To *you*, you mean. She never said that to *you*?"

"Yes, that's right. Never to me."

"But she could have told her *attorney* that, without your hearing it—isn't that correct?"

"Yes. I never meant to imply that I knew *everything* she said to Mr. Wahl."

"You weren't listening to them through the keyhole? Were you?"

William Thackery Scott spoke up. "Your Honor, I hate to interrupt my learned friend, eliciting the perfectly obvious information that Mrs. Connor only heard what she heard, but he is badgering the witness."

"It doesn't sound like badgering to me," ruled Otto Hammer. "Go ahead, Mr. Raymer."

"Thank you, Your Honor," said Raymer in a gloating tone, "I'm nearly through. And Mrs. Connor, you weren't listening in on the intercom either?"

"Of course not."

"Then, as a matter of fact, you wouldn't have the slightest idea what Mrs. Stevens told Mr. Wahl when you were not present, would you?"

"No, but . . ." Cathy answered meekly, as if she had been caught in a lie.

"Your Honor, I have no further questions of Mrs. Connor. I'm sure she has told the truth, so far as she knows it. Mr. Scott's problem is that she knows very little."

William Thackery Scott stood up like a shot. "Mr. Raymer, I don't need you to tell me what my problems are. No one is pretending that Mrs. Connor heard Priscilla Stevens say anything other that what Mrs. Connor herself just testified to."

"Gentlemen, gentlemen. I shall be the one to decide the facts in this courtroom. You can save your analysis of this young woman's testimony until closing argument. In the meantime, Mr. Scott, I would suggest you call your next witness."

To Mark, it seemed that Cathy Connor's testimony had helped very little.

"Very well, Your Honor," continued William Thackery Scott. "I call Mr. Henry Enfield."

It was clear that Henry had not expected to be called as a witness. He looked questioningly, first at Wahl, then at Raymer. Raymer shrugged his shoulders and nodded toward the witness stand.

Henry walked to the stand and paused while the bailiff administered the oath. "Do you swear to tell the truth, the whole truth and nothing but the truth, so help you God?"

"Yes, I do."

"State your name, please, for the record."

"Henry Enfield." Henry appeared apprehensive. He tried to conceal his trembling hands.

"Mr. Enfield, you are the father of Priscilla Enfield?" began Scott.

"Yes. I was, before she died."

"Of course. Did it surprise you that her last will named you as sole heir?"

"Actually, it didn't. I knew she was unhappy with her husband. Before she married Mark, we had each named each other in our wills. Mine still does, as a matter of fact." Henry was calmer now and was answering the questions confidently.

"I see. Mr. Enfield, would you mind if I take you back a few years?"

"I suppose not."

"You were born in England?"

"Yes."

"Do you mind if I ask what year you were born?"

Joseph Raymer started to rise to object, but then sat down again. It sounded to him as if Scott were on a fishing expedition, but he didn't want Hammer to think he feared his client's answer.

"Eighteen ninety-eight."

"And how old are you today, sir?"

"Eighty-two."

"Congratulations, sir."

"Thank you."

"When did you come to America to live?"

"Nineteen thirty-seven. I came to San Francisco in 1937."

"What had been your business in England?"

"I was an investment banker there. Just as here."

"Nineteen thirty-seven is a long time ago. What prompted you to come to America?"

"My firm was then Dempster and Blaney, in London. I wanted to start a branch office here in San Francisco."

"And did you?"

"At first it was a branch, but then it became my own firm. It was my own capital, you see."

"And you prospered in San Francisco?"

"After a time, yes. I've been very proud of Enfield & Co. I did it all on my own. Never had partners."

"You married here?"

"No, I had married in England."

Raymer, who had been tapping his fingers impatiently, finally rose. "Your Honor, I object. I don't know where all this is leading. Mr. Enfield's life history is hardly what this case is about."

"Never mind, Mr. Raymer. I assume Mr. Scott has a purpose."

"Thank you, Your Honor," said Scott. "My purpose will soon become evident. And your wife died when?"

"Nineteen fifty-four. May 19, 1954."

"And you had a child?"

"Yes, of course. Priscilla."

"When was Priscilla born?"

"Nineteen forty-five. Just at the end of the war."

"And you loved your daughter very much?"

"Of course I did."

"And she loved you?"

"She lived with me for many years after her mother died. I don't know what I would have done without her."

"Now, going back to 1937 . . ."

"Yes."

"Whose idea was it for you to come to America?"

"As I say, my company wanted to commence branch operations in San Francisco. They had started one in New York the year before."

"So it was your company's idea?"

"In actual fact, it was my idea. It was I who persuaded the managing director at that time. I remember it very well. Parsons was his name."

"Was there any reason for your coming to America, other than the one you've given us here this morning?"

"No, of course not."

"You are sure?"

"Of course I am sure." Wondering what Scott was driving at, Henry was apprehensive.

With careful deliberation, William Thackery Scott picked up a yellow pad from the table and read to himself the notes he had taken from his telephone conversation with the London investigator. He put down the pad and asked Henry his next question.

"Mr. Enfield, I remind you that you are under oath."

"I don't need reminding, Mr. Scott."

"Isn't it true that early in 1937, whilst still in England, you were arrested for child molestation?"

Henry gasped inwardly. So that was Scott was driving at, he thought. His mind raced, trying to know what to say, what to do.

"It certainly is not true. Whatever are you talking about?" Henry's face dramatically reddened. He turned his head in Mavis's direction. What all did Mavis know? he wondered.

"Your Honor, I fail to see what this has to do with this case," complained Raymer.

"Then you object?" said Hammer.

"I most certainly do."

"Wait," said Henry. "I want to answer this monstrous charge."

William Thackery Scott lost no time asking his next question before the judge could rule otherwise. "Mr. Enfield, I put to you that you were arrested for attempting to molest a child."

"That's not true!"

"That this unsavory event occurred during a weekend at the country home of family friends, who shall remain nameless. That . . ."

"I tell you, that's a lie! Where did you ever hear such slander? It was my sister, wasn't it? I was not arrested. I was not charged." Henry was terrified about what his questioner might know about Priscilla and himself.

"The whole matter was hushed up, was it not?" Scott continued. "Your friends promised not to bring charges, but only after your father promised them you would leave the country. You . . ."

William Thackery Scott never finished his question.

The red in Henry Enfield's face changed to ashen white.

His eyes remained open, while his eyeballs rolled upward.

He slouched forward, but did not fall from his chair because his knees were wedged in the witness stand.

Henry Enfield looked as if he were dead.

"Mr. Enfield?" Scott inquired. "Mr. Enfield, are you all right?"

Startled, Mark stared at Henry.

"Bailiff, get him some water!" said Otto Hammer, panic in his voice.

"Henry!" cried Mavis, rushing from the spectator area through the low swinging doors toward her half brother. "Oh, my God! Henry!"

Henry did not move.

"This court is in recess," commanded Hammer, who nervously headed toward the door leading to his chambers. "Bailiff, call the paramedics."

Henry was still conscious as they waited for the paramedics. They laid him on the floor by the empty jury box, and put a pillow under his head. His eyes were open, but dazed. His breathing was very shallow.

Mavis bent over him. "Oh, Henry, if only you had stopped this foolish lawsuit!"

Henry stared at Mavis. Clearly, he recognized her, but he said nothing, his face devoid of expression. Finally, he murmured feebly: "Mark. I want to speak to Mark."

Mark was standing behind the counsel table. "Mark," said Mavis. "He wants to speak to you."

"He wants to speak to me?" Mark asked incredulously. Mark's feelings about Henry's apparent heart attack were suspended. Strangely, he felt neither joy nor sadness. He simply felt nothing as he stood there in disbelief.

Kneeling, Mavis turned and motioned with her hand for Mark to come forward. "Quickly," she commanded.

Mark bent his head close to Henry's face, and could see that Henry recognized him. "Mark, I'm dying."

Mark felt guilty over still being angry with Henry, but he could not bring himself to say anything comforting. "I'm here, Henry."

"You hate me, I know." Henry was making an ominous wheezing sound.

"We've had some bad times between us, Henry."

"You knew, didn't you?" Henry asked weakly.

Mark did not know what Henry meant. "Knew what, Henry?"

"Priscilla told you, didn't she? That was why you hated me all these years."

"I didn't hate you, Henry."

"I could tell. I knew she had told you."

"Told me what, Henry?"

"You mustn't blame her. She was just a child."

"What? Tell me what?" Mark was still puzzled.

Henry closed his eyes and then reopened them.

"It wasn't her fault," Henry said.

Then he died.

Exactly what Henry had confessed to had not dawned on Mark.

Within five minutes of Henry's death, Derek Harden, Thomas T. Wahl and Joseph Raymer headed back to Raymer's office to decide what step to take next.

The others, not comprehending what had happened, blankly watched as the paramedics came.

"He's gone," one of the paramedics said. "Somebody call the coroner's office."

"What happens next?" Mark asked William Thackery Scott.

"I don't know. What is your opinion, Rolf?"

"I'm not sure either. I suppose it depends on Henry's will. I suppose whoever his executor is will decide what to do about this lawsuit. Does anyone know who inherits his property?"

"He never confided in me," said Mavis, "but he just testified it was Priscilla."

"But now that she's dead, what happens?" asked Rodney.

No one answered.

-66-

Like his daughter's, fewer than two months earlier, Henry Enfield's funeral was held at Grace Cathedral. After the ceremony, a large crowd of San Francisco notables gathered outside the church. The morning fog had begun to dissipate. Mavis, Rodney and Mark found a place near the parking lot where they could be away from those wanting to offer condolences.

"I hadn't expected to feel this way about Henry's death," Mark said.

"And how is that?" Rodney asked.

"Pity, I guess. I feel sorry for him," Mark answered.

"I wouldn't pity him too much. He got just what he deserved," said Rodney.

"Henry was an important part of all of our lives," Mavis said.

"I'm sorry, Mother, but I'm not very sympathetic," said Rodney.

"When I was sitting in the church, I was thinking: What if Henry had made me a partner?" Mark mused. "I probably never would have started my own company. I wouldn't be where I am today."

"That's right," said Mavis. "Life works that way."

"Mother, what was that on the witness stand about Uncle Henry's having molested a child?" Rodney asked.

"Yes, what was that all about?" inquired Mark.

"He didn't think I knew, but I had heard talk," Mavis answered. "I wasn't stupid. I figured out what had happened."

"I never heard a whisper," said Rodney.

"Father loaned him money to start all over again in America. That story about starting a branch office in San Francisco was complete rubbish. I know very well they sacked him. The child's family agreed not to press charges if he left the country."

"But how did William Thackery Scott know about it?" Mark asked.

"I told him," said Mavis. "I was not going to let him ruin you, Mark. He brought it on himself."

"I can imagine how difficult that must have been," said Mark.

"We had a terrible row. He wouldn't stop the takeover attempt."

Silence ensued while Mark absorbed the magnitude of what Mavis had done. She had turned against her brother in order to protect him.

"Mavis, I don't know what to say."

"Don't say anything. His hatred had blinded him. I'm sorry he died, but he was doing an evil thing."

"Well, it was an amazing turn of events," said Rodney. "So you are to see Henry's lawyer tomorrow afternoon?"

"Yes. The one who prepared his will," said Mavis.

"I'll stay over, if you want me to."

"There's no need, Rodney. You have business to attend to in London. I may have to stay here for some time."

"Are you sure you'll be all right?

As they were talking, a bearded man with thick glasses approached Mark. He was Van A. Goodwill, Ph. D., Priscilla's psychotherapist.

"Oh, yes, Dr. Goodwill," said Mark. "You're the doctor Pris had been seeing."

"I just wanted to pay my respects, and tell you what a marvelous lady your wife was."

"That's very thoughtful of you. Thank you for stepping forward."

"Not at all, Mr. Stevens. I wish you well."

"Strange," Mark said to Mavis and Rodney as Goodwill walked away. "I had the feeling he wanted to tell me something more."

Mavis and Mark sat opposite Manley J. Davis, the head of the probate department of Joseph P. Raymer's law firm. Davis had drawn Henry's will.

"This is an awkward situation for us, Lady Ashley." Manley Davis was nearly 70, but had chosen not to retire. Davis had drawn the wills for many older wealthy clients, and as far as he was concerned, the fees for probating their wills would be like clipping coupons from investments made years ago. The wills were "maturing," to use a phrase used in private by probate lawyers.

"Why is that, Mr. Davis?

"You see, my partner, Joe Raymer, was handling this litigation against Mr. Stevens, and now there is the will. Normally, I would be expected to act as the attorney for your brother's estate."

"I don't understand," said Mark. "What does the will say?"

"You don't know the contents, Lady Ashley? I thought you would know."

NOT BY BREAD ALONE

"No, Henry never discussed such things with me."

"Henry's will names you as the sole beneficiary, Lady Ashley."

"Me? The sole beneficiary?" Mavis was shocked. "Why me? What on earth for? The last thing I need is Henry's money."

"You are his only heir, after Priscilla, poor woman."

"What does it mean? I really don't understand what it all means."

"He names the bank as executor. I'm sure they'll handle things very properly."

"What about the lawsuit?" Mark asked. "What do we do about that?"

"I've already taken the liberty of conferring with Joe Raymer about that. We agree on the legal aspects."

"And what is your opinion?" Mavis asked.

"After Priscilla, you are the sole heir, Lady Ashley. As the sole heir, you inherit everything. By that I mean *everything,* right down to any stock that Henry might have inherited from Priscilla."

"But . . ." Mavis was overcome by what she had heard.

Mark interjected: "Do you mean that if the court had held that Pris owned my stock, Mavis would . . ."

"Yes, that's the point," said Davis. "In the eyes of the law, any community property, stock or otherwise, that Pris might have legally owned, has come to Lady Ashley."

"I think I understand, but it's difficult to absorb," said Mavis. "You mean *I* hold the controlling interest in Mark's company?"

"That's precisely what I mean. The stock, and everything else Pris legally owned, was willed by her to Henry. And then, Henry in turn willed it to you. Don't you see, if Raymer wins the law suit . . ."

"Mavis would control my company?" Mark said incredulously.

"That's preposterous!" said Mavis. "That whole lawsuit was ridiculous. Henry never should have started it in the first place. And now you say I end up inheriting control of Mark's company? Absolutely ridiculous!"

"I agree, it is startling, isn't it?" asked Davis.

"My God, that would mean that Mavis and I would control the company, and Derek would be out in the cold. How ironic!"

"I won't hear of it. I don't want Mark's company. We must stop that lawsuit. Tell Raymer to stop the case."

"That's where the embarrassment comes in," Davis said. "Technically, Wahl is Joe Raymer's client. Wahl's the executor of Pris's will, and our firm must take its directions from him, not you. He's the one to make the decision to keep on with the lawsuit, even though if the lawsuit were won, all the benefits would be yours as the sole heir."

"Now you listen to me, Mr. Davis." Mavis was upset. "As you say, I'm the one who inherits my brother's estate, not Mr. Wahl."

"There must be some way to stop him." Mark asserted.

"I'm sure there is," agreed Davis. "But you will need to consult other attorneys. If Wahl persists, we cannot represent you. If Joe can't talk some sense into him, we may have to resign from the case entirely."

The next day, Joseph Raymer, Jr. met in his office with Derek Harden and Thomas T. Wahl. Raymer had just explained that under Henry's will Mavis had inherited everything, and for all practical purposes the case was lost. The two were stunned.

"There would be absolutely no chance of Lady Ashley's joining forces with me?" Derek pondered aloud. "Oh, of course not," he answered his own question. "Her son being Rodney—I can see that there would be no hope."

"What about me?" asked Wahl. "Where in the fuck does that leave me?"

"Tom, it still leaves you with a substantial executor's fee," said Raymer, distancing himself from Wahl.

"But after all, I *am* still the executor. I can choose to keep on with the litigation if I want."

"If you do, Lady Ashley will ask the court to oust you as executor, and there goes your nice, fat fee."

"You'd better give up, old fellow," said Derek. "Can't you see, it's time for an orderly retreat?"

"I think that's good advice," said Raymer. "I'd suggest you do what Lady Ashley tells you."

The wheels in Derek's head were swiftly turning. He could see that Lady Ashley would vote her shares the way Mark wanted. With Mark solidly in control of the company, the stock market would have renewed confidence, and the price of the stock would be apt to rise. Here was his chance to recoup his losses. As soon as possible, he would telephone his broker to begin selling his shares in The Stevens Group.

Alex pulled Mark's Rolls-Royce to a stop in the parking lot of Sonoma's Mountain Cemetery. Mavis and Mark walked up the hill to Pris's grave. They looked down on her new headstone:

Priscilla Enfield Stevens
1945—1980

The old cemetery, with its silent graves, was peaceful. Mark and Mavis each wore coats against the chill air.

"What do you suppose Henry meant when he was dying?" Mark asked. "It was as if there were some secret about him that Pris knew. Henry thought Pris had told me."

"I remember."

"Did Pris know about that little girl he molested in England?"

"No, I don't see how she could have."

"Someone could have told her."

"Mark, don't you know what Henry was saying?"

"No, what?" Mark looked at her quizzically.

"Mark, dear, I don't know how to tell you. I knew right away."

"What, Mavis? Tell me, what?"

"When she was small, they would come to Castle Enfield for Christmas. I remember worrying, but I dismissed it from my mind."

"Mavis, what are you driving at?"

"I didn't think of it again until Henry lay there on that courtroom floor, asking for your forgiveness."

Mark, still not getting what she was talking about, waited impatiently for her to continue. Mavis could see that she would have to tell him straight out what she had on her mind.

"Mark, listen to me. I think Henry had molested Pris."

Her words hit Mark like a thunderbolt. Never had he imagined such a scenario. Of course, he thought, that would be what Henry was babbling on about. He was swept over by a wave of near-nausea. He staggered, and put his hand to his stomach. "My God, that filthy old man! No wonder Pris was the way she was!"

Mavis touched his hand. "What way, my friend?"

"It was personal . . ." At first he was reluctant to answer her. It seemed like a betrayal of Pris to tell anyone. But then, he wanted Mavis to know. "Pris could never bring herself to let go, sexually I mean. To really love me. Not until the very end in Las Vegas."

"In Las Vegas?"

"Yes. She changed."

"The poor child."

They walked up the side of the hill to look at Jonah's grave. "Do you think you're right about Henry and Pris?" Mark asked. "It's hard to believe."

"I'm afraid I am."

"It's awful! I don't know whether to push it out of my mind—that's what I'd like to do—or just accept it as true."

"You'd better look at it. Clear it all out. Not hide from the truth."

They looked down at Jonah's tombstone:

Jonah Stevens
1915—1964

"Have you ever made peace with Jonah?"

"I don't know. He doesn't bother me the way he used to."

"Good."

"He's just a man I knew once who used to be my father."

"Do you think you have forgiven him?"

"Forgive? I don't think about forgiveness any more."

"What do you think about him right now, as you stand here?"

"You know, it's odd."

"Odd?"

"Yes. I wish he were here. I wish he could see me now."

"You mean your success and all?"

Mark laughed. "No, I didn't mean that. I wish he could see what kind of a man I've become." Mark turned to her. "You know, I think you're right. I think I have forgiven him."

Otello Bagliani had not wanted to go to the hospital. He always told Christina he wanted to die at home. Since last night it looked as if that time were very near.

"Mrs. Bagliani, Mrs. Bagliani," the nurse cried out. "Come quickly! The end is near." Christina was walking on the grounds to get a respite from the depressing death scene. She had completely confined herself to the house for the past two weeks, since Otello had taken such a bad turn. Since returning from America, she had gone out in her car only for brief periods. She had thought frequently about Mark, but in returning to Italy she had done the only thing she felt she could have done.

Christina rushed up the grand staircase to Otello's bedroom. The other nurse had turned off the oxygen equipment. "I'm sorry, Mrs. Bagliani," she said. "Your husband has died."

Christina Movelli Bagliani walked to the bedside and took her dead husband's hand. "I've done what was right," she said.

Derek Harden showed the real estate broker around his condominium.

"I'll not be returning to San Francisco," Derek said. "My business here is concluded. I leave for London this afternoon. I want you to dispose of this place for me as soon as possible."

"Yes, sir."

"I've got pressing business waiting for me at home."

.   .   .

Amanda was beside herself with joy over having a genuine English lady dine at the Movelli compound. While she happily outdid herself in the kitchen, Mavis and Mark saddled two of the horses for a ride. As they rode the trails and back roads so familiar to Mark, he reminisced. Who would have thought it all would end with Henry Enfield's death, and the disclosure of his sexual aberrations? He recalled racing over these roads with Christina. He pointed out to Mavis the corner where the accident had left him with his limp. What a wonderful friend Mavis had become: a mentor, a confidant, indeed such a true friend. He wondered if their relationship would have grown to what it was today if they had never made love. Mavis was in her 60s now, but still very beautiful. Mark still had sexual feelings toward her. He simply did not act on them. The truth was he loved Mavis. It was a love that few others would understand. He hoped he would know her forever.

After their horseback ride, they bathed and changed clothes for dinner. It had been a delightful meal in the dining area of Amanda's kitchen. They laughed and joked. Amanda even told a slightly off-color, traveling-salesman joke. It seemed to Mark that he had never been so relaxed.

After dinner, Mavis and Mark went up to the mansion. Mark still had one of Rodney's cigars. As they sat in Antonio's den, he poured them each a brandy and lit up the cigar.

"I used to play chess here as a boy."

"What kind of a lad were you?"

Mark thought for a moment.

"As a boy, I was impressed, very impressed, with Antonio."

"Yes."

"I wanted to be like him some day. Rich, respected."

"Don't you think you've gone far beyond that?"

"Perhaps I have."

"I think so. You're what a man should be. You're not afraid to show your feelings. You think about life . . ."

Mark got up from his chair. "I have an idea." He went to the record player. "I keep some of my Beatles records here. Remember how we listened to the Beatles at Castle Enfield?"

"I'll never forget," Mavis laughed.

"I've been thinking a lot about what Hollingsworth said."

"He's had quite an impact on you, hasn't he?"

"This ambition thing. I often think about John Lennon. I think toward the end he gave up playing the ambition game. Remember, he was spending so much time with his family?" Mark blew smoke from his cigar, carefully turning away from Mavis.

"Do you think Lennon found what he was looking for?"

"He didn't have time. They shot him first. But that's what I want to do. I've made some decisions."

"What?" Mavis sipped her brandy.

"I've got a proposal for you." Mark was light-hearted.

Mavis smiled at her friend. "A *proposal*? Really, Mark!" she laughed.

"You know the company stock that *we* own?"

"It's not *our* stock. I'm not taking anything. It all belongs to you."

"You listen to me, Lady Ashley. Here's my proposal: We—you and I—we take our stock in the company, and we put it in trust."

"A trust?"

"Yes. We use all the dividends to help my mother."

"Help your mother?" Mavis laughed. "Whatever are you saying?"

"Mother wants to do something with Antonio's mansion. She's been talking about some of her church work. Well, I have a better idea."

Mavis looked at him with anticipation.

"I say you and I establish a center for abused women."

"I like the idea," said Mavis. "Research, education."

"Yes. Maybe a home for battered women."

"Let's do it! Mark, that's a brilliant idea.

Suddenly, Mark laughed out loud.

"What is it?" Mavis asked, laughing in return.

"I was thinking of Ecclesiastes." He was still laughing.

Mavis laughed along with him.

"At the end of Ecclesiastes, it says something like, 'The secret to life is doing the Lord's work.' Something like that. I don't remember exactly."

"But what's so funny?"

"I was thinking. Maybe this abused women program would be the Lord's work. Mavis, you don't suppose that, after all this, I'll get into heaven after all, despite all my money." Mark's eyes twinkled.

"Who knows. Maybe because of your money."

Just then Amanda came into the den.

"Mark, they called with a telegram."

"Who?"

"The telegraph company. Here, I wrote it down for you. It's from Christina Movelli." Amanda handed Mark a piece of notepad paper.

"From Christina? How did she know I was here?"

"She probably didn't," Amanda responded. "I imagine she figured I'd get the message to you. It's very short."

Mark's hand was shaking as he read aloud from the paper:

"Mark. Otello has died. I am free. Cristina."

Still holding the paper, Mark sat down. "Good Lord—Christina . . ." He was stunned by the telegram.

"What are you going to do?" Amanda asked.

"It's too late now. I've changed so much. The timing has always been wrong for Christina and me."

"The timing?" Mavis asked.

"Two months ago, I would have done anything to have her. But the time for us has passed." He shook his head sadly. "Now I would need something far more than we had then."

"But Christina seems to have changed too," Mavis commented.

Mark looked at Mavis questioningly. "Christina . . . changed?"

"Certainly, Mark. Look what she did. I have no doubt she loved you and wanted to be with you, but she did what she thought was the moral thing to do. She stayed with her husband. That wasn't an act of some flippant sex object."

"I keep thinking of Ecclesiastes," said Mark.

"What?"

"Everything has its time and there is a time for everything."

"I remember now that you remind me," said Mavis. "It does seem to be the way of life."

"Right now it's time for me to do some serious thinking about my future," said Mark. "Perhaps one day I'll contact Christina—to see if she still cares. Who knows—perhaps there will come a day when it will be time for me to love again. It would be to love in some other way. But for now it's time for me to discover a new path. A path my soul wants to follow."